TRUSTED MOLE

Milos Stankovic was born in Salisbury, Southern Rhodesia in 1962 – a British citizen with Scottish and Royalist Yugoslav parents, themselves refugees from Yugoslavia. Educated in England, he enlisted in the Parachute Regiment in 1981; the Army commissioned him and sent him to university where he studied Russian at Manchester and in Minsk in the Soviet Union.

Since then he has served with the British Army in Belize, Northern Ireland and Africa, and with the UN in post-war Kuwait and Iraq. Between December 1992 and April 1995 he served two long tours in Bosnia with the UN. Prior to his arrest at Staff College in October 1997, Major Stankovic served as a company commander with the 1st Battalion, Parachute Regiment.

The effects of the Ministry of Defence investigation destroyed his military career. He resigned and left the Army on 31 July 2000 to pursue his case against the MoD in the civil courts. The case continues...

Further reviews for *Trusted Mole*:

'By far the best book to have come out of the Balkan wars, not because it explains the conflict simply, but because Stankovic demonstrates with wit and eloquence that simplicity was never part of the equation ... This is not, however, a bleak book. Far from it. There is humour, lots of it, often (inevitably) black, but also reflecting the accidental idiocies and genuinely comic scenes that occurred in the midst of organised chaos.'

PETER MILLAR, *Sunday Times*

'Stankovic's book is far more than the outcry of an innocent man foully accused. He has a wonderful eye for detail and a natural storyteller's gift, and passion, to get across the bizarre and terrible cruelty of what the people of Bosnia went through. At times, I laughed out loud; at times, horrible moments of my spells there came swimming back, brilliantly evoked in Stankovic's fresh prose ... *Trusted Mole* is rich in comic scenes ... But the comedy switchbacks with the tragedy ... this man was a hero, caught in the middle and discarded by a military bureaucracy that should be shot at dawn for its betrayal.'

JOHN SWEENEY, *Observer*

TRUSTED MOLE

*A Soldier's Journey into Bosnia's
Heart of Darkness*

MILOS STANKOVIC

HarperCollins*Publishers*

HarperCollins*Publishers*
77–85 Fulham Palace Road,
Hammersmith, London W6 8JB

www.fireandwater.com

This paperback edition 2001
3 5 7 9 8 6 4 2

First published in Great Britain by
HarperCollins*Publishers* 2000

Copyright © Milos Stankovic 2000
Maps by Jillian Luff

The Author asserts the moral right to
be identified as the author of this work

ISBN 0 00 653090 7

Set in Sabon by Rowland Phototypesetting Ltd,
Bury St Edmunds, Suffolk

Printed and bound in Great Britain by
Omnia Books Ltd, Glasgow

This book is dedicated to the memory of two people. First, it is for my father, who led a full, varied and productive life. Second, it is for Dobrila Kalaba and countless others like her who were denied the realisation of those basic aspirations by the horror that was Bosnia.

Contents

Author's Note

This book had its genesis as long ago as 1993, long before most of the events in it had happened. The idea was sown by Keith in a restaurant in Split. Since then it has germinated and, weed-like, grown in all sorts of ill-defined directions. Initially it was nothing but a hobby and a dalliance, during which I pottered with early drafts of amusing anecdotes only. I found it almost impossible to address the more tragic and serious aspects of my time in the Balkans. All that changed on 16 October 1997 when I was arrested by the Ministry of Defence Police. That alone forced open the lid on my Balkan Pandora's box and compelled me to re-examine in minute detail the events of those years. This book is a result of that examination.

Trusted Mole was written exclusively while I was on police bail. Fortunately, the MoD Police saw fit to extend that bail three times and this book was written 'on the hoof' – in London, at Chanter's House in Devon, in the bush in Zimbabwe and on yachts *Te Aroa* and *Rockin' Billy* while crossing the Atlantic between Antigua and Falmouth.

This is a personal account of what happened to me from January 1992 to the present day. The opinions expressed in it are therefore mine and mine alone. They are not in any way representative of the opinions or policy of the British government (past and present), its Ministry of Defence or its Foreign and Commonwealth Office.

I learnt one very valuable lesson in the Balkans. There is no Truth. There is only Perception. This book does not claim to be an accurate portrayal of what was true and what was not true in the Balkans – no book can be, despite the best efforts of the author to convince the reader that he or she is the sole guardian of Truth. *Trusted Mole* is therefore a true story based on my *perceptions*. Throughout, I have been less interested in the nitty gritty and frequently boring details of the war and the negotiations in it. Who said what to whom, when, where and how is, to say the least, dull. It is guaranteed to send the reader to sleep.

Of much more interest is the nature of human relationships. In that sense, there is nothing that happens in war, other than legitimised killing, which does not happen to all people in their everyday lives. It's all there: courage and cowardice (moral and physical), charity and selfishness, humility and pride, sloth and industry, petty jealousies, greed, envy, self-seeking and aggrandisement, hate and love. It is my perception that these traits, good and bad, lurk within us all; some to a lesser, others to a greater extent. Some are propelled to visibility by the circumstances in which we find ourselves, while others remain hidden. It is also my perception that in peacetime we have more control over which of these aspects of character we, chameleon-like, choose to present to others. It's a subconscious bluff. That luxury of choice and control does not exist in war. The extreme nature of violent human conflict heightens our level of awareness and diminishes the control we have over our emotions and the ability to conceal our true nature. For better or worse war opens a window on our souls. *Trusted Mole* is my perception through that window. I hope that in the pages of this book the reader will recognise something of himself or herself, and ask, 'How would I have been?'

A word on accents and pronunciation. Most books dealing with the Yugoslav wars of the 1990s tend to include the appropriate accents above hard and soft consonants – presumably in the hope that either the reader will pronounce the unpronounceable (to Westerners) correctly or that it will lend authority to the text. I have not bothered, for two very sound reasons. First, Yugoslavs themselves instinctively know what the accents are, whether the notations appear in the text or not. Furthermore, literary tradition and custom in former Yugoslavia allow both for the printing of accent markings or otherwise. Second, it has frequently been my experience that Westerners, however well-schooled, however well-meaning, of whatever age and seniority of position, have and still do display an uncanny aptitude for managing to pronounce whatever word or name every which way but correctly. I was often amazed by the resilience and self-control displayed by Bosnians when verbally assaulted by hopelessly mangled variants of their place and personal names. I would rather the reader glide through the text making up whatever version he or she is comfortable with, than try to apply phonetic rules to words and letters with which the eye is not comfortable. Go on. Make it up. Everyone else did!

Were this a book about the war in Croatia, life would be easy in the sense that one could refer to the two belligerents as 'Serbs' and 'Croats' without risking offence to either party. Sadly, that is not the case when dealing with Bosnia where nomenclature is a minefield of political correctness. One risks blundering in and detonating someone's sensibilities. The confusion arises in that of the three parties to the conflict in Bosnia, two were commonly labelled with their ethno-tribal categories rather than their religious ones, namely 'Bosnian Serbs' (Orthodox) and 'Bosnian Croats' (Catholic). Unfortunately, the third party to the war in Bosnia has conventionally been labelled according to its religious orientation, namely 'Bosnian Muslims'. To even out the balance the term 'Bosniac' was fabricated to denote 'Muslims'. It is an offensive label in that it would never have arisen had this war not happened. Bosnians are Bosnians irrespective of whether they are Orthodox Christians, Muslims or Catholic Christians. The label 'Bosniac' was not widely used during my time in the Balkans. It seeped in during my last few months there. From the outset of war Bosnia's Muslims were burdened with the label of 'Muslim' not because they chose to be but because the internationals, particularly the media, created that convention. It was unfair. It would have been very easy in this book to have slipped into this familiar convention by referring to 'Serbs', 'Croats' and 'Muslims'. Mindful of the offence this might cause to the last-named group, I have deliberately referred to the first two groups by their ethno-tribal labels, while the other I have variously, and probably confusingly, tried to call 'Bosnians', 'Bosnian Muslims' and 'Muslims'. 'Bosniac' is a term which I never used out there and do not use in this book. No offence is intended to any group. I hope all parties would agree that had I bowed to the ultimate absurdity of political correctness and called the groups 'Bosnian Orthodox people', 'Bosnian Catholic people' and 'Bosnian Muslim people' – terms never used during the war – the reality of events and their impact would have been ludicrously diluted.

The writing of a book is not a solo endeavour. From the sowing of that initial seed, through agonising reflection and feverish tapping on a keyboard to the final product's appearance in the hands of a reader, there occurs a bizarre process of shaping which draws together, mentally rather than physically, a phalanx of people without whom the book could not have appeared in its final form. Each in their own way has added something to its shaping. *Trusted Mole* is, therefore, as much theirs as it is mine. There is no pride of authorship here. I cannot mention everyone involved, but I am deeply thankful to the following:

First and foremost, to Keith for the idea. To Patrick and Catja Mavros for their encouragement over five years: 'Write it. Turn disadvantage into complete advantage.' To Nichola Vickers without whom all this would have been so much harder. To *Vecernje Novine* and Martin Bell OBE, MP for the title. Also to Martin and his wife Fiona for their enthusiasm and invaluable advice. Without Barbara Levy there would have been nothing – from her ceaseless encouragement and prodding: 'Write it as you tell it, not as you think you should write it.' Equally, Richard Johnson at HarperCollins for his patience, and Richard Collins and Marian Reid the final shapers. Steven Barker, Desmond de Silva and Qaiser Khanzada for their measured and sensible comments. Bernardo Stella for his stark and moving poem. Equally to Harold Pinter for 'American Football'. A very special thanks to Geordie for his unswerving support and biting encouragement: 'Take 'em to the cleaners!'

and to Maria Vlahovic whose ideas helped shape the end. There are others too: Bill and Pam Coleridge, Sarah Jackson, Nicole Hope-Allan, Robert Adams, Bob 'Active' Edge, Mark Etherington, James Stewart for the elephants, Ian for listening, Jamie Lowther-Pinkerton without whose diaries I'd have been lost, Colin for providing a much needed break, and Paul Vallance, Dom McCully and Tim Bradshaw for their good humour at sea. And finally, to Oivind Moldestad, for whom I hope this book will lay to rest a ghost and right a wrong.

All photographs are from the author's collection, apart from the following: Brigadier Andrew Cumming in conversation with Indian General Satish Nambiar © AAJR Cumming; Bosnian Army soldier with sniper's rifle in trench © Steven Chapman-Bertelli; Dead Croatian HV soldier with medics © Steven Chapman-Bertelli; Corpse of unknown Serbian soldier, Gradacac, 1993 © Steven Chapman-Bertelli; Little girl in Tuzla hospital bed © Oivind Moldestad; Little girl and vulture, Sudan, 1994 © K. Carter/Southlight/Network.

Milos Stankovic
London, May 1999

Foreword

BY MARTIN BELL OBE, MP

In January 1993 in Central Bosnia I met a British officer who was introduced to me as Captain Mike Stanley of the Parachute Regiment. There was something quietly out of the ordinary about him. He was not in the usual Sandhurst mould. He was reserved, self-contained, intense and fiercely loyal to the cause he was serving, which was to save as many lives as possible under the inadequate mandate of the UN peacekeeping force. He was at that time the interpreter and adviser to Brigadier Andrew Cumming, the first commander of British Forces in Bosnia. He went on to work for Lieutenant Colonel Bob Stewart of the Cheshire Regiment, Brigadier Robin Searby and Generals Rose and Smith, the British commanders of UNPROFOR in Sarajevo. He served longer in the Bosnian war than any other British soldier.

His real name was Milos Stankovic. His father was a Serb and his mother was partly Serb and partly Scottish. Both had served the Allied cause in Yugoslavia in the Second World War, and had been lucky to escape to England with their lives. Their son, a British citizen, chose a military career. He was accepted by the Parachute Regiment, and served in Northern Ireland, Mozambique and the Gulf. When the Bosnian war broke out he was one of only three soldiers in the British Army who spoke the language fluently. It seemed an advantage at the time – or at least an advantage to everyone but himself.

His value to successive British commanders was that he could translate the people as well as the language. Tito's illusion of 'Brotherhood and Unity' fractured into barbarism, and competing warlords dragged their peoples into an abyss of psychotic savagery and primeval horror. These leaders were as indifferent to suffering on their own side as on the others'. Betrayal, mendacity and manipulation were their common currency. At prisoner exchanges they traded in bodies both dead and alive – and the dead, it seemed, mattered more to them than the living. Stankovic called this *necrowar*. He did not share their values but he understood their mentality. The Balkan warlords on one side and the International Community on the other glared at each other with incomprehension across a great divide. The captain from the Parachute Regiment could make sense of each to the other across that barrier.

He also saved lives. He rescued a wounded Muslim woman under fire in Vitez. With another British officer of similar background, known to us as Captain Nick Costello, and with the approval of the UN Commander, he smuggled scores of people out of the besieged city of Sarajevo – Muslims, Croats and Serbs alike – to join their families abroad. He helped to unblock UN convoys and to negotiate cease-fires. His mission was to win the trust of the Serbs, and he did so. They knew of his origins, but they also knew that he was not 'one of them'. 'Captain Stanley is a nice enough guy,' the Bosnian Serb Vice-President Nikola Koljevic was quoted as saying to a colleague, 'but you must always remember that his loyalty is to his Queen and his Commanders.'

He served with honour and distinction and received the MBE from the hand of the Queen. He was the outstanding liaison officer of his time. He did for Britain in the 1990s what Fitzroy MacLean had done in the 1940s, and in the same turbulent corner of Europe. Whenever Milos Stankovic crossed over into Bosnian Serb territory he described it as going to the 'Dark Side'.

In April 1995, after serving in Bosnia for the greater part of two years, he returned from that theatre of operations and resumed his military career. By this stage he had been promoted to major while in Bosnia. He served as a company commander with the 1st Battalion of the Parachute Regiment and was accepted into the Joint Services Staff College at Bracknell.

It was there on 16 October 1997, two and a half years after leaving Bosnia, that he was arrested by the Ministry of Defence Police under the Official Secrets Act, on suspicion of having spied for the Bosnian Serbs. Neither the origin nor the precise nature of the allegations was ever made clear.

By that time I had embarked on a new career as a Member of Parliament. He would not have been allowed to speak to me had I still been a journalist, but as an MP I could contact him. I offered to help because I knew the man and was convinced of his innocence. I also knew he was totally alone. There is no lonelier soul on the planet than a British soldier arrested under the Official Secrets Act. The Army at that stage had not even provided a 'soldier's friend', the basic right of any soldier facing a serious charge.

His treatment at the hands of the MoD Police is a story in its own right. He was extraordinarily well served both by his lawyer, Steve Barker, and by his 'soldier's friend', Brigadier Andrew Cumming, who was eventually appointed, as Milos Stankovic's choice, into that role. All I will say at this point is that the conduct of the inquiry was hostile and prejudicial, and should be used in our police academies for years to come as the textbook case of how not to conduct an investigation.

One of the many injustices of the police inquiry, in which an innocent man's rights were flagrantly violated, was the sheer inordinate length of it. Stankovic was thirty-four when it started, and thirty-six when the papers were finally passed to the Crown Prosecution Service. One advantage of this, however, was that it gave him the time to reflect on his years as a soldier of peace in Bosnia and to set down his account of them.

That account is what follows. It is the best book yet written on the Bosnian war, certainly including my own. It is more than that. It is the most extraordinary soldier's story that I have ever read.

MOTHER BOSNIA

Independence, the dream of man.
Independence, the goal of nations.
Why for Bosnia is this a contradiction?
Mother to three major creeds,
Whose devotees fight for spoils
In each other's gardens.

Horrified is the gaze of the world
While Mother Bosnia tears herself apart.
Offspring, brothers and sisters
Are set along the route to destruction
Deaf to Reason, blind to facts.

Mother Bosnia – a cradle of riches
Now becomes the spring of discord,
History repeating itself
Maiming, killing, displacing,
Robbing of land, the rule of the gun.

Seeds of a future conflict are sown,
Mother Bosnia is torn apart.
The atomic age is with us,
But Bosnia is just another name for Lepanto:
Creeds disunited and waging war.

I often wonder how God must feel
When three sons with different flags
Crave for his attention:
'In your name I kill,
Thy will be done.'
How? By killing the other son?

Mother Bosnia is bleeding
No quarter is given.
Hate is a chameleon of chauvinistic meanings,
And the World at large watches on TV
With an attitude of:
Provided it is you and not me
You can have my sympathy.

And so, Bosnians are
The perpetrators and the victims.
While the World watches on
Mother Bosnia is torn apart.

                              Bernardo Stella, London 1994

PART ONE

1992–1993
Baby Blue

You must leave now, take what you need, you think will last
But whatever you wish to keep, you better grab it fast
Yonder stands your orphan with his gun
Crying like a fire in the sun
Look out, baby, the saints are comin' through
And it's all over now, Baby Blue.

'It's All Over Now Baby Blue', Bob Dylan, 1966.

ONE

Operation Bretton

Thursday 16 October 1997 – Joint Services Command and Staff College, Bracknell, UK

'Are you Major Stankovic?' I catch the flash of a silver warrant badge encased in black leather and glimpse a pair of shiny handcuffs in one of the open brief-cases on the table. I nod – *what the hell's going on here?*

'I'm Detective Chief Inspector —, Ministry of Defence Police. I have a warrant for your arrest under Section 2.2b of the 1989 Official Secrets Act . . .' he's reading from the warrant, '. . . on suspicion of maintaining contact with the Bosnian Serb leadership, of passing information which might endanger the lives of British soldiers in Bosnia, of embarrassing the British government and the United Nations . . .'

My stomach lurches. Instinctively I cross my arms.

'. . . You have the right to remain silent, but anything you say can and will be used in evidence against you. Do you understand?'

My mind is racing – *say nothing*. 'Mmm' is my only response.

The day had started normally enough. I'd spent the previous night at home in Farnham reading up on various articles and reports in preparation for the following morning's syndicate room discussion on getting women into front-line units. Normal Staff College stuff.

The alarm wakes me at seven – quick shave, throw on the leathers, twenty minutes threading my way through solid early morning traffic on the M3. My thoughts are given up to taking a radical line – *get 'em into the Paras and Marines first*. I leave the Suzuki in the car park, dump the leathers in my room, climb into Barrack Dress – brown shoes, green plastic trousers, shirt, green woollen jersey – *don't forget the wretched name-tag, they're so anal about them here*. I wander over to the syndicate room and leave my bag. Still ten minutes to go. Time for a quick coffee and a smoke.

It's 0820. I'm standing outside the Purple Hall smoking a cigarette and chatting to James Stewart – something about women sticking bayonets into people and could they do it. Brigadier Reddy Watt walks past. He catches

3

my eye and gives me a funny look. I carry on chatting to James for another couple of minutes. The Brigadier is back again.

'Milos, could I have a quiet word with you?' Nothing unusual in that. Probably something to do with last Friday's syndicate room discussion which he'd sat in on.

'Sure, Brigadier.' I put out my cigarette and follow him in silence. It's slightly uncomfortable and I'm wondering why he's saying nothing. We round the corner of one of the large unused prefabricated lecture halls. He opens the door and motions me inside. The lights are on. The place is almost empty, but not quite – two men in dark suits on the left, brief-cases open on a desk. At the far end of the hall two more men in dark suits, also with open brief-cases on a desk. They're chatting quietly. I take a couple of paces forward and turn to the Brigadier to say, 'We can't talk in here. There are people here.' But I don't – his right hand is stretched out, palm open. There's a strange expression in his eyes, almost apologetic.

I walk towards the two at the far end. They're watching me now. The one on the left is short and tubby with a pot belly hanging over his belt. The one on the right is slightly taller but not much. He is also slightly portly but not as flabby. Both men are wearing cheap, dark blue off-the-peg C&A-type suits. There's a puffed up, officious air about the pair of them. As I approach the one on the right produces a warrant badge. Pot Belly does the same. The first one then starts reading from a piece of paper. Time stops dead.

The Taller One produces a warrant for the search of my house with authorisation to seize just about anything they want. It's signed off at Bow Street Magistrate's Court. I'm forced to hand over my house keys, car keys and motorbike keys. I sign some bit of paper to that effect.

'You'll now be taken to your room where you'll be able to change. We want to minimise any embarrassment.' *That's kind of you!* I'm not really interested in them. *Spying for the Bosnian Serbs! Where has this come from?* I feel faint.

I change quickly – trousers, shoes, shirt, tie and blazer, all a bit grubby but so what. Pot Belly and The Taller One are in there with me. I'm told not to touch anything. They're talking into their Cell phones, '. . . is the car ready yet? . . . no! . . . ten minutes! . . . yes, that's right, side entrance . . .'

There's time to kill. They're not ready for whatever's coming next. I sit on the bed and smoke a couple of cigarettes.

The Taller One turns to Pot Belly. 'What did the suspect say when he was arrested?'

Pot Belly checks his notes. 'He said quote "Mm" unquote.'

'Is that with two Ms or three?' his companion asks.

Pot Belly looks confused.

I rescue them. 'It's three "Ms".' *Jesus! These boys really are Keystone Cops. And they're flapping too, nervous almost. Curious.*

Eventually they're ready. I'm bundled into the back of an unmarked car along with The Taller One. There's a woman driving. Pot Belly follows in another car. Apparently we're off to Guildford Police Station – quite what for I still don't know.

The Taller One asks what my neighbours are like and whether they're likely to cause trouble. I tell him that they'll all be at work. He continues asking questions about the house almost bashfully.

'Is there anything we need to know about your house before we enter?'

'Like what? What do you mean?' Now he's got me baffled.

He says almost shyly, 'Well you know ... some people leave things in their homes, when they're out ...'

'What sort of things?' Now I'm interested.

'Well ... unexpected things ...'

'Unexpected things?'

'You know ... booby traps and things like that,' he says quickly. *Booby traps! Does he really think I've dug a bear pit in my mid-terrace two-up two-down?*

'No, no, don't worry. Just turn the key. You'll be fine,' I reassure him.

With nothing else to talk about he tries to engage me in idle conversation, 'So, you're a biker then. What type do you ride?'

'Suzuki ... eleven hundred,' I reply automatically.

'Eleven hundred, eh. What's the servicing interval then?' I'm stunned. I can't believe this is happening. *Motorbikes! Servicing intervals ... who gives a shit! Here am I arrested for spying and this clown wants to know about servicing intervals.*

I make a huge effort, '... er ... every six thousand miles ...' He nods knowledgeably and the stupid conversation continues. He's got an accent, West Country or something. I ask him.

'Devon actually.'

'Oh, right.' *What next?*

'Have you come far?' *Now I'm doing it, asking stupid questions,* 'Do you come here often?'

'From Braintree, in Essex. Early start this morning. We were up at five.' *Poor thing! Must have been terrible for you. It's the early copper who catches a spy. Braintree? Essex? What the hell happens there? And, anyway, who are these people? The only MoD Police I've ever seen are those rude, unfriendly uniformed knobs who lurk at the main gates of MoD establishments. Those buggers at Shrivenham are particularly odious – gits without a civil word in their heads.*

On the outskirts of Guildford the inane conversation stops. The Taller One's voice changes, goes up by perhaps half an octave, quicker too. 'Right, when we get to the police station this is what will happen ...' He quickly

5

outlines a sequence of events adding almost breathlessly, '. . . I don't want to make a mistake at this stage!' *I don't want to make a mistake at this stage!? You're flapping.* For the first time I realise he's nervous. *You've just made your first mistake . . . never reveal a weakness.*

The car swings right through a rear entrance followed by Pot Belly. We're out of the cars. Flanked by both suits I'm marched into a dark entrance leading to a custody suite with a long, raised counter. There's an unshaven scruffy drunk slumped against one end of the counter. There's a large desk sergeant and a young PC behind the counter. The Taller One approaches the PC who is partially hidden behind a computer screen. He produces him his warrant card and explains who he is. The PC looks a bit bewildered. *The civilian police don't know anything about this. They're not expecting us.*

The Taller One starts to read out the arrest warrant. The PC taps furiously on his keyboard – 'Hold on. Slow down. I've got to type all this in.' He slows down . . . Official Secrets Act . . . Bosnian Serbs . . . passing information . . . endangering lives . . . blah, blah, blah . . . The PC glances at me. His eyes are popping out of his head. Even the drunk perks up.

I'm told to empty my pockets of everything. Wallet is emptied, coins, an old train ticket, Zippo lighter, twenty B&H – ten left. Everything is itemised and recorded in triplicate by the sergeant. My meagre bits and pieces are stuffed into plastic bags.

'Please remove your belt and tie.' I do as I'm asked. *I can't believe this is happening!*

'Do you want my watch?'

'No. You can keep that and your cigarettes. Not the lighter. You'll have to buzz if you want a light.' *What the hell do they think I'm going to do? Set fire to myself with a Zippo!*

'Have you ever been arrested before?' asks the PC, eyes still popping. *What do you think?*

'No. Never.'

'Didn't think so somehow.' He casts an eye over my blazer with its brass buttons of the Parachute Regiment.

All puffed up, The Taller One pipes up, 'We don't want him to make any phone calls at this stage . . . because of the seriousness of the arrest . . . not until we've searched his house . . .' *What! What does this asshole think I'm going to do? Pick up the phone to some fictitious contact and say 'The violets are red'! They really do think I'm a spy.*

The PC looks uneasy. 'No phone call?'

The Taller One nods, '. . . because of the serious nature of the arrest . . .' *Oh, you're so bloody sure of yourself aren't you!*

The PC looks troubled and turns to me. 'Who would you call?'

I shrug my shoulders. 'Dunno.'

'Well, don't you want to phone a lawyer?'

'A lawyer? I don't know any lawyers. What do I need a lawyer for?'

'Is there anyone you want to call?'

I think – Mum? *'Hi Mum, I've just been arrested by MoD Plod for being a spy . . . how's the weather in Cornwall?'* Sister? *She'd freak out.*

I shake my head, 'No. No one.'

The PC frowns again and hands me a booklet. 'You might want to read this in the cell . . . your *rights.*' He stresses the word, glancing at The Taller One. Something clicks – *you've just made your second mistake, you plonker – two in less than half an hour!*

The Taller One and Pot Belly go one way, back out, and I go the other. I'm led down a linoleum-floored passage, the left-hand side punctuated by grey steel doors. The sergeant stops at the last, selects a key from the long chain on his belt, turns it in the lock and heaves open the solid door. I step into the cell.

'Want anything just press this button – coffee or a light, just buzz for it.'

The door slams heavily shut. The key turns in the lock. Silence. For the first time in my life I find myself on the wrong side of the law and the wrong side of a cell door. I feel weak and sick. My knees tremble. I'm sweating slightly. Delayed shock starts to creep over me.

The cell stinks. Shit, piss, puke, stale smoke, disinfectant. I stare in shock at my bleak surroundings. The cell measures maybe twelve by twelve feet, painted a faded, chipped blue-grey. There are two fixed wooden benches; on top of each of them a blue plastic mattress is propped against the wall. To the left is a small alcove with a toilet – chipped and dirty porcelain, no seat, no chain.

I sit down heavily on the right-hand bench. It's cold and hard. Dumbly, I stare down at my leather brogues – so out of place – and then fish around in my pockets for a light. *I need a cigarette. Shit. No light.*

I press the buzzer. Nothing happens. I wait a minute and buzz again. Still nothing. I'm about to try again when a little metal grate, half way up the door, scrapes open. A bored voice says, 'Yeah. Whaddaya want?' *Whaddaya want!!! . . . YOU . . .* somehow, my criminalisation is now complete.

'. . . Er . . . do you have a light, please?' I'm trying to be polite here.

'. . . Yeah . . .'

As if by magic a cheap red lighter appears between fat fingers. For a second there I think it's Pot Belly's hand, but he's busy ransacking my house. A dirty thumb strikes a flame. Gratefully I bend and suck in my first lungful of smoke.

'Thanks very mu—' The grate slams shut. Silence again. I exhale noisily and sit back down. My mind is now going bananas. *What? Why? Who? When? How?*

The tip of the cigarette glows angrily. I'm smoking hard. I light another one from it. *What to do with the stub?* I hold it in my hand and search for an ashtray. There isn't one. Above the other bench there's a barred, thick, frosted glass window. On its ledge there are five or six Styrofoam cups lined up like soldiers. I grab one. It's brimming with cigarette butts. So's the next, only these are smeared with garish red lipstick – *I wonder who you were?*

I sit and chainsmoke five cigarettes. Blue smoke hangs in the cell. The nervous, sinking feeling in my stomach gets worse. My bowels are churning furiously. My head is bursting. Pain straight up my neck, around my brain and down into my teeth. *How did this happen?*

One minute you're a student half way through a two-year Staff Course, one of the so-called 'elite' top five per cent; doing well, head above water, bright future. And the next, here you are, career blown to smithereens by an arrest warrant for espionage – *for spying!? . . . espionage? . . . a traitor? How the fuck did this happen? How? How? How?*

Despite the pain, ache and worry I'm thinking furiously. *How?* Connections, seemingly unrelated snippets from the past year and a half.

I'm trying to connect. Random telephone calls. A mysterious major from MoD security. Taped conversations. Jamie's telling me that people don't trust me. I voice my concerns. Nothing happens. No one gets back to me.

And then there are the watchers, followers. Horrible, uncomfortable feeling that I'm being watched, followed . . . for a long time. Eighteen months perhaps. I've seen them occasionally – just faces, out of place, people doing nothing, with no reason to be there. Who were they? Croats? Bosnians? Serbs? Someone is watching me. Paranoia? I know I'm being watched. Who's doing it? Why?

The cell door crashes open, severing my train of thought. I leap to my feet not quite knowing what to expect. It's the young PC. He's looking at me, uncertainly, almost sympathetically.

'We're not happy about this. I've been upstairs to see the Inspector. He agrees with me. We think your civil rights have been abused. You're entitled to make a phone call. It was obvious to me that you had no one in mind when I asked you who you'd like to call, so, who do you want to call?'

I'm stunned. I can't believe it. Good on him for doing his job properly.

'Dunno. Don't know anyone,' I stammer.

He's adamant. 'Look, it's only advice, but you do need a lawyer. Really you do.'

'But I don't know any lawy—'

He cuts me short. 'We'll call you a duty lawyer if you like.' I nod. He disappears and the door clangs shut. I glance at my watch. Over two hours since I was booked in. *Bloody heavy-handed MoD Plod – GUILTY, now let's prove the case!*

Ten minutes later the PC is back. 'We've got you a lawyer. She's on the phone right now . . . come on!' I'm led from the cell and shown to a phone hanging off a wall. The handset's almost touching the floor. I pick it up and put it to my ear.

'Hello, I'm Issy White from Tanner and Taylor in Farnborough. I understand you need help . . .' *Help. What can you do for me?*

'Yes, I suppose I do.'

'What can you tell me?' *What can I tell you? What should I tell her? How much? All of it? Some of it? Which bits to leave out?*

'Er . . . well . . . it's all very sensitive . . . I can't . . . well, not on the phone . . .'

'I'll be round shortly.' She's curt.

I'm pathetically grateful that someone, anyone, has shown interest. Face to face she's as brusque as she was on the phone. In three hours she has my story, all but the really sensitive stuff. She doesn't need to know about that at the moment. I tell her about my time out there, about the List, the gong, the phone calls, about everything that matters. She scribbles furiously throughout.

'Does all this sound unbelievable to you, Issy?'

She looks up and quite matter of factly says, 'No. It all sounds true. I can spot a liar a mile off.' She's very serious.

'No. I don't really mean "unbelievable", I suppose I mean "weird".'

'Weird? . . .' She pauses, '. . . I've never heard anything like it.'

'Yeah, well, it's all true, every word of it . . .' I feel tired '. . . It's all true. It happened.'

Issy promises to get me some more cigarettes. She thinks they'll be finished with my house by two o'clock. She leaves and tells me she'll be back for 'question time'.

Back in the cell I've got nothing to do except mull over the same old thoughts. Two o'clock comes and goes. Nothing. Three o'clock. Still nothing. I'm dog tired but still thinking, sick and churning but still thinking. *What should I tell them? All of it? That would implicate Rose and Smith. Keep it from them. Tell them the minimum. I know what this is about. It's about phone calls. It's about a lot more than that. But for now, it's about phone calls. I'm not about to bubble away Rose, Smith and the others. Not yet anyway. Keep the List out of it.*

I'm sitting there staring at my shoes again, my elbows on my knees, head in my hands. I've smoked my last cigarette. There's nothing else to think about. There's nothing left anymore. Staff College and all that's happened in the last two and a half years – a dream, a lifetime ago. And now they're utterly irrelevant to me. Reality is where the illusion is strongest. *This* is where it's strongest. Reality is *this* cell. Nothing else exists and I'm so tired, so, so tired. I have to sleep. Get some strength. Must sleep.

I take off my blazer and lie down on the bench. I can't be bothered with the mattress. I cover my head with the blazer. It's all so cold and dark, just like it was then, a thousand years ago – cold, dark, unknown and terrifying. I close my eyes. The tape starts playing and I'm back there. Reality. I can hear the shouts and screams, feel the cold, the panic and the terror. I'm there again.

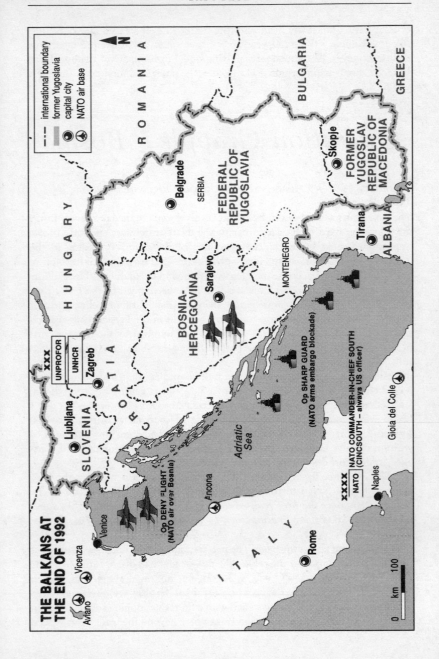

THE BALKANS AT
THE END OF 1992

international boundary
former Yugoslavia
capital city
NATO air base

N

R O M A N I A

BULGARIA

GREECE

H U N G A R Y

Belgrade

SERBIA

FEDERAL
REPUBLIC OF
YUGOSLAVIA

Skopje

FORMER
YUGOSLAV
REPUBLIC OF
MACEDONIA

Tirana

ALBANIA

MONTENEGRO

C R O A T I A

Zagreb

UNPROFOR
UNHCR

xxx

Sarajevo

BOSNIA-
HERCEGOVINA

Ljubljana

SLOVENIA

Adriatic
Sea

Op DENY FLIGHT
(NATO air over Bosnia)

Op SHARP GUARD
(NATO arms embargo blockade)

NATO COMMANDER-IN-CHIEF SOUTH
(CINCSOUTH – always US officer)

Gioia del Colle

Ancona

Venice

Vicenza

Aviano

xxxx
NATO

Naples

Rome

I T A L Y

0   km   100

11

TWO

Operation Grapple – Bosnia

8 January 1993 – British National Support Element Base, Tomislavgrad

The Americans were about to bomb the Iraqis again. On the hour, every hour, the television fixed high in a corner of the dusty warehouse spewed out the impassioned, near hysterical commentaries of the drama unfolding in the Middle East. Iraqi non-compliance with some UN Security Council Resolution seemed to be the issue; cruise missiles were poised to fly, midnight the deadline. In another place at another time we'd all have been glued to the box as we had been in 1991, eagerly anticipating the voyeuristic thrill of technowar. But not this time, not here and not tonight. The crisis in the Persian Gulf seemed so remote, so distant, so unreal. Shattered and numbed by the day's events, nearly all the soldiers had shuffled off to their makeshift bunk beds, stacked four high around the warehouse.

Being less tired and having nothing more appealing than a sleeping bag on a cold concrete floor to look forward to, I'd delayed getting my head down. I was alone at a small wooden table, determined to finish recording the day's hectic events in an airmail 'bluey' to a stewardess friend at British Airways. I glanced at my bedspace and marvelled that Seb had somehow managed to stuff his massive frame into his doss bag. Even more astonishingly, he'd managed to doze off despite the freezing concrete.

2225. The time flashed on the TV screen as the latest news from the Gulf came in from CNN. I turned back to the letter. Over the page and I'd be done, '. . . so, once the Boss realised what was going on, the three of us spent most of the day driving like madmen to get down here, but it was all over when we arr—.'

Ink splattered across the page. The pen sprang from my fingers as I leapt out of my skin knocking over the table. The newsreader had disappeared from the TV screen, obliterated. My ears were ringing, my mind stunned as a deep *WOOOMF* slammed into the warehouse, rattled the filthy windows and rolled over and around us. The air was filled with a fluttering, ripping sound and then another shockingly loud detonation somewhere beyond the wall. I was rooted to the spot. My legs started trembling. Adrenalin gushed through my veins.

'Fuck! Shit! Oh, Christ, not again!' Expletives echoed around the warehouse.

Pandemonium. All around me soldiers cursing, grunting, wild-eyed, tumbled from their bunks clutching helmets, flak jackets, stuffing feet into boots, laces flying, others scampering off with boots in hand, determinedly dragging their sleeping bags behind them into the darkness of the back of the warehouse.

Seb was on his feet in the same state of stunned confusion as I was. Within seconds the warehouse had emptied. The soldiers seemed to know precisely what to do. Why didn't we? The greater terror of being left behind seemed to unfreeze me. A corporal raced past. I grabbed at him.

'Hey! Where do we go? We've just arrived.' Panic in my voice.

He wasn't going to be stopped. 'Just follow me, sir!' he yelled over his shoulder as he disappeared into the gloom. We bolted after him. Ironic that he should be our saviour at that moment; officers were supposed to lead the men. Ridiculous really, but I didn't care, just so long as he took us to wherever it was everyone else was going.

Cramming ourselves through a small door at the back of the hall, we emerged onto a raised walkway of a loading bay. Turning left we hurried after fleeting, bobbing dark shapes. I hadn't a clue where we were going and blundered on regardless, driven by panic. We raced through a cavernous, dank boiler room. Another salvo of shells screamed in. Through a door at the far end we were hit by a wall of freezing air. It had been below minus twenty during the day. Now it was even colder.

We were now slipping and stumbling over uneven and frozen gravel. Ahead, stooped and crab-like, dragging doss bags, the black shapes of soldiers darted and weaved – like ghosts caught in the chilling glow of a half moon. Another whirring and ripping of disturbed air. We flung ourselves down grazing palms and knees, cheeks were driven into rough and frozen stones. I clung to the earth as an oily, slithery serpent in my stomach uncurled itself. The night was split for an instant, spiteful red and white followed by a deafening, high-pitched cracking, ringing shockingly loud. Then a deeper note, a rolling wave through the ground beneath, the air swept with an electric, burning hiss.

The desire to remain welded to the earth, panting and cowering, was overwhelming. Although the brain screamed 'no!', no sooner had the pulse washed over us than we were up, stumbling across the gravel. With horror I realised we were running towards the impacts. It made no sense. *Surely we should be legging it in the opposite direction?*

Far in the distance, beyond the broad, flat and featureless plain, now cloaked in darkness, behind a distant, rocky escarpment, two soundless halos of dull yellow flickered briefly. Moments passed and then two flat reports.

'Incoming!' screamed a breathless, hysterical voice somewhere ahead.

For seconds, hours, nothing . . . nothing . . . then a fluttering warning which sent us diving headlong into the gravel again. More cringing and tensing, detonations, ringing – closer this time. *What the fuck are we doing running towards it?*

We moved forward, staggering and diving in short bounds for what seemed like an eternity, keeping the edge of the warehouse to our left. In the darkness it was difficult to tell how far we'd gone – time and distance distorted by panic and fear. We rounded the far corner. Beyond a concrete V-shaped ditch was a row of maybe five or six armoured personnel carriers, APCs, neatly parked, squat and black.

I still had the corporal firmly in my sights. In a single bound he vaulted the ditch, raced up to the rear of the left-hand APC, yanked open the rear door and hurled himself inside. Others flung themselves in after him. Another flash on the horizon. Shit!

I was the last into the vehicle and feverishly pulled the door to before the shell landed. It wouldn't shut. Too many people and too many sleeping bags. It was the bags or me.

'We don't need this sodding thing,' I hissed in desperation, hurling one out into the night. I wrestled the door shut and hauled down on the locking lever just as the shell exploded somewhere to our front.

Inside the APC it was pitch black. Nobody said a word. Nothing could be heard save ragged, terror-edged panting as each man fought to recover his breath. Someone in the front flicked on a torch with a red filter. What little light managed to seep into the back cast eerie patches of dull red across strained, pallid faces. There were far too many of us crammed into the vehicle – knees and elbows everywhere. On my left was a slight youth clad in a boiler suit, who didn't look like a soldier at all. Opposite me I recognised one of the batch of colloquial interpreters, a staff sergeant in the REME,* evidently posted up to Tomislavgrad, TSG, and now stuck in this APC. He looked terrified. It was his sleeping bag I'd slung out. Two down from me and next to the youth was Seb, still panting furiously. There were others too. Seb's driver, Marine Dawson, had somehow ended up in the commander's seat, and somewhere up there was the Sapper corporal, whom we'd blindly followed. There must have been about eight or nine of us stuffed into the small APC.

Our private thoughts were interrupted by a wild banging on the door and muffled shouting. Reluctantly, I eased up the lever and opened the door an inch.

---

* Royal Electrical and Mechanical Engineers. All acronyms and abbreviations are explained in the Glossary on p. 447.

'Fuck's sake! Lemme in. Lemme in!' A helmeted shadow was trying to rip open the door. I held on grimly, not wishing to expose us any more to the outside world.

'Sorry mate. No room in here ... try the one next door ...' I barked through the gap. The shadow swore savagely and disappeared into the night. I slammed the door shut just as another shell screamed in, shattering the night.

'Oi! You! Get the fucking periscope up!' It was the corporal, up front somewhere. What was he on about now? Deathly silence. Nothing happened.

'You in the commander's seat! Get the periscope up and let's get a fix on those flashes ... work out where the bastards are firing at us from ...' *Has he gone mad?*

The unfortunate Dawson, who clearly had never been in an APC in his life, frantically started to tug at the various levers and knobs around him. He had no idea what he was supposed to be doing. I'd have been just as clueless. Another shell screamed in.

'Fuck's sake, fuck's sake ... get out, get fucking out!' The corporal had finally lost his rag. A scuffle broke out up front as the shell exploded. In the darkness all you could hear above the high-pitched ringing in your ears were thuds, grunts and the occasional blow as Dawson and the corporal struggled with each other. Somebody whimpered, the APC rocked softly on its suspension, a few more grunts and blows and the unfortunate Marine was ejected from his seat.

Settled in the seat the corporal expertly flipped up the periscope and glued his forehead to the eyepiece. 'Compass ... somebody gimme a compass!' he yelled without removing his eyes from the optic. His voice rose a note, 'Shit! 'nother two flashes on the horizon ... two rounds incoming!!'

I stared down at the luminous second hand of my watch ... *five seconds* ... it swept past *ten seconds*. Someone started to whimper, another's breathing rose in volume, great gasping pants ... *thirteen seconds* ... my watch started to tremble. I was mesmerised by it ... *fourteen* ... *fifteen* – the air was ripped; two double concussions which rolled into each other. A collective sigh of relief swept through the APC.

'Where's that fucking compass?' The corporal was at it again. Either he was barking mad or had simply been born without fear. He was still determined to get a fix on the guns. I dug out a Silva compass from my smock pocket and passed it up the APC.

'Time of flight's about fifteen seconds,' I shouted up at him.

'Good. Fifteen seconds, yeah?' He seemed pleased. What difference did it make? Flashes, bearings, time of flight? The facts couldn't be altered. We were stuck in this APC. Shells were landing somewhere to our front. A direct hit would destroy the vehicle. A very near miss would destroy it as well, and, with it, us. But I had a sneaking admiration for that unknown corporal. He was one of Kipling's men, keeping his head and his cool while all around him were losing theirs. At least he was doing *something*, keeping his mind busy, warding off the intrusion of fear and panic – pure professionalism. I felt useless, unable to contribute in any way, jammed as I was in the rear and prey to my fears and imagination.

What were we doing sitting in an aluminium bucket *between* the building and the incoming rounds? Surely we'd be safer in the lee of the building, behind it? Another dreadful thought came to mind: the CVR(T) series of vehicles, of which this Spartan was one, were the last of the British Army's combat vehicles which still ran on petrol. All the others – tanks, armoured infantry fighting vehicles, lorries, Land Rover and plant – ran on diesel. We were sitting on top of hundreds of litres of petrol 'protected' only by an aluminium skin. We'd sought refuge inside a petrol bomb. My mind imagined a near miss – red hot steel fragments slicing through aluminium, piercing the fuel tank, which we were sitting on, and *wooooosssssh* . . . frying tonight! Fuck this! This was not the place to take cover.

'Hey! Why don't we just drive out of here, round the back of the building where it's safer?' I shouted at the corporal and anyone else who might care to listen.

'No driver in the front,' he shouted back, seemingly unconcerned. I don't suppose the fuel thing had occurred to him.

'We had this for four hours this afternoon . . . just sat here, froze and waited . . . shit myself,' mumbled the staff sergeant opposite and then he added savagely, 'I've fucking had enough of this shite!'

'Another flash!' screamed the corporal. Bugger him! Why did he have to be so efficient? I didn't want to know that another shell was arcing towards us. *This is the one that's going to fry us! . . . three seconds . . .* the panting started . . . *five seconds* . . . where were Corporal Fox and Brigadier Cumming? Where had they taken cover? . . . *seven seconds* . . . How had we got ourselves into this? How eager and consumed with childish enthusiasm we'd been, desperate not to miss out! How we'd raced down to TSG – and for what? . . . *nine seconds*. . . . Idiots! The lot of us.

We'd been in Vitez that morning. In fact we'd just left the Cheshire Regiment's camp at Stara Bila when it happened. We'd driven there from Brigadier Cumming's tactical headquarters in the hotel in Fojnica. He'd been incensed by an article in the *Daily Mail*, written by Anna Pukas, which had glorified the British contribution to the UN and had damned, by omission, everyone else's. We'd dropped by the Public Information house in Vitez late the previous night after a gruelling eleven-hour trip up into the Tesanj salient. Cumming had returned to the Land Rover Discovery clutching a fax of the article. He'd been livid but it had been too late to do anything about it at that hour so we'd

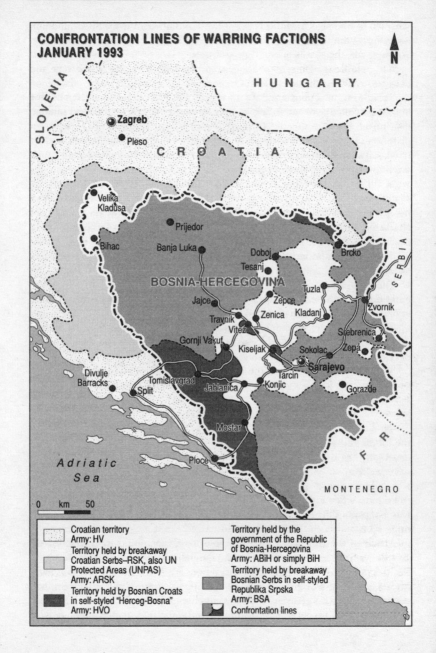

**CONFRONTATION LINES OF WARRING FACTIONS
JANUARY 1993**

N

SLOVENIA

HUNGARY

◎ **Zagreb**
• Pleso

C R O A T I A

SERBIA

• Velika
  Kladusa

• Prijedor

• Bihac

Banja Luka •

Doboj

Brcko

Tesanj

BOSNIA-HERCEGOVINA

Tuzla

Jajce •

Zepce

Zenica

Kladanj

Zvornik

Travnik

Vitez

Srebrenica

Gornji Vakuf

Kiseljak

Zepa

Sokolac

Sarajevo

Divulje
Barracks •

Tomislavgrad

Tarcin

Split •

Jablanica

Konjic

Gorazde

F R Y

Mostar

*Adriatic
Sea*

Ploce •

MONTENEGRO

0   km   50

Croatian territory
Army: HV

Territory held by breakaway
Croatian Serbs–RSK, also UN
Protected Areas (UNPAS)
Army: ARSK

Territory held by Bosnian Croats
in self-styled "Herceg-Bosna"
Army: HVO

Territory held by the
government of the Republic
of Bosnia-Hercegovina
Army: ABiH or simply BiH

Territory held by breakaway
Bosnian Serbs in self-styled
Republika Srpska
Army: BSA

Confrontation lines

returned to Fojnica. The following day we shot back to Vitez where Cumming had words with the Cheshires' Commanding Officer, Lieutenant Colonel Bob Stewart, who had been quoted in the article.

We were heading back to Fojnica and had been on the road some ten minutes. The Brigadier was silent. Corporal Fox was concentrating on keeping the vehicle on the icy road and the accompanying UKLO team – an RAF flight lieutenant called Seb, his driver, Marine Dawson, and their wretched satellite dish in the back of their RB44 truck – in his rear-view mirror. Next to his pistol on the dash the handset of our HF radio spluttered and hissed into life. It was always making strange noises and 'dropping' so I never paid much attention to it. Corporal Fox grabbed it and stuck it to his ear.

'Sir, I'm not sure, but it sounds like something's going on in TSG ... signal's breaking up and I can't work out their call sign ... sounds like they're being shelled or are under attack.' Corporal Simon Fox was a pretty cool character, never flustered, always the laconic Lancastrian. I couldn't make much sense with the radio either. Static and atmospherics were bad. All we could hear was a booming noise in the background. We decided to head back to Vitez.

The Operations Room at Vitez was packed. We entered to a deathly, expectant hush as everyone strained to hear the transmissions from TSG.

'... that's forty-seven and they're still landing ... forty-nine, fifty ... still incoming ...' There was no mistaking it: TSG was definitely being shelled and some brave soul was still manning a radio, probably cowering under a desk, and was giving a live commentary as each shell landed.

'How long's this been going on for?' snapped Cumming, now hugely concerned that his logistics and engineer bases were being attacked.

'About twenty minutes.'

'Any casualties?' His tone was unmistakable.

'None as yet. Too early to tell. Everyone's under cover except ...' except the loony under the table.

'Right, I'm off to TSG. Get hold of the Chief of Staff in Split. Tell him what we're up to.' And with that we swept out of the Ops Room. The Brigadier was right of course. He could hardly sit around in Vitez or, worse still, retire to Fojnica, while his troops were under fire. I told Corporal Fox and Seb what was happening. They'd had the presence of mind to get the vehicles fuelled up.

Ahead of us stretched a long journey: Route Diamond to Gornji Vakuf, around the lake at Prozor and then the long climb up over the 'mountain' on Route Triangle. This was the worse of the two main supply routes into Central Bosnia, a hell of frozen ruts, tortuous bends, precipitous slopes and broken-down and stranded vehicles. It would take us hours.

I doubt there was a man among us who didn't feel a buzz of anticipation.

The military is a peculiar profession. It's crammed full of frustrated people – highly trained, frustrated professionals. Unlike any other profession we rarely actually put into practice what we train for ad nauseam. In a sense, we're untried, untested, and always there's that little nagging doubt, that little question – how would I cope? Would I do the right thing? Would I freeze? Panic?

Sometimes there *are* incidents and soldiers *are* shot at, attacked, bombed, and they *are* tested. But it doesn't happen to everyone. Most of the time nothing happens. I've done three tours in Northern Ireland, one in the bandit country of South Armagh, and I've never been shot at, heard a shot fired in anger or heard a bomb go off. There are the occasional blips – the Falklands and Gulf Wars, where people really are tested and really do 'see an elephant' as the Americans refer to combat: *'Few people have actually seen an elephant, most have only had one described to them.'*

It's an odd arrogance that underpins opinion on being in combat. The US Army is almost obsessive in this respect. As a visual manifestation of this, soldiers who have 'seen their elephant' wear on the right sleeve of their fatigues the patch or emblem of the unit or division with which they served on operations – 'look-at-me-I've-been-there' symbolism. Those unlucky enough not to have been on operations can only wear on their left sleeve the patch of the division with which they are currently serving; their right sleeves remain bare. Fortunately, we have no such rites of passage badges in the British Army, just medals which we're required to wear so infrequently that most people can't remember where they've put theirs.

As a very young soldier I remember well one night in McDonald's in Aldershot. It was June 1982 and 2 and 3 PARA had just returned from the Falklands War. The place started to fill up with a gang of Toms from 2 PARA, all wearing 'Darwin and Goose Green' sweatshirts. All were drunk.

'An' where were you fookin' craphats while we were scrapping wi' the Argies?' snarled one of them aggressively (some of us had missed out). And then they all rounded on us.

'Watch who you're calling a craphat, boyo. I'm 1 PARA,' spat back Taff Barnes, our corporal, who was from 1 PARA mortar platoon. He was a hulking great bloke – crazy to pick a fight with him.

'You 1 PARA? Oh, well, that's okay then.' Instantly they were mollified and we were all suddenly the best of friends.

'So, what was it like then?' I asked our original assailant. I was curious to know.

He looked at me. The drunkenness in his eyes seemed to evaporate. They became focused and intense. 'It was shit,' he said evenly. 'It was pure shit . . . you're lucky you weren't there.' And then he was gone, staggering off to order his 'fookin'' Big Mac and mega large chips.

His answer had floored me. What had he seen and done that had been so terrible as to humble him in that way, to knock the bravado out of him so completely? I remember feeling pure jealousy at that moment, jealousy born out of a weird frustration that we now had nothing in common. He'd seen his elephant up close.

The majority of people in the Army have never seen an elephant. There are senior officers, even generals, who haven't got a single campaign service or operation medal. Some only have a Queen's Jubilee Medal. It's not really their fault. Put it down to fate or luck. It doesn't make them any less professional or useful to the system. But it is a source of personal frustration. So much training, so many years learning your profession and yet never been tested. So, it's not at all surprising that we were all gripped by a horrid fascination to get down to TSG as quickly as possible, in case we missed seeing the elephant.

By the time we'd passed through Gornji Vakuf, skirted Lake Prozor, crawled up the 'mountain' beyond, shaken ourselves to bits on the winding and hellish Route Triangle, darkness had fallen. At a UN checkpoint, the last British outpost along the route before TSG, a burly Sapper corporal waved us down outside a small cluster of Portakabins in a bleak, rocky and windswept landscape.

Cumming stuck his head out into the freezing night air.

'Sir, you can't go any further. There's heavy shelling in TSG,' the corporal informed us gravely.

'I know,' answered Cumming without a hint of frustration in his voice, 'that's why we're here.'

'Sorry, sir, I've got my orders. No soft-skinned vehicles beyond this point.'

'But I'm the Commander. No soft-skinned vehicles? Not even me?' I could tell Cumming was highly amused by the proceedings. The corporal was adamant.

We were saved by the shrill ringing of the car phone.

Evidently, from the conversation which followed, it was someone on the phone from TSG. An arrangement was made to proceed as far as the Croat checkpoint at Lipa in the Duvno valley. There we'd cross-load into an APC for the final couple of miles to the NSE (National Support Element) logistics base.

At Lipa the Brigadier and I donned helmets and leapt into one of two 432 APCs. Corporal Fox would wait at Lipa and only proceed to the base once summoned on the radio. As we clattered along in the APC I felt faintly ridiculous, surrounded by all this armour. Ten minutes later we rocked to a halt in 35 Engineer Regiment's part of the NSE to be met by the Commanding Officer, Lieutenant Colonel John Field. It rapidly transpired that the shelling had ceased some time ago.

We could see little in the darkness but were given a quick guided tour of the warehouse and the offices where some of the windows had been blown in. Colonel Field described the events of the day. The Serbs had 'walked' their artillery fire around the town and it was believed that they had been targeting a Croat gun line which had been set up behind the UN base. A total of one hundred and forty-eight 152mm shells had been counted. A number of buildings in the town had been hit, some of the NSE's 'B' vehicles – soft-skinned trucks and Land Rovers – had been damaged, but no one in the base had been injured. Very lucky. Well-rehearsed drills in the event of such an attack had paid off. The 'loggies' next door had had the luxury of taking cover in a huge bunker, while the Sappers had had to seek protection inside their armoured vehicles.

I spotted Corporal Fox emerging from the shadow. 'How the hell did you get here?'

'Oh, I came in with you . . . followed your APC in. I wasn't going to miss this sitting at that checkpoint!'

'Nothing here to miss. It ended hours ago.' I think we both felt a bit deflated. Worse still we were now 'war tourists', hanging on every word of those who had undoubtedly seen their elephants that afternoon.

As there wasn't much else to do, Seb and I found a patch of concrete to kip down on in the TV room. I bought a box of Rowntree's Fruit Pastilles in the canteen for the journey back the next day and then wandered off to the TV room where CNN was reporting another crisis in Iraq.

The sweep of the second hand jolted me back to the present . . . *twelve seconds* . . . frantic heavy breathing in my ears. It was infectious, unnerving. Others' terror compounded your own . . . *thirteen seconds* . . . it was hopeless. We were helpless. Unable to do anything to influence fate, to save ourselves. We were completely at the mercy of the Serbian gunners and their thunderbolts, which hammered the earth around us . . . *fourteen seconds* . . . shit! I felt myself slipping into unchecked panic, muscles taut and trembling . . . *fifteen* . . .

The shell hissed in and missed. We were still alive and not burning to death. Intense relief.

The corporal was still doing his thing up front. 'Think I got a fix on 'em that time,' he shouted. 'Be able to confirm it next time.'

Next time! He was barking mad. But he was keeping himself together by occupying his mind. I doubted I could stomach much more of this. I had to do something quickly. Anything. The fruit pastilles! I clawed at the crushed box in my pocket.

'Anyone want a sweetie?' I produced the box in the red half-light expecting to be told to sod off. Absurd really. The reaction was quite the opposite. Hands appeared from nowhere. Passed down the APC – even the corporal got one – the pastilles were feverishly devoured. The chewing seemed to help and at least brought some saliva back to dry mouths. It was a short-lived respite.

'Here we go again! 'nother one incoming. Should get a fix this time.'

Another fifteen seconds of clock-watching, bowel-churning gripped us. I was raging. We had nothing to fire back at them with. Where was DENY FLIGHT? Where were the jets that were supposed to be somewhere up there? Why couldn't a couple of Sea Harriers whip off *Ark Royal* in the Adriatic, zip over here and drop a couple of cluster bombs on the bastards?

It then occurred to me that this was only my tenth day in theatre. Snuffed out on day ten by the Serbs of all people. My parents would love that one! Day bloody ten. This hadn't been part of the plan at all. Mentally, I cursed my youth, my wretched impetuosity, and my pig-headed unwillingness to listen to my father, whose dire words of warning were spinning around in my head – *'Son, listen to your father. You don't know what you're getting into. You don't know the mentality of the people there . . . all of them, they're rotten, rotten, rotten . . . dangerous people and they'll get you, they'll kill you in the end just for what you are.'*

I hadn't listened to him. And now that arrogance had led me up this blind alley and there was no way out.

I felt myself slipping off the edge of sanity. Again the earth rocked. Another miss. Someone grunted in relief, another whimpered. Perhaps me.

'They'll send a runner round soon.' The staff sergeant sounded as though he was being strangled.

'A what?' A runner! He must have cracked. A runner, round all the vehicles? During the shelling?

He nodded. 'They did it this afternoon . . . to find out who was in each vehicle in case one of them got hit.' It sounded mad but also made sense.

'Right, I want everyone's ID card now. Pass them down.' I got out my notebook, stuck a Maglite torch in my mouth and started scribbling down numbers, ranks and names. At last I was doing something positive. It was a great tonic and, I'm convinced, stopped me from losing it. As I scrawled my mind retreated a step or two back from the edge of panic. There was one card missing.

'He hasn't got one. The boilerman's a local.' The staff sergeant nodded towards the youth next to me.

'*Kako se zoves? What's your name?*' The boy was trembling. He half whispered something, Darko, Dario, Mario or something. I couldn't quite get it so simply wrote down *boilerman – local*.

The shelling continued sporadically, the gaps between the salvos increasing. Five minutes passed. Nothing. Another couple of minutes. Still nothing. For the first time I noticed it was freezing in the vehicle. Suddenly the door lever sprang upwards. A helmeted soldier poked his head in.

'Who's in this one?'

'Here you go. It's all there, if you can read it.' He grabbed the slip and tore off into the night.

We sat there in silence waiting for the corporal's words to throw us into terror. They never came. Eventually, the door was opened. It was the runner again.

'All clear,' he announced cheerfully. 'It's all clear. You can come out now.' I was stunned. All clear? Just like that! 'I suppose someone's rung up the Serbs and asked them if they've finished for the night!' I quipped, more out of relief than sarcasm. But he'd already disappeared.

Stiffly we eased ourselves out of the Spartan. I expected devastation. There was nothing. The sky was cloudless and the moon had risen higher, casting its chilling rays, illuminating soldiers who were clambering out of other vehicles and walking slowly back to the warehouse clutching their sleeping bags.

'Well, I don't know about you, but if they do it again I'm not taking cover in that fucking thing – it's full of petrol.' I was shocked at what we'd done. The staff sergeant mumbled his agreement. There was more to it than just the petrol and the exposed position of the vehicle. The worst of it had been the claustrophobic and narcotic effect of being in close proximity to other people's terror. We'd all set each other off.

Next to the boiler room door stood a large square chimney running up the outside of the building but offset from the wall by about two and a half feet. Where it disappeared into the ground, between wall and chimney, was a concrete-lined well about four feet deep. Perfect for two people. That's where we'd be going next time.

Together we found a couple of hefty slabs of concrete, a manhole cover and some sandbags, enough to create some form of overhead cover against splinters. Twenty minutes of grunting and heaving warmed us up considerably. I was pleased. The chances of a shell actually landing on us were slim. Satisfied that we knew where we'd be going next time, we retraced our steps into the warehouse and parted company.

In the warehouse I spotted Brigadier Cumming, Colonel Field and his RSM, Graeme Furguson. They were chatting and laughing, an encouraging sign. Someone had produced an urn of sweet tea. There was plenty of nervous chatter and laughter, a strange but perfectly normal reaction to stress. I asked the Brigadier where he'd got to.

'Oh, I had a marvellous time. I was in the command APC. They even made me a cup of tea!' He seemed quite relaxed about things. I recalled the 432s clustered somewhere round the back of the building. At least he would have been spared the running commentary and the clock-watching.

The CO and RSM were doing their leadership bit, moving among the soldiers and chatting. It all helped. It was time to try and get some kip so I wandered back to my sleeping bag only to be confronted by a disturbing sight.

Standing in the half-shadow, just beyond our bergens and sleeping bags, were three soldiers. With them was a young Sapper lieutenant supported by two others. He seemed to be trying to get away from them. But, they weren't so much trying to restrain him as calm him. One was holding his left arm and patting his shoulder while the other was attempting to soothe him. He seemed oblivious to them both. His eyes, unfocused, wild and staring, said it all. His lips trembled slightly. Occasionally he'd gulp hard and nod his head, but his eyes just kept staring. He'd had it. Genuinely shell-shocked.

'He all right?' I asked, approaching.

The one on the left shot me a glance. 'He had a bad time of it this afternoon. This last lot . . .' He didn't bother finishing the sentence.

'He'll be fine,' chimed in the second, which really meant 'leave us alone'. I was only too glad to. It was unnerving seeing someone's soul stripped bare, so starkly reminding me of my own terror.

I thought the Serbs were bound to shell us again so I didn't bother taking anything off. Somehow I managed to cram myself into the sleeping bag still wearing the flak jacket, but I couldn't zip the bag up over the bulk. It was a wretched night and I suppose I was still edgy. I dozed fitfully on the cold concrete while freezing air seeped into the bag. They had the last laugh: there was no more shelling that night.

Breakfast was a subdued affair. I found a place opposite Seb at one of the wooden trestle tables in the makeshift canteen in one of the halls. He was talking about the shelling, banging on as if none of us had been there. I suppose it was just a delayed reaction or just his way of getting it out of his system but it was irritating and he was making me distinctly nervous. I didn't need an action replay over breakfast.

'Seb, it's over, it's passed. Just drop it.' It was precisely the wrong thing to say. He rounded on me angrily.

'Yeah, that's right, rufty tufty Para. Easy for you to play it cool, especially if you've been through it loads of times. For some of us it was our first time.'

I was stunned by his presumption. Suddenly, I didn't feel like breakfast, got up and walked off. In the following six months Seb and I could barely stand to be in the same room as each other. The atmosphere would always be tense and uncomfortable. Was it because he thought I'd seen him lose it that night? Who knows. It's strange and sad what these things do to people.

Before we left Brigadier Cumming inspected the night's damage. In the compound where we'd taken cover in the Spartans stood a row of four-tonne trucks some thirty metres forward of the APCs. Nearly all were shrapnel-damaged and sagging forlornly on punctured tyres. The walls of the warehouse were deeply scarred. To one side of the warehouse two Land Rovers had been completely destroyed. A shell had landed fifteen metres on the other side of the compound fence and shrapnel had ripped through their soft aluminium sides, turning them into sieves. It was a sobering sight.

Not one shell had landed within the compound. Further analysis revealed that the shells had landed some 100 metres forward of the camp with the nearest landing about seventy metres away. How could the Serbs have managed to converge all their guns on one spot and yet drop all the rounds short? Maybe it had been deliberate, a warning – stop allowing the Croats to fire their guns from behind UN buildings. Another suggestion was that they'd intended to hit the warehouse but had been working from old and inaccurate maps. I doubted it; they'd recorded that particular DF during the day and would have known to 'add one hundred'.

In all some thirty-three 152mm shells had been fired that night. Astonishingly, no one had been hit. Two things had saved us. The first was the row of four-tonne trucks which had absorbed some of the shrapnel, the second that the Serbs had been using old stocks of shells which had burst into large lumps of jagged metal. Although these looked menacing, they travelled less far and quickly lost their energy. Modern artillery rounds fragment into splinters one third of the size and travel three times further. We'd been lucky. The TSG incident so disturbed the politicians back home that a Naval Task Force, including a regiment of 105mm light guns, was quickly dispatched to the Adriatic.

We departed TSG at 0900 hours. Brigadier Cumming was keen to get back to Tac in Fojnica as quickly as possible. Another crisis was brewing. While we'd been racing down to TSG, a French APC transporting the Bosnian Deputy Prime Minister, Hakija Turajlic, to the airport in Sarajevo had been stopped by Chetniks, Serb irregulars. After a stand-off, they'd gained access to the APC through the rear door, machine-gunned the interior and murdered the Deputy. The UN's future in Bosnia looked short-lived.

We crossed the almost featureless Duvno plain before picking up the road which ran along the plain's eastern edge. At the Lipa checkpoint the Brigadier decided that we'd reach Fojnica quicker if we took Route Square along the Dugo Polje valley and thence drop down off the 'mountain' to Jablanica. It was a favourite route and spectacularly beautiful. We drove for half an hour in silence. Eventually Corporal Fox broke it.

'Well, I don't know about you ... ,' he drawled, addressing no one in particular, '. . . in a way I'm glad we went there, but I wouldn't ever want to go through that again.' We said nothing. There was nothing to say. He'd spoken for us all.

We'd begun the descent into a breathtakingly steep valley – a wild, almost prehistoric place of towering black mountains, jagged rocks and shimmering ice, both bleak and forbidding. Some of the previous night's terror entered my thoughts. How on earth had I got myself into this mess? Almost a year earlier, amid the arid wastes of Iraq and Kuwait, I'd been desperate to get to Yugoslavia. Now I wasn't quite so sure I hadn't made a terrible mistake – one all of my own making.

THREE

Operation Bretton

October 1997 – Ian, UK

I'm sitting down, leaning forward, my stomach a fire of anger and fear. Legs crossed, one foot kicking uncontrollably.

I'm fiddling like mad with my watch strap. I can feel the fire welling up about to engulf me. I'm struggling to suppress tears of rage and frustration. I'm trying to explain but I'm just burbling incoherently. The man opposite me is a saint. I've met him before – in a past life. I mean, he's *seen* me before, after the first time. He's a lieutenant colonel, also a psychiatrist, the only one worth seeing. His name is Ian. He's got a clipboard and a pen, but he's not writing. He's just looking at me, listening to me ranting.

'I should have come to see you a long time ago, but I couldn't. You just can't . . . I mean, you try and get on with your life, put the past in a box and sit on the lid by busying yourself . . . of course, *they'll* always tell you that the support is there – all you have to do is ask. But it's not really there at all . . . let me tell you, your sort of help is virtually inaccessible.'

'How do you mean, Milos?' He's frowning.

'It's the culture . . . it's a cultural thing.'

'Culture?'

'Culture, macho Army culture. Can you understand what I'm saying? Y'know, you're a major in the Parachute Regiment or whatever. In that culture you can't show weakness or flaws. No one can. You're supposed to be strong. So you wander around keeping it all inside, pretending everything's okay . . . you bluff those around you, you bluff yourself . . .' I'm close to tears now, '. . . but deep down you know you're not well. You're ill and need help but you can't ask for it because you're trapped in a straitjacket which is put on you by your peers, by the culture, by yourself . . . because you *are* the culture . . .'

'So, why are you here now, Milos?' his voice is soft and gentle, probing. 'Why did you ask to see me?'

I stare out of the window at the sea. *Why indeed?* It's choppy and green-grey. The waves are flecked with white horses. *Why?* The nightmare of the last five days flashes through my mind. It had been an unimaginable nightmare – it still is – and had it not been for Niki, my girlfriend, I'm not sure I'd be sitting here with Ian.

I'd held myself together long enough to answer their questions. They hadn't finished with my house until past six in the evening. The questioning – in an interview room, all taped – had started at six thirty. Fortunately Issy, my solicitor, and I had been able to see the questions beforehand. It was all about phone numbers, phone calls to the former Yugoslavia, just as I'd expected. Most were instantly explicable and innocuous. It boiled down to three which weren't. I told them the truth, but not all of it. I couldn't bring myself to start talking about the List and about Rose and Smith. They'd have to find that out for themselves. The interview had lasted for no more than about twenty minutes, after which one of the policemen unexpectedly announced that I was on police bail. Just like that.

Curiously, he'd looked at his watch. 'We'll get this thing wrapped up by Christmas, so, let's say bailed until eleven o'clock on 11 December – back here at Guildford police station.' I was stunned. *Oh, you're confident of yourself, mate. Think you'll get this cracked in a couple of months? You're about to open up a real can of Balkan worms.*

Before Issy left and I was handed back to the Army, she let slip two snippets of information – something about the Bosnian ambassador making a complaint and that the police had mentioned that they'd seized my diary from Bosnia, which apparently contained 'evidence of disaffection with the West's policies'.

After the questioning, I was led to another room where two colonels from Bracknell were waiting. One was in a suit and the other, a very tall, thin Guards officer, was in uniform. The Guards officer simply read out a typewritten statement from Bracknell to the effect that, due to the serious nature of my arrest, my vetting had been revoked and I therefore could not continue on the course. Forthwith I'd be posted to the Parachute Regiment's headquarters in Aldershot. With that he dropped the paper into his brief-case, snapped it shut and brushed past me without so much as glancing in my direction. I felt like dirt, a leper standing there with no tie or belt.

The other colonel, Dennis Hall, was kinder. He explained that he'd been tasked to look after me. He asked me not to discuss the case with him and, with that, his driver drove us the ten miles to Farnham. It was dark and raining heavily.

My house had been taken apart. They'd removed just about anything they could lay their hands on. On the table lay a number of blue seizure of property forms. The words 'OPERATION BRETTON' were printed across the top of each. They had mounted an operation against me.

I'd quickly scanned the house. None of it really made sense. Why had they left that? That would have been useful to them. Why had they taken a whole pile of novels and Latin textbooks, and a sheaf of sandpaper? What possible purpose could they serve? Why had they taken that picture but left that one? Then I spotted it.

They left a Coke can in the kitchen. I don't drink Coke at home – ever. They were drinking and eating while ransacking my house and then left their rubbish behind. A specialist search team? Nothing but a bunch of incompetents. They're not professionals, they're just Plod from the MoD.

I'd found a bottle of red wine in the fridge. At least they hadn't touched that. Having opened it I then rang my mother. I had to. She was alone in Cornwall.

'What!! Milos, I don't believe it! After all you've done for them . . .' Her voice was cracking and breaking over the connection. Then she got angry, 'It's the Muslims, Milos, the Muslims and the Americans!'

Things happen either by cock-up or by conspiracy. In my experience, usually the former. In any event the phone was probably tapped so I asked her not to jump to any conclusions and told her that a mistake had probably been made. I didn't believe a word of it and neither did she. We agreed not to tell my sister.

Half an hour later L-P, a friend from the Army, called from a bar in London. He'd been interviewed by the MoD Police while I'd been in my cell. 'Milos, don't worry. I'm behind you all the way. One hundred per cent.' He couldn't discuss anything, certainly not over the phone. I didn't want to know anyway. All he had to do was tell the truth. I trust him with my life. His call perked me up slightly.

As I polished off the wine I stared at what was left of my house. It wasn't mine anymore. It was theirs now – they'd taken my life, my mementoes, dismantled my museum and carted off a large part of me. I was a squatter in my own home. I felt hollow and sick – *this is what it must feel like to be violated!*

I awoke the next morning curled up in a little sweating ball. I'd had another of those vivid dreams from over there. Everything was an effort; dragging myself out of bed, shaving – I'm staring at myself in the mirror, mindlessly pulling the razor across my face. I'm staring into my eyes. I can still look at myself in the mirror, because I know the truth. But I feel like shit. I've got this horrible squirming, sinking feeling in my stomach. I feel weak, sweaty and queasy. I stare at myself, razor frozen in mid stroke – *Traitor? No.*

I smoked a couple of cigarettes. At nine-thirty Colonel Hall arrived to take me to Bracknell to clear out my room. Before we reached the car he stopped, looked around and said in a low voice, 'Look, I'm breaking the rules by saying this . . . don't feel as though you're on your own in this. You're not. A lot of people are backing you on this but they can't tell you. People like Rose and Smith cast long shadows.' It was something to cling to.

When we arrived at Bracknell the students were in a lecture. Just as well because I didn't want to see any of them. Plod had gutted my room – laptop, printer, keyboard, monitor, books, books, books – all issued – gone. Gone also one copy of *Playboy*, my Service Dress jacket and my medals. They'd even unpicked my miniatures from my Mess Dress jacket.

It took me less than half an hour to pack up my room. We then drove back to Farnham in convoy. I dumped my stuff without bothering to unpack it and jumped in with Colonel Dennis. Next stop Regimental Headquarters, The Parachute Regiment in Aldershot to see my new Commanding Officer, Lieutenant Colonel Joe Poraj-Wilczynski, the Regimental Colonel. We're old friends. He was shocked, didn't really know what it was all about. All he'd heard was that I'd been arrested, kicked out of Staff College and that I was to be under him for welfare matters. Joe gave me a cup of coffee and Colonel Dennis returned to Bracknell saying he'd send his driver back for me. I still had to collect the motorbike.

Joe and I chatted for about an hour. He explained that, as my CO, he couldn't be privy to any details about the case and that we'd have to confine our conversations to other matters. This was a blow. I was rapidly running out of people to talk to.

The driver took me back to Bracknell. When we arrived I discovered that I had to go and see my Divisional Colonel, Colonel Hamish Fletcher, also a Para and an old acquaintance. As I walked into his office he stood up and just stared at me. It looked as though he'd been crying, but he hadn't – bad flu. Concern and worry were etched across his face.

'Has someone stitched you up, Milos?'

'Don't know, Colonel.' Really I didn't.

He continued, 'I'm not supposed to say this to you or talk to you about it but, when you were arrested we had a meeting with them and I told him in no uncertain terms. I told the spook that . . .'

'Spook? Y'sure, Colonel? It was MoD Police who arrested me.'

'No, this guy was definitely a spook and I told him, "You better make sure you've got this right. He's thirty-four, last chance at Staff College, and you've just blown his career apart. If you've got this wrong he could just turn round, resign and sue the MoD!"'

I blanched. *Thanks for the support, but I wish you hadn't said that. Now they'll be under added pressure to prove a case, to fabricate something.*

'Your posting order's being sorted out now. I'm popping over to Aldershot this afternoon with it. Where will you be?' I told him I'd wait in Joe's office and with that I went, collected the bike and sped off to Aldershot.

Colonel Joe had some more unpleasant news for me. He produced a long secret signal which he'd received from someone in the MoD. It was a set of Draconian instructions detailing what I could and couldn't do. I was forbidden from having any contact with anyone in the Services and discussing the case. If I did they'd be obliged instantly to record the details of the conversation and report them to the MoD Plod. But I was free to organise my own defence!

Colonel Hamish arrived at five with the paperwork. He told me that General Rupert Smith had phoned him from Northern Ireland and that his first question had been, 'Has he been spying for the Serbs?' Colonel Hamish had told him 'no'.

'Well, you told him right, Colonel. I haven't been spying for the Serbs!'

Before I left for Farnham, Joe asked me if there was anything he could do for me on the welfare front. I'd thought about it long and hard in the cell and throughout the day.

'There's only one thing I want right now, Colonel. I want to see a doctor, and not just any doctor.' I told him about Ian. Joe wanted to see me on Monday. Till then I was free to do my own thing.

I arrived home at five-thirty with a splitting headache. I hadn't eaten for forty-eight hours but I wasn't in the least bit hungry. I tried to turn the key but the front door was already unlocked. Niki was lying on the sofa with Frankie, her dog. She'd come down from London for the night. She had a christening in Camberley the next day and we'd made the arrangement the previous weekend. She smiled brightly at me. 'I'm bored with this revision. How's your day been?' She had an Open University exam to sit on the following Wednesday.

I sat down heavily in the armchair, loosened my tie and just stared at her. She frowned.

'Notice anything different about the house, Niki?'

Her frown deepened. 'No, not really. Well, sort of cleaner, less junk. Come to think of it, have you had a clearout?'

'Sort of . . .' I closed my eyes and took a deep breath – *here goes!* – 'Nix, I was arrested for espionage on Thursday . . . I'm on police bail . . .'

She stared back at me uncomprehendingly. The next four days were a nightmare, so bad that I can't recall them.

And now I'm sitting in front of this bloke Ian, who's asking me why I'm here. I'm staring out of the window wondering why there are no yachts out there on the sea. Must be at least a force six – perfect day for a sail . . . *Why am I here?*

'Why am I here, Ian? . . . I'll tell you why. I'm here because I've got nothing left, nothing. That's why I'm here.'

'Nothing at all?'

'That's right, nothing!' I struggle to control my voice. 'Look! The Army's a great life-support machine. It provides you with all sorts of crutches . . . well, life-jackets really. They keep you afloat and everything looks fine to the casual observer . . .'

'Life-jackets?'

'Precisely that. The uniform is a life-jacket, so is the job. They prop you up and keep you going . . . you know, you stick on the uniform and the beret and bingo! You're a company commander. But when you take off the uniform, when you get home in the evenings or at the weekend and you step through the front door – alone – you step back into the museum and the pause button on the machine in your head gets pressed. The tape starts running again, and you're back there. You're somebody else and you're back there. Everything else is irrelevant because being back there is more real.'

'Where's there, Milos?'

'The Dark Side, Ian. You're back on the Dark Side. That's what we called Serb-held territory. That's it then, by day or during the week you're a major, Parachute Regiment, MBE, company commander or student. But at night or during the weekends you're somebody else, you're Stanley again . . . Mike Stanley, fixer, useful tool. You won't believe this, Ian, but people still ring me up and call me "Mike". Geordie does all the time. And I still get letters dropping onto the carpet addressed to this person called Mike Stanley . . . there are still people out there who don't know me as anything other than Mike Stanley!'

'And now? Who are you now?' he asks gently.

I think hard. I'm not sure of the answer. 'I'm both, Ian. Or maybe I'm nothing . . . a hybrid, a monster.'

I lapse into silence. I'm fiddling with the bezel of my watch – round and round and round, click, click, click, click, click, click. Ian's waiting for me to say something. A thought enters my head and makes me instantly furious. I look directly at Ian.

'I still can't believe it, really, I can't . . . I mean, you can't dream up a more tragic joke. It's a sick joke!'

'What is?'

'Names, Ian. Our names! I mean, I can't believe it. We've got thirty years experience in Northern Ireland, thirty years of living with the terrorist threat, thirty years of developing systems and procedures for personal security, of protecting people's identities . . . and what do we do with all that experience? Do we transfer it to the Balkans . . . ?' I'm gulping for air. I didn't wait for him to answer, '. . . do we hell!! D'you know what names they gave the three of us? The first two they called Abbott and Costello. Can you believe it? And then I flew out as Laurel and then they changed my name to Stanley . . . Abbott, Costello, Laurel and Stanley. Big joke, Ian. Very funny if it wasn't so serious. It's our lives they're playing with!' I'm breathless, furious, almost shouting.

And then quietly, 'Ian, Abbott was blown after only three months there. The Croats found out who he was, threatened to kill him, just because he was a Serb. He was removed from theatre within twenty-four hours. He never came back.' I lapse back into silence. Staring at my boots. *Big joke.*

'Has it always been like this, Milos?'

'Like what?'

'This double life of yours. Has it got progressively worse or has it stayed the same? You've been back two-and-a-half years now . . .'

I'm not sure what to say. I think hard for a moment, '. . . '95 was quite bad, the last half of '95. I had a naff job with the Territorial Army up north, did a parachute refresher course, my Company Commanders Course. It sort of kept me busy, but I was back there when I wasn't busy. 1996 was so busy, that's when I was Company Commanding in 1 PARA – twice in the States, once in Northern Ireland, once in France, in between exercises. Just didn't stop, I wasn't on the Dark Side much. Thought I'd cracked it. Put all my demons in the box and locked the lid.'

'And?'

'And then, Ian, I went to Shrivenham. Nightmare. Suddenly you're a student along with ninety-nine others, all on an equal footing. No responsibility, except for yourself; no soldiers to look after; no careers to manage. This year has been a nightmare. It's just got worse and worse. More and more polarised. It's the routine.'

'Routine?'

'Predictable, bloody routine. Monday morning to Friday afternoon you're a student. Live in a room there. Work hard. Drink Diet Coke only, watch the diet and become an obsessive fitness fanatic.'

'And then?'

'And then, get home Friday evening. Walk through the door of the museum. Tape starts playing and I'm there again on the Dark Side. Sink a bottle of red wine, stagger up to the pub, few pints of Guinness . . .'

'How many?'

'Five or six maybe. Sometimes I get a kebab, sometimes I forget to eat all weekend. Saturday's the same. So's Sunday. I'm there on the Dark Side with all my friends, dead and alive. And then Monday morning I drive to Shrivenham where I'm a student again, for another four and a half days. And that was my life. You keep it all inside you.'

There's a long silence. 'That's why I'm here, Ian. I'm here because when something like this happens, something big that explodes your fragile world, something that removes all your crutches and life-jackets . . .' I can feel tears welling, that's when you realise that all those things were nothing, that you're still where you've always been – on the Dark Side . . .'

'Is that where you are now?'

I shrug, not trusting myself to speak. Not really knowing the answer.

Another long silence. Ian very quietly, 'Do you want to come back?'

I can't speak. I nod my head and then shake it. *I really don't know.*

Ian's scribbling something. I try to get a grip of myself.

'How do you see the future?' he asks quietly.

'Sorry?' He's suddenly changed tack and caught me by surprise.

'Do you see a future for yourself? I mean how do you see your future?'

'I don't. There isn't one. There is no future on the Dark Side. I suppose I've been drifting ever since I got back. I'm still there, but I'm back. Does that make sense?'

Ian nods. We've been at it over an hour. Me burbling, him listening and making the occasional note.

I'm staring out at the sea again. It's getting dark there. Winter's definitely on its way. It's dark, cold and lonely out there. Ian's asking me a whole load of practical questions: sleep patterns, dreams, panic attacks? Alcohol intake, diet? How's your libido? Sex life? Steady relationship? I answer him as best I can, but I don't take my eyes off the sea. My answers are automatic. I know myself so well by now, I don't even have to think about the answers.

'If we're to do any meaningful work we need some sort of structure to work from. When did you last see me?' He sounds quite businesslike now.

I'm still looking at the sea. 'November '93 after my first year there.'

'That's right. I've got the notes somewhere, but I think it would help if you took me through it . . . from the beginning . . .'

'The beginning?' *The beginning? When was that? Where did it begin? This century? Last century? When I was born? The recruiting office in Plymouth? It began all over the place. Where to start? Kuwait in the desert, that's as good a place as any.*

'Milos?'

'Yes.'

'Where did it start? What was it like?' *What was it like?*

I tear my eyes from the sea and stare at Ian. I don't really see him. *What was it like?*

I'm speaking slowly now, more measured. 'It started in Kuwait and turned into a living nightmare. It was a completely upside down world – Alice-Through-the-Looking-Glass – warped, weird, back-to-front. I can't begin to explain what it was like.'

'Well, why don't you just tell me about the job? Start there.'

'Job? Interpreter?' I pause for a moment. *Was that it? Just that?* 'Only for a short while, Ian, just at the beginning.' I'd hated interpreting. It had given me hideous headaches and in any case I just didn't have that computer-like brain that the job requires.

'Well, what *was* your job then?' *What was it? How do you describe it? It doesn't exist in any job description that the Army has ever heard of. What was it . . . in a nutshell?* I'm thinking hard now and it comes, absurd though it sounds.

'Ian, I was a fixer.'

'A fixer?'

'Yeah, that's right – a fixer, a sort of go-between . . . for the UN, for Rose and Smith . . . you know *"go-and-wave-your-magic-wand"* stuff.'

'That's the job they gave you?' He sounds incredulous.

'No, not really. It sort of just happened by accident. It evolved I guess . . . by accident.'

'Okay then, but what exactly did it involve?' I can see he's not getting it.

'Involve? Just about everything. As I've just said: *"go and wave your magic wand at the Serbs . . . fix this . . . sort that problem out . . . get 'em to see it this way . . . get the hostages released . . ."* on and on and on. There was no job description, just sort of made it up as I went along.'

'How?'

'History, that's how. By prostituting myself, not my body . . . but my history, my family history . . . I was a sort of historical prostitute. I prostituted my background and my soul to get close to those people.'

'Which people?'

'The Serbs. Just them. Hid it from the others, the Muslims and Croats. They'd have killed me had they found out. They tried to kill Nick Abbott. This is serious shit, Ian. You don't fuck around with these people.'

'Did it work? I mean, this prostitution.'

'Did it work? Did it! Why do you think I spent two years out there? It worked all right . . . worked a treat. It was a sort of Barclaycard, y'know, gets you in anywhere. Gets you into their mentality and into their minds. Problem is, once you're in you end up playing mind games with them.'

'Mind games?'

'That's right. Three-D mental chess. Trouble is, once you're in their minds, they're in yours too . . . they're still there, that lot . . . and you engage in this bizarre struggle of wills. Did it work? Too bloody well. It worked too well and that's the problem. It just never ends.'

'How do you mean *too well*?'

'*Too well* means that you become a sort of useful tool and everyone wants a bit of you. As I said, it's never over. It never ends.'

'But you've been back a while now, Milos. Surely it's over.'

'It's never over. You know, you come back. No one bothers to debrief you. No one grabs you and tells you it's over. So, you drift along never really sure whether you're going back or not. No one tells you a thing. You just don't know.'

'But surely you'd started a new job, done your courses. Surely that's enough?' This is getting exasperating. He's just not getting it.

'No it isn't. Listen,' I can feel the anger rising again, 'I come back and guess what? Two months later I'm at this wedding. Mark Etherington's marrying Chelsea Renton, the MP's daughter. I'm at this wedding, this is mid-June 1995, and General Mike Jackson comes up to me, he's the bloke I delivered all those parcels for, on behalf of his au pair . . .'

'What parcels?'

'I was Postman Pat out there, but I'll tell you about that later. I even fixed up a meeting for him with Mladic once, but anyway, so he comes up to me at the wedding and slaps me on the back and says, *"Ah, Milos, well done, good to see you back . . . done more than anyone could have asked of you . . . no need for you to go back . . . got a good career to crack on with . . . get yourself to Staff College etc etc etc . . ."* and then what?'

'Go on.'

'Six and a half months later, on 2 January 1996, on the day that I've taken over command of A Company 1 PARA in Aldershot, I get this phone call. It's Will Buckley, the Regimental Adjutant, and he says to me, *"General Jackson's been pinged to be the IFOR Commander Multinational Division South West in Bosnia and has asked for you to go out with him."* Can you believe it? One minute it's one thing and the next it's quite another. So, you see, it's never really over. You just don't know . . .'

'Why didn't you go back out?'

'Simple. The Muslims would have killed me. Jackson's not the only one. Three months after that we get a new second-in-command in 1 PARA – Paul, who has just come from a staff job in the MoD and he tells me that, at the same time Jackson was asking for me, his boss, who is also pinged to deploy his HQ into Sarajevo also asks for me – *"let's get Stanley out. He'll give us the inside track on the Serbs."* See what I mean . . .' I'm shouting at him again, '. . . which is it? I mean, what do these people want? One minute they give you an MBE for your work out there. The next they arrest you as a spy! Who's mad here? Me or them?' I lapse into silence, exhausted.

We stare at each other. 'No, Ian – that's the way we did that. Historical prostitute . . . funny if it wasn't so tragic, being a prostitute.'

Ian's picked up his board again. He doesn't bother writing while I'm raving at him. He's talking softly now, 'Let's forget about Bosnia for a moment. Why don't you tell me about your family? Let's start with that, shall we. That seems to be the root of all this.' His voice is very soothing, compelling, almost narcotic.

'My family! Have you got all night? There's more history here than anyone can cope with. Sure you're up to it?'

'Only if you are.'

'We've been at it for most of the century. All over the place. Even the Army can't figure out what I'm supposed to be. On my PAMPUS computer record they've got me down as "BRIT NAT/FOREIGN" for my nationality at birth and current nationality. What's that supposed to mean? "FOREIGN"?'

Ian just shrugs. There's no answer to that sort of question.

'I suppose it's their way of labelling someone if they can't work out where they're really from. You've got to sympathise with them to a certain extent. It's a nightmare trying to work out what's what in our family this century.'

'So, tell me about it.'

'Okay. Best place to start is with my maternal grandmother, Jessie Constance Millar Rowan. A Scot. I suppose that's what the Army means by "FOREIGN". She was from a wealthy Ayrshire family who were shipping-line owners in the last century. Of course, she had the best schooling – Paris and Cheltenham Ladies – and pretty much did nothing other than look after a menagerie at home and drive around Scotland. She was somewhat eccentric, though. She had no brothers, so in a peculiar sort of way became the son her father never had. She'd sit there with him after dinner, at the age of fifteen, smoking cigars and drinking port. She also wore a monocle for some reason. When the Great War broke out she nursed with the VADs in France and then in Malta during the Gallipoli campaign. After that she had a brief but disastrous driving job in London with the War Office from which she was sacked for being rude to an American general whom she'd accused of coming into the war three years too late. That wasn't the end of her driving career, though. She ended up as a Scottish Women's Hospital ambulance driver on the Salonika front in the Balkans where the British, French and Serbs were holding the line in the Macedonian mountains. There she met her future husband, a Serbian officer called Vladimir Ilija Dusmanic.

'He was from a grand Belgrade family. His father had been Minister for Education in Nikola Pasic's government in Serbia. Both Vladimir and his younger brother, Branko, were educated at the Pazhovski Institute in Russia. He went on to study law in Moscow but was recalled to Serbia in 1911 when the Balkan war against the Turks broke out. Branko never returned from Russia. He was at one of the Tzar's cadet academies and disappeared in the Revolution, no doubt eliminated by the Bolsheviks. My grandmother met Vladimir Dusmanic on the Salonika front. He was close friends with Prince Alexander, who later became King of Yugoslavia. He was in uniform for the best part of eight years, by the end of which he'd been decorated with the Milos Obilic Gold medal for Valour, the VC equivalent. Nice, but his education had been blown to bits by all these wars.

'He and my grandmother lost touch at the end of the war. She went back to her pets in Scotland and he was sent to Paris to finish off his law studies. After that he joined the diplomatic service and was posted to London where he was the Third Secretary at the Serbian Legation. From there he tracked down Constance, pursued her to Scotland and they were married in Ayr in 1920. That was just the beginning of it.

'He left the diplomatic service because the thought of rushing around Europe with my grandmother's pets was too much for him. He went back to law in Belgrade where they built a home in Dedinje, just opposite what is now Milosevic's palace, and settled down. They had four children – three daughters, of which my mother was the second, and a son. Most were actually born in Scotland.'

'How come?'

'Oh, don't think they lived in penury in Belgrade. They had an extraordinary life. At least once a year they'd jump into the Bentley and drive from Belgrade to Ayr. It only took four days. On one occasion my grandmother was escort for ten days to the Duchess of York, when she and the future King George VI were visiting Belgrade in the early 1920s. So, all in all, they were pretty well-connected at court. The children received English and then Swiss finishing school educations, though they were removed from Switzerland as Nazism took hold of Germany and it looked as though Europe was heading towards another war. At the end of March 1941 they had to escape from Yugoslavia.'

'Why?'

'It's obvious. Germany was about to attack in the Balkans. My grandfather was back in uniform as a lieutenant colonel and was the Royal Yugoslav Army's liaison officer in the British Embassy in Belgrade. A few days prior to the German bombing of Belgrade and the invasion of Yugoslavia the Brits warned my grandfather and told him to get his family out of the country. Any family with connections at court was earmarked for liquidation by the Nazis. So he rang my grandmother, told her to get the children packed – one suitcase each – and to leave that very day. And that's exactly what happened. They grabbed what they could and fled south by train that same night. My grandmother never saw her husband again after that call from the British Embassy. He stayed on to fight the Germans and died in 1943.'

'What happened to your grandmother?'

'She and the four children escaped by train, south to Istanbul initially and then over the Bosphorus into Asia Minor and down to the port of Mersin in southern Turkey. They stayed in Mersin for nearly a week hoping to catch a refugee ship across the Med to Palestine. Half of middle Europe was mooching about in Mersin having fled from the Germans. Eventually, they got passage on the *Warshawa*, a chartered refugee ship that was crammed with all sorts of aristocracy on the move out of Europe. Four days later they landed in Haifa, Palestine, where the British gave them refugee status and provided them with accommodation.'

'And that's where they sat out the war?'

'Sat out? Hardly. All four children joined up with British Forces Middle East. Yvan, the youngest, lied about his age and got into the Royal Signals. The youngest daughter, Tatjana, joined the Royal Navy as a Wren, while my mother and her elder sister both joined the ATS and were posted to Cairo. My mother became a driver, initially moving tanks about large depots, then graduating to motorcycle dispatch rider and finally ending up driving ambulances during the battle of El Alamein. Her sister worked in SOE Cairo, on account of her Serbo-Croat, where she married a British officer called Rocky. He was an SOE agent and member of Force 133 which fought for Tito against the Germans in the Adriatic. Even got an uncle who fought there in the last war.'

'So, your aunt was the only one involved on the Yugoslav side of things?'

'Initially yes, but eventually my mother was roped into it too, again because she could speak the language. She was posted to a large refugee camp in the Sinai desert which was packed with Croat refugees. From there she was moved into Dr McPhail's "Save the Children" Unit. By the end of 1944 they were in southern Italy preparing to go back to Yugoslavia with their ambulances as part of UNRRA, the United Nations Refugee Rehabilitation Administration. The first ever UN mission. Ironic that my mother should have been sent to Yugoslavia. In March 1945 she landed in Dubrovnik with her ambulance and spent the remainder of that year driving around Bosnia, Hercegovina and Montenegro dispensing aid to orphans. At one stage she managed to get up to Belgrade to check on the house. There was nothing left of it. German nurses had used it during the war but when the Russians arrived in Belgrade they'd used it as accommodation for a platoon. The Russians had stolen everything and defecated in every conceivable corner of the house.

'She was eventually demobbed and returned to England to join her mother, sisters and brother, who were also now "out". They lived for a while in Godmanchester in Cambridgeshire. Mum did Russian at the School of Eastern European and Slavonic Languages and even got a job as an interpreter in the 1948 London Olympics. Grandmother's health wasn't good, though. It was a combination of ill-health and poor English weather which forced them to emigrate to Rhodesia. They bought ten acres just north of Salisbury, built a house and settled down to grow flowers. My grandmother died in 1957, well before I was born. I never knew her, nor my grandfather who was left behind in Yugoslavia and died before the end of the war. In fact I never knew any of my grandparents, not even on my father's side – all because of the last war really.'

'And you end up in Bosnia fifty years later with the UN.'

'Correct. Three generations, all fiddling around in the Balkans during three different wars. A novelist couldn't have written that one.'

'I suppose you're going to tell me that your father was in the UN as well.' Ian's laughing.

'No. That side of the story's quite different. There are parallels with my mother's side of the family, but nothing as grand and aristocratic. His father also fought on the Salonika front in the First World War, but as a warrant officer in the artillery. But that's not to say he was a peasant or anything like that. In fact he was an agricultural specialist who'd been university trained in Prague before the War. They came from a small village in Sumadija called Mrcajevci, in Central Serbia. No great connections at court. My father was born in Kraljevo in 1920. His mother died when he was very young and he was brought up by his two older sisters, the eldest of whom was killed during an Allied bombing raid in 1943. He was educated in Skopje in Macedonia where he was studying law when the Germans invaded. He'd been politically active throughout the 1930s and had been a staunch anti-Communist and supporter of the King.

'When the Germans invaded King Peter fled to London in April 1941 and set up a government in exile. The likes of my father stayed on to fight. You could write a book about what went on in Yugoslavia during the war and still not understand it. Although the Germans occupied the Balkans and fostered Fascism in Croatia, which included in those days all of Bosnia and Hercegovina, they were quite happy to allow the locals to fight it out amongst themselves in a bloody civil war. My father joined the Serbian Volunteer Corps, a Royalist outfit fighting Tito's Communists. He was one of the original volunteers. By the end of the war he was a company commander in an infantry regiment. The commanding officer of his battalion, Ratko Obradovic, eventually became my godfather but was assassinated in an underground car park in Munich in 1968 by Tito's UDBA assassins.'

'Assassinated!'

'That's right. Tito couldn't tolerate anti-Communist opposition from the émigré community, so he had them murdered. The Royalists and Chetniks, under Draza Mihajlovic, were forced to fight a rearguard action withdrawing from Yugoslavia. Some went north to Austria, others, like my father's battalion, went west into Italy. In fact, his war ended on 5 May 1945 when he conducted the last bridge demolition guard of the war. They were holding the bridge over the river Soca, which marked the border between Slovenia and Italy. The bridge had been prepared for demolition and my father's company was on the Slovenian side holding that end of the bridge in order to allow as many refugees as possible to get across into Italy. Russian tanks eventually appeared and they were forced to leg it over into Italy and blow the bridge. End of his war.

'The next day they handed over their weapons to the British in Palmanova and were then carted off to a concentration camp at Eboli, south of Naples. No one really knew what to do with these people so they stayed in that camp for the best part of two years before being moved to other camps in Europe. My father was moved to one near Munich where, in 1947, he was selected by the British as suitable for labour in Britain. The Belgians had already rejected him. At the end of 1947 he stepped off a refugee ship at Southampton docks. No socks, no money and not a word of English. Each person was given a pound as they stepped off the gangplank; my father remembered his first purchase, a pair of socks, and his first meal, fish and chips, wrapped up in newspaper. I remember him laughing about this, how shocked and horrified that such a cultured people could eat their food with fingers from newspaper.

'The deal for all these displaced people from Eastern Europe was simple. Three years labour in exchange for the right of abode but not citizenship. For three years my father, ex-law student, ex-officer, was a hod carrier at the London Brick Company factory in Bedfordshire. That did his back in. Still couldn't speak a word of English and by the time he'd worked off his obligation to the British government he still wasn't integrated into society in any way. To put that right he lived with an English family in Ealing and gradually learned the language. He also put himself through night school and taught himself electronics. By day he swept the floors of the Rank Bush Murphy television and radio factory at Chiswick. By night he studied for his degree. By the end of the 1950s he'd qualified as an electrical engineer and was employed by Rank as a TV design engineer.'

Ian's puzzled by something. 'But I thought your mother's lot were in Rhodesia by this stage. How did your parents meet?'

'In 1960 Rank sent him out to Southern Rhodesia to help set up the black and white TV system there. He and my mother met in Salisbury and they married in the Greek Orthodox church. I was born in 1962, my sister fifteen months later. Then, in 1965, Ian Smith declared UDI. My father sniffed another war and wanted no part of it whatsoever. You could hardly blame him. Branko, my maternal grandfather's younger brother, was lost in Russia during the civil war. My mother's father died in 1943 in Yugoslavia. My father never saw his father again after 1945 – he died in 1957 in Serbia. That's why they decided to leave Rhodesia before things got worse.

'We returned to London but most of my cousins stayed on in Rhodesia and fought their Communists in that war. In fact, we've still got the property in Harare. Mum's eldest sister, the one who worked in SOE Cairo, lives there, has a beautiful house.

'My father continued working for Rank in Chiswick. I received a pretty bog standard education. They pumped every penny they could into it; prep school in Leicestershire, minor public school in the West Country where I was head boy and head of the Combined Cadet Force. Father, of course, wanted me to be what he never was – a lawyer. I had other ideas. The day after my last A level – I did Latin, Greek and Ancient History – I walked into the Army recruiting office on Mayflower Street in Plymouth and enlisted in the Parachute Regiment. My father hit the bloody roof. Real drama.'

'Drama?'

'Like you wouldn't believe. But you've got to see it from his point of view. So many upheavals, so much misfortune in both families for so long, it's hardly surprising that the one thing he wanted for me was security. But you're wilful at that age. At eighteen you know best and he just had to live with it.'

Ian has been listening patiently, only asking one or two questions.

'Why didn't your father return to Yugoslavia after the war?'

'Oh, that's because of the code.'

'What code?'

'There was an unwritten code, a rule, among the émigrés. There was to be no returning to Yugoslavia while Tito and the Communists were in power, not for any reason whatsoever. Some weakened towards the end of their lives and went back. He never did. A die-hard to the day he died. I suppose it was because of the assassination of my godfather. He didn't even go back when his own father died. None of us did, except my mother who'd trip out there every couple of years to look after Dad's sole surviving sister, Bisenija. She'd been declared "mad" and an "enemy of the state" by the Yugoslav authorities; she had no state pension, so we had to keep her alive from the UK.'

'That determination never to go back to Yugoslavia is a hard attitude to take, Milos.'

'Hard, but understandable too. It's all a product of history and personal experience.'

'That's a lot of history you're carrying around on your back.'

I'm silent for a moment. 'It's like a sodding monkey hanging off you. Can't complain, though. It's beyond my control. I suppose Trotsky was right in the end.'

'In what way?'

'Well, he said that anyone who wanted a quiet life should not have been born in the twentieth century.'

'Do you think he was right?'

'Looks that way now, doesn't it?'

Ian doesn't reply to that one. He's turned the page on his note pad. The pen's poised again.

'Let's get back to Bosnia, to the present. Pick it up from the start.'

'Even that's all over the place. I could pick any bloody starting point and it still wouldn't make any sense. I mean, I could start in Iraq and Kuwait if you wanted me to, because that's where this mess really began.'

'All right then. Let's start with something concrete.'

'Like what?'

'A date. When exactly did you go out to the Balkans?'

'That's easy! 29 December 1992. How about that, then? There's a date for you.'

'Okay then. Tell me about that and Kuwait if it's relevant.'

'It's all relevant, in its own way.'

I take a deep breath, pause, and then begin.

FOUR

Operation Grapple – UK

Tuesday 29 December 1992 – UK Airspace
The cavernous hold of the C130 was a cacophony of rattling and jangling fittings. As the propeller pitch of the four massive turboprops altered and the blades bit hungrily into the air, the aircraft strained and heaved against its wheel brakes. The vibrations seemed to pummel the eardrums and reach into the very fillings in our teeth. Suddenly the aircraft surged forward, rapidly overcoming its own inertia, and gathering speed as it raced down the runway. The two white Land Rovers strained against the shackles and chains lashing them to the deck. The human cargo in drab, mottled camouflage, stuffed into the impossibly narrow gap left between the wall of the aircraft and two Land Rovers, strapped shoulder-to-shoulder on webbed seats, was thrown rearwards in unison restrained only by primitive seat belts. There is nothing glamorous about flying by Herc. The RAF really is a classless outfit. There's only one class of travel in its aircraft – cattle class. Bump . . . bump . . . bump . . . heavy, solid pneumatic tyres transmitted the force of contact with each join in the runway's slabbed concrete surface, blending with speed into a single continuous battering in the seat of your pants. With a final lurch and a change in attitude tonnes of Herc broke its natural bond with gravity and Flight Lyneham-Split lumbered into the sky. It never ceased to amaze me. Hydraulics hissed, a motor whined and, with a sickening thump, the undercarriage retracted, wheels still spinning into the wheel well. We were airborne. 'Captain Laurel' was finally on his way.

Around me soldiers unbuckled, donned Walkmans, stuffed their heads into the hoods of their Arctic windproof smocks and tried to settle themselves comfortably for the duration of the flight. While they did so, white cardboard boxes were passed down from the front of the aircraft; another delight of flying 'Crab Air' is the interesting in-flight cuisine.

I didn't wait to find out what surprises lurked in my white box. Although I'd been up since half three in the morning, I knew I wouldn't be able to sleep, not with my knees jammed up against the side of the Land Rover. I unbuckled and struggled over knees and legs, made my way to the rear 'port' para door and stuck my nose up against its small, round Perspex window.

We had already reached about 5,000 feet and were still climbing steadily. The sky was cloudless. As far as the eye could see southern England was covered in a crisp coating of icing sugar. A low winter sun cast long shadows, defining perfectly every frozen detail. I could make out the M4. We were just to the south of it, flying due east rather than south, which surprised me. Apart from the colour, the splendid desolation below reminded me so much of the wind-blown wastes of Kuwait and southern Iraq. Was it possible that almost a year had passed? I remembered the day in February when I'd been summoned up to UN Headquarters at Umm Qsar in Iraq. I'd received the bollocking of my life from Major John Wooldridge and been told to 'wind my neck in' about Yugoslavia. I wonder what he'd think if he could see me now?

It had been quite a good one as bollockings go. We'd strolled around the headquarters with its strange blue pyramids. Built by the French, it had been the only working hospital in that part of Iraq. It had survived the Gulf War but not the UN, which had requisitioned it from the unfortunate inhabitants of Umm Qsar and turned it into a headquarters. John never raised his voice once, an effective technique when you're giving someone a roasting. In fact he was positively friendly.

'Look, believe me, I've got your best interest at heart here but I have to warn you,' John had continued, '. . . you're in danger of damaging yourself . . .'

'What do you mean, John? How?' I knew perfectly well what he meant, but I wanted it spelt out.

'Listen to me. What you've got to understand is that Colonel Garret is an old school officer. In his world one just accepts one's lot, bites the bullet and gets on with it. He doesn't take kindly to people bucking the system. It's that simple.'

'Yes, but John, he doesn't understand . . .'

John cut me short, 'Yes he does. He understands perfectly well. And it's not him. He's done his best for you. It's General Greindle. He's the one who's put the chop on it. It's his decision who goes and he's not letting you go. Nothing to do with Colonel Garret at all.'

'But what's Greindle's problem?' General Greindle was an Austrian. He was also the Chief Military Observer of UNIKOM – the main man. A professional UN general, he had quite a record of heading up one UN military mission after another, and knew the 'light blue' system inside out.

'It's almost not even him. It's the UN . . . their rules. It's precisely because you *do* speak the language and because you have a background from there that the UN says you can't go.'

This drama, the cause of my angst, had sprung up out of nowhere six weeks earlier. Just as the novelty of UNIKOM had begun to wane and the boredom of driving round the desert had set in, it had been announced that a number of observers, two of them from the British contingent, were to be sent at short notice to Croatia. Cyrus Vance, the American Secretary of State, had achieved the impossible and secured a permanent cease-fire between the Serbs and Croats, ending a vicious six-month civil war. The UN Security Council had resolved to send a peacekeeping force to Croatia and various UN missions around the globe were hurriedly being stripped of surplus observers in order to carry out an initial recce for the force's subsequent deployment.

Aching to escape the monotony of the desert each of us had speculated wildly as to who would go. Since I spoke Serbo-Croat I'd assumed I'd be the natural choice. It didn't quite work out that way; Major Andy Taylor and Captain Hamish Cameron went and I stayed behind. The logic escaped me: surely it made sense to send someone who could talk to the locals? I was furious but John Wooldridge placated me somewhat and assured me that more observers would be sent and that I'd be sure to go at some point.

Sure enough, a month later UNIKOM announced that an additional fifty observers would be sent to Croatia. Three Brits were selected, including, much to my dismay, Guy Lavender, the only other Para in the contingent. Evidently, my rantings and railings in the desert wastes of the Wadi Al Batin could be heard as far north as Umm Qsar. Someone's patience ran out and I was summoned for an 'interview without coffee'.

'Is it because I can't be trusted? Is that it, John? What about the old officers' integrity thing? You know, I *am* an officer in the British Army. Doesn't that count anymore?' I'd almost convinced myself that was the case.

'It's got nothing to do with that. It's to do with protection – yours and the UN's. It's nothing personal. It's not you.' John really was being quite patient. 'They'd no more send you to Yugoslavia than they would a Greek or Turkish officer to sit on the Green Line in Cyprus. That's the logic of it.'

'I see.' I didn't really, but there was little point in pushing a bad position. I'd never ever considered myself as being from an ethnic minority group. Born in Southern Rhodesia, raised and educated in England, in the Army since eighteen, I'd never had a problem. Suddenly there was one. Now I'd reached the age of twenty-nine my parents' background had risen up and slapped me in the face. Was it as simple as John's argument or was there something else, something to do with trust? It bothered me.

'I'm glad you understand. So, get it into your head that for as long as the UN is in Yugoslavia you won't be going. You will never be going to the Balkans in uniform. Banish that idea from your mind for ever. Get it?'

It all seemed so logical. Anyway, I had no option. There was absolutely nothing more I could do.

'Yes, got it, John.' It didn't make me feel any better though.

'Right, then. Look, you've got your promotion exams in March, so my advice to you is to stop razzing up Colonel Garret and just go back to the desert, get into your books, and just shut up about Yugoslavia.'

That's exactly what I did. Watching our five heroes return from Croatia in April, full of the most incredible stories, had been galling. By that stage we were due to depart for the UK and I'd resigned myself to a six-month course in England. I was also resigned to not going to Yugoslavia.

Somewhere over Reading the Herc banked right and took up a more southerly course. From 10,000 feet the ground detail was crystal clear. We drifted over the M3. I strained to make out familiar features. There was the A325, Farnborough, Queen's Avenue. My eye followed the well-known geography of Aldershot: home of the British Army and of the Paras. I could see Browning Barracks, the Parachute Regiment's Depot. The aircraft outside the museum was just visible, as was the parade square. I could imagine some beast of a platoon sergeant 'rifting' his platoon of recruits, sweating and terrified, around the square.

We'd slipped past Aldershot. I was now straining for a better look through the Perspex, following the network of roads leading south to a small town nestling in a valley. The Herc had climbed higher but it was still possible to trace out the streets. There! My eye fell on a tiny row of seven small terraced houses. Three in – my house. Colin and Melanie would be there. Colin was sure to have made it back from Lyneham by now. At least it would be in good hands. He was a mate from the Regiment.

As I strained to get a better look, Farnham slipped beyond the periphery of the window. I was sad – my first house and I'd barely lived there. I'd arrived back from the Gulf not exactly dripping with money, but I had saved six months of pay. In an uncharacteristic moment of madness I'd blown the lot on the deposit on the house instead of doing something sensible like buying a fast, new motorbike. My parents had been delighted, confident that their son had finally grown up. It made me break out in a cold sweat: mortgage repayments equals commitment equals entrapment equals lack of freedom! I took possession of the keys the day before disappearing on a six-month course and had barely had time to haul over from the Depot two large cardboard boxes containing my worldly possessions, buy a bean bag and a cheap phone.

There was of course the odd weekend off when I tried my hand at painting, but other than that the course was long and thoroughly absorbing, so much so that I barely registered the fact that a war was raging out of control in a place called Bosnia. It seemed to be as bloody and as confusing as the Croatian one. In October the TV reporting in the UK intensified – the British had deployed an armoured infantry battalion out there as part of a new UN force. Barely a day passed when the lunchtime news didn't carry pictures of the Cheshire Regiment's white-painted thirty-tonne Warriors charging down some Bosnian road, or their CO, the flamboyant Lieutenant Colonel Bob Stewart, instantly elevated to a household idol, issuing a statement. It all seemed so distant and I viewed the proceedings with the detached interest of one who knew he wouldn't be going.

The course ended in November. I was sitting in front of the course officer receiving my final interview. I finished reading the report, handed it back to him and stood up.

I stared at him. What was he on about? He must have sensed my confusion.

'Yeah, in fact if I remember correctly, it was September when your postings branch, PB2, rang us up and asked to get you released from the course. They needed interpreters or something to go out with the Cheshires . . .'

'What! You're joking!'

'No . . . interpreters, you know, anyone who can speak the lingo. They'd scoured the Army for them . . . found two others and you. Anyway at the time it was felt that you should stay on the course. Send us a postcard, you lucky bastard.'

I was stunned and couldn't get his words out of my mind as I drove home. By the time I'd arrived I was more than curious to get to the bottom of all this. I rang PB2 within moments of opening the front door.

'I do remember something about that,' the desk officer seemed dubious, '. . . oh yes, that's right, but that was in September. Anyway the moment's passed.'

What did he mean, 'the moment has passed'? The Cheshires had been in theatre barely a month. I rang the Regimental Adjutant, David Bennest. He hadn't actually lined me up with my next job and agreed that he'd speak to somebody at the Army's HQ at Wilton, which was controlling the Bosnia operation. He also ordered me to take three weeks leave.

'You probably need it. Just leave us a contact number. Any ideas where you might go?'

I told him Zimbabwe. I hadn't been back since the Mozambique job. The course had been long and tiring, English winters were revolting and I couldn't think of a better place to recharge the batteries than Zim. It was the natural place to go – back to my birthplace.

The weather was a dream. The garden at Braenada was basking in the heat of a Zimbabwean summer. Elat, the gardener, was capering about in one of the flowerbeds while Tilly, my aunt's Staffie, savaged one of his gumboots. I'm sure she was doing that the last time I'd been to Braenada. Nothing ever seemed to change in Africa. It was an enchanting time warp.

'Do you think they'll send you?' my aunt asked over tea.

'Perhaps . . . who knows, the way this year has panned out I'd say anything is possible.' I blew an almost perfect smoke ring and watched it rise slowly, expanding and distorting until it was a mere wisp of blue.

'Do Mum and Dad know anything about this?' I glanced over at her. Her cup was frozen half way to her lips. She raised a quizzical eyebrow and her grey eyes twinkled knowingly.

'No. Nothing. I haven't told them a thing.'

'Just as well,' she continued, 'you know what your father's like. Such a worrier. He won't like you going to the Balkans one bit.' She was right. It was going to be a very difficult subject to broach.

I stared out over the perfect lawn. Now and then something yapping wildly darted from the shrubs, deftly avoiding Elat's half-hearted kicks.

'No, he won't like it one bit.' She was off again, telling me what I already knew.

'They ruined his life and forced him to flee as a wretched refugee. He's hated them all his life, the Communists . . . and then when they assassinated your godfather . . . no, he'll take this very badly . . .' Her voice trailed off and suddenly perked up, '. . . of course your mother will be delighted. It'll appeal to her sense of adventure. You know what she's like!'

'Oh well, I wouldn't worry about it too much. It's hardly likely to happen. You know what the Army's like. I've a friend in the Regiment who speaks fluent Arabic. Studied it at Cambridge and in Egypt. When the Gulf War broke out he was posted to Northern Ireland!'

Zimbabwe proved to be just the tonic I needed. After three weeks soaking up the sun, visiting the camp up at Inyanga where we'd trained the Mozambicans, and catching up with old friends, I was ready to return to the gloom of a British winter. I arrived home on 8 December wondering what the future held. I didn't have to wait long to find out. Amidst a pile of unopened letters was an official looking brown HMSO envelope marked *On Her Majesty's Service* with *Orderly Room – Depot Para* stamped across the back. It felt flimsy and insubstantial – probably a Mess bill. A sixth sense told me it wasn't. My heart pounded as I tore it open. It was a Memo from the Chief Clerk dated almost a week earlier:

Sir,
You should have been in Bosnia a week ago. Where have you been? We've been trying to get hold of you. Get in touch ASAP. Your joining instructions are with the Adjutant.
    Chief.

Exactly as my aunt had predicted, breaking the news to my father was not easy.

'You don't know what you're doing, what you're letting yourself in for.' There was a horrible pause. The phone felt like a brick in my hand. 'Son, please, you're making a terrible mistake . . . a huge mistake.'

My father died in March 1996. I think he died of a broken heart. I will always remember him: for his love and his support, for his unfailing encouragement and for his wisdom. I will remember him for his industry and his utter honesty, as a husband, as a father and as head of the household. But more than all those things I will remember him for those haunting and prophetic final words. I wish I had listened to him and heeded his advice. But I didn't. I was youthful, impetuous, callow and cruel.

Around me in the Herc everyone seemed dead to the world. I stared at the white paint of the vehicles inches from my nose, hoping to sleep. My mind was racing and I was slightly depressed as England and its familiar comforts slipped away. The unknown lay ahead and that curious mix of regret and apprehension squeezed me.

The three weeks since arriving back from Zimbabwe had been frantic. I learnt that the first group of some thirteen volunteers had just finished a crash course in colloquial Serbo-Croat at Westminster University. I was to join them since the Commander British Forces, COMBRITFOR, Brigadier Andrew Cumming, based in Split, had no objections to my coming out. Our imminent departure had then been delayed when some kind soul in the MoD or at the UN office in Wilton had decided that the interpreters could spend Christmas at home, and that we'd all fly out to Split on one of the civil charter R&R flights leaving Gatwick on 29 December.

This breather had given me time to tackle the monstrously large kit list found in an annex to the Op HANWOOD deployment instruction. This was somewhat confusing since the Bosnia deployment had been given the operational name GRAPPLE. The kit list was exhaustive and might just as well have said everything but the kitchen sink; my house quickly began to look like a quartermaster's stores. Piles of military junk sprang up in every room – socks, shirts, trousers, boots, shoes and trainers, towels and washing kit, webbing and mess tins, helmet and Combat Body Armour, polish and brushes and a plethora of bits and pieces gathered and hoarded over the years. I managed to stuff the whole lot into a bergen, a large sausage-shaped kit bag, a grip bag and a daysack. Each item weighed a ton. I should have heeded my instincts. I barely used a quarter of this baggage in all my time in Bosnia.

While I'd been struggling with the kit list the gang of interpreters had been undergoing some sort of brush up military training at the Guards Depot at Pirbright. Foot drill had not been on the agenda but pistol training, first aid, mine awareness and basic fitness had been. On 21 December we gathered at HQ United Kingdom Land Forces for a briefing. I'd met none of my new colleagues before and was curious to see just who these people were who'd been brave or foolish enough to expose themselves to the little-known Balkan language of Serbo-Croat.

They turned out to be quite a mixed bunch drawn from the Army and Navy. Their self-appointed guru was an elderly, plump and slightly fussy major from the Royal Army Pay Corps called Martin Strong. The other officers were mainly captains: Neil Greenwood, a keen medal collector from the Gunners: Nick Short, an infantryman from the Gloucesters, and a number of others, including Sue Davidson from the Woman's Royal Army Corps. The Senior NCOs were even more curious: a Scottish Warrant Officer called 'Jock' McNair, and a thin, wiry Colour Sergeant with black, mischievous, ferrety eyes – Bob Edge, also a Gloucester. There were others of various ages, ranks and backgrounds. Seeming to have nothing in common save the course they'd just attended, they reminded me more than anything else of the cast of *The Dirty Dozen*.

The briefing was a fairly traumatic affair delivered by a worn-out looking watchkeeper, Major Windsor, who'd just finished the night shift. With the aid of a huge map of the Balkans and Bosnia-Hercegovina, across which snaked an impossibly contorted front line drawn in red, he attempted to explain what was going on out there: Serbs here, Croats there, Muslims here, Bosnian Croats there, Bosnian Serbs here and here, Krajina Serbs, Croat Serbs, Croat Croats, Serb Serbs, HVO, HV, JNA, JA, ABiH, BSA, UNHCR, ICRC, BRITBAT, BRITFOR, COMBRITFOR, BHC, UNSC, NGOs, ICFY, ECMM, Route Circle, Route Diamond, Route Square, TSG, GV, blah, blah, blah, blah. It was all gobbledegook, meaningless confusion that went straight over our heads. I don't think they really understood it either.

Christmas at home had been strained. My father had worked himself up into a real lather over the whole thing. 'You don't know what you've let yourself in for. You don't know what they're like, those people down there, the mentality. They're not like us here in the Diaspora. All the decent people were either killed off or fled into exile ... Tito might have gone but they're still old Communists. They're born and bred that way and they're rotten – Yugovici, all of them. And you can't trust them. They're cheats and liars and they'll use you if they can. I haven't suffered here in the West for fifty years, struggled to bring you up and educate you, just to watch you disappear off to the Balkans and be killed ...'

On and on it went. He was distressed, inconsolable. It was dreadful and I felt guilty that I was causing him such pain by opening up old wartime wounds and bitter memories. Suddenly, I was no longer sure I was doing the right thing. My plans started to look less like a great adventure designed to keep at bay the dreaded desk job and were beginning to take on a much more sinister hue. The thought that I might be killed, particularly in a UN mission, hadn't even entered my head.

'And that blue beret won't protect you and they won't be fooled by that Laurel name they've given you. They'll see through that immediately.' I had to agree with him on that one. The Laurel thing was particularly absurd and unfunny.

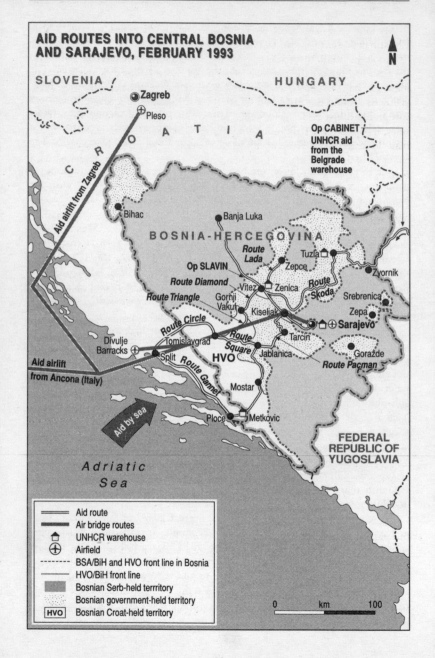

AID ROUTES INTO CENTRAL BOSNIA AND SARAJEVO, FEBRUARY 1993

N

SLOVENIA

HUNGARY

Zagreb

Pleso

C R O A T I A

Op CABINET
UNHCR aid
from the
Belgrade
warehouse

Aid airlift from Zagreb

Bihac

Banja Luka

BOSNIA-HERCEGOVINA

Route
Lada

Tuzla

Op SLAVIN

Zepce

Zvornik

Route Diamond

Vitez

Zenica

Route
Skoda

Srebrenica

Route Triangle

Gornji
Vakuf

Kiseljak

Zepa

Route Circle

Sarajevo

Divulje
Barracks

Tomislavgrad

Route
Square

Tarcin

Aid airlift
from Ancona (Italy)

Split

HVO

Jablanica

Gorazde

Route Gannet

Route Pacman

Aid by sea

Mostar

Ploce

Metkovic

Adriatic
Sea

FEDERAL
REPUBLIC OF
YUGOSLAVIA

Aid route
Air bridge routes
UNHCR warehouse
Airfield
BSA/BiH and HVO front line in Bosnia
HVO/BiH front line
Bosnian Serb-held terrritory
Bosnian government-held territory
HVO Bosnian Croat-held territory

0   km   100

My mother was far more pragmatic about it all. 'Here you go, son, a little Christmas present for you to take out to Bosnia.'

I took the small, soft package from her. It felt like a handkerchief. Mothers! I wasn't too far off the mark. It was an old Second World War silk escape map, the kind issued to aircrew and SOE agents. Although slightly frayed, yellowed around the edges and musty through decades of storage, it was still soft and had lost none of its rich colour. Printed in exquisite detail on both sides, it depicted the Balkans and middle Europe – Sheets F and G. The legend read 'Frontiers as at September 1943 . . . owing to frontiers being constantly changed in Eastern Europe, those marked on the map must be accepted with reserve.' The scale was 1mm:1km. It was all there: Vitez where the Cheshires were, Gornji Vakuf, which was also featuring in the news, and Split on the Dalmatian coast, where we'd be going in four days' time. I'd never seen the map before.

'Where did this come from?'

'Oh, we were each issued with one,' my mother replied cryptically.

'What! In the desert?' I was mystified. I knew she'd been in North Africa, but what on earth was she doing with an escape map of the Balkans? The only ones issued with those had been the Cairo-based SOE agents. 'You weren't in SOE were you?'

'Well, not exactly. For a while I worked for Colonel James Klugmann, the head of SOE Cairo . . . that Communist traitor!' she'd almost spat out his name, '. . . but no I wasn't SOE. But I was sent to Yugoslavia with Dr McPhail's Save the Children.'

Her story was all completely new to me. I'd vaguely been aware that she'd finished her war somewhere in Italy, but not that she'd been part of the first ever UN mission to the Balkans in 1945. The candles flickered on the table as she spoke. Recruited into Dr McPhail's unit in 1944 she'd acted as an interpreter in a large Croat refugee camp in the Sinai desert. In late 1944 the unit had moved to Italy and in March 1945 my mother and her three-tonne ambulance had landed in Dubrovnik. She'd spent the rest of that year driving around Bosnia, Hercegovina and Montenegro looking after orphaned children.

'. . . anyway, we were each issued with one of these maps and I think you should have it out there.'

I looked carefully at the silk and found Dubrovnik some way to the south of Split; to think that this had been in her pocket in that place nearly half a century ago! My father had never mentioned his war and my mother rarely hers. Now it was as if my imminent departure for the Balkans had spurred them both into revealing things that had for decades been locked away.

Another peculiar thing happened that evening. Mark Etherington, an old friend from the Regiment, rang up to wish us all a happy Christmas. He'd been out of the Army for over a year and had last been seen heading out of

Wandsworth in south-west London bound for Cape Town on a motorbike. On the phone his voice sounded faint, distant, distorted by terrible static and a hollow, irregular thumping sound. I had to shout down the phone.

'Mark! Where are you?' No doubt he was stuck somewhere in darkest Africa.

'Bihac . . . I'm in Bihac . . .' He too was yelling.

'What? Sorry? Where did you say?'

'Bihac . . . in Bosnia . . . thought I'd ring and wish you all a happy Christmas.'

'Mark! What're you doing there . . . and what's that banging noise?' The thumping in the background was incessant.

'Shelling! It's shelling.'

'What!' Had he gone mad?

'Shelling. I'm in a basement with my Muslim interpreter and the Serbs are shelling us!' The random thumping took shape in my mind. Mark was never prone to exaggerations.

'What're you doing there? Thought you were in Africa?'

'. . . ran out of money . . . dumped the bike in Nairobi . . . got a job now as a European Community monitor . . .' the line was getting worse, 'gotta go . . . on my mobile . . . not good reception in this cellar . . .' And then he was gone, cut off in an instant.

I searched for Bihac on the silk map and found it, a dot in the top left-hand corner of Bosnia. As I stared at the silk, I was chilled by the incongruity of it all: me enjoying Christmas in the warmth and security of a house in the West Country, listening to the sound of battle hundreds and hundreds of miles away, where a friend was cowering in a cellar.

I've always hated goodbyes. The following day we repeated a ritual that had been going on for the past twelve years. I'd kiss my parents goodbye and stuff my head into the helmet saying 'don't bother coming out' – but they always would. They'd traipse out after me; my father would grab my arm and say 'be careful on that thing' and my mother would say 'I wish you'd get rid of it'. They hated the bike. Then I'd roar off down the road and they'd stand there waving until I was out of sight. It never changed.

But this time it was different. We were on the road. My father grabbed me. 'Be careful out there.'

'Yes, son, be careful and God bless.' My mother was never one for grand emotions.

I fired the engine and clicked the bike into gear glancing across the road as I did so. They looked small and vulnerable in the December chill. My mother was waving, smiling encouragement, as mothers always do, masking her true feelings. My father was just standing there staring. What was in those eyes? I couldn't quite place it. Regret? Compassion? Pity? It was something deep and sorrowful and it cut me to the quick. His lips were quivering. Quickly I glanced over my left shoulder, rolled the throttle and roared off down the road. In the mirror I could see them standing there, waving madly – two small old people standing in the road. They waved until I rounded the corner and could see them no longer. That image burns in my mind today. I have often wondered what happened next as they turned and went indoors. Did he put his arm around her? What did they say to each other? What did they think? What were their private and miserable thoughts?

For some reason sleep continued to elude me, which is peculiar as it's quite normal for a Herc load of ninety paratroopers to nod off immediately after the aircraft has taken off. SOP. My stomach was still knotted with apprehension. How was I going to get out of the airport at the other end? Had the 'movers' there been briefed? A week ago it had seemed funny. Now, stuck in limbo at thirty thousand feet, it was anything but.

After being thoroughly savaged by Major Windsor's barrage of Op GRAPPLE abbreviations, route names and a plethora of confusing place names, we'd staggered out of the Wilton briefing room and made our way up several flights of stairs to see another major called Francis Brancato. He ran the UN office at Wilton. I'd met him once before when he'd come out to visit us in Kuwait. In his office he'd taken me to one side and announced that I'd be flying out as Captain Laurel.

'Pardon me?' What was he on about?

'Captain Laurel. That's who you're going out as and that's who you'll be,' he repeated matter of factly.

'Laurel! Why?' I was bemused.

'Do you know the other two who're out there now?' He was deadly serious, '. . . both Serbs . . . like you . . .' he rattled off their names. One was a lieutenant in the Light Infantry, the other a corporal in the Royal Anglian Regiment.

'Nope. Never heard of them . . . didn't know there were any others in the Army.'

Now I was genuinely surprised.

'Well there are and they're out there. Apparently there's some sort of threat to them from the Muslims and Croats. It's not very healthy being a Serb of any sort in Croatia and Bosnia these days. Anyway we've changed their names . . . Abbott and Costello!' he sniggered . . .

'And you want me to be Laurel!' I was almost shouting, '. . . and what happens if you find a fourth Serb? What's he going to be?'

There was a horrible pause. Francis could barely contain himself, '. . . how about Hardy?' he spluttered. I stared at him in disbelief and then we both burst out laughing. What else could we do?

The day before our departure there'd been yet another unexpected change in plans. I was telephoned by someone in Movements in Wilton (they co-ordinated movements of personnel going abroad) and informed that I wouldn't be flying with the others from Gatwick.

'Why not? What's the problem?' The obstacles seemed endless. What now?

'Problem is you haven't got a passport in the name of Laurel and you'll be stopped by Croatian customs if you go civil.'

'Does that mean I'm now not going?' More frustration.

'No, no, you're still going. There's a "Herc" flight to Split early tomorrow . . . departing RAF Lyneham. You've got to be in uniform and you're to be there at 0500.'

'Why so early?' It was always early report times with the RAF.

'Dunno, those are the timings. Oh yeah, when you report just tell them you're Captain Laurel . . . they'll know. At the other end you'll be met by movers, our people who've got access to the pan. They'll get you through one of the side gates. Okay?'

Next morning Colin and I got up at a grotesquely indecent hour. It was bitterly cold but despite the darkness and the frosty roads we reached Lyneham with fifteen minutes to spare. Between us we lugged the bergen and bags into the terminal building where other bleary-eyed fellow travellers were sprawled over hard plastic seats.

'Come on Col, let's see if the Captain Laurel shit really works.' I nodded towards the counter where a lone and youthful leading airman was tapping away furiously at a keyboard. I dumped the bergen heavily on the electronic scales next to him.

'Ninety-five and a half pounds!' I announced. Startled, he looked up.

'Oh right, morning sir.' He was slightly flustered.

'I'm flying to Split this morning. This where I check in?'

'It is, sir. Could I see your ID card?' He'd recovered his composure.

'I'm sorry but I'm afraid I haven't got one.' Which was true, not in the name of Laurel anyway.

'Oh well . . . I'm afraid you can't fly if you haven't got ID.' I glanced over at Colin who was enjoying himself immensely.

'Look . . . I'm Captain Laurel if it'll help.' Somewhere to my left I heard Colin snigger. I was doing my best to contain myself and make the best of this charade.

The airman suddenly became very tense, his eyes almost feral. Carefully he looked from left to right, checking that no one else was within earshot before leaning towards me. His words were husky, deliberate, almost conspiratorial.

'Captain Laurel is it? Yeeeees . . . it's okay . . . we know all about you.'

'Excellent. I knew you wouldn't let me down,' I whispered back. Keeping a straight face was hell. Colin had given up. He was outside, laughing into the cold, inky blackness.

That had been then. Seven hours and many hundreds of miles later it wasn't such a laughing matter after all. Would the movers be there? What if they weren't? I thought of my father's dire words of warning. Had I just made the biggest mistake of my life?

With a thump, the Herc hit the runway. The wheels bounced and bumped and the hold rattled and jangled madly as stressed metal and engines strained to slow the cumbersome aircraft. The slumbering soldier beside me woke with a startled grunt. He'd dozed the whole way, snorting fitfully, and had dribbled saliva down his combat jacket. Rudely awakened, hair dishevelled, headphones askew, puffy red-rimmed eyes, he stared about him in wild, unfocused confusion. After a few minutes of lumbering and bumping, the Herc slowed and lurched to a standstill. One by one the four turboprops were starved of fuel and, with a dying moan, fell silent.

The silence in the hold was shocking. It seemed to last for ages. Gradually soldiers came to life, unbuckling seat straps, packing away their Walkmans, yawning, stretching and scratching their heads. With a dull hydraulic whine the Herc's tail gate split laterally in two and opened up like a giant TV screen. Bright light flooded in and tired soldiers blinked owlishly, screwing up their eyes and straining to get a view of the world outside. Through the opening I got my first glimpse of the Balkans – a barren, rocky, forbidding escarpment of high jagged peaks. My gloomy thoughts of a few hours ago had gone. *This* was exciting! I thought of General Greindle, of Colonel Garret and John Wooldridge, and of the many other curious twists and turns of the previous eleven months. I thought of my father who had last seen this country nearly half a century earlier. Somehow, against the odds, I'd made it to the Balkans. I should have turned back there and then.

FIVE

Operation Grapple – Croatia

Tuesday 29 December 1992 – Divulje Barracks, Split

'Once you've been checked off, grab your kit and take it off to your relevant messes and then be seated in the briefing room at 1700 hours. Right then, excuse ranks . . . Davidson.'

'Here.' Sue Davidson pulled her baggage from the mountain of kit which cluttered one of the corners of the foyer entrance to the HQ BRITFOR block. We were grouped around a youthful looking cavalry captain called Sam Mattock, one of the staff officers at the HQ. He'd met us at the airport and seen us onto a coach, which had ferried us the mile to Divulje barracks. As luck had it my fears had been unfounded and I'd been met off the Herc by one of the movers. Having dumped my gear into his Land Rover he'd clipped a pass onto my pocket and spirited me through one of the airport's side gates and deposited me outside the Arrivals lounge. Sam had been waiting for me there along with another staff officer, Captain John Chisholm, whom I knew well from the Parachute Regiment. We'd had an hour's wait before the R&R flight landed, bringing with it some of the Cheshires returning from R&R and the thirteen interpreters.

'Edge.'

'Sir.' The Gloucesters colour sergeant retrieved his bags and disappeared into the darkness beyond the glass doors. Quickly the group thinned out, eager to seize a decent bunk and unpack.

'Stanley.'

Silence.

'Stanley.' Still no one answered. Sam looked up from his clipboard staring directly at me, 'Stanley's you isn't it?' he said pointing with his pen.

'No. It's Laurel, Captain Laurel,' I answered, wondering what was going on.

Sam scratched his head again with his pen. 'There's no Laurel on the list, just Stanley. That's who we've got you down as, so that's who you are. So, you're present then?'

'I suppose I must be,' I mumbled, still thoroughly confused. After the last of the group had left I tackled Sam over the name. He said he'd never heard of a Laurel and insisted that I was to be Stanley. 'Is that "ly" or "ley"?' he'd asked. 'ley', I'd replied off the top of my head.

'And what's your Christian name?'

I told him 'Milos' and he just chuckled. 'You can't be that, I mean, it just doesn't go ... you know that and Stanley. You'll have to have an English Christian name. What'll it be?'

I was caught on the hop. It isn't every day you're asked for an instant Christening. I thought for a moment before blurting out, '*Mike Stanley*'. It sort of rolled off the tongue.

'Mike Stanley it is then.' Sam looked pleased as he annotated his list. 'See you in the briefing room in half an hour ... Mike!' And that was it, just like that. Bye, bye Laurel, hello Mike Stanley.

Five o'clock turned out to be less a briefing, more an introductory session with a difference ... in Serbo-Croat. Nick Stansfield, a highly capable captain in the Education Corps, led the proceedings. He spoke excellent Russian and good Serbo-Croat. He'd gone out to Zagreb earlier in the year and had migrated to Bosnia in October to work for Bob Stewart as his interpreter. Under his supervision the novice interpreters struggled through a few sentences while I sat at the back chatting to Nick Abbott, the corporal from the Anglian Regiment. Most of his extended family were Krajina Serbs and most of his cousins were in the ARSK, the Krajina Serb Army around Knin. He looked every bit a Dalmatian – swarthy, with black hair and dark eyes. He told me that Nick Costello, the 'other one', was also from Knin, also had cousins in the ARSK, and was currently up in Vitez as Bob Stewart's interpreter.

'What do you reckon? Do you think these people see through the Abbott & Costello nonsense?' I was keen to learn the rules of the job as quickly as possible.

'Well, people ask you where you've learnt the language, and you have to trot out the same old lie about university and coming here on holiday before the war. Throw in a few deliberate errors, struggle a bit and you might get away with it ...' He paused for a moment's thought and then added, '... if I were you I'd keep your mouth shut here in Croatia. Save it for Bosnia.'

I was slightly alarmed. 'Why?'

'Simple. You speak with an *ekavski* accent ... obvious you're from Serbia, whereas here they speak with an *ijekavski* Dalmatian accent. And the words are different too. What's "bread"?'

'*Hleb*,' I replied.

'No it isn't. Here it's *kruh* and in Bosnia it's *hljeb* or occasionally *kruh*. They've become so politically correct here in Croatia. Serb words are out. Croatian words are in. And where there isn't a dual, they've simply made up a new word rather than use one that the Serbs are also using . . . all politically correct words, thousands of them.'

'For example?'

'For example . . . *helikopter* . . . you know, in Serbia or Bosnia, but not here. Here it's a *zrakomlat!*'

A what! A something-beater? I'd never heard the word *zrak*.

'An *air-beater* . . . *zrak-o-mlat* . . . *zrak?* You'd know *zrak* as *vazduh* – air.' Suddenly I felt completely out of my depth. Not only was my accent 'Cockney' while theirs was 'Geordie', but they had a range of words, old and invented, which I'd never heard before in my life.

'Gets better than that. How about this, then? What's a "belt"?' He was really enjoying himself now.

'I'm tempted to say *kajs*, but I'm sure I'd be wrong.'

Nick smirked, '*Kajs* in Serbia or Bosnia, but here in Croatia it's a – wait for it – an *okolotrbusnipantolodrzac!*'

'An around-the-stomach-trouser-holder! You're kidding me!' I was astonished.

'Spot on. Got it in one. They're at it all the time, making up new words. They're creating a whole new language here. They've even got a huge Croatian to Serbo-Croat, Serbo-Croat to Croatian dictionary, just as if they're two separate languages.'

'Bad as that then?'

'Yep. So, if you don't know New Speak keep your mouth shut here in Croatia and Hercegovina, especially with your accent.' That was enough for me; I made a mental note there and then to play the dumb foreigner in Croatia.

That evening Nick Stansfield dragged me off to a bar in Trogir, an enchanting fifteenth-century fishing town about four miles north of Split airport and Divulje barracks. Trogir is a mini-Notre Dame, perched on an islet linked to the mainland and to the island of Ciovo by two bridges. At its heart lies a labyrinth of narrow, twisting alleys, small continental-style bars and a variety of restaurants. Before the war it was a haven for tourists and drug addicts. While none of the former was in evidence, Trogir still featured as one of the main nodal points on the drugs route from the East into Europe. Not only was trade prospering, but the war had, according to Nick, allowed the local mafia to flourish and spread its tentacles into every bar and restaurant, including the small corner bar, King Bar, in which we were quietly drinking.

Nick was leaving theatre in a couple of days' time, after almost a year in the Balkans. He was unsure what the future held for him once he got home. He even had the option to stay on, one which I was rather selfishly encouraging him to take as he was just about the only person out here that I really knew.

'Trouble is, you can only play the odds game so long and then your luck's up . . .' I wasn't sure what he was getting at but let him continue, '. . . I've followed people into the most frightening situations . . . Bob Stewart drove us straight into a fire-fight . . . I crapped myself . . . then in Sarajevo there was that much metal flying through the air that you spent most of the time cowering in a bunker . . .' He paused. He was thinner than I remembered him. His voice trailed off, '. . . No. Eventually your luck just runs out.' I knew he wouldn't be staying.

At the bar a fat German was shouting something in his mother tongue. He was waving a wodge of Deutschmarks at an uncomprehending bar girl and stabbing a sausage-like finger at a crucifix and rosary beads hanging behind the bar.

'I thought there were no tourists here, Nick, you know, the war and all?'

'There aren't. He's probably one of those German businessmen who nip down from Munich in their Mercs for a spot of hunting for the cause.' He laughed dryly.

'How d'you mean?'

'They think nothing of spending a long weekend down here with the hunting rifle taking pot shots at the Serbs on the Knin front line. Solidarity with their Croatian brothers. And then zip back to the office in Munich. Weird, but it happens. There's weirder yet, but you'll find out. Whole place is fucked up.'

The following day we once again found ourselves in the briefing room for a day of orientation briefings. As Brigadier Cumming was indisposed, we were welcomed instead by Major Richard Barrons, the Brigade Chief of Staff and a Gunner. His address was really an overview explaining that the UN's mandated presence in the Balkans was to facilitate the delivery of humanitarian aid to whomsoever the United Nations High Commissioner for Refugees, UNHCR, the lead aid agency in the Former Republics of Yugoslavia, FRY, saw fit. The UN Protection Force, UNPROFOR, was mandated to protect UNHCR and the aid. Then it got a bit more complicated. UNPROFOR 1 was the UN force charged with maintaining the peace in the four disputed UN Protection Areas, UNPAs, in Croatia, while UNPROFOR 2 was concerned solely with the protection of humanitarian aid in Bosnia-Hercegovina, B-H. Both UNPROFORs were commanded by an overarching HQ in Zagreb, the capital of Croatia. UNPROFOR 2's headquarters, known as HQ Bosnia-Hercegovina Command, HQ BHC, was located in a hotel in Kiseljak in Central Bosnia. It was run on a day-to-day basis by BHC's Chief of Staff, Brigadier Roddy Cordy-Simpson. The actual commander of BHC, the French general Philippe Morillon, had established himself in a small tactical HQ in Sarajevo in a building known as the Residency.

If that wasn't enough, UN deployments within B-H were even more confusing. The French had two battalions, the Egyptians and Ukrainians one apiece in Sector Sarajevo. The Spanish had a battalion based in Mostar in Hercegovina and outposts up the Neretva river valley. The British battalion, BRITBAT, based on the Cheshires' Battle Group, was centred on Vitez in Central Bosnia and had the largest Area of Responsibility, AOR, with a company in Gornji Vakuf, GV, and B Squadron of the 9/12 Lancers in a base at Tuzla airfield way up north. Not far from the British base at Vitez, the Dutch had a conscript transport battalion at Busovaca.

In addition to BRITBAT, which numbered about 800 troops, the British had insisted on the deployment of a National Support Element, NSE, logistics battalion and 35 Engineer Regiment, which was located at Tomislavgrad, TSG, in the south in Hercegovina. Their primary tasks were to open, widen and maintain routes running northwards and to keep the Cheshires supplied from points of entry at Split airport and harbour, where the Royal Fleet Auxiliary supply ship *Sir Galahad* was moored. The controlling HQ for the NSE was in Divulje barracks: based on Cumming's 11th Armoured Brigade HQ, now called HQ BRITISH FORCE, BRITFOR, (he himself being Commander BRITFOR, or COMBRITFOR), it answered to the Joint HQ, JHQ, in Wilton. Thus the total British strength came to a shade over 2,400 troops.

Co-located at Divulje barracks was half a squadron of Royal Navy Sea King helicopters from 845 Naval Air Squadron, 845 NAS, who were known as 'junglies' and their French equivalent with their Pumas, known as DETALAT. Although they were unable to fly over the Croatian border into B-H, the junglies and DETALAT busied themselves conducting navigational exercises in preparation for the day when diplomatic clearance and the situation in B-H would permit the first proving flights north.

Somewhere over the horizon lurked the ships of a multinational flotilla, Op SHARP GUARD. High above both of us ran yet another operation, Op DENY FLIGHT, which consisted of two E3A Sentry AWACs, one above Hungary and the other above the Adriatic, which controlled fighter aircraft from NATO's 5th Allied Tactical Air Force, 5 ATAF, who were charged with preventing the warring factions in B-H from using their fixed and rotary wing military aircraft.

All this military effort was in support of United Nations High Commission for Refugees, whose in-theatre head, Jose Maria Mendeluce, a Spaniard, was based in Zagreb. He was charged with the provision of humanitarian aid throughout Croatia and B-H. UNHCR's logistics operation was even more complex than UNPROFOR's. Bought by the UN's World Food Programme, WFP, using donor countries' money, aid would be moved into theatre by a variety of means, most usually by sea or road, to UNHCR's primary depots at Zagreb and Metkovic in Croatia, and Belgrade in Serbia. From those nodes the aid would be trucked into Bosnia. Aid from Belgrade travelled through Serbia, crossed the River Drina into B-H over the Karakaj Bridge near Zvornik,

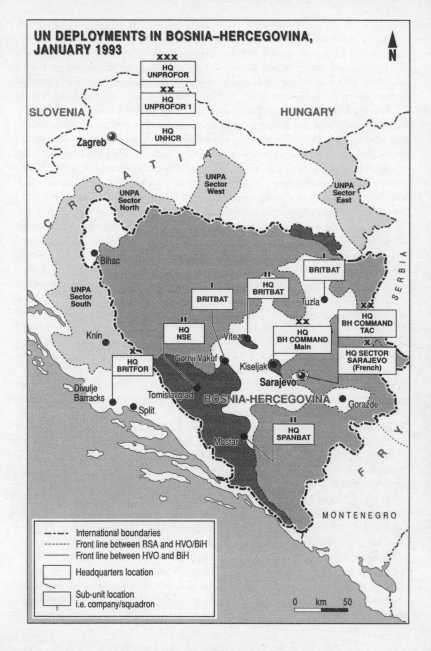

UN DEPLOYMENTS IN BOSNIA–HERCEGOVINA,
JANUARY 1993

International boundaries
Front line between BSA and HVO/BiH
Front line between HVO and BiH
Headquarters location
Sub-unit location
i.e. company/squadron

moved through Serb-held territory to the front line at Kalesija just east of Tuzla, where it was escorted over the line and into Tuzla by B Squadron 9/ 12 Lancers. That operation had been unofficially christened Op CABINET by an exasperated Major Allan Abraham, the Squadron's OC, who had been heard to comment that it would take a Cabinet decision to get a line crossing approved by the Serbs.

The aid from Zagreb travelled south into B-H destined both for the Serbs in Banja Luka and the Bosnians in Central Bosnia. These convoys, bound for the UNHCR warehouse in Zenica, were frequently frustrated by the Bosnian Serbs and rarely managed to cross the front line at Turbe, just west of the Cheshires' Vitez base. That crossing operation was christened Op SLAVIN after a footballer who never quite managed to get the ball over the line. The aid from the warehouse in Metkovic, a small town south of Mostar and just inside the Croatian border, usually made good progress up the Neretva valley but, because the road into Sarajevo disappeared into Serb-held territory, it slowed down as it negotiated a mountain route into Kresevo and onwards to the warehouse in Zenica. A second, and much more tortuous, route into Central Bosnia went via Split, TSG, along a mountain track which had been widened by the Royal Engineers, known as Route Triangle, through Prozor, GV, Vitez and thence to Zenica.

Aid almost never reached Sarajevo by road and had to be flown in by transport aircraft operating a Berlin Airlift-style shuttle from Ancona in Italy, Zagreb and Split and the USAF base at Ramstein in Germany. The airlift was by far the riskiest of operations. Sarajevo airport lay astride a hotly contested front line and was reputed to be 'the most dangerous place on earth'. Aircraft were intermittently hit by small arms fire on approach and take off. An Italian transport aircraft had been shot down in August by a surface-to-air missile fired from somewhere in Central Bosnia and had crashed in the Fojnica valley killing the crew. Confusingly, the RAF contribution to the airlift was known as Op CHESHIRE – nothing to do with the Cheshires in Vitez.

Thus, UNHCR had distribution warehouses and offices in Sarajevo, Tuzla, Banja Luka, Metkovic, Split, Zagreb and Belgrade. From the B-H warehouses UNHCR handed over the aid to the local authorities who disposed of it as they saw fit. In addition to UNHCR there was a host of Non Governmental Organisations, NGOs all doing their bit; the International Committee of the Red Cross, ICRC, Medicines Sans Frontieres, MSF, Caritas, Merhemet, to name but a few. Wackier still, there were one-man-band, go-it-alone outfits bringing aid from across Europe in broken down old lorries and vans. 'The Serious Road Trip' was one of these. In short the aid effort seemed to be a loosely co-ordinated patchwork of well-meaning do-gooders who exposed themselves to horrible risks for no return other than the satisfaction of having delivered some aid.

In addition to the military component, UNPROFOR also had a legion of civilians welded into the organisation: Civil Affairs officers, financiers, accommodation officers, communications officers, mechanics etc. all of whom were professional 'UNites' who seemed to drift around the globe from one mission area to another. We even had two civilians in HQ BRITFOR to assist Brigadier Cumming. Both were 'ours' in the sense that David Arnold-Foster, the Civil Secretary, was a senior MoD finance officer who controlled the purse strings and the Civil Adviser, from the Foreign Office, advised the Commander on political matters.

Richard Barrons completed his address by telling us that somewhere, high above this tangle of military and civilians, Lord Owen and Cyrus Vance of the International Conference on Former Yugoslavia, ICFY, were conducting a frantic shuttle diplomacy effort to end the war in B-H and were currently negotiating with the leaders of the warring factions in Geneva. A Vance–Owen Peace Plan, the VOPP, would shortly be announced.

It was time for a break. That was lecture one over. It couldn't possibly get any more complicated, could it?

Wrong. Within five minutes Major Chris Lawton, the SO2 G2 Intelligence, or Military Information as the UN euphemistically calls it, had us in a double arm lock. He was attempting to explain the background to the conflict, which seemed to have started with the Battle of Kosovo in 1389 and was giving us a detailed picture of who was doing what to whom – how, where and why. The UN/international community side of it was bad enough, but what the locals were up to and why was almost impossible to follow.

The universal bogeyman was the Serb, but it seemed there were three different types of Serb. There were the Serb Serbs, from Serbia proper beyond the River Drina, led by their president, Slobodan Milosevic. Their army was still called the Jugoslav National Army, JNA, or what was left of the Federal Army now that Slovenia, Croatia and B-H had seceded. There were the Krajina Serbs of Croatia who, refusing to acknowledge Croatia's secession, had revolted, fought a six-month war with the Croats, and were now established in their breakaway Republika Srpska Krajina in the UNPAs: UN Sectors North, South, East and West. Their army was known as the Army of Republika Srpska Krajina or ARSK. Finally, there were the Bosnian Serbs who, like the Krajina Serbs, had refused to recognise the secession of B-H and were now locked in a civil war with those who had voted for secession. Their leader was Dr Radovan Karadzic and the army commander of the Bosnian Serb Army, BSA, was General Ratko Mladic. Received wisdom suggested that the revolts of both the Krajina Serbs and Bosnian Serbs had been orchestrated by Milosevic himself in order to achieve a dream of creating a Greater Serbia. All three were universally termed the aggressor, particularly by the media.

The Croatian president was Franjo Tudjman and the Croatian army was

called the Hrvatska Vojska, HV. Then there were the Croats of B-H led by
Mate Boban in his Hercegovina HQ at Grude, not far from Mostar. Their
army was called Hrvatsko Vece Odbrane, the Croatian Defence Council or
HVO. Politically, they aspired to the creation of their own mini-statelet called
Herceg-Bosna and closer ties with Croatia proper with whom they shared a
common border, the western border of B-H. They therefore effectively controlled the access into B-H and access to the Adriatic from B-H. They were
in alliance with the Muslims of Bosnia led by President Alija Izetbegovic whose
army, Armija Bosne i Hercegovine, Army of Bosnia-Hercegovina, ABiH, was
commanded by General Sefer Halilovic. The alliance was shaky in the extreme
and only held together in the face of the common enemy – the Serb.

Along an impossibly long and convoluted front line, in red on the map,
which snaked through Croatia, swung north into B-H near Split, meandered
northwards creating bulges and salients, looped around Tuzla and then wandered south-westwards to the east of Mostar before swinging south towards
Dubrovnik, the HV and ARSK stared at each other across a bleak no-
man's-land in Croatia, while the HVO and ABiH fought the BSA in World
War One-style trench warfare in Bosnia. Sarajevo was besieged by the BSA.
To the east the Muslims were besieged in a large pocket backed up against
the river Drina at Gorazde, while in the north-west corner of B-H they were
holding out in a sizeable but isolated pocket called Bihac. Somewhere in and
amongst all this the UN was either attempting to keep the peace in Croatia
or trying to deliver aid in B-H.

It was all thoroughly confusing.

The greatest shock was the revelation that the UN was not particularly
popular in Croatia. In fact the Croats called it 'Serbprofor' on account of the
fact that they viewed the UN as protectors of the Krajina Serbs in the UNPAs.
The British in particular seemed to have been singled out for particular hatred
and a number of off-duty soldiers had been set upon by local louts in Trogir
and Split. Officially the UN was tolerated, mainly because of the huge sums
of hard currency being injected into the local economy through the hire and
leasing of barracks, warehouses and port facilities. Indeed, the local hotels up
and down the Dalmatian coast survived only because the UN was desperate
for over-spill accommodation. Thus it was a love-hate relationship – they
loved the colour of our money but hated us.

To complete our confusion, we learnt next that a number of independent
organisations were floating around FRY, each with its own reporting chain
of command. The Brussels-led European Community Monitoring Mission,
ECMM, which had been monitoring the collapse of Yugoslavia from the start,
had small teams of ECMM monitors, all seconded or retired military officers,
dotted throughout FRY and its bordering countries. Dressed from head to toe
in white, their remit was to hob-nob with local politicians, assess the political,

economic and military situations in their areas and to report back to Brussels via their Zagreb HQ in the Hotel I. In parallel, the UN had its own unarmed Military Observers, UNMOs, again, dotted about in small teams and reporting the military situation up their own separate chain of command to HQ UNPROFOR in Zagreb.

Finally, not to be outdone, BRITFOR had its own version of information gatherers and liaison officers called United Kingdom Liaison Officers or UKLOs. They were armed and consisted of eight teams each of one captain, one Royal Marines driver and a peculiar mini four-tonner known as a Renault-Bowden 44 (RB44). Each carried a satellite communications dish in the back which, in theory, could track satellites and communicate on the move. The cab resembled Concorde's flight deck and sported radios, computers and a fax machine. Each of the teams was thus independent, could range throughout Bosnia and communicate with Split. The concept was flawed, however, as there was no room to carry an interpreter. The Cheshires, who had their own liaison officers, unkindly christened them 'Cumming's Commandos'. Lastly, there were the international mass media, for the most part reporting from Sarajevo or Central Bosnia, each to their own editors or desks.

From what we could gather from the blizzard of information presented by Richard Barrons and Chris Lawton, Croatia and B-H were full of people either trying to kill each other, or trying to stop them doing it, or trying to feed those being killed; and, lastly, there were lots of people charging around gathering all sorts of information and telling disparate groups and organisations all about it. A perfect nuthouse.

All we really wanted to know was who we'd be working for, where and when we'd be off.

Sam Mattock, our original contact on arrival at Split, brought us all down to earth. We were all farmed out to various locations. To my intense disappointment, I was to stay in Split as COMBRITFOR's interpreter. 'Up country' was where things were happening and the last thing I thought I'd be doing was hanging around Divulje barracks kicking my heels. Fortunately, I kept my mouth shut.

The remainder of the day was spent drawing Arctic clothing from the quartermaster's stores and being processed into theatre, largely a matter of paperwork and queuing: the issue of blue UN ID cards, the filling out of next-of-kin forms and the surrender of our medical records to the Orderly Room. In return we were given a UN PX card which entitled us to buy spirits, wine and tobacco each month. Another card recorded the receipt of the only financial allowance in theatre – telephone money rated at $1.28 a day. This was supposed to offset the personal costs of phoning home. We were also issued, as medical aid, a 15mg morphine autojet syrette in its green polythene sleeve, which lived around one's neck taped to the ID disc chain. Finally we signed for a pistol and thirty-nine rounds of 9mm ammunition, though these were kept locked in the armoury and only issued when needed.

Divulje barracks was a large camp situated between the airport and the bay. Pre-war it had been home to a JNA air defence regiment and a seaborne special forces unit. As the rump of the JNA withdrew from Croatia into Bosnia and Serbia they had smashed up their barracks, ripped out fittings, broken windows, and, to ensure that they remained uninhabitable, had mined and booby-trapped the buildings and un-Tarmaced areas. When BRITFOR had first arrived the entire force, less the Cheshires' Battle Group, which deployed straight up country, had been accommodated in the Hotel Medina while the Royal Engineers made Divulje habitable and safe in a rudimentary way.

BRITFOR occupied five large, three-storey buildings in the north-eastern corner of the camp. Three were Messes – officers', warrant officers' and sergeants', and 845 NAS. Another served as the HQ building while the fifth belonged to the HQ's signal squadron. A central cookhouse fed all ranks on a rotational basis. Each of the long rectangular blocks was identical in build: three storeys high, at the end of each floor a large room, accessed by stone stairs, with a walk-out balcony. The room led to a long, gloomy corridor off which were a mass of rabbit hutch rooms or offices, depending on the function of the building. In the south-western corner of the camp was the helicopter dispersal area, hangars and 845's Portakabin offices.

The remainder of the camp's buildings were given over to an HV unit of dubious identification. At least part of the unit was HOS, reputed to be the fanatical element of the HV and identified for the most part by its predilection for black uniforms and even blacker operations. A number of their members were foreigners from European countries including the UK and Eire. We were warned to keep well away from them. All official business was conducted between HQ BRITFOR and the camp's HV commandant. The relationship was never an easy one and I suspect the Croats tolerated the British only because the latter had cleaned up the camp and were now paying through the nose for the privilege of using it. The pretence of mutual tolerance was only ever evident in that British and HV troops jointly manned the front gate.

Sam Mattock was immensely friendly, cheerful and likeable, and always did his best to make me feel part of the team. When he told me of a New Year's Eve party to which I was invited, I wasn't too keen to go. I knew no one except John Chisholm, who, I discovered, was in charge of the United Kingdom Liaison Officers, UKLOs. Sam assured me that the Villa Sanda, on Ciovo island, was 'an interesting place' and that the evening would be a good laugh. On the grounds that it would at least be a good way to meet people, I reluctantly accepted his invitation.

The restaurant was humming, crammed to capacity. The BRITFOR group was seated at a long table running the length of the room. Brigadier Cumming was at the far end, barely visible through a haze of smoke and a forest of green wine bottles. The more junior staff officers were seated at the other end, noisily cracking into the most enormous lobsters I'd ever seen. The rest of the restaurant was given up to two equally large parties of Croats who were doing their best to ignore us. The evening had started in the Mess, then a minibus had shuttled the party of about thirty to the Villa Sanda, about twenty minutes drive from Divulje. By the time we reached the restaurant, we were pretty well lubricated.

The waitresses were all stunning, absolutely gorgeous, smiling and grinning, plump breasts bouncing above platters as they skipped between the tables. Must be something in the water I decided. They were all like that even in Split itself. With nothing to do during the day, five of us had begged a lift into Split, some twenty kilometres away, on the pretext that we needed 'to look for dictionaries' and had spent most of the afternoon sitting at an outdoor café on the southern harbour, watching the world and the women of Split sauntering by. There hadn't been one who couldn't have instantly appeared, without cosmetic alteration, on the front cover of a Western glossy. Small wonder that a Split girl had won Miss Europe that year and that the city would hang onto the title for the next four years, despite the war. It was definitely the water.

'Hey, Sam.' I caught his attention. He was sitting three down from me. 'These women! What do they do with the ugly ones? Send them up to the front line?'

His mouth full, eyes laughing, he said, 'You haven't worked it out, have you? Why do you think they keep disappearing upstairs?'

I had no idea. 'I suppose there's a restaurant upstairs . . . I dunno.'

Sam sniggered. He could barely contain himself. 'They're pros, Mike, y'know, whores . . . restaurant downstairs, knocking shop upstairs. Probably doing the bizzo with their clients between courses!' He was almost shouting.

'You're kidding!?'

'Nope. It's true. Whole place is mad. It's the war. They're not even locals, these girls. They're Ukrainians, Latvians, Lithuanians, y'know . . . The Wall comes down, nothing at home but a depressed economy and . . . flutter, flutter, flutter down here to the war where there's easy money . . . place is run by the mafia like everything else . . . ,' he paused for a moment, his fork hovering inches from his mouth, '. . . but it's still the best restaurant in Trogir and it's got its very own night club.'

As if on cue the door burst open and one of the local yobbos barged his way into the restaurant. He was a Neanderthal – six foot four, thickset, huge head with black, close-set, unintelligent eyes and a skinhead crop. He wore jeans, trainers and a cheap blue and white donkey jacket with a fluffy white fake fur collar. The black FN assault rifle, which he slammed down on the small wooden bar, completed this picture, but the bar girl seemed to know him and a glass of beer miraculously appeared in his paw. He glared around the restaurant, fixing those horrid little eyes, so full of contempt and hatred, on the British table. Clearly his entrance hadn't caused the stir he'd expected as celebrations continued unabated. He gulped down his beer and demanded another. Sitting at the end of the table I was nearest him. I just hoped he wasn't going to go mad with that rifle and demand that we empty our wallets.

Fortunately not. Moments later he grabbed the FN and lurched past us out onto the patio where he pumped four rounds into the night sky. The hubbub in the restaurant eased momentarily but quickly picked up again, much to the man's annoyance. Then he resumed his position at the bar and continued drinking. So did we.

With dinner over we were on our feet, mixing and chatting, pints of beer in our hands, all waiting for midnight. I found myself standing in front of a man dressed in tartan trousers, dinner jacket and bow tie. The Brigadier! I forced sobriety into my voice and introduced myself. The Brigadier was without doubt the most charming, easy, urbane man I'd ever met.

'Don't worry about Split,' he said as though he'd read my thoughts, 'we won't be spending much time here. I'm deploying a small tactical headquarters to Fojnica in a couple of days' time and we'll be doing a lot of travelling, you, me and Corporal Fox.'

As midnight approached we found ourselves out on the patio. It was freezing. Neanderthal-man was out there, too, pumping the odd round skywards between swigs of beer. I just prayed he'd keep that thing pointing in the right direction. At midnight the sky erupted with multi-coloured streaks of tracer arcing into the air. As far as the eye could see, right down the coast to Split, a madness of gunfire heralded 1993. That night nine people were killed by spent rounds falling to earth. They even found one stuck in the skin of one of 845's Sea Kings.

Nearby, Trogir was rocking with automatic gunfire. Our man went berserk. He'd flipped onto auto and was spraying the night with long, raking bursts of automatic fire. His body shook and juddered in sympathy with his weapon as he staggered around the patio. The magazine empty, he dug a fresh one from his jacket pocket and, once he'd inexpertly loaded it and wrenched the cocking lever back, he continued to blast the opposite shoreline with another long, raking burst. Then the FN jammed. Neanderthal-man was hunched over it, furiously tugging at the cocking handle, his face black and contorted with the effort. It had jammed solid.

John Chisholm sallied forth to his rescue, grabbing the weapon from the startled hood. 'Issallaright mate, I know about these things, lemme help you.' He flipped off the magazine and tugged at the lever. Nothing. 'Weapon's filthy, bet he's never cleaned it ... jammed solid...'sno problem ... jus' needs a little force.' With that he placed the butt on the ground and stamped on the cocking handle as hard as he could; with such force, in fact, that the weapon broke, the working parts shot out of the back and smashed against the wall, cracking and shattering the breech block.

The world went silent. We gazed in horror at the broken rifle, then at the smashed breech block and finally at its owner, who was staring in shock and amazement at the bits and pieces. Oh, shit! That's it. We're dead. He's going to rip us apart. Slowly he sank to his knees, collected up the pieces and, turning, sat down heavily, cross-legged, clutching the FN's shattered innards. He looked up at us in utter bewilderment. We stood there transfixed by the ghastly horror of it all, dreading what was to come. His gaze went back to the broken metal that his massive paws were nursing. Then his shoulders heaved and he let out a huge sob and burst into tears, blubbering over his broken toy.

Seizing the moment, we fled into the night before his grief turned to blind fury.

SIX

Operation Bretton

October 1997 – The Nelson Arms, Farnham, UK

'You'll love this one, Nix . . .' I'm reading the list of instructions I've found in the box of pills that Ian's given me, telling her about the side-effects – nausea, excessive sweating, mood swings and so on. I'm exhausted from the ride back from seeing Ian in Gosport, exhausted from digging up the dead.

She doesn't laugh. 'How did it go?'

'It went, Nix. Hours of insane rambling and a packet of pills.'

'They'll do you good. Honestly they will. I'm *so* pleased you've taken this first step. Everything will get better. I promise. It will.'

'Yeah, well, we'll see.'

Will it get better? 'You know, Nix, you take a rifle out of the armoury. You use it and eventually if you don't clean it it'll stop working. So you clean it: you pull the barrel through, scrape off the carbon, oil up the working parts, and it works. Easy. Humans aren't any different . . . how do you clean this shit out of your mind? I mean, what do you use to pull your brain through with?'

'Ian will help you do that. He's your pull-through . . . you must stick with him.' Nix was an Army officer for seven years so she knows all about pull-throughs. I'm bored of psychobabble. I've had it all afternoon, evening and now here in the pub. I want a rest from it. But I can't help it and I start rambling again.

'Wait! Milos, stop! Where does that fit in? Was that with Rose?'

'Rose! No, Nix! I've already told you . . . with Cumming . . . at the beginning.'

'Oh. Right. With Cumming.' She's confused.

'That's right. Cumming, Nix . . . when we were travelling around in January 1993.' I'm getting edgy.

Nix looks exhausted – huge bags under her eyes. She's trying to understand, but it's confusing. *I* know it's confusing – so many people, so many stories. I have to take it slowly. If she can't get it, what hope have Plod got?

'Right. We start touring. Brigadier Cumming, Simon Fox the driver, and me. The three of us in the Discovery plus that ridiculous little RB44 truck with the satellite dish that doesn't work. It followed us around like a puppy. After that New Year's Eve party on Ciovo island we were supposed to drive straight up to Fojnica where this Tactical HQ is established on one of the floors of a hotel there. But we don't, because that day, the 4th, we wake up to discover that someone has blown up one of the bridges on Route Pacman just north of Mostar. Pacman is the major aid route north and now no aid is running. No one's sure how the bridge has been destroyed so we jump into the Discovery and zip down the Dalmatian coast. Absolutely spectacular – the Dinaric Alps just drop vertically into the Adriatic and this road is simply a scar on the rock, sometimes hundreds of feet above the sea. Offshore are these enormous long, flat, grey islands lying there like hump-backed whales. They've got names like Hvar and Brac ... there are more further north, hundreds of islands. Forget Mozambique, this is the most stunning coastline in the world. At Ploce, which is a big marshy port, we cross the Neretva river and swing north following the river valley. At Metkovic we cross into Hercegovina and stick on our body armour and helmets; it's SOP for all troops in B-H to wear the stuff.'

'And the bridge?'

'It was buggered. We get to it eventually after passing Mostar, which was pretty trashed itself. It's not hard to see why; the Serbs are sitting on a massive escarpment to the south and dominating the town and the road. They can drop a shell or mortar round just about anywhere they want. The road we're on is pitted with craters. But they don't dominate the bridge because that's in a tight gorge with sheer rocky sides rising hundreds of feet. We reach the bridge which is a concrete affair, one span of which the Jugoslav National Army had dropped as they had retreated over it, so the bit that's been blown up is the wooden repair to the span which the Royal Engineers have constructed. We get chatting to the HVO soldiers there. One, a battalion commander, blames it on the Muslims on the other side, which baffles me because they're supposed to be allies. One of the soldiers then tells me that the Chetniks (an extreme wing of Serb irregulars) came down the gorge wall at night and did it. That's scarcely believable because it's sheer and covered in ice and is hundreds of feet high. So how did they get back up?

'We don't hang around for long. Colonel John Field, the Engineer Regiment CO, turns up to assess the damage. It's bitterly cold. This icy wind just howls down the gorge and cuts right through you, so it's time to get back to Split.'

'What has all this got to do with anything? What's the relevance of this bridge?'

'Nothing and everything. Just illustrates what it was like out there. Something blows up and the UN has to crisis-manage the problem. Secondly, the date is fundamentally important: that's when I started working and it marked the end of the honeymoon period between the Croats and Muslims in Central Bosnia. Obvious now but it wasn't so obvious then. We reached Split that evening just in time for the 1700 O Group. The whole HQ is crammed into the briefing room. Chris Lawton tells us that someone had tossed a grenade at someone else in Mostar that day, and then Richard Barrons briefs us on ICFY's Vance–Owen Peace Plan, which has just been announced.'

'Which was?'

'Which was never going to work, in my opinion . . . now. But not then. I didn't know anything about these wider plans then or their significance. But in essence the VOPP map divided B-H into ten cantons; two for the Croats, three for the Serbs, three for the Muslims, one a mixed Muslim/Croat (number ten). The last canton (number seven), around Sarajevo, was mixed and of special status, having some sort of UN/EU administrator running the place. On paper it all looks fair and square, but in practice, on the ground, different groups are all mixed up in each other's cantons-to-be. Worse still, all three parties have completely different aspirations, none of which can be stuffed into that VOPP map. The 4th of January 1993 is the day it all went horribly wrong.

'The next day we start touring and travelled up to Tac stopping off at all the British locations – TSG, 'Fort Redoubt' on Route Triangle, the company base at GV and the main Cheshires' base at Vitez. All the routes were iced over – vehicles and aid trucks stranded all over the place. It made operating virtually impossible.'

'Well, we managed it in the Arctic.' Niki had been the Assistant Adjutant in 29 Commando and had done a winter deployment to Norway.

'You may well have done, but there's a huge difference. You lot stopped training at –30°C and went into survival mode, didn't you?' She nods.

'We're not talking about –30° here, Niki. We're talking *freezing*. It was the coldest winter for decades. The lowest recorded temperature was –67° with the wind-chill factor. Everything froze. Nothing would work. Diesel jellied up in fuel tanks, but guess what? The locals kept on fighting. We were sort of all right with a lukewarm Discovery wrapped around us. But the locals kept on at it. They're the hardest bastards I've ever seen. Just beyond Fort Redoubt, on Triangle over the mountain and through the forest, there was an HVO checkpoint – big Croatian flag hanging vertically off a wire stretched high across the road. We're stopped by this soldier, a mad longhair with broken teeth and wild eyes. He's wearing trainers, cammo trousers and a lumberjack shirt open at the neck and with rolled-up sleeves. He's clutching some bottle of poison and he's waving and grinning like mad at us. And, we're freezing *inside* the vehicle! We think we're hard as nails in the Paras, but these boys are in a completely different league.

'We're based on the fourth floor of this hotel in Fojnica, which is at the

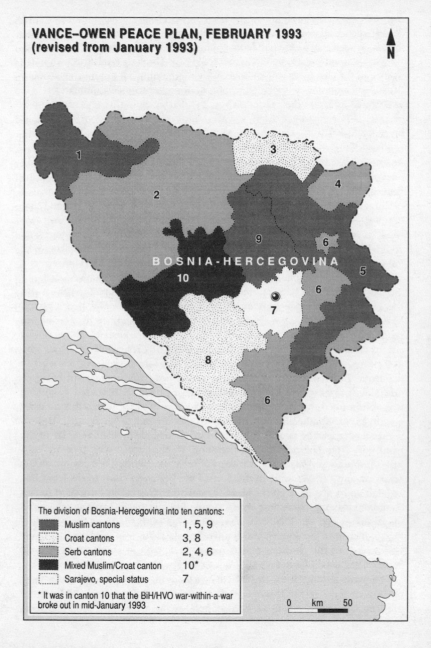

**VANCE–OWEN PEACE PLAN, FEBRUARY 1993
(revised from January 1993)**

N

BOSNIA-HERCEGOVINA

The division of Bosnia-Hercegovina into ten cantons:

▓	Muslim cantons	1, 5, 9
░	Croat cantons	3, 8
▒	Serb cantons	2, 4, 6
■	Mixed Muslim/Croat canton	10*
░	Sarajevo, special status	7

* It was in canton 10 that the BiH/HVO war-within-a-war
broke out in mid-January 1993

0   km   50

top end of a valley. The rest of the hotel has been given over as some sort of convalescence centre. So, all you see are blokes hobbling around on crutches, legless, armless, all war-wounded – youngsters and old men for the most part. But, it's a good location for Tac with BHC in Kiseljak only fifteen minutes away and the Cheshires half an hour. We end up doing a lot of touring around. Brigadier Cumming never failed to pop in and chat to local commanders. He was trying to assess their mood. Thus, I ended up doing quite a lot of interpreting. It is vital to get to grips with military speak when your language is virtually domestic. 'Pass the bread, Mum' hardly prepares you for 'anti-aircraft artillery'. Had to learn that fast.

'I met Nick Costello on that first trip. We overnighted at Vitez and sat in on Bob Stewart's O Group that evening. Nick was sitting just in front of me wearing one of those green shamaghs, which he gave to me when he left. We called it the interpreter's shamagh. Someone pointed him out to me and that evening we're in the Cheshires' Officers' Mess, an ex-night club on the main road. It still had one of those glittery balls hanging from the ceiling. You could just imagine it being a sort of speak-easy before the war. The 9/12 Lancers had even shipped in their leather furniture from their Mess in Germany and everyone's drinking from Cheshires 22nd of Foot silver goblets.

'On 7 January we were on the road again. Cumming wanted to get up into the Tesanj salient so we took along the Cheshires' LO for the area, Captain Matthew Dundas-Whatley. He'd already fixed up a number of meetings to go to with all the local commanders. All for me to translate. The first was with this horrendous creep – a really nasty piece of Croat work in Zepce who at the time was making life intolerable for the Muslims in the town. He wanted them out. D-W had warned us that he was thoroughly unpleasant, but even that hadn't prepared us for a torrent of racist invective. Brigadier Cumming was so outraged that he simply said to us all in English, which this monster couldn't understand, 'I'm not listening to this anymore. We're off!' And off we went, deeper and deeper into this salient, this light bulb-shaped bit of the front line, attending meeting after meeting. By the time it was dark my head was thumping and my teeth aching; I'd been interpreting for almost eleven hours on and off. We were in this sort of bunker quite close to the front line at Jelah and I just gave up the ghost. I remember Cumming's question to this commander being something really simple but my brain ran out of oil and the engine seized up. The Serbs then opened up with the most almighty firefight which just got louder and louder. It was their way of saying "Happy Christmas" to the Muslims and Croats – "Happy Christmas . . . we're still here!" That was a long day. I fell out of love with interpreting that day.

'The next day the Serbs shelled TSG throughout the afternoon and we just tore down there in the Discovery, all over those dreadful roads and iced-up bottlenecks. That's when we had to hole up in a Spartan with the Serbs dropping shells all around us. And the Bosnian Deputy Prime Minister was murdered. Bloody awful, the whole thing.

'After the incident in TSG we went back to Fojnica, then down to Split where Richard Barrons had been holding the fort and fielding a barrage of questions from the UK. Cumming had to get back for that. The day after, the 11th, while we were down in Split, the storm breaks with a vengeance. The bubble burst in GV where the HVO and BiH went for each other's throats with poor old B Company 1 Cheshires caught in the middle of it. We were getting horrifying reports from Split: one hamlet after another around GV was being obliterated, mostly by the Croats. The worst of it for us was that the Main Supply Route to Vitez and Zenica went right through GV which meant that nothing – no aid, no convoys – could get up country using that route. GV became a "hard" area; i.e. no "soft-skinned" vehicles allowed through unless escorted by a couple of Warriors and only then if the situation permitted. At the GV base itself only "armour" was allowed out in an attempt to mediate, assess the damage and help wounded civilians.'

'But I just don't understand why they started fighting. You've told me they were allies fighting the Bosnian Serbs.'

'We could scarcely understand it ourselves at the time. It didn't make any sense. They needed our aid but by fighting each other they were depriving themselves of that. We were naïve. But now I know why it happened. Two reasons. First, the Bosnian Croats wanted Hercegovina for themselves. They even called it Herceg-Bosna, claiming Mostar as their capital. This had all started long before I got there. In October 1992 they'd hoofed all the Muslims out of Prozor which is on the route to GV. They hadn't just asked them to leave. They'd forced them out. It was a scary place to drive through – some homes intact, others bullet-ridden and burned out with Nazi swastikas and the Croatian Ustasa "U" daubed all over them. Secondly, I reckon they interpreted the VOPP as a green-for-go: *"This'll be a Croat canton. We don't want the Muslims here, so, let's fuck 'em off before we have to put pen to paper."* Well, that's what it looked like at the time, on the ground at any rate.

'I remember we were in the BBC house in Kiseljak once. We used to pop in there either for tea or supper, courtesy of the BBC, if we were passing through. We'd meet the lot of them that way. That's where I'd first met Martin Bell. He'd just come out of Sarajevo where he'd finished making a *Panorama* documentary. He'd been badly wounded there in August 1992 but he'd gone back into that hellhole four months later. He's the only one of them to have got under the skin of the bigger issues. The rest of them were quite content to hang onto the coat tails of the British Army. We were having supper there one night with some of the UK press when Cumming just ups and says, "Why don't you get yourself down to Prozor where the Croats are pitchforking to death the Muslim farmers around the town whom they failed to cleanse out in October." '

'And did they?'

'Don't know. Doubt it though, because it's not worth it for them. The editor in London would probably have said "Too difficult. Give me Serbs doing bad things. We can't sell this mess to the public, they'll never understand." So the Croats crack on wielding their pitchforks and no one knows.'

'And you were in the middle of all this?'

'The UN was but I wasn't personally. For some of it I was in Split with Brigadier Cumming. I went where he went. But others were and paid dearly ... two days after it blew we got our first casualty. Not a helicopter but a real live human being. The 13th of January – even the date makes my skin crawl. We're in Split and we start to get this sitrep through – a Brit casualty in GV, no more than that. That's the way initial sitreps are, and usually wildly inaccurate. We didn't know who it was, what's gone on or where. We're all in the Ops Room listening to the reports as they come in. Cumming is extremely anxious. They're his boys you know, and he cared for them because they were his responsibility. And, as these reports come in he looks more and more shaken. He's close to tears. We're all close to tears. And then it's confirmed ...

'... Dead, Nix. Corporal Wayne Edwards. Shot in the head and killed ... and do you know what he was doing? ... he was driving his Warrior through GV escorting an ambulance full of wounded civilians. He was doing his humanitarian duty and some bastard shot him. When it was confirmed the whole Ops Room went silent. It's bad enough in Northern Ireland where there's a real threat, but not on a peacekeeping operation where you're trying to help people and save lives ... the only thing worse than being shot at by the enemy is being shot at by people you're trying to help. I loathe the lot of them – Serbs, Croats, Muslims. Taking our aid and goodwill wasn't enough for them. Wayne Edwards, Warburton, all the others. They had to have our lives as well.'

Niki is looking at me in horror.

'I remember seeing his coffin in a hearse outside the Officers' Mess block. It had a Union Flag draped over it and I remember thinking, *"What on earth do you tell his parents?"* The strangest thing about his murder was the reaction back home.'

'I think I remember it.'

'No! Not the public – the politicians. They sweat buckets over casualties. We get this daft question from JHQ to answer, *"Why was Corporal Edwards killed when he was in a Warrior?"* Shall I tell you where that one came from? It came from the very top, from the Secretary of State for Defence who ups and asks someone on the 6th floor of the MoD just that. You can see it now, *"You've told me Warriors are impregnable to small arms fire. So, why was someone killed in a Warrior?"* I mean for God's sake! Anyway, this question bounces all the way down the chain of command and instead of someone in Wilton fielding it, it's passed out to us and lands on some watchkeeper's desk.'

'But why was he killed?' Sometimes I think Nix spent the whole of her Army career skiing.

'Simple, Nix, the driver's the most vulnerable person. The commander and gunner can get their heads down and see everything through sights and periscopes. Blokes in the back are safe unless *they* toss a rocket up your arse. But the driver has to see where he's going, so he's got a bit of his head up, that's all. Someone was a good shot equals deliberate shot equals murder in my book.'

'Don't you think you're being a bit harsh on people? In a way, if you don't know what you know it's not that unreasonable a question.'

'Maybe,' I mumble. 'But there were other stupid questions: "How many tonnes of aid were moved today?" would land on the watchkeeper's desk at 3 a.m., just so that some Minister could be told at his or her morning briefing. But who is the poor old watchkeeper going to ring at 4 a.m. local? Everyone in UNHCR is asleep because they're human beings who need their sleep . . . it's not doing me any good all this, Nix. I mean, talking just makes me furious. It doesn't help.' I *am* furious. I've half forgotten these snippets, but somehow, starting at the beginning, it all floods back.

'I suppose the fighting put a stop to your touring then?'

'Did it hell. We were up country and back down again like a bloody yo-yo. If it wasn't visiting the troops or BHC then it was always because we had a visitor on our hands. They flocked out from the UK, and they weren't small fry either – three-star and upward. Two-star downwards? Forget it – too junior, wait your turn. The other UN contingents thought we were crazy. The Spanish battalion in Mostar was just sent out for a year and told to get on with it. No one came from Spain to visit them. Visiting is very much a British pastime. We were the most visited people in the Balkans.'

'Like who?'

'Like everyone. PM came out at Christmas clutching a little plastic carrier bag of CDs to give to the troops. Then we had Chief of Defence Staff, Field Marshall Inge, who I remember was accosted on Route Triangle by a chain-saw-wielding Sapper who came staggering out of the woods like something out of the *Bosnia Chainsaw Massacre* all wild-eyed, buzzing and billowing plumes of blue smoke. To the inevitable question he'd said, "Enjoying myself, sir? This is fookin' great – in Germany you can't snap a twig without getting bollocked, I've just chopped down twenty-five trees this morning!" And with another "fookin' great" off he charged back into the forest trailing smoke. Next in the queue was CinC UKLF, a mere four-star, General "Muddy" Waters. That one was a horror story. It nearly went horribly wrong.'

'How?'

'First of all, he's a man with a fearsome reputation. Bob Edge was his house sergeant for years and told me one horror story after another. They didn't care in the least what the situation was like on the ground. They were coming out regardless. General Waters was due to fly into Sarajevo on the airlift on 17 January and would be met there by Peter Jones whose four-man team of "loggies" was in the city assisting UNHCR. BRITDET Sarajevo was the jewel in the crown of the whole operation. You've got this "Reputation" flying in and Peter has to meet and entertain him until Brigadiers Cumming and Cordy-Simpson, and Victor Andreyev, the BHC head of UN Civil Affairs for B-H, can get in from Kiseljak to pick him up. The plan then is to whip him around Sarajevo, out to BHC and thence to Vitez to overnight with the Cheshires. It nearly didn't happen.

'We're in the foyer of this monstrously overcrowded and over-multinationalised hotel-cum-UN HQ. The three of them are about to hop into an armoured Land Rover and disappear off to Sarajevo. But, there's a flap on from hell. Waters is about to land at Sarajevo but the mad women of Hadzici don't care. They've decided that the 17th is the day they want to do their sit-down protest.'

'Who? Mad women of where? Why?' I've thrown her.

'Look. Let me explain. You've got to understand the geography. This beer mat is Sarajevo and the lighter is BHC in Kiseljak. Right?' She nods. I dip my finger in my drink, join them with a wiggly line and slash it in two places, one near the lighter and one even nearer to the mat. 'In between is Serb-held territory. The mat is Muslim-defended Sarajevo and the lighter is the Croat-held Kiseljak pocket. Well, this is how it goes . . .' my finger starts moving from the lighter, '. . . this is the only way into Sarajevo by road for UN vehicles, convoys and the like. It's only twenty-one kilometres but it's a fearsome drive. First few kilometres east out of Kiseljak are okay. Then after some tight, uphill S-bends you hit an HVO checkpoint, Kilo 1, "K" for Croat, logical eh? Usually no problem there and you sail through into a very quiet no-man's-land. Simple. Then round a sharp left-hander you arrive at Hell, Kobiljaca, the first Serb checkpoint, Sierra 1. The most obnoxious, obstreperous and difficult people. They haul over convoys, rip through possessions, confiscate "illegal items" just like that. They hold up convoys of food or wood for weeks. Nightmarish. That's S-1. It's a bit like Dungeons & Dragons. Then, if you're lucky, you proceed down the road for about ten kilometres to a Y-junction at Hadzici – Sierra 2 – sometimes activated sometimes not, depending on whether they want to trap convoys between S-1 and S-2. Get through that and a bit further on you're into this vile hornets' nest of a place called Ilidza, a Serb-held suburb of Sarajevo full of people who hate *everyone,* including all the other Serbs on account of them being virtually isolated. Once you've braved the insults, abuse, stones and gob it's right and down a horribly bumpy and long alley to Sierra 4 . . .'

'Where's three?'

'Funny, but I can't really recall there being an S-3. Must be in Ilidza somewhere . . . anyway, S-4 is the last and it's about half way down this alley. Once through and to the end and you hit a T-junction. Right takes you to the airport. Left takes you through a really dangerous no-man's-land with a destroyed T55 tank and recovery vehicle. Before that there's a French UN checkpoint, an APC blocking the road. It drives back two metres, lets you pass, and then forward two metres blocking the road again. Most interesting job in the world, eh? And then you drive as fast as you can along this totally exposed road with trashed houses, I mean completely levelled, on either side. After about 700 metres you hit BiH lines, scoot down a tight right-hander which loops you around a tiny cemetery to the first BiH checkpoint under Stup flyover. And then you're in. That's what it's like normally.'

'And what about *ab*normally? Sounds bad enough as it is.'

'*Ab*normally, anything can happen – hi-jackings, severe fighting and mad women! As it was that day. The mad women of Hadzici decide it's Protest Day and they all sit in the road at S-2 with their kids and babies and won't budge until their demands are met. Nothing goes in and out of Sarajevo all day long. Convoys are stuck on both sides of these women. It's *the most* effective way of blocking a road. Soldiers are no good for such a showdown because you can always shoot them or, as Brigadier Cordy-Simpson did once, when one of these oiks pointed his weapon at him, fly into a rage, grab 'em by the scruff of the neck and shake them to bits. But with women and kids you can't do that, certainly no one from the UN is going to run them down, particularly as they'll always have their own press there to record the event.'

'Why were they doing it?'

'We didn't know. But there's a huge flap on; nothing's moved in or out of the city because of these women, and we're staring at the prospect of Waters being stuck on one side and us on the other. The fastest way of screwing up your career is to stuff up a visit programme for one of the Brass. He won't blame the women; he'll blame you. Cordy-Simpson turns to me and says, "You'd better come along and earn your pay today." I was supposed to be left at BHC – too junior. So, I'm sitting in this closed-up vehicle and wondering just what I'm supposed to do about all these women. Eventually, the vehicle stops and we all hop out and there they all are – all these women dressed in black and sitting in the middle of the road screaming that they won't budge until they get word that their husbands and sons, who are POWs in a Muslim prison in Tarcin, are alive.'

'What did you do?'

'It ended up with me and Victor in a tiny room with their representatives.

We made a deal: only our vehicles in and out in return for Victor promising to get the International Committee of the Red Cross to look into the matter immediately. Sounds easy, but it required a load of play-acting, sympathetic nodding, and, basically, grovelling. But we did it and got to the airport to find Peter chatting to the "Reputation". Did he look relieved! There were no more flights out and he'd have had to look after an irate four-star all night in the PTT building's more than squalid accommodation.

'We jumped into the vehicles and zipped him around Sarajevo. I remember that tour because I saw nothing, being in the back of an armoured Land Rover. We were told not to stick our heads up through the hatch because somebody would shoot them off. But, we did stop at this cemetery by Kosevo hospital, called the Lion Cemetery. It's a regular feature on the Balkan tourist route, a staggering place brimming with graves. There are Muslim head and foot stones, but they're not stones, they're coffin-shaped wooden boards. And just as many Christian crosses. But the spookiest thing is that all the graves are freshly turned, hundreds, thousands, and they've even started in the corner of a football pitch below. That place leaves you with a huge lump in your throat. You only have to see it once and you'll never forget it.

'The rest of the visit was pretty straightforward. We overnighted in Vitez and the next day tried to get Waters through GV by Warrior, but the fighting was too severe. It was good for him to see that plans do go wrong simply because the locals couldn't give a damn about your visit programme. We took him the long way to TSG instead, via Kresevo, Jablanica, and Route Square. We slept at TSG and the next day two 845 NAS Sea Kings picked us up and tried to fly us into the warehouse at Metkovic. They damn near succeeded as thick fog forced them to fly along the Neretva river, but even then it was no good as the fog was sitting on the water. So we aborted and flew up the coast past those whale-shaped islands to Split where he eventually met as many members of the Gloucesters as they could find. You know, Nix, the funny thing was that throughout the trip Waters never said a single word to me. Never once even acknowledged my presence. But, just as he was stepping into a car to be driven to Split airport he turned to me, and do you know what he said?'

Niki shrugs.

'He just ups and says, "Thanks for getting me through that checkpoint. Don't go native out here. We don't want to lose you." His very words. He completely floored me. Wise old bird. He knew. He knew what might happen and was the only one to see that danger.'

'And did you go native? Is this what this is all about?' She's looking at me anxiously.

'I hate that expression "going native". It's dirty. It belongs to the last century, to the Raj. Going native – what does it really mean? You tell me.'

'Well, I suppose it means . . .'

'I'll tell you what it means. To my enemies, to my detractors, to most people who don't know me, including these Keystone Cops, it means "siding with the Serbs". That's what they'll tell you because it's a natural conclusion, a racist one, to jump to. Being partisan. That was and is their spin. But!'

'Milos! Keep your voice down.'

I hardly hear her. 'But to me it means something else. Sure I did go native, I admit it, native as they come. But it's not entirely my fault and it's not what people think. I went native all right, but in a weird way. You won't ever understand. You're English. You can't understand . . . it's all to do with parcels and history . . .'

'Parcels? History?' She's lost again.

'Look, the parcels came first and our family history fed the process of "going native".' Niki is just staring at me. She probably thinks I've finally flipped.

'You can listen to this, but you'll never ever understand what I'm going to tell you – simply because you're English. You come from a country that was last invaded in 1066. No invader has ever set foot in Britain since. Sure, the Spanish and Germans have tried in the past. It's madness to try and invade this island – first you've got to brave hideous seas, then you've got to overcome treacherous rocks and cliffs, and, if you manage all that, you've then got to deal with 60 million people with "bad attitude". So, none of you know what it's like and your family has always lived in England.'

'So what?' Now she's getting angry.

'So a lot. You've had your last civil war nearly four hundred years ago. You've got the oldest and most respected democracy in the world. It's a democracy which has come about naturally through *evolution* and not *revolution*. You people don't even know what you've got here! You take it all for granted. But, remember, no other country in Europe has got what you've got . . .'

'But, what're you driving at? Get it out!'

'All right. This is the way it is. I'm the son of refugees who've lost everything they had in Yugoslavia. My father began life in Britain as a displaced person, as a hod carrier. Growing up was a nightmare. There was no money. Endless arguments over making ends meet. We were the only kids at school without pocket money. When you grow up in that environment you adopt the same mentality. You become a sort of Scrooge, a hoarder. My mother won't throw anything out, ever. She works at Dr Barnado's and buys half the shop for herself! The house is full of rubbish; the family motto is "mend and make do". Why? Because she once lost everything. It's recorded in her memory banks. You become like that yourself.'

'How does all this tie in with Bosnia and going native?'

'Simple, Nix. Here's the rub. You've got everything. Life is comfortable financially. You've been careful as hell and have thousands stashed away – thousands that will never be spent – just in case . . . and then you go out there and something massive happens in your life. Something so huge that it makes you go native . . .'

'What?'

'You meet the Little People, as General Rose used to call them. You meet these Little People because you're in a privileged position. You speak the lingo and you have this *curse* of understanding, a sort of secret passageway into their minds and mentality. You have the curse because you're born with it. You *are* one of them. And when you meet them you're staring into a time warp. You're staring at the way your parents once were. You're looking at people who ten months previously had a life, a family, a house, comfort, electricity and gas at a flick, possessions and things that make life tick along. Everything *you* now take for granted. And suddenly *BANG*, they've got nothing. They've lost members of the family killed, the kids have been evacuated and they're somewhere in the West – but where? They don't know. They haven't heard from them for a year. They've got no heating, no light, no gas and it's freezing cold. They're cowering in their miserable little flats that used to be homes. Some of the rooms they can't go into because shrapnel and bullets come in through the window. In a dirty backroom, where it's safer, they huddle over a jam jar of water which has an inch of oil floating on top, and a piece of string suspended in this thing is burning with a yellow sooty flame. And they're scared out of their tiny minds because they have no future. But, they do have their dignity, which they cling to desperately because it's all they've got. When you see *that* for the first time and you're staring at your parents through a hole in time, you're touched by something, which I can't adequately explain. And it's only then that you realise that all you have, your comfortable home in Farnham, the car, the bike, the emergency dosh – all of it is meaningless. Because you have everything and they have nothing and you're ashamed. And these were people whom I loathed because they were "Communists"! Up close they're just human beings who want what you and I want – a life. When that happens, you're presented with a choice – do something or do nothing. Walk on by on the other side or cross the street . . . I chose to cross the street. I went native, simple as that.'

Niki has gone terribly silent. Neither of us is saying anything. A million thoughts, none of them good, are turning over in my mind. If that couple over there, sitting quietly with their drinks, minding their own businesses, could read my mind. Christ Almighty. I'm seeing them in Sarajevo, in Hell, going through what people out there go through. They haven't the faintest idea what it's all about. Niki breaks my train of thought, thank God.

I can feel her tugging on my arm. 'Milos! You're staring at those people. Are you all right?'

'Do you think there's such a thing as Fate, Nix?'

'I do. I've always thought there was such a thing.'

'Well, there is. I know it exists because I've experienced it. I sound like a bloody raving missionary. It comes out of nowhere, it leads you down a path and yet you don't know you're being led. And it starts with something totally innocuous.'

'For example?'

'Well, in my case it was a small parcel from the UK. Y'know, I didn't just up and decide to be a do-gooder. As I've explained, my instincts are quite selfish. Had that first parcel not come out I'd probably have done a couple of six-monthers out there as a regular Joe interpreter. I'd have come away from that place clean, but none the wiser. I got pushed into it by that first parcel.'

'I don't understand this thing about parcels.'

'That's because I haven't told you about it. Listen, as I've told you, the fighting between the Muslims and Croats intensifies throughout January. The tension spreads north-eastwards right up to Vitez in the Lasva valley. Checkpoints spring up all over the place – BiH and HVO checkpoints. They're like dogs marking their territory, staking claim to their villages and hamlets. The road linking Vitez with Kiseljak through the Busovaca valley is riddled with these checkpoints and very shortly the fighting erupts there at a place called Kacuni. By now Bob Stewart is spending every day trying to keep the lid on all this. He's shuttling the various commanders up to Kiseljak for talks at BHC. In front of the UN they agree to cease-fires that collapse before the ink is dry. The situation gets so bad that eventually Brigadier Cumming is summoned back to London on 22 January to attend a Prime Minister's working supper at Number 10.

'That morning he's up in the MoD briefing various people and he bumps into Major General Mike Jackson, who has some job in the Ministry at the time. Jackson's a Para. He was CO in the mid-1980s when he commanded 1 PARA in Bulford. We call him PoD, the Prince of Darkness, because although he's English we reckon that he actually comes from Transylvania and needs at least a litre of fresh human blood every day to keep him going. We adored him, but he was dangerous – if you drink with Jackson you die! Jackson hands Cumming this small parcel. Apparently, he's got an au pair, a young girl from Sarajevo, who was stuck in London when the war started and hasn't had any contact with her parents in Sarajevo. Jackson gives Cumming this parcel and asks him to see if he can get it delivered. That evening he attends the supper at Number 10. They're all there: John Major, Lord Owen, Douglas Hurd, Malcolm Rifkind, etc.

'Later, I asked Brigadier Andrew how it went, so I've only got this second hand. So, they're all there pontificating about how to make the VOPP work and banging on about "lines-to-take" and "ways-forward". They completely ignore Cumming. Eventually, towards the end Cumming is asked his opinion since he's the man on the ground. Cumming tells them straight, same as he told the press back in Kiseljak: "As we speak the Croats are pitchforking to death Muslim farmers around Prozor . . ." Douglas Hurd is incredulous and apparently says, "I don't think we want to hear that." Well, of course they didn't; it blows their plan to bits. But Cumming did say that Hurd approached him afterwards and said, "Is that really what's happening?" Even they couldn't believe that these "allies" were turning against each other.

'A few days later Brigadier Cumming is back and five of us drive up to Kiseljak in the Discovery. That's the three of us plus the Civil Adviser and Captain David Crummish who is the SO3 G3 Ops in the Split HQ. General Morillon has decided it's time for a big pow-wow on how to withdraw the UN from B-H. As you can see, we were full of self-confidence. We called it the "Running Away Conference". Cumming and all the COs have to attend. Come the day of the conference at BHC we're all pretty redundant so Cumming suggests that, rather than hanging around the foyer of the hotel all day long, we take a trip into Sarajevo. He asks me to take along Jackson's parcel and give it to Peter Jones to deliver. That morning the four of us – Simon Fox, the Civil Adviser, David Crummish and myself – leap into one of the Danish M113 APCs which run a couple of regular daily shuttles between the city and BHC. And off we go along that Dungeons & Dragons route of unpredictable checkpoints into Sarajevo.'

SEVEN

Operation Grapple, Bosnia

Thursday 28 January 1993 – Sarajevo

She was quite the most fearsome woman I had ever seen. It wasn't the one-piece blue camouflage 'frontier guard' uniform, nor the short-barrelled AK47 carbine slung over her shoulder. It wasn't even the gruff manner of her questioning. It was the moustache, the beard and the horrible black hairy mole. I was quaking.

For ten minutes or so we'd clattered along the road out of Kiseljak. Since we hadn't stopped we'd evidently sailed straight through K-1. The four of us were crammed into the back of the M113 along with one other passenger, a Ukrainian grinning like a maniac. Conversation was out of the question: the clattering of tracks, crashing of gears and high-revving engine all conspired to obliterate any other sound and threatened to loosen our fillings. Like rush-hour commuters we clung grimly onto leather straps as the tin can bounced and lurched alarmingly around corners and bends.

'What's in your bag?' demanded the bearded woman after she'd inspected our ID cards.

'Just personal effects . . . you know, for shaving and washing . . .' I prayed she wouldn't inspect it. Wrapped in a towel was the brown paper parcel. It was addressed to *Pijalovic, Ulica Romanijska, Sarajevo* and even had a photocopied map of the centre of town glued to it showing our destination. It was strictly against the rules by which the shuttle operated to smuggle letters or anything into the Muslims of Sarajevo. Fortunately, she didn't seem too interested in the daysack and the door of the APC slammed shut again.

You have successfully negotiated the Bearded Woman of S-1 at Kobiljaca. Proceed to S-2!

After another twenty minutes of discomfort the APC once again lurched to a halt. We had no idea where we were. The journey in was utterly disorientating – no frame of reference, no windows. Just the incessant racket and the crazy Ukrainian. Again the door opened and this time an enormously bearded and long-haired Serbian soldier demanded to see our IDs. We were in a tight alley – S-4 – and close to the front line. As we set off, the Danish commander closed his hatch, rolled his eyes and with a sickly grin yelled, 'Heavy shelling and fighting.'

First stop the airport. No one got out but a couple of UN soldiers squeezed in and off we sped again, racing through no-man's-land. Even above the APC's din the dull booming of mortar and shell rounds impacting somewhere could be heard. The APC swerved dangerously around the Stup graveyard and then accelerated down Sniper's Alley. A couple of minutes later we ground to a halt. 'PTT Building' announced our taxi driver.

Stiffly we clambered out of our Tardis and blinked around at the unfamiliar surroundings. The experience had been disorientating, as if we'd stepped into an inefficient and sluggish transporter at Kiseljak. After much discomfort we'd popped out at the other end into another world. Gone were the steep sided, heavily forested, snow-covered valleys of Central Bosnia. Suddenly we were dumped into an unfamiliar world of urban warfare littered with burned-out high rise buildings, crumbling concrete, rusting and abandoned bullet-riddled trams, sagging, broken electric wires. And the incessant, dull booming of impacting shells and the popping of small arms which echoed up and down the valley that was Sarajevo.

Directly in front of us loomed a concrete monstrosity that resembled the superstructure of an aircraft carrier. Being some four or five storeys high and therefore open to shellfire damage, its windows were criss-crossed with brown masking tape. The edifice, something like an imaginery Willy Wonka's Chocolate Factory, was crowned with a shattered but still legible sign – PTT INZINJERING. The former Postal, Telephone and Telecommunications building was now UN HQ Sector Sarajevo.

To our left, beyond some dirty brown warehouses and what appeared to be a dilapidated cable-making gantry, rose a steep-sided hill. This was Zuc. To this clung myriad houses all with square brown roofs. With little apparent regard for town-planning, these houses had been carelessly and densely scattered across the hillside. Some were burned out. Most of the roofs sported gaping black holes which exposed shattered skeletal timbers. As we stared, one erupted in a cloud of dust. A boom echoed across the valley and bounced off the PTT building. It filled me with terror. This was worse than the valleys where the danger zones and front lines were at least known. This was completely random. A man could get killed here by accident.

We scuttled up a steep concrete ramp, past a French guard and across a raised car park filled with an odd assortment of vehicles, French APCs, armoured Land Rovers and Toyota Land Cruisers. All dirty off-white and adorned with various emblems – UN, UNHCR, UNICEF, ICRC. For such an imposing building, the back entrance was surprisingly modest: a small glass and aluminium door set into the far corner of the car park. The front, on Sniper's Alley, was far too dangerous to use. A burly French Foreign

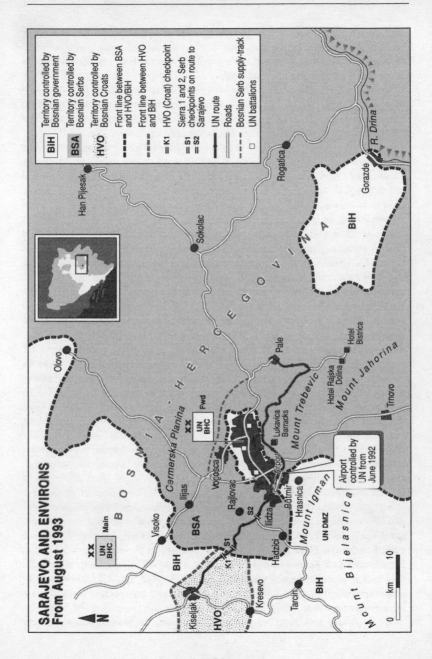

Legionnaire Para from 2eme REP blocked our further passage to safety. Patiently we lined up and showed our IDs. The fact that we were in uniform and wearing blue helmets seemed to matter not a jot. This was the land of checkpoints, of ID cards and of hard men 'with orders'.

Once we'd penetrated this UN citadel we found ourselves in a large foyer, at journey's end. We hadn't a clue where to go next. All the BiH and BSA liaison offices, as well as aid agencies, had been stuffed down a narrow, gloomy corridor. I was vaguely aware of civilians scurrying between offices, ID cards around their necks. I was sure I'd find Peter Jones here. It surprised me that all the aid agencies had been isolated in such a small part of the building but I later discovered that they were engaged in a bitter defensive battle with the military. Quite simply, the French wanted the civilians out of their military citadel. It seemed to me that we soldiers had already forgotten precisely why we were in Bosnia.

We went in search of somebody to brief us. David Crummish wanted to talk to someone, anyone, in Ops. The interior of the PTT building almost defied description. A wide, square, dark central well of cold stairs ran from the top of the building right down into its subterranean depths. A hawser of cables of varying degrees of thickness, all taped together into a knotted black snake, hung down the well. It was the core of the building's central nervous system. At each level it sprouted nerves of black worms which meandered along gloomy, wooden-partitioned corridors leading to offices, Ops rooms, and, further up, accommodation. The inhabitants of the citadel were all escapees from *Blade Runner*. Coal-scuttle helmeted Legionnaires, FAMAS rifles strapped across their chests, long bayonets slapping loosely against their thighs, the buckles on their boots jangling, menaced the entrances like members of a Praetorian Guard. Elsewhere in the dim corridors the camouflage uniforms of a plethora of nations vied for attention. Weaving their way between the uniforms, civilians – locals, interpreters and internationals – darted about their business. One thing united them all: everyone seemed to be clutching a Motorola walkie-talkie into which they would scream in whatever language seemed appropriate.

The Ukrainian Ops Officer's English was limited. David Crummish nodded politely, understanding nothing. I couldn't be bothered to listen to his gibberish. It reminded me of Kuwait. All I wanted to do was to find Peter Jones. I'd popped into UNHCR and politely asked where he could be found. I'd met a wall of hostile faces – they didn't like soldiers in their enclave – and had been informed that he was out in a place called Dobrinja, that he'd be back in an hour or so. Eventually the Ukrainian's English ran out. We were left none the wiser, but in true English fashion thanked him profusely for a most informative overview of the situation in Sarajevo.

Rumour had it that the Praetorian Guard had a coffee shop somewhere in the bowels of the citadel. We set off in opposite directions and I found myself on a lower level, in a narrow corridor, my path blocked by a huge Legionnaire with a lantern jaw and shaven head.

'Excuse ... me ...' I spoke no French so took it slowly, '... is ... there ... anywhere ... where ... a ... man ... can ... get ... a ... coffee? ... *Café?*'

'You a Brit?' he replied in an accent straight from the mid-West cornbelt. Dumbstruck, I nodded slowly. 'Sure, buddy. One floor down, same corridor, turn right at the end ...' And then he was gone. Later I got to know him well – Tom Iron, ex-US Ranger, now Corporal-Chef, 2eme REP.

The four of us regrouped and descended into the depths in search of the elusive coffee shop. Not there. Oops, that's a hospital. *'So sorry';* two Legionnaires glared at us malevolently from their card game. We were in yet another corridor, still hunting, opening doors and apologising profusely.

Suddenly, the cloistered quiet of the corridor was shattered by a wild, animal scream and a babble of desperate voices, which surged around the corner and stopped us in our tracks. Moments later a gaggle of perhaps fifteen or twenty people, some uniformed, choked the passage ahead and advanced towards us. Unsure what to do, we flattened ourselves against the walls. A young girl of perhaps fifteen or sixteen was shrieking her head off. She was howling – a horrifying animal scream of madness. She wasn't so much being helped and supported as actually being carried. Arms and legs firmly gripped, she was carried aloft, struggling and fighting like a *beserker* while the crowd babbled in concerned and anguished 'polyglot'. The mob, flailing limbs and all, swept past us and turned the corner towards the hospital. The girl's screams echoed back down the corridor. We stood there, rooted to the spot, horrified, speechless. Something in those unhinged, feral screams had touched us all. I looked across at David and the Civil Adviser. Their eyes were staring and the blood had drained from their faces. I can hear those screams today and I can still see those ashen, horrified faces. We looked at each other for what seemed an eternity. No one moved. No one even murmured. Corporal Fox was the first to react and save us. I felt him jab me in the ribs and I could see his face in front of me. His eyes were twinkling slightly and I could see his lips, half-smiling, move in laconic slow motion.

'You know what, sir? I know exactly what she is going through.'

'How's that then, Corporal Fox?' I heard myself say.

He chuckled then laughed slowly. 'I hate going to the dentist as well.'

The spell was broken. The screams receded. We laughed nervously and self-consciously, aware that we had been, momentarily, somewhere dark and awful. We abandoned our search for coffee and, in silence, went back up to the foyer. We didn't know it at the time but the girl, a local, had been walking past the PTT building with her father. A mortar round had landed very close to them. It had decapitated him but had left her unscathed, splattered and standing in a warm pool of his brains, gore and blood – screaming her head off in terror . . . . . . Welcome to Sarajevo.

Cumming's instructions had been quite specific. 'Give the package to Peter. Tell him to deliver it only if and when he can. He shouldn't go out of his way or risk himself.' When I eventually located Peter he looked at the map on the package and told me the address was in the middle of town. Since I spoke the language, he said, I could deliver it myself.

We clambered into his battered old Range Rover, which had belonged to the British Ambassador in Athens. It had found its way, courtesy of Ms Glynne Evans of the FCO's UN Department, into Sarajevo for BRITDET's use. Until its appearance Peter and the others had only had the protection afforded by a soft-skinned Land Rover. Their job required them to cross front lines every day.

Peter Jones is an exceptional man. He is also extremely lucky to be alive. I first met him in July 1987 when we were both 'sickies' at RAF Headley Court, an RAF/Army Rehabilitation unit in Surrey. I was there rebuilding arm and shoulder muscles after a routine shoulder operation. Peter was learning to walk again having lost six inches from both legs after he'd fallen several hundred feet off a Scottish mountain. It had nearly killed him but he was making a full recovery. I only ever heard him complain once. Sucking on a Marlboro he whinged, with a smile, that the accident had cost him a small fortune in new uniforms! It came as no surprise to me that the ex-six foot two officer had been selected to lead a tiny detachment of three other soldiers in Sarajevo. I know of no one who could have done the job better.

In November 1992 UNHCR Sarajevo had asked the British to lend them some logistics advice. At the time Peter was the Ops Officer of the National Support Element at TSG. He was tasked to select and take into Sarajevo a team of three other logistics experts to help and advise UNHCR on the finer points of setting up a logistics operation for the delivery of humanitarian aid. He chose WO2 Don Hodgeson, SSgt Allan Knight and LCpl Caroline Cove. Together they drove into Sarajevo in a soft-skinned Land Rover towing a trailer. They were due to remain for two weeks but stayed for 110 days. For UNHCR they found three warehouses in the city and established an efficient system of secondary and tertiary distribution of aid. The aid was in-loaded from the warehouse at the airport to the city warehouses from where, in consultation with a four-man Bosnian commission, it was further distributed to eighty-four 'communes' (defined as a street, apartment block or area) on a fortnightly basis. In addition they strove to keep Kosevo hospital supplied with fuel oil. This brief description of their efforts does absolutely no justice to their success. On arrival they met with hostility from the local Sarajevan UNHCR staff. When they left there was scarcely a dry eye in the house.

The conditions they endured daily were far more extreme than any endured by British troops in Bosnia. BRITDET Sarajevo was the jewel in the crown. It was a flagship operation which was monitored closely by the FCO and which, rightly, accorded Peter 'favoured son' status in Split.

As we drove east along the main drag towards downtown Sarajevo the geography of the city both in terms of terrain and buildings changed markedly. The valley became narrower and the buildings older. For the most part, Sarajevo is a prime example of the dreariest Communist high rise architecture and reminded me vividly of the buildings I had seen in Minsk and Moscow, where the Army had sent me to learn Russian in the 1980s. There was scarcely a single building that remained unscathed. On the left – a grotesque concrete battleship, the TV building. Further on, the Holiday Inn hotel, a foul-looking six-storey square of yellow. Three-quarters of it was still functioning for the press, to whom rooms were charged at pre-war prices. Behind it were the twin UNIS tower blocks of glass, miniature versions of New York's World Trade Centre. Both were virtually gutted with not a single pane of glass left unbroken. On the right – a huge oblong skyscraper, which had served as B-H's parliament. Now completely gutted, it was home to snipers and sharpshooters. In some instances buildings had ceased to exist at all. Peter tried to explain the layout of the front lines but it was too confusing to absorb. I remember being surprised when he said that the Serbs not only held the hills around but also parts of the city where the line came down almost to the River Miljacka, which paralleled the main drag east-west through this long and thin valley city. Where the front line cut into the city, as it did opposite the Holiday Inn, the threat from snipers was greatest. Here ISO containers had been stacked upon each other as a barrier to view if not to bullets.

From the gutted parliament onwards the architecture became nineteenth-century Austro-Hungarian – much more pleasant on the eye, though just as battle-scarred. We were now driving along an embankment. To our right, the Miljacka was spanned at intervals by small, arched bridges. We drove over the spot where Archduke Ferdinand had been shot dead by Gavrilo Princip in 1914. On the left was the famous Europa hotel, now a grotty refugee centre. On the right, over the river, an area of tight, winding, narrow alleys and rocket-shaped minarets. This was Bistrik.

At the end of the embankment the city virtually stopped dead at the narrowest and oldest part of this steep-sided valley. High to the right – Serbs. High to our front – an old Turkish fort, and higher yet, an Austro-Hungarian barracks, both of which were Muslim-defended. At the extremity of our journey the road virtually looped back on itself, curving tightly to the left. In the centre of the loop stood the most beautiful building of all, the *Vijecnica*, or Public Records Library, which until August 1992 had been maintained in the

Austro-Hungarian style. Like so many other buildings, it was now a hollow burned-out shell. Even its great marble pillars had cracked and splintered in the savage heat which had devoured its precious contents.

We were now heading west again. The area between the embankment and us – Bascarsija – was the oldest part of Sarajevo and the heartbeat of Bosnian Muslim tradition. To our right a number of tight alleys led uphill. Suddenly, we swung right up one of them. Peter slowed and checked the map on the parcel. He stopped the vehicle. 'Ulica Romanijska, Apartment Block 2. This is it. That's your entrance. We'll wait for you. Good luck.'

I stepped out of the vehicle clutching the package. The armoured door closed with a clunk and I suddenly felt very alone, teetering on the cusp of two cultures. One lay in the Land Rover. Up some steps and through a dirty glass and metal door lay another. My heart started pounding.

Trudging up several flights of cold stairs I could have been in any one of hundreds of thousands of examples of hastily built 'people's accommodation' which littered Eastern Europe. At the top of each flight was a small square landing. To the left and to the right, blue apartment doors, each with a small brass plaque. On the fifth floor the door on the right bore the plaque engraved *'Pijalovic'*. I banged on the door. My heart started beating even faster. *What do they look like? What shall I say?* No answer. I banged again. Still no answer, no sounds of movement from within. I was about to give it a third try when a woman poked her head around the stairs from the floor above.

'They're not at home. They're both out . . .' Her voice trailed off when she saw me. Her hand flew to her throat and her eyes bled confusion. The two aliens stared at each other. I realised I was still wearing the flak jacket and helmet.

I cleared my throat, 'Er . . . I'm looking for the Pijalovics . . . for Minka Pijalovic . . . I've got a parcel from her daughter in London . . .'

'Aida!! You know her? Where is she? How is she? . . . quick, come upstairs.' She beckoned urgently. I wasn't sure what to do, but I couldn't admit defeat now. Hesitantly, I followed her upstairs and into her flat. *Who is Aida? Is that her name, the girl in London?*

'How do you know Aida? How is she? . . . they haven't heard word from her since the start . . .' She had recovered her composure somewhat, '. . . I'm sorry, but . . . well, we've never had a visitor from UNPROFOR here before.' *There! She does think I'm an alien!*

'Well, she's fine . . . I mean, I don't know her . . . all I know is that she's the au pair to one of our generals in London . . . this package is from her, I'm only the postman here . . .'

'And Arna? Where's she?' *Who the hell is Arna?* I shrugged my shoulders and shook my head, 'Fine, I suppose . . .'

We were standing in her tiny kitchen. It was sparse and bare. The window had been smashed in and replaced with a sheet of plastic. The walls and ceiling were gouged and pitted in several places where shrapnel had flown in. *How can people live like this?*

She promised to deliver the package. I wasn't sure. I didn't know her. How could I trust her not to keep it for herself? She told me her name was Greta and that she was a Serb. The Pijalovics were Muslims. Could I trust her? I had no choice and handed the package over. She looked up at me. There was hurt and sorrow in her eyes. It was as if she'd read something in mine.

'You see. The war has even touched you. The first demon of war is suspicion . . . we're all friends here in this block. We look after each other . . . we have to . . .'

I felt sick at having been exposed. Guiltily, I fished out a cigarette. It didn't occur to me to offer her one. She was middle-aged, proper looking, clean and smart. She didn't look like a grubby smoker, but her eyes followed my cigarette with a desperate hunger.

'Do you mind if I have one of your cigarettes?' Her voice was small and hollow.

I was shocked and suddenly, for the second time in as many minutes, embarrassed. She was embarrassed for asking and I was embarrassed because she was, '. . . I haven't had one for . . . I mean . . . we have nothing . . . I can't offer you coffee . . . I can't even light this fire . . . we've nothing . . .' Her voice started to quaver and I could see her eyes beginning to mist over. Shame engulfed me. All these trinkets I had, these guaranteed comforts of life, all taken for granted by me were gold dust to her, and she had been reduced to begging for a cigarette.

I dropped the packet and the cheap plastic lighter on the table. 'Please, have these, I've got plenty more.' I dug around and found a box of matches in a pocket. *What have I got in my wallet?* I fished it out. *Only 40 Deutschmarks!* But I dropped those on the table as well. I wished then I'd had more. She stared at the fortune on her table, but she didn't reject it. If it was probably the most humiliating moment of her life, it was my most shameful. I wished I'd had more to give her.

'You're one of us . . . one of *"ours"* . . . I mean, the language.' *Ti si nas! One of ours! Am I? What does she mean . . . one of 'ours'? What shall I tell her? I can't lie, not to her.*

I told her straight. I told her the truth. I couldn't be bothered to lie, not to a woman who had almost burst into tears in front of me. As I explained, the blood drained from her face, replaced by a look of horror.

'Don't ever breathe a word of this!' She was breathless, eyes pleading and concerned. 'Don't tell anyone . . . it's not safe for you here. You're from over *there*. You don't know what we're like *here*.' Her voice became sad, '. . . they should never have sent you. Go home and save yourself!'

'They didn't . . . I sent myself. It was my choice.' Her words had echoed my father's. *Are they all that wicked here? All of them? Have I missed a trick here?*

'Here!' she announced triumphantly as she rummaged about in a cupboard and fished out a bottle of something pink. 'We've got no coffee, but we've all got drink. That's something we're never short of. At least I can offer you some cherry brandy!' She was laughing now. At least they still had their dignity and sense of humour. We started drinking and chatting.

There was a bang on the door. Greta looked startled and suddenly frightened. Cautiously she opened the door and caught her breath. 'More UNPROFOR!'

Peter and David stood at the door, Peter looking both worried and relieved at the same time.

'Mike! We were worried about you . . . thought you'd been kidnapped or something.'

I laughed, looked at Greta and then at her pile of gold dust on the table. 'I have been, Peter . . . in a manner of speaking.' I finished the drink, kissed Greta on the cheek and left her. I didn't see her again for two and a half years.

Peter continued his guided tour, this time up to Kosevo Hospital and the Lion Cemetery for David's benefit. I didn't register the rest of the tour (my mind was elsewhere) but eventually we found ourselves back at the PTT building. We dropped David off; he was going to overnight there and catch the airlift down to Split in the morning. The Civil Adviser and Simon Fox were still in the building somewhere and David promised to make sure they caught the last APC shuttle back to Kiseljak. Peter offered to drive me back in the Range Rover. He had something to buy in Kiseljak and added that it would be useful for me to see the Dungeons & Dragons route through glass.

As we drove he told me about the difficulties of the job, how he was stretched having to deal with problems in the city and with difficult people on the Serb side. 'You're wasted in Central Bosnia. This is where you should be . . . you'd be most useful on the Serb side unblocking problems there. This is where you should be . . .' He'd just planted the idea in my head. I mulled it over – *This is where it's at . . . where it's really happening. But how?*

'Peter, why don't you mention it to Brigadier Cumming. He's at Kiseljak now. I can't ask . . . besides he'll say "no" anyway.' I also knew that I was shortly to be posted up to the Cheshires in Vitez. Bob Stewart had been asking for me for several weeks now. He needed both Nick and me, one of us up in Tuzla to cover the Op CABINET crossings, the other in Vitez to cover the Op SLAVIN crossings. As it was Nick was having to dash between the two. Stewart had a point, and within days, in fact on the back of the Minister for the Armed Forces and the Adjutant General's visit, due to happen on 8 February, I'd go up country for the last time and be left in Vitez. It didn't appeal much. But the idea of working in Sarajevo did.

We sailed through all the Sierras. Even S-1 was no problem. The bearded monster recognised Peter, broke into a huge, toothy smile and forced a glass of Slivovica onto us. The penny dropped – *the key to all this is the personal contact.*

Predictably, Brigadier Cumming said no. He could read us like a book – two naughty schoolboys, plotting. 'No, he's needed in Central Bosnia . . . and he's still my asset.'

At half-six Peter departed as the Sierras closed down for the night at seven. There was still no sign of the APC shuttle or of the Civil Adviser and Simon. Unbeknown to us Sarajevo was being subjected to an intense and sustained barrage. Both men were trapped in the PTT building and were consequently being subjected to an all-night barrage of red wine from Peter. Somehow he'd made it back through the shelling. That's what he was like.

'Driver's let us down! Stanley! You're driving, let's get back to Fojnica.' Cumming wasn't bothered. He would have been had he known I'd never driven a Discovery before and certainly not on iced-up roads in the dark.

It had started snowing again. We stopped for an hour or so at the BBC house in Kiseljak where Martin Bell, 'the Man in the White Suit', entertained us. We fell into deep conversation. I wanted to know more about the place.

We arrived back in Fojnica before midnight. I'd driven in silence and listened as the Brigadier told me how the conference had gone. It had been something of a jamboree during which it had been discovered that the British were the only contingent in theatre with the command and control assets – radios – necessary to effect a UN withdrawal. As we drove somehow I knew we wouldn't be leaving. I pictured Greta in her flat, in the dark, in the freezing cold, with no future and only despair for companionship. We wouldn't be going. We couldn't abandon them – the Little People.

EIGHT

Operation Bretton

October 1997 – Ian, UK

'So, that's it, Ian. You stand on the cusp of two cultures. You cross that bridge to the Little People and you're hooked. Like Caesar and the Rubicon, there's no going back. Once you've done it, you've done it . . .'

Ian's listening carefully. I'm calmer this time round. He says I look calmer. Perhaps it's the pills. Sixteen days have dulled the edge off the 'shock of capture'. I'm starting to get this stuff out, bashing Niki and him with it. In a way it has started to help and very slowly I'm beginning to climb that rope which Ian has dropped to the bottom of the pit I'm in.

It didn't all happen at once. I wrote to General Jackson in London to tell him that the package had been delivered successfully, that Aida's parents were all right and that she was not to worry. I didn't tell him about Greta. Aida would only have flapped. I'd taken Greta at face value and trusted her. Fortunately, I wasn't wrong. I didn't hear anything from the Jacksons for another few weeks. In fact I pretty much forgot about the whole thing. Events in Bosnia just moved on as they do.

I'm laughing now. An absurd image has entered my mind. The British really are the most peculiar people. They might find themselves in the most God-awful situation, but they'll always make the best of it; they'll ignore what's going on around them and cling to their culture and their ways.

I'm thinking about Burns Night, 25 January, in Split. The entire canteen has been converted into a dinner night. Brigadier Cumming and his replacement, Brigadier Robin Searby, and one or two other visitors from JHQ, are sitting on a high table on the stage. Searby is over here on his recce. He's a brigade commander in Germany and he and his HQ are to take over from Cumming in May. He's another cavalry officer, 9/12 Lancers. I'm looking at him and feeling a bit scared. He looks as dangerous as a shark and he's as mad as hell because his luggage has been lost. We're all sitting there eating haggis, swigging whisky and listening to the bagpipes. Young officers and sergeants stand up and recite Robert Burns. Weird, because you're also aware that fifty miles away people are slitting each other's throats and burning and raping each other out of their homes.

The next day we take Searby and the others up country – TSG, Triangle, we even get through GV, and on to Vitez. I wasn't in the Discovery but in the backing Land Rover TDi and I'm giving a running commentary to this lieutenant colonel from Wilton who runs the G3 Ops desk in JHQ, Jamie Daniel. He became Rose's MA in 1994. We reach Vitez, get a brief from Bob Stewart and that evening we leave Daniell and the others in Vitez. I'm back in the Discovery along with Cumming and Searby and we're driving along the Busovaca valley to BHC. It's dark outside and we're negotiating one checkpoint after another. All along the valley, high up on both sides, houses are blazing away, chucking sparks and smoke into the night sky. It's straight out of Dante's Inferno. We drive to Kiseljak almost in silence.

In the foyer of BHC people are scurrying around in a panic. Apparently, the 'Mujahideen' are on their way to do the place. The Muslim-owned pizza restaurant has already been blown up. Searby's standing there puffing on a cheroot and he turns to me and growls out of the corner of his mouth, 'Is it always like this?' I assume he's referring to this picture of multinational madness. A helmeted and flak-jacketed Danish guard races past us with *two* weapons – a G3 rifle slung over his shoulder and an MG42 machine gun, its ammunition belt trailing along the floor. 'Yes, it is, sir. This HQ is an utter nuthouse.' 'I don't mean this . . .' he snaps back, '. . . I mean that – the valley, the burning houses. Is it always like this?'

It's weird. We've just driven down a valley of burning houses. To me it's no more than that, a valley of burning houses. But to him, to a fresh pair of eyes, it's horror. We'd got used to it; we'd already become slightly desensitised to it. It hadn't occurred to me until Searby had said that. I'd only been there a month.

That was pretty much the last event with Brigadier Cumming. I stayed in Vitez. I didn't really work for Bob Stewart, not directly and then rarely as an interpreter. He had his own and some of them were quite outstanding.

The whole business about interpreters is interesting. When the Cheshires arrived in mid-October 1992 they selected a schoolhouse at Stara Bila just outside Vitez as their main operating base. No one knew then that the road running through the Lasva valley would become the Muslim-Croat fault line, and this schoolhouse was right on it. You wouldn't know the place was a school. The blockhouse or schoolhouse was furthest from the road. It was a two-storey concrete affair, long and squat with its flat roof now bristling with antennae. Between the schoolhouse and the road was a playing field, which had been converted into Portakabin accommodation and a Warrior/vehicle park. Originally it had been tents but the Royal Engineers had put down hardcore and built a mini Portakabin City, with a fine canteen. A one-way circuit for the vehicles surrounded all this like a moat. Along the left side of the circuit were civilian houses, some occupied by the locals, others hired by the UN. The UKLOs had one, the doctors and medics another, the lieutenants yet another and the one nearest the road and the mess was the captains' house. It was all pretty chaotic. Electricity was supplied by a camp generator, but that was it. There was no heating in the houses save wood-burning stoves. If you wanted a bath you had to wait for hours while a huge galvanised iron bucket of water heated up on the stove. There were even some houses outside the wire and on the other side of the road – the CO's and the PInfo house. It was all fairly strung out, but no one was fighting when the place was set up and the mission was to escort aid convoys. The Cheshires and Engineers set all this up but none of it was any good unless you can speak to the locals. Almost immediately, therefore, the Cheshires recruited a pool of local boys and girls who spoke good English, some of them quite superbly. They were recruited on an equitable basis – Serbs, Muslims and Croats – all locals from Vitez, Novi Travnik, Travnik and Turbe down the road. Without them there would have been no operation. There must have been about fifteen of them.

You might think that was quite a number, but anyone who had contact with the locals had to have an interpreter. Not just Bob Stewart. The Quartermaster had to negotiate the purchase of materials, hardcore and so on. Every single liaison officer, all Cheshire captains, had their own 'patch' and were responsible for liaising with local commanders. The BRITBAT area of responsibility was huge. Each of these LOs needed an interpreter. So did the battalion Padre, Tyrone Hillary. Most of these interpreters, of varying ability, were held in a pool. There was even a tiny office, a sort of standby room, where the door might suddenly open, someone would shout, 'Need an interpreter' and one of these boys or girls would jump up and go. For the most part though, each LO had his favourite with whom he'd work permanently. The best, of course, were retained for the difficult interpreting with the CO and the company commanders.

I had a small room at the bottom of the captains' house and shared it with one of the local interpreters, Edi Letic, a Muslim from Novi Travnik. He was an outstanding linguist, a brilliant guitar player and singer and all he ever wanted to do was to drive around the world in a battered Renault 4 with his guitar. He had qualified as a civil engineer at Sarajevo University and spent most of his time working for the QM or the Engineers. The Padre also had a room downstairs. The rooms at the top were occupied by the doctor, Captain Mark Weir, and a couple of LOs. I had nothing to do so latched on to Martin Forgrave, the LO for Travnik, Novi Travnik and Turbe. Each day we'd jump into his Land Rover and go visiting and chatting with the local commanders.

The first thing we had to deal with was the mysterious death of two British mercenaries, who had been killed in Travnik. The whole place was mad with suspicion. Something very odd was going on right across Bosnia and Croatia at the time.

The war was so accessible. It was only a two-hour hop from London. The fighting attracted a bizarre collection of people who flocked down to the Balkans: aid workers, go-it-alone journalists hoping to make their names and, inevitably, mercenaries. Some were genuinely ex-services, others were bluffers and Walter Mittys and some were just utterly naïve and lost. They came from just about every country in Europe and beyond. When I left Split, Bob Edge was dealing with the local police over the case of a Brit in the HOS who had been found with his throat cut. The police reckoned it was something to do with drugs. I'm not so sure. Another three British mercenaries were found dead in Mostar that week and then we had these two in Travnik to deal with. For some reason the locals were popping off British mercenaries.

These two in Travnik weren't dogs of war or anything like that. All they were doing was running first aid courses for the BiH 7th Brigade in Travnik. One day they're found face down in a field, hands tied behind their backs and riddled with bullets . . . from behind . . . an execution.

Who knows what the motive was. My guess is that they'd been seen coming to the camp at Vitez once or twice for a meal or a chat or whatever. Someone put two and two together and came up with five . . . British spies, and bang, executed. Martin and I flapped around for a few days trying to track down the bodies. They'd been taken to the mortuary in Zenica but we couldn't find them. We spoke to Djemajl Merdan the BiH 3rd Corps Deputy Commander, who didn't know where the bodies were. And no one knew exactly what the status of these people was anyway. What was Britain's obligation to dead mercenaries? We weren't really interested in that and all we felt at the time was that they should at least have a Christian burial. We looked around the cemeteries and graveyards of Zenica and eventually found them in graves with Muslim head boards. Bob Stewart and the Padre and one or two others went up there and Christian crosses were placed at their graves and they were given a proper send off. Bloody sad. That's what it was like there – the place stank of suspicion and death.

In the evenings I'd sit in the Mess drinking and chatting with some of the interpreters. We fed off each other, explaining the intricacies of idioms in both languages. There wasn't really a pecking order amongst them but the best two, Dobrila Kalaba, a Serb from Novi Travnik who had studied English at Novi Sad University, and Ali, a Muslim from GV, whose home and family were being trashed by the Croats there, were the best. They worked almost exclusively for Bob Stewart. Then there was Edi Letic my roommate, who was almost their equal and was also Dobrila's boyfriend. They'd been childhood sweethearts. Finally, there was Suzana Hubjar, half-Serb, half-Muslim from Travnik. She was exceptionally bright and brave. She'd been in her final year of medical studies at Sarajevo University, had returned home to Travnik to cram for her finals and bang, war – no finals, no qualifications and she winds up working for us. Tragic, all of it.

It was Edi to whom I got closest. We'd spend hours in the kitchen chatting, him strumming his guitar and telling me what it was like to grow up in Yugoslavia. I learned a lot from him. He had a mouthful of the world's most rotten teeth, but he was a real window into the mentality of the locals. I remember him saying, 'Here was I, a Yugoslav, born to Muslim parents, never stepped into a mosque in my life, never considered myself to be anything other than a Yugoslav and then suddenly this war comes and I'm pigeon-holed "Muslim".' He horrified me once when he told me of an incident back in October 1992 when the Croats and Muslims of Novi Travnik started fighting, 'I'm in this trench with a radio and with a whole load of other Muslims. The Croats are charging us, firing, and we're firing back and then suddenly something snaps. Everyone around me leaps up screaming and shouting, mad with red rage. They drop their rifles and charge forward with axes, knives, meat cleavers and bayonets and they hack away at each other. That's what it's like here. It's not enough to shoot. Better to make a real job of it with axes and knives. I just cowered in the trench and thought "fuck this" . . . that's why I'm an interpreter.' The Padre used to sit and listen to us rambling on but I think it was all beyond him, the mentality I mean.

As for what was going on in the rest of Bosnia at the time I didn't have a clue. When you're back in one of these valleys that's your frame of reference. You meet the locals, the commanders in Travnik, like Commander Kulenic – young, charming, very bright, terrific sense of humour and an expert ski instructor from his JNA days. He'd point up at this enormous mountain at the head of the valley which we called the Vlasic feature. The Serbs held it and looked down on the whole valley. Kulenic would say, 'I know that mountain like the back of my hand. I've spent my life skiing it. It's as much mine as it is theirs. One day I'll ski it again.' He used to slap me on the back at parties and his eyes would twinkle, 'Ah, Mike, *ti si nas*, you're one of us, I know.' He knew. He was no fool. You can't hide your soul from these people. But as for the rest of Bosnia – I hadn't a clue what was going on behind the scenes. All I knew was that valley; you could feel this terrible tension hanging over it. Croats and some Muslims in Vitez, Croats and Muslims in Novi Travnik and in Travnik and it was all going to blow sky-high. The Lasva valley was a giant pressure cooker waiting to blow. And there we were, sitting in the middle trying to keep the lid on things, but knowing secretly that something was coming our way. It was just a question of time.

Then one day in February this enormous 25-kilo parcel arrives for me. It's from General Jackson in London. There was a note too, *'Well done for delivering the parcel. Here's another. This is your own personal humanitarian mission.'* So that was it. I became Postman Pat but the problem was, how to get it into Sarajevo. Although it was nearer than Split it was harder to get in. You had to have a damn good reason to go into that French colony. You couldn't just hop off to Sarajevo and besides, apart from their Mortar Platoon, the Cheshires rarely went in there. So the parcel stayed in Vitez.

In the meantime I had to go up to Tuzla and cover the Op CABINET crossings while Nick Costello was away on R&R. The Cheshires had just acquired a new 2IC, Major Bryan Watters, who had come from commanding the Jungle Warfare Centre in Brunei and he and OC HQ Company, another major, wanted to visit Tuzla, so, the three of us drove up in a Land Rover. The journey was indescribable, horrendous – them in the front with a heater and me in the back shivering in a sleeping bag – along the worst routes over the worst mountains in the world. At one point the route comes within sight of the Serb front lines at Bomb Alley, which you have to scoot along as fast as possible while they fire mortars and cannons at you. Monty, a lieutenant in the 9/12 Lancers, was the first to return fire at them from his Scimitar and just hurled 30mm shells back at them. But most of the time the Serbs had the upper hand – Land Rovers and aid trucks don't come furnished with 30mm RARDEN cannons.

Tuzla was a real break from Vitez. First off, it was B Sqn 9/12 Lancers all on their own up there in a few blocks at Dubrave military airfield. They shared this with the BiH who operated their Hip helicopters from there and thus attracted Serb artillery fire. The airfield was overlooked by a hill called the Vis feature about ten kilometres away. The Serbs were on that too – the name of the game in war is 'grab the high ground'. This airfield was huge, flat and had plenty of redundant runways. Tuzla itself was half an hour's drive away. Most of the aid agencies were up there trying to help this rather large and beleaguered town. The centrepiece was the Tuzla hotel, home to all the internationals including the press.

Conditions at the airfield were spartan. There was no fresh food as there was no refrigerator, so we were all on compo permanently. B Sqn were a very relaxed and professional bunch. Captain Tim Hercock had been left in charge while Alan Abraham was on leave. Dave Bennett was the Ops Officer and Mark Cooper was the LO in Tuzla and knew the place and 'smells' inside out. But the weird thing was there was no work for me there either. Not a single convoy was crossing the front line at Kalesija. One day the Mayor of Tuzla, Selim Beslagic, just ups and says, 'We're not accepting your UN aid until you do something about our Muslim brothers in Cerska. We can't accept your aid while they're being ethnically cleansed by the aggressor.' Just like that. It floored us. Each day we'd drive down to Kalesija to escort an aid convoy from Belgrade across the line and each day zip, nothing. The BiH refused to let anything cross into their territory. Clever tactic, but they had a point – morally they couldn't allow food aid convoys from Belgrade, transiting Serb-held territory, to enter Tuzla, be unloaded and then scoff the food while Muslims in Eastern Bosnia were being cleansed out of their homes.

This didn't come out of nowhere. It had its origins back on 7 January. The Muslims weren't just holed up in Gorazde. There was an enclave in a deep valley at Zepa and another in a valley at Srebrenica. On 7 January a BiH fighting patrol hoofs it out of Srebrenica and trashes a number of Serb villages along the Drina. Then the Chetniks in Sarajevo murder the Bosnian Deputy Prime Minister. Serbs in Eastern Bosnia go wild at the trashing of their villages which triggers a wave of ethnic cleansing around Zvornik, Cerska and in a broad valley called Konjevic Polje. Most of this goes unreported simply because there's no press to report it. So the first we really hear of it is when the Mayor of Tuzla forbids UN aid.

The UN effort in Tuzla ground to a halt. Hercock, Cooper and I popped down to the UNHCR office where Anders Levinson, a Danish ex-footballer and now head of office in Tuzla, shows us his plan to relieve the town. I'm not sure he'd quite grasped what was going on. They didn't want our food. His plan horrifies us because he's planning to fly Herc-loads of food into the airfield, just like that. None of this has been cleared with anyone and it would have ended in disaster. The Serbs would have shelled the shit out of the airfield, destroyed the aircraft and claimed that the UN was gunrunning for the Muslims. At Sarajevo there were Serb inspectors, who checked the aircraft and the aid, but at Tuzla there were none. You just couldn't up and do an airlift into the place, and even then you can't *force* people to eat your food.

After a week of this there's no point me hanging around Tuzla so, one night, Mark Cooper and I hoof it down to Vitez in his Land Rover. He's off on R&R. A lot starts happening very quickly. We're into the beginning of March now. The snow has begun to melt, Nick and Alan Abraham come back from R&R and that night we're having a huge dinner in the Bosna restaurant because quite a few of the Cheshires' officers are leaving early, posted to other jobs in the UK. Either Nick or I have to go back up to Tuzla; we agree that it should be me. But the next morning Nick's up before me. I'm in tatters and not ready to catch the transport but Nick's not bothered. He likes it up in Tuzla and agrees to take my place. That was pure fate. That's how delicately your life hangs in the balance. Anything can affect the course of events including a hangover!

Meantime, because of the business in Srebrenica, General Morillon's touch paper has been lit. He blasts off from the Residency in Sarajevo, comes screaming out of the city like an Exocet, turns right and disappears up to Tuzla and Zvornik, trailing hot gasses. He grabs Alan and Nick and they probe south through Serb territory, trying to make contact, to halt this wave of ethnic cleansing. Without Nick and Alan he somehow makes it into Srebrenica with his interpreter, a giant Macedonian/Frenchman called Mihajlov, and his British MA, a fluent French speaker called Major Piers Tucker. Once in Srebrenica he hoists the UN flag over the small PTT building, promises solidarity and pledges that Srebrenica will never be abandoned. Very brave, but he's marooned there with no contact except through the Muslims' ham radio. C130s then start dropping food aid right across Eastern Bosnia, mainly into Goražde, Zepa, Srebrenica and Cerska.

Confused reports start coming out of Srebrenica. No one's quite sure what Morillon's status is there. BHC is in a flap and there's a rumour that Morillon and his gang are actually hostages of Naser Oric, the BiH commander in the pocket. Another report suggests that Morillon, who has been in there a week or so by this time, is in dire straits – no food, nothing. And then this little message slips out of Srebrenica, 'Send more Davidoff cigars!' Cool! But you've got this general stuck in this pocket barking for more cigars while down in Split there's this unit of French Special Forces all set to bust into the valley and rescue him. Madness! After about nine days he makes it out and reappears in Zvornik where the enraged population goes insane, kicks his car, spits at him and screams, 'Morillon is a liar!'

He fails to get back into Srebrenica so returns to Sarajevo to plan the relief of the pocket. I remember driving up to BHC one day with Bob Stewart who tells me that one plan is to drop paratroopers into the enclave. He asks me what I think. I've already looked at the map and tell him, 'Madness! Only if you want them all to get broken legs. It's a steep-sided and heavily wooded valley, not a frigging drop zone. Can only be done by free-fall or by steerable "squares" but then not in sufficient numbers. Plan's barking!'

In and amongst this little lot, I've still got Jackson's bloody parcel to deliver. Again, the opportunity comes out of nowhere on the back of the PWO's visit. Lieutenant-Colonel Alistair Duncan and some of his staff who'll be taking over from the Cheshires in May are out doing their recce. One day Bryan Watters takes his opposite number, the PWO's 2IC, Major Richard Watson, into Sarajevo. BRITBAT had a responsibility under the UN withdrawal plan called Plan 006 whereby the route through the Sierras into Sarajevo would be held by them while the city is evacuated of UN personnel. It was a distant prospect but the plan existed. Brian and Richard decide to go in and review the plan with whomsoever in HQ Sector Sarajevo. I offer to go with them as interpreter for the checkpoints. Neither of them has been into Sarajevo before. The day before, I grab the SQMS and liberate the stores of as much food as I can stuff into my bergen: whole Edam cheeses, blocks of UHT milk, bags of sugar, coffee, tea, matches, candles, just about anything I can lay my hands on. So I'm sitting in the back of this Land Rover, bergen weighing a ton, the parcel hidden away under a blanket. We bluff our way through the Sierras and get into Sarajevo.

As before, Peter Jones takes us all to Ulica Romanijska, where the Pijalovics live. I'm hoping Minka Pijalovic will be in. Bryan Watters insists on accompanying me up the stairs. This time they are in. A plump, middle-aged lady with a sweet face opens the door, sees me, and starts wailing, 'My Aida! My Aida has come!' We're in her tiny kitchen and she's hugging me, wailing and crying, asking me one question after another. We've only got a few minutes so I'm unpacking the bergen like mad, dumping everything on the floor. Minka is crying her eyes out. Her husband, Munir, a thin man, is weeping silently and all the while Bryan is just standing there shocked and shattered, gawping. There's no time to hang around and we depart but not before she's given me a bottle of Slivo and a letter for Aida. We leave them crying over the pile of food on their kitchen floor and the parcel. The experience was gut-wrenching. That's the first time I met Minka and Munir Pijalovic and we didn't even have time for a proper conversation. Shortly after that yet another parcel came out to Vitez and sat there until I could deliver it. Peter Jones' BRITDET were leaving on 30 March and he'd invited me to their leaving party on the 27th. That offered me an opportunity to deliver the parcel, but whether I'd be able to get into Sarajevo was another matter.

We're now into the second week in March. The Lasva valley pressure cooker is bubbling away. Up north Alan Abraham, Nick Costello and a few 9/12 Lancers have managed to get into Konjevic Polje where there are some 2,000 Muslim refugees holed up and on the run from the Serbs who are closing in. They've got into the valley, assessed the situation and got out again. UNHCR is desperate to get aid to them and a second trip in is planned. Meanwhile the Army system has caught up with me. Despite all this madness, the cogs of the wheel have been grinding on and I find myself having to report to Split on Friday 12 March to sit the Staff Selection Test exam on the following Monday. I'd sat my Promotion Exams in Umm Qsar in Iraq. I'd passed them but failed the SST and now had to re-sit the paper. There were about five British officers across Central Bosnia who were in the same boat, among them Ken Lonergan, a Cheshire, Lee Smart the PInfo captain, and Dave Bennett from Tuzla. Exams don't stop for any war, so we jump on this Sea King at Kiseljak and hop down to the sunshine in Split straight into a disaster.

All hell has been let loose over the last forty-eight hours in Konjevic Polje. Nick and the others have got back into the valley but the situation has changed dramatically. The Serbs had closed in and the Muslims are desperate and panicking for their lives. Naser Oric is there too with some of his fighters and they've surrounded all the UN vehicles with bales of burning straw and the group has been held hostage like that for nearly two days. Oric has told Nick and Sasha Vassiliyev, a Russian Special Forces/UNMO major, that if they're to die then the UN will die with them. Nick and Sasha have been out of the vehicles trying to calm the crowd and negotiate. They've been doing this for nearly two days. Eventually the thing splits open and the Serbs start shelling the valley. People are dropping everywhere. Simon Mardell, a WHO doctor, assisted by WO2 'Jock' McNair, the medic interpreter, whom I'd first met at Wilton, is conducting roadside surgery and amputations without anaesthetics. The shelling intensifies. A Muslim woman rushes up to Nick and tries to make him take her decapitated baby, only seconds before a shell fragment removes her own head and leaves Nick splattered with blood and gore. And I've just walked innocently into the Ops Room in Split at the height of this tragedy. The only link with them is with Major Alan Abraham giving regular sitreps from a Spartan APC. Cumming is just standing there, tears of frustration in his eyes as he listens to his men dying more than a hundred miles away. And there's absolutely nothing he can do about it except listen.

I escape from the Ops Room. I can't listen to it. I can't listen to Nick dying, knowing that if I'd been able to get up that morning I'd be there instead of Nick. He was due to get married in a couple of months' time. I'm sick inside and go up to the Mess where I sit and wait. An hour or so later I can't help myself and I return to the Ops Room. The atmosphere has changed, relief mixed in with nervous tension. Cumming is shaken. They'd got out . . . just, and in appalling circumstances. As the shelling had intensified the crowd had disintegrated, an opening had been formed and the vehicles just went for it, driving like mad. Nick and Sasha were nearly left behind along with a destroyed Spartan and a recovery vehicle. I remember Cumming swearing blind that he would never again allow any British troops to be abandoned in a situation where they couldn't be reached, helped and supported. He swore blind and he meant it.

Shortly after that we had a minor drama of our own in the Vitez area. Bob Stewart was concerned about complaints made by the BiH and HVO in the Tesanj salient that the Serbs were using their helicopters in defiance of the No Fly Zone, Op DENY FLIGHT. He tasked John Ellis, his LO for the area, to take in a patrol and establish an OP to confirm this. It fell to me to go along as the interpreter since it was unreasonable to expect any of our locals to sleep out for a week.

We set off after lunch on Saturday 20 March – John and his driver, with me and a Fusilier, Corporal Stone, in the back of the Land Rover. Behind us was a Spartan APC with a few more blokes. We got through Novi Seher, but just short of Tesanj we were met by the HVO liaison officer to the BiH, Colonel Josic, a former JNA Naval officer. Despite the dramas in GV and elsewhere the HVO and BiH in the salient were still rock solid. They had to be for mutual survival, just as in Tuzla. Josic was hugely charismatic and made a point of wearing boots with no laces to show he had no intention of running away. He told us that it was too dangerous for us to drive through

Tesanj as the town was under heavy shell and rocket fire. More than that, the entire 'light bulb' (we called it that because of its shape) was being pressed on all sides. That same day some 600 shells impacted in Sarajevo and Tuzla was also being shelled. The war had gone mad. We could hear it all going on and just sat it out and waited all afternoon.

At twilight the shelling eased. Josic scooped us up and we scooted through Tesanj, the gateway to the 'bulb'. Then the shelling started again and we were effectively trapped inside this 'light bulb' which measured about ten by ten kilometres. They wouldn't let us select our own OP, but told us exactly where to put it and even provided us with two young military policemen to 'watch over us'. It was quite dark when we occupied this bit of high ground and parked the vehicles up in some bushes. We set up the HF radio, a PRC 320, but couldn't get through to anyone because the allocated frequency numbers were too 'high' for night-time transmission. After much bleating and re-positioning of the wire we finally got through to Tuzla and gave them our exact grid reference. In fact we gave it to everyone in the world because UN comms were not encrypted. We had no choice: tell no one or tell everyone.

By this time, the shelling had intensified. One landed about 500 metres from us, and that was enough for me to get a bit flaky and to suggest we dig a couple of deep four-man trenches. That didn't go down too well. Soldiers don't like digging and this lot were keener to take cover in the Spartan. Shades of TSG, and I told them so in no uncertain terms. After much muttering and dragging of shovels and picks from the vehicles we set about split-locking and de-turfing the two trenches. There was little enthusiasm for the work until something exploded ferociously above our heads and we found ourselves hugging the ground. The two policemen roared with laughter, 'Luna rocket – Tesanj!' they howled just as this missile impacted and the town glowed orange. The rocket had just passed overhead going supersonic. It was enough to galvanise the men into frenzied, mole-like activity. We worked like slaves. I remember begging Corporal Stone to take a spell holding the torch and let me do some digging, 'No, no, sir. I'm just fine down here, just fine.' He was scooping up dirt like crazy and hacking away with a pick like a man possessed. He'd been blown up twice in Northern Ireland and had recently been trapped for hours in an overturned Warrior surrounded by leaking battery acid and ammunition. This probably explained his stutter. I wondered then if I'd picked the right bloke to share a trench with.

After a night spent listening to shells landing and staring at the stars from the bottom of our trenches, we awoke to discover that the OP location was absurd. It was too far away from any front line for us to be able to observe anything accurately with a pair of binoculars and we had no proper surveillance equipment with us. We could hear the helicopters but couldn't see them. Colonel Josic wouldn't allow us to move the OP so it really wasn't worth staying there. Konjevic Polje was still uppermost in my mind and John Major wouldn't thank the UN if we all got killed or trapped in this 'light bulb'.

It seemed pointless to stay up there for a week, as Bob Stewart had ordered. John Ellis didn't want to disobey his CO, but at the same time we were risking the soldiers' lives needlessly in the pursuit of nothing. During the day we watched Luna rockets landing in the town of Jelah a few kilometres away. They didn't really explode so much as produce a huge orange mushroom cloud. Could have been incendiary or it could have been chemical and we had no NBC equipment. That night John and I sat on the hillside smoking and watching the world burning. The whole rim of the 'light bulb', especially around Teslic in the west, was burning as fighting and fire raged through the forests. We agreed then to get the blokes out the next day. It seemed that the shelling of Tesanj eased around lunchtime, presumably while the Serbs had their lunch. We'd do it then.

The next day we informed Josic that we had heard but not seen the helicopters and that we'd report that fact. The two Muslim policemen smirked as they watched us fill in the trenches, carefully replacing the squares of turf – just as we do on Salisbury Plain – and, in extended line picked up every scrap of litter. We left the place just as we'd found it. They probably thought we were off our heads.

At midday we shot through Tesanj like rabbits and popped out of the neck of the 'light bulb' mighty relieved at having done so. That night I was back in the Mess chatting to Edi Letic. The log fire was burning merrily and I was hugely relieved to be out of Tesanj.

Out of the blue a runner came into the Mess and handed me a scrap of paper, 'Sir, from the Ops Officer.' I read the message: 'For Mike Stanley. Report to BHC tomorrow at 1700 for a briefing. Helicopter evacuation of Srebrenica wounded planned for Wednesday 24 Mar 93. You're to go along as interpreter for 845 NAS.' That was it. Nothing more. What did this mean other than the para drop option seemed to have been sensibly abandoned? I showed it to Edi. He chuckled. I remember it so well. Then he threw his head back and laughed, muttering darkly and shaking his head, 'Srebrenica, eh? Helicopters is it? *Joj, covece, ti ces ostaviti kosti na Balkanu* – Man, but you're going to leave your bones in the Balkans!'

NINE

Operation Grapple, Bosnia

Tuesday 23 March 1993 – BH Command, Kiseljak
The plight of the Muslims in Srebrenica had finally and unexpectedly come to a head. Somehow, General Morillon had managed to cut a deal with the Serbs to evacuate Srebrenica's wounded by helicopter in exchange for the authorities in Tuzla allowing 240 Serbs to leave the town and move across to the Serb side. The Serbs themselves had agreed to silence their guns and co-operate.

The plan was relatively simple. Four Super Pumas from the French DETA-LAT, already in position at Tuzla airfield, would lead in the first wave, land at Zvornik and submit to an inspection by the Serbs, who were paranoid that the UN would use the opportunity to smuggle in arms and ammunition. Concurrently, three of 845's Sea Kings, commanded by George Wallace, would transit to Tuzla and make for Zvornik once the French had departed the town for Srebrenica, from where the wounded would be flown direct to Tuzla. The Brits would then do the same and the staggered, triangular routing, including the Zvornik inspection, would be repeated until all the wounded had been transferred to Tuzla. The first wave would also take in Lieutenant Colonel Jean Richard, DETALAT's CO, along with 845's Royal Navy MAOT, Lieutenant Tim Kelly. They would remain on the ground on the football pitch at Srebrenica, which was the designated and only HLS in this steep-sided valley town. They would maintain a constant radio link with inbound aircraft and with 'Magic', the AWAC aircraft over the Adriatic. At the same time they would run the HLS and organise the wounded into groups for extraction.

The evacuation completed, Alan Abraham's B Squadron would escort the 240 Serbs from Tuzla over the front line at Kalesija and hand them over to the Bosnian Serb authorities. The operation would last a day and we'd be back in Kiseljak by the evening. It all seemed pretty straightforward particularly as the French had successfully conducted a number of proving flights up to Tuzla airfield over the past few days. Serb artillery had remained silent and bombardment of the airfield had ceased. In general, confidence was high and it appeared that the operation would go ahead. The world's oldest, boldest and smelliest names in international journalism had flocked to Tuzla, commandeered the hotel and were waiting with bated breath and whirring cameras at the airfield. What could possibly go wrong?

Unbeknown to us in Kiseljak, the authorities in Tuzla had already announced that they'd only be releasing forty-six Serbs. General Morillon felt let down. Worse still, although the Bosnian Serb political and military leaders had given their blessing to the operation, no word had come back from their staff HQ with details as to how the operation would be conducted. There was, therefore, some niggling doubt as to whether Dr Karadzic and General Mladic would be able to exercise control over the local Serbs besieging Srebrenica. Despite this lack of firm commitment and guarantee of control, a view prevailed that the plight of the wounded civilians was such that the operation could wait no longer.

George Wallace, the Squadron boss, didn't share in the general euphoria. His mood was sombre and serious. The consummate professional, he was not prepared to hype up feelings. The small briefing room in the bowels of the hotel was packed with aircraft commanders, pilots and crewmen, about twenty in all including the standby crews. They'd spent the past hour hunched over their notebooks intently scribbling down details of the operation. Wallace let it be known that he considered it an extremely high-risk operation. There would be two Air Commanders, himself and his French counterpart. If either commander felt it necessary to abort the mission, the other followed.

The O Group broke up and crews shuffled quietly out clutching sleeping bags, looking for a space in which to sleep for the night. I asked George exactly what he wanted me to do. He nodded at the two loudhailers I had managed to prise from the Danish stores: 'You come in my aircraft and sweet-talk the Serbs at Zvornik. As for Srebrenica . . . God knows what we'll find on the ground, but if we're swamped by a rabble desperate to escape from the enclave, then you just bellow at them through those things . . .' He added with a smile, '. . . not that it will help much.' He lit a cigarette, picked up his papers and wandered out of the room in search of a bed.

0945 hrs, Wednesday 24 March 1993 – Dubrave Airfield, Tuzla, Northern Bosnia

It couldn't have been a more perfect day for it: warm, a cloudless sky, crystal clear visibility. As the airfield broadened to fill the view from the cockpit, I strained to look over George's shoulder and could make out the Vis feature, barely ten kilometres away. Atop it sat Serb forward observers watching our every move, the same who had relentlessly brought down artillery fire onto the airfield. Vis was what the military call *Vital Ground* – you couldn't take a piss in the trees without the Serbs knowing about it.

'Will you look at that!' The intercom between pilot and commander hissed softly.

'Every man and his bloody dog! Look at them!'

The helicopter was close to the ground now, heading into a concrete dog-leg, a dispersal pan, at 90° to and halfway down the main runway. Measuring some 100 metres wide and 400 metres long, it was surrounded on three sides by thick walls of towering silver birches. To our left were UN vehicles, a couple of Warriors, a Spartan command vehicle and an assortment of jeeps, French-type, bristling with antennae and surrounded by groups of UN troops. I strained to see if Nick was amongst them, but they were too far off. Members of the press were at the far end and beyond them a fleet of ambulances, parked off to one side, waited to whisk the first evacuees off to hospital. This was a big scene. Judging by the size of the press corps, it was also the only show in town.

'And where are the bloody Pumas?' crackled the headset which was clamped over my ears.

'Dunno. Must've already buggered off to Zvornik,' someone guessed.

The Sea King pivoted smartly through 90° and sank to the ground. Behind us the other two aircraft followed suit, all three lining up facing the vehicles across the pan.

'What now? Close down?'

'Hang on! I'll find out.' I ripped off the headset, leapt out of the Sea King and raced across the pan. No Nick. Lots of French and 9/12 Lancers. I spotted Alan Abraham talking to Commander John Rooke, the boss of CHOSC, Commando Helicopter Operations and Support Cell, and George Wallace's superior officer.

'Stanley!' Alan Abraham pounced on me, 'What're you doing here?' Didn't he know?

'I was told to accompany 845 to Zvornik, do the inspection and then continue to Srebrenica . . . in case there's any interpreting to be done . . . with the casualties . . .'

'Too late for that. Costello's already over there in Zvornik. We sent him in with the French, who are, as we speak, being ripped to pieces by the Serbs . . . so, you can just stay here in case we need to make any phone calls.'

'But–'

'No! You're staying here.' He turned away.

All change! One minute this, the next that. Worse still, I could just picture the chaos at Zvornik. Four Pumas being strip-searched, Serbs going through everything, tempers fraying and poor Nick rushing around like a blue-arsed fly. Dejectedly I made my way back to the Sea King to retrieve my daysack. John Rooke was briefing George Wallace.

I grabbed the daysack. 'Sorry. They want me to stay here and make phone calls.' I shrugged my shoulders and ambled back to the vehicles. Alan Abraham had disappeared. A French Foreign Legion major was issuing orders and his radio operator, who had the name Fraser on his tag, was barking into his radio in pure Glaswegian. Didn't they have any Frenchmen in the Legion? I slung my helmet and daysack on the grass and squinted over at the press. There they were. Kate Adie, Sasha, Anamarija, who else? Brigadier Cumming! He was chatting and joking with Anamarija. What was he doing up here? Was there anybody who hadn't come to the party?

The beat of the Sea Kings' rotors changed and in a flurry of wind and blown kerosene they lifted, hovered off down the pan and, in line astern, rose gracefully into the air, headed for Vis and Zvornik beyond. I watched them become tiny specks, then disappear behind Vis. I smoked as I wondered what to do. Five minutes later a single Puma appeared from the direction of Vis and disgorged a section of Legionnaries.

'Where are the evacuees?' I asked the French major.

'Srebrenica,' he replied matter-of-factly.

'But, what about that?' I cocked a thumb at the Puma, which was taking off again.

The major rolled his eyes, 'The Serbs. Big problems at Zvornik. We're having to shuttle back a platoon they wouldn't allow to go to Srebrenica.'

I was on my feet, 'Y'mean ... that one's off to Zvornik ... now?' The major nodded.

'Look. I'm supposed to be there ... as an interpreter ... but I was sort of left behind. Can you get me on that one?' The Puma had all but disappeared.

'No problem,' said the major casually as he turned to Fraser, who in turn spoke into his mouthpiece. I was on my feet and sprinting down the pan clutching helmet and daysack. After all, I was Cumming's 'asset' and he must have had a hand in dragging me out of Vitez and into this mad operation. Zvornik was where I was supposed to be and that's where I was going. Ahead of me the Puma turned and like a giant vulture swooped back down onto the pan. Crewmen hauled me into the hovering aircraft, threw me onto the floor and slid the door shut. The helicopter lifted into the air and made for Zvornik.

Once we'd gained height and levelled out I scrambled onto a seat and buckled up. Below us I could see the Vis feature sliding past. The forward slope, facing the airfield, was devoid of any movement. Behind the crest, it was a different story. It was crawling with troops and equipment; D30 field artillery pieces, M84 main battle tanks, modern ones and not the old T55s one usually saw. These boys meant business. Suddenly I was chilled by the prospect of what we'd set out to do. Beyond Vis was a range of hills, which dropped abruptly into the Drina river valley. On this side Bosnia. On the other side Serbia.

Perched precariously on the Bosnian side clung a town of jagged and jumbled apartment blocks looking like a mouthful of dirty, broken and rotten teeth – Zvornik. On the other side of the broad, glassy river was its smaller sister town, Mali Zvornik. Unlike Zvornik, somewhat incongruously its mosque was still intact.

As Zvornik grew in size it was difficult to see where a helicopter could be landed amid the clutter of Titoist architectural junk. Where was the football pitch? We hopped over one tatty block, looped around another, and there below us appeared a small sunken football stadium. Like a Greek amphitheatre, the top of the terraces was level with a road, which ran between the stadium and the river. Along one side of the pitch were the three Sea Kings, closed down and surrounded by gaggles of soldiers. In an opposite corner, huddled around a satellite dish, French soldiers were waiting to be ferried back to Tuzla. As we sank into the pit below the level of the road we could see that the stadium was surrounded on four sides by a militant mob of several thousand. This was worse than I'd imagined.

The Puma settled in front of the French troops. I hopped out and searched frantically for Nick. Above the hissing of the Puma's turbine and its buzzing rotor I was aware of chanting. Soldiers were grouped around the first Sea King. The crewmen looked harassed and stressed-out. A Serb was crawling around inside the helicopter, looking under the seats, pulling open medical packs, opening the GPMG's ammo boxes. I suddenly saw Nick, sweat pouring off his face, dashing from one inspector to another vainly attempting to translate.

'Nick!' I grabbed him. He stopped short and spun round. His dark eyes were wild, his flak jacket stained dark brown in places. Blood from Konjevic Polje.

'Mike! Thank God you're here. It's chaos ... they're ripping everything apart ... tore the French to pieces!' He was breathless and sweating heavily.

'Yeah, well, nearly didn't make it here ... anyway, what's the problem?'

'UN's fucked up again. Not kept to the agreement.'

'What do you mean?'

'... deal was ...' he continued quickly, '... empty helis into Srebrenica. Wounded out ... simple. But no! First thing the Serbs found was four Pumas stuffed full of troops with a satellite dish all bound for Srebrenica ... went fucking insane and now they're ripping the Brits to pieces.'

The Puma lifted off. Its buzzing receded. The chanting from the crowd rose in volume. *MORION LAZE! ... MORION LAZE! ... MORION LAZE! – MORILLON LIES! ... MORILLON LIES! ... MORILLON LIES!* Stones were lobbed into the stadium. One bounced off a rotor blade.

'... rent-a-crowd isn't helping matters, and if that's not bad enough then those two are the icing on the cake!' Which two? What was Nick on about?

'Which two? What, Nick?'

'The press. Those two!' He pointed up the steps leading to the clubhouse where two rather subdued civilians, a man and a woman, were standing quietly next to the entrance. '. . . BBC cameraman, Brian Hulls, and she's Maggie O'Kane from the *Guardian* . . .'

'How did they get here? Thought no press on this one!'

'Yeah, well, that was the deal, but they jumped onto the helicopters at Tuzla. Someone must've let them on. He filmed all those Serb positions on the Vis feature. They've found that on the film, so he's been arrested for spying, and when we got here she just ran around the HLS like a mad thing interviewing everyone. Serbs went mad and told me to stop her, but every time I turned my back she was off again. So, they've arrested her as well.'

At the far end of the stadium, daubed in black paint across a wall, was a huge skull and crossbones, the old Chetnik symbol, with *Sloboda ili Smrt* – Freedom or Death – scrawled in uneven foot-high Cyrillic letters. It loomed over us adding a depth of menace to the monotonous chanting, the stone-throwing and the exertions of the prying inspectors. This was rapidly turning into a five-star fuck-up. The only consolation was that three of the French Pumas had made it to Srebrenica.

'And what are these?' One of the inspectors held up a pair of PNGs.

'Night flying goggles,' answered Nick.

'Night flying goggles, eh? What do you need those for if you're flying by day? No! You're supplying these to the Muslims in Srebrenica. Smuggling!'

'Look! Grenades! They're smuggling grenades to the Muslims as well!' another inspector roared triumphantly as he brandished a green cylindrical canister. PNGs were momentarily forgotten . . . *MORION LAZE!* . . . *MORION LAZE!* . . . *MORION LAZE!* . . . bayed the crowd, tossing even more stones at the aircraft and us.

'It's marker smoke for marking HLSs,' protested a crewman to Nick. *GRENADES! . . . GRENADES! . . . MORILLON LIES! . . .* howled the mob. More stones rattled off the aircraft.

'It's marker smoke, coloured marker smoke . . . not grenades,' stammered Nick.

'Prove it then. Let's see that it's smoke!' ordered the inspector. Nick grabbed the canister, yanked out the pin and hurled the grenade away from the heli-copters. It popped dully in mid flight, the lever pinged off and the canister landed fizzing and spluttering. Then it belched out an acrid cloud of green smoke. *GRENADE!* screamed the crowd.

'Look! Green smoke! Muslim colour! It's Muslim smoke! It should be red smoke – Serbian colour . . . proves you're pro-Muslim!' roared the inspectors, laughing their heads off and winking at Nick. They were enjoying themselves immensely.

'Mike, for fuck's sake! Get them to stop throwing stones . . . pitch is covered in FOD. It'll be thrown up when we take off!' George was hugely under-impressed with the proceedings. I grabbed one of the inspectors and urged him to tell the crowd to stop throwing stones. He shrugged his shoulders, ambled off half-heartedly and said something to the crowd, which responded with more hissing, booing and cries of *MORION LAZE!* It was hopeless. One thing was clear: Zvornik was the dead weight which would sink the day. I forgot about going to Srebrenica and resolved to stay with Nick in the hope of sweet-talking the Serbs before the Pumas reappeared. There was also the problem of Brian Hulls and Maggie O'Kane to resolve. As they hadn't been carted off perhaps there was still a chance that we might slip them onto the Tuzla-bound Puma. There was just a small group of French soldiers left, one more lift with room for two journalists.

'Nick! Who's the boss here? Who is actually in charge?'

Nick was holding his own and they were half way through finishing with the third Sea King. 'Colonel Pandjic. An air force colonel from Han Pijesak. He's in one of the offices in the clubhouse. I think he's had enough of the chaos out here!'

I climbed the steps to the journalists. 'You two all right?' I asked.

'Not really . . .' mumbled Hulls, '. . . they've arrested us.'

'I'm aware of that. I'm going to try and have a chat with their boss. I can't promise anything, but I'll try.' The pair of them were pretty uncommunicative.

'No, they're spies!' Pandjic was adamant.

'They're not spies, Colonel. They're journalists. They're just doing their jobs.'

'No! They're spies. We've inspected the film and he was filming our positions.' There wasn't much I could say to that. That bit of it was true. But it wasn't spying.

'Look, Colonel, it was a mistake. They shouldn't have been here. We can just throw them onto the French helicopter and fly them back to Tuzla. You can keep the film.' It didn't sound very convincing.

The Colonel sighed heavily. 'It's out of my hands. Pale has ordered me to hold them for questioning. They've got no press accreditation here and so an investigation has to be conducted. Sorry.' I sensed that he'd have loved to be rid of them. He was as much a victim of old-style Communist bureaucracy, secrecy and paranoia as the two journalists. 'They won't come to any harm. If they're innocent they'll be released. But an investigation must take place.'

I wasn't going to win this one. It was like talking to a brick wall. 'Of course, Colonel, we'll report the fact that you've arrested them and that they're being held by you.' It was the best I could do.

I went back out to the journalists. 'Sorry. Nothing I could do. They're determined to have their little investigation. Nick and I will be staying here so we'll try again once things calm down. If not, at least we'll be able to report where you are and who's holding you.'

The journalists were pretty calm. They'd been in much tighter scrapes. Part of the job. I can't say I had much sympathy. They'd caused part of this chaos. But then, so had the UN for allowing them to come along and do their jobs.

The French Puma had landed and was filling up with the last of the troops. The inspection of the Sea Kings was over and they too had flashed up their engines and were building up rotor revs. I grabbed a headset in George's aircraft.

'Sir. I'm staying here with Nick if that's all right with you. This is where the problems are and we've still got these two journalists to sort out.'

'Okay then, Mike. See you next time round.'

I handed the headset back to the crewman and watched them take off. Nick had disappeared inside to try his luck with Colonel Pandjic again. The French Puma lifted off first, rose to about fifty feet and then rapidly descended. I watched it, idly wondering why. A crewman leapt out and sprinted towards me frantically waving his arms. I ran to meet him half way. His eyes were bulging and he was jabbering in French.

'What? What are you telling me?' I screamed into his ear above the din of turning rotors and howling turbines. He realised I spoke no French, took a pace back and flung his arms theatrically into the air.

'Boom! Boom! Srebrenica. Boom! Boom!' he yelled into my ear.

'What the fuck are you saying to me?' I shouted back, now quite alarmed.

'Boom! Boom! Srebrenica . . .' and then he pulled a grotesque face, extended his neck and drew his thumb across it several times. With that he turned and sprinted back to the Puma, which rose quickly.

I spun round and saw George's aircraft tremble as it started to pull power and lift. I started running, shot through with adrenalin, but my feet seemed stuck in treacle. I watched in horror as the nose came up and the weight came off the front wheels. The crewman was hanging out of the door. I waved frantically at him as I ran screaming, 'Stop! For fuck's sake stop!' which of course he couldn't hear. But he did see me and I could see his lips moving against his boom mike. The Sea King sank again. I grabbed the crewman and yelled into his face, 'Srebrenica's being shelled!' but he just shook his head not understanding anything. I clamped both hands over my ears and mouthed, 'Gimme a headset.' He handed me one, which I stuffed on my head.

Out of breath, I had to gulp several times to calm myself, 'Sir! I don't know how to say this but I've just had this mad Frenchman from that Puma try and tell me something . . . I'm not sure . . . but I think Srebrenica's being shelled!'

There was a pause and then George swore violently. There was another long pause and then, 'How accurate is this information?'

I was still breathing hard. 'Not very. He was screaming and shouting "Boom! Boom! Srebrenica", rolling his eyes and waving his arms about . . . then he made a cut-throat sign a couple of times and cleared off . . . but they did take off and land back down to tell us . . . must've heard it on their radio.'

'Well, we've got no comms here on the valley floor. We're deaf down here.' George paused again for what seemed like an age and then wearily asked, 'What do we do now? What do you reckon?' I wasn't sure whether he was talking to me or just thinking aloud.

'I don't know.' I really didn't. Do you scrap an op on the sketchy info presented by a gesticulating Frenchman? 'Sir, it's your shout.' It was. He was one of the two Air Commanders.

After another long pause, George was in charge of the situation. 'Mike, get in and see that Serb colonel. I want a one hundred per cent guarantee that nothing is going on in Srebrenica and that we've got a guaranteed clear route in. Got it?'

I bounded up the steps and collided with Nick in the corridor. 'Srebrenica's being shelled . . . I'm pretty sure, but the boss wants Pandjic to guarantee that nothing's going on and we're clear to go.' We confronted the colonel. He was surprised, irritated and angered all at the same time. He swore blind that nothing was happening and gave a personal guarantee for our safety.

I was back on the headset to George, '. . . swears blind that Srebrenica's quiet and we're good to go.'

'You believe him?' George sounded sceptical. Did I? Didn't I? I wasn't sure.

'No, sir. I mean, he's not lying . . . he just doesn't know . . . he would say that anyway.'

'That's it then. Get in. We're aborting back to Tuzla.' It was the only shout he could make.

'Just a second, sir. Lemme just grab Nick.' Nick was still on the steps near the two journalists. I waved him over. 'Come on Nick. We're off back to Tuzla . . . the mission's over.'

'What about those two?' He indicated the two journalists, who had been joined by two military policemen.

'Fuck 'em. They'll be all right . . . get in!'

We scrambled aboard and lifted off, leaving behind the baying crowd, the stranded journalists and the nonchalant inspectors. Despite the juddering of the helicopter, it was remarkably peaceful in our cocoon, isolated from the nightmare below us. We were all subdued, deflated in the knowledge that the operation had been a disaster. I was worried. Now a little calmer, I wondered whether I'd heard it right, if I'd misread the Frenchman's message. Suppose M. Stanley had got it badly wrong and was personally responsible for screwing up the biggest operation the UN had undertaken in the Balkans! My stomach started churning. It didn't bear thinking about. I felt sick and fretted for the rest of the ten-minute hop to Tuzla.

I didn't wait long to find out. No sooner had the aircraft settled on the pan than John Rooke had sprinted over. He was wearing a headset and didn't even bother climbing aboard but stuck the jack plug in the external socket. Through the Perspex windshield I could see his face, strained with concern. There was a desperate edge to his voice.

'George! Srebrenica's being shelled. It started just after the French lifted off. Tim Kelly and Colonel Richard are still on the ground . . . two Canadians have been wounded . . . splinters . . . head injuries . . . VVSI . . . they'll die if we don't get them out . . .' he caught hold of himself and added, '. . . better speak to you outside, George.'

It was worse than I thought. My short-lived relief at having been right was now eclipsed by news of the casualties. Add a sixth star to this screw-up.

'Shut her down,' George instructed the pilot, a hint of resignation in his voice. By the time we were on the tarmac the rotors had stopped spinning and the turbines had run down. Nick joined our group.

'The casualties are bad, George. The French can't do it. They've had to go back to Kiseljak to refuel, so really it's up to us.' John looked pale and almost apologetic. George was listening intently, stony-faced, staring impassively at the ground. I had a ghastly feeling I knew what was coming next. 'Look, I can't order you to do it. It's your Squadron, you're the boss and mission commander. I'm not going to order you in any case, but, the situation's critical. It's your call . . .' His voice trailed off. George said nothing but took out a cigarette, lit it and exhaled noisily. He was staring at the ground deep in thought. I was aghast. Surely we weren't being asked to fly into a valley that was being shelled?

'What's the situation on the ground now?' asked George finally.

'Still being shelled as far as we know . . . Tim Kelly's got comms with Kiseljak . . . seems every time they re-emerge onto the HLS the Serbs lob in more shells.' It didn't look at all good. There's no way we'd be going. George wandered off, smoking thoughtfully. John Rooke, Nick and I walked over to the vehicles. Major Olivier, the French major who'd called back the Puma to pick me up, turned quickly to Nick. He was livid, chopping at the air with his hands in fury.

'Tell them, tell the Serbs there are wounded in Srebrenica and we're flying there direct. Two helicopters. No Zvornik. No inspections . . . the shelling must stop immediately . . . I don't care who you have to tell!' Nick nodded furiously and sprinted off in the direction of the British HQ block.

I glanced across the pan. George was stalking about in front of the Sea Kings, scowling alternately at ground and sky – wrestling with logic and conscience. He looked alone and worried. You often hear people in the Army banging on about the 'loneliness of command'. Watching George pacing up and down, for the first time in my life I saw what it was all about. He alone was responsible for the aircraft and the lives of the crews. Logic said don't do it, it's suicide. But what of the Canadians? Could anyone with a shred of decency turn their back on them? No one was going to thank him for losing two aircraft, but no one was going to thank him for allowing two Canadians to die either. Catch-22.

Eventually he signalled to the crews of both helicopters to join him. I heard the turbines flash up and the rotors slowly begin to turn. We were off to Srebrenica. Nick arrived back; he'd spoken to Colonel Andric, the BSA brigade commander in Sekovici, and had received guaranteed approval to proceed direct to Srebrenica.

'Oh yes? And where have we heard that before?' snapped George sardonically. I felt distinctly queasy as I slung my daysack in the back of the aircraft and followed George in. I was half inside the door when he turned to me.

'I don't want you on this aircraft, Mike. Nothing personal. I just want as few people as possible on this one.' He smiled and turned back into the aircraft. It hit me like a bolt. *He really believes that they're not coming back.* I retrieved my daysack. I was both sad and immensely relieved I'd been bumped off the aircraft. I'd have given them only the slimmest of odds of pulling it off.

From the grass verge by the vehicles I watched George's and Lt Kev Smith's Sea Kings disappear off to the east. I took off my helmet and flak jacket. Both were soaking. I sat down against my daysack and lit a cigarette. There wasn't much else to do other than try to calculate how long it would take them to get back, assuming they were successful. I figured half an hour to Srebrenica, say, five minutes on the ground and then half an hour back. They'd been gone ten minutes so should be done within the hour.

Half a packet of cigarettes later the hour had passed. Nothing. Not a speck in the sky. People were milling around, saying little. Some could be seen squinting at the eastern horizon or scanning it with binoculars. Nothing. Ninety minutes into the mission I'd given up hope. Nobody's eyes met lest they confirmed the worst. I started to doze off.

'Look! It's them!' someone with a pair of binos shouted nearby.

People were suddenly on their feet, straining for a glimpse. I couldn't see anything other than a leaden sky pressing down on the hills and on Vis. A moment later I made out two specks, which grew in size with every minute until the pan was filled with angry buzzing as the two Sea Kings jockeyed for position. No sooner had the wheels touched than we sprinted forward to assist with the casualties. A French APC reversed up to George's aircraft.

The first off were the two Canadians, both wrapped in blankets. One was walking wounded. The other, with bloody bandages wrapped around his head

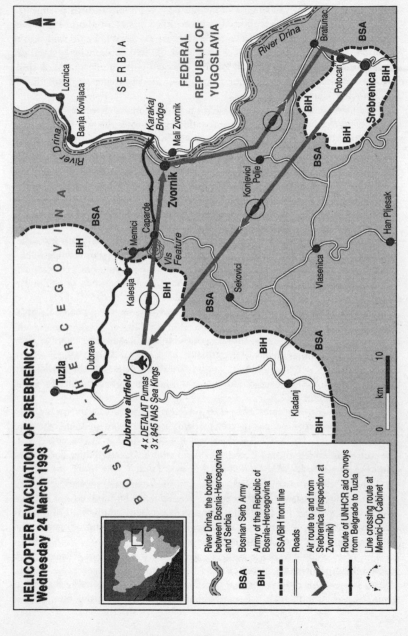

HELICOPTER EVACUATION OF SREBRENICA
Wednesday 24 March 1993

and a drip in his arm, was on a stretcher. Both were bundled into the APC and whisked off to be stabilised and X-rayed. The next off were Tim Kelly and a small French officer in a blue leather air force jacket, Lt Col. Jean Richard. Both were ashen-faced with a wild, hunted look etched into their eyes. As the aircraft closed down George emerged looking even more gloomy than when he'd left.

'Somebody give us a fag!'

In clipped sentences he explained what had happened when they'd got to Srebrenica. Kev Smith's aircraft had remained circling at altitude as top cover, trying to spot any artillery fire. George had dropped down to the football pitch and had found it deserted. He'd then hovered off up the main street to a pick-up point, which Tim Kelly had chosen in front of the hospital. Initially, Tim had contemplated an extraction from the roof of the PTT building, but it had a large antenna, which would have needed chopping down. Moreover, the only access to the roof was through a trap door, through which the casualties could not have been passed. In addition Tim was carrying a small girl with very bad splinter injuries, whom he was determined to bring out. So he chose the spot in front of the hospital, from which they'd all been winched up one by one. This had taken the time.

'Where's the girl?' someone asked. George took another drag on his cigarette.

'We had to leave her behind . . . she died before we could winch her aboard,' he said simply.

The plan now was to fly the casualties to Kiseljak just as soon as they reappeared. I wandered back to the grass to retrieve my kit and to say goodbye to Nick and the others. A camera crew had been quicker off the mark. One was jammed in Tim Kelly's face and he was stumbling through a brief résumé of the day's events.

'. . . about three minutes after they took off we were still on the landing site organising more people to come down, more injured people, when we were shelled . . .' He looked shaken and his voice had a husky edge to it, '. . . the shell landed about fifteen yards from where we were lying. There were about eight shells and one landed right in the middle of the football field . . .' he faltered momentarily, '. . . we were supposed to have winched up three people . . . the third was a little girl . . . she died . . .' he croaked out the last two words, shaking his head and biting the corner of a trembling lip as his eyes misted. I felt for him and was almost beside myself with anger at the intrusive nature of the camera and the interviewer.

The news people weren't going to get much more out of Tim, so they turned their attention to Colonel Richard, who was standing next to a sombre John Rooke. 'Our only protection is our white paint . . .' he cocked a thumb over his right shoulder at a Puma behind him, '. . . and I think that people who are in charge of people who are going to shot [sic] us will take a large responsibility in front of everyone . . . because we have only our hands!' He spread his open palms before the camera. He couldn't have stated it more clearly.

The Sea Kings had already flashed up and run up their rotors when word came that the doctor had deemed both casualties fit for onward flight to Kiseljak. They were expected on the pan at any minute. The APC reversed up to the helicopter and the casualties were quickly loaded. I grabbed my things and started across the pan.

Half way across, a fluttering, scraping sound ripped through the air, clearly audible above the engines. A shell exploded in the trees behind the helicopter. A second one screamed in but I couldn't see where it landed because I was face down, hugging the concrete. I looked up at the crew in the cab of the aircraft, who both had their palms up and a bemused expression on their faces. Commed up and deaf in their cockpit, all they could see were panic-stricken soldiers diving into vehicles or throwing themselves to the ground. Unable to shout loud enough I picked myself up and raced back towards the vehicles. All the best seats had been taken. There were too few vehicles for the mass of sweaty and swearing flesh trying to cram itself in.

The aircraft started to close down. I could see a helmeted crewman trying to pull a stretcher out of the helicopter. *The casualties!* Before I knew it, and much against my better (cowardly) judgement, four of us had sprinted up to the helicopter, grabbed the stretcher and were racing across the pan to a Warrior, which had roared on and executed a perfect 180^0 neutral turn. We'd just stuffed the stretcher into the back when the crewman arrived supporting the walking wounded. He too was bundled in and the Warrior took off.

Eventually the Serbs got bored and stopped the shelling. The helicopters weren't going anywhere now. Another attempt to take off would be met with more shelling, so the decision was made to leave it for the day and try again tomorrow. Nick was nowhere to be seen. I guess he'd been back in the Ops Room ringing Colonel Andric and asking him to stop shelling us, please. The signaller in the Spartan stuck his head out of the back door and shouted at me, 'Sir! Are you the interpreter?'

'No. Lieutenant Costello is, but he's not here.'

'I know. It's him on the net. Wants the other interpreter. You're needed to do the line crossing. They're leaving as soon as you can get to the HQ block.'

Line crossing! What were they on about? And then I remembered: the other half of the deal – the forty-six Serbs to be escorted over the line at Kalesija. Surely they weren't still going ahead with that? I looked at my watch – half-four. It would be dark in an hour. And anyway, why couldn't Nick do it? I ran out of the pan, turned left and sprinted the 500 metres to the Squadron HQ block. There wasn't even time to find out what was going on.

'Come on, sir! Jump in! They're waiting for us at Kalesija.' The driver of a Land Rover, its engine running, urged me in. I hurled myself into the back as it started moving and collapsed in a sweaty, breathless heap on one of the plastic seats. We raced out of the airfield, turned right and drove at breakneck speed down to the Kalesija forming-up point where a bizarre convoy sat waiting. A couple of Scimitars were at the front, behind them a Spartan APC. Behind that was a soft-skinned Toyota Land Cruiser. Next in line was a rickety old Centrotrans coach crammed full of glum and exhausted looking civilians. Finally, another couple of Scimitars brought up the rear. We pulled up next to the coach; I hopped out and bumped into WO2 Sterenberg, B Squadron's Sergeant Major.

'Who's the boss here, Sergeant Major?'

'Lieutenant Beddard, sir. He's up front somewhere.' There was more than a hint of anger and irritation in his voice.

'Everything okay, I mean with the civvies . . . are you all right?'

'No, sir! It's not all right. It's disgusting! I've never seen anything like it in my life!' He was fuming, barely able to contain himself, '. . . I've never seen abuse like it. These people have been badly mistreated.'

'How? What do you mean?' I was definitely out of the loop on this one.

'They went through all their possessions. We stayed with them as best we could, but then they were taken off and strip-searched. Some have been beaten! Most of them are just old people!' There wasn't much time for this. A red-haired lieutenant had joined us.

'Mike Stanley?'

'That's right.'

'We've got to get going. You're in the Spartan, okay?'

I climbed into the APC and off we clattered; through Kalesija, shattered beyond repair, left at the edge of town and along a horribly rutted D-shaped track, which led us over a small river, the front line, and then on up a rise to Memici and the Serbs. It seemed to take for ever as we could only go as fast as the coach in front. It was dark and oppressively hot in the Spartan and I must have dozed off because I awoke with a start as the APC came to a grinding, swaying halt.

As we clambered out I was half expecting to see the usual motley crew of Memici front-line Serbian soldiers and was not prepared for the pandemonium that immediately engulfed us. The coach had quickly been surrounded by a throng of soldiers, civilians and press. Flash bulbs burst in the gathering gloom and powerful halogen lamps illuminated the front of the bus. Traditional Serbian folk music was blaring through tinny loudspeakers nearby. A hulk of an officer with a wild, black beard seemed to be in charge of off-loading our passengers. As each of the civilians emerged from the coach he or she was met with kisses and words of welcome from Black Beard. With camera and microphones thrust in their faces each would be asked a barrage of questions about their treatment in Tuzla. At this rate it was going to take hours to off-load the coach.

The 9/12 boys busied themselves with shunting and turning the vehicles around and forming up the convoy to face the direction we'd just come from. Ben Beddard grabbed me. 'Mike, any chance of asking the Serbs to hurry up with the bus? We've got to get going before it gets completely dark.' From his tone it was obvious he was worried. Line crossings by day were risky enough, but to attempt one at night would be pushing it too far. Besides, no one had ever attempted one at night. Just too risky.

I wasn't optimistic of getting anything speeded up. The Serbs were deter-mined to milk this one for all it was worth. I pushed through the throng and grabbed Black Beard's arm.

'Do you think you could speed this up a bit. We've got to get back across the line while there's a little light left.' There was no polite way of putting it.

Black Beard forgot the woman he had been kissing and turned to me. His eyes full of fury he stabbed a finger in my chest and bellowed for the benefit of the cameras and folks back home, 'We've waited a year for this! Now it's your turn to wait!' There was little to be gained from having a stand-up row in front of the cameras, so I retreated back to Ben.

'Not a chance, Ben.' He looked even more worried and disappeared, mum-bling something about getting on the radio. The light had completely gone now and this bizarre scene was illuminated only by the lamps of dancing TV cameras and the dirty yellow headlamps of the vehicles. The coach had only half emptied and it looked as though we'd be in for quite a long wait.

'Fucking civvies!' I swore aloud in frustration at no one in particular.

'Pardon me?' It was a woman's voice, small, with an accent. I looked around in surprise but she now confronted me. Petite, she was burdened with an enormous light blue flak jacket and blue helmet, from under which sprang strands of long dark hair, framing a delicate oval face with high cheek bones and flashing, dark, angry eyes.

'Pardon me?' she snapped again.

'Well, you know . . . that,' I waved a hand at the bus, feeling guilty now. Who was this woman, this girl, who looked so out of place amid this mayhem?

'That's no excuse!' She snapped again. 'I expect better behaviour from an officer in the British Army.' With that she spun round and stalked off to the other side of the road where she stood with a group of UNMOs, arms folded across her chest, eyes hurling daggers at me. I felt about an inch tall and stood there smarting from her tongue-lashing. She was obviously an interpreter working for the UNMO team based in Banja Koviljaca on the other side of the Drina in Serbia. There was no point in making enemies of everyone so I shuffled across the road.

'I'm sorry. I didn't mean anything by it . . . it's been a very long day . . . you know, Srebrenica . . .'

'You were there?' Her tone had softened.

'No. Zvornik . . . with the helicopters . . . and then we were shelled at Tuzla . . .' I nearly said 'by you' but caught myself. We moved away from the UNMO group.

'Speak English!' she insisted.

'Why?' I obliged her.

'Because . . . because, you give yourself away too much. It's not safe for you, not even here amongst these people.' She nodded in Black Beard's direction. And before I could point out that it was my job she added, '. . . you're Nick's friend, aren't you? He's told me about you.'

'Nick? You know him?' She nodded.

Ben Beddard interrupted us. He was quite agitated. 'Mike! The coach. What do you reckon?' I glanced across. It was nearly empty, but it was also pitch black. We had two options. Stay here the night and cross in the morning or risk it and go now.

'You're the boss, Ben. For what it's worth, I don't particularly fancy spending the night over here. Let's get back.'

He paused for a moment's thought. 'Right! Let's go.' And then shouted up the line, 'Sergeant Major! Mount up. We're off.'

The girl grabbed my arm. 'Please say hello to Nick . . .' she faltered, '. . . you two shouldn't be here. They should never have sent you. If you can, go home and get away from this place. It's not your war . . . just look after yourselves and watch your backs!' She was almost pleading. There was no time to argue or to find out what she was banging on about. She sounded just like Greta in Sarajevo.

'Okay then, I'll tell Nick. Anyway, sorry about . . . you know.' I didn't know what I was sorry about. It wasn't until I was back in the stultifying Spartan that I realised I didn't even know her name. But it was too late. We were already rolling, leaving the absurd pantomime behind us.

As we lurched and bumped along, above the clattering of the tracks I was aware of stones being thrown up against the metal sides of the vehicle. Once or twice, through the tiny rectangular vision block of thick, armoured glass, I thought I saw an angry flash of red. But I was so tired I thought my eyes were playing tricks and in any event my thoughts were filled with the image of the girl with no name wearing that stupid helmet.

We stopped in Kalesija so that UNHCR could take their Land Cruiser and the coach back to Tuzla. Wearily, I stepped from the APC on the scrounge for a cigarette. Sergeant Major Sterenberg was at the wheel of the Toyota behind. His eyes were bulging and his white-knuckled hands were still gripping the steering wheel. In fact he looked as though he was in a trance.

'You okay there, Sergeant Major?' I opened the door. He was trembling slightly.

'Okay? Okay? . . . no I'm not fucking okay!' His voice was shaking.

'What's the problem?' But he was too far gone to answer.

'Did you see that?' someone nearby was shouting, '. . . fucking tracer everywhere. I reckon every vehicle must have been hit . . .'

Tucked up in the noisy Spartan, consumed with thoughts of women in helmets and flak jackets, I'd been oblivious to the battle raging outside. We'd driven right through a fire-fight. Miraculously no one had been hurt. The Muslims and Serbs together had conspired to spoil Sergeant Major Sterenberg's day still further. They hadn't had the good grace to let the UN get away safely.

Back at the HQ block a party was in full swing. The briefing room was packed with uniforms of all descriptions; British camouflage, flight suits, a gaggle of BiH officers, including the airbase commander and his staff. He was a thoroughly charming and measured man who'd been a fighter pilot, instructor and display pilot prior to the war. I suppose the party had been organised in advance on the premise that there'd have been something to celebrate.

I was desperate for a smoke and went on the scrounge. Nick was chatting to Tim Kelly and a couple of the pilots. I couldn't see George Wallace anywhere.

'Where's George?'

'Oh, he's been invited to dine with Morillon in Tuzla. Cumming's there as well. Seems Morillon wanted to meet the pilot who flew to Srebrenica . . . anyway, how did the crossing go?'

'Crap, Nick. Chaos. Serbs made a big deal of it . . . music, press, lights . . . all pretty fraught . . .' suddenly I remembered, '. . . by the way, who's that girl, the UNMO interpreter on that side . . . small, dark hair . . .'

'Oh, so you've met Biljana. Biljana Sretenovic. Lovely, eh? If I wasn't getting married . . .' Nick smiled.

'Well I don't think I left her with a brilliant impression. She kept banging on about it being unsafe for us and that we shouldn't be here . . .'

'She's right!' Tim Kelly snorted, 'it is unsafe. What a fuck-up! I mean, we were being shelled, people being killed and wounded and they wouldn't have any of it, wouldn't believe me . . .'

'Srebrenica?'

'Yeah, they had it pretty well taped. Every time we came back onto the football pitch they'd lob in another couple of shells. They knew exactly what they were doing . . . bastards . . . and that lot in Kiseljak didn't help. They just didn't believe it was happening . . . they were the only ones I had comms with and when I told them they just kept coming back with "we've had assurances ... the operation will continue" ... and I'm there saying, "I'm telling you, we're being shelled ... one's landed fifteen metres in front of us ..." but they wouldn't have it. They kept bleating on about assurances and signatures ... I mean, what a cock-up!' He shook his head in disbelief. The little girl's death had really got to him.

Eventually, sheer exhaustion and lack of food drove us to bed. I followed the air crews upstairs to the TV room where they busied themselves unrolling sleeping bags. Only then did it dawn on me that all my kit was in Kiseljak. It had been naïve of me to assume that the operation would go swimmingly, that we'd all now be back there. The daysack full of medical kit was quite useless to me now. I cursed myself for having broken the most basic rule of soldiering – never get separated from your kit. I had nothing but an electric razor and a toothbrush in my flak jacket but I knew we'd be back in Kiseljak in less than twelve hours and one night of discomfort wasn't going to kill me. I threw the flak jacket onto the linoleum floor and curled up on it. As I drifted off I remembered distantly that it was my sister's birthday.

'. . . but that did not impress the men with the guns, and they're the people you must impress if you're going to do business here. This operation went wrong in exactly the way everyone feared it would; when the Bosnian Serbs' political leaders could not control their men on the ground. It wasn't all bad news; a few people did make it out on the three French helicopters that got away safely. After months of terror they were transported to relative safety in under half an hour. Some would not have survived much longer in Srebrenica. Others, perhaps have a chance to start again. But the overwhelming sense of the day is that of good intentions cruelly dashed. Justin Webb. BBC News. Tuzla.'

Thursday 25 March 1993 – Dubrave Airfield, Tuzla, Northern Bosnia

Something was wrong but I wasn't sure what. Just that feeling that things weren't quite right. Time? 0630! Around me green maggots snored. What was it? Beyond grunting and snoring it was deathly quiet. No birdsong. Nothing but heavy silence. Odd. Stiffly, I hauled myself off the jacket and stretched. I was aware of a bright uniform white light streaming in through the window. I stared in disbelief. *Oh my God! We're never going to get out of here!*

The world outside was blanketed in the thickest snow I'd ever seen and it was still falling so heavily that it almost obscured the row of trees barely twenty metres away. I watched mesmerised as great sides of snow slithered off overburdened conifers and tumbled silently to the ground. There'd be no flying today. No one would be going anywhere. Now I was doubly depressed.

The chances of making it into Sarajevo for Peter Jones' and BRITDET's leaving party on Saturday had suddenly been dramatically reduced. I cursed silently. *You just can't win in this place. If it's not the warring factions, then it's the bloody weather!* Glumly, I fished out the razor.

The atmosphere in the Ops Room was tense. Just about everyone was there, trying to figure out what to do. First there were the casualties. Then there was General Morillon: the taciturn French general was puffing away furiously on one of his Davidoff cigars, filling the airless room with choking smoke. His face showed no emotion as he listened to the various options. He had a meeting with President Milosevic in Belgrade and no way of getting there. Suddenly, he stood up. The Ops room went silent.

'Git me ma flakker jacket and fly me to Belgrade!' he growled, waving his cigar at a stunned George Wallace. It was hard not to laugh. *Go on George. Let's see how you're going to get out of this one!*

There was a deathly pause while George gathered himself. Very deferentially and with the utmost reverence and patience he explained that there was no diplomatic clearance to fly into Serbia, that there wasn't enough fuel, that *... the idea is barking mad. Go on! Say it like it is, George!* But he didn't and continued gently to explain that it couldn't be done.

With a flourish of his cigar Morillon silenced him and announced instead that he intended to fly immediately to Kiseljak. From there he would drive across Serb-held territory, cross the Drina and proceed to Belgrade. Major Olivier started issuing orders to get the two French Gazelle pilots stood-up and readied. It was an even more improbable plan. I had to get out of the Ops Room and get some fresh air.

'Come on, David, let's take a wander out onto the pan and see how bad it really is. Besides, I'd hate to miss Morillon's departure.' I'd found David Bennett lurking in the corridor. He too was trying to get out of Tuzla as his tour was over. He had to report back to his Regiment, which was departing for a six-month tour in West Belfast.

The snow was falling harder than ever. The pan was completely deserted and in deep snow. The Sea Kings and Pumas looked particularly forlorn, their blades drooping heavily under the weight of the snow. I clambered into George's aircraft and retrieved the two loudhailers. To the right of the pan a French crew was clearing snow off the tiny Gazelle and readying it for flight. From somewhere David had produced an old-fashioned witch's broom.

'See this, David!' I smirked, grabbing the broom and shoving it between my legs, 'Morillon's got more chance of getting out of here on this than in one of those!'

The snow was so bad that the end of the pan was barely visible. A French jeep pulled up next to the Gazelle and out hopped Morillon, still puffing on his Davidoff. The Gazelle flashed up and the rotors began to turn.

'Five minutes. That's all I'll give them . . . five minutes before they're back, if they haven't crashed into the mountain.' One couldn't help but admire their determination though. Then the Gazelle lifted off, windscreen wipers swiping madly at the snow, which was packing up on the Perspex. The aircraft hovered just above the ground and, as it glided slowly past us, barely ten metres away, David and I braced and threw up two perfect salutes at Morillon; he acknowledged us with a flick of his cigar and a slight inclination of his head.

'Do you think he knows we're taking the piss?'

'No. They love saluting each other in the French Army. Y'know, all that thigh-slapping and shouting of *"Mon General!"*'

Within moments the tiny Gazelle had been gobbled up by the blizzard. There was nothing else to do on the pan and it was far too cold to hang around waiting for Morillon's return. We'd barely slithered three-quarters of the way back to the HQ, however, when we heard the Gazelle returning. As we staggered off up to the cookhouse to grab some breakfast I wondered what Plan C would be. One thing was certain. Morillon being Morillon, he was not going to get beaten by the weather.

Plan C had swung into action even before we'd finished breakfast. Determined to get to Belgrade, Morillon had decided he'd drive over the front line at Kalesija and head off into Serbia over the Karakaj bridge. Returning to the Ops Room I discovered that they'd grabbed Nick and were down at Kalesija waiting for the UNMOs to fix up a line crossing.

Not to be defeated by the snow either, the Serbs decided to keep us all on our toes by blindly lobbing more shells onto the airfield. This time no one was caught in the open and we were able to take cover in the Ops Room or in the shorn-up bomb shelter, which was really just another room but reinforced with beams and joists of wood.

Alan Abraham grabbed me. 'Mike! Ring up Colonel Andric and tell him to stop the shelling this minute!'

I dug out my notebook and hunted for the long INMARSAT number, which Nick had given me. Brigadier Cumming, as usual, was taking the whole thing in his stride and was sitting quietly on a wooden bench, helmet on, quietly puffing away on a cigarette.

As I jabbed at the keypad on the handset, and waited for the required tone, before continuing to punch out the impossibly long number, I noticed that my hands were trembling. I don't think anyone ever gets used to being shelled, however lacking in intensity it is. The whole ghastly experience leaves one helpless. After several failures I made a connection; somewhere in Sekovici a telephone was ringing. No answer. I was about to give up when a crackling voice came through at the other end.

'G'day. How can I help you?' I was slightly stunned that the voice spoke English.

'It's us at Tuzla. The British. Stop the shelling will you?'

'Sorry?' The voice sounded odd and distant. Another shell screamed in.

'The shelling! Stop shelling us!'

'Sorry mate. This is Texaco, not Shell.'

'What?'

'Texaco!' I could barely hear him. What was this English-speaking berk in Sekovici on about?

'Who are you, anyway? Where's Colonel Andric?' I could seen Alan getting irritated as he was only getting half the conversation.

'I'm the petrol attendant . . . Texaco, not Shell.'

The penny dropped. 'Sorry, but where are you?'

'Look mate! This is the Texaco garage. Perth.'

'Perth where?'

'Perth . . . Western Australia! Who are you anyway?' I *almost* forgot we were being shelled. Perth!

'Well, I'm a British soldier . . . think we've got a crossed line here . . . we're in a place called Tuzla, in Bosnia . . . and the Serbs are shelling us . . .'

'Oh yeah, what's that like then?' he asked in a bored voice. I don't think he believed me.

'Not very pleasant . . .' I could see Alan hovering, '. . . sorry, got to go.' And I broke the connection.

'Who were you talking to?' demanded Alan.

'Crossed line,' I replied quickly, redialling the number. By the time I finally got through to Sekovici, the shelling had ceased. A rather irritable duty officer informed me that Colonel Andric was 'in the field' and unavailable. He promptly hung up. I had to get out of the Ops Room.

Things had not gone well down at Kalesija. The Serbs had basically stuck two fingers up at Morillon and told him he wasn't crossing. The whole party was now on its way back to the HQ to hatch Plan D and there weren't too many more options left. Brigadier Cumming came to my rescue and suggested I accompany him into Tuzla where he was due at a meeting between the Mayor of Tuzla, Selim Beslagic, and the ECMM representative, Tom Colbourne-Malpas, a former Irish Guards officer. I think Cumming was quite keen to disappear before Morillon and gang reappeared.

It was good to be back in my familiar seat in the Discovery. Sam Mattock had come up with the Brigadier from Split. Corporal Fox was as laconic as ever. The Brigadier was interested to hear about the details of the Zvornik inspection and what had gone on over the line. I filled him in on the salient points. It was a golden opportunity to get my oar in.

'Sir, you know Lieutenant Commander Wallace?'

'George Wallace? Yes. What about him?'

'Well, it's just that I was with him nearly the whole time and . . . well . . .

was there when he had to make some really tough decisions . . .' I poured it all out, explaining how George had bumped me off the flight and that as far as I was concerned he wouldn't be making it back. I felt it was important that Cumming knew, just so that the facts of that extraordinary decision were lodged somewhere. The Brigadier listened in silence, only occasionally asking a question, but for the most part letting me tell the story. It wasn't lost on him.

Back at the airfield Nick was grappling with a furious Morillon and the INMARSAT phone. Morillon had stormed into the Ops Room bristling with indignation and had hurled a Belgrade number at Nick, telling him to ring it and fix the crossing. The phone behaved itself this time and, much to Nick's horror and surprise, the rasping voice at the other end was that of President Slobodan Milosevic himself. Nick, who had come through on his direct line, stumbled through the introduction, then explained how Morillon was being prevented from getting to Belgrade by the Serbs at Memici. Milosevic assured him that it would be fixed and that they could cross now. By the time the party got back down to Kalesija, the Serbs there were all sweetness and light and Morillon sailed through without a hitch.

With Morillon gone and the snow continuing unabated, the frenetic atmosphere at the airfield ebbed away to be replaced by boredom and endless debates about the weather. The problem still remained as to how to get the casualties down to the Canadian base at Visoko. Eventually it was decided that if it was still snowing the next day, Brigadier Cumming would attempt to drive the route in convoy along with an ambulance and a Land Rover. Major Olivier, David Bennett and I managed to secure places in the vehicles. It offered me my best hope of getting into Sarajevo on Saturday to attend the party and deliver General Jackson's latest parcel to Minka Pijalovic. There was no way on earth I could miss that.

That evening I was able to hear Nick's account of the Konjevic Polje incident. I was horrified by what he told me. As he talked, Nick's voice grew quieter and quieter. It was obvious that all those who had been involved in the incident were still deeply affected by the experience.

'It's funny you know . . .' continued Nick, '. . . when I realised we were going to die in that place the only thing that kept going through my mind was "not now . . . not like this . . . I'm not going to make it to my wedding." There was just this huge feeling of regret and disappointment.'

'What about this Naser Oric character, Nick? Where is he now?' I didn't much like the sound of him.

'Srebrenica. He made it to Srebrenica where he's still the commander in the enclave.' Hearing it from Nick, I wondered about fate and how easily it could have been me. It should have been me, but it wasn't. It should have been my flak jacket caked in dried blood. But it wasn't. Fate.

Friday 26 March 1993 – Dubrave Airfield, Tuzla, Northern Bosnia

Weather – no change! If anything, worse. Now we'd almost certainly be trying to drive out to Visoko. By nine o'clock Brigadier Cumming had appeared from Tuzla. The casualties were collected in an ambulance, and a third vehicle, a Land Rover, was readied. Dave Bennett was to command it – in the front with the heater. I'd be in the back with the two loudhailers – and no heater. Major Olivier would travel with Cumming and Sam Mattock. I steeled myself for yet another hellish journey. There was no guarantee we'd make it. No one knew what state the roads were in, but it was the only way of evacuating the casualties. At 1030 we were good to go and set off from the airfield in a driving blizzard.

Eleven hours later we pulled into BHC in Kiseljak. We'd made it – just. The trip had lived up to the worst of Bosnian expectations. Most of the journey had been spent out of the vehicles shoving, grunting and cursing in the cold as we pushed stranded lorries and cars off the narrow mountain track. By the time we'd dropped down to more level going, we were soaked and frozen and still being held up, this time by slow-moving cars. As it was essential to get the casualties to hospital quickly Cumming ordered that our vehicle should lead and get the road cleared ahead of the ambulance. The loudhailers saved the day.

'Here, stick this out of the window, David!' and then when we spotted a slow-moving Yugo or Zastava, I'd blast them with a quick, 'You in the Yugo!' which resulted in violent skidding and sliding of the target vehicle, 'Critical casualties on board! Move over!' And they'd oblige by driving straight off the road and into a ditch. Worked a treat every time.

By the time we'd got to Kakanj it was pitch black. The Canadians met us with an ambulance and an APC escort. The casualties were quickly cross-loaded and we departed for Kiseljak. There, we found the standby Sea King crews dead from boredom and frustration. Three days hanging around the UN's HQ, trying to find out what was going on in Tuzla, had just about finished them off. They were desperate to escape. I handed in the loudhailers, retrieved my bergen, and joined Cumming and gang in the dining room. The Danes had rustled up a meal and a few bottles of red wine. We toasted Major Olivier. He'd been the perfect LO – cool as a cucumber. Within half an hour we were on the road again, Vitez-bound. I'd reclaimed my seat in the Discovery and had managed to prise a cigarette out of the Brigadier.

'You seem pretty keen to get back to Vitez, Mike. Any particular reason?' I was fairly sure he knew I hated it there. I was tired, not thinking straight and enjoying the cigarette. Before I could check myself I'd blurted it out.

'I've got to get into Sarajevo tomorrow.'

'What business have you got going there?' His antennae were twitching.

'Another of those parcels from General Jackson, you know, for his au pair's family . . .' which was perfectly true.

'No other reason?' He was fishing now.

'Oh, yes, well . . . Peter Jones and his team are leaving on Tuesday and they're having a party . . . tomorrow night.' It sounded a bit thin.

'A party, eh? Well, give them my regards. I expect I'll see Peter on his way through Split. In fact, tell him to come and see me.'

The drive to Vitez went quickly. The one good thing about the sudden freeze was that the fighting between the Muslims and Croats had been suspended. There wasn't a soul about. We pulled into Vitez in time to dive into the Mess.

'That's it then for you, David. When are you off to Northern Ireland?'

'Couple of weeks time.' He paused and swigged his beer. 'In a way I'll miss it here, the madness.' He almost sounded nostalgic.

'No you won't. Exactly the same in NI, the entrenched mentality, I mean. You'll feel quite at home there.'

That was the last I saw of David until we met up again by chance in June 1995 on the Isle of Wight. David was at Staff College in Shrivenham. We talked of Morillon and the Gazelle; of George Wallace, who had been awarded the Air Force Cross for his actions in Srebrenica; of the two press people – one of whom turned out to be Kate Adie's cameraman – who'd been left behind in Zvornik. We supposed they'd made it out of there. We hadn't heard anything more of the incident. Nothing stood still out there. Things just moved on in the Balkans.

TEN

Operation Bretton

October 1997 – Ian, UK

'So, there you are, Ian. I came within an ace of not getting that package into Sarajevo, but someone dropped me off at Kiseljak and I caught the Danish APC shuttle into town. My only companion in the M113 was a local employee of Civil Affairs, who worked in the PTT building. She was only in her thirties but looked fifty. Her hair was all shot through with grey and her face was quite badly disfigured. She'd been hit by mortar splinters when the building had been shelled and had been evacuated to a French military hospital in Paris. I couldn't quite work out why she was coming back. "Family," she'd said simply. She unnerved me a lot. You could tell she was a bit crazy from her eyes.'

As soon as I arrived at the PTT building we were off again, Peter, his interpreter Lejla, and me. Peter was saying goodbye to everyone he'd worked with. We then went to the bakery to pick up pies for the party. It was an extraordinary place, a cavernous multi-storeyed affair of conveyor belts, drop-through hatches, spiral chutes and mechanical racks. It was almost eighteenth-century – water, flour and yeast in at one end, hundreds of thousands of loaves out at the other. It had been derelict until Peter had arrived and getting this thing producing bread had been one of UNHCR's major successes. The extraordinary thing was that it was so exposed and attracted mortar fire. One of the workers had been killed there the previous day. But they still kept at it. I don't recall it ever not producing bread.

The party – held in BRITDET's bedroom on the fourth floor at the top of the civilian wing of the building – was a manic affair. The military had considerately accommodated the local staff and Peter's team in the most exposed part of the building, flush with the roof. The windows had been smashed by splinters and shrapnel. Sandbags had been piled up to head height. The team slept in doss bags on cots, which had now been pushed to one side to make room for the revellers. More than seventy of them crammed into this room, one wall of which was stacked high with cases of beer. It was like the Intergalactic Bar in *Star Wars*. There were the local and international UNHCR staff; there was Peter's team, Caroline Cove, Allan Knight and Don Hodgeson. Then there were five or six 2eme REP Legionnaires, some in uniform, others in regimental tracksuits. Tom Iron, the American, was there. The rest were Brits – George Wallace, Tommy and one or two others. Then there were other aid workers, radio technicians and guests from elsewhere in the building, none of whom I knew. This wasn't some Yuppie London drinks party; this was a wild session-from-hell, an imbibing of vast quantities of beer and an outpouring of emotional stress. Nearly everyone was smoking, guzzling, jostling and shouting above music while outside artillery and mortar rounds thumped into the city and streaks of tracer arced across the sky. It was the Mother of All Parties.

At 11 p.m. the building's MPs, in accordance with the Citadel's rules, tried to close down the party. One of them was a Ukrainian, whom one or two of us serenaded with the Red Army's Second World War song, 'Katyusha'. I remember one of the office staff, a slight girl, mid- to late twenties, oval face, long brownish hair and glasses, grabbed me. She shouted above the din, 'See what this war has done to me already!' She selected her only grey hair, holding it out almost reverently. I thought she was crazy. Her name was Una. They all struck me as half mad, these girls and boys, the local Sarajevans, but there was something vital about them all. These were no hillbillies from the backwoods. These were sophisticated, highly educated people; degrees in this, that and the other. Fluent in English, French, Danish, Italian, German and just about any European language. Bright people, and it became patently obvious to me months later that it was they who made UNHCR Sarajevo tick. They had names like Lejla, Meilha, Mica, Amira, Suad, Alija, Rajko, Njonjo, Rale. Ethnically, they were all mixed up and didn't care who was what. They all needed one thing – dollars to keep their families alive. They were real Sarajevans and I liked them immediately.

By 8 a.m. we were still at it, a few of us survivors – Peter, Una, Lejla, Mica, and George and Tommy, two of the Legionnaires. Tommy staggered off blind drunk to drive his CO to the airport and nearly killed them both by missing a turning at the front line. Sunday was a complete washout: we just lay about trying to de-tox. It was pointless even trying to go and see Minka in the state I was in. At 11 a.m. a cease-fire came into effect. A few minutes prior to it the Serbs lobbed in one last big shell, which killed three people downtown.

Towards evening two new Brits appeared – an RAF flight lieutenant called Nick and an Army WO1 called Brian. They comprised the new BRITDET. We were all crammed into Peter's room watching a video when these two turned up. It was a bit embarrassing. No one really spoke to them. The locals, especially the girls, cold-shouldered them. It was obvious that no one wanted Peter's team to go and they resented these two imposters.

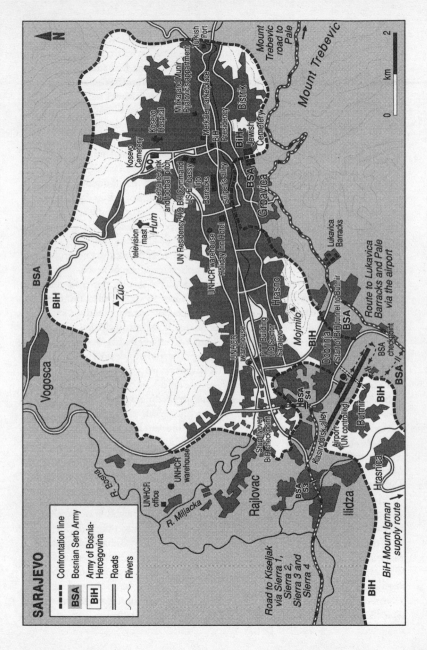

SARAJEVO

- ▪▪▪ Confrontation line
- BSA Bosnian Serb Army
- BiH Army of Bosnia-Hercegovina
- Roads
- Rivers

N

Mount Trebevic road to Pale

Mount Trebevic

Turkish Fort

Minka and Munir Pijalovic's apartment

Markale marketplace

Bistrik

Kosevo Hospital

BiH Presidency

Jewish Cemetery

Kosevo Cemetery

BiH

Zetra ice rink and football pitch

BiH Command HQ

US Embassy

Tito Barracks

Sniper's alley

BSA

Grbavica

Hum

television mast

UN Residency

Holiday Inn Hotel

UNHCR warehouse

Lukavica Barracks

Zuc

Hrasno

Route to Lukavica Barracks and Pale via the airport

BSA

BiH

BSA

UNHCR warehouse

PTT Building HQ Sector Sarajevo

Mojmilo

Dobrinja

Start of BiH tunnel to Butmir

BSA checkpoint

BiH

BSA

BSA S4

Vogosca

R. Bosna

UNHCR warehouse

UNHCR office

Stup flyover BiH checkpoint

Kasindolska alley

Airport (UN controlled)

Butmir

BiH

Rajlovac

BSA S3

R. Miljacka

Ilidza

Hrasnica

BiH

Road to Kiseljak via Sierra 1, Sierra 2, Sierra 3 and Sierra 4

BiH Mount Igman supply route

BiH

km 0   2

One of the girls – Una or Lejla – told me that when Peter's team had first arrived they'd treated them the same. They resented soldiers coming in and telling them what to do after they'd all survived that first terrible summer in 1992. They'd been evacuated to Zagreb when the war had started, when the original UN building had been destroyed, although UNHCR's office had been downtown at that time, and the UN had withdrawn. They'd returned in June, established the airlift of aid into the city and had worked, driven by the crusader-like and bearded Larry Hollingworth, to get that aid delivered even to places as far away as Gorazde. Una had been wounded in the head on that trip when their APC had hit a mine. She'd been arrested and molested by Serbs in Ilidza, who had confiscated her passport. Her crime? Being a Serb *and* working for UNHCR *in* the city. But she always maintained that she was a Sarajevan and Bosnian first. They all had similar stories and experiences. Small wonder then that they resented BRITDET's arrival. Small wonder too that they now wouldn't talk to these newcomers. Shared experiences bind people strongly.

The next day, Monday, Peter dropped me off at Minka's. I'd rung her to check she'd be in. Peter was busy doing his hand-over with Nick and said he'd come back for me in a few hours' time. The second trip was different from the first, when I'd only had a few minutes to dump everything on the kitchen floor. Minka did start crying when she saw me, but then we sat down and opened this enormous parcel. Her husband, Munir, was away at work, so it was just the two of us . . . three if you include her canary. It was singing its head off. 'See!' cried Minka, 'A good sign! She's happy now . . . she hasn't sung for weeks.' We were in this small sitting room – carpet, sofa, two arm-chairs, coffee table, TV and bookshelves – could have been England. Except that the windows had been smashed in and the ceiling and walls were scarred. Minka was a bag of nerves. She couldn't apply herself to the parcel. She'd read a letter from Aida, burst into tears, recover and ply me with more Slivovica. Then she started grinding coffee in one of those traditional brass grinders. When it came it was as dark as midnight, thick as treacle and just as sweet, poured from a small copper pot into tiny porcelain cups on little saucers. Coffee was 150 Deutschmarks a kilo on the black market. Sugar was more.

Minka asked me about Aida and what the Jacksons were like. The stories she told me about the hardships they'd endured since the start of the war horrified me. I knew that Aida had been caught in London but I didn't realise that there was another daughter, Arna, who had been evacuated to Paris at the start of the war. Minka and Munir hadn't heard from her either. It was scarcely credible what had happened to this family and yet here she was squandering her precious coffee on me . . .

I'm smiling now, thinking about Minka and our meeting. Until then you could have put me down as the world's greatest sceptic. Not any more. Minka had second sight; she could *see* things. I'm sitting there on this sofa. I've finished my thimble of coffee and she bustles in from the kitchen with the pot to top me up. She's bending over about to pour and suddenly stops and says, 'Oooo, I see a little bird!' I'm thinking she's gone mad because all I can see is black glutinous sludge in the bottom and coffee grounds sticking to the sides. Now she's picked up the cup and is telling me about things in my past. I don't mean the sort of garbage you get in horoscopes where you can read anything you want into it. This stuff is dead accurate. She scares the shit out of me. She tells me that four years earlier I'd had a blonde-haired girlfriend, that I'd been sent to Africa for a year and that our relationship had fallen apart after three months ... it's not that it was vaguely true ... it was one hundred per cent true. Every detail.

And she couldn't have known, not someone who has lived in a besieged city for a year. No international calls in or out. No post. And I've only met her once before and I've never told her anything. And let's just suppose that just somehow she'd got a letter from Aida – which I know she hadn't – Aida couldn't have known because the only Army people she knows are the Jacksons. And I haven't seen Mike Jackson since the mid-1980s and we're talking here about something that happened in 1989. Besides, no one knew that girl. She saw it all and other stuff too. Then she upends the thimble and the residue forms a pattern on the saucer and she's reading into it and then I have to stick my finger into the muck and make a fingerprint, which she also reads. And all the time her voice is different, growing huskier and breathless. Her eyes, her pupils are pinpoints and she's staring at me, '... danger ... danger ... be careful!'

I told my father about it all once. I remember he went quiet and then told me that there were soothsayers in the Balkans who saw things in coffee. But then he wagged his finger at me and told me that it was un-Christian and that I should stay away from it ...

Everyone wants to know the future, don't they? She never got it wrong. Just before I left Bosnia I remember her telling me that I'd travel a lot, remain in the Army but that I'd be out and free by the time I was forty. She said life would be difficult, but I'll bet even she could never have known that I'd get arrested as a spy! I was astonished and none too sober because she kept plying me with Slivo and coffee, both of which gave me a banging headache. It was getting dark outside. The whole day had slipped away and I was beginning to flap that Peter had forgotten me. In fact he had. He'd been so engrossed in handing over that he'd actually forgotten me. Fortunately, he remembered and scooped me up at half-five. I left Minka armed with letters to send to Paris and London. I remember ringing Aida that night and telling her that everything was okay. So that was my first real contact with the woman who would become my Muslim mother, as she called it.

The next morning we left Sarajevo in a couple of vehicles. Peter and his team could have just flown down to Split on the airlift, Maybe Airlines as it was called, but he wanted to drive back down the route they'd come up 110 days ago. We also had this girl Una with us, who wanted a lift down to Split. I think she had some business with the UNHCR office there. I'll never forget that drive out. The Motorola just didn't stop squawking messages for Peter and the team – UNHCR callsigns were based on people's initials – 'Papa Juliet, this is Lima Hotel, thank you and good luck.' On and on it went as we drove through Ilidza and the Sierras. There was a huge lump in my throat. You can imagine how Peter and his gang were feeling. We stopped briefly in Kiseljak. Minka had been devastated that Aida had forgotten to send food for the canary, so we bought several kilos of the stuff and Una promised to deliver it to Minka just as soon as she got back to Sarajevo. She did too.

As we drove through the wreckage of burned-out houses and trashed villages that littered the Busovaca valley, Peter couldn't believe his eyes. 'This was all intact four months ago!' I remember saying something to the effect that there were a couple of wars going on outside Sarajevo, which was something the Sarajevo-centric international media tended to forget. They dropped me on the road outside the Mess at Vitez. Peter and I shook hands and promised to keep in touch. I said goodbye to Una and told her not to forget the bird seed. She promised she wouldn't and then dug an envelope out of the bag and thrust it into my hand. 'I wrote this last night. I couldn't sleep.' And then they were gone, leaving me walking back to the captains' house trying to decipher her atrocious spidery writing, all on one page of writing paper.

Before I could read it I was grabbed by Major Martin Waters and SSgt Mackenzie from PInfo. They were leaving theatre and had acquired this horrid yappy little Yugoslav mountain dog. I hated it – all teeth and claws with malevolent little eyes. They were taking it back to Germany and needed an interpreter to go with them to the local vet to get the thing inoculated. I remember instructing the vet to really stick the needle in hard, but this bloody thing called Dfor – D for dog – didn't even whimper once. Tough as old boots, like the people. Can you believe it? You go from sitting exams in Split, to being trapped in Tesanj, to that mad heli op in Tuzla, to the party-from-hell, into the hands of a soothsayer and then you end up taking a dog to the vet. Some place.

The police have got Una's letter now. It was a very sad letter, all about her feelings, how the war had destroyed her future, devastated her family and how she felt adrift in a rudderless boat ... how she hated soldiers, men with guns who'd wrecked their lives, but how through meeting Peter and people like him, who had come to help, she'd revised her generalisations and saw a ray of hope. I guess the letter was the beginning of our friendship.

I went to bed after that and didn't get up for four days. I fell horribly ill with flu. I didn't know it but I was totally run down. If you work it out, I hadn't had a proper meal for eleven days. I'd existed on snacking and a diet of Slivo, beer and cigarettes. The next ten or so days were exceedingly dull. Virtually nothing was going on other than the pressure cooker valley was set to explode. The Muslims and Croats in Travnik were at each other's throats. The LO for the place, Matthew Dundas-Whatley, spent much of his time mediating between the two. Eventually it blew and a sort of gunfight at the OK Corral erupted in Travnik. We tore down there in a couple of Warriors to maintain a presence and be ready to intervene to prevent a war crime from happening.

A war crime can be a family being dragged out of its home, lined up and shot. Under international law we were obliged to respond to prevent it. I remember sitting all night in the back of that Warrior, gassed out by smoking soldiers. It was weird because you were commed up but couldn't see anything. So, you just listened to the commander and gunner's endless commentary. When we returned to base I discovered that someone had left a message for me in the communications centre. The girls from UNHCR Sarajevo had rung to ask when I'd next be popping in to town.

There was one dark cloud, however. I'd fallen out with Dobrila. We were barely speaking to each other. She'd been involved in an accident when a Land Rover had skidded off the road. She'd been knocked out and needed stitches to her head, and was now in our MST Bravo, the surgical hospital on base. I remember going to see her parents in Travnik. Both Serbs, they were a terribly sad couple. Their son was somewhere in Serbia and they had grave reservations about Dobrila working for us. They'd been devastated by the accident. One night she and Edi confided in me, telling me how one of the officers, who has since left the Army – not a Cheshire – had 'sleepwalked' into her room one night and had woken her up by sitting on her bed. She'd rejected him but had not reported the incident. A couple of weeks later when Dobrila was in hospital this officer irritated me so much in the Mess one night that I obliquely referred to his 'sleepwalking'. He went running to berate Dobrila while she was ill and the moment she was discharged she came at me like a banshee, slapped me across the face and accused me of betraying her confidence. She was right. But the damage had been done and I was too stupid to apologise properly.

Things moved on quickly and I soon forgot the incident with Dobrila. One day Bryan Watters and I flew up to Tuzla to pay Nick and Phil Jennings a visit. Major Phil Jennings' C Company had replaced B Sqn 9/12 Lancers at the airfield and I reckon Bryan just wanted a quick change of scene. The BiH at the airfield loved C Company because of the company flag that hung outside the HQ block. It was green for C Company with a white letter 'C' on it.

Green's the Muslim colour and the 'C' could be interpreted to be a crescent moon! They loved that.

Nick had fixed up a line crossing, so the four of us crossed and drove on to Sekovici for a meeting with Colonel Andric. Nick did all the interpreting as he knew Andric better. It was strange meeting the commander whose guns at Memici and Vis were shelling the airfield and town of Tuzla, the very man we'd ring to get him to stop it.

After that we moved on to Karakaj to do business with Majors Vlado Dakic and Pandurevic. We were trying to recover the Spartan and the recovery vehicle, at a quarter of a million pounds, which had been abandoned at Konjevic Polje. At the time the Srebrenica issue was still high on the agenda. The Serbs were rapidly eating away at the pocket. UNHCR, and in particular its Head, Larry Hollingworth, had somehow managed to get a convoy into the valley. Only one convoy of refugees got out to Tuzla. It had made a huge splash. They'd been packed in like cattle, desperate to escape the town. One little boy had fallen out and had been photographed running along the convoy crying. Then this Serb major was photographed picking him up and lifting him back onto the truck. The picture had made the front cover of *The Times*. That man was Vlado Dakic. We called him the 'King of the Bridge' because he controlled the convoys crossing from Serbia into Bosnia over the Karakaj bridge. We gave him a copy of the newspaper and he promised to look into the issue of the two vehicles. As nothing could be done until the next day, so we pushed over the Drina into Serbia and booked into the Hotel Podrina at Banja Koviljaca where the UNMOs had their HQ.

Biljana Sretenovic, whom I'd last seen at Memici, was there and we were all drinking tea in the restaurant when the head of the UNMOs, a Dutch officer, marched up to the table and informed us that we had no right to be on this side of the front line. Bryan Watters damn near exploded and informed him that BRITBAT's AOR extended to the Drina and that we had every right to be there. The Dutchman was abrasive and rude. Biljana was embarrassed as he was her boss.

The following day Dakic directed us to a scrapyard in Karakaj, where we found the Spartan hidden under a cover: it was completely burned out and useless and not worth recovering. There was no sign of the recovery vehicle, so we removed the Spartan's registration plates and a wing mirror, which Phil Jennings later presented to Alan Abraham. We then zipped back up to Memici to try and get through on the radio and fix up a line crossing for us to get back. It was then that we heard that SSgt Bristow, the PInfo photographer in Vitez, had been shot in the head in Turbe while sitting in a Warrior with the back door open. It was therefore imperative that we now get back to Vitez. The line crossing was fixed for mid afternoon and would allow us a precious few minutes to get back to the airfield and hop onto a helicopter bound for

Kiseljak. It was Senator Joe Biden's flight. He was over from the States on a mission to visit the refugees in Tuzla. The rest of the day was filled with Vlado Dakic serving us lunch on the Serb side of the Drina.

We only just managed to get across the line and catch the helicopter in time. Bryan and I stuffed ourselves into this French Puma along with a number of baseball-capped Americans. When we landed at Kiseljak our lift hadn't arrived. The Puma needed refuelling before going on to Split with the Americans. We fell into conversation with one of Senator Biden's aides, one of those bright young Ivy Leaguers. He claimed he'd been studying the Balkan problem for two years and knew what the solution should be. Bryan and I were all ears as this bloke explained his theory: that the UN was useless, should be removed and that a huge logistics base should be established in Croatia from where arms would be pumped up into Bosnia. Bryan's eyes nearly popped out of his head. It would have been the fastest way of filling up more cemeteries – guaranteed that the Croats wouldn't have allowed the Muslims to have those arms. It would also have dragged the JNA into the war and probably precipitated a wider Balkan war. So much for two years of studying the problem. I think we parted company shouting at each other. They weren't interested in what anyone on the ground had to say.

During the second week in April, I again flew up to Tuzla, this time with Bob Stewart. He was on a quickie one-day visit. This time I had my bergen with me and was determined to stay up there. We flew up with the Russian head of Civil Affairs, Victor Andreyev, and the new BHC Chief of Staff, Brigadier de Vere Hayes. Other passengers included a number of aid workers, one of whom was wearing a baseball cap emblazoned with AMERICARES, an NGO I'd never heard of. As we hovered over Tuzla airfield this bloke's eyes were everywhere – unusual behaviour since it was only an airfield.

First stop was a meeting at the Tuzla hotel between Brigadier de Vere Hayes and Selim Beslagic and other representatives of the ABiH's II Corps. A deal seemed to be in the offing to get more wounded out of Srebrenica and more Tuzla Serbs out and over to the Serb side. The Little People really were just pawns, bargaining chips, in a much bigger political game.

Next stop was lunch downstairs in the restaurant. I was down at the far end of the table with the BiH airfield commander and the NGO bloke from Americares. They were chatting about the airfield and I was interpreting. He was asking the airfield commander a whole lot of technical questions; depth of concrete, length of runway, alternate runways, average air temperature and density for the time of year etc. etc. It meant nothing to me. When you're interpreting you don't pay too much attention to the overall conversation.

Phil Jennings managed to convince Bob Stewart that he needed me up in Tuzla while the convoy and refugee crisis in Srebrenica was gaining a head of steam again. The CO agreed and departed for Vitez where the wheel had finally come off the wreckage that was the Lasva valley and the place was apparently in flames. But, where we were in Tuzla, with our own focus, what was going on in some other valley to the south, not to mention the fighting that had erupted between the Muslims and Croats in Mostar, seemed so remote. As Bob Stewart dashed off I was left wondering whether it was just another gunfight that was going on down there.

That evening Phil Jennings came into the Mess looking worried. BHC were in a flap because an NGO calling itself Americares, having apparently done a thorough recce of the airfield, was threatening unilaterally to 'bust in' with medical aid. As Phil stood there scratching his head, the penny dropped. I told him about the bloke in the baseball cap. His jaw dropped and he rushed off to the Ops Room.

You might wonder at all the fuss about one NGO. There were loads of them. The Serious Road Trip, hippies, Caritas, Merhemet etc. etc. But none of them had their own aircraft, so this was no ordinary NGO. We discovered that Americares had a reputation for busting into war zones aggressively and unilaterally, usually without diplomatic clearance. They'd been very active in supplying the Mujahideen with medical aid during their war against the Russians in Afghanistan. Some of the press who seemed to know more even claimed that Americares was the baby brother of Air America, the CIA front airline that was so active in Vietnam, Cambodia and Laos. Who knows ... but they were threatening to fly into Tuzla airfield with medical aid, which would have resulted in shelling of the airfield and of the town. More than that, it would have wrecked delicate plans to get more aid into Srebrenica and more wounded out. At the time the Mixed Military Working Group at Sarajevo was attempting to come up with some sort of cease-fire for the Srebrenica crisis. This sparked a diplomatic crisis right across Europe as one country after another refused to allow Americares' chartered aircraft to operate from their airports. The long and the short of it was that the flight never happened.

Most days were spent hanging around at Kalesija waiting for convoys full of Srebrenica's wounded to appear. They never came. Only once did a vehicle bring people out – three old Muslim women, who had somehow managed to wander out of the enclave and were by chance placed on these empty vehicles by the Serbs, who didn't want them. That was it. In the evenings we'd drive down to Tuzla hotel for a scoff and a chat with the press or with the ECMM team or anyone we could find.

Then a disaster happened. On 12 April the Serbs intensified their bombardment of Srebrenica. One of the shells landed in a schoolyard and killed fourteen kids and maimed countless others. About fifty-five people were killed in that attack. All this was witnessed by some sixteen internationals, soldiers and civilians, whom Morillon had taken in there a month earlier and left behind.

Word got out of what had happened. Larry Hollingworth went insane and very public. He delivered a blistering attack on the Serbs, which I remember to this day. It started off with something like, 'My first thought is for the commander who gave the order to attack. I hope he burns in the hottest corner of hell.' The rest of his invective was directed at the shell-loaders, the lanyard pullers and he made special reference to the Bosnian Serb leadership. It was a gut-wrenching diatribe from a man who cared.

The world, including UN HQ in New York, went into a frenzy. We watched it all on the box in the Mess. On 14 April Naser Oric in Srebrenica announced he'd be surrendering the pocket. The credibility of the peace process, of the UN mission in Bosnia, of Morillon's promise to defend the place, hung in the balance. The surrender was announced on 15 April. The UN rapidly formulated some sort of demilitarisation plan for the enclave, and it was agreed at the Mixed Military Working Group in Sarajevo that 140 Canadians would be permitted to enter the enclave to effect the demilitarisation. In addition the evacuation of some 500 wounded by helicopter was also agreed, as was the principle of freedom of movement for those who wanted to leave the enclave and flee to Central Bosnia. We watched all this unfolding on the TV, aware that something big was happening, but not quite sure how it all fitted together. The fate of Srebrenica was being decided thousands of miles away in New York by the Security Council. On 16 April the Council passed Resolution 819 declaring Srebrenica to be a 'Safe Area'. No one knew what that meant, least of all me. But it was now a Safe Area. It must have been, because men in New York said it was so.

One morning I was woken at 6 a.m. It was 17 April. Sergeant Philpott had come up from the Ops Room below and was shaking me roughly. I was in my doss bag on a camp bed upstairs. He was shaking me and screaming into my ear, 'Sir, sir . . . get up! You're going to Srebrenica, get up.'

ELEVEN

Operation Grapple, Northern Bosnia

Sunday 17 April 1993 – Dubrave Airfield, Tuzla

'What do you mean, Srebrenica?' I was trying to make sense of this while rubbing the sleep from my eyes.

'I don't know, sir. That was the message.' With that Sgt Philpott disappeared back to the Ops Room leaving me to roll up my sleeping bag, dress and shave, all at breakneck speed.

No one in the Ops Room could enlighten me further. Phil Jennings and Nick were still asleep. There were no details other than 'Stanley to go to Srebrenica'. Its origin and details remained a mystery. By 8 a.m. I was still none the wiser and got onto the INMARSAT phone and rang the Ops Room in Vitez. They knew nothing more than I did, nor could they chat for long as a major crisis had blown up on their doorstep. Their hands were full dealing with massacres.

The Ops Room in Split was more helpful. I was to hook up with a Canadian company, which had departed Visoko bound for Srebrenica. They'd be passing through the airfield bound for Kalesija, crossing the line there and then heading down to Srebrenica via Zvornik. No one could tell me when they'd set off. There was some vague idea that this reinforced company of five platoons' worth of M113 APCs would be stopping at the airfield. Maybe they were still here. However, Split gave me two specific instructions. First, I was to act as interpreter for the Canadians as they had no military interpreters of their own and none of their locals could or would go into the enclave. Secondly, I was told that no matter what happened or what the circumstances were I was to be back out of the enclave by 5 p.m. on Wednesday 20 April. This was a direct order from Brigadier Cumming.

By 9 a.m. the airfield and in particular the helicopter pan had become the scene of chaotic activity. DETALAT Pumas and 845 Sea Kings were arriving by the minute. The same familiar faces from a month ago were popping out of the woodwork – David Lord, 845's Senior Pilot, Tim Kelly and Lt Col. Jean Richard. Another attempt to evacuate Srebrenica's wounded by air was on the cards, all apparently agreed at Sarajevo airport. The press too had flooded in from the Tuzla Hotel in numbers that I'd never before seen. This time they were corralled at the end of the pan, kept at bay by white mine tape. Again, a fleet of ambulances was standing by to scoop up the wounded. None of this helped me as I scooted about the airfield in search of five mechanised platoons. The Canadian company was nowhere to be seen. I wondered then if there'd been a crossed wire and if I was supposed to have met them down at Kalesija. Maybe they didn't even know about me.

By 10 a.m. we got word that they'd passed through Kalesija hours before, had got through Zvornik and were making good progress towards Srebrenica – minus their interpreter. Too bad. I went back to the HQ block and dumped my kit off, cursing the UN's inability to pass information accurately.

My frustration was short-lived. Within minutes Phil Jennings had told me that the Canadian battalion's CO and RSM would shortly be arriving in Tuzla bound for Srebrenica by air and that I'd now be going in with them. A copy of the airport agreement had been faxed up to II Corps HQ in Tuzla and it needed to be delivered personally to Naser Oric. It was also widely believed that a second document, a direct order for Oric to surrender and comply with the airport agreement, was also to be delivered. There was no sign of these two documents and we waited in the conference room for a courier to deliver the envelope. The helicopter operation couldn't begin until it arrived. I was told that I'd be couriering the letter in and that my first task would be to track down Naser Oric. Once done, I was to report back to confirm delivery.

Nick was sitting opposite me. Rolling his eyes he said, 'Rather you than me. Give him my regards . . . see if he remembers me from Konjevic Polje.' I think Nick was mighty relieved that his role would be confined to the helicopter inspections at Zvornik.

The conference room was packed to capacity with air crews, commanders, aid officials, Larry Hollingworth of UNHCR, and just about anybody who thought that he or she would be scrounging a lift into Srebrenica. I nipped off to the mess room and grabbed as many packets of Benson & Hedges as I could lay my hands on.

'Only going for the day then I see!' said Mick Fenton, Phil Jenning's Warrior Captain, who not only hated my smoking but also had the driest sense of humour.

The Serbs had banned the press and cameras from Srebrenica: clearly they didn't want images of that place to be added to eyewitness accounts. For their part, the press was dying for images and digging around for a way of getting a camera in, and an ITN reporter pestered us so much that I agreed to take in a camcorder. I wasn't particularly keen to do this but, after a quick cadre on how to use the thing, I stuffed it down the back of my flak jacket. It was the least likely place that would be searched.

Back in the conference room debates were raging as to exactly how this thing was to be done. Essentially, it was a repeat of 24 March. The first lift in would take the Canadian CO, his RSM, Lt Col. Richard and Tim Kelly to run the HLS, two Muslim doctors and me. We'd pick up two Serb doctors in Zvornik and, after the inspection, push on to Srebrenica. The evacuation of wounded would proceed as it had been planned in March. Almost everyone in the room had an acceptable reason for hopping onto the flights but most were turned down. Tempers flew and no one was quite sure whether any of our names, ID cards etc. had been cleared with the Serbs. This had all the hallmarks of another five-star fuck up. I looked across at Tim Kelly. He looked distinctly uncomfortable.

The evacuation would run for a day. The most critically wounded would be brought out by air. Thereafter, the principle of freedom of movement for those who wished to leave Srebrenica would come into effect, and they could be moved out by road. I felt a bit hollow. I didn't relish the prospect of being trapped in the enclave, the only Brit there, without a radio or any means of contacting my own people. I kept reminding myself of Cumming's directive – out by 5 p.m. on 20 April.

Eventually a courier arrived with a white envelope addressed to Naser Oric. It was sealed and taped at the back, the flap stamped in several places with the BiH II Corps stamp. We assumed it contained the airport agreement and the surrender document. I tucked the envelope away inside my smock.

As we walked past the press on the pan to the waiting Pumas, I was stopped by Kate Adie of the BBC. A camera was thrust into my face and she began asking me about my mission and what the envelope contained. It was an unpleasant experience and the first time I'd ever been ambushed by the press. I fished out the envelope and mumbled that I was just a messenger boy. Sky TV got pretty much the same answer.

The Pumas had already flashed up and run up their rotor revs, blasting hot air and kero around the pan. Two Canadians joined us. The taller one was the CO, Lt Col. Tom Gebert, a dark-haired, fit and serious-looking officer with a neat moustache. His RSM was a shorter, thin and wiry professional type. As I introduced myself a runner raced onto the pan and informed us that the Serbs had not cleared the two Canadians into Srebrenica. Clearance would have to be obtained for them to go in the next day. Gebert was furious at being bumped off. Squatting on the tarmac he rapidly scribbled out some orders for his company commander in the pocket. It half occurred to me that I too didn't have clearance and would be kicked out at Zvornik. I decided to bluff it out and if the worst came to the worst I could always give the letter to Tim Kelly.

With that we piled into the Puma and headed off towards Vis. My last view of Tuzla was of the chaotic goings-on on the pan where aid workers and others were venting their fury at being left behind. I'd gladly have swapped my seat with them. I wasn't looking forward to being pelted with stones again by a howling mob in Zvornik.

Surprisingly, the stone-throwers and boo-boys weren't there. The football pitch was deceptively quiet as the three Pumas closed down and we stepped out. No crowd, no press, no stones – just the skull and crossbones staring down at us. The UNMO team from Banja Koviljaca was waiting for us, as were the inspectors. No rude Dutchman either. The boss seemed to be a large Norwegian officer who had Biljana Sretenovic in tow as his interpreter. She was delighted to see me and began by scolding me quietly.

'Why are you going to Srebrenica?'

'It's my job – I have to.'

'No you don't. Don't go in there. They'll kill you.'

'No they won't. I'm only a messenger in all this.'

She grabbed my arm and led me away, 'Why don't you just marry me? Take me away from this place . . . we could have lots of children!'

I was stunned. 'Are *you* asking *me* to marry *you*, Biljana?'

'Why not?' She laughed, 'Why not since you obviously won't ask me!'

I didn't know how to answer her. *She's joking. Surely, she must be!* Marriage, babies etc had never entered my head. It was now the furthest thing from my thoughts.

The inspection seemed to be progressing smoothly, far less dramatic than before, but no less thorough. The crews were lined up beside their aircraft with their bags and bergens at their feet. Serb inspectors were even asking them to empty out their pockets and delving deeply into the bags. When they got to Colonel Richard they met their match.

'I am a colonel in the French Army. I will only submit my person and my bag to inspection by an officer of equivalent rank!' he snapped, his eyes flashing.

The Serbs were stunned and unsure how to deal with the protocol. One of them scampered off and returned with an embarrassed-looking Colonel Pandjic, whose eyes flicked once over Colonel Richard's open bag. 'That's fine. Sorry to have offended you.' I smiled to myself. He was the first Westerner I'd seen who'd managed to click into their mentality. But, the rest were thoroughly searched. I knew that I too would be frisked and started flapping about the camcorder.

'Where's your daysack, Nick?'

'In the UNMO's vehicle,' he replied hesitantly.

'Come on.' Together we walked over to the vehicle's open rear door. Shielded by it I fished out the camera and stuffed it into Nick's bag. 'I'm not jeopardising this op for some press bloke, Nick. Just make sure he gets it back.'

Colonel Pandjic informed me that he'd been on to Pale. There'd been no request for me to go into Srebrenica and one would have to be raised, and perhaps I could go in tomorrow. We started to argue. I didn't tell him about the letter but rather stressed that the Canadians were in there without an interpreter. We reached a compromise whereby I could proceed in but had to return to Zvornik on the last lift out that evening. By the following day Pale should have agreed to me staying on in the enclave. He floored me. He'd made this dangerous decision all on his very own, without bleating for orders and instructions from above. I told Nick to wait for me to come back out and we'd re-cross to Tuzla together.

Two Serb doctors in white coats clambered aboard one of the Pumas. We climbed out of Zvornik in a three-ship stream. The hop to Srebrenica to the south was short and took perhaps ten minutes. The Pumas flew low and fast keeping just above the crest lines of wooded and meadowed hills, which rolled past below us. In many places the greens and browns of spring were spoilt by the acne of war. Dotted across the landscape were the shattered remnants of remote villages, accessible only by twisting tracks. They looked as though a giant fist had thumped down and squashed them flat into white rubble. These were not the burned-out husks of Central Bosnia. Like Lidice in Czechoslovakia, each and every house had been reduced to dust and broken brick by systematic dynamiting. Not a wall was left standing.

We dropped rapidly into a tight valley. Its wooded sides had been hacked back leaving splintered stumps like broken teeth sticking out of the ground. Along the bottom snaked a long thin winding dirty yellow town, a curious mixture of old houses and tatty apartment blocks. The main street was packed solid with a river of milling humanity. Here and there a white vehicle sparkled, disturbing the drab scene. The Puma hopped over a high-tension cable, which spanned the valley, and dropped neatly into a walled football stadium. It hovered momentarily, side-slipping to the right to avoid a huge crater in the middle of the pitch and then settled. The second Puma landed to the left of the crater and the third slipped in behind us. We'd arrived in the Vale of Tears.

As we sprinted from the aircraft, hunched low to avoid the spinning disc, I was aware that we'd dropped into a scene of almost uncontrolled chaos. To the left a twelve-foot wall separated the stadium from the street. Atop it sat several thousand refugees clapping, cheering, shouting and screaming. To the left were terraces, half full of more people. At the top end were a couple of Canadian M113s and one or two UN 4x4s including a huge armoured GMC. Milling around these were more locals, youngsters strutting about with an air of self-importance. Dotted around the pitch a number of helmeted Canadian soldiers stood guard facing the crowds. The entrance to the stadium, in the corner, was guarded by an M113 and secured by a roll of barbed wire to prevent access. Beyond it a seething mass of people. There was not a single casualty in sight. No one was available for evacuation.

Quickly we set about our various tasks. Tim Kelly, Colonel Richard and their signallers swiftly established comms with the AWAC aircraft 'Magic' and with Kiseljak. The two Serb doctors ambled off to one side and stood there chatting quietly, hands thrust deep into the pockets of their coats.

I wasn't quite sure how I was going to track down Naser Oric. The commander of the M113, to whom I passed Colonel Gebert's orders, had only arrived some hours previously and had never heard of the BiH commander. I opened the door of the GMC, which revealed a lanky and swarthy Dutch UNMO. He'd been in Srebrenica for a few weeks. You could tell, simply from his drawn features and distant, uninterested eyes.

'You won't find him. He's always in the field,' he muttered.

'You know him though?'

'Oh yes, I've met him.'

'Then you're going to help me find him.' I explained about the letter. He seemed even more uninterested and indifferent but eventually he agreed to drive me through town in the hope that Oric might be at one of a number of houses, which he was known to use as headquarters.

We pushed beyond the wire and very slowly ground our way through thousands of people clogging the street. It was estimated that some 55,000 refugees were crammed into this small town. To the left, people hung over every balcony of the shabby apartment blocks, the walls of which were pocked by scars and shell holes. Further up and on the right was a wired compound crammed full of Canadian vehicles. A little beyond that was a three-storey square building also surrounded by barbed wire and sporting a tatty and faded UN flag – the PTT building. As we continued the street narrowed as it twisted through the older part of town, which was no less clogged with people.

'He might be in the house we're going to.' The UNMO didn't sound hopeful, but continued, 'He's supposed to have been wounded and is resting up somewhere.'

I was curious to know more about him. 'What's he like, this Naser Oric?'

The Dutchman paused for a moment. 'He's seen too many Rambo films. You'll see.' This wasn't the most helpful briefing I'd ever had. 'He's good at minor tactics in the woods. He's surrounded Serb patrols and chopped them to pieces. He's a good guerrilla fighter.' This was better.

We stopped and the UNMO pointed to a nondescript house with two steps leading to a door. 'In there is where he sometimes is.'

I asked him to wait and bounded over to the door. I paused and then knocked. It opened almost immediately, revealing an enormous man with a huge black bushy beard, dark eyes and hair drawn into a ponytail held by a black bandanna. His uniform too was black – boots, trousers, T-shirt and a black combat vest festooned with dangling grenades. An MP5K swung loosely in his hand. He was bigger than I expected and not wounded.

'Naser Oric?'

'Who wants to know?'

'Me. I'm a messenger. I've a letter for you from II Corps in Tuzla.'

He pushed the door to, leaving it slightly ajar. I could hear voices inside. The door swung open again and the giant stepped aside. 'Enter!' he commanded. I did so and stopped dead. My heart was pounding and my eyes popping out of my head. There were more of them, five in all, dressed much as the giant – black, bandannas, vests, grenades, beards, piercing eyes and MP5s. Five pairs of eyes glared at me. Immediately to my left was a young man sitting on a sofa. His right leg was stretched out in front of him propped on a low coffee table. He was short, squat and muscled under his black T-shirt. He turned his head and looked at me. He was young, no more than twenty-six, fresh-faced, deep dark brown eyes and short fuzzy black beard.

'I'm Oric,' he said simply.

'I've a message.' I unzipped my smock, fished out the letter and handed it to him. He examined the address and then the seals. Satisfied that it hadn't been tampered with he tore it open. The room went deathly silent. There was no second document, just one fax copy of the airport agreement, perhaps ten or eleven paragraphs in all. But scrawled in red biro at the bottom were three or four sentences, which I couldn't read. He read carefully and in silence. When he'd finished he folded the paper and looked up at me. His dark eyes sparkled.

'We will do everything to comply with this agreement and co-operate fully with the United Nations . . .' he paused, smiled and continued slowly, '. . . but as for freedom of movement. There is none. No one will leave this enclave, not even the United Nations.'

His companions sniggered.

I nodded. He might just as well have said we were all his hostages. But he didn't need to. The message was perfectly clear. No one would be leaving Srebrenica.

'By the way, Nick Costello sends his regards. He's in Tuzla.'

Oric's black eyebrows knitted together.

'Konjevic Polje?' I reminded him.

He smiled wickedly. 'Costello! Tell him nothing personal . . . it's war, the way it is.' He finished with a chuckle.

I nodded again and left. My heart sank as I returned to the GMC. I had to get a message out of this place fast.

Back at the football stadium the three Pumas were still turning and burning, gobbling up hundreds of litres of fuel. Still there were no casualties. Tim Kelly and Colonel Richard were worried that the Pumas would have to depart empty to refuel. It didn't appear that anyone was in charge of collecting the casualties, wherever they were. Amongst the locals who were milling around

I spotted a grizzled old man standing on top of a pile of rubble. He was filming with a camcorder.

'How long have you been here?'

'Since the start,' he replied, sweeping the scene with his camera.

'How do you keep that thing going?'

'Batteries? No problem. I charge them using a water wheel in the river. But I'm short of tapes.'

Here was an opportunity. 'How about a deal? You stay right here and film all this. Give me the tape at the end of the day. We'll fly it out and then . . .' What? What would he want? Money? '. . . well, you can have whatever you want.'

'More film and cigarettes. Money has no value in here.' The deal was struck.

I dug out a bluey from the top of my bergen and penned Phil Jennings a quick sitrep – no freedom of movement, implied threat to keep everyone hostage, send as many cigarettes as possible! I stuffed the letter away in my pocket.

Eventually the barbed wire was pulled aside and a rickety old blue lorry, high-sided and with no cover, chugged through the entrance and pulled up behind the goal posts. The first casualties had arrived. No one was sure what to do. Canadian soldiers stood around staring at the lorry and its hidden contents. No one wanted to approach it, to find out what lay behind its wooden sides. The spell had to be broken. I tore at the catches of the tail-gate. It dropped with a loud clang. I nearly puked when I saw what lay inside. The stench was overpowering, a mixture of stale sweat, faeces and sweet, rotting putrification. Clambering up I stared down at this mass of living dead. They looked like corpses – gaunt, hollow-eyed, swathed in dirty yellow bloody bandages. Some were limbless. Some looked dead. There must have been about twenty of them crammed in there. The stronger ones weakly raised an arm, clawing at me with open fingers, gasping for a cigarette. The stink was overpowering. I gagged. Still no one beyond the boards had moved. *Which one first?* At the far end were two little girls, no more than five years old, one crying hysterically. The other, dressed in a little red jump suit and fawn woollen bonnet, stared at me dumbly with her big brown eyes. *She's the first* something said inside me. Carefully, I picked her up, not sure exactly where she was wounded.

'Come on, give me a hand,' I shouted at the soldiers. They sprang forward, dropped the sides of the lorry and I handed down the girl in red. She weighed nothing. She didn't even whimper. The second girl was lowered and then the moaning and groaning were stretchered off and placed in a line where the Muslim doctors and ICRC reps tended to their worst wounds. Once the most urgent cases had been triaged they were raced onto the helicopters which lifted off Tuzla-bound. Throughout this the two Serb doctors stood around with their hands stuffed in their pockets. I was boiling over with rage.

'Aren't you going to help?'

One of the doctors looked at me as though I was stupid. 'They're the enemy,' he replied with a shrug. How could a five-year-old girl be the enemy?

'No they're not, they're civilians!'

'They're still the enemy,' he reiterated, unconcerned.

'And you're a piece of shit!' I shouted. 'I don't suppose your Hippocratic Oath counts for anything here, does it?'

He shrugged again and turned away from me, not bothering to answer. He was a disgrace to the white coat he was wearing.

Three 845 Sea Kings swooped in over the electricity cable, one popping decoy flares much to the amusement of the crowd. Another vehicle load of casualties arrived. This time an ancient two-stroke tractor belching black smoke pulled a flat trailer full of near dead into the stadium. The tractor's hysterical engine beat a manic note, which I can still hear today.

I grabbed David Lord, stuffed the bluey into his hand and begged him to hand it over to Phil Jennings at Tuzla. I urged him to find Phil as soon as possible; it was vital that this information got out and that BHC knew that the freedom of movement clause would not be adhered to.

Tom Gebert and his RSM had made it in on one of the helicopters and I quickly briefed him on the results of the meeting with Oric. I added that I didn't know much about what his boys were up to but that I believed his company commander was in the PTT building. With that they dashed off to come to grips with the situation.

The evacuation continued throughout the afternoon at a painfully slow pace. Casualties couldn't be moved from the hospital as fast as the helicopters were able to turn around. Towards late afternoon the flow of casualties dried up completely. We were supposed to evacuate some 500 but at best had only managed a couple of hundred. An entire wounded family was somewhere up at the hospital and their evacuation to the football pitch was being prevented by a howling mob. Colonel Gebert grabbed me and together we walked up to the hospital to see what the problem was.

The lorry was blocked in by a large crowd of men, all of whom were missing one or both legs. We waded into them and Gebert started talking to the nearest of them. 'What's the problem?' I translated. In an instant we were mobbed by this crowd of near hysterical men. Their fury was directed at me. Nick had warned me from his experience at Konjevic Polje that the instant they realised you could speak the lingo you became the 'point of focus', as he called it. I was overwhelmed by a tide of anger and noise. Their point was simple: no more casualties out unless they too could be evacuated. We couldn't promise anything as this had to be cleared by BHC. Somewhat mollified they allowed the family to proceed, but they pursued us down to the wire where they remained clamouring and begging and waving their sticks, demanding to be evacuated.

Colonel Richard passed all this back on the radio and eventually got word that the evacuation would be extended for one more day. It promised to be a nightmare, particularly since we knew that not all of these legless men would be going out. I grabbed the camcorder man and relieved him of his tape, which I gave to Tim Kelly and asked him to pass it to Martin Waters of PInfo. He was up at the airfield and it was his job to dispose of it as he saw fit to whichever network was next in line. Colonel Gebert was not hugely pleased that I wouldn't be staying but I promised that I'd be back the next day and would stay on.

Tim Kelly, Colonel Richard and I flew out on the last hop leaving behind the Canadians, the football pitch with its huge crater and the mob still choking the street and crowding the wall. During the transit to Zvornik, where the Serbs could check I had indeed left the pocket, I was assailed by a mix of feelings – relief that I had got out of that place without having been ripped to pieces by the legless mob, and regret at having abandoned Colonel Gebert. I was also aware of something else. I stank. My clothing reeked of death. I was infested with it and felt dirty and drained.

At Zvornik Nick told me that I had clearance to go in the next day and stay. He also told me that he would be spending the night in the Hotel Podrinja in Banja Koviljaca and suggested that I do the same. The UNMOs would bring us back to Zvornik in the morning in time to hop onto the first flight into Srebrenica.

'Nick, I stink!'

'I know. I can smell it.'

I clambered out of the uniform and dumped it on the floor of our tiny hotel room. It had two narrow beds built into the walls. Although I showered thoroughly I couldn't get rid of the smell and pulled on the reeking garments before going down to the restaurant.

Biljana had gone home to Loznica, so Nick and I ate alone. I told him what had happened in Srebrenica, of my own grave misgivings about going back in. In fact I was scared but stopped short of actually telling him that. Throughout the meal we were watched by two young men from a table across the room. Both were alert, carefully groomed, casually dressed and they talked quietly as they eyed us up. Eventually, they sauntered over and sat down with us. I didn't like them one bit.

'Were you in Srebrenica today?'

I nodded. They identified themselves as Zoran and Goran.

'What's it like in there?' *Who are you and why do you want to know?*

'It's a hell hole.' I said no more.

They invited us to join them in a local bar. We both declined. I was shattered, wanted to sleep and besides, I didn't really like these two. They were too smooth, too alert and too sober.

'What do you reckon, Nick?' Goran and Zoran had returned to their own table.

'Secret policemen,' Nick replied.

'Yes, I agree. But whose?'

Monday 18 April 1993 – Zvornik, Drina Valley, North-Eastern Bosnia

An engines running inspection was underway. Tim Kelly hopped out of one Sea King and handed me a bluey and a carton of 200 Benson & Hedges. I tore open the bluey. It was from Phil Jennings and read 'Well done for the sitrep . . . it's been passed to Kiseljak . . . keep the info coming . . . recharge your mags with 200 B&H'. The tape had been delivered to Martin Waters who'd passed it to CNN or one of the networks. But there were no blank tapes in return. I felt sick at letting the old boy with the camcorder down.

'Well, this is it, Nick. I was hoping the helis wouldn't arrive . . . must admit. I don't want to go back in there . . .'

'Can't say I blame you.'

'Y'know, the last time we did this Edi Letic warned me that I'd be leaving my bones in the Balkans. Maybe he's right . . . see you whenever. Enjoy your football, eh?'

With a heavy heart I climbed into the Sea King's black interior. There were other passengers on board – Larry Hollingworth and UNHCR Sarajevo's press spokesman, John McMillan, every inch a Texan, clad in cowboy hat and appropriately buckled belt. There were also a couple of BiH officers from II Corps HQ on their way into Srebrenica to try and knock some sense into Naser Oric.

As soon as we arrived I spotted Mr Camcorder and unloaded 180 B&H on him apologising profusely about the replacement. The scene seemed even more chaotic than the day before. An atmosphere of desperation hung over the valley. People knew that this was the last day of evacuation and the last chance to get out. The limbless were still clamouring at the wire, demanding to be let into the stadium, but there were still more wounded to be flown out and they took priority.

At one stage Colonel Richard threatened to shut down the operation. He was furious that wounded soldiers, still in camouflage, some with weapons and grenades were brazenly being stretchered into the stadium in preference to wounded civilians. He stated flatly that no one was going anywhere unless they were civilians and wounded – that meant no soldiers. While this was going on the poor old ICRC rep was holding the wire and agonising over which of the limbless should go. It was impossible for him to prioritise people who'd had limbs amputated months previously. Arbitrary selection was forced on him by those who shouted the loudest and by the pressure of time. Throughout, Larry Hollingworth and John McMillan were present at the stadium, doing what they could to help. Larry was hugely pleased with the effort. To him, every person out was a life saved.

At one stage I went up to the hospital to help unblock a problem. As I emerged an old man handed me a brown briefcase. He pulled me to one side and begged me to get the brief-case out to Tuzla. It was stuffed full of diaries, typed and handwritten accounts of the siege and of the attacks – all testimonials to what had happened. He was almost in tears. A side pocket contained a pink envelope and personal letter addressed to someone in Tuzla. It also bore the phone number of the recipient of the brief-case.

I took it and promised to get it delivered. Not once had the man asked to be taken out himself. His only interest was that the testimonials should reach the outside world. Back at the football pitch Tim Kelly was more than delighted to act as courier. He was the man to do it simply because of the little girl who had died in his arms. We hid the brief-case in the back of one of the M113s where a Canadian guarded it until Tim took it out on the last flight.

By 6 p.m. it was all over. No more evacuations. I had no idea how many people we'd got out. Certainly not enough, but that was it. Larry Hollingworth slapped me on the back and said 'well done' and added, 'Do me a favour. As we lift off, get on the radio to UNHCR Ops and tell them we've departed.'

As their Puma lifted I grabbed the mike in the UNMO's vehicle and passed the message. At that precise moment, I felt empty, alone and very scared. *All right for you, you bastard* ... I thought bitterly ... *I've got to stay in this shit-hole!*

The Dutch UNMO drove me up to the PTT building. The entrance was guarded by a couple of Canadian soldiers, who maintained the integrity of the wire. The ground floor was a hollow square with offices leading off it. A wooden counter over which letters and stamps had once been passed now served as a makeshift canteen table. One bare office had been converted into a rudimentary Ops Room – map on the wall and soldiers manning a radio. Other rooms were full of personal gear – bergens, sleeping mats and so on. I slung my bergen down into a corner and joined Colonel Gebert and his company commander in the Ops Room. A meeting had been arranged for 8 p.m. between the UN and Naser Oric, the main issues to be discussed being the process of demilitarisation and the priorities for the in-loading of aid into the pocket.

The meeting was held in a small conference room on the first floor. It was a disaster fraught with tension. I shared the interpreting with a professor of geology called Enver, a charming, likeable man with a bald head and a startling white beard. The only other interpreter in the pocket was a shifty teenager – one of Oric's men – whose English was virtually unintelligible. He seemed to do nothing other than skulk about the building listening to other people's conversations. Oric had brought along a team of three. One of them was the Chairman of Srebrenica's Defence Council. Although he was older than Oric, there was no doubt who was in charge.

Tom Gebert tried to control the proceedings in a calm and measured manner. The MSF and ICRC reps stated that the priorities for the enclave were first medical and second food aid. Regardless of this Oric rattled on with demands for so many hundreds of metric tonnes of concrete, so many hundreds of square metres of sheet glass etc to be brought in immediately to rebuild the town. He was way off mark and hugely disruptive. The II Corps officers were clearly embarrassed by his outbursts. Proven fighter he no doubt was; reasoned negotiator he certainly wasn't.

The issue of demilitarisation proved to be even trickier. Everyone present knew it was impossible to achieve, because there were simply too few UN troops in the enclave to effectively demilitarise it. The task would have gobbled up a whole brigade. Agreement was ultimately reached that the town itself would be demilitarised. Weapons held in town were to be surrendered at weapons collection points, while soldiers returning to town from the hills would be required to surrender their arms on entry in exchange for a ticket. Weapons could thus be retrieved on exit. It was the only practicable solution and the very best option the Canadians could come up with. I knew that the Serbs would never accept anything less than full demilitarisation of the entire enclave. The Canadians agreed to push their M113s, which mounted TOW anti-tank missiles, into OP positions to the south where the greatest threat from Serb tanks lay.

Something was achieved that night, but, secretly, we all knew we'd been sent into Srebrenica to fulfil a UN mandate with wholly inadequate resources. As the meeting broke up Enver thanked me for helping him with the translating and then disappeared into town to visit a relative.

Shortly afterwards, Tom Gebert, his company commander and I squeezed ourselves into the back of a command M113, which was parked flush with the building. We needed to talk in private. What followed was something of a Chinese parliament. Tom Gebert confirmed that the demilitarisation task had to be completed within seventy-two hours, which, clearly, was impossible. He seemed to imply that the duration of the mission as a whole was seventy-two hours, after which Serb, BiH and UN representatives would arrive to check that the enclave had been demilitarised. We all knew it couldn't be done.

I hadn't had a proper chance to brief the CO, so I outlined what Oric had

Left: Vladimir Ilija Dusmanic, the author's maternal grandfather. Educated in St Petersburg, Moscow and Paris and holder of Serbia's highest award for valour, he met his future wife, Constance, on the Salonika front in 1918.

Right: Constance Jessie Millar Rowan, the author's maternal grandmother, in the uniform of a Scottish Women's Hospital driver on the Salonika front, 1918. Prior to this, as a VAD, she nursed in Flanders and on Malta. She and Vladimir were married in Ayr, Scotland, in 1920.

Left: Stose Stanko Stankovic, the author's paternal grandfather. Educated in Prague, he served in the Serbian artillery: here seen in 1917 on the Salonika front.

Left: Radomir Stanko Stankovic (left), the author's father, who served as a Royalist officer in Yugoslavia during World War II: here seen with his company sergeant major at Valjevo in 1943.

Right: Danitza Constance Dusmanic, the author's mother, in British Army ATS uniform serving in Montgomery's 8th Army in Egypt as an ambulance driver at the battle of El Alamein, 1942.

Below: Dubrovnik, Dalmatia, March 1945. As adjutant of UNRRA's Save The Children unit, the author's mother returned to Yugoslavia with her ambulance, which she drove in Bosnia and Montenegro for the best part of 1945.

Wadi Al Batin, Kuwait, January 1992. First brush with the UN: the author as a UN Military Observer with UNIKOM in post-war Iraq and Kuwait.

Split, Croatia, November 1992. Commander British Forces in UNPROFOR, Brigadier Andrew Cumming (left), in discussion with UN Force Commander, Indian General Satish Nambiar, at Divulje Barracks.

Bosnia, 9 January 1993. Typical of Bosnia's mountainous terrain, this is the icy view from Route Square down towards Jablanica.

Left: Terrain and harsh weather conditions during January and February 1993 frequently frustrated aid delivery.

Below: Slow-moving modern and ancient transport also clogged the aid routes.

Below: Kalesija, Tuzla, March 1993. UNPROFOR's primary mission was the escort and protection of aid delivery. Here a Scimitar of B Squadron 9/12 Lancers leads a convoy out of Tuzla back across the confrontation line with the Serbs.

Zenica, Bosnia, February 1993. Arctic conditions caused numerous accidents – underway is the recovery of a BRITBAT truck which has skidded off the bridge and plummeted into the River Bosna below.

Tuzla, March 1993. Hostile fire from the warring factions also took its toll of vehicles and peacekeepers. This BRITBAT Land Rover strayed too close to the confrontation line and was destroyed by the Serbs.

Travnik, February 1993. The author (left) with Dobrila Kalaba (centre), one of our BRITBAT local interpreters, and Captain Martin Forgrave of the Cheshires in a Travnik café. Dobrila was shot dead by a Croat sniper on 5 July 1993.

Sarajevo, March 1993. Minka Pijalovic (right) and her 90-year-old mother proudly display their singing canary. Minka's daughter Aida, stranded in London, was au pair to General Mike and Sarah Jackson. Through them and the author, Aida was able to keep her family supplied and alive throughout the war.

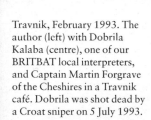

Above: Ulica Romanijska, Sarajevo, March 1993. Minka Pijalovic (centre) serving coffee to the author (left) and to Captain Peter Jones, OC BRITDET UNHCR Sarajevo.

Below: Tuzla Airfield, Thursday 25 March 1993. Following an abortive attempt the previous day to evacuate by helicopter wounded Muslim civilians from Srebrenica, Sea Kings of 845 NAS are paralysed as much by snow as by Serb shell fire.

Above: Srebrenica, 19 April 1993. Thousands of desperate Muslim refugees crowd the wall of the football stadium as their wounded are evacuated by UN helicopters.

Above: Srebrenica, 19 April 1993. The wounded were moved from the hospital to the stadium on rickety local transport. Here, Canadian peacekeepers help to off-load the sick and injured.

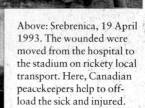

Left: Tuzla Airfield, 22 April 1993. Major Phil Jennings, OC C Company of the Cheshires, briefs Bianca Jagger over a can of Boddingtons.

Left: Central Bosnia, May 1993: the 'Man in the White Suit', Martin Bell of the BBC, reporting the war from the front line filmed by Sebastian Rich.

Right: Zepa, May 1993. Lieutenant Tim Kelly RN, 845 NAS's MAOT (left), and Colonel Jean Richard, DETALAT's CO, establishing comms with 'Magic' from within the enclave during heli evacuations of yet more stricken civilians.

Below: Vitez, June 1993. The effects of ethnic cleansing on BRITBAT's doorstep during the Croat-Muslim war-within-a-war of 1993–94.

told me about no one leaving the pocket, including the UN. I explained that General Morillon had been trapped here for nine days, blockaded in by mobs of women and children. I then described what had happened at Konjevic Polje. Given the dispersed nature of the Canadians' positions it was highly unlikely that any form of organised withdrawal could be effected before Oric sniffed a rat and filled the streets with women and children. From a purely military point of view, Oric's and his fighters' continued survival depended totally on there being a UN presence. From a wider politico-strategic point of view, as seen by the Bosnian government, the maintenance of Srebrenica was vital. If it went it would trigger a domino effect and Zepa and Gorazde would go too. We were caught in an impossible Catch-22, unable to fulfil UNSCR 819, while at the same time trapped, as hostage as the wretched refugees. What of the option of withdrawal after seventy-two hours? Possible, but not without considerable bloodshed.

Tom Gebert listened quietly to all the arguments. When the arguments ran dry he paused and made his decision.

'I was at Nicosia Airport in 1974. We had the option then to withdraw, to run away. But we stayed. We're not leaving this enclave. We're staying come what may.' It was the gutsiest decision I'd ever heard anyone make, but it filled me with terror and foreboding.

Our situation was made worse by appalling communications problems. Here we were at the epicentre of the most delicate and precarious politico-military operation at the time. The eyes of the world were on us, but we couldn't even communicate with our controlling HQ in Kiseljak. All HF transmissions had to be relayed via the Canadians' Ops Room in Visoko. It was a wholly inadequate arrangement, and one that only served to increase our isolation. At a personal level I was even deafer. I had no means of reaching any Brits.

I chucked my sleeping bag on the concrete floor. Although exhausted, I couldn't sleep. My thoughts were filled with images of panicked crowds, babies being placed underneath the tracks of APCs and of Serbs fighting through the town.

Tuesday 19 April 1993 – Srebrenica, Drina Valley, Eastern Bosnia

I was ravenous. I'd come into the pocket without a single ration pack. The Canadians fed me breakfast, boiled up in aluminium bags containing sausages and beans. As I wolfed down this gastronomic delight I wondered what dramas the day would bring. I didn't have to wait long.

A crisis was brewing. Reports from the Canadian M113 OPs to the south were flooding in at an alarming rate. Serb tanks had appeared on the crests of hills and had traversed their barrels on to the Canadians' vehicles. Serb tank gunners had their fingers poised, ready to send tank rounds hurtling into the M113s, while Canadian gunners had their fingers poised set to launch TOW missiles in the opposite direction. They were staring at each other through the cross-hairs of gun sights. The situation was explosive. It was simply a question of who would fire first. Regardless of who it was it would precipitate a bloodbath and the pocket would collapse. Something had to be done fast. The greatest problem was that we had no way of contacting the Serbs whatsoever.

Tom Gebert grabbed me and together we tore off north towards Potocari, the northern extremity of the enclave where the valley flattened out. The front line, which was essentially marked by a small bridge called *Zuti Most* – Yellow Bridge, lay a few kilometres from the town of Bratunac, where the Serbs had a headquarters. We parked the jeep just short of a chicane barrier and jumped out. After about ten minutes a couple of scruffy looking Serb soldiers popped out of their trench and demanded to know who we were and what we wanted. I explained that we had to speak urgently with the Serb commander in Bratunac. One of them disappeared to make a call. We waited a further half an hour before a car arrived from the direction of Bratunac. An officer stepped out. He also wanted to know who we were and the nature of our business. Time was slipping by so rapidly and we had no way of knowing whether or not a dreadful fire-fight was in progress to the south. After more phone calls and more waiting we were escorted into Bratunac, a drab little one-horse town. As ever, the HQ was to be found in the administrative building of a factory complex. In all it had taken us the best part of three hours to meet the Serb commander face to face.

The meeting was a difficult one. The Serb commander accused Colonel Gebert of aiding the Muslims by reinforcing their front with APCs. In a way, this was true. Each time an M113 parked, within a minute or two one of Naser Oric's units would appear and dig in around the vehicle, using its white paint as protection. This too had been reported by the OPs. There wasn't much that could be done about this trick but Gebert promised to raise the matter with Oric that evening. He went on to state that the presence of the tanks was both unnecessary and menacing and likely to result in an accidental fire-fight. The Canadians would open fire if threatened, which they were, and added that pointing tank barrels at the town served no purpose. He suggested, as a gesture, that the tanks traverse their barrels in the opposite direction. The Serb commander flew into a rage. 'Do you really expect us to point our tank barrels at our own people?' We'd got almost nowhere and departed hugely worried. The Serbs of Bratunac were seething with fury.

Back at the PTT building we discovered the situation to be no better. Each time an APC moved location, another BiH platoon would appear and dig in and another Serb tank would appear and point its main armament at the UN vehicle. It was almost certain that a disaster could now not be prevented. In desperation I suggested to Colonel Gebert that I could best serve him by establishing myself in Bratunac with a driver and radio. This would speed up communications considerably. Gebert agreed and I was provided with a jeep and driver/radio operator. Together we shot down to the Potocari chicane and again were subjected to the laborious tedium of phone calls to Bratunac. An hour later a white Mercedes pulled up. I was told to get in and leave the jeep and driver behind. I had no choice. I told him to wait and that I'd be back. With that the Merc whisked me off to the factory HQ in Bratunac.

The commander, a major called Cvijetin Vuksic with a huge walrus moustache, was still hopping mad. Present also was a colonel called Lazic, but he seemed not to be in charge and confined himself to listening. I explained my proposal and suggested it would be sensible for the driver and me to locate ourselves in the car park in order to diffuse any problems quickly. Vuksic wasn't in the least bit interested. When Bratunac had been besieged by Naser Oric in 1992 he'd lost his entire family: wife, sons and daughters. They were all buried in a cemetery in Bratunac along with several hundred others. 'I have nothing left to live for!' he bellowed, his moustache twitching violently, 'except revenge.' He added that he was quite prepared to die in this war. Unusually, he had a Belgian FN assault rifle as his personal weapon. He snatched it up and shook it in my face to make his point. He was almost beyond reason, driven half mad by grief and a desire for revenge.

Colonel Lazic was more reasonable and spoke in measured tones. He said that they were not keen to have any LO on their territory and thought the idea impractical. Again I explained my reasons.

'Who exactly are you? And where did you learn our language?' He smiled at me.

I had no option but to lay most of my cards on the table.

'Well, Milos, that's who you claim you are. But how can we be sure? How do we verify that? How do we know that you're not a clever Muslim spy?' I had no answer for him, but he continued, '. . . we can't make that sort of decision here. We have to seek approval from Pale. We need to know something that will convince us that you can be trusted to be neutral.'

I thought very hard. I didn't want to do it. After all, these people were Communists. Their fathers had been my father's bitterest enemies. I didn't want to prostitute my past, but now I had no option. With a heavy heart I began.

'If you go to Mrcajevci near Cacak in Sumadija, Serbia, you'll find a graveyard. There's a large black marble gravestone. On it are the names of my father's entire family this century. These are . . .' I felt sick as I listed what they'd find. In a way it was a betrayal of family and of a century's worth of ideals. But the situation in the enclave was so critical that it was a last-ditch measure.

'We *will* check,' said Colonel Lazic, eyeing me curiously, '. . . but there'll be no reply before tomorrow . . .' he paused, thoughtfully stroking his own neat moustache, and then, '. . . come on, I'll buy you lunch.'

We left Vuksic fuming and climbed into the Merc. I was wondering exactly where lunch would be. Instead of turning right back to Potocari we turned left and passed an Orthodox church. Its graveyard contained hundreds of fresh graves. When we crossed over an iron bridge over the Drina and drove into Serbia I started flapping. *These buggers are kidnapping me!* A little way on we reached a town called Ljubovija where we stopped at a café. Colonel Lazic ordered two beers and hard-boiled eggs. He didn't say much other than to curse when the waiter produced a bill. 'Least he could do is treat us to a free beer considering we're fighting their war for them!'

It transpired that Lazic was an LO from General Mladic's HQ. Clearly, they didn't trust Vuksic to manage the situation all on his own. Tacitly he agreed that the idea of having a radio link with the UN in Srebrenica was sound. But, as ever, every decision had to be referred to the top. He even seemed confident that there would be a positive answer once my 'credentials' had been checked. He told me to drive direct to Bratunac the next morning. We recrossed the Drina and he and his driver dropped me off at the Serb positions at Potocari. The Canadian driver was still there and relieved to see me again. The feeling was mutual.

I briefed Tom Gebert and told him there was a fair chance that we'd pull off the LO thing. That being the case we'd need to provide him with another interpreter, and the only person who could do it was Nick Costello. And yet, after Konjevic Polje and with him having only a couple of weeks left in theatre, I felt guilty about suggesting this option, but there was no other way to make this thing work. Colonel Gebert agreed to ask Kiseljak, via Visoko, to get Nick sent in.

The stand-off between the Serb tanks and the Canadians seemed to have eased, though they were still glued to their respective gun sights. I had another problem on my mind, which concerned the duration of my stay. If the LO plan was to work then 'out by 1700 on 20 April' was no longer feasible. Cumming's instructions had been crystal clear, but I now needed to get a message to the Brits. The UNMOs were the only option. One of them was up in the hills talking to the UNMO HQ in the Tuzla Hotel. I grabbed a Motorola and spoke to him, requesting that the Tuzla UNMOs somehow get a message to Phil Jennings asking him to seek an extension to my stay. The UNMO in the hills was African. He did his best to relay the message, but in my heart I knew that the Tuzla end would screw it up. The chances of Phil hearing any message were almost nil. I was right.

That evening's meeting went much more smoothly. Naser Oric had been ordered to stay away on account of his being a disruptive influence. The Chairman of the Defence Council was a much more measured man and issues critical to the health of the people of Srebrenica were at the top of the agenda. The ICRC rep stated that unless something was done quickly to restore the flow of water into Srebrenica then an epidemic of cholera was likely to break out. The Serbs had captured the water-pumping facility at Zeleni Jadar to the south and the population in the enclave was reliant on dirty river water. Again, Enver and I did all the interpreting. I wondered, not for the first time, why a professor of geology was sitting in this dump wearing ill-fitting camouflage fatigues.

Colonel Gebert reported that the demilitarisation of the town was under way. A substantial number of weapons had been handed in, although most of these were broken or lacked the necessary ammunition natures. The best stuff had been kept in the hills. That was the only sensible military option but we knew it was one that would not satisfy the Serb inspectors, who would be flying in the next day along with BiH and UN officials.

At about 10 p.m. I stood outside the PTT building watching the nightly ritual. Thousands of people, waifs and shadows, shuffled silently down the street clutching candles and torches: they were on their way out to the hills and DZs where aid would be dropped to them. This torchlit procession reminded me of Christmas or New Year's Eve in the Alps where descending skiers bore torches and flares in an endless winding and glittering snake. But these people of Srebrenica were not on their way to guzzle Gluwein and make merry; they were off to scavenge for food dropped from the air. They were on their way to hack each other to pieces with knives and axes, which they concealed beneath their robes. They were off to compete with each other in a gruesome and bloody fight for food and survival, where only the fittest and most cut-throat would triumph and scamper back to their hovels clutching their bloody morsels. Slightly later the drone of an unseen stream of C130s, flying at 10,000 feet, could be heard. They'd finished the drops into Gorazde and Zepa. Srebrenica was the last enclave on the circuit. I wondered then, as I listened to their droning engines, whether the dispatchers from Ramstein in Germany, clad in flight suits and helmets, tethered to strong-points in the aircraft and shovelling out food as they stood on lowered ramps, had any idea of the savagery erupting below them as desperate human beings scampered about hacking at each other in order to survive another day.

Wednesday 20 April 1993 – Srebrenica, Drina Valley, Eastern Bosnia

I'd slept badly again. I'd dreamed of people killing each other for food, for a brown plastic American MRE. My eyes felt gritty. I had a meeting in Bratunac to get to but needed some more ammunition for leverage. I asked the ICRC rep about the risk of cholera breaking out. He said it was high. I asked him then for the very worst that could happen. He mentioned typhoid.

'Look, give me something so infectious, something so dreadful ... like bubonic plague, that could happen here and sweep through Bratunac.'

'What's your point?'

'Simple. If we can scare them enough with something so awful that will affect them also, maybe they'll allow UN engineers to repair the water pumping station and run it.'

He saw my point. It was a long shot, but anything was worth trying. He gave me the name of some hideous plague, which had such a bizarre name that I had to write it down in my notebook. My driver and I then shot off, sailed through Potocari and the Serb front line as arranged and parked up at the factory. At least we now had a radio link.

Major Vuksic was not, as I might have guessed, in the least bit impressed with my apocalyptic prophecies of doom. He couldn't care less. He asked me whether the enclave had been demilitarised yet and added that it better have had been by the time the inspectors flew in. I replied that weapons had been collected and that the town had been demilitarised, which was true.

He scoffed, 'We know what they've got in there . . .' and proceeded to list an almost unbelievable itinerary of weaponry by numbers and type, which I faithfully copied into my little blue notebook. As I wrote I thought, if they had all that then it would be Bratunac and not Srebrenica under siege. Vuksic informed me that no word had yet been received from Pale about the LO proposal, but added that a message had been sent. As he spoke and ranted they fed my driver steak and chips. Having delivered his sermon Vuksic grabbed his rifle, shook it in my face once more, uttered something dark about dying, and then announced that he was off to the hills.

By midday there was still no word, so we departed for the football stadium to await the arrival of the inspecting delegation. First off the helicopter were three Serb colonels in camouflage, graced with Sam Browne cross belts and those Commie leather officers' satchels hanging off their shoulders. One I recognised as Colonel Lazic, another, with silver hair, was called Milosevic, and the third's name escapes me. All looked distinctly nervous as they clambered into an M113. Next off were three BiH officers from Tuzla accompanied by Brigadier de Vere Hayes, the BHC Chief of Staff. In separate APCs we shot up to the central weapons collection site in the Canadian compound.

Naser Oric, leaning heavily on a stick and accompanied by an entourage of bodyguards, was waiting for Brigadier de Vere Hayes. During this meeting the Serbs stayed out of sight in their APC. Oric and de Vere Hayes spoke for almost an hour. The latter impressed on the younger man that in his hands lay the responsibility for the people of Srebrenica and that the eyes of the whole world were on him. After the talk de Vere Hayes grabbed me and insisted that he must now go to Bratunac and, in the interest of impartiality, be seen to be talking to the Serbs as well. He was convinced that they were watching him from the hills talking to Oric and that he needed to even up the balance. He was probably right. I could just imagine Vuksic glaring through a pair of binos at the spectacle below.

As we walked to the APC he asked me straight, 'You've been in here a few days. What's your assessment?'

Suddenly I felt drained. What to tell him? That the Resolution was unworkable? That we needed more troops? That the Serbs in Bratunac were burning, smouldering away and bent on revenge? What? I was irritated and frustrated by the situation and exhausted through lack of sleep. So, I just told him straight. Not a logical analysis. I just told him as I felt it from the gut.

'Sir, these people . . . everyone in this pocket, including the UN, are . . . dead meat.'

We climbed into the M113 in silence. I half regretted what I'd said: not exactly a proper military assessment devoid of passion and emotion. He was deep in thought and looked worried. Half way down the road he leaned forward, hanging off a strop, and shouted above the clattering of the tracks. He was angry and concerned at the same time.

'Those words you've just used. They're highly emotive. We're trying to make this thing work and words like that will not help. When you get out of this enclave you're never to repeat them again . . . not to Bob Stewart . . . not to anyone. Understand?'

I nodded. I felt sorry for him. He was the man with responsibility for this absurd operation. It wasn't his fault, but he was left holding the baby. At the time his instructions made perfect sense. Now they no longer matter.

At Potocari the Serbs informed us that there was no one in Bratunac. Vuksic had taken to the hills. Brigadier de Vere Hayes had to settle with talking to these grubby Second World War-type trench rats, who'd emerged from cover unshaven, smelly and unquestioningly hostile. They were the wrong people, but the only ones available.

Fortunately, Biljana and her UNMO had turned up and between us we did the interpreting, for what it was worth. A military policeman then turned up. He spoke some English.

'I know Naser Oric. We were policemen together at President Milosevic's presidency in Belgrade. I trained him so you can't tell me anything about him. It's him and two hundred and fifty of his fighters we're after. As far as the rest of them are concerned, they can go. We won't stop them.' *Yeah, that would suit you wouldn't it? But it also suits him to keep them trapped in the world's largest concentration camp. You're both two of a kind aren't you?*

During a quieter moment Biljana grabbed me by the arm and led me over to the stream.

'How many babies should we have?'

'Oh, I don't know. One or two I guess.'

She was stunned, 'One or two! I want ten at least!' She didn't look like the breeding type. It was an amusing conversation, which to my mind had no relevance to the current situation.

'How much longer will you stay in that place?'

'Don't know. A week or so I suppose, at least until they can find another interpreter to replace me.' I wasn't too sure. There were only three hours left until my deadline expired.

We had a meeting to get to in the PTT building. The finer points of demilitarisation had to be ironed out. On the way there I told the Brigadier of our efforts to establish an LO in Bratunac, that I'd been ordered out by 1700 hours, which would leave Tom Gebert with nothing. I told him I was quite happy to stay on for a week or so until a replacement could be found. He agreed to fix it with Cumming.

The Serbs had brought along their own interpreter and insisted on using her. She was a wee slip of a thing, a primary school teacher from Bajina Basta from up the Drina on the Serbian side. She was scared out of her mind and shaking with terror throughout the meeting. I helped her as much as I could and told her she was doing well, which gave her confidence. Two hours later the meeting was over, leaving everyone threatening each other, but it was quite clear that the crisis of the past few days was over. An uneasy though acceptable status quo had been maintained. The Canadian and Serb gunners took their fingers off the triggers.

As the meeting broke up and de Vere Hayes and the others headed downstairs to catch the APCs down to the football stadium, I told Tom Gebert that I'd be staying another week. He looked relieved.

I pulled out a cigarette and as I lit it the Chairman of the Defence Council sidled up to me.

'Milos! We know all about you!' He wasn't shouting, more whispering. My heart leapt into my throat. *How does he know my name?*

'No. There must be some mistake,' I mumbled unconvincingly as we stared into each other's eyes. There was no hate in his, more like pity or compassion.

'No, Milos . . .' he said slowly and evenly, '. . . we know about the graveyard in Mrcajevci . . .' Edi Letic's words thumped through my head – 'Man, but you're going to leave your bones in the Balkans.'

'. . . you're not safe here anymore. You'll die,' he finished, still looking at me curiously. A thousand thoughts tumbled through my mind. *How? Radio intercept? Surely the Serbs couldn't have been so stupid as to pass that information by radio or telephone! They must have been. How else?*

I rushed into the toilet, drew my pistol and, pulling back the slide half way, checked that a round was still chambered. *I'm not going to get caught here like those two signallers in Belfast in 1988!* The Browning went into my pocket where I could get at it quickly.

When I emerged he'd gone. I took the stairs two at a time. I could hear the APCs revving up and beginning to pull away. I grabbed Tom Gebert.

'I'm sorry, Colonel, really I am . . . I've got to go . . . I've just been compromised . . . sorry!' I didn't wait for his answer but tore down the stairs, scooped up my bergen and threw myself into the last APC as it was pulling away. 'Just drive!' I hissed at no one in particular. I was clutching the butt of my pistol in my pocket, imagining a crowd forming rapidly to block our route and baying for my blood. It didn't happen and I dived into the last helicopter out of that place. Slumped in a seat, fiddling nervously with the safety belt and breathing heavily, I was aware of a rather surprised looking Brigadier staring at me. Enver was doing the same. *Does he know? Will he tell them in Tuzla? He's bound to! It's over!*

As the helicopter headed towards Zvornik I calmed down. *Why did he warn me? He didn't have to. So, why did he? Why did he save my life?*

I felt someone nudge me in the ribs. It was the primary school teacher. She was shouting something above the din.

'What?'

'Have you read *Fathers and Sons*?'

'Who? . . . No!'

'You remind me of the son in the book . . . you're trapped between two cultures!'

She wrote the name of the book on a slip of paper. I'd never heard of it and I didn't see her again. They all got out at Zvornik and we proceeded to Tuzla with the BiH officers. Enver was still staring at me, but not with any hostility. I wondered if he knew.

We landed on the pan and disgorged ourselves. De Vere Hayes strode towards the black, glowering storm of waiting press. I trotted along a couple of paces behind. From nowhere we were joined by Phil Jennings and his CSM, 'Blue' Rees. The Brigadier stopped and addressed the press. As I listened my mind was raging, burning with the memory of a madman waving an FN rifle in my face. I wanted to scream *You don't understand! They're all dead meat in that place. Dead meat!* But I didn't. I'd given my word.

'Blue' Rees slapped me on the back and whispered, 'Welcome back, sir. It must have been terrible in there.'

I smiled and nodded. 'Thanks. It's good to be back.' *Terrible? You'll never know.*

TWELVE

Operation Bretton

October 1997 – Ian, UK
'Dead meat, Ian! Those were my words then. It's what I've always known and bang, two years later it happened . . . the largest massacre in Europe since the end of the Second World War. Dead meat.'

I'm seething with rage. I've remembered something my solicitor had said. 'Y'know, they made a comment in the police station. They said that they'd seized my diary because it *"contained evidence of disaffection with the West's policy"*. Those were their words . . .' I'm almost boiling over with anger and I'm shouting again, '. . . exactly which policy am I supposed to be disaffected with? There wasn't one! Just a whole load of competing agendas and a lot of waffle, indecision and hot air from the UN in New York and from various governments. Whose policy am I supposed to be disaffected with? The American? The French? The Pakistani, perhaps? Or perhaps the Malaysian? Can't have been the British one. They never have one . . . not in the sense of shoring up rebuild contracts like the French!'

I'm thinking now. In a way they're right, those coppers . . . I *am* disaffected, hugely disaffected . . . with the international community as a whole, not just with the West. When that Safe Area policy came into effect UN commanders on the ground assessed that 34,000 troops would be needed to make it work. The Secretary General of the UN went to the world and asked for them. After a lot of umming and ahhing, guess what we got? Seven thousand troops . . . pissing in the wind. Two years later Srebrenica and Zepa fall. It could have been prevented.

And don't let anyone tell me it was too expensive. The moment the last bullet flew in that war and Dayton came into effect, what happened? Sixty thousand troops flooded into the place, half of them American. There's no escaping it. The international community is guilty of physical and moral cowardice. Sure, the Serbs were the trigger-pullers at Srebrenica, but the international community loaded their magazines for them. Moral and physical cowardice equals dead meat.

General Rose ran into the same problem in February 1994 when a window of opportunity appeared to flood Sarajevo with troops and demilitarise the place. He asked for those troops and the international community sat on its hands, chewing its lower lip, wracked with indecision. The window closed and the war continued, cemeteries filled up ... more dead meat. I tell you, the answer can always be found somewhere in history. Someone's worked it out before. Thomas Hobbes summed it all up in *Leviathan* – 'Covenants without swords be but words.' Pretty good epitaph for that whole bungled Bosnian affair.

Nothing really went right. The brief-case we got out was sent to Split where it was declared to be of no intelligence value. It was flown back up to Tuzla minus the letter so no one knew who to deliver it to. And the little girl in the red jump suit and fawn bonnet ... that one really gutted me. Two years later I'm visiting Nigel Bateson in his London home. He was a BBC cameraman out there. We're sitting there with whiskies and looking through some of his footage of the op which he'd shot from the Tuzla end. And there she was on film, limp little body being carried from the helicopter by a Muslim doctor who's in tears. 'Shame,' says Nigel, '. . . she died.'

The weirdest people popped up all over Bosnia. The night I got out of Srebrenica we had a meal in the Tuzla hotel. I'm sitting opposite a Latino woman. I thought she was an aid worker or something. But she wasn't. It was Bianca Jagger, Clinton's special ambassadress, out on a fact finding mission. She announces that she's going to recommend to Clinton that all the bridges over the Drina should be bombed. Can you believe it? The next day we get her up to the base and Phil Jennings disabuses her of this idea – 'Drop the Karakaj bridge and the Muslims in Tuzla get no aid from Belgrade.' Her jaw dropped. They just didn't ever realise how complex and interlinked it all was.

Strangely enough a letter from Una in Sarajevo had somehow made its way up to Tuzla. Most of it was about her successful delivery of the bird seed to Minka. The next day Nick and I get this mysterious message – 'Costello to go to Vitez and Stanley to go to Split.' No one could explain why. It just didn't make any sense as it left Phil Jennings with no military interpreter cover. The next day we drive down to Vitez and straight into pandemonium. Bob Stewart and Andrew Cumming have their hands full leading around a large group of UN ambassadors, who have flocked in to have a look at the site of the Ahmici massacre. While we had been messing about in Srebrenica the lid had finally flown off the Lasva valley pressure cooker, as we thought it would. The HVO in Vitez had trashed a small Muslim village nearby. They'd blown up the mosque, burned whole families alive in their homes and shot dead fleeing civilians. They'd even shot dogs, cats, sheep and cows. The Muslim-Croat war had finally come to the base in Vitez.

That evening I saw Cumming in the Mess. He seemed relieved to see me and I asked him why I was being summoned to Split. He told me that he'd been worried about me and felt I should have a break. He'd resisted an initial request for both Nick and me to go into Srebrenica because of the Konjevic Polje incident but under considerable pressure he'd been forced to make a compromise choice – me. The next day we drove down to Split where I was given my Confidential Report and then told to have a week's rest locally. I wasn't really sure what to do so Martin Strong, the Pay Corps major, who was Mr Visits (coordinating the visits of VIPs from the UK) and also in charge of interpreters, fixed it for me to spend four days in a rented villa in the fishing village of Bol, on the south side of the island of Brac. It sounded all right, but four days on my own in an apartment would drive me crazy. On the spur of the moment I rang Una in Sarajevo and asked her if she wanted to join me. To my surprise she took four days leave and we met up at Split's southern harbour. We caught the ferry to Supetar on Brac and then a taxi over to the south side.

It was a very strange experience for both of us. She got the room with the en suite bathroom and I had the other. It was the least she deserved. The UNHCR girls in Sarajevo were all cooped up in a communal room in the PTT building – there was virtually no water, absolutely no privacy, nothing except that mad building in which you couldn't get away from anyone. It was odd. We hardly spoke to each other during the four days. She read a lot on the balcony and I just stared out over the Adriatic watching the Sea Kings and Pumas doing their navigational exercises. It was peaceful. These islands hadn't been touched by the war at all, a huge contrast from the chaos of Srebrenica, which I couldn't get out of my mind. Bol was small, quaint and the people friendly, not at all like their manic countrymen on the mainland. There's something about island folk . . . they tend not to give a damn about world events.

By the time we returned to Split we'd become good friends. I wasn't quite sure what to do next. Cumming's HQ was in the throes of packing up and leaving. Newcomers were flooding in, including the advance party of the PWO Battle Group, which would be replacing the Cheshires. All my gear was still up in Vitez and so was my job. Somehow I had to get up there, but strangely enough there was no hurry so Una and I went shopping and we both bought as much food as we could for her parents and Minka respectively. Una took some of it up on the airlift that day and I flew up the next in a French C130.

That was a terrifying experience. It was the first time I'd flown into Sarajevo on the airlift. The Herc takes off and climbs to flight level 180, that's 18,000 feet, in order to keep out of SAM range, and then it scoots across B-H to a position over Kiseljak where it turns right and begins a rapid descent over Ilidza and into Sarajevo airport. We're not talking here of some nice little gentle glide path. This thing virtually dives from 18,000 feet at the airfield, twisting, turning and spiralling to avoid lock-on by missiles and being hit by small arms fire. It's like a rollercoaster ride, the worst, like Nemesis at Alton Towers. At the last moment it pulls up and bangs down hard on the runway. The Herc is an amazingly robust plane. This punishing technique was developed by the Americans during the siege of Khe San in Vietnam – Khe San landings they're called. The bizarre thing is that after all this effort to protect the plane it just sits on the pan engines running while fork-lift trucks off-load the pallets of aid *first*! We don't take priority; we just sit in this plane full of fuel waiting for the aid to be off-loaded and praying that no one's going to lob a mortar onto the pan or fire at the aircraft. I never did find out why the people were off-loaded last. That was the worst bit, worse than the descent. That pan was dangerous. I remember on one occasion a group of UNMOs, new arrivals in theatre, were machine-gunned as they scuttled from the aircraft to the bunker.

Minka was delighted to see me again. Like all good mothers, she wagged her finger in my face and scolded me – 'Danger, terrible danger. I saw it in the coffee. You've been in terrible danger!' I told her about Srebrenica, about Naser Oric and about my escape. She scolded me again as we had another of those coffee-reading sessions. It was the future this time. She told me that I'd meet a girl with short dark hair. I wondered if she meant Biljana Sretenovic. Her soothsaying still spooked me a lot. There was something of the Romany in her. She gave me a small green flower, like a clover, which she said would protect me. I never scoff at these things. If you reject it someone might stick a curse on you. I tucked it away in my little blue notebook. It's still there, though the police now have that too.

That evening Una took me out to see, as she put it, the 'real' Sarajevo. We were dropped off somewhere downtown in the Austro-Hungarian bit. First stop was to see some of her friends. Two of them had got married in one of those weird underground wartime weddings. The pictures had made it into *Le Monde* magazine, which Una gave them. A third person, a lame girl who looked gaunt and thin, was lying on a sofa-bed. She'd been hit in the leg by a sniper and was bedridden, virtually crippled. I kept my mouth shut and just listened.

Next stop was to be Una's parents, she announced, as we left the flat and started to walk. It scared me, I can tell you. Here I was, rufty tufty Para, escapee from Srebrenica, and I'm walking down the street with this girl, who is dressed in a tight navy blue dress, stockings and high heels. It's dusk, the light is fading and the city is rumbling with the growls of impacting mortars. *No! Don't walk down the middle of the street. Snipers will get you, you fool! ... stick to the walls and the shadows.* Her urban fieldcraft and savvy were much more advanced than mine. I felt naked – no helmet, no flak jacket, and completely out of my depth. There was a loud rumble somewhere ahead. Moments later there was another behind. *Shit! We're being bracketed. The next one's going to land in this street!* But Una wasn't in the least bit bothered. *These people are mad. They've lost it!* We passed a couple of rusting ISO containers, which blocked a street to our left. She stopped at the edge and squatted down – 'Come look! Look quickly through the gap. You'll see where the war started.' I did. All I could see was a wide street, a concrete bridge and beyond it the French UN compound at Skenderija.

We dived into a dark and gutted bookshop on the corner of one of those large Austro-Hungarian apartment bocks. Crunching our way over broken glass, she led me through a back door, up some dark steps leading into a dim hallway and then through a metal doorway, which scraped horribly and slammed shut loudly. We were now climbing a series of wide stone stairs. To the right, shattered windows exposed a tatty inner quadrangle – more smashed glass, twisted and rusting metal pipes and UNHCR sheet plastic flapping in the wind. We stopped on the second floor and she banged hard on a solid red door. After an eternity, a latch scraped, a chain jangled, a key turned and a wizened old woman, small, frail and wrinkled, opened the door cautiously – 'Una!' she gasped.

We were hustled into a dark and dingy room. The old woman shuffled in behind us. Grouped around a table on which burned a low candle were three other people – an old pensioner, male, and a couple, perhaps a generation younger. I was introduced to Una's parents, Bobo and Natasa, and her grandparents, Tomo and Vera. As Una chatted away with them I glanced around the room with its high ceiling and creamy-brown walls. It was quite tatty and gloomy. A grey, scruffy-looking canary shuffled silently about in its cage. The furniture was old and seemed to have been there for decades or so it seemed – a divan and a couple of old armchairs, a large old TV in the corner, old map of B-H on the wall and books all over the place and tumbling out of an over-burdened cabinet. Beyond the wartime squalor, one could see that this had once been a smart apartment. The room we were in was obviously the safest and was probably inhabited all day long. Tomo and Vera were well into their eighties. He seemed almost childlike, animated and full of enthusiasm. She, by contrast, was quiet and serene and had a sort of ancient wisdom about her. The parents looked drawn and haggard. I reckoned they were in their fifties. Natasa was thin and looked ill, while Bobo seemed in a way sad, disconsolate, almost listless. He couldn't hide it in his voice. They treated me with kindness, but I felt a bit like an interloper.

We stayed half an hour and then went off to a restaurant. I was wondering whether such a thing existed in this dreadful city. It certainly did. Like everything, it was underground. Down a flight of stairs and suddenly we were in a different world – a restaurant called Boemi. Plush red carpets, tables set in alcoves, waiters in bow ties, a musician and soft lighting. The menu too was impressive – mixed grill, pancakes, good wine from Serbia and from Mostar. Hard currency buys anything in Sarajevo. I was shocked by the contrast between life above and below ground. Above people were being butchered in the streets by an unseen hand, scavenging for food and cowering in their dirty flats. Below, in Hades, you could sip fine wine and fill your belly.

Una explained that her parents had lived in one of the new apartment blocks in Dobrinja, which had been built as the Olympic village in 1984 and was now the scene of vicious front-line fighting. Access in and out of the place was strictly controlled by its BiH commander and the mafia, even though it was part of the city. It was an enclave within an enclave. While at college Una had lived, grown up, with her grandparents in the apartment in the centre of town where we'd just been. Her mother had suffered kidney failure and on that pretext she and Bobo had managed to get out of Dobrinja to get treatment at Kosevo hospital. They never returned to Dobrinja and were now squatting with Bobo's parents. They weren't just squatting, they were in hiding. Being under sixty, Bobo was liable to be grabbed off the streets and stuck into unarmed trench-digging gangs, where the survival rate was low. They were virtual prisoners in the flat. Una explained all this in a very low voice. She seemed sad and vulnerable. She admitted that there were pipelines out of the city, methods of escape. She'd tried twice to get them out but on both occasions had failed. It was just too risky and would spell death for her parents if it went wrong. It sounded unbelievably tragic. All that kept her in the city was a sense of filial duty, nothing else. *Pity families in Britain aren't this tight.*

As we chatted a rowdy group swaggered into the restaurant and filled up a long top table. The men were decked out in tailored combats which stretched across their fat bellies. Pistols in leather holsters hung from their hips. Young, teenage dollybirds in tight Lycra pants, tank tops, permed blonde hair and bright lipstick, hung from their arms. The table filled up quickly with bottles of wine and mountains of food. The men shouted, argued, smoked, stuffed their faces and fondled their compliant girls. I had to pinch myself hard to remind myself that I was not in the Chicago of the 1930s. I wondered who really ran this city.

That was an eye-opener, a real education; it showed me that all was not as it seemed. The bottom line is that bandits, gangsters and hoods prosper in war. I stayed on four days in Sarajevo. I actually slept on the floor of the girls' room. Six of them slept on cots in one room. They tried to give me a spare bed but it belonged to someone and it was their only bit of private space, so I had the floor and a blanket. I remember Lejla tutt-tutting one morning – 'Mike Stanley! What are we going to do with you?' It was peculiar; anyone hearing this would probably think 'Lucky old him!' But it wasn't like that – we were friends and that's all we were. War and shared discomforts tend to break down mores and taboos. They couldn't care less that they had a man squatting on their floor. And I couldn't really give a damn about their outrageous male pyjamas. That's the way it was. I longed to work in Sarajevo.

Reluctantly, a sense of reality pulled me back to Vitez. I half expected people to demand where I had been but no one did – I hadn't been missed in the least. The Cheshires were in the dying throes of their departure, preoccupied with saving a bear they'd found half-starving in a cage in Vitez. They'd called it MacKenzie The Bear after General Lew MacKenzie, the 1992 Canadian UN commander in Sarajevo. An animal welfare group, Liberty, which specialised in rehabilitating bears, had flown into theatre to facilitate Bob Stewart's last mission. At the same time you've got this war raging up and down the valley. The camp at Vitez was surrounded on four sides by warring factions. The road in front of the Mess was quite literally the front line. Croats over the road cleansed out the Muslims who had fled to our side and sought shelter among the houses closer to the camp. From the high ground to our left the BiH fired rockets, cannons and small-arms rounds over the camp at the HVO, who fired back with equal ferocity. Elsewhere, in the surrounding countryside, there were tit for tat trashings of each other's villages and wholesale butchery.

Into this chaos appeared Lt Col. Alistair Duncan and his PWO (1st Battalion, Prince of Wales's Own Regiment of Yorkshire) Battle Group – bright new uniforms, new Warriors gleaming white, bright blue unsullied cloth helmet covers, innocent and fresh faces. Exhausted, the Cheshires departed in their chipped and scarred Warriors, in their dirty and torn uniforms, their minds etched with images of horror, mayhem and blood-crazed lunatics. They couldn't get down to Split fast enough. I couldn't blame them in the least.

They left behind a handful of us – me and the Royal Marines UK Liaison Officer teams, which occupied one of the houses. Captain Mike Buffine was the boss and Lieutenants Matt Bray and Jules Amos commanded a team each. Theirs was a ghastly but vital job. On a daily basis they'd drive out patrolling and probing the hills, trying to identify the state of isolated hamlets and communities. Often they'd return shattered, wrecked and gutted after discovering another outrage. They'd spent a lot of time searching for and clearing up the rotting, stinking and maggot-ridden bodies which had been left scattered about fields in the wake of the Ahmici massacre. It was gruesome work, which left a horrible mark on them. In the evenings we'd gather on their balcony and, in the process of drinking a crate of beer, get it all out of their system. Next day they'd do it all over again. Sometimes I'd go out with them to interpret, but my main preoccupation was being mother to the local interpreters, of whom I'd been put in charge. None of them had had a break in six months, while each of the Cheshires had enjoyed a two weeks of R&R.

Quite rightly they'd done something about this prior to leaving and had set up a system whereby each could have a free flight to Germany or the UK and two weeks off. Dobrila was the first to use the system and was away in London. I hadn't seen her since our bust-up. The project was slightly risky in that no one could be certain that these people wouldn't abuse the system and, having gapped it, seek asylum in the UK. It fell to me to work out the roster for their leave – very dull. Suzana Hubjar was next to take leave once Dobrila had returned.

It's the strangest thing but you'd have thought that the newcomers would have been glad to have some old hands knocking around, if only for continuity's sake. But they didn't much like us being there. It's difficult to explain why. It's not that they didn't like us. It's just that they couldn't understand us. They were looking at us through fresh, untainted and naïve eyes and I think they didn't much like what they saw. To them we appeared to be madmen on the ragged edge, drinking too much. On one occasion Alistair Duncan pulled me out of the Mess and told me that he was worried about me, said I'd had no leave, had been run ragged and was drinking too much. I remember telling him: 'In six months time you'll be like us, but I'll bet you we'll be no worse.' You reach a sort of mad operating plateau and you stay there. But they couldn't see that and wanted us out, in case we infected them with whatever disease it was we had. He also mentioned that he'd be speaking to Brigadier Searby about me. I knew that my cards were marked so I mainly stuck with the UKLOs; we understood each other.

Almost daily some unfortunate civilian would be shot by HVO snipers, be rescued if possible and if lucky end up on the operating table in the MST. Battles raged around the camp. We'd watch them from our balcony as we drank beer. We'd just sit there watching tracer flicking over the camp, RPG 7 rockets whooshing by, giving marks out of ten for hits. And we'd also watch the PWO soldiers below us in their sports gear and Walkmans jogging round and round the one-way circuit just as they would in Germany or Northern Ireland. The five o'clock conferences were even stranger. One hot topic for discussion was where the soldiers should wear their morphine syrettes. Six per cent of the Cheshires' ones had been damaged because they were worn taped to their ID disc chains. The hunt was on for a better solution. Each evening a new method would be discussed; we'd sit at the back and listen to all this. Once Matt Bray leaned across and whispered in my ear, 'Why don't they just stick 'em up their arses!' One day even the RSM piped up and said he was most concerned for the safety and health of troops bathing in the river and washing down their vehicles there. 'Thank God someone's finally woken up to what's going on round here!' It was Matt again. The river was below the BiH-held hill and bullets, rockets and shells whizzed over the bathers. The RSM wound up by expressing his concern that no one knew what chemicals or pollutants may have been dumped into the river. Matt and I just looked at each other in amazement.

Ian's interested in all this mainly from a psychological point of view – new arrivals in Hell so shocked by their surroundings that they fall victim to cognitive dissonance and block it all out. It's a classic reaction – focusing on trivia in order to block out the horror. What do I remember of the horror? What sticks in my mind?

I think hard. The tractor's noise at Srebrenica . . . the smell of all those wounded people . . . we all saw dead bodies, corpses in differing degrees of decomposition . . . I remember the green, severed head of a Muslim, which the HVO had cut off in Kiseljak and stuck on a railing . . . but they're just memories. I don't dream about that stuff. It's the little things, the poignant things that really stick in your mind . . . the stuff that reminds you of the human tragedy of it all . . .

I remember Nerko, a young Muslim soldier. I dream, of him, of the whole thing, sometimes. It's always there like a video tape. Matt Bray and I had spent the morning in Vitez, which by this stage had been completely devastated by a lorry bomb . . . place looked like Stalingrad. There was a small BiH enclave holding out in the town and completely surrounded by HVO. We'd been lured there by the commander to go and find a body, which had supposedly been buried under rubble for a few weeks. When we got to the site of this destroyed house, right on the edge of town, there was no body. You'd have smelled it. Then we got shot at by a sniper. Should have seen us jump! The round just missed Matt and me . . . passed straight between us. We'd been set up. Off we scampered back to base all shot through with adrenalin and giggling like schoolchildren. After listening to another session of where to put the morphine syrettes we repaired to our balcony to watch the evening's battle rage over the camp while chatting and sinking a couple of cans. I remember we had to be in the Mess that evening because Brigadier Searby was up visiting from Split. I was quite sure he'd been invited all the way up by Alister Duncan just to sack me . . .

Operation Grapple. Thursday 20 May 1993 – Vitez, Central Bosnia

The Mess was heaving. Every officer in station was crammed into the place. Most of the interpreters were there, too. Scale A. This was a big scene – COMBRITFOR's first visit to Vitez since assuming command from Brigadier Andrew Cumming and he had the new CinC UKLF, General Sir John Wilsey, in tow.

We fought our way to the bar, bought our drinks and then fought our way back into one of the corners. As mere minions and 'undesirables' it was unlikely that we'd be sought out and introduced to the good and the great, who were in any case busily being steered from one important personage in the Battle Group to another. Since none of us was a PWO we didn't count as important people.

Sensing that buttonholing Brigadier Searby and engaging him in a discussion based solely on my future would have been wholly inappropriate and utterly futile in such surroundings, I made no effort to place myself in a strategic position where our paths might cross as he was ushered from one group to another. I did, however, keep a sharp eye out and followed his meanderings closely, while chatting idly with Matt and the others. Had we been set up that morning or had we merely fallen victim to a Balkan bungle? I spotted my moment. Instinct told me it was now or never. The good and the great had had enough of bumping gums with the masses and had made a move for the exit, intent on dinner in the canteen, to which none of us had been invited.

I pushed my way through the crowd, which had mysteriously relaxed and was baying at the bar now that it was no longer on show. Once outside, I found the group just ahead of me. The CO was walking ahead with the CinC. Searby was a pace or two behind. Perfect. I fell in step with him.

'Hello, sir.' I wondered if he'd recognise me from January. He was puffing away on one of his cheroots. He paused and glanced at me. It was quite dark by now.

'Stanley, sir.'

'Ah, yes, Stanley . . .' It sounded like a swear word as he dragged it out slowly, '. . . I've been meaning to have a chat with you. Crowded in there though.' He nodded back at the Mess.

'Sir.'

He spoke as we walked. 'How are you?' *Odd question!*

'Fine, sir.' I knew where this was going. *Now, what are those answers?*

'Y'sure?'

'Yes, sir . . . positive.' I tried to sound chirpy, which is a bit difficult if you've been shot at that day.

'Mmmmmmm.' He was thinking. Not a good sign. There was a long pause and then, 'How long have you been out here now?' *I know where this is going.*

'Only five months, sir . . . not even a full tour.' I was gossamer thin. Pathetic really. He wasn't going to be bluffed either.

'Five months, eh? How did your R&R go?' *Dammit! How does he know I haven't had any?* How could he have known that every time I'd tentatively fixed up dates, some crisis had happened and I'd had to cancel? Or did he suspect the truth, which is that I hadn't really bothered?

'Well, sir, I haven't . . .'

'Had your R&R?' He knew. This verbal fencing was getting painful. Mercifully he got straight to the point.

'This place is a shit-hole! . . .' he announced. We'd rounded the corner and were walking past the Warriors towards the canteen. In the distance bright red tracer, three blobs at a time every ten or so seconds, flicked across the valley from one hill to another. It all looked so normal. '. . . this is not a healthy place. Why would anyone in their right mind want to stay on out here?'

He meant, why did I want to stay on? I hadn't even considered this to be one of the Twenty Questions. My mind started racing, grabbing at snippets and threads that might be woven into something plausible . . . Nick Costello had gone with the Cheshires . . . Abbott had been hounded out of Croatia by the HOS . . . continuity for the PWO . . . *dare I tell him about the parcels? About Minka or worse still about Una and the UNHCR girls?* What could I say? But it had been a rhetorical question.

'Because you're a good bloke.' He answered his own question. I was stunned. It wouldn't have been my answer. What was he getting at? We were nearing the canteen and my time was nearly up. Searby finished the conversation quickly.

'I think you're tired. You've been at it too long without a break and you're in need of a rest. You've done more than enough out here . . . ,' he paused probably trying to gauge my reaction. I was glad it was dark. '. . . this isn't the place to talk about it. So, in a week or so, once I've settled in, I'm going to call you down to Split. We'll talk about it there. All right?'

And then he was gone. I felt hollow. Somehow the encounter had not quite turned out as I'd expected. Not as bad, but, then . . . what? I turned and walked slowly back to the Mess, turning his words over in my head and trying to analyse their meaning. *Does he mean that I'm for the off?* It seemed like it. *That's it then . . . another week and curtains!* I plunged down into the gloom.

'You all right Mike? Another beer?' Matt asked.

'I'm fine . . . I mean, no I'm all right. Enough for one day.'

'Y'sure?'

'Long day . . . twats in Vitez! No body. Fuck 'em, eh?' I was angry about the incident.

'Yeah, bollocks to 'em.' Matt was slightly mellower about it.

'Right. That's me – bed.' I felt tired and quite crushed.

'See you tomorrow then. Fancy coming out again?' He was laughing now.

'Fuck off! I've had enough of the Corps today to last me a lifetime.'

'Paras can't hack it, eh? Is that it? Ha, ha.'

'Something like that. Anyway, you just go off with your bucket and spade and play gravedigger without me. 'Night.' I waved over my shoulder as I pushed my way through.

The captains' house was in darkness save for a Tilly lamp burning in the grotto. No electricity again. It occurred to me that I'd be leaving soon and there were a few loose ends to tie up in Sarajevo – Minka, Una and others. I'd probably not see them again so it would have to be done by letter. The tiredness seemed to have gone so, despite the fact it was past 10 p.m., I decided to make a start.

By the light of the Tilly lamp, hunched over a Formica table, which was burdened with tins of mouldy Stilton, half-consumed pots of jam and Marmite, and liberally dusted with crumbs of cheese and broken bits of Jacob's Cream Crackers, I penned a quick letter to Minka. I explained that my time was up and that I'd try and find somebody from the PWO to act as Postman Pat. Then I started on a letter to Una. She was planning to take some leave and go to London to visit her brother, Dusan, who'd been evacuated at the start of the war and was stuck there as a refugee. To get to the UK she needed a letter of guarantee from a British Citizen offering assurance that she wouldn't do a bunk. I'd agreed to be her guarantor. Una had also become distant, more detached. I sensed it was something to do with the plight of her parents and her inability really to help them. What to say? Words, words . . . how to craft them and not to offend.

'Mike! Quick!' I looked up from the page, startled, pen frozen in mid-sentence. I found it difficult to focus on the figure standing in the door.

'Mike! *Molim te, molim te . . . pomozi me!* Please, please help me!' It was Edi Letic.

'Edi! What is it? What's the time?' *It was nearly two in the morning!*

'Come quickly please!' He was visibly upset, not panicky or distraught, more pleading with his eyes.

'Right . . . well, what's the probl–what's happened, Edi?' I'd never seen him like this.

'Come quickly, please! I'm just a local . . . I need your help . . . I can't do it on my own!' He'd gone, vanished down the stairs. *Has he gone mad?* At two in the morning! I dropped my pen, grabbed my Maglite and chased him down the stone stairs.

In front of a small kiosk outside the house a small group of five or six soldiers had gathered. Illuminated only by a fullish moon they cut a ghostly scene, standing soundlessly, motionlessly, like statues, mesmerised by an untidy heap lying at the base of the kiosk. Among them I recognised Carson Nicholson, the PWO's padre.

At first glance I thought the heap was a blanket until I saw a pair of camouflaged, booted legs sticking out at odd angles from under it.

'How did that get here?' I asked.

'He's just been killed . . . shot, five or ten minutes ago.' Edi's voice was breaking.

'What! Here?' I hadn't heard a shot for the past hour or so at least.

'No. He was killed in front of his home . . . they just pulled up in a car, started shooting . . . he ran out to defend his house . . . three bullets in the chest . . .' Edi's voice trailed off.

'But how did he get here? What are we supposed to do?' None of it made any sense. The group was spellbound, still staring at the heap.

'His family brought him here . . . asked if the UN could help . . .'

'Do what, Edi? What? What can we do? He's dead.' It was desperate.

'. . . to take him to the mosque. It's too dangerous for them on their own. They'll get shot,' he added quietly.

Nobody had moved. They were still staring, still shocked, shuffling their feet in the dust. I felt sorry for them.

'Well, where's the mosque then?'

'Just up the road. About two kilometres . . . not far . . . can we do it?' He was almost pleading. I felt the anger rising.

'Of course we can bloody well do it. You!' I pointed to one of the group, 'get down to the Ops Room and get the duty Warrior down here.' The spell was broken. The soldier raced away leaving us standing around the body.

'Do you know him, Edi?' I had a sneaking suspicion.

'Nermin is his name . . . was his name . . . a Muslim,' he said simply.

Within five minutes a Warrior had ground to a halt in front of the kiosk. We placed the body on a stretcher and tried to stuff it into the back, but it wouldn't go without tipping the stretcher on its side, which made the body slide off. We binned the stretcher and hauled him into the bottom of the Warrior through the rear door, pulling his arms and pushing his legs. The blanket fell away. Although it was dark we quickly replaced it before anyone could see his face.

There was considerable discussion as to exactly where this mosque was. The Warrior commander didn't know. No one knew except Edi, who also explained that we had to pick up some other people on the way. It was impossible for Edi to sit in the back in pitch darkness and guide the vehicle via the intercom. The only logical solution was to put Edi in the turret next to the commander in place of the gunner. Totally illegal, but we did it anyway and the gunner clambered into the back of the vehicle and joined me and the body. The Warrior lurched off and turned sharply right. I guessed we were headed towards Travnik.

It was as black as doom in the back of the Warrior. Somewhere on the opposite bank of seats sat the gunner, consumed with God alone knows what thoughts. Between us, in the foot well, lay the body. I tried to ignore it and kept my feet propped up on the far seats for fear of touching the body.

After a few minutes the Warrior swayed to a halt. The commander activated the rear door, which hissed and swung open on its hydraulic arm. Two men leapt in.

'*Pazi! Pazi! Nemojte da ga gazite . . . !*' I hissed. But it was too late. They were terrified and leapt in, ignoring my warning, trampling all over the body, falling over and collapsing against the sides of the vehicle as the door closed and it sped off. There were feet, arms, grunts and curses everywhere. One of them lost his footing on the body and crashed into me. Angrily, I pushed him away. Didn't these people, whoever they were, have any bloody respect for the dead!

There wasn't enough time to disentangle ourselves before the Warrior again stopped short, heaving on its suspension. The body slid forward. As the hydraulic arm whirred I could hear somebody clambering out of the turret. Edi was standing by the door as it opened.

'Quick, we're here!' he whispered urgently.

We pulled the body out feet first, dragging it over the raised lip of the doorway. Hurriedly each of us grabbed a leg or an arm and hustled the dead weight through the front door of a mosque. Somebody grabbed the blanket, which had again fallen off, and dragged it with him.

In contrast to the warmth of the night outside, the mosque was cold and gloomy. Immediately inside, on the left, was an alcove, a small atrium, white-walled and smooth-tiled. In the centre a raised marble plinth rose from the floor like a flower, supporting an oval marble dais – human sized. A single arched window, through which the moon shone, cast a cold, eerie, green hue about the alcove. We heaved the corpse up onto the dais. That done, the urgency of our efforts seemed to melt away. We stopped and stared.

His head lolled to the left. Sightless, opaque eyes stared through me. His mouth hung open and his tongue slipped out. The skin on his face, taut, glowed green and slowly, very slowly, a thin rivulet of blood slipped down his tongue and drip, drip, dripped onto the marble and collected in a small pool about his cheek. I could feel my bile rising. I felt weak, sad, angry, more than anything, horrified. I wondered who it was exactly who had termed the dead 'glorious'. What was glorious about this? He looked eighteen. He was eighteen.

Someone stepped forward and closed the eyes and tried to close the mouth; it wouldn't close because the poor boy's tongue was hanging out. The blanket was thrown over him to spare us all. His arms were placed by his sides and his feet were placed neatly together. Under the blanket he looked like bodies should look – lumpy and unseen.

The man next to me, scruffy and unshaven, middle aged, wearing slippers, let out a sob and sagged against the wall. He was sobbing and sobbing, shoulders heaving up and down, while his whole being shook uncontrollably. His right hand was pressed to his eyes. Through his fingers tears flowed onto the floor. It was the boy's father.

It was so utterly base and cruel, so awful and so degrading. It was inhuman.

It was upside-down, pervertedly back-to-front. Sons were supposed to bury fathers, not the other way round. Not like this. Killed, and half an hour later dumped in secret, with no decorum, onto a cold slab in a cold, dark, green place to be stripped and washed as a prelude to a hurried, furtive nocturnal burial – lest the snipers get the grieving too – and dumped in an unmarked grave. Back home the bereaved could rightly expect a polite knock on the door, a visiting officer and female help, armed with platitudes and sympathy. There was none of that civilisation here. Far worse than the boy, far in a way worse, was the father.

I didn't know what to do. It was beyond my experience. What do you do? Put your arm around his shoulder? Pat him in sympathy? Say 'Don't worry. It'll be better.'? How could it be? Ever.

I put my arm around him to stop him sagging to the floor and shoved him as hard as I could out of that mosque, supported him to the Warrior and pushed him into it before leaping in myself.

The Warrior stank. The well was wet – sticky yet slippery. The boy's blood had emptied onto the floor and the father, somewhere in the lurching darkness, was sobbing and sobbing, slithering about in his son's blood.

We dropped the father and his friend – the boy's father-in-law, as I was soon to discover – and sped back to camp as quickly as possible. As they slipped and stumbled their way out of the Warrior, mumbling pathetic thanks between sobs, I wondered what the CinC and Searby, tucked up and sound asleep, would have thought of our nocturnal caper. Lucky for them they didn't. Lucky them.

Barely had I returned to the grotto and lit a cigarette than Edi reappeared, imploring me to help him. 'The widow is in a state. No one knows what to do. She will die ... of shock.' *What bloody widow? What now?* It was past three.

Edi led me round to a house which was just behind ours. It was one of those full of Muslims who had been shot, burned and terrorised out of their own homes by the Croats over the road. We, the UN, had merely watched it all happen.

The kitchen area was full to bursting, maybe sixteen people of all ages and both sexes – old crones and ancient men, middle-aged women and young women with children. No middle-aged men or young men. You could smell their distress and anxiety. It was overpowering. They just stared at me, an alien who'd dropped in from next door, from outer space. I felt very uncomfortable, stepping beyond the UN world into their world. No one said hello, but some nodded. A few of the women were weeping. The room reeked of stale sweat and Turkish coffee.

Stepping over these people Edi led me through a back door and into a sitting-room. On a dirty brown sofa sat a young woman; a teenager, she looked forty. She was dressed in a pink towelling track suit. Her feet were bare and she was heavily pregnant, perhaps eight months gone. Her stomach bulged against the pink. She looked Buddha-like but quite wild. Lank, matted, greasy hair straggled over her shoulders. In the corner of the room, at the foot of a mattress, where she evidently slept, was a small cot waiting to be filled.

I'd expected to find her wailing and crying and flinging herself around the room. None of it. It was far worse. She was in deep shock. Her body trembled and rocked slightly. Wide, sightless eyes stared at nothing. Her hands, which were held firmly to her stomach, were gouged and bloody. As some sort of reaction gripped her, she nervously raked her hands with her fingernails. She sat there quivering, trembling and scratching, oblivious to her surroundings.

We put a shawl around her shoulders and Edi found some slippers for her feet. We sat on either side of her and each took a hand to prevent her from scratching herself further. Her hands were ice-cold and slightly clammy. There was absolutely no reaction from her. It was as though we didn't even exist.

Very quietly Edi started talking to her, soothing her. 'Be strong. You must be strong for the baby.' He kept saying this over and over again but to no avail. He was unable to penetrate her trance. There was nothing I could say, so I just sat there holding her torn hand. After a while Edi's voice started cracking. He was crying. To my horror, even today, I didn't, despite seeing him and that girl in that abject state. I was an unwilling voyeur to all this.

Once in a while the door would open and someone would poke their head through. Seeing the pitiful sight unchanged, a pained look would crease the face before it quietly disappeared.

After a while Edi started cooing and soothing, all the time stroking her hand and saying words which I have now forgotten. Somehow he must have penetrated her terror. Her lips moved. She was trying to say something. Edi put his ear to her lips.

'Mike, have you got a pen and paper?'

I fished into my flak jacket pocket and produced my blue notebook and a felt pen. I handed them to Edi. He placed the book on her knee, holding it steady, and the pen in her hand. She held it loosely, still trembling and staring sightlessly ahead. He whispered something in her ear. She bent her head and with great effort slowly scribbled four deformed and shaky words, and then released the pen, which rolled onto the floor. She was staring ahead again. Edi glanced at the words and handed me the notebook. He was crying again. I glanced down at the scrawl. Suddenly everything was clear – '*NIJE ISTINA ZA NERKA.*'

'It *is* true.' Edi was now whispering to her. 'It *is* true about Nerko!' She shook her head in denial, but he kept at her, '. . . it is true about Nerko.'

Her trembling suddenly stopped and her body seemed to relax. The spell had been broken. Her staring eyes misted over, filled up until there was no room, and big fat tears streamed down her cheeks, dripped off her nose and chin and fell onto her swollen pink stomach, soaking into the towelling. I watched in horrified fascination as the patch of soggy grief spread over her belly like a giant cancer infecting the unborn child beneath.

I knew then that there was no hope. None whatsoever. That baby, born out of grief, no doubt a son as fate would decree, would be tainted for ever, would probably be named after his dead father, would grow up being told that his father had been killed by the 'filthy Ustasa' in the war – the next generation perfectly prepared, twisted and bitter, primed for the next bloodletting. How many times was this hideous scene being repeated this night, on the Serb side, on the Croat side, on the Muslim side? There has been a war in the Balkans once every generation for the past fifty generations and I understood in that soggy patch of stretched pink towelling exactly why. No agreements, no treaties brokered in the hushed corridors of Geneva, London, Washington or Paris would ever, could ever, break this vicious, elemental cycle of revenge and hatred. They are doomed for eternity.

Someone must have heard her sobbing. Two of the elder women bustled into the room and took control of the distraught widow, who was now wailing and blubbering. There was nothing left for us but to go.

'Nerko? Edi?' We were outside in the cool sweet pre-dawn air gulping down lungfuls of the stuff.

'Diminutive of Nermin,' he said simply. He paused and added, 'I think I'll stay a while longer with them.' I nodded and told him I'd try and get the doctor to have a look at her tomorrow . . . today! See if he couldn't prescribe some sedatives or something.

In the grotto the Tilly lamp was still burning. My pen lay on the sheet of paper where I'd dropped it. The nib had dried up so I squeezed some ink into it and looked down at the unfinished sentence, blotted out the past four hours, and continued writing. I didn't tell Una anything of what had happened. There was enough misery and horror in her life in Sarajevo without adding to it.

Later in the morning, after daybreak, the doctor visited the widow. Edi thanked me for helping him; and someone complained that one of the Warriors had been left in shit state, full of dried blood, and that it had taken several hours to clean it out.

THIRTEEN

Operation Bretton

November 1997 – Ian, UK

'There's more, Ian. A day after we put the Muslim boy in the mosque a woman was shot in the field next to the captains' house. I heard the shot, but you hear lots of shots and you pay no attention. I was drinking a cup of tea in the kitchen and chatting to an Int Corps captain, Rob, who was up visiting from Split. I heard this shot and just carried on drinking my tea. But then I heard this babbling and wailing outside – *"Ranjena je! . . . Ranjena je! She's wounded! . . . She's wounded!"* I poked my head out of the kitchen door to see what was going on. About thirty metres away lying squirming in a field lay an old Muslim woman. She'd been hit by a Croat sniper from seventy-five metres away across the road. A group of Muslims were huddled behind a breeze block shed just outside the kitchen. They were weeping and wailing and wringing their hands in frustration, wanting but not daring to rush out and help her. Amongst the group were the woman's husband and children. The sniper was still firing, trying to finish her off. The rounds were kicking up dust around her.'

I was in uniform and half toying with the idea of rushing out myself, hoping that the light blue might prove bulletproof. But you never can be sure whether the bloke behind the rifle is drunk, drugged up or just crazy. Then I spotted Jules Amos coming back from a shower wearing only flip flops and a green issue towel, wash bag in one hand and rifle slung over his shoulder. He seemed to be the only one not frozen with panic, unlike the PWO guard. There was a Warrior parked by the Mess and its turret was actually pointing across the street. But it was empty, there was no one at home. I rushed into the Mess and grabbed two PWO lieutenants who were drinking tea. I told them to get the Warrior started up and to park it between the sniper and the woman. Unfortunately it was locked up so they had to dash off and find the keys. Meantime Jules had galvanised one of the Toms on guard into sprinting down to the MST to summon an ambulance. Both of us joined the distressed family at the blockhouse. The keys had been found and the Warrior's engine fired up; then it lurched forward only to be blocked in by an ambulance which had come screaming round the corner. All the time we're just like the locals watching this poor woman grovelling and moaning thirty metres away. We were hopping up and down and burning with frustration and just as I'm saying to Jules – *'You've got the gat, cover me'*, which sounds brave now but I'm not sure I'd have done it, to be honest, the Warrior lurches forward and blocks the sniper's view. He stops firing. We rush out and scoop her up. She's light and frail and making this mewing noise. We stuff her into the back of the Warrior, close the door and the vehicle neutral turns and bounces off.

We're frantic now because she's gone grey. We rip off her top, exposing her chest. There's a huge exit wound in her back. Jules is checking her airway, breathing and pulse and I'm ripping open a shell dressing and taping it over the wound with black masking tape. The Warrior is bucking wildly and lurching about and I'm not sure the subaltern knew how to drive the bloody thing. We're searching frantically for the entry wound but just can't find it anywhere – not a spot of blood anywhere. When it happens it's not nice and easy like on the floor of the classroom during a First Aid lesson where you always find the entry wound. But we don't. The lack of light in the back doesn't help either. I remember she had big black hairy armpits and we're rummaging through that lot and lifting up her saggy breasts. But nothing. So I then start sticking together a drip and stuff the giving set into a bag of saline solution. I've got the canula ready but there's no chance of finding a vein or of sticking the needle in accurately in that bucking Warrior. The vehicle then suddenly stops and the commander shouts down that it's stuck trying to go round a corner. So we hit the open button but the sodding microswitch in the hydraulic arm fails and we're stuck in the vehicle with a dying woman on our hands. Frantically we throw open the top hatches and drag her out over the top, risking even more injury to her. Her spine could have been hit, we don't know. She's gone a white-grey and is no longer moaning. She's barely breathing and her pulse is almost non-existent. There's a medic outside the vehicle with a stretcher so I give him the drip set as he's the expert. But he mucks it up and tries to stick the canula into a vein in her hand, à la classroom. But there's no vein because it's collapsed, as veins do in the extremities when someone's in shock. Anyway, this needle goes in and produces nothing more than a bloody great bubble of saline solution under her skin. There's nothing going into her system. Then the medic faints. I tell you it's never just one thing. It's always a combination of factors that mount up against you exponentially. In desperation Jules and I race her to the MST and dump her on the operating table. The surgeon and his team are there all dressed up and ready to go. He orders us out. I take a last glance at the woman. She looks dead.

I wander back to the kitchen. My mug of tea is still warm. I'm soaked with sweat and very surprised to see that only about ten minutes have elapsed since I heard the shot. Rob is staring at me as I gulp down the tea. I'm panting and shaking like a dog and just as sick as one because we've helped kill this woman.

You're not going to believe this, but despite our best bungling efforts to kill her, we didn't. She lived. I was convinced she was a goner. But that night I bump into the surgeon in the Mess and he tells me that they saved her, but only just. He reckoned another thirty seconds and it would have been all over. The bullet had entered, almost slipped in, through her left armpit – no blood – even the surgeon admitted that it had taken them an age to find the entry wound. Then it had gone through her left lung, bounced off her spine – mercifully no damage there – turned right and exited out of her back. Sad thing in all this is that night PInfo put out that she had died. God knows why. Crossed wires I suppose. So, officially she's still dead. But she isn't. I went to see her in hospital only to discover that she was mad as a hatter, quite literally; she was known to be a bit of a village idiot and that's why she had been wandering about in that field. Five days later she's back on her feet and up and about. I took Chris Stephen from the *Guardian* to show him our living-dead zombie. *'There you go, Chris. There's your dead woman.'* The next day she and her family were evacuated to Zenica.

A couple of weeks later I got my marching orders – 'Stanley to move to Split with all his kit. Interview with COMBRITFOR on Monday 31 May.' I knew what that meant – end of tour. Why else pack up all my kit? Stanley's out of the Balkans. I have to say, I was quite depressed for my last week or so in Vitez. Throughout May I'd made it into Sarajevo a couple of times. One occasion an English cameraman, Seb Rich, who was working for NBC News, needed to deliver an armoured car into Sarajevo to NBC, but he didn't know how to get through the Serb checkpoints. Now, we're not talking here of any old armoured car. We're talking about the German Chancellor's cast-off armoured Audi, a great big black thing with grey tinted armoured windows, a prize for the Serbs if ever there was one. I struck a deal with him that I'd get him and the vehicle through if he'd buy me a bergen load of food. He was delighted and spent nearly US$100 on food in a shop in Kiseljak on our way through. We drove into Sarajevo with all this as well as with another of General Jackson's aid packages. Getting through the Sierras required a hefty amount of drinking with the Serbs at S-1, whom I'd got to know quite well. Minka had been delighted with the food. I told her that I was leaving and we had a very tearful parting. I was distraught at the thought of not seeing her or Munir again.

All was not well with Una. She'd changed somehow and was distant, withdrawn and seemed nervous in some way. I couldn't work it out. The situation in the city was appalling now that the heat had come. With a desperate lack of water there was a high chance that the place would be ravaged by some hideous epidemic. It affected everyone's mood.

I packed up my gear in Vitez. I'd arranged a lift into Sarajevo airport on Sunday 30 May as I was intending to fly down to Split. Unlike Peter Jones I had no desire to shake my bones to bits on a final drive down those terrible routes. I'd also rung Una and arranged to meet her and Danko at the airport to say goodbye. The day before I left Vitez I suddenly felt guilty at not having said goodbye to Una's parents and grandparents. I imagined that they'd be having a hard time of it in that filthy, humid flat. I knew I wouldn't be seeing them again either. For some peculiar reason, which I still can't really explain, I drew out 1000 Deutschmarks on the acquittance roll in the pay office, which would be deducted at source from my pay at the end of the month. I stuck it in an envelope along with a letter to Bobo telling him I hoped the money would see them through the war. I taped the envelope to a carton of 200 Marlboro.

On Sunday 30 May I left Vitez and was driven to Sarajevo airport. In a strange way I was sad to be leaving the PWO. They'd suddenly got over their first few difficult weeks and were now forging ahead with what was to be an extraordinarily hard, stressful but successful tour. Una and Danko were at the airport to see me off. I gave Una the cigarettes which she promised to give to her father. I didn't tell her about the money, but I did tell her that I felt sure that I was about to be sacked. We agreed to meet up in England in July when she'd be visiting her brother.

And that was it really. I hopped down to Split where it was boiling hot. Being a Sunday, there was no one around. Most people were off on the islands getting their sun tans sorted out. It didn't really matter as I hardly knew any of the new crowd. I just hung around kicking my heels and fretting over what Searby would say to me the next day.

For the occasion I stuck on a clean uniform, then loitered on the balcony smoking and waiting for the appointed hour. It's funny, but things never quite work out the way you think they will. Instead of me going to see him, he suddenly wandered out onto the balcony smoking one of his cheroots. 'Ah, Stanley! There you are. I'll interview you when I get back from Trogir. I'm off for a haircut.' I shot back, 'Then you'll need me otherwise they'll fuck it up and scalp you!' I remember he looked at me wickedly through slitty narrowed eyes behind a cloud of cigar smoke. 'All right then. But if you fuck up my hair I'll sack you!' Those were his words and I knew then that my time wasn't over. He really was a good man. He simply ordered me back to the UK for six weeks' leave, barked at me '. . . and don't you dare come back a day earlier!' And then told me that I'd be working for him when I returned. I hung around for an extra day waiting to catch Wednesday's VC10 shuttle to RAF Brize Norton. Amazingly, I bumped into Dobrila in the Mess and we chatted for a few hours. She'd just returned from London looking fit, refreshed and full of plans for the future. She'd used her time in London wisely, staying with an English girlfriend, Fleur, and organising a course at the University of London in September in order to finish off her English degree. The plans sounded great: leave Bosnia in a month or so's time and move to London. But she spoke with no real conviction. It was odd. Neither of us raised the issue of my betrayal of her confidence. I had my chance then to bury the matter but blew it. More fool me. After five and a half months in the Balkans I flew in to Brize on 2 June.

You might think it was a welcome break. You'd be wrong. It was a living nightmare. No one will ever really understand. Most people think 'lucky sod, six weeks' leave'. But it was hell. Looking back on it, the problem was the transition from Bosnia to southern England, to quaint old Farnham basking in a glorious English summer. It was too quick. If I was to do it again, I'd spend two weeks loafing about the Adriatic islands to calm down from Bosnia and then four weeks in the UK. But to pop up in Britain just like that after all that had happened was unsettling. It was difficult to talk to anyone. Colin and Melanie, who were looking after my house, were okay, but you couldn't explain anything to them. What do you say? I spent a lot of time in the pub listening to stupid conversations about football scores or whatever. It bored me. On one occasion I met some mates from the Regiment in the pub. 'Oh yeah, it's not a real war. Not like the Falklands. You're not fighting anyone. All you're doing is escorting aid convoys!' That's the sort of stuff they'd come out with. It really irritated me. What did they know? You couldn't tell them though. You couldn't tell them that in a way it was worse . . .

The Gulf and the Falklands wars were identical. Both were pretty much fought over bits of wasteland. The protagonists were by and large all military, so the majority of the bodies were those of soldiers. Also both wars, on the ground that is, were over pretty quickly – three weeks and 100 hours respectively. Both had clearly defined political and military goals and everyone knew where they were going. Relatively speaking, there was very little collateral damage to civilians and infrastructure. Don't get me wrong. I'm not in any way demeaning the efforts and achievements of those who fought in those two wars. It must have been horrendous for them. But people have got to understand that we weren't just escorting aid convoys. We were piggy in the middle of a vicious, chaotic and bloody civil war. Most of the corpses we saw were those of old men, women and children, rarely actual combatants. And there we were 'area cleaning' someone else's dead bodies for them. There were no real political and military aims and we didn't know where we were going. All around us people were dropping like flies and we were able to do almost nothing about it. What do you think that does to you? Drip, drip, drip, every day drip-fed stress, continually and endlessly. Sure, you can scoop up the odd wounded woman, feed the odd poor family in Sarajevo, but it's a drop in the ocean. It makes no difference really. The slaughter just continues regardless . . . 'escorting aid convoys' . . . what do they know?

I went to see my parents almost as soon as I got home, but even that was difficult. They were delighted to see me but it was difficult. I ended up arguing with my father. It was dreadful! He saw things differently. His generation . . . their clocks stopped in 1945 when they became refugees. But then they started ticking again in 1991 when the wars of Yugoslav succession began. So they saw it all through 1940s eyes and memories. They based their preconceptions on their experiences then. So Serbs – angels, Croats – Ustasa Fascists, and Muslims – evil demons from the Levant threatening Europe and Christendom. Black and bloody white. So, when I started talking about Srebrenica, he wouldn't have it. Wouldn't accept that his son had a different view. It upset him so much that I just shut up and didn't bother. So I couldn't really get anything off my chest. Nothing I was doing seemed to be right. 'Why are you spending so much time looking after Muslims in Sarajevo?' Or if it wasn't that it was the other. When I told him about the 1000 Deutschmarks to Una's father he went mad: 'Why are you squandering your money on Communists?' I was in tears at that one. I remember crying in the kitchen asking my mother exactly what it was that I'd done wrong. But she understood. Mothers always do: 'It's fate, son. You're just paying back the good that complete strangers did to us when we were refugees. It's out of your hands.'

But it wasn't easy. Bosnia was my frame of reference, my reality, where the illusion was strongest. I watched the news every day, read every article. I even went to Germany for two weeks and stayed with Peter Jones and his wife, Jane. That was better because all we talked about was Sarajevo. It was good too because all the B Sqn 9/12 Lancer boys were also in Herford. On another occasion I went down to Somerset where Commander John Rooke, the boss of CHOSC, threw a party at his home. All the gang were there. Rooke, Tim Kelly, Nick Costello and many others from the Srebrenica ops. That was good too. But back in Farnham it was TV, newspapers, pub and ticking off the days till I went back. Nothing really, when you think of it.

The low point was 5 July. I was watching the BBC 6 o'clock news. It led with a report of an aid worker from Edinburgh Direct Aid, who had been shot dead in Sarajevo that morning. That dovetailed into a second report which stated that one of the local interpreters had also been shot dead. I froze in my seat. There were pictures of this girl being stretchered out of the captains' house. Despite the bloody bandages wrapped around her head I could see that she had long black hair. I nearly threw up on the spot. It was Dobrila. I knew it. I went to the pub, got drunk and watched it again on the 9 o'clock news. Same story. I had to know for sure, so I rang the watchkeeper in Split. He confirmed it. It's the worst thing. You argue with somebody, you betray a confidence, you're too proud to apologise properly . . . and then they're killed. And you've blown it. Too late. You can never undo that wrong or put right that mistake. I rang David Arnold-Foster in Cambridge because I knew that Suzana Hubjar was spending her R&R with his family. He'd been the MoD financier, the Civil Secretary, in Cumming's HQ and it was largely he who had fixed up the financing of the interpreters' R&R scheme. He broke the news to Suzana and she came down to Farnham for a couple of days. She was distraught . . .

I remember what Suzana said to me at the time. Even now it raises the hair on the back of my neck. She told me that when Dobrila had arrived back in Vitez she'd talked a bit about her plans to finish her degree in London and that she'd be finishing her interpreting job in a month or so's time. All rather unconvincing and then she just upped and told Suzana that she'd be killed soon, that she wouldn't survive the war and would never leave Bosnia again. Horrifying isn't it? Apparently, the fighting was so bad around Vitez that she had to be buried hurriedly and in secret at night. Her grave is unmarked and to this day I don't think anyone knows where she's buried. At least I've never heard anyone claim to know . . . that's right. All we did was escort aid convoys!

I saw Una for only half a day in Farnham. After Dobrila's death I wasn't exactly in a brilliant mood. Nor was she. I'd never seen her in such a nervous state, pale, drawn, completely changed. I don't even think we particularly liked each other at that stage. In a way we were from two separate cultures and, worse still, the war had pushed us apart.

I just longed for that six-week nightmare to end. I was irritated by people's endless prattling in the pub, their endless whinging about trivia . . . you just felt like slapping them about a bit and saying 'Morons! Assholes! You don't have any problems.' But instead you just get yourself another pint and keep it in.

As soon as I got back to Split, everything was fine again. Keith, the FCO's UN Department rep in the HQ, took me under his wing and out to restaurants in Split. The Chief of Staff, Patrick Roberts, told me to get myself thoroughly briefed up again as I'd been away for so long. This took about two minutes with the Mil Info people – more fighting, more destruction and more cemeteries filling up. Mostar was in ruins, the Lasva valley still in flames. Situation no change.

I made a new friend too, Captain Carole Burnell, married to a Royal Marine. She was one of a batch of new replacement interpreters. She'd been given the job of Protocol or visits officer and occupied Martin Strong's old office in the Split HQ. She became a staunch ally when things started to go wrong later.

For about two weeks I found myself doing just what I'd done when I'd first started working for Brigadier Andrew Cumming in 1992. I'd hang around

Split and then a visit would wind up, some politician or general would trip out and off we'd all go up country. We were still the most visited contingent in theatre. In fact it had got worse and Carole's plate was full juggling one VIP visit after another for people who wanted a sniff of what it was like – war tourists. They'd all come out with their Instamatic cameras and take photos to show the wife and kids back home. It was dull, tagging along as unused interpreter.

The only one of those trips I really remember was when the Defence Secretary, Malcolm Rifkind, and Douglas Hogg from the Foreign Office came out and we went up to Vitez. It was the first time I'd seen Edi since Dobrila's death. Standing in the kitchen of the captains' house he told me what had happened. The pair of them had been sitting on the step outside eating strawberries. It was late afternoon. He was still in uniform while she had changed into jeans and a top. As she stood up a sniper from across the street shot her clean through the head. The bullet had passed through the open doorway of the kitchen and punched a hole through the internal door. The hole was still there. Edi was curiously calm about the whole thing. He told me about the funeral at night and then told me that he had moved heaven and earth to get her poor parents transferred across the front line to Sipovo on the Serb side. The double tragedy in all this is that Sipovo fell to the BiH-HVO assault in summer 1995. No doubt her parents were either killed or became refugees.

Secretly, I was searching for a way of escaping up to Sarajevo, but it was proving almost impossible. There was no real job for me there and BRITDET had a new boss in the form of Matt Bray, the Royal Marine UKLO from Vitez. The Chief of Staff was resistant to my leaving Split where I was kept on quite a tight leash. I even started to behave like an REMF – shorts, T-shirt, top up the tan, out to the islands etc. Fortunately I was saved from this by the Commander of the Bosnian Serb army, General Ratko Mladic himself.

Towards the end of July an opportunity suddenly presented itself and I grabbed it instantly. Mladic had launched a massive offensive from way south of Sarajevo towards the city. The aim was to capture Trnovo, cut off the Muslim supply route from Central Bosnia to Gorazde, and finally capture mounts Bijelasnica and Igman, thus completing the encirclement of Sarajevo. Despite a spirited defence in depth and tenacious fighting withdrawal by BiH forces, they proved no match for the Serbs' superiority in artillery. When Trnovo was captured, Serb TV showed Mladic remonstrating with anyone he could find by the gutted Orthodox church there. When asked by a journalist where the mosque was – for there had been one but since the town's capture it had disappeared – he flew into a rage and shouted 'Time to move on!' Mount Bijelasnica was on the verge of being taken. Panic gripped Sarajevo. Its only pipeline out via the tunnel under the airport linking Dobrinja and Butmir, and thence over Igman and Bijelasnica, was about to be cut. Almost certainly the Bosnian government would be forced to sue for peace. The international community was gripped by yet more frenzied spasms and now a real threat of massive NATO air strikes loomed large on the horizon. As all this approached crisis point Matt Bray found himself alone in the city. For some peculiar reason his whole team was either on leave or out of the city. He was completely on his own and hadn't a clue what was going on.

Patrick Roberts suggested I fly up and see how he was. Carole Burnell too was extremely concerned as to his well-being. I stuffed a bergen full of Coke cans, beer and food and shot straight up there on the airlift. Matt picked me up from the airport. I remember him saying something like, 'I'm no coward, Mike, but this place isn't worth dying for or in . . . I've got a wife back home and I want to see her again!'

I couldn't blame Matt in the least. He was virtually isolated in the PTT building and doing the job on his own. I'd never seen him so angry, on such a short fuse. Every aspect of his life was riven with frustration. The situation was pretty bad: heat, lack of water, Mladic's imminent seizure of Bijelasnica and the incessant roar of NATO jets flying at low level over the city all combined to create a desperate and frenetic atmosphere. UNHCR was contemplating withdrawal but had no coherent plan. In the event of having to scuttle off we'd not only have to get the internationals out but also all the local workers and their families – hundreds of people. I was quickly roped into working on a collection, movement and withdrawal plan. In the end it was a reasonable one but it would never have worked as it relied on the airport remaining open. Fear and uncertainty pervaded every corner of the PTT building. We were woken one morning at 4 o'clock by the continual rumble of battle and shelling, the worst to date. Savage flashes ripped through the pre-dawn sky. The UNMOs recorded nearly 3,000 impacts. It looked as though Mount Bijelasnica had fallen.

I spent a lot of time with Minka and with Una's parents and grandparents. Una was still away on leave. One afternoon I popped round to the grandparents with some milk and sugar. Bobo and Natasa were asleep next door. A third person was sitting with Vera and Tomo, a neighbour from upstairs. Well into her seventies, with perfectly groomed, straight white hair and a sweet, kind, wise old face, she was serenity and calmness themselves. We fell into conversation. She was fascinating, highly educated and what she didn't know about the archaeological history of Bosnia wasn't worth knowing. It had been her lifetime's passion and she'd been head curator of Sarajevo's museum of history for forty years. I told her about myself. She listened quietly. She seemed to have this way of making you trust her. Eventually she said, 'I've a brother who was with your father's group. He also left in 1945.' 'Oh,' I said, 'I'd imagine that he either lives in Birmingham or London where most of the émigré community of his vintage finally settled.' She even had his address but added that she'd last seen him seventeen years ago and had had no contact whatsoever since the start of the war. I told her to write him a quick letter and that I'd post it to him through our BFPO system and that he'd get it within four days. Her eyes sparkled with pleasure as she scribbled away to her brother Jovica Miletic.

The next day I flew down to Split and penned him a quick note telling him that I'd met his sister, Nada Miletic, that she was well but that like all people her age she was finding it impossible to make ends meet since a monthly pension barely covered the cost of an egg on the black market. I told him that she needed Deutschmarks desperately and in small denominations. I also told him he could feel free to send her letters, parcels and money via me, but warned him not to send anything until he had verified my credentials with my father in Cornwall. I stuck her letter in with mine and posted them.

A couple of days after sending that letter I decided to ring my father to warn him that Jovica Miletic would be ringing about me. I explained that I'd met a pensioner in Sarajevo called Nada and that her brother Jovica would be ringing him ... 'That's not Jovica Miletic, is it?' It was like being hit in the stomach with a sledgehammer. I replied that it was and he said, 'Jovica and I were at school together in Skopje before the war. His father taught me law. During the war Jovica and I were in the same unit, we came to England as refugees together and ... I was best man at his wedding!'

That completely blew me away. What were the odds of me meeting the sister of a man whom I'd never met before, the sister of my father's friend whom he hadn't seen for seventeen years? She only went down to Vera and Tomo's at 3 p.m. to watch the news. It was a fluke that I popped in at that time of day. And think of the chain that led to this: Cumming meets Jackson in the MoD, Jackson's parcel to Minka, Peter Jones happening to work in Sarajevo, his leaving do, meeting Una, then her parents and then this Nada Miletic. Fate. That's all I can put it down to. It exists. Now my Postman Pat role widened even further as did an overwhelming desire to find a permanent reason for basing myself in Sarajevo.

One other thing happened which was to alter dramatically the course of some people's lives. I'd asked Lejla precisely what the matter was with Una. She told me that it was her parents. Her father in particular was beginning to suffer psychological trauma from being cooped up in a single room and sleeping on a mattress on the floor. I'd spend time with them, often hours at a time. We'd share a bottle of wine and chat about what life was like before the war. But it was true he was listless, quiet and withdrawn. He seemed to have lost his purpose in life and reason for living. Here he was aged fifty-five or whatever, squatting with his wife in a grotty, dingy room in his father's flat. I remember one day, 7 August, I was sitting there with them. It was stinking hot and he was in a vest. We were sitting at their small table having a glass of red wine. Our conversation was incessantly interrupted by the howling of low-flying jets. They irritated me, and I wondered if those jet-jockeys from Italy really knew what life was like beyond their cockpits. I noticed two small suitcases by the door. 'What're they for?' I asked. 'Oh, just in case . . .' he replied unconvincingly. 'In case of what?' He went very quiet and then said, 'In case there's an opportunity to go. We keep them packed . . . more out of hope than any real expectation . . .' His comment left me feeling a bit odd – *poor sods*. All their hope lay in those two miserable little packed suitcases.

That evening Matt and I were having a beer in our room. I couldn't get the suitcases out of my mind. They plagued me. Suddenly, I just said, 'Matt, I need your help.' 'Whatever you want, just name it.' So I did and we hatched a plan on the spur of the moment. 'Yeah, fuck 'em all. Let's just do it!' Matt was all for it.

We didn't tell a soul, not even Una. Especially not her. She'd have flapped like a good'un. We were risking her parents' lives here . . . and if it went wrong she could genuinely have denied all knowledge. The PTT wasn't exactly the most secure environment. Information, however sensitive, has a way of moving around of its own accord. People can't help talking. It's human nature. It's what we all do best – talking. No, Matt and I just hatched this plan and decided we'd go for it in the morning.

I fretted all night. You don't just up and risk people's lives lightly. If it went wrong, if we got caught at any one of a number of checkpoints, they'd have been lifted and probably killed.

The next morning I had such severe misgivings that I squirted out my guts into the toilet and just sat there thinking, 'I can't go through with this . . . cancel now. Easiest option as no one's hopes will be dashed.' I told Matt. He was much cooler. 'Nah, bollocks. Let's go for it!' I think he saw it as his last act of revenge before leaving Sarajevo. He hated the place.

The plan was pretty simple really. Jump into Matt's UNHCR vehicle. Zip into town, checking out the checkpoints along the way and then drop me off. I'd wake them up while Matt drove the route out again to check the alertness of the checkpoints going the other way. If he sailed through he'd be back in twenty minutes, pick us all up and off we'd all go. If he got stopped we'd abort and he'd pick just me up. Simple.

On the way into town we were stopped at a Bosnian checkpoint. As the policemen glanced into the vehicle my heart sank. *'That's it. No point continuing with this,'* I said. Again it was Matt who suggested he drop me off anyway and continue out. If he wasn't stopped outbound then we'd continue.

Vera's eyes nearly popped out of her skull when she opened the door. It was 8 a.m. I barged my way in. Natasa was in a panic. She was still dressed in her night clothes. 'Quick. Get dressed. We're off out of here in twenty minutes.' I remember she started shaking, quite panic stricken. 'Just fucking get dressed!' I was pretty panic stricken as well. Matt was on the radio checking in using a simple code we'd agreed the previous night. He'd sailed through every checkpoint as far as the airport and was now on his way back – 'Piece of cake!' crackled the radio and then he confirmed he was in position for pick-up. I virtually had to shove them out of the flat. There was barely enough time for them to say goodbye to Vera and Tomo who were in tears and also in a real dither themselves. Bobo and Natasa were trembling with fear. They hadn't been out of the flat for months.

Matt had reversed the vehicle up to the bookshop entrance. We bundled ourselves in, all arms legs and suitcases. 'Fucking 'ell, mate!' roared Matt laughing, '. . . if you'd been a minute earlier you'd have found this vehicle surrounded by policemen all going to work!' In the back we had two blue flak jackets and two UNHCR baseball caps, which I made them put on. At a glance they looked like aid workers. Matt floored the accelerator and we hared off down Sniper's Alley and just tore through all the checkpoints. After the no-man's-land at Stup we swung right down Kasindolska and into Ilidza. 'That's it then. You're free now.' They still had the 1,000 Deutschmarks I'd given Bobo and we just dumped them in a side street in Ilidza where they claimed to have a cousin. There wasn't even time to say goodbye. We left them standing there and shot off to the airport so that I could catch a flight down to Split. That was the last I saw of Bobo and Natasa.

I gave Matt a bluey to give to Una. I'd prepared it in case we were successful. I told her what we'd done, not to breathe a word to anyone and just to carry on as normal. The whole thing had taken less than half an hour. An hour later I was sitting on the pier in Split with my feet dangling in the Adriatic.

Ian's now looking at me strangely.

'I know what you're thinking . . . that's not even an issue . . . others were doing it all the time . . . some even made money out of it. As far as I'm concerned our mission was the provision of humanitarian aid and this was the way we chose to interpret it. I don't give a damn what anyone thinks. They were human beings and they needed help.'

FOURTEEN

Operation Bretton

November 1997 – Ian, UK

'In the end, Ian, I got what I wanted – a posting to Sarajevo – by accident rather than by design. There'd been much hue and cry in the West about the twenty-four per cent of aid arriving at the airport, which was handed over to the Serbs to feed those in need on the Serb side. It was widely believed that because the distribution of that aid was unmonitored, it was going straight to Mladic's army. From the airport the Serbs' slice of aid was trucked to a warehouse in Rajlovac, a large industrio-agricultural complex to the west of the city. A portion of that twenty-four per cent was trucked direct to another warehouse in Grbavica, a Serb-held part of the city where the front line dropped down to the Miljacka river, the Serb side of Sniper's Alley opposite the Holiday Inn. That was it. There was no monitoring of secondary or tertiary distribution of that aid. No one knew what the Serbs did with it.'

For a year and a half UNHCR Sarajevo had been trying to establish an office on the Serb side in order to find out where this aid was going so as to satisfy donor countries. Glynne Evans of the FCO's UN Department was particularly interested in finding out, largely, I think, because the Americans were insisting that it was going straight into the bellies of Mladic's fighters.

At the time, the situation around Sarajevo had eased slightly and under threat of air strikes the Serbs had been forced to withdraw from Mount Bijelasnica, but not before blowing up the communications tower on top. The Mixed Military Working Group, chaired by Brigadier de Vere Hayes, had agreed to the creation of a Demilitarised Zone running over mounts Igman and Bijelasnica, the integrity of which was to be maintained by UNPROFOR troops. The Bosnians in the city now had a lifeline running out through the tunnel under the airport and over the mountains into Central Bosnia.

With the situation somewhat calmer and the threat of the UN scuttling away from the city diminished, I suggested to Tony Land, the head of UNHCR, that if he could somehow get an office opened on the Serb side then I felt sure I'd be able to run it. Nicholas Morris, the head of UNHCR for FRY, was also in favour of this plan. The donkey work actually fell to Colin Price, UNHCR's logistics officer at the airport. His job was supervising the unloading of aid from the aircraft, its initial storage at the airport and its subsequent movement into the city or to the Serb warehouses in Rajlovac and Grbavica. Colin was a Zimbabwean salt of the earth type: he had good relations with everyone including the Serbs. Full credit must go to him for actually persuading the Serbs that a monitoring operation was a prerequisite if they were to continue to receive aid. Colin negotiated the hiring of two Serb women as UNHCR staff members and monitors and subsequently these two women and I found a tiny corner office on the first floor of an agricultural administrative block in the Rajlovac complex. We hired it for $70 per month and hoisted the UNHCR flag on the first day.

The younger of the two monitors, in her mid twenties, was a wild dark-haired and dark-eyed banshee from Ilidza called Ljljana Elez. She had the shortest fuse in the world. The other, Ljerka Jeftic, was a mother of three from Ilijas, on the Serb side of the front line from Visoko north of Sarajevo. She spoke excellent English as she'd taught the language in a Visoko school before the war. Now, many of her former pupils were busy lobbing mortar rounds into Ilijas from Visoko. Both were grateful for the job and the salary, which was paid in US dollars. I got on with both immediately.

My most pressing problem was that I had no vehicle. UNHCR couldn't give me one. Monitoring required a lot of travelling, frequently close to front lines, and it became a matter of considerable importance that BRITDET some-how acquired its own vehicles. Interestingly, it was Glynne Evans in the FCO who came to the rescue. She waved her magic wand in Whitehall and two brand spanking new Kevlar armoured Land Rovers, known as snatch vehicles in Northern Ireland, were flown out to Split in late August. Such was the importance attached to the monitoring of aid by the FCO.

Matt Bray's tour ended at pretty much the same time. He couldn't get out of theatre fast enough. What with picking up dead bodies in Ahmici, dis-covering an atrocity in Miletici and topped off with a nerve-wracking time in Sarajevo, he'd had enough. His replacement was another UKLO, Captain Piers Hankinson, a cavalry officer from the Queen's Royal Lancers. Piers and I flew down from Sarajevo and together drove the two snatch vehicles up from Split, but not before I'd been forced to sign for £100,000s worth of vehicles, which made me break out in a cold sweat. Because Mostar was a virtual no-go area we had to take the other route over the mountain, through Gornji Vakuf, which was raging, then Vitez and Kiseljak and finally through the Sierras into Sarajevo. We did this one Sunday, by the end of which BRIT-DET had become autonomous and independent on both sides of the front line.

Soon after Peter Jones' team had departed the gauleiters of the PTT building had moved BRITDET's accommodation from the civilian wing to the third floor of the military wing. They'd given us two poky little rooms. Piers and I occupied the smaller one and the rest of the team, WO2 George MacAlister, Cpl Andy Gibbons and Marine Smith, had the larger one which they shared with a mountain of compo rations, the INMARSAT telephone and the TV/video. I can't really claim that we 'lived' there: it was more like camping. Basically, we were squatting in these hovels with boarded-up windows and sandbags piled up above head height. Occasionally snipers from the Alipasino Polje flats over the road would pop rounds into the PTT building just to remind everyone that they were dissatisfied with the UN. I can't remember one ever coming into our room, but I do remember a burst being fired into the room next door. It was occupied by the French, who never spoke to us, so when it happened we cheered – they'd forever been defacing the Union Jack stickers on our two doors.

Life as squatters was grim. There was no running water in the building. We were rationed to one litre per person per day of cartoned drinking water. We pooled this and every day observed an unchanging ritual. At 8 a.m. we'd congregate in the larger room. One bowl of water served all five of us for a shave. Feet and so on would be washed in that water. We'd then make a communal brew to start the day off. It was a cardinal sin for anyone to drink pure water, all of which was used for brews and some left for the evening treat – one of George's superb curries. His father had served in the Indian Army and George took his inherited curry-making skills extremely seriously. Anyone going to UK on R&R went armed with a list of spices, herbs, powders and Basmati rice to buy and bring back. Onions and garlic were a must. We insisted that any visitors flying up from Split would not be given a guided tour of the city unless they came armed with onions, garlic, bread, other luxuries and at least a bottle of whisky. After the morning's ritual we'd go our separate ways and do a day's monitoring. I'd drive out through Ilidza, pick up Ljljana and drive a horrendous back route to Rajlovac, which avoided the front line. Piers would disappear into the city with 'Smudge' Smith, while George and Andy would scoot around the airport or be out of the city trying to get fuel into Sarajevo.

Evenings were the dullest. We'd climb out of our stinking, sweat-soaked uniforms and hang them up on a line running across the grott. By the time we awoke in the morning the night's heat would have dried them to white crispy boards, which would have to be scrunched up before being pulled on. We'd sweat into these garments all day long. The heat in the city was terrific. There was no air-conditioning in our vehicles, and, being armoured, the windows couldn't be lowered. Clad in flak jackets and helmets we were virtually driving around in mobile ovens. After a week of this, when all the uniforms had gone white and were quite honking, we'd stuff them into a bin liner and dispatch Smudge or whoever down to Split on the airlift to chuck them into the washing-machine.

The French wouldn't allow us into any of their bars in the PTT building, so we usually frequented the civilians' international bar, which was much more interesting and congenial than some stuffy military bar. It was the strangest thing. You couldn't get drinking water for love or money but there was as much beer for sale as you could drink. Some of the aid workers were so shot-away that they'd become permanent drunkards. One of these soaks was Colin's assistant at the airport, a large Scandinavian. To my surprise I discovered that he'd worked in UNHCR Tuzla during the March helicopter operation. It was he who had driven the coach back across the front line at Memici that evening when we'd had to escort forty-six Serbs across the line. His heavy drinking seemed to have started once the coach had come under fire.

Some evenings I'd pull on a pair of jeans and off we'd go to one of the restaurants for a pizza or pancakes. Usually I'd go with Mica or Lejla. Una and I were keeping a respectable distance from each other since one or two of the girls in the office had noticed that her parents had disappeared and were asking whether they'd moved back to Dobrinja. She couldn't say much at all and in many ways was herself at risk, simply because she had been labelled a Serb while at the same time holding down the pivotal administrative job in the office. Like all the local staff, she was indispensable to the operation. Since she now had no reason to stay the main push was to convince her to get out of Sarajevo. She was too bright to fester away in that place. Cautiously, she investigated the prospect of moving to UNHCR's head office in Zagreb, but Tony Land's successor, Michael Phelps, a lawyer, was panic stricken at the prospect of losing her. She made the place tick.

Mica really became my best friend there. I was fond of them all but she and I were very close. She was small, impish with black spiky hair and an enormous personality, a wicked sense of humour and a vicious cackling laugh. On Sundays, a day of rest for all but those being killed, we'd visit her mother who lived on the fifteenth floor of a partially destroyed tower block. I'd be used as a pack mule, lugging a bergen full of food up fifteen flights of stairs, exhausting and sweaty work, which served merely to remind me how unfit I'd become on my diet of cigarettes and beer. Mica's mother, who had become involuntarily separated from her husband by war and a front line, made the best potato and onion pies in Sarajevo. Either that or we'd visit one or two of her friends, which was less physically strenuous but much more stressful and dangerous.

One couple, Micky and Tanja, lived in a flat in the most dangerous part of the city, Hrasno, an area frequently subjected to vicious sniping and mortaring. Just getting to the flat was hazardous and required much ducking and diving between doorways. But it was well worth it. Tanja was a Serb, lively, attractive and friendly, he a Muslim, thin as a rake but with a wild sense of humour and wickedly flashing and intelligent eyes, and also a soldier in the BiH. The first time we met he'd just returned with his platoon over Igman and through the tunnel for a spot of R&R. How absurd – retreating into a besieged city for a rest! The interior of their flat had been wrecked by shrapnel. Tanja had collected this and kept it in a glass fruit bowl rather as people in England keep glass trinkets in bowls – 'Just for decoration,' she said. There was no electricity. Light was supplied by candles and a bizarre and dangerous gas affair. A rubber hose brought Russian gas into the flat. At the end of the hose was taped a giving set from a drip ending in a sharp canula needle. From this danced a sooty yellow flame, which gradually oxidised and consumed the needle.

Micky and I cracked a bottle of whisky. He had me in stitches telling me what life as a pre-war conscript in the JNA had been like. It didn't seem any different from life as a Tom in our grotty barracks in Aldershot. He was incredibly lively, the master of the punchline and more than anyone else he opened my eyes to the absurdity of the war. He told me that just about everyone was reluctant to die for the mafiosos and their unscrupulous leaders. His unit frequently traded not fire with their Serb opponents but goods and money – mortar bombs emptied of explosive and full of cigarettes would go one way and others would be fired back containing money.

Micky's unit had just returned from protracted operations far to the south near Mostar where the BiH was fighting the HVO. The BiH offensive had made extraordinary ground and had come to within eight kilometres of Grude, the HDZ HQ. At one stage, he said, they'd run out of artillery rounds – '. . . we did a deal. You see we had money but no shells and the Serb Hercegovina Corps had shells but no money. Since we weren't fighting them down there we did a deal and bought 1,000 shells at 100 Deutschmarks apiece. But the problem we had was we had no means of transporting these shells, so the Serbs fired the fire-missions against the Croats for us. All we had to do was to get our observers to flick to the Serb artillery net and adjust the fire . . . it went so well that the Serbs threw in an extra 100 shells *za kafu* – for free!' When he told me that my jaw dropped because while that was going on fifty miles to the north in Sarajevo the BiH and Serbs were kicking hell out of each other. It was really a war about money, of wheeling and dealing, of local warlords making money hand over fist at the expense of the Little People. Small wonder that there wasn't a single offspring of any of the leaders on any of the sides who fought. The precious ones were all away in the West or in Turkey or in Belgrade studying at university or whatever. You only had to listen to stories like these to realise that policy makers in the West would never be able to sort this problem out.

I kept up my Postman Pat role with Minka, Tomo, Vera and now Nada. Money or parcels would come from the UK and Pat would deliver them. Visiting the grandparents became problematic. Una was terrified that someone would have worked out what had happened and that I'd get lifted or perhaps killed. A part of that was paranoia, but some was true so I only ever went there in darkness or let Mica make the deliveries. Amazingly, Bobo and Natasa had somehow made it to Belgrade where she had family. They'd got there within four days of escaping from Sarajevo. The great fear had been that, having got them out of the city, Bobo would have been lassoed by the Serbs, stuck in uniform and given a gun since he still had five years of 'military service' left in him. He'd been a TV producer before the war, not a soldier. That had been a double risk, though one which fortunately came to nothing.

Without doubt the best bit of the job was ... the job. En route to the Rajlovac office each morning Ljljana would give me a whole load of verbal abuse about being an AfroBritishChetnik spy and I'd tell her she was a myopic one-sided bitch from Ilidza. This mutual verbal abuse went on for months. We'd meet Ljerka in the office, who would have been dropped off by her husband, Zdravko Jeftic, the Commissioner for Humanitarian Aid and Refugees for Serbian Sarajevo, as they called it. We'd start off with coffee and then hit the road and go monitoring. We literally put in hundreds of miles a week of driving over dreadful routes.

The Serb distribution system was highly efficient. UNHCR would truck aid into the Rajlovac warehouse where it would sit until there was enough for a monthly distribution to six warehouses serving the communities of Ilijas, Vogosca, Centar, Rajlovac, Ilidza, and Hadzici. We also had to keep tabs on the aid that went direct from the airport to Grbavica. Each sub-warehouse had a Serbian Red Cross representative, who was responsible for tertiary distribution. In all, some 148,000 people received the aid. For the most part, the job required Ljljana, Ljerka and me to pore over their books and records checking inloaded against outloaded quantities. Once that had been done we'd go banging on people's doors to check the validity of their signatures and to confirm that they'd indeed received such a quantity of aid. The bookkeeping was staggeringly and mind-numbingly accurate and detailed, painfully so. Clear evidence of how thinly spread the aid was over 148,000 people. Not once were we denied access to a warehouse or to books and ledgers. Basically they had nothing to hide because the end user received so little. In that sense the job was easy. In contrast, Piers was finding it difficult to gain access to some 'communes', which were widely believed to be shadow military units.

Nobody really abused the aid because there wasn't enough of it to be abused. Every month we were able to track down and account for about ninety-eight per cent of the inloaded aid, but those are just figures. Neither side had a professional standing army; basically they were comprised of citizen militias with men up to sixty years old in the front trenches. In a family of four you might have a father and son spending two days in the trenches, two days at home. At home of course they'd eat the aid food the wife has signed for, ergo you feed half of Mladic's army. You can put any spin on it you want. But by and large, none of it went to Mladic's manoeuvre units.

The other interesting thing was that these people had a siege mentality themselves. Serbian Sarajevo, especially anything west of the airport, was virtually, but not wholly, cut off from the remainder of 'Republika Srpska'. What's more, they loathed Pale with a passion. They hated Karadzic who hadn't visited Ilidza, for example, since the start of the war. They felt they were being treated as convenient tools in the siege. Each sub-warehouse boss had one horror story after another about aid from the Serbian Red Cross in Serbia destined for them, which mysteriously disappeared in Pale. Some even went as far as to accuse certain individuals in Pale of war profiteering. To be honest, in terms of mentality and outlook you couldn't put a credit card between the besieged and besiegers. Brigadier de Vere Hayes was once pilloried in *Private Eye* for saying as much but he was right.

The most interesting part of the job was meeting the local mayors, politicians, commanders and aid workers. I soon got to know them well. Even the hornets' nest of Ilidza became less daunting. We started driving up to Pale to talk to Mr Ljubisa Vladusic, the Serb Commissioner for Humanitarian Aid and Refugees. He was a suave, urbane, well-educated, also over-stressed man. He was assisted by a Mr Simic, whom I didn't care for much and who more often than not seemed drunk.

Split wouldn't stop interfering with us. HQ BRITFOR was still at Split. We were forever being pestered by the Chief of Staff who'd suddenly ring up and retask me, wiping out a day of monitoring: 'Go to Kiseljak. Marry up with 845. Fly to Srebrenica and arrest a prisoner . . .', or 'So and so or such and such a Minister is flying up to Sarajevo. Pick him up and give him a guided tour of the city.' It used to drive Piers and me mad, particularly when it became obvious that they were war tourists, who'd appear empty-handed. Our favourite guest was without doubt Keith, the FCO's UND man in Split. He'd fly up armed to the teeth with bottles of whisky and bags of fresh food. He took a keen interest in the monitoring operations as it was the only place in B-H where this was done, and was particularly grateful for being taken up to Pale to discuss aid with Mr Vladusic.

Every ten days or so I'd hop down to Split to brief Brigadier Searby on the military, political and aid situation on the Serb side. It was all useful information. He was grateful for it, but the Chief of Staff resented the free rein I had, although he didn't once bother to fly up and see how we were. In Peter Jones' time, Richard Barrons used to do it all the time. As a result of no one bothering to come up all they'd ever see of us would be dirty, scruffy, sweaty blokes appearing in Split. I remember once popping into the cookhouse; they tried to throw me out for being covered in huge white patches of salt. I told them to sod off: how dare they sit there at their al fresco tables all dressed up in their Bermuda shorts, T-shirts and Ray-Bans all set for the beach! The serious grafters in the HQ like Searby were always in uniform, but a lot of the support people looked as though they were on some sort of Club Med holiday. And there we were rationed to one litre of water per person per day and stinking to high heaven. They would get sitreps from the UNMOs in Sarajevo that so many hundreds of shells had been recorded hitting Sarajevo; they'd sit there in Split imagining they'd all landed on us and therefore concluded that we were all mad and shell-shocked. But that wasn't the case at all. These detonations became background noise. They didn't bother you and you just got on with your job, but you couldn't tell them that in Split. And so Stanley was labelled as mad.

My real allies down in Split were Bob Edge and Carole Burnell. Carole would often ring us in Sarajevo to chat or to ask if we needed anything or to warn us if the Chief of Staff was plotting something. Keith would also make me laugh. He travelled around and saw a lot. I remember once in September, when a big Bosnia-wide cease-fire had been engineered and fighting had stopped as a precursor to the mammoth peace talks on HMS *Invincible* in the Adriatic. Lord Owen was to chair it and all the hoods were to be present – Milosevic of Serbia, Tudjman of Croatia, President Izetbegovic, Mate Boban and Dr Karadzic. The whole first XI! The weekend before all this Lord Owen arrives in Split with Jeremy Braid, his map and bag carrier. They're booked into one of the hotels for a relaxing working weekend prior to the talks. Keith attaches himself to them to help Lord Owen relax. One morning they take him onto the Adriatic in a boat. He looks over the edge of this boat and his glasses fall off and sink to the bottom of the sea. When they get back to the hotel room they start work and Owen orders Braid to fetch him the map. There are hundreds of maps in this case. It was all about maps, that war. Eventually the right one is produced and Lord Owen realises he can't see it. He sees Keith standing there and orders him to go and get him some glasses. Keith starts flapping and fussing about enquiring into what dioptic corrections Owen requires. He tells him not to be so stupid, that he's a sixty-year-old man with a sixty-year-old man's short sight. Keith rushes off to find some glasses. In the corridor he bumps into a Croatian cleaner, a Nora Batty-type with scarf and curlers. She's also about sixty . . . and she's got glasses. With a quick apology he whips them off this startled woman's face and disappears back into Lord Owen's room. Owen puts them on and immediately starts examining the map. He even wore those glasses during the peace conference on the *Invincible*, which caused a huge stir . . . they were enormous, pink-framed, Dame Edna Everidge spectacles with huge gull wings! These sorts of stories kept our morale up.

The job in Sarajevo just ground on. We virtually had to prise Una out of that place with a crowbar. She didn't want to leave, despite having got the job in Zagreb. Like everyone else she had got hooked on the madness and manic atmosphere of the place – very difficult to tear yourself away. At the end of September she left to take that first step to a new life. Mica, myself and others promised to look after Tomo and Vera and, anyway, she was only an aid flight away from Sarajevo.

After the failure of the peace talks on HMS *Invincible* the wars resumed with a vengeance. Sarajevo went mad and my existence became more and more peculiar. During the day I'd be on the Dark Side monitoring or sitting in our office going through the figures. The windows would rattle and shake all day long as a nearby Serb artillery battery lobbed shell after shell into the city. Then I'd jump into the vehicle, drive back into the city and find myself on the receiving end of that fire. Inevitably we found ourselves drinking more and more.

We're pretty much into October now and one day Brigadier Searby summons me down to Split. He's not interested in the usual sitrep but tells me that a young Royal Marine UKLO, Rob Bucknell, is to replace me, that I'm to work out a hand-over programme and then be out of Sarajevo by 2 November, my end-of-tour date. Then he drops this bombshell on me – 7 November I'm to report to HQ 8 Infantry Brigade in Londonderry to begin a two-year staff job. Just like that. Do not collect leave, go straight to Northern Ireland. I'm astounded. He tells me that he thinks it sucks but that's the system, as ever hiding behind the magic words – 'in the interest of the Service'. We all know that the interests of the individual come below that of the Regiment, which is below that of the Service. That has to be the way but sometimes it's fundamentally wrong, particularly since CinC UKLF had issued a directive stipulating that all troops leaving theatre were to have one week's admin in barracks followed by three weeks' leave, mandatory. That only applies if you're part of a formed unit or a deployed HQ. If you're a single capbadge individual in theatre, like me or any UKLO, you simply get forgotten and fall through the cracks. I'm devastated: after nearly a year in the Balkans, living that weird life, the last thing I need is to go straight to another fucked-up part of the world, equally riven with ethnic and religious hatreds, and for two bloody years.

My morale goes rock-bottom and I slink back up to Sarajevo thoroughly pissed off and seething with fury at a callous system. I've got nothing to look forward to once I get out of that hell hole. The worst aspect of all this is that, once in Northern Ireland I know I'll never be allowed back to the Balkans, simply because the brigadier there would never release a principal staff officer to leave one operational theatre and go to another. Inevitably you become an asset and once people have got their claws into you that's it, you're trapped. Where would that leave Minka, Munir, Tomo, Vera and Nada? The other thing Searby said to me was that I was to visit Captain Paula Webster, the psychiatrist in Vitez. It was his policy that anyone in the 'high-at-risk' category must see the psycho prior to departing from theatre. In a way he was one of the most enlightened commanders out there and recognised the dangers.

Bosnia had gone bananas. In Bihac, Fikret Abdic, a Muslim wheeler-dealer, businessman cum politician, had declared UDI. During the March 1992 Bosnia-wide elections he had in fact won more votes than President Izetbegovic but had not been allowed by the SDA to take office and had thus reverted to his entrepreneurial activities in Bihac. By declaring UDI, and sticking two fingers up at the Sarajevo government and at General Atif Dudakovic's 5th Corps in Bihac, he installed himself as leader of the breakaway Bihac Muslims in a castle in Velika Kladusa. His Muslim forces controlled the northern half of the Bihac enclave; another absurd war within a war, this time Muslims against Muslims.

In Central Bosnia the HVO in Tesanj and Maglaj over at the 'light bulb' just upped and defected over to the Serbs, leaving the Muslims hanging on there on their own. Then the BiH 7th Muslimanski Brigade swept through Vares and kicked out the HVO and Croat civilians. These fled over the Serb front line and flooded into Vogosca where the Serb Red Cross manager emptied his warehouse of aid to see these people on their way. Some were bussed through Serbian Sarajevo, down through the Sierras and injected into the Croat pocket at Kiseljak. Others flooded east to Sokolac where they established a large tented refugee camp and gave Mr Vladusic an even bigger headache as he struggled to further spread his aid resources. The strangest thing in all this was that the Serbs, Mladic, allowed whole HVO units to transit Serb-held territory and re-inject themselves elsewhere in Croat-held areas of Central Bosnia. It wasn't too long ago that they'd been selling and firing shells for Micky and gang against the HVO. That place was enough to drive anyone mad.

Towards the back end of October the Sarajevo mafia warlords start a war against each other in the city. The Sarajevo BiH brigades are all commanded by pre-war mafia hoods. The most famous of these was Juka who organised the defence of Dobrinja, then fell out with his bosses and cross-loaded to the HVO and sold his services in Mostar. His body was found dumped on the Dutch-Belgian border in December 1993. When war breaks out it's not lawyers, teachers and academics who grab guns first and fight in a Territorial Defence force. It's the hoods, the old pre-war mafia, who go for it first. Izetbegovic had no choice in April 1992 but to rely on them to defend the place. In doing so he basically ends up with hoods running the city, controlling the tunnel, the black market and ripping off people like Minka.

Above: Gradacac, 1993. A Bosnian Army (ABiH) soldier takes aim with his Dragunov sniper's rifle assisted by Gypsy 'observers' in his trench. Devastatingly accurate sniper fire characterised the war and terrorised civilians and soldiers alike.

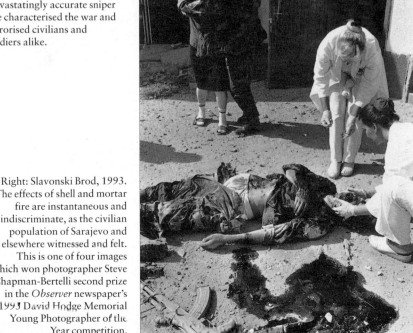

Right: Slavonski Brod, 1993. The effects of shell and mortar fire are instantaneous and indiscriminate, as the civilian population of Sarajevo and elsewhere witnessed and felt. This is one of four images which won photographer Steve Chapman-Bertelli second prize in the *Observer* newspaper's 1993 David Hodge Memorial Young Photographer of the Year competition.

The face of war. The corpse of an unknown soldier has lain in the open for ten days reclaimed only by nature. In the aftermath of the Ahmici and other massacres, such sights were commonplace in the Lasva valley. This image was one of Steve Chapman-Bertelli's portfolio of four prize-winners.

Right: Vitez, July 1993. Malcolm Rifkind, the British Secretary of State for Defence, is interviewed during a live link-up with the UK from the back garden of the BBC's Vitez house.

Left: Vitez, July 1993. The second Commander British Forces, Brigadier Robin Searby, chats to Martin Bell of the BBC.

Maybe Airlines, Sarajevo Airport. As with the Berlin Airlift, the multi-national airlift of aid into the airport was critical to the city's survival. UN aircraft were frequently subjected to hostile fire from the confrontation lines abutting the airfield.

Left: Sarajevo Airport, May 1993. The author (left) with UNHCR Sarajevo local staff, Una (centre) and Danko. Both are now married and live in the West.

Below: UNHCR Sarajevo, 1993. Cosmopolitans all, it was the local staff members, irrespective of religious background, who made the whole operation tick. L-R: Lejla, Mica, Gordana, Meliha, Sandra and Lejla Hrasnica.

Left: PTT Building, Sarajevo, 1993: BRITDET UNHCR Sarajevo's Spartan but adequate accommodation. Captain Piers Hankinson and the author shared this grott.

Right: The 'Dark Side': the author with local UNHCR staff members, Ljiljana Elez (left) and Ljerka Jeftic (right), at our Rajlovac office.

Below: The 'Dark Side': on the heights of mount Trebevic overlooking Sarajevo, Serb besiegers relax at their bunker, the Café Chetnik. Behind them is the treacherous road to Pale.

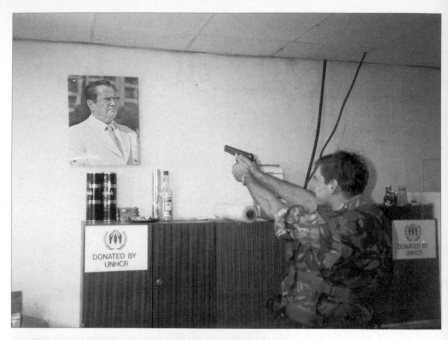

Above: Sarajevo Airport, October 1993. In a moment of fantasy and wishful thinking the author takes revenge against his godfather's murderer – Josip Broz Tito.

Above: Sarajevo, 9 November 1993. The author with Una's octogenarian grandparents Vera (left) and Tomo (right).

Right: Sarajevo, 9 November 1993. The author with Nada Miletic, Tomo and Vera's neighbour. Her father had taught the author's father mathematics in Skopje in the 1930s.

Above: Mostar, July 1994. Jennifer Brush of the US State Department leads retired SACEUR General Galvin's entourage across the makeshift bridge constructed by the UN after Croat shell fire had destroyed Mostar's medieval Ottoman span in November 1993.

Above: Mostar, July 1994. General Rose and Goose (right) on the makeshift bridge.

Right: Mostar, July 1994. General Galvin (right) with the CO of the Spanish Battalion on another of Mostar's makeshift bridges linking the Muslim-held east bank with the Croat-held west bank.

Right: Koran Hospital, Pale, Thursday 28 July 1994. A Serbian nurse and newborn baby demonstrate the 'sun bed' donated by the British Red Cross and delivered by General Rose's wife, Angela.

Below: Visegrad, Thursday 28 July 1994. Having delivered a British Red Cross incubator to the Bosnians in Gorazde (who made novel use of it), Lady and General Rose inspect Ivo Andric's famous 'Bridge Over the Drina'. L-R: Serbian Colonel Masal, his interpreter, Lady Rose and General Rose.

Right: Haircuts! The Residency, Sarajevo, Friday 29 July 1994. One of the author's more bizarre duties was to install Muhamed the barber in the General's bathroom. Here, on orders from Angela Rose, the General prepares to be scalped. Curiously, Muhamed had also struggled with Dr Karadzic's hair before the war.

What sparked the mafia war is still a mystery, but in essence it's gangland turf warfare. One of them called Celo I is sitting in Boemi and someone shoots him in the heart. But he doesn't die because the bullet lodges between the two ventricles of his heart – miraculous, but it happened that way. The UN flies him across to Ancona on the airlift so that he can be treated in an Italian hospital. He recovers and then refuses to return to Sarajevo ... sometimes I have to pinch myself hard to remind myself it was all real. In August the RAF had flown in a special Herc at the behest of Prime Minister John Major, who had been goaded into action by a BBC report about a young girl called Irma Hadjimuratovic, who was dying of cerebral cancer in Kosevo hospital. All this to evacuate her to the UK for treatment. Very noble, but that act was met with howls of derision from the girls in UNHCR, they all knew that the French and Americans had been quietly doing that sort of thing for months. It was called Operation Irma and the RAF even commissioned a painting of a Herc diving at the airport in celebration of the op. There's a print of it in the canteen at RAF Lyneham. Then two months later the UN uses one of its Hercs to fly a gangster out to Italy to have a bullet removed from his heart!

The "turf wars" continued. Another warlord, Caco, by all accounts the worst, and who commands the 10th Mountain Brigade in the Bistrik area, fires mortars at the Serb barracks at Lukavica. The Serbs respond by rolling forty-four gallon oil drums packed full of explosives down the hillside in the early morning. These lodge in the BiH trenches and blow them to smithereens. We hear that little lot as far away as the PTT building. The next thing Caco does is to kidnap some French soldiers and hold them hostage. The French in the PTT building and at Skenderija go mad and start threatening all-out frontal assaults. Caco releases the hostages and immediately grabs a whole bunch of civilians and policemen again as hostages. In retaliation the 9th Mountain Brigade around the Holiday Inn mortar their brothers in the 10th, who of course then respond in like manner. The press in the Holiday Inn really haven't got a clue, or daren't confuse their editors and audiences, and simply report that it's Serb mortars.

The Serbs aren't shelling anyone. They're just howling with glee. Then another of these characters, Celo 2, ups and takes pretty much a whole street hostage near Bascarsija in the old part of town. The streets fill up with troops all loyal to one gang leader or another. They man every corner and stop any vehicle or foot movement. UNHCR's vehicles are stopped and the drivers' helmets and flak jackets are grabbed at gunpoint. Some are beaten up. Others are held and we rush around like mad things trying to get them back. Sarajevo is tearing itself to pieces and there's a good chance that the government will finally lose control. In desperation Izetbegovic orders the police onto the streets to sort out the problem. They're still pretty much loyal to the government. Pitched battles rage throughout the city. The UN Sector Sarajevo commander,

General André Soubirou, orders no UN vehicles east of the PTT building until further notice. Piers can't do his job but it doesn't really affect mine and I just carry on with my working hand-over to Rob Bucknell, who basically shadows me around and meets all the personalities.

The battles continue for four days and it's touch and go as to who will win. Gradually the police gain the upper hand and Caco is cornered with his hostages. He starts killing them and mutilating them, gouging out their eyes and cutting out their tongues. One of them is a young policeman. In all over ten policemen are killed before it's all over and Caco surrenders. But he doesn't live long. The young policeman's father, also a policeman, shoots him dead on the spot.

Celo 2 is cornered with his hostages in a flat in that street, but that one ends less bloodily. The Bosnian Prime Minister, Haris Silajdzic, takes to the street and personally negotiates the release of the hostages and the bloodless surrender of Celo 2 and his gang. After four days the crisis is over and the government retains control of the city again. To this day it baffles me as to why the Serbs didn't take that opportunity to attack and end the war.

Because all this is going on I've got myself an extension in the city till 10 November. Searby has departed from theatre and COMBRITFOR 3, Brigadier John Reith, a Para who'd been my CO when I'd been a platoon commander in 1 PARA in the 1980s, tells me to stay on and wait until he can fly into Sarajevo where he wants me to brief him about BRITDET. He can't fly in because of fog so we drive to Vitez and meet there. That afternoon I obey Searby's last command and hunt down the psycho. Paula Webster's not there so I end up on the couch for four hours talking to another doctor. I had no idea then that he wasn't a qualified psychiatrist. The result is that he writes a damning report (Keith told me this) stating that I'm mad and should be FMED 8ed immediately on my return to the UK. You know what that means? Psychiatric referral equals destruction of career. I don't know at that stage what he's written and sent down to Split. Brigadier Reith arrives in the early evening and Lt Col. Alistair Duncan, who is also about to leave with the PWO, briefs him first. Then I get half an hour or so alone with him. He assures me that the staff job in NI would be good for my career. He tells me that he's working on some sort of deal whereby I still go to Northern Ireland within five days of leaving Sarajevo, do a three week hand-over–take-over there, and then get Christmas leave. It's the best compromise deal available. I'm not interested. You know what NI is like? One shot fired on the border, the whole world goes mad and ministers are briefed in London. You can't really take that sort of stuff seriously when you've just stepped out of a Wild West city like Sarajevo. Some Ops Officer rings up in a panic to tell you that a mortar bomb has just landed in their SF base. How do you think you'd react? Probably just tell him to grow up and not to pester you with anything less than ten rounds landing! John Reith tells me that he'll see me again in Split on the 10th.

My last few days are spent monitoring and travelling about saying goodbye to people on the Serb side. It's a sad time: I've got to know these people well and particularly like the Red Cross workers, who were just little people like those in the city, as much victims of circumstance as anyone.

On the 9th Keith flies up and he, Ljerka, Ljljana and I take a last trip up to Pale to say goodbye to Ljubisa Vladusic. He takes us to the Hotel Panorama, the annex to which is Dr Karadzic's presidency. It's a curious looking, round, three-storeyed building with lots of smart new grey-tinted windowed Mercs and BMWs parked outside. We have lunch with Ljubisa Vladusic and his assistant, Mr Simic. Simic is drunk and banging on about Muslims and so on. I'm doing the interpreting along with Ljerka for Keith's benefit. 'You see, that colour of theirs, green, it was originally ours. They stole it. Green is a Serbian colour!' 'But I thought your colour was red.' 'It is. That's ours as well!' He makes me sick. Keith is grinning like mad and asks, 'What about black?' 'Oh yes! . . .' says Simic '. . . black's ours too.' That's pretty much how my tour ended . . . listening to a raving lunatic laying claim to every colour in the sodding rainbow.

That puts me in a furious mood, that and the wine. On the way back Ljljana has a go at me – 'Your problem is that you've got too friendly with those Muslims in Sarajevo, and with traitors like Una. That's your problem!' She makes me so mad that I just drop her in Ilidza and as she steps out of the vehicle, the last time I'll ever see her, I refuse even to shake her hand or anything and we part with me shouting, 'I hope you enjoy the rest of your shitty war!' and she just slams the door. We don't learn a bloody thing, not a sausage! If I'd learned anything from Dobrila's death I wouldn't have allowed us to part like that. But we don't ever really learn these lessons in life properly, which is why, I suppose war will always be there . . .

Keith and Ljerka have gone silent in the back. On the way to Rajlovac, Ljerka bursts into tears and begs me to go home with her, at least to let her cook me a meal. I tell her no, that I've got others in the city to say goodbye to. I know that Tomo, Vera and Nada have prepared some sort of last supper for me. Ljerka gives me a hug but is still crying her eyes out as she steps out of the vehicle and disappears into the darkness cloaking Rajlovac. Keith says nothing and I reckon he thinks I've gone mad.

I spend a couple of hours with Tomo, Vera and Nada. They're sad I'm going but insist that I've done enough for them. We drink a couple of bottles of wine and eat some pancakes all by the light of a couple of candles. It's cold in the room. Winter's on its way and I wonder what chances these old folk have of surviving a second winter under siege and with a monthly pension that can't even buy an egg. With a heavy heart, knowing I'll never see them alive again, I leave. One of the drivers picks me up and I hop into the back where Mica's waiting for me. As we pull away I'm staring through the small, dirty, armoured window at the back with silent tears streaming down my face. Back at the PTT building Mica, myself and others spend a long time at one of the canteen tables drinking wine. I've grow so fond of these genuine Sarajevans, who've given me an oil painting of the Vijecnica as a going-away present, that parting from them is equally difficult. The remainder of the evening is spent drinking whisky with Keith and the team at one of our favourite haunts, on the roof of the PTT building amid the satellite dishes. In a last gesture of defiance and drunkenness we drop our trousers and moon at Sarajevo!

The next morning I ring Carole Burnell to let her know I'm on my way. She's almost hysterical on the other end of the INMARSAT, telling me that the Chief of Staff, my loyal old ally for all these months, has been jumping up and down in his office threatening that if I'm not standing in front of him by midday he'll post me as a deserter.

I'm booked on to a 10.30 flight which God willing should get me to Split before I'm cast adrift as a deserter. I've got one last thing to do. Minka and Munir. We shoot down there. I feel a bit guilty because I haven't seen them since the turf wars started. When I get there Minka's almost hysterical. It was Ulica Romanijska and their flat and in particular themselves who'd been held hostage by Celo 2 for four days. They'd been bound and gagged and had lain on the floor living in terror of having their throats cut. She described in graphic detail what had gone on and how only Haris Silajdzic's intervention had saved them from certain death. I listened to this in stunned silence. Here's the rub. My parents, basing their observations on what they saw on the TV, always claimed that Haris Silajdzic was a slimeball. To me he's someone who had the balls to confront the Mafia and thus saved Minka's and Munir's lives. Of all of them, Silajdzic was a true Sarajevan whose family had lived in the city for over four hundred years. That's why he did what he did. He was the only one who could, while the rest of them were panicking in their offices.

I also discover, too late, that it's Minka's birthday. For the first time I hadn't brought a thing with me, and I now feel doubly guilty. She does one more session of coffee-reading. She's in the mood. She tells me that she sees a cross-shaped medal. I tell her I've already got my UN medal for service in Bosnia and that it's round. For the first time I doubt her sight, but she's insistent. I don't have too much time to argue and after a tearful goodbye I tear myself away. She told me to come and visit after the war and that I was to treat her home as my second one. With a second winter on its way and no end to the war in sight I doubted I'd ever see her again either.

I was running late and in danger of turning myself into a deserter. Rob rushed me to the airport. There wasn't even enough time to stop by the bus station where Mica was organising some sort of chaotic evacuation of people, so we had to say goodbye on the radio. That was it. My last view of Sarajevo was of the white minarets in Butmir glinting in the cold rays of a low winter sun as we shot down the runway. As we lifted off I unbuckled, moved across the aircraft and stuck my nose to one of the windows. I could see our office in Rajlovac with its little UNHCR flag. I could imagine Ljerka and Ljljana sitting there drinking coffee. I wondered what they'd be saying to each other. I felt sick and suddenly very sorry that I'd been so harsh with Ljljana Elez.

I walked into the Chief of Staff's office with fifteen minutes to spare. He was all sweetness and light. I didn't mention the deserter bit. He'd just have had a go at Carole. Brigadier Reith had blown his top at the doctor's report and ordered me to re-go with Paula Webster who was available in Split just for me. So I had to go through yet another four-hour session with her, at the end of which she declared that I was perfectly all right but that unless I got some leave there might be a problem. That didn't satisfy the system, which ignored her advice.

My flight out to the UK was scheduled for 13 November. I spent the next two days clearing from theatre, handing in my pistol, ammunition and morphine. Then I remembered that I'd never touched any of the telephone money I was supposed to draw. It came to about 700 Deutschmarks which I stuck into an envelope addressed to Mica along with instructions to give it all to Minka as a sort of belated birthday present. I gave the letter to the girls in the Split UNHCR office who had it flown up to Sarajevo the next day.

On my last full day, the 12th, Carole and I wandered over to the canteen for lunch. I was in scruffy civvies without even a pair of socks on. I hadn't cut my hair for months and I suppose I looked like a greasy aid worker. I felt pretty grim. I'd lost eighteen kilos in Sarajevo – cigarettes, booze, stress and infrequent eating had all conspired to turn me into a waif.

That fate thing I've kept banging on about – it just happened again, that very day. This one really freaked me out.

Carole and I are standing in the queue for lunch and as we shuffle along we move past a table, with four foreign officers seated around. Nothing unusual: every man and his dog used to eat in that canteen, but one of them looks somehow familiar. I ask Carole who they are. 'Oh. Some sort of group of UN investigators who've just arrived . . . looking into allegations of UN corruption . . .' But as we shuffle further along I recognise one of them. He's the Austrian general, Greindle, from my Kuwait days. I just shot over and asked him whether he remembered me. He simply said that he'd had so many MILOBs working for him that he couldn't remember them all, but he did remember my boss in the desert, a Kenyan lieutenant colonel. Afterwards, as we're sitting on the low wall outside having a smoke, Greindle and gang emerge from the canteen. He spots me, comes over and asks me to remind him who I am. At that point I just can't resist it any longer: 'General, perhaps you'll remember if I was to say that I was that British officer whom you wouldn't allow to go to Yugoslavia in January and again in March 1992!' Well, his jaw dropped and his eyes damn near fell out of his head. 'But this is Kroatzia,' said he. 'That's right sir, but I've just spent a year in Bosnia, mostly in Sarajevo.' Carole was gawping at me. Greindle composed himself and asked me when I'd left the British Army. I told him I was still in, at which his eyes opened even wider. Eventually we had one of those nervous laughs together and parted on amicable terms.

The next day I was smuggled through Split airport the way I'd come in, through the back entrance posing as a mover. The Herc wasn't ready to go so I was told to loiter discreetly over by the aid pallets. At one stage I had to hide in an ISO container when I spotted a Croatian policeman wandering over with his AK slung over his shoulder.

As a special treat I flew back the whole way first class in the cockpit. No cattle class for me on my homeward-bound leg. They even gave me one of those nice hot oven meals that the cattle in the back never see. It was pitch black as we crossed the south coast of England. Ahead lay the whole of Greater London spreading out like a giant orange glowing spider. It was strange to see a city with lights on at night. It looked and felt utterly alien. Over Biggin Hill we turned west and half an hour later had banged down at RAF Lyneham – nice little glide in lining up with the runway lights. No manic dive in from 18,000 feet. I was quite disappointed.

Brian Nicol, my boss from my Africa days, and his wife, Peeps, were there to meet me. We drove east to Surrey in virtual silence. I don't think either of us knew what to say to each other. I was miles and miles away, mulling over that peculiar train of fateful events which had anchored me firmly in the Balkans for nearly a year. That anchor was still embedded in Sarajevo and the links of the chain, which still tethered me to that place and its people, were like joins in a circle of fate – Jackson's parcel, Peter Jones, Minka and Munir, Una, her grandparents, Nada Miletic and then General Greindle. I couldn't even begin to describe all that to Brian and Peeps. It's too much to take in let alone let out. There you have it. Fate. Circles in history. And so it is in everything.

> You have noticed that everything an Indian does is in a circle
> And that is because the power of the world always works in circles
> And everything tries to be round . . . The sky is round
> And I have heard that the earth is round like a ball
> And so are the stars.
> The wind in its greatest power whirls. Birds make their nests in circles
> For theirs is the same religion as ours . . .

Even the seasons form a great circle in their changing
And always come back again to where they were.
The life of a man is in a circle from childhood to childhood,
And so it is in everything where power moves.*

* John G. Neitrardt, *Black Elk Speaks*, William Morrow.

PART TWO

1994–1995
The Mad Hatter's Tea Party

'Have some *peace*,' the March Hare said in an encouraging
tone. Alice looked all round the table, but there was nothing
on it but *war*. 'I don't see any *peace*,' she remarked.
  'There isn't any,' said the March Hare.

Adapted from *Alice in Wonderland*, Lewis Carroll.

UN DEPLOYMENTS IN BOSNIA–HERCEGOVINA, JUNE 1994–APRIL 1995

N

HUNGARY

Zagreb

xxx
HQ
UNPROFOR

xx
HQ
UN CROATIA

HQ
UNHCR

CROATIA

UNPA
Sector
West

ARSK

UNPA
Sector
North

UNPA
Sector
East

ARSK

ARSK

SERBIA

Bihac
Battalion

Bihac

x
HQ
Sector
North-East

BSA

BSA

UNPA
Sector
South

x
HQ
Sector
South-West

BSA

Tuzla

ll
Srebrenica
Battalion

xx
HQ
BH COMMAND
Main

xx
HQ
BH COMMAND
Forward

Srebrenica

ARSK

xx
HQ
BH COMMAND
Rear

Gornji
Vakuf

Kiseljak

Zepa

**Zepa
Company**

Divulje
Barracks

Sarajevo

BiH/HVO

Gorazde

ll
Gorazde
Force
Battalion

Split

CROATIA

BOSNIA-
HERCEGOVINA

x
HQ
Sector
Sarajevo

F
R
Y

BSA

MONTENEGRO

United Nations

Sector Sarajevo	6 battalions
Sector North-East	1 Scandinavian battalion
Sector South-West	7 battalions
Bihac	1 battalion (French then Bangladeshi)
Srebrenica	1 battalion
Zepa	1 Ukrainian company
Gorazde Force	1 composite battalion (British battalion, minus 1 company, plus 1 Ukrainian company)

Warring Factions

ARSK	Army of Republika Srpska Krajina
BSA	Bosnian Serb Army
BiH/HVO	Federated Army of the Republic of Bosnia-Hercegovina and Bosnian Croat Army

0   km   50

International boundaries
Confrontation line
Inter sector boundary

FIFTEEN

Operation Bretton

November 1997 – Ian, UK

'The first time I clapped eyes on him I thought he was one of the bodyguards!'

'Who?'

'General Rose. He just stepped out of this car on the tarmac at Naples airport. He was wearing a pair of those green-grey Army issue trainers, faded blue, baggy cotton trousers and an tatty old polo shirt hanging out of his trousers; and he was wearing a pair of Ray-Bans. The other bloke was equally scruffy, much heavier build, and was dragging bags out of the car boot. I swear, I thought they were both bodyguards. But when no one else got out I realised that the taller, thinner one was General Rose. I was a bit shocked. You don't expect three-star generals to be dressed like that, do you?'

'You're jumping ahead a bit here, Milos. When was that?'

It was Sunday 26 June 1994. I'd had about six months in the UK. I can remember it so clearly now, when the posting to Northern Ireland was abruptly stopped. That's when I'd first met you, Ian, in Woolwich, the end of November 1993 or thereabouts.

I'd been miserable in those first few days after Brian Nicol had picked me up at Lyneham. I spent the days unpacking from Bosnia and repacking for two years in NI. On the third day the phone had rung. It was Major Simon Barry, the Regimental Adjutant in Aldershot, asking me to come in and collect my flight ticket for Belfast and to have a chat. I'd walked into his office and he'd taken one look at me and come to the very swift conclusion that the NI posting was all wrong. Within the hour I'd been marched in front of the CO of 23 Parachute Field Ambulance, who'd reiterated Simon's words and added that I should see a psychiatrist to get a second opinion on the posting. So I did and had driven all the way to Woolwich in south-east London and redid the on-the-couch bit for the third time. Your recommendation had been that I must get a decent amount of leave immediately otherwise there'd be a problem. This time the advice was heeded by the system and I was called to the Regimental Colonel's home where Colonel David Parker was resting, having just broken his leg on a parachute jump. He'd told me to take two months leave immediately, that the NI posting would be stopped and a job would be found for me somewhere on the mainland. It's strange but, being tribal, it's always your Regiment and not the Army that ends up really looking after you. As far as the Army's concerned you're just another plug to be used to block a leaking hole.

Leave wasn't as bad as that period in June, but not much better. I was listless. It followed a predictable pattern. Potter around during the day. I organised my slides, created a sort of pictographic, retrospective diary. But that only made the isolation worse. My mind was still on the people out there. I spent a lot of time on the phone to people in UNHCR Sarajevo, fretted a lot about how the monitoring was going on the Serb side. In early December there was a sort of Op GRAPPLE 1 reunion in a bar in Soho with most of the old crew – Brigadier Andrew Cumming, Richard Barrons, Glynne Evans, Larry Hollingworth, Jeremy Braid. That was good, but by and large I was alone and drinking a lot – the pub and then whisky at home. I shudder when I think of it. I reckon I was getting through at least half a bottle of whisky before I could get to sleep, to blot out the thoughts and images. It got so bad that I even went out to Germany and spent Christmas and New Year with Peter and Jane Jones. That was better, but of course, what did we do? We talked about Sarajevo the whole time. It must have driven Jane mad. I was also slightly worried at the time. I'd got this order posting me as a grade 3 staff officer, SO3 G3 Training/O&D, to a place I'd never heard of nor knew existed – 49 (East Midlands) Brigade, a TA brigade headquarters, staffed by regulars but managing a number of TA battalions.

I didn't much like the sound of it. Fear of the unknown, I suppose. What I knew about staff work, paper shuffling and pen pushing could have been written on the back of a stamp. I'd never been an Adjutant or an Ops Officer in a battalion. I'd spent nearly all my time either on operations or in the field. In many respects my profile wasn't exactly balanced. What did I know about that side of the Army? More to the point what happened in Nottingham? I didn't even know that we had TA brigades. Also, Nottingham was 150 miles from Farnham, from the museum, so several years of weekend commuting didn't appeal. I bought that bloody house specifically because it was only four miles from Aldershot and I had never really lived in it.

I was due to start there on 10 January 1994, but something happened on 4 January. Nick Costello rang me in Farnham to say that he'd just been pinged to go out with General Rose to Sarajevo at the end of the month. It blew me away, not least because I hadn't a clue that Rose had been nominated to replace the Belgian Commander of BHC, General Briquemont, who had himself replaced General Morillon in 1993, but was for some reason being short-toured after only about seven months out there. I knew that Nick had never been to Sarajevo, that none of them had. The only real institutional knowledge of the place rested with those who'd served in BRITDET. Sniffing an opportunity to get back out there, I wrote directly to General Rose in the hope that he'd take the both of us out, and thus spare me the anguish of flying a desk. It didn't work. Some colonel in the personnel branch at Wilton wrote back a snotty letter reminding me that I'd forgotten to date mine with 1994, adding that Nick had been selected because he'd had nine months rest back in the UK but that I'd be borne in mind should the situation require it. I was fuming. So with a heavy heart I drove north on 10 January to the Land That Time Forgot, Chilwell, Nottingham, home of 49 (EM) Brigade HQ. Home also to an outfit called the Military Works Force and to a whole lot of odds and sods. It was a real backwater and, worse still, the camp was hugely depressing as it had been a First World War shell-filling factory. I can't even bring myself to talk about the place.

It was a dreadful place. First off, everyone in the HQ was married and they lived on the 'patch', so I only ever saw them during working hours. I lived in this creaky old mansion building, whose sole occupants were older commissioned-from-the-ranks Military Works Force types, also weekend commuters. They insisted on candlelit dinners every evening. It's okay once in a while, but not every sodding night. There were only about five of us. Eventually I just stopped eating with them and took to eating in my room. None of them, either at work or in that mausoleum of a Mess, had been to Bosnia so you couldn't talk to anyone about it. Just weren't interested. You kept it all inside, and drank, and wished away the week to escape day – Friday – when I'd hare down the M1 to the sanctuary of Farnham. The early Monday morning run up north was depressing and bitterly cold on the bike. The work was undemanding and I'd wrestle with such momentous decisions as to how to divide up seventy 66mm HEAT rockets between five bickering TA battalions. You couldn't imagine a job more diametrically opposed to Bosnia.

There was just nothing there to get the pulse racing. The Chief of Staff described it as an ideal posting for relaxing and getting into hunting, shooting and fishing. He would: he was a cavalry officer. But since I've never done huntin', shootin' and fishin' I couldn't have given a stuff about those opportunities. My main aim was to produce paperwork that would not come back from the Brigadier covered in red ink. He'd even circle in red a staple which was not exactly at forty-five degrees to the corner of the page. It was a nightmare, straight out of *Blackadder Goes Forth*. My only amusement, which was also a huge frustration as well, was to follow Bosnia on the television. General Rose seemed to have gripped the situation, especially after the 5 February Merkale marketplace massacre, which left me fretting about Minka because she lived just round the corner and used to shop there frequently. Nick used to ring me regularly from Sarajevo, which further increased my sense of isolation and frustration. During that period I was dragged down to

Wilton for two weeks to work in the J2 Int cell because they knew nothing about the city nor of the personalities on the Serb side. That infuriated my Brigadier, who resented my absence from his centre of the universe.

Then, in April, came the crisis over Gorazde when Rose initiated air strikes against the Serbs, who were attacking the place (a UN safe area) – the first air strikes of the war. That caused a storm, especially when a Royal Navy Sea Harrier was shot down over Gorazde. That was the worst moment, by far it was the worst moment for me.

One day my father rang me in the office. He was beside himself with excitement that the Serbs had shot it down. He saw Rose as the enemy and told me how thankful he was that I wasn't out there with him, how sorry he felt for Nick. How do you think that made me feel? You're part of the British Army, but your father sees one of its generals as the enemy. Madness. After that I too was secretly pleased I wasn't out there, simply for my father's sake. He'd had a massive heart attack in March 1992 and I'd been rushed back from Kuwait, Cat A Compassionate, as they thought he'd die. He survived, just, but he was never the same and the stress of following the wars in Yugoslavia was going to get him in the end. At the time I figured I wouldn't do anything to add to that stress and just bit my tongue there in Chilwell.

Then it all changed. Towards the beginning of April I got a surprise phone call. I was fiddling around with some rubbish, how many bullets to each battalion or whatever, and the voice at the other end of the phone says, 'This is Colonel Jamie Daniel on the J3 desk at Wilton. Nick Costello's got to come back at the end of June to attend Junior Division of the Staff College. We're looking for someone to replace him for the last seven months of General Rose's tour. Would you be prepared to go back out?' Knocked me out. I weighed up the effect it would have on my father against the benefits for Minka, Nada Miletic, and Tomo and Vera. For better or worse I said yes. Jamie Daniell seemed pleased and told me that he too would be following me out a month later to go and be Rose's MA, Military Assistant.

You can guess what happened next. I made the dreaded phone call. My father went ballistic. He told me that I was no longer his son and he cut me off for a whole week. That's the way it was. I immediately regretted my decision, but there was no going back. You make your own choices in life and have to live with them. It's that simple. My Brigadier was none too pleased either and resented me being pulled away. He had no choice though. Operational requirements take priority over peacetime soldiering. Secretly, I was delighted to be leaving Chilwell and to be getting back to doing what I'd joined the Army to do. But there were still three months of living in the mausoleum left.

Fate played its hand again in Chilwell, one Monday in early May. I'd just come back from the dentist in Melton Mowbray. I'd had three injections and a mouth that felt as though Mike Tyson had laid into me. I was summoned to the Chief of Staff's office; he gave me a bollocking for missing Monday morning PT, wasn't interested that I'd had a dental appointment. He warned me that the Brigadier was none too pleased and that I was now to go in front of him for another bollocking. In I went, thinking how pathetic it all was, then the Brigadier just pulled a bottle of champagne from his drawer, popped the cork and congratulated me for picking up an MBE on the operational list. An MBE for that work I'd done in 1993.

I was astonished. There I was trying to sip this bubbly but, because I had no feeling in my mouth, it was dribbling down my pullover. A cross. A bloody cross. Minka saw it. She said I'd get a gong in the shape of a cross, the last time I saw her I hadn't believed her. She was right. She *saw* it! She saw it all.

By mid-June my father and I had more or less patched things up. He'd become reconciled to the fact that I'd always do what I wanted to do and that there was no point kicking against it. I even went and saw my parents a week before my departure. Our parting was nowhere near as emotional as the first time. On the way back to Farnham I stopped by General Jackson's house in Tidworth. They lived next to the Roses and I met Angela Rose and Nick Costello's wife, who was visiting Lady Rose. She took her duties of looking after the General's staff's families very seriously and I felt then that I'd be going back out into good hands.

Nick and I had cooked up my arrival between us, a cunning plan which would fly me straight into Sarajevo on the aid flights from Ancona. For that I'd need a new UN ID card. I'd sent him a couple of passport photos and he'd sent back another *Stanley* ID card. The plan was simple. Jump on Friday 24 June's Herc at Lyneham. Fly via Gioia del Colle to Ancona. Cross-load to an aid flight and go straight into Sarajevo. Met by Nick and a four-day hand-over–take-over. Couldn't be simpler, eh? Talk about the best laid plans of mice and men.

Just about everything went wrong. The first thing that happened was that the car I'd hired to drive to Lyneham was hit by a big black crow, which cracked the windscreen, a bad omen if ever there was one. Then the Herc broke down before we'd even got into it, so the flight was delayed. We got to Gioia del Colle, from where the RAF Op DENY FLIGHT Jaguars were operating. The Herc packed up there as well, delaying us even further. By the time we'd landed in Ancona the last aid flight had gone.

I was met by an RAF flight lieutenant who told me that there was a change of plan. Things had calmed down in Sarajevo after the post-marketplace massacre showdown between the Serbs and threatened NATO air strikes. The Serbs had withdrawn their heavy weapons outside a twenty-kilometre Total Exclusion Zone or corralled them in weapons collection sites supervised by the UN. The situation in and around the city had relaxed to such an extent that Blue Routes had been opened in and out of Sarajevo allowing virtual free movement for the Serbs and the Bosnians. Trade was starting up and aid convoys were beginning to replace some of the costly aid flights into the airport. None of this helped me. There were no aid flights out of Ancona during the weekend, so it looked as though I wouldn't be getting into Sarajevo until Monday morning, which would give Nick and me approximately one day to hand-over and take-over the job.

We rang Nick in Sarajevo, who had cooked up a hair-brained plan to get me into Sarajevo by Sunday evening. General Rose, his bodyguard, a monster called Goose, and an American Special Forces signaller, Dave Pitts, were in Naples for the weekend, where Rose was meeting with CINCSOUTH (Commander in Chief Allied Forces South), an American Admiral called Leighton Smith. Somehow, I was to get myself to Naples, find some obscure hotel, meet up with Dave Pitts on Saturday night and then hook up with General Rose and Goose on the Sunday morning for their hop back to Split. It seemed absurd to go all the way down to Naples, hundreds of miles away, in order to fly to Split, which was only fifty miles from Ancona across the Adriatic. But that was the plan.

The next day I set off in a hire car with the flight lieutenant and drove south, crossing the Apennines, skirting Rome, passing Monte Cassino and arrived in Naples in early evening. That was the easy bit over. It took ages to locate this seedy one-star hotel opposite a US Navy compound. We even managed to locate Dave Pitts' room. A short, swarthy and athletic looking soldier in shorts opened the door. It was Pitts, but he hadn't a clue who I was. No one had told him and it was obvious that I wasn't even expected. Goose was off somewhere at a function with Rose. The worst thing was that Dave Pitts told me that the aircraft taking them back to Split the next day was one of those little white American cigar-shaped executive jets and that there'd probably be no room for me and my luggage. All of this was unhelpful and I dreaded the drive back up to Ancona. We decided to stay the night and see if I could be squeezed in the next day.

The next day Dave Pitts and I were sitting in the sweltering heat on the dispersal pan at Naples airport. The little US Navy Lear exec-jet was parked off to one side. This car pulls up and out jump these two scruffy blokes, General Rose and Goose. I introduced myself to Rose. He was completely unfazed and said something like 'Welcome aboard. Right, let's go!' Mercifully, we managed to squeeze me and my kit in and then took off almost immediately.

We circled higher and higher over Naples gaining altitude. Goose was sitting opposite me. He was enormous with a battered craggy face and short, black, greased-back hair. Not the sort of bloke you'd like to find peering at you through the bushes on a dark night. Our knees were virtually locked together due to the cramped confines of the cigar. The General was on the other side of the aisle peering intently through the window. Suddenly he stiffened up, 'Look at that, Goose!' Goose craned forward and peered out of the window at Naples' football stadium some 14,000 feet below. 'Perfect for a lob-in, eh Goose?' said Rose with some satisfaction. 'Yes, Boss,' replied the BG dutifully. Apparently the Boss was a mad keen free-faller. I just sat there listening to this little lot, lost for words and wondering whether this looney was suddenly going to give us all parachutes and lead us out of the door! That was my introduction to the helter-skelter life of the next seven months. It wasn't exactly normal.

Within the hour we'd landed at Split airport. Goose and I had chatted on the way over. I remembered him from his days in the early 1980s when he was a Tom in A Company 1 PARA. He asked me a lot about the state of the Company and the Battalion, did I know so-and-so. His ominous size and appearance belied an unexpectedly soft nature, which was evident in the tone of his speech. To my surprise we were whisked through arrivals and straight into the VIP lounge. No showing of passports or ID cards, much to my relief. I didn't have a passport, not in the name of Stanley anyway. The wheels were definitely well greased for this general. Without further ado, we were picked up by the BHC Rear protocol officer in a fleet of cars.

Much had changed since my departure. COMBRITFOR and HQ BRITFOR had moved up country to Gornji Vakuf under Brigadier Reith and had become a proper UN HQ in its own right – HQ Sector South-West. The old HQ BRITFOR block in Divulje barracks had become HQ BH Command Rear – logistics support. HQ BH Command Main was still in the hotel in Kiseljak and Rose's BH Command Forward, an expanded tactical HQ of Portakabins, was in General Morillon's and Briquemont's old Residency HQ in Sarajevo. Rose had been horrified at the bloated size of the Kiseljak HQ compared with the spartan Forward HQ in the city and had stripped out what was essential, relocated to the Residency and had created an efficient functioning HQ there. Kiseljak ceased to figure very much at all.

The most important change of all was that the Croats and Muslims in Central Bosnia were no longer fighting. A peace deal brokered by the Washington Accord of March 1994 had ended that 'war-within-a-war' and created a being called the Federation. Tensions were still high, but there was no fighting. Their focus, after a year of ghastly and pointless bloodshed, was now fixed firmly on the old enemy – the Serb.

We spent the whole afternoon hanging around COMBRITFOR's villa on Ciovo island. Our hop in one of 845's Sea Kings into Sarajevo wasn't booked until late afternoon. Rose sat in the sun reading a paper. Goose and Dave Pitts sat around doing nothing and I was at a complete loose end. No one said a word. At the time I thought they were the most unfriendly bunch of people I'd ever met. It wasn't that, though. They were an incredibly close team and I was still an outsider.

The first attempt to fly to Sarajevo ended in near disaster. One of the Sea King's engines packed up, overheated, and we had to return to Split to get into another one. It was early evening by the time we flew over Ilidza and then skipped low and fast down the length of the city. I was astounded. Seven months earlier no one would have dreamt of flying a helicopter down the length of Sniper's Alley. Now it seemed so commonplace. As we neared the eastern end of the city Goose nudged me and pointed out of the port window. 'The Boss takes us running up that each day.' I gazed at the steep hill called Hum, which I knew to be just behind the Residency. My heart sank. I knew that Rose had a thing about fitness.

The Sea King flared on finals and dropped into Zetra football stadium. An armoured Range Rover and armoured snatch Land Rover scooped us up and whisked us off to the Residency some 600 metres away. As we swung in, a Danish guard saluted smartly. I was immediately struck by the double-storey, white Portakabin City which had grown, cancer-like, around the Residency building. During my time there'd just been the building, the former Delegates Club, which had boasted one of the finest restaurants in Sarajevo. It had been hired as Morillon's and then Briquemont's Residency. During their time it had been just the building and the walled garden, chosen because it was five minutes walk from the Bosnian Presidency on Marshal Tito Street. Now it was a bustling headquarters.

The bottom of the Residency was given over to a reception area, a large dining-room and kitchens. The first floor contained the General's office and bedroom, Victor Andreyev's office and, sandwiched between the two, the Outer Office. This was a large room shared by the General's and Victor's personal staff. On our side of the house desks were occupied by Lt Col. Simon Shadbolt, a Royal Marine who was Rose's MA, Captain Jeremy Bagshaw ('Baggers'), his ADC, by Jean, a Wren, who acted as the PA, and by Nick's desk. At the other end of the room were Andreyev's MA, a Canadian captain called Pat Drey, and a couple of Civil Affairs staff. It didn't look like any senior officer's Outer Office I'd ever seen before. There was an almost manic air about the place; an expensive looking portrait of a nude hung behind the MA's desk, while on the other side of the room this young Canadian was screaming his head off. A second door opened to the outside and led to a wooden landing which in turn connected to raised wooden duckboards running the length of the top row of Portakabins.

Above the Outer Office were three rooms in which the General's staff squatted. One was given over to the bodyguards, Goose and a Royal Military Police sergeant called Frank, and to the second driver, UJ, and the General's house sergeant of five years' standing, Sergeant Mick Daly. A second room was occupied by the MA, ADC and Nick. The third was occupied by Victor Andreyev's driver, Mac, a lance corporal from 216 Parachute Signals Squadron. Although it amounted to indoor camping again, it was leagues more luxurious than my previous grott in the PTT building. The remainder of the HQ's staff were accommodated in spartan conditions in an annex.

The next day Nick whipped me around the city, introducing me to all his contacts. Among them were a bunch of shady mafiosos who seemed to be the point of contact for the Sarajevo football team, which Rose was keen to get to the UK for a fixture. Next stop was to a home-grown children's aid organisation called 'Flowers of Love'. Apparently some brigadier in the UK was in contact with them and one of Nick's duties was to act as postman – not an unfamiliar one to me. One of the Flowers of Love was a Muslim lady, Jasna Pandurevic, who clearly adored Nick. As we left the place Nick muttered something about her being desperate to get out; her husband, Ranko, was a Serb in hiding and they had a four-year-old daughter, Maja, who, coming from a mixed marriage, had little hope if they stayed. It all sounded depressingly familiar. Nick added something about having made Jasna a promise of some sort. Much of the day was spent rushing around with Nick saying goodbye to various people. We even went to the Presidency where Nick tracked down Haris Silajdzic, the Prime Minister, and got him to stick his signature in a book all about the shelling of Sarajevo. The weird thing was that Nick had collected signatures from Karadzic and Mladic and all the Serbs in the same book and Silajdzic didn't bat an eyelid when adding his own.

As we walked back to the Residency for lunch, Nick turned to me and just said, 'There's one other thing you should know . . . we run an operation and get people out of the city . . . just drive them out, those who want to go . . . those with no money and no hope . . .' I was a bit stunned, recalling how dreadful it had been getting Una's parents out and how I'd sworn never to do it again. Nick seemed to read my thoughts, '. . . it's all right. The General knows, we tell him each time we're doing it. He sees it in the spirit of the humanitarian mandates and so long as we do it on an equitable basis, for those who are desperate, then it's okay. No one gives a shit as the Blue Routes are open and we just zip 'em out onto the Serb side from where they make their own way.' I still wasn't sold on the thing, which sounded risky, and asked him what of the Muslims and Croats who were dumped on the Dark Side. 'Simple, they go unmolested because the Serbs know that if they interfere with them then none of their people get out.' It seemed that just about everyone was in some way involved – the drivers, Pat Drey, Goose, even the American communicators, and all with the General's and Victor Andreyev's nod.

Nick justified it. 'Look, there are four ways out of this place. If you've got money then you can buy your way out with the mafia who control the tunnel under the airport, or you can bribe one of the more unscrupulous UN contingents who charge 1,000 Deutschmarks per head. If you've got no money you're pretty much fucked, and if you're still desperate you can take your chances and try and leg it over the line ... it's usually fatal as the landmines or snipers get you ... and then there's us ... Schindler's List.' I remember asking him, 'You don't call it that, do you?' 'Oh yeah we do ... Schindler's List ... whose name is on the List today?' Nick had laughed. 'How many?' I'd asked. 'Loads so far ... but we don't keep a list, it just gets done and then forgotten about ... Jasna and her family are next, I've promised them, but haven't managed it so far as it's difficult to get all three of them together at the same time when we've got the time.' I didn't press Nick too closely, but it looked as though I was inheriting a promise as well as this Schindler's List thing, all of which seemed to have been sanctioned from above. At the time, I just remember logging it and hoping that the problem would disappear as soon as Nick left. I wasn't massively keen on doing any of it.

The only other thing of any significance was that I met Ljljana and Ljerka again, the two Serb women with whom I'd worked when monitoring the aid distribution on the Dark Side. I'd left Ljiljana in Ilidza having hurled some insult at her, and Ljerka in tears. The evening of the hand-over Nick, Pat Drey and I went over to Ilidza and had a meal with Ljerka and Ljiljana in a café. Pat Drey had a girlfriend over there, Sonja, only eighteen, but she was also one of the police people on the S-4 checkpoint into the city. I half expected to get the sharp end of Ljiljana's tongue, but she was all smiles and hugs. She'd completely forgiven me and our contretemps was never mentioned again. That's what people are like out there – at each other's throats one minute, the best of friends the next ... the errant Slav gene ... up, down, up, down, up, down ... nothing new to me. I've been that way all my life. Every nation has an errant gene, something that marks the ethnic or national characteristic ...

The next day Nick departed with all his bags, all set to see his wife again and get stuck into JCSC. General Rose went too, on eighteen days' leave. They both flew out together from Split in one of those RAF exec-jets, HS 125s, which are laid on for the Brass and operate out of RAF Northolt in north-west London. In theatre for twenty-four hours, then the man I'm working for ups and takes two and a half weeks' leave. It gave me a chance to get my feet under the table. Simon Shadbolt suggested I grab a vehicle and spend the time renewing all my old contacts; he even suggested I shoot off to Serbia and visit my family graveyard, which I'd never seen. I wasn't keen on that, driving around on the other side of the Drina on my own in a white UN vehicle, so I didn't bother. There were people closer to home to see. I spent the first few days visiting Minka, Nada, Tomo and Vera and the gang at UNHCR Sarajevo, who had moved out of the PTT building into plush and hushed offices in the Cenex building, a mirrored glass affair, which looked like a bordello from outside. UNHCR had civilised itself but in so doing had also lost some of that appealing mania, which had so characterised its existence in the PTT building.

Before he'd left, Nick had told me that I wouldn't recognise Sarajevo. He'd meant that things had got better since my time there in 1993. True, there was no shelling, the trams were up and running, shop windows were being replaced, the Blue Routes were bringing trade into the city and restaurants were springing up all over the place. You'd scarcely believe there was a war going on. In a funny sort of way all this had made Sarajevo into a ghastly place and not the sophisticated city I remembered . . .

These improvements were all superficial. Any place is the sum total of its people. Sarajevo used to be this cosmopolitan mix of sophisticates who couldn't have cared less who was who. The trams were running but beneath that superficiality a lot had changed for the worse. Anyone with any sense, and who was young enough, had legged it as soon as the Blue Routes had opened up. They just cleared off to the West or elsewhere as fast as their little legs could carry them. In their stead a torrent of ethnically cleansed peasants from the hills and from Sandzak had flooded into the city bringing with them their goats, cows and chickens. You'd see cows grazing on the grass verges along Sniper's Alley; you'd see peasants with their goats and chickens on the trams. As far as I could see Sarajevo had lost its soul and had become a giant village.

Nick had told me that getting to know the Serb liaison officers to UNPROFOR, who hung out in a couple of offices in Lukavica barracks at the eastern end of the airport runway, was absolutely essential. The most immediate day-to-day business – i.e. anything – with the Serbs was done through them. During my time with BRITDET I'd stayed well clear of the place unless we'd had to go up to Pale and had needed stamped papers from them to proceed up the mountain. Even then I'd let Ljerka do all the talking as the head man, Major Milenko Indjic, had a fearsome reputation as an arch manipulator. He'd been an officer for sixteen years in the JNA's Counter Intelligence Service, KOS, and was well versed in the art of manipulation and in the dissemination and implantation of ideas into people's minds . . . all designed to cause doubt . . .

Each UN battalion in Sarajevo had liaison officers all of whom swung through Major Indjic's office every day on some business or other. He'd see them all individually over a Slivo and coffee and would tell each of them different things – all calculated according to some worked-out scheme. He was bloody good at it. On one occasion in 1993 he'd so manipulated the two LOs from FREBAT 2 and FREBAT 4 that both French battalions ended up not speaking to each other for a week. Clever bastard, and dangerous too, but everything went through him. If you wanted to drive vehicles from Sarajevo through the Sierras to Kiseljak you had to ring him up in advance with the number of vehicles, the registration numbers, the names of the passengers and their bloody ID card numbers. If you didn't do it you just didn't get through.

Even General Rose came up against it. Freedom of movement for the UN simply didn't exist, not on the Dark Side. It all had to be haggled for. Nauseating, but that's the way it was. Indjic even had the looks to go with it – everything dark and black – eyebrows, moustache, neat swept-back hair, all black . . . but his eyes, black-brown, glittering, feral, darting . . . penetrating . . . and his voice – deep, monotonous, bass . . . gravelly . . . this bloke wasn't just manipulative and cunning. He was extremely adept at playing complex, exhaustive mind games. In 1993 I had avoided him like the plague but now I had no choice.

One day I went over to Indjic's to establish my credentials, fully expecting to be mentally savaged like the Sector Sarajevo LOs, whom he treated like shit . . . in the nicest possible way. Instead he was all glittering, toothy smiles, simply because I was now Rose's man and spoke with Rose's voice. The bigger the fish you represent, the more they sit up and take notice of you, so it was all pretty cordial in that office at the end of a dark cold corridor, in that grubby little office with cheap furniture and walls that stank of tobacco and Slivo. There were three of them in that office – Indic, his oppo Major Brane Luledzija, and their 'secretary', Biljana Andjeljkovic, who remembered me from 1993. She'd run the Serbian Red Cross in Grbavica and had since cross-loaded to the Serb liaison office in Lukavica. That was the beginning of a fascinating, complex relationship, all personality driven, all mind games.

In the evenings I'd go out for a pizza with Mick Daly, a Coldstream Guardsman. That had been Rose's original Regiment so it followed that his staff, including the house sergeant and the ADC, came from the Coldstream Guards. Mick had been with the General for five years and was coming to the end of his time in the Army. When Rose came back from leave he'd be bringing with him a new batman. I had two weeks in which to pick Mick Daly's brains and find out what my new Boss was like. It was important really because once you get over the shock of working for a three-star you realise that you're working for a 'personality'. This particular 'personality' had a big reputation. If you've never met these people then you've only ever heard of their reputations. If the Boss doesn't like you you're out.

I picked Mick's brain shamelessly. He was a Geordie and, more importantly, one of that dying breed of Kipling's Tommy Atkins, a rogue and a scoundrel, but utterly loyal and devoted to his general. Mick's insight into the Rose personality was gold dust to me, but daunting too. The son of an officer in the Indian Army, educated at Cheltenham College, Oxford and the Sorbonne, failed to make it into the RAF as a pilot (he'd tried to land an Air Training Corps light aircraft on the runway as a Shackleton had been taking off) Mike Rose had been commissioned into the Coldstream Guards. From there he'd joined the SAS, during which time he'd served as a troop commander in Aden and had risen to command the Regiment. His tour as CO had seen both the Iranian Embassy Siege of 1980 and the Falklands War of 1982, during both of which he'd deployed himself to theatre. He'd gone on to command an infantry brigade in Northern Ireland and then the 2nd Infantry Division in York. Then he was Commandant of the Army Staff College at Camberley followed by Deputy Cin CUKLF, in which job he'd been pinged to be Commander Bosnia-Hercegovina. He was an operational soldier, non-Germany, non-NATO, all brush fire wars.

All this was good bloody intelligence from Mick Daly. 'You'll be all right, you've got wings on your arm!' was one thing he said which sticks in my mind; the other was the best bit of advice I ever got from anyone: '. . . don't take any shit off him. He hates yes-men and sycophants . . . he'd much rather hear the bitter truth than a whole load of brown-nosing grovelling this-is-what-I-think-the-General-wants-to-hear bollocks. Works with other generals, but not with him. Tell him the truth and battle to have it heard and although he might not agree, he'll respect you for fighting your corner and being forthright. He hates wafflers.' When Mick told me that I took it all in but I reserved judgement. You can never be sure whether you're being fed a line by a salty old SNCO, being stitched up, only to find the first time you lock horns with the Boss he rips your head off!

Everything Daley said was one hundred per cent accurate. You could see it at work even in Rose's absence. Most evenings you'd see these two journalists, Kurt Schork of Reuters and a much younger bloke in his early twenties, Joel Brand, a freelance stringer for *Newsweek* and *The Times*, perched on chairs in front of Simon Shadbolt's desk sharing a whisky and chinwagging for an hour or so about the General's line and the situation. Both were Americans and both were pretty incisive, hostile even, to Rose and the UN. They'd both been in the city since the start of the war, were deeply immersed in the whole show and, not to put too fine a point on it, emotionally attached to the situation. I couldn't believe my eyes when I first saw these two guzzling the General's whisky, pontificating and holding forth. I couldn't understand why Rose allowed it, particularly in his absence.

To the casual observer it looked pretty strange but that's to misunderstand the point completely, which is that he deliberately patronised these two precisely because they took opposite points of view to him – they were foils, if you like. Daly was right. And to get on in that environment you had to understand that simple basic psychological fact: Rose was confrontational, and he thrived on it.

That was one small example of his unconventional approach. The other was in the nature of the relationship between the individuals in the 'team'. On my first day Simon Shadbolt told me to stop calling him 'Colonel' and to call him Simon. It was all first name terms except with the General, who was 'General', 'Sir' or, if you were Goose, 'Boss'. In a nutshell Rose preferred to operate the Outer Office as though it was a small SAS team. Coming from the red ink nightmare of staples at forty-five degrees in Chilwell, for me the whole set-up was positively relaxing – unusual, but relaxing. All that mattered were results, not how you achieved them. Rose would frequently storm at wafflers, 'Don't tell me how a fucking watch works! Just tell me what the time is!'

The HQ set-up took some getting used to. It didn't consist just of the Outer Office: there was much more crammed into the grounds. Broadly speaking, it consisted of three parts. There was the building itself, but also a large conference/briefing room and an area tucked away where a British Army signals detachment, hidden away like troglodytes, beavered away providing strategic communications back to the UK. The Portakabins nearest the Outer Office and linked by wooden duckboards consisted of the most critical cells. On the bottom were the G3 Ops cell, run by Lt Col. Nick Magnell, the G2 Mil Info cell and the Air Operations Co-ordination Cell, AOCC, which dealt with any 'air' over Bosnia and had a direct link to NATO's 5 ATAF in Italy. Above them were Portakabins occupied by the BHC Chief of Staff, Major General Van Baal. He was Dutch, as was his entire staff. Next to them were the JCOs, the Joint Commission Observers, in a single Portakabin. Beyond them were the G4 Movements people, convoys and the like, and finally there was a Civil Affairs office. There were other Portakabins elsewhere in the compound given over to such activities as Geo-Survey . . . maps to you and me.

That wasn't the end of it. There were yet more people secreted away in another annex – Claire Grimes and her Public Information team, the Plans people, the G5 Civil-Military relations people, who worked at re-establishing utilities on both sides of the line . . . pretty much unsung heroes. Then, on one floor of the annex was another team of bleepy troglodytes, a gang of US NATO, not UN, communications specialists. They rarely showed themselves and yet their antennae and mysterious boxes festooned the annex. Their precise function at the time was a mystery to me but later it became painfully obvious. There were other Americans knocking around too. Lt Col. Gordon Rudd, US Army Special Forces, was the NATO liaison officer who provided the direct link to CINCSOUTH, Admiral Leighton Smith in Naples. Lt Col. Clifford Schroeder worked in the G2 Mil Info cell and Major Michelle Stinton, long time in Bosnia, worked in the G5 cell. Then there were the American communicators, Special Forces again, from Stuttgart in Germany. Dave Pitts was one of them, the other was a sergeant called Studervant. They accompanied the General everywhere. Their sole job was to carry around the TACSAT, Tactical Satelite radio, so that Rose could have instant, secure satellite comms with whomsoever, wherever he was . . .

The TACSAT had a US 6th Fleet crypto in it in order to allow communications to Admiral Smith in Naples. The Americans weren't going to allow the Brits to walk about with one of their secure codes without supervision. These communicators were changed about every three months, so that they wouldn't go native. Dave Pitts left shortly after my arrival and was replaced by a sergeant called Jim Lenski. Whenever we were on the road there'd be two vehicles. Leading was Rose's armoured Range Rover, always driven by Goose. Backing that was the armoured snatch Land Rover driven by UJ, a Brit signaller, with me as the passenger in the front so that I could leap out and leg it to catch up with Rose whenever he decided to stop and get out to talk to some local, which he loved to do. It made me into quite a good sprinter as you had to be on his shoulder by the time he'd exhausted his entire vocabulary of Serbo-Croat, which was pretty much limited to 'dobar dan – good day'!

In the back of the snatch would be Sergeant Frank Cannon, the Royal Military Policeman and second bodyguard, and one or both of the American communicators. That was our little group on the road. The only thing that varied was whom Rose decided would accompany him in the Range. Usually it was the MA, who acted as his scribe during meetings, or it might include the ADC, Captain Jeremy Bagshaw – if he needed a break from wrestling with three telephones all making demands from Zagreb, Italy, New York, the UK and keeping control of the General's rolling programme. If you ask me it was the worst job of the lot. The phones never stopped ringing and he never stopped pulling his hair out.

That was the set-up. Everyone had their job and responsibilities. Goose was protection and the vehicles, I was the mouth, the MA was the scribe, the Americans provided mobile secure comms, Baggers sorted the Generals admin and Jean was the PA. It all functioned pretty well.

The JCOs were yet another bunch of LOs, just to add to that list of ECMM officers, UKLOs, UNMOs and the various UN battalions' LOs. When the Muslim-Croat cease-fire was brokered in Washington in early 1994 this lot, all Brits, were established to act as observers for the Joint Muslim-Croat Commission, chaired by the UN. Their main function was to map, monitor and report back on the state of the cease-fire line in Central Bosnia. When they'd come into existence someone in UK had used his head and ensured that the JCOs were not a repeat of the UKLOs, who were by and large much too young, untrained and not selected. The JCOs were all selected from across the Army and Services for their psychological suitability for working in small teams. Not only were they specially selected, but they were also adequately trained for the job and structured properly with officers and NCOs. Consequently they were older, more mature and more self-confident in what they were doing than the rest of the UKLOs and UNMOs drifting around the Balkans. Many were Paras who'd all volunteered to escape the drudgery of life in Aldershot and Northern Ireland. Definitely a good adjunct to any peace support operation.

It didn't take long for Rose to spot their wider utility and he quickly stuck a team into Gorazde and elsewhere where accurate info was needed. When the Serbs had attacked Gorazde in April, one of the JCOs, a corporal from 2 PARA called Fergus Rennie, had been killed in crossfire and his officer, also a Para, wounded in the arm. Despite that, they were the most efficient of the eyes and ears on the ground, which is why Rose stuck their HQ in a Portakabin opposite his office. The whole gang was commanded by a major, with a captain who acted as the second in command. Unlike the UKLOs, the JCOs were a particularly useful force multiplier; they had high grade comms, credibility and were robust in facing up to local commanders.

On 4 July 1994, while Rose was still away, the Americans opened their Embassy next door to the Residency. The last shell to land in Sarajevo had done so months previously, so it was now safe enough for the State Department to hoist the Stars and Stripes above the building. It was only ever a part-time embassy in the sense that Ambassador Victor Jakovich and his staff, which included a John Menzies and a Jennifer Brush, still operated from the Vienna embassy and would only fly into Sarajevo when they needed to. Big party on the lawn, flag raising and a rousing speach from Victor Jakovich in Serbo-Croat which included the words, '. . . so long as that flag flies above the Embassy, we will never desert you . . .' Nice and rousing, good illusion, but the flag did come down when they all hopped off back to Vienna for strudels.

The British and the French also had embassies, but the British was run on a shoestring without anyone of ambassadorial status in charge. Our representative in Sarajevo was a Mr Bean type, whose sole interest seemed to be running the Bosnian-British friendship society at the embassy on Monday evenings. The number two was Steve, who was younger and brighter than Mr Bean. He basically cracked the whip and Mr Bean jumped.

While General Rose was still away I had to take the Foreign Secretary, Douglas Hurd, up to Pale. He and Alain Juppé, the French Foreign Minister, suddenly came out needing to go and talk to Karadzic and gang. The background to all this is that, as I arrived, the Contact Group, which consisted of an ad hoc, solve-the-Bosnia-crisis gang of five ambassadors from Britain, France, America, Russia and Germany had drawn a map for the settlement of the war in Bosnia – the Contact Group Plan, as it was known. It was a final, take it, or leave it and be bombed, plan. This was a powerful group that included Charles Redman representing the US, Pauline Neville-Jones the UK, and Vitaly Churkin the CIS. Their map was promulgated in June and the message went out loud and clear that there'd be no further movement on it. The Bosnian Serbs were making loud noises about rejecting it, so Hurd and Juppé arrived in Sarajevo bound for Pale in order to persuade Karadzic to accept it. Simon Shadbolt was busy so he told me to take Hurd up to Pale in a helicopter and then report back on what had happened.

It was a lot easier than I expected. We flew up in a Sea King. Hurd was all trussed up in a seatbelt so I got him to unbuckle, gave him a set of headphones and stood him up behind the pilot. As we flew east across the city I described for him where the front line lay, where it came down into the city, and where it ended beyond Bascarsija. Direct line of flight, Pale was only some ten miles and as many minutes away. By vehicle, winding over Mount Trebevic along a dreadfully narrow and twisting road, it took the best part of an hour, on a good summer's day. Within minutes we'd landed on a small football pitch in Pale, which was nothing more than a scattering of rich people's weekend homes nestling in an emerald-green valley. A cavalcade of Mercs and police cars, sirens blaring, picked us up and tore off to some hotel in town.

At the entrance to the hotel Dr Karadzic, hair all over the place, and one or two others met the Foreign Secretaries. Among them I spotted the man whom Nick had told me would be my main contact in Pale. He wasn't hard to pick out – smart suit, Jermyn Street double-cuffer shirt, expensive silk tie, round gold-rimmed glasses and bald head. Scholarly looking, donnish almost. That was Jovan Zametica, Karadzic's political advisor and press spokesman. Nick had said, 'You'll keep him sweet if you take up British newspapers and a copy of *Yachting Monthly*.'

Apparently, although born Omer Zametica to Muslim and German parents in Banja Luka, he'd completed a doctorate at Cambridge and had lived in academic splendour in England for eighteen years, during which time he'd Anglicised his Christian name to John, and then Balkanised it again to Jovan when he'd cross-loaded to the Karadzic camp from King's College London in 1993. Having taught at Marlborough School and in various other academic institutions in Britain, he spoke perfect English. Quite what this dapper man in his late thirties was doing mixed up with the Pale gang was beyond me, but, if it took a few papers and *Yachting Monthly* to keep him sweet, it was a small price to pay for gaining a foothold. I remember he took the papers from me without a murmur, almost as though they were some sort of tariff, and then imperiously announced that I'd be doing the interpreting. I told him to sod off, politely of course, saying that I was Hurd's escort not his interpreter. Zametica scowled at me, sunk his neck into his collar and skulked off after

**CONTACT GROUP PLAN
PROMULGATED JULY 1994**

N

BOSNIA-HERCEGOVINA

This map represents the last division of Bosnia-Hercegovina "offered" to the Bosnian Serbs by the international community, represented by the five-nation Contact Group (US, UK, France, Russia and Germany).

Bosnian Serbs

Federation of Bosnian Croats and Muslims

Sarajevo area under UN control

Over 27–28 July 1994, a general referendum was held across the Republika Srpska Bosnian Serb-held territory. The result was an overwhelming "no" to the Contact Group Plan.

0   km   50

the party into the dining-room. I sat right at the end of the table and took notes. Zametica was saddled with the interpreting.

The meeting accomplished nothing. Karadzic told the Foreign Secretaries that the Contact Group Plan was unacceptable to the Serbs and that they'd never accept it. He also announced that he'd be throwing the decision to the people in a referendum and that the people would decide. For his part Hurd urged him to say 'Yes and . . .' and not 'Yes but . . .' to the Contact Group Plan. The finesse of this wording, exactly what it meant and how the international community would interpret it were completely lost on me. Judging by his glazed eyes, Karadzic was equally baffled and seemed uninterested. After a quick lunch we packed up and flew back to Sarajevo where the Sea King dropped me off at the airport. I didn't have much to report to Simon, only that the Serbs looked likely to reject the CG Plan. Quite apart from the momentous ramifications that the decision would have on my life, none of which I was remotely aware of at the time, the meeting was my first exposure to the Serb politicians in their 'mountain stronghold of Pale' as the press called it.

General Mladic wasn't at the meeting – only politicians attended – but I had met Mladic a couple of days earlier during a separate meeting at Lukavica barracks. For some reason the Force Commander, a French general called Bertrand de Lapresle, who was Rose's immediate boss in Zagreb, had flown down for a meeting with Mladic. Again, Simon sent me along as the BHC representative to listen and take notes. The meeting was in this long conference room in the barracks. All the French along one side of the table, including General Soubirou the Sector Sarajevo commander who was still there, and the Serbs along the other side. I only got half of the meeting as the French did everything through their own interpreter in French. All I remember was Mladic banging on about the Muslims violating the DMZ on Igman and Bijelasnica and how the French were turning a blind eye to it all.

It was fascinating watching and listening to Mladic. Unlike the politicians in Pale he had *presence*. He was short and squat like a fist fighter, barrel-chested, broad-shouldered but with virtually no neck. His head seemed to be welded onto his shoulders. His fingers were short and fat, one of which sported this large gold ring with a black stone in it. His hair was close-cropped, silvery-grey, but his eyes were his most striking feature – pale blue, duck-egg blue, with little pin-point black pupils. They pierced like lasers, roving all over the place, as cold as a shark's. De Lapresle had said something, Mladic retorted and then finished, '. . . but that's war, isn't it?' but he did it by raising his eyebrows and furrowing his brow, nodding curtly as though to drive home his point. And all the while his eyes fixed unblinkingly on the Frenchman as the statement hung in the air. It was weird, but fascinating.

Next to him sat a major general, Zdravko Tolimir, who was their intelligence guru and doubled up as Mladic's note taker. Hazel eyes, receding, swept-back hair and little pot belly which strained against his Sam Browne cross belt. 'Who're you? You're not French!' he scribbled on a note to me. I scratched back who I was and whom I'd replaced. The next note simply read, 'I hope you do as good a job as he did!' I caught him staring at me, almost with hostility. I could see it was going to be an uphill struggle with this lot.

One evening I was having a beer at the UN fire station on Sniper's Alley. They were an interesting bunch, a complete home-grown organisation. Led by a hulking ex-US Marine Corps officer-turned-fireman called John Jordan, GOFERS, or the UN Emergency Medical and Fire Service, had grown from almost nothing in 1993 to a fully-fledged fire brigade service. It had been Big John's inspiration and he'd been the driving force behind the Rhode Island Volunteer Group, now renamed GOFERS. They'd shipped in old 1970s fire engines from Chicago and elsewhere and had dedicated themselves to putting out fires on both sides of the line. His gang were all volunteers and among them I found George Whitfield, who'd left 2eme REP at the end of 1993 and joined John's mob.

Their work was extremely hazardous. Not only did they find themselves tackling fires caused by Heath Robinson gas plumbing but they were frequently shot at in the course of doing this. In 1993 John had been badly beaten up by the Sarajevo mafia, who had objected to him putting out fires on the Serb side. His relationship with the Muslim authorities was never easy for precisely this reason. Unlike any other fire service in the world they were armed to the teeth with snipers' rifles, carbines, sub-machine guns and pistols. Their armoury made any British Army infantry company's look modest. When I'd left Sarajevo in November 1993 John had given me a Beretta 90 pistol. I'd refused it, saying I'd have no use for it in the UK. He'd laughed and just said, 'You'll be back. When you do, look me up and you can have it.' He was true to his word. Having arrived in theatre without a weapon I hunted him out and he produced it immediately.

Nearly all the people gathered that evening were firemen and -women, including locals. One or two were guests, officials, civvies from the US Embassy. One of them, Jennifer Brush, was banging on about the shelling in the city during 1993. She was irritating everyone, mainly because she was talking nonsense. George Whitfield was rolling his eyes – the Legion had decorated him for bravery during that period. John looked bored and just listened to this drivel. Eventually I said, 'You're talking through your arse. What the fuck do you know about it anyway? You lot weren't even here then.' She went off like a rocket and launched into a blistering anti-Serb, anti-UN, anti-Rose tirade. After she'd left, John told me that she was another State Department person at the embassy. Both she and Ambassador Jakovich had been educated in Sarajevo, had a long-standing affinity with the place, and had been selected for their current posts on that basis. Both reputedly spoke the language. Funny how no one could get it right. We sent Mr Bean to Sarajevo and they sent a bunch of rose-tinted-spectacle-wearing-less-than-objective-agenda-driven types to the place. I took an instant dislike to that woman. None of the firemen liked her either.

Suddenly, on Sunday 17 July, this bloody whirlwind stormed back into Sarajevo, all full of energy and ready to go. Rose had returned and the honeymoon was over. That Monday evening I was in the British Embassy during one of Mr Bean's Anglo-Bosnian love-ins and I found myself talking to Paddy Ashdown, who was over visiting his 'Liberal constituents'. I didn't recognise him immediately because he was dressed in a checked lumberjack shirt, fawn trousers and buckskin boots. He was pleasant enough and asked me what I did. When I told him he remarked that he'd just spent half an hour in Rose's office and commented that the General looked absolutely exhausted. It irritated me because it was not his place to make such comments and fish around for confirmation from one of Rose's staff. I put him straight – that Rose had just returned from over two weeks leave and was fully charged. Rose *was* fully charged up and ready to go, but it's interesting how perceptions sometimes seem to count for more than the truth.

He certainly didn't behave as if he were exhausted. The next day he popped his head out of his office and said, 'Fancy coming for a run with an old man?' It wasn't really a question. It was a direct order. It was baking hot in Sarajevo, nearly 40°C, really gopping and humid. So what did we do? Did he wait until it was cooler in the evening? No! We – Rose, Goose and me, followed by the backing vehicle – set off for a five-miler at two in the afternoon. Two and a half miles up this hill and then back down again, most of it in full view of Serb snipers, with the only thing protecting Rose from their bullets being Goose's sweating bulk. On the run back down the pace increased and I remember Rose muttering something like, 'This is what it's all about. This is what sets us apart. It's what makes us the best.' He was a driven man. I can't think of any fifty-five-year-old lieutenant generals in the Army who can do that, not in the way he did it. We're talking here of a full-blown run with a 500 metre sprint at the end. Half an hour later he was back in uniform behind his desk. Awesome! We did that four or five times a week, regardless of what was going on.

A few days later we were up on Mount Jahorina for a one-to-one meeting with General Mladic. I was supposed to be the interpreter. In fact it was the first time I'd done it for Rose. Mladic had brought along Major Brane Luledzija from Lukavica barracks as his. General Tolimir was there taking notes. I can't remember the exact details except that one of the topics was bloody incubators, for God's sake. Apparently, during the Gorazde crisis, letters and cheques had flooded in to Lady Rose as a result of the TV pictures of the plight of the hospital there. She'd hooked up with the British Red Cross and some £5,000 had been raised. The plan was that she'd come out with two incubators, one for the Serbs in Pale and one for the Muslims in Gorazde, all in the interests of impartiality. Mladic was pro the idea, guaranteeing full co-operation and remarking that Rose's predecessor, General Briquemont, had done a similar thing for all sides.

I wasn't too fussed about the incubators. When you're struggling to interpret you can barely remember a bloody thing that's been said. From my point of view the meeting was a total disaster. I just couldn't keep up with Rose. He rattled away like a machine gun, almost without pause. Forget being able to speak a language. That has no relevance whatsoever when it comes to simultaneous interpretation. You've actually got to be trained to do that and then you've got to have an almost computer-like brain to do it. I had neither the training nor the brain. It was a nightmare – you'd miss something, panic about missing it and before you know it you've missed the next bloody sentence and then you'd be locked into an unrecoverable, terminal death dive. Horrifying. And, all the time Rose is getting frustrated because you can't keep up. It was almost like translating verbal diarrhoea, except it wasn't because he wasn't talking shit, but it came out just as fast.

I hated every second of it and was fuming with the humiliation of it all ... fuming also about the fact that languages in the British Army are consigned to the lunatic fringe and given no weight. It all comes from that arrogance that believes that if you bark loud enough at a foreigner you'll make yourself heard. Here's the problem in a nutshell: what do you call someone who speaks lots of languages? A polyglot. Someone who speaks two languages? Bilingual. Someone who speaks only one? English. It's ignorance. Pig-headed, Anglo-Saxon ignorance. But it didn't quite apply to Rose who spoke fluent French ... I often used to fantasise about him being my interpreter at a French checkpoint and I'd just speed up and up and up until his brain tripped out. Sadly it only remained a fantasy. When we got back Goose took me to one side and said, 'Don't worry, Mike. Nick used to have off days as well.' Just before he'd left I'd asked Nick how he had coped. He'd laughed and said, 'I just make it up. I just invent words ... use English words and Balkanise them. Funny thing is the Serbs all seem to understand.'

I couldn't do that. I like to get things right. The bluff would freak me out just as much as not keeping up. It was the experience with Mladic more than any other which made me determined to avoid formal interpreting at meetings, high-level meetings, and to make myself useful in other ways, just to survive in that environment. I was comfortable being the 'mouth' informally or during low-key affairs, but the truth is we had two locals, Lana and Darko, in the HQ working for the Chief of Staff and for Victor Andreyev who, without exaggeration, were exceptionally gifted simultaneous translators. They could do it. And Darko did.

A couple of days later we were on the road in Central Bosnia touring around so that Rose could recce likely trout-bearing rivers. Fly-fishing was his thing. We were up in Zepce talking to the BiH commander there and for some reason all the interpreting just clicked into place. I don't know why. Perhaps because the environment was less stressful and the context of the conversation less critical . . . all about good local trout rivers. But really, it was General Galvin's visit where I recovered some Brownie points. Galvin was a senior, retired four-star American general. He'd been the Supreme Allied Commander in Europe, SACEUR, in the 1980s. President Clinton had dug him out of retirement and dispatched him to Bosnia to find out what was going on. The last time I'd come across one of these special Presidential envoys it had been Bianca Jagger in Tuzla. This saga came out of nowhere. In fact it began with a pizza.

SIXTEEN

Operation Grapple, Bosnia-Hercegovina

20 July 1994 – Sarajevo

It was a balmy Sarajevan evening – still air, soft light, warmth still radiating out of old brickwork, and high above a dark blue sky, which would soon give way to stars. I was about to dig into a pizza. Steve, the number two at the British Embassy, stared at his in wide-eyed fascination. Since the Blue Routes had been opened all this was possible and the small pizza restaurant on the corner of a steep, narrow street, which was within spitting distance of the Residency across the park-with-no-trees, had become a favourite haunt for the UNites.

I was about to pop the first piece into my mouth when the General's Range Rover appeared and screeched to a halt. Out leapt Goose and Mac, Victor's driver, looking flustered and concerned.

'Mike! For Christ's sake! Where's your radio? We've been driving all over the city looking for you. The Boss wants you to go over to Lukavica barracks and pick up an urgent message . . . now!'

With a slight pang of guilt I realised I'd left the Motorola, my ball and chain, on my desk. It wasn't unreasonable to assume that by nine in the evening there'd be no more work. Wrong assumption. I was fast learning what it was like to work for General Rose. The slice of pizza fell from my fingers. I mumbled an apology to Steve and jumped into the Range. At the Residency I cross-loaded into one of the JCO's Land Rovers and shot straight off with a bloke called Jack.

The flog right down to the western end of the city, through the BiH check-point at Stup flyover, across no-man's-land, haggling through S-4, which nor-mally shut at seven, and then through two French checkpoints at the airport, through a final Serb one beyond that and into Lukavica took about twenty-five minutes. It was getting dark by the time we got there. There was a quicker way, which shortened the distance and time by two-thirds: half way down Sniper's Alley was the Bridge of Brotherhood and Unity across the Miljacka linking Muslim Sarajevo with Serb-held Grbavica. It was guarded by the BiH on one side, Serb policemen on the other and the French in the middle. To use it required prior notice to Major Indjic of vehicle plates, ID card numbers and names. Generally speaking only the General and Victor were allowed to use it if they were going up to Pale. Minions like us had to take the long way round.

As soon as I stepped into Indjic's grubby office Biljana Andjeljkovic started laying into me.

'Look at you, Mike! You're a disgrace! No uniform . . . General Rose wouldn't be happy if he saw you now . . . you look like a tramp!' The faded jeans, maroon T-shirt and grubby deck shoes I'd worn for my night out clearly weren't her idea of LO's attire.

'Hello, Biljana. Where's this message that's so vital that I've missed my meal?'

Major Indjic handed me a small envelope, taped at the back, with General Rose's appointment hand-written on the front. I asked what was in it, but Indjic just gave me one of those conspiratorial looks as he stroked his moustache.

'All right then, if you won't tell me what's in it, who is it from?'

'It comes from the highest level,' he said cryptically and added, 'and we need an answer tonight . . . and not by phone.' I looked at Jack and swore inwardly, knowing that the pizza would never be eaten as we'd be repeating the drive a second time.

'Any chance of using the bridge?' I asked, hoping that the apparent urgency of the letter might soften Indjic's heart. The look in his eyes confirmed that I'd wasted my time asking the question.

In the Outer Office General Rose scanned the message once, nodded with satisfaction at its contents and said, 'Good. Tell them seven o'clock's fine . . . at Lukavica barracks.'

By the time we'd re-driven the route, passed on Rose's equally cryptic reply, had a cup of coffee and a Slivo and returned to the Residency, it was past midnight. I was still none the wiser as to what it was all about and was left wondering whether it had all been worth the price of a pizza.

21 July 1994 – Sarajevo, Bosnia-Hercegovina

These little helicopters were new to me. Norwegian Air, NORAIR, Arapahos hadn't been in theatre in 1993. Essentially they were old US UH1s, known as Hueys, from the Vietnam era, which had been extensively retroengineered: four blades instead of two, two engines instead of one, and a suite of avionics which made them the most agile and all-weather-capable helicopters in theatre. They also had pilots whose Wilco, can-do attitude perfectly complemented the airframes.

True to form, the US Embassy, which had no logistics infrastructure in Bosnia, had come cap in hand to the Residency and asked us for help with

241

moving General Galvin around theatre. De facto General Rose became the visitor's host and Galvin's trip had effectively been hijacked by the UN. Two thousand feet above Bosnia's forested hills and mountains two Arapahos were beating their way northwards through a blazing blue sky to Tuzla. The first aircraft contained Rose, General Galvin, Goose and, mysteriously, Jennifer Brush, who had, much to everyone's irritation, invited herself along unannounced. She wasn't going to allow Galvin to go gallivanting unchaperoned around Bosnia with the 'untrustworthy' UN. In the second aircraft were Simon Shadbolt, Jim Lensky, one of the US communicators with his TACSAT, and me.

First stop Tuzla. Much had changed there too. Whereas in 1993 there had been a somewhat beleaguered British sub-unit at the airfield, under the restructuring Tuzla had become home to HQ Sector North-West, which was exclusively a Scandinavian affair, a composite mix of Norwegians, Swedes and Danes, all commanded by a Swedish general called Ridderstadt.

After a quick briefing from him at the base we all hopped into Swedish APCs for a drive north to visit one of a chain of Swedish-manned OPs, which clung to the edge of a range of hills overlooking the much contested Posavina corridor.

To my secret satisfaction I noticed that Jennifer Brush was already encountering some local difficulties and was having problems clambering in and out of the APC. She'd come inappropriately dressed for the occasion – her tight, short black dress was one thing, but the brown leather handbag and high heels proved more of an obstacle to quick APC entry and exit drills.

By contrast, Galvin wore a loose-fitting, turquoise, short-sleeved polo shirt, baggy fawn slacks and black shoes. He was small in stature but fit looking, with wispy white hair. His silver-rimmed spectacles covered bright, intelligent blue eyes. Relaxed and casual, he listened a lot and, unusually for an American, was on 'receive' rather than 'send'. You don't get to be Supreme Allied Commander in Europe unless you have something about you. We liked him immediately.

It was stinking hot. It wasn't Jennifer I felt sorry for. It was the poor old Swedish soldiers who seemed to be cooking away slowly inside their Arctic camouflage boiler suits and were further burdened by heavy flak jackets and helmets. In the stillness of the heat, as we laboured on foot up a rutted track, in which Jennifer's high heels would periodically stick, all that could be heard was the chirping of summer birds.

Slightly forward of the crest of the hill we came upon a rudimentary affair of sandbags, wooden poles and a sheet of corrugated iron, which served to ward off the elements more than hissing shrapnel. Its occupants, two more overdressed Swedish soldiers, were gazing through their binoculars at the enormous flat panorama ahead of and below them, which stretched out northwards towards Serb-held Brcko and the river Sava. For as far as the eye could see yellow-gold wheat awaited harvesting. Somewhere down there, indiscernible to the naked eye, was a front line. Galvin and Rose fell into conversation with the soldiers who briefed them on the lie of the land. Jennifer Brush hung on their every word.

Somewhat disinterested in all of this I wandered off a few metres . . . and then I spotted him. *Surely we haven't come to exactly the same OP?* About 100 metres further down the slope, resting peacefully in the shade of a tree was an ancient cowherd. His fat cows milled about chomping grass, oblivious to the high-ranking visitors on their hill.

With a jolt I recalled Nick's story. Several months earlier Rose had been ferrying CinCSOUTH, Admiral Leighton Smith, around theatre on a similar visit. They'd been standing on this very spot and had spied the cowherd, as Nick had it a real Worzel Gummidge. Nick had been dispatched to bring him over as Leighton Smith had wanted to 'talk to a local Muslim'. Paraded in front of the Admiral, Worzel Gummidge had been asked how long he had lived in the area. 'For all of my seventy-five years . . . except those when I was away,' he'd announced proudly, confirming that he was indeed a local and a Muslim, which had satisfied the Admiral. Showing suitable interest, the Admiral had asked what he'd done when he'd been 'away'. To everyone's astonishment, Gummidge had broken into a big toothy glittering smile and had announced with great pride, 'Oh, that was during the war when I was in General von Paulus's Sixth Army at Stalingrad . . .' and had then proceeded to prove it by throwing up his arm in a Nazi salute and screaming, 'Heil Hitler! Heil Hitler!' The Admiral had looked on bemused and muttered something like, 'The least said about that the better . . .' while Goose and Nick had split their sides with laughter.

There I was, gazing at this historical relic wondering whether we'd be treated to a repeat performance. I didn't have long to wait. The conversation at the OP had soon exhausted itself: there was only so much that could be said about a flat bit of ground.

'Mike! Go and get that bloke.' Rose had spotted him as well. He didn't miss a thing. I scampered off down the hill to rouse the recumbent cowherd.

He took some rousing. When he didn't respond to words I shook him. Still nothing. Only his snoring and the sprig of grass, which was lodged in his mouth and moved backwards and forwards like a metronome in harmony with his rasping breathing, told me he was still alive. A couple of hefty kicks to his backside eventually roused him. He struggled into a sitting position, wiped the sleep from his eyes, which automatically scanned his cows.

'There are some very important visitors who want to talk to you . . . General Rose and a very important American general who represents the US President . . .' I could see from his glazed expression that it meant nothing to him. His world was a million miles away. '. . . remember the last time? Heil Hitler? Stalingrad?' Something clicked in his memory and he broke into a huge grin and began to struggle to his feet. I helped him up and, leaning on his staff, grass still in his mouth, he set off up the hill.

'They're very interested in you. They're particularly interested in history, so don't hold back . . . give 'em everything . . . you know, a few salutes and a couple of Heil Hitlers . . .' I was whispering to him, trying to prime him. *This'll show Jennifer that things aren't quite as they seem here.*

Gummidge was grinning away like mad, clearly enjoying his celebrity status and fully aware of what was required of him. We stopped in front of the group – medieval East meets the good and the great of the West. Rose had a half smile on his face and a twinkle in his eye. I was willing Gummidge to give a star performance.

It never happened. Rose carefully steered the conversation into the present. He must have second-guessed what I had been whispering into the old man's ear. Galvin asked him about his family and Gummidge replied that his three sons were out on the front line and that he looked after the cows. Galvin, ever astute, asked how the harvest was gathered in, given that it basically straddled the line. Without batting an eyelid the old man admitted that it was done by collusion between the two sides – down guns, pick up scythes and take to the fields. To my disappointment there was no mention of the Second World War.

Very quickly the old man was forgotten as Rose started to explain something to Galvin about harvests. As they moved away I saw Jennifer move in for the kill and hung around within earshot. She was talking to him in Serbo-Croat: lots of *'dobar dan, kako ste vi* – hello, how are you'. Her accent was good, as it should have been with a Sarajevo education. But it irritated me. *Cheek of it. First you muscle in on the trip and now you're fucking showing off your godamned Serbo-Croat – all for Galvin's benefit no doubt. He's your General. Why don't you do the interpreting?* I was seething, but said nothing.

Next stop Travnik for a big meeting between Galvin and the local BiH and HVO commanders in the area – General Mehmet Alagic commanding the ABiH's 3rd Corps, and General Filipovic commanding the Croats in Vitez. All this was to prove that the Washington-brokered Federation was in fine fettle and that the bloodshed of the past year a forgotten thing of the past.

As we flew south over Central Bosnia the shadows of the Arapahos flitted over an almost endless succession of smashed mountain villages and hamlets. In the lead aircraft Jennifer Brush started banging on to General Galvin about the devastation caused by the Serbs. Rose leapt in to disabuse her of that notion and to point out that what they were looking at was the result of what the Muslims and Croats had done to each other during 1993, that the Serbs had never set foot in that area. She wouldn't have it, though. Couldn't have it, as it didn't harmonise with the State Department view of what had gone on in the Balkans. It rather exploded the simplistic cowboys and indians view held in Washington.

In Travnik the jamboree began. We landed in the field behind BRITBAT's base at Stara Bila. The PWO had been succeeded by the Coldstream Guards who, in turn, had been replaced by the Royal Anglians, which meant that we were in Op GRAPPLE 4 time. They scooped us up in a fleet of vehicles and sped us off down the road to Travnik, where we were deposited at the front entrance of a large warehouse complex – Mehmet Alagic's HQ. A gaggle of smartly dressed BiH officers met us with many salutes. Brand new uniforms, stiff peak caps, leather satchels slung over their shoulders completed the illusion. It all looked highly professional. Where were the ragtag embattled fighters of 1992–3?

We were led into a large conference room on the first floor, which was dominated by a long, wide wooden table. Sitting in the middle of his staff officers, who were arrayed along the opposite side, was General Alagic. He was an enormous, broad-shouldered man with a massive head and a shock of swept-back hair. His face was large, oval and slightly jowly with dark, deep-set eyes. But it was his arms and teeth which fascinated me. His arms were like powerful tree trunks, his teeth, exposed when he flashed a genial smile, were as large as old tombstones, slightly crooked but just as discoloured. He greeted General Galvin warmly. We sat ourselves down opposite the BiH officers. I sat on Galvin's left and Jennifer Brush to his immediate right.

To the right of the BiH were a number of empty seats. The Croats were late and the meeting couldn't begin until they arrived. Five minutes passed – nothing. Ten minutes – still nothing. We talked quietly amongst ourselves. Alagic looked hugely pleased with himself, licking his lips as if he were the cat with the last of the milk. Eventually the Croats turned up and trooped in looking highly embarrassed and apologising profusely. A wide grin spread across Alagic's face. We discovered later that General Filipovic and his officers had been deliberately delayed en route at various BiH checkpoints and at the entrance to the 'joint HQ', precisely so this late arrival could be engineered.

I turned to General Galvin. 'General, I know I'm your interpreter for the day, but Jennifer Brush here speaks excellent Serbo-Croat. It would be a good demonstration of Washington's interest in the Federation if you were to use one of your own countrymen as interpreter.'

'You think so?' said Galvin, slightly taken aback.

'Oh yes, sir. It would create such a good impression.' Beyond him Jennifer's eyes were hurling daggers at me. A light sweat had broken out across her brow.

Galvin paused for a moment's thought and then turned to Jennifer, 'Good idea. You're now the interpreter.' Her face dropped and eyes bulged, barely concealing her rising panic. I cheered inwardly. I settled back in my seat. The pressure was off and I was going to enjoy every second of this.

My respite, predictably enough, was short-lived. Within five minutes she was in one of those interpreter's nose-dives. As I listened to her struggling away, my vindictiveness was quickly replaced with guilt and shame at having stitched her up so horribly and so publicly. As she squirmed to get the right words out, I was acutely reminded of my own recent disaster at the Mladic meeting. I put her out of her misery and took over the interpreting. I'm sure she's never forgiven me for what I did. Too bad. At least the point was made.

Of course, the healthy state of the Federation was discussed in detail. Alagic smirked as he detailed one success story after another. Filipovic said very little. His eyes couldn't conceal the fact that things were not quite as rosy as Alagic alleged. They were both on the same agenda – curry as much favour with the Americans and get as much out of them as possible. Rose said absolutely nothing. His view was that this was Galvin's show and that, in public at least, he was tour guide only. Besides, he'd heard all this blathering before.

The moment the meeting was over the HVO officers were given the heave-ho by the BiH. Phase two of the visit was upon us and we were all off, guests of General Alagic, to view one of his front-line units at Turbe down the road. A strange-looking Range Rover was waiting to whisk us away. Its once proud paintwork had been hand-painted over in green and brown. Here and there tiny patches of white poked through. *Liberated from some aid agency, no doubt!* There wasn't enough room for us all so Rose graciously (thankfully probably) declined and opted for a backing vehicle muttering that I should get in as interpreter. Since the Range Rover had a driver and a BiH bodyguard in the front, the three of us had to cram ourselves into the back. General Galvin found himself sandwiched between me on one side and the tombstone smile on the other.

The doors slammed shut and we sped off at high speed. Alagic wrapped a big friendly paw around the unfortunate General's shoulders, and, fixing me with a blank stare, barked '*Prevodi!* – Translate!'

'*Sada, ti reci Bilu da nam da . . .*' Alagic flashed his teeth at Galvin. I was so taken aback that I forgot to translate.

'What did he say?' Galvin looked helpless and vulnerable, pinned as he was by the friendly tree trunk, which enveloped his shoulder.

'Err . . . he said . . .' I tried to concentrate, '. . . he said "you tell Bill to give us . . ."' I was struggling to keep a straight face.

'Bill? Who the hell is Bill?' snapped the General.

'Well, sir . . . I think he means the President of the United States . . .'

'Oh! Right! . . . Bill?' Galvin lapsed into thoughtful silence.

And so the conversation carried on, with Alagic issuing instructions to Bill via General Galvin as though Bill and he had been great high school buddies. General Galvin was the epitome of diplomacy. He listened quietly – no doubt seething inside – and answered politely that squadrons of F16s were probably not possible at this stage. He never lost his cool once. I loved every minute of it – Galvin the thoughtful diplomat, fielding masterfully each high-speed ball that was hurled his way, all the while in a vice-like grip – and within frighteningly close proximity to those enormous gnashers millimetres from his nose.

Fortunately, this performance didn't last too long. Within ten minutes we'd scooted down the road to the front-line village of Turbe, had swung off and bumped up a track, which drew us towards a dark and slightly spooky-looking wood – Murk Wood of Bosnia. A ragtag 'guard of honour' was drawn up next to the track and as we alighted from the vehicle there was much throwing of salutes, stamping of feet, screaming and shouting of orders as the 'guard' was presented to Alagic and Galvin.

Unlike their compatriots in Travnik, these soldiers were dressed in an odd assortment of ill-fitting JNA conscript gear, the sort of stuff Tito's Partisans might have been dressed in fifty years earlier: woollen trousers tucked into socks, civilian hiking boots, baggy jerseys full of holes and a peculiar selection of headwear. This was much more like 1993. It seemed that all the good gear, the new uniforms and badges, went to the staff officers down the hill.

Military formalities over, we were guided into Murk Wood to view the dispositions, which were the forward edge of the BiH front line. Somewhere beyond the wood, across an emerald green field, which sloped away steeply, lurked the Serbs. We couldn't see a thing. Dug in and camouflaged, some ten metres from the wood's edge, were several 30mm PAT anti-aircraft cannons. Their twin barrels were depressed in the 'ground role' and pointing at the trees directly in front, and indirectly at the Serbs through the trees.

The gun's crews, another ill-clad assortment of middle-aged men, were drawn up in line awaiting inspection. As we approached, their commander detached himself and with right hand welded firmly to his temple in a permanent salute, goose-stepped towards us Soviet-style while at the same time shouting at the top of his voice as he presented his command. These theatrics were all a bit sad and completely out of place in such a tactical setting. Although amusing, I felt a bit sorry for these troglodytes, who, judging by their grubby appearance, were a permanent feature of Murk Wood. Galvin took all this in his stride asking good-humoured and relevant questions.

Before we knew it General Alagic had seized Galvin and dragged him off to the eastern edge of the wood. Through the trees, across a valley, could be seen the Vlasic feature, a high, steep-sided rocky mountain, which dominated the Lasva valley and prevented any further military movement northwards.

Pointing a stubby finger at Vlasic, Alagic roared, 'Serbs!' and then launched into a soliloquy about how he came from Banja Luka 100 kilometres up the road and how he, Alagic, would personally liberate the place. The obvious precursor to this would be to dislodge the Serbs from their dominating position atop Vlasic.

'Tell Bill that he must give us F16 fighters, he must give us tanks and artillery . . .' The speech was touching and his list of demands almost endless.

Galvin quietly explained that he would be sure to pass on Alagic's request but cautioned him that such demands were in contravention of the arms embargo and that it would probably not be realisable.

Alagic lapsed into thoughtful silence, mulling something over in his mind, and then burst out with, 'Well, in that case, could you ask Bill to send us some rock-climbing equipment?'

I almost choked. Galvin was quiet and pensive for a moment, staring up at the mountain, before muttering, 'I think you're gonna need more than rock-climbing gear to get them off the top of that!'

We left the troglodytes of Murk Wood to their own devices and departed in a cloud of dust to Stara Bila where the helicopters were waiting to whisk us off on leg three of the tour. Next stop Mostar in Hercegovina.

Mostar looked like Stalingrad at the height of its destruction. It was by far the worst example of concentrated, wholesale annihilation in Bosnia. There was scarcely a single building either on the cluttered Muslim east bank or the more extensive Croat west bank which had not been virtually completely destroyed. The ancient fifteenth-century Ottoman arched bridge which had finally succumbed to Croatian shell fire on 10 November 1993 had been replaced by a rickety wire and wooden board footbridge which swayed alarmingly 100 feet above the turbulent green and white Neretva river below.

As a tourist you hadn't really done Mostar unless you'd braved the bridge. Led by the CO of the resident UN Spanish battalion, we dutifully lined up and began the perilous journey. The CO, Galvin, Rose, Goose and I made it across without mishap. Glancing back I was both alarmed and amused to see that a huge gap had opened between us and Jennifer, whose heels were making the gaps between the planks difficult to negotiate. Although her dark form virtually blotted out the sea of blue berets lined up behind her, I could just make out Simon Shadbolt's face over her left shoulder. He was laughing his head off as the bridge swayed threateningly from side to side. I took a quick picture for posterity. High heels and high, swaying bridges clearly weren't a good mix.

The destruction on the west bank was no less complete than on the east. Whole residential apartment blocks had been reduced to gutted shells. Amazingly, in one of these, an old Croat woman lived in an apartment, one side of which was exposed to the elements. She'd simply refused to move out. In theory joint Muslim and Croat police teams patrolled the bridges and town junctions. Despite this evident show of solidarity the air was still thick with suspicion and mistrust. The pretence and the boisterous words of 'let bygones be bygones', which tripped merrily off various tongues were, as ever, merely calculated to assure the enquiring observer that the Federation was sound in body and spirit. We all went along with the pretence and departed Mostar with a warm and yet unconvincing glow in our stomachs.

Back to Sarajevo airport. Evening was upon us, we were running late and had a 7 p.m. appointment to keep in Lukavica barracks. Frank Cannon, the second BG, had the vehicles waiting at the airport for us. Jennifer Brush tried to tag along but I think General Galvin's patience had worn thin and she was packed off back to the US Embassy in a sulk. It seemed that Galvin had become bored with having his every word and gesture subjected to Jennifer's scrutiny. It had been a long day and we were all tired. Quite what awaited us in Lukavica barracks was still a mystery to me. The previous night's cryptic exchange between Indjic and Rose had revealed nothing to me, and had not been mentioned during the day, at least not in Jennifer's presence.

I got the shock of my life when Major Indjic, who'd met us at the HQ block entrance, led us into the conference room. I should have guessed that something was up. He was not his usual blustering self. Instead, he was courteous and polite. The entire opposite side of the conference table was lined with Serbian officers, some of whom I recognised – Tolimir and one or two others among them. Most were unknown to me, except of course Mladic who walked round the table and greeted General Galvin. Indjic slunk into the background giving me one of those you're-on-your-own-here looks. He hated interpreting as well and we'd always try and stitch each other up as much as possible prior to the start of a meeting. I suddenly developed a massive headache.

Galvin was an interpreter's dream. Like most Americans he spoke quite slowly and, for some reason, on this occasion spoke in bite-sized, manageable chunks ... with pauses. He would even stop in mid flow and ask me, 'Am I going too fast for you? ... did you get all that? ... do you want me to repeat that?' I wondered briefly if Rose would take a leaf out of his book.

As ever with interpreting, the specifics of the meeting eluded me. Mladic basically set out the Serbs' position, complained about NATO and the UN turning a blind eye to the Muslims' violation of the Igman/Bijelasnica DMZ, and made it quite clear that the Contact Group Plan was unacceptable. But he added that he was a soldier, not a politician and that the issue of acceptance or otherwise of the Plan was in the politicians' hands. Galvin listened to all this and, as with Alagic, guarded his response with diplomatic pleasantries.

Three years after this meeting a book, *General Mladic – The Serbian General*, written by a Belgrade correspondent, Jovan Janjic, who had interviewed

Mladic extensively, appeared in Cyrillic in Serbia. In it Mladic referred to the meeting but not to Galvin by name. In the book, no doubt for domestic consumption only, he claims to have berated 'the American general' and threatened that Mount Igman would be soaked in the blood of American soldiers. No such utterances were ever made. The meeting was congenial and the two parted on cordial terms.

As we dropped General Galvin off at the Holiday Inn it was clear that he'd thoroughly enjoyed his day, and, as a result of having met a broad cross-section of military commanders and listened to their views, had a clearer picture of the complexities of the Balkans. Whether anybody bothered to listen to the retired SACEUR back in the States is another matter entirely.

Operation Bretton, November 1997 – Ian, UK

'Are you telling me that Rose cooked up that meeting between Galvin and Mladic?' Ian's flabbergasted.

'No. Quite the opposite. Rose merely responded to a message from Mladic saying he'd be available to meet Galvin. Rose put it to Galvin. It was his decision. Rose merely facilitated it . . . that's what that rushing around with messages was all about.'

Ian still doesn't get it. 'The first message was from the Serbs to Rose and the second message was Rose's confirmation, correct? So how did the Serbs know that Galvin's programme ended at seven? How did they know to suggest a meeting at seven in the evening?' Ian's choosing his words carefully, speaking slowly as he pieces it all together.

'You've got half of it . . . pretty close. Look! It's simple. Rose's office was bugged . . .' That's floored him.'

'Bugged. By whom?'

'Obvious isn't it? By the Bosnians . . . perhaps. By the Americans . . . absolutely certainly.'

'By the Serbs as well?' Ian's eyes are popping out of his head.

'No . . . well, yes indirectly. That's the whole point of the story . . . the Serbs were bugging the buggers . . . if you'll excuse the pun. Everyone was bugging each other. No secrets in the Balkans. The only people not playing that game was the UN. It's simple: Rose is discussing Galvin's programme in his office the previous day, the Yanks, or Bosnians, bug that conversation, and then the Serbs listen in to what the Bosnians are saying to each other. Before you know it, that little titbit has landed on Mladic's desk and in a jiffy we're rung up by Indjic saying there's an urgent message for Rose, which has to be picked up by hand. Obvious really, when you think of it.'

I sniff, wipe my nose and register Ian's disbelief. I remind him of the time the Muslims in Srebrenica intercepted that message to Pale about my family graveyard in Serbia, in April 1993. If they can do that there, why not vice versa in Sarajevo? He's staggered that the Americans would bug the UN Commander's office, but the nice little symbiotic relationship that held good during the Cold War ended when the Wall came down. There's a different set of rules now . . . New World Order rules.

No one's really got a good definition of the New World Order. All one can do is discern some of the hallmarks, such as there being only one global superpower and therefore the old checks and balances have gone. The most noticeable characteristic is that two sovereign states can at the same time be allies in one part of the world, where their mutual interests coincide, and antagonists in another part where they don't. Those are the new rules. We'll happily jump into bed with the Yanks if there's a bit of Saddam-bashing to be done, but in Bosnia the US viewed the British as the 'enemy'. You can read it in some of the British journalist Ed Vulliamy's stuff. The Yanks have publicly admitted that was the case . . . New World Order rules. We've got to learn to live with them, that's all.

We had the place 'swept' regularly, but it made no difference. That building was the Delegates' Club – top Commies' Sarajevo bordello. It was built around bugs. You can sweep as much as you like but it won't do any good if your security's bad, which it always is in the UN. Before I arrived, someone entered Rose's office at night, accessed his laptop and stole some of his diary. And he was sleeping next door! But if you think about it, it's dead easy . . . all you have to do is reverse the polarity of wires going into any telephone handpiece and it becomes a live microphone even when it's cradled. You can pick that one up with a hand-held compass. Or you stick a laser on Rose's office window – which is what they did – and it picks up every tiny vibration. That's how the Soviets 'attacked' the US Embassy in Moscow in the early Eighties. It's not a new trick.

Then there were the troglodytes, the American NATO cave-dwellers in the annex. The Hidden Ones. You don't think their forest of antennae and funny boxes were for show do you? They were busy hoovering up every single little electronic bleep and fart, every single electronic emission to come out of the Residency . . . and . . . funny old thing . . . but the BiH intelligence set up under General 'Taljan' Hajrulahovic just happened to be in the annex too. As time went by they got neckier and neckier. When General Smith was in the chair they virtually had a sign in his office saying 'Hi General, but we're bugging your office!'

In Rose's day those trusted EUCOM American communicators who carried the TACSAT everywhere were pretty good blokes. Not so in General Rupert Smith's day. One of them wasn't even US Army. He was a Langley bloke dressed up as a soldier . . . but he couldn't carry it off very well . . . couldn't answer simple questions about where he'd served or which career courses he'd done. Lousy cover. Smith's pair of goons were so concerned that the General's every communication need should be catered for that out of the goodness of their hearts they set up the TACSAT in his office . . . only their TACSAT had an extra little box bolted onto it. That's how brazenly they 'attacked' Smith, and everything he said was listened to and taped in a room on the ground floor of the US Embassy next door. Shabby! And what was Mr Bean's successor up to? Still obsessed with running the Anglo-Bosnian friendship society.

We knew all this was going on but it didn't matter in the least. Both Smith's and Rose's attitude was that the UN mission was transparent so what did it matter who listened to what? It could even work to your advantage. You could cook up anything you wanted on the phone, lie as much as you wanted, and they'd never know what was kosher and what was deception. Bugging really is a double-edged weapon, which only works when the bugged don't know about the buggers.

It's an old story. There were other ways round it, ways which really did make me public enemy number one in the Yanks' and Bosnians' eyes, much more so than Jennifer's nose being put out of joint. Just imagine that you've got so used to hearing every fart in the Residency, so used to it that you've become complacent, and then suddenly someone comes along and cuts off both your ears and you can't hear a damn thing. That's what we did to them and it drove them mad. It's a huge American weakness, their total and utter reliance on technology. They base everything on electronic emissions – it's their God, but it's their eternal Achilles' heel. They're useless at HUMINT, human intelligence. That's where the real art is – what you read in someone's eyes, in the catch in their voice, in their nervous mannerisms. Those are the real point-scorers. They've none of it and we had it all and it drove them mad.

As with all things out there the programme was so busy that as soon as the Galvin visit was over it was forgotten. That had been Simon Shadbolt's last fling as general Rose's MA. He was leaving theatre shortly and only had to hand over to his successor, Lieutenant Colonel Jamie Daniel, who'd rung me up from Wilton and asked whether I'd be prepared to replace Nick Costello and work for Rose. Simon wasn't the only one to be leaving. Peter, the OC of the JCOs was also due for the off. His replacement, an Army officer called Martin, had just arrived in theatre and they were busy conducting their hand-over. Just about the whole of Rose's original team had left or were about to leave with the exception of Goose, who would be staying on to the bitter end. In fact he was the only one to stay. Even Frank Cannon, the second bodyguard, was departing to be replaced by another RMP sergeant, Clive Davies.

All this pretty much happened around me, almost seamlessly and without too much screaming and shouting. The nature of that HQ was such that people were rotating in and out almost daily. None of it was really of much interest to me. I still loathed interpreting and concentrated on developing my survival plan. During days when Rose was confined to his office I'd take myself off to Rajlovac to visit Ljiljana and Ljerka, or to the Cenex building to chinwag with the UNHCR girls such as Mica who were still plugging away at 'protection'. Most importantly, I'd spend hours over at Lukavica barracks talking to Indjic, Brane and Biljana. Getting on with these people was critical. The Muslims never gave us any problems with regard to freedom of movement. But the Serbs controlled so tightly any vehicle movement across their territory, particularly where the General's movements were concerned, that sticking a few credits in your back pocket was vital.

The spin-off, which resulted from hours of sipping rancid coffee chased by Slivovica while chatting about the war, how it started, what the Serb concerns were, etc, was that I began to build quite a good low-level HUMINT picture: mental attitudes, perceptions, views – all these things mattered. Occasionally you'd pick up an interesting snippet. Sometimes you'd be fed a line, particularly by Major Indjic, in the hope that it would be passed on to the General so that it might in some way influence him. I'd try to disregard the rubbish, but most of that stuff I wrote up in the evenings in a short report, marked it CONFIDENTIAL, because the HQ was so leaky, and passed it across Rose's desk. All of it was qualified with COMMENT, in the sense that 'In conversation with the BSA LO today he revealed that . . . or commented on . . . COMMENT: This is bullshit . . . or this indicates such and such a frame of mind . . . or, shows that there's a grass roots mood to reject the CG Plan.' It all helped to build a picture which no amount of electronic hoovering could produce.

You might ask if this couldn't be defined as spying, but what you hear in conversation and the fact that you formalise it in a report can hardly be construed as espionage per se. I had the responsibility of passing it on to Rose. Indjic himself was a seasoned spook; you don't imagine for a minute he'd willingly or otherwise pass on their innermost secrets. That's not what we're talking about here. More than anything it was a way of interpreting the mentality. Rose found it useful, but what I produced for him was simply one of many sources of information to which he was privy and upon which he'd make decisions. To suggest that I exerted some sort of disproportionate influence over him is absurd. Sometimes he'd read these reports and not pass comment. Sometimes he'd say, 'Well, I just don't agree with that!' That was his prerogative. He was the Boss. Anyway, it all started from small beginnings over coffee and Slivo.

When I wasn't doing that I was visiting Minka, Nada, Tomo and Vera. Since the opening of the Blue Routes their situation was less acute, not life-threatening at least. Minka, in particular, was pleased to see me back. She admitted that the 700-odd Deutschmarks I'd sent up to her via Mica as I'd been leaving in November 1993 had seen her and Munir through yet another winter. Tomo and Vera seemed in fine spirits and Nada, as ever, was her usual gentle intelligent self. Her knowledge of Bosnia's prehistory was exhaustive. During a spare hour or so I'd take Goose up to see her and we'd sit there drinking tea and eating biscuits. For some reason she and Goose got on well. It was bizarre, watching them together – hulking great bruiser of a BG and this demure, white-haired lady in her seventies. What they both had in common was a gentleness of soul.

Jamie Daniel arrived about a week after the Galvin visit in the midst of high drama in the Outer Office. A VIP was arriving and this particular visit had to go like clockwork. Nothing could be left to chance, nothing could go wrong. The media would be part of the trip, which would involve getting this VIP up the routes from Split and into Sarajevo and thereafter by helicopter to Pale and thence to Gorazde and then back to Sarajevo by road across Serb territory. We worked feverishly to make sure that every detail was boxed-off. Baggers tore his hair out fixing all the travel arrangements from the UK to Split and up to the Serb front line by road. I was responsible for squaring up every detail of transit on the Serb side of the line, which involved considerable LOing both with Indjic and with General Mladic's HQ. If ever a VIP visit had to go without a hitch, this was it. If ever there was one which had huge scope for going wrong, this was also it. The Prime Minister? Royalty? Much more important than that. Lady Rose was coming out with her Red Cross incubators.

Left: Sarajevo, September 1994. A visit to an Egyptian UN observation post. L-R: Sgt Clive Davies, Major Jamie Lowther-Pinkerton (background), General Rose (facing), Lieutenant Colonel Jamie Daniel (back) and Lieutenant Colonel Tim Spicer.

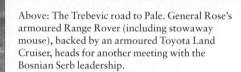

Above: The Trebevic road to Pale. General Rose's armoured Range Rover (including stowaway mouse), backed by an armoured Toyota Land Cruiser, heads for another meeting with the Bosnian Serb leadership.

Left: Goose: General Rose's bodyguard, a tough and loyal paratrooper, ever vigilant and ready for anything. He stayed with his General throughout.

Right: Maljevac, Krajina, August 1994. General Rose on the secure Tactical Satellite radio to US Admiral Leighton Smith in Naples generates an airstrike. L-R: Goose, Jim Lenski, and (right) Lieutenant Colonel Jamie Daniel.

Above: Hat trick! Banja Luka, Friday 27 August 1994. After a tortuous meeting between US General Wesley Clark and Bosnian Serb Army Commander, General Ratko Mladic, hats were swapped. L-R: Major Kralj, General Mladic with Clark's hat, General Clark with Mladic's, and General Rose not amused.

Left: Sarajevo Airport, September 1994. UN Force Commander, French General Bertrand de Lapresle (right), in conversation with US Admiral Leighton Smith who was visiting from Naples.

Right: Mojmilo hill, Sarajevo Airport, September 1994: General Rose (centre) briefing Admiral Leighton Smith.

Left: The 'Dark Side' – Lukavica Barracks. At the centre of the spider's web, Major Milenko Indjic, the Machiavellian Bosnian Serb Army LO to UNPROFOR, 'manipulates' by phone one of any number of UN LOs in the Sarajevo area. Without his say so, no vehicles could transit Serb-held territory.

Right: Pale. Up at the Bosnian Serbs' 'mountain stronghold', as press jargon had it, there was seldom much unity. L-R: Dr Karadzic, Professor Nikola Koljevic and General Mladic squabbling.

Left: Pale. After a meeting with the Bosnian Serb leadership in their 'mountain stronghold': L-R: Captain Michel Bruketa (ADC to the UN Force Commander), General Milan Gvero (Mladic's deputy), General Bertrand de Lapresle (UN Force Commander), General Ratko Mladic and General Sir Michael Rose.

Right: Mixed Military Working Group, Sarajevo Airport. General Rose (left), Victor Andreyev (centre), the Russian UN Head of Civil Affairs for Bosnia, and the MA, Jamie Daniel, plotting during a lull in negotiations.

Right: Jinxed – Rose's Boys: sorting out the press line in the Outer Office. Whatever happened to them all? L-R: Tim Spicer, Hervé Gourmelon (back to camera), Rose and Jamie Daniel. With the exception of Rose, all (including the photographer – author) were destined for trouble.

Left: Operation BLUETIT 1, Pale, November–December 1994. In a scene from *'Allo 'Allo* the author (left) takes instructions from General Rose via secure Tactical Satellite radio while Geordie elevates the antenna to get better reception. During the battle for Bihac, Geordie and the author remained on station in the attic of the UNMO's house in Pale.

Left: Christmas Day 1994, The Residency, Sarajevo. The author is comforted by Residency local staff Goca (left) and Nada (right) after the trauma of translating Rose's joke about a prostitute during the staff and their families' Christmas lunch.

Right: Bosnian Government Presidency, Sarajevo, December 1994: at one of numerous meetings during the run-up to the Cessation of Hostilities Agreement, L-R: The UN's SRSG, Yasushi Akashi, Bosnian President Alija Izetbegovic, and ABiH supremo, General Rasim Delic.

Left: Bosnian Government Presidency, Sarajevo, December 1994 After a meeting concerning the Cessation of Hostilities Agreement, Bosnian Vice-President, Ejup Ganic, and UN SRSG, Yasushi Akashi, confront the press. Second and third from the right are Kurt Schork of Reuters and Bob Simpson of the BBC.

Right: Operation BLUETIT 2, Pale, 31 December 1994: Cessation of Hostilities negotiations. L-R: General Tolimir (hat), Jovan Zametica on the TACSAT to General Rose in Sarajevo, Biljana Plavsic (standing), Nikola Koljevic, Karadzic, the author, Mladic and Major Kralj.

Left: Operation BLUETIT 2, Pale, 31 December 1994. During Cessation of Hostilities negotiations a furious argument breaks out among the Bosnian Serbs: General Mladic (right) berating General Tolimir (left, with hat), Karadzic paralysed and Geordie trying to hide behind the TACSAT.

Right: Operation BLUETIT 2, Pale, 31 December 1994: Cessation of Hostilities negotiations. The author (right) reading back to General Rose the exact text of his last message which clinched the agreement.

Above: Sarajevo Airport, January 1995. Following the Cessation of Hostilities Agreement, negotiations for the establishment of a Central and two Regional Joint Commissions resulted in more signatures. Seated L-R: General Blaskic (for the Bosnian Croats), General Mladic (for the Bosnian Serbs), General Rose (for the UN) and General Rasim Delic (for the Bosnian Government).

Below: Sarajevo, February 1995. A moment worth waiting for: after two years of helping to keep alive his au pair Aida's family, General Mike Jackson finally meets Munir and Minka Pijalovic. Without the personal intervention of Jackson and his wife Sarah, this family would not have survived the war.

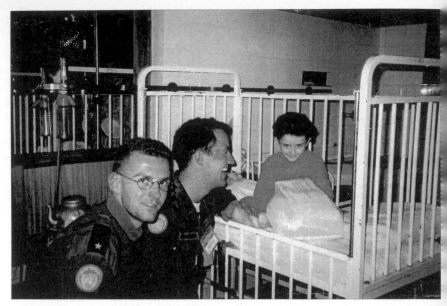

Above: Lucky. Tuzla hospital, 1994: thanks to the undaunted efforts of Norwegian peacekeeper Major Oivind Moldestad, six-year-old Fauda Sukic was rescued from Srebrenica and her life saved.

Below: Unlucky. Sudan 1994: Fauda Sukic's younger African cousin, too weak to help herself, awaits her fate. The colour of her skin, the location of her country and Western apathy all counted against her survival. War photographer Kevin Carter received the Pulitzer Prize for this image and then took his own life. The note left behind said: 'I am haunted by the vivid memories of killings and corpses, of starving or wounded children…'

SEVENTEEN

Operation Grapple, Bosnia-Hercegovina

Wednesday 27 July 1994 – BH Command, Sarajevo
The Outer Office was a hive of frenzied activity. The bulk of the planning donkey-work had necessarily fallen on the ADC's desk. Task: get Lady Rose and two incubators, the latter packaged in four large brown boxes, from the UK to Sarajevo and thence to Pale and Gorazde. The only clues to help him on his way had been vague hints from the General who'd stick his head into the Outer Office, suggesting, 'It would be nice to fly to Pale and Gorazde and then drive back along the river Drina . . . a picnic along the way . . . and I think we'll take some press . . . but they won't drive with us . . .' and then he'd dive back into his office.

Direction from the MA was more specific: 'This has got to go like clockwork. Not a single hiccup or we'll all find ourselves as the only members of Fence Repair Unit, Outer Hebrides.' The pressure was on. Baggers spent hours on the phone to all manner of people – the RAF in UK, BHC Rear HQ in Split, JHQ at Wilton, and not least Lady Rose herself. Increasingly he took on the appearance of a mad professor as he wrestled with telephones, sketched flow charts and endlessly tweaked the ever-changing plan. His tousled hair looked even more troubled than usual.

Gradually the plan took shape. Frank Cannon, UJ and Liz Wichelo, the JCOs' interpreter, would drive to Split in two vehicles on Tuesday 26th where they would meet Angela Rose off the HS 125. The party would overnight at COMBRITFOR's villa and then drive via Mostar to Sarajevo, arriving in time for dinner with the General and Victor Andreyev. Concurrent with this the incubators would be delivered to RAF Brize Norton and would be flown out to Split on Wednesday 27th's regular VC10 shuttle. 845 NAS would scoop up the boxes, shove them on their Sea Kings and ferry them up to the Zetra stadium HLS on the morning of Thursday 28th. The General, his wife, Baggers, Goose, two press and I would jump on the aircraft and fly first to Pale, drop off the first incubator, then fly on to Gorazde, deliver the second to the Muslims, and then drive back to Sarajevo in the Range Rover and backing Land Rover. These would have departed Sarajevo at six in the morning, driven by Frank Cannon and UJ, and prepositioned themselves in Gorazde in time for our arrival by helicopter. Timings throughout were extremely tight and there was huge potential for the unforeseen, though depressingly inevitable, Balkan spanner in the works.

None of this was helped by a marked deterioration in the general security situation. No sooner had Frank Cannon and his team departed for Split on the Tuesday than the General received a formal letter from Dr Karadzic stating that, because of continued and incessant Muslim offensives, in direct violation of the 8 June Geneva cease-fire, he would be withdrawing from the Blue Route agreement and would henceforth *not be able to guarantee the safety* of any Muslim convoy coming down the Igman route and across the airport from Butmir to Dobrinja. The respite that the people of Sarajevo had enjoyed throughout the spring and summer was effectively at an end. That night a 20mm or 30mm AAA cannon firing from a position in Ilidza engaged a Muslim convoy. The Serbs meant business.

Worse was to come. The next day, on Wednesday 27th, the appointed day of Lady Rose's arrival in Sarajevo, a British resupply convoy from Kiseljak to Sarajevo took a wrong turn, got lost and ended up coming down the Muslims' Igman route – *Alahov Put*, or Allah's Way as the Serbs called it. Confusion surrounds what actually happened and the Serbs later claimed that they couldn't see that it was a UN convoy because the lead truck had been Muslim and was not painted white. This was true and it appears that a civilian truck may have seized the opportunity to come down the route in daylight thinking that the Serbs might mistake it for part of the UN convoy. If that was the thinking, it proved to be flawed. As the convoy slowed at a sharp right-hand bend at the base of the route, just short of the cover offered by the built-up area of Hrasnica, the Serbs opened fire with their cannon from Ilidza at a range of just over 1,000 metres. The burst of fire killed Corporal Bottomley in his cab and pierced a UN fuel tanker, causing a torrent of burning fuel to rage down the road, gutting a further three vehicles.

I was oblivious to this as I'd spent the morning at Lukavica barracks fretfully double-checking with Major Indjic that Frank Cannon's group bringing in Lady Rose had the necessary clearance to get through the Serb checkpoint at Hadzici. Once I'd satisfied myself that all was in order I returned to the Residency where I learned of the morning's tragedy. This was not a good start to the visit.

Moreover, the ADC's carefully crafted plan had already begun to go wrong. At midday, by which time the road party should have reached Mostar, we discovered that they hadn't even left Split. By mid-afternoon they'd barely reached Mostar. Tension mounted in the Outer Office. Baggers and Simon Shadbolt struggled to devise alternative options. Once it was realised there was no hope of getting the party into Sarajevo by last light and before the

Serbs shut down the Sierras, the MA, keen to avoid an Outer Hebrides posting, made a command decision to pluck Angela Rose and Frank off the Mostar road and deposit them by helicopter in Kiseljak where the General, Goose and I would meet them and bring them through the Sierras. This would leave Liz Wichelo and UJ to bring the vehicles, which were critical to the following day's plan, in through Hadzici at night. G3 Ops were thrown this fastball and within an hour had informed the MA that the helicopter would land at Kiseljak at 1830 hours, which meant that we had to be on the road by 1745 hours at the latest. I spent most of the afternoon smoothing the changes with Major Indjic at Lukavica, eliciting from him a promise that Liz and UJ would be allowed unhindered passage through the Hadzici checkpoint at about 2100 hours.

'Right! Let's go! How're we off for time, Mike?' I chased after the General as he vaulted from his office, beret in hand, and dashed down the wooden stairs to where Goose was waiting by the Range Rover, doors open and engine running. Throwing myself into the back I glanced at the time as Goose gunned the engine and we swept past a saluting Dane and out of the gates. 1800 hours!

'We're late, sir. Got half an hour before they land.'

'Half an hour, eh? What do you reckon, Goose? Can we make it? Don't want to be late.' There was a hint of urgency in the General's voice. I wondered what sort of grip his wife had on him.

'No problems, Boss,' drawled Goose laconically, flooring the accelerator and sending five tonnes of armoured Range Rover hurtling westwards down Sniper's Alley and the fast-track road towards Stup flyover. In the west a setting sun bathed Igman and the surrounding hills with a deceptively soft golden mantle. As we bumped painfully along the hideously rutted Kasindol-ska Street, through gaps in the anti-sniper screens we could see a heavy black pall of oily smoke drifting vertically into a motionless dusk and rising above Igman. From almost two kilometres away it looked like a Kansas tornado. The base marked the spot of the morning's disaster where three trucks were still burning fiercely.

Rose craned his head to the left silently taking in the scene. Suddenly he snapped his head round and spat, 'That's outrageous! Right! There's only one thing for it. Demilitarise Sarajevo . . . the whole lot. No weapons. Nothing. That's the next step.' And that became the thrust of his policy. At the time I doubted that either side would see things Rose's way – too many vested interests, none of which coincided with his quest to alleviate the suffering of the Little People, whose destinies were not in their own hands, but whose interests the General was trying to represent. I was gloomy about the prospects of achieving the total demilitarisation of the Sarajevo area. But, staring at that deathly pall of smoke, I had to admire the Boss for one thing – his sheer drive.

Free of Ilidza we raced Time itself; Goose pushed the Range faster than it had gone before, deftly swerving to avoid slow-moving Yugos, horse-drawn carts burdened with hay, and soldiers with rifles slung lazily pedalling bicycles to or from the front. The General cruelly piled on the pressure by continually glancing at his watch.

'Whadya reckon, Goose? Make it, will we?'

'No probs, Boss.' Predictably confident.

Indjic was as good as his word. The border guards at Sierra 1 recognised the Range Rover and raised the barrier, allowing us to sweep through without slowing. A couple of kilometres from Kiseljak, silhouetted against a deepening evening sky, I could see a tiny black speck clearing the mountain range south of the town and beginning its descent into the UN base. 'There they are!' I said, pointing over Rose's shoulder, 'we're going to make it.' And we did . . . just, pulling up next to the helipad in a cloud of dust as the rotor blades of a DETALAT Puma died and dipped. I hurried forward to grab whatever bags needed carrying and almost bumped straight into Lady Rose as she stepped off the aircraft.

'Hello, Mike,' she said thrusting her hand forward, 'how's it going?'

I hadn't seen her since that evening at General Mike Jackson's place when I'd first met her and Nick Costello's wife. I was stumped by her easy and friendly manner, and surprised that she'd remembered my name.

Within an hour we were back at the Residency where another task awaited me. 'Mike, I'm worried about Liz Wichelo and UJ getting through Hadzici. Their vehicles are vital for tomorrow and without them we're stuffed. Get over there and wave your magic wand if required.' The MA had a point, and despite my earlier assurances it was just as well that he sent me back out. When I got to the checkpoint Liz and UJ were indeed stuck on the other side of the barrier. They were prevented from passing through by the police guard who was claiming that he'd received no instructions to let anyone through. Despite my protestations to the contrary he insisted that I accompany him to the police station in Hadzici. I had no option but to follow. This was turning into yet another of those long and exasperating Balkan days.

'We've got an UNPROFOR officer here . . . British captain . . . claims he works for Rose . . . speaks our language . . . what? . . . wait a minute!' The police chief lowered the phone and turned to me, 'What's your name again?'

'Stanley.'

'He says it's Stanley and he wants you to ring Major Indjic at Lukavica, who will sort things out . . . well no, we know nothing about it . . . okay, five minutes.' He put the phone down. 'That was my boss, the police chief in Ilidza. He'll speak to the Army. If you say it's been cleared then everything will be okay. No doubt it's the off-going shift not telling us about it.'

And that was that. Nothing for it but to wait. The guard from the checkpoint fished out a crumpled packet of Drina cigarettes and offered me one. Gratefully I accepted. I hadn't had one for hours and in the panic to pick up Lady Rose had virtually forgotten I smoked.

'Something strong perhaps?' A sly smirk flickered across the police chief's face as he slid open a drawer and produced a bottle of homemade Rakija.

'Just a small one. I'm driving.' With a collective chink of glasses and a 'ziveli' we downed the tot.

'How's General Rose these days? His wife's here, isn't she?'

I explained that we'd just picked her up and that the two vehicles at the checkpoint were part of the plan and were needed to deliver an incubator to the Koran hospital in Pale. I added that the whole thing had been cleared by Mladic himself, hoping that this name-dropping would help get Liz and UJ through. They in turn said that they knew all about the incubators as the subject had received wide coverage on Serb TV and in the papers.

Two cigarettes and several tots later the telephone jangled. I tried to look unconcerned but inwardly I was worried. What if they said no? Liz and UJ would have to turn around, make their way over the mountain via Kresevo and overnight at Kiseljak. The Sierras didn't open until 0700 so they'd never get the vehicle to Gorazde in time. I could see everything collapsing before my very eyes.

'Stanley! . . . yes . . . Indjic . . . Lady Rose . . . incubators . . . yes, yes we know . . . well, it's not our fault that the message wasn't passed . . . okay?' The police chief gave me a wink and nodded his head. I breathed easier.

'You were right . . . ,' he conceded, '. . . looks like those fools on the off-going shift were told but didn't pass the message on. We've got to abide by our orders, you understand?'

'No problems, orders are orders no matter which army you're in.' I fought off another offer of one last tot and headed back to the checkpoint with the guard where Liz and UJ were patiently awaiting rescue.

By the time we got back to the Residency it was nearly 2230 hours. The Office was deserted. I headed for the bar wondering gloomily what disasters the following day would bring. I felt particularly sorry for Frank Cannon and UJ who, having driven all the way from Split, would be leaving Sarajevo at 0530 the following morning bound for Gorazde, and they'd have the pirates of Rogatica to deal with on the way. There was plenty that could still go wrong.

Thursday 28 July 1994 – BH Command, Sarajevo

We awoke to another brilliantly hot Balkan summer's day; still air, cloudless azure-blue sky but still the stinking, oppressive humidity in the city. I was less concerned about the weather and more fretful about the fate of Frank Cannon, UJ and the road party. During the run up to Angela Rose's arrival there had been some discussion as to where I should be. At one moment the General had said I should go with the road party to ensure that there'd be no problems at Rogatica. But that would have left him with no interpreting cover in Pale and I'd further put my neck on the block by guaranteeing that there'd be no problems for the road party and had given General Mladic's assurances. It had therefore been decided that I would fly with the incubators and the General's group.

A nagging doubt remained. The previous night's cock-up at Hadzici had left me feeling less than confident and I awoke with a terrible feeling of trepidation. I fully expected to discover that the road party would be stuck at Rogatica being worked over by its pirates. This would no doubt be hailed as another Stanley balls-up. Amazingly, not only had they sailed through unmolested but had, as we were waiting for the arrival of the helis at Zetra, already reached Gorazde. A good omen.

Our lift to Pale and Gorazde arrived on the dot at 1000 hours clattering, juddering and flaring as it descended on finals into the stadium. The four boxes containing the incubators filled most of the interior thus restricting room for passengers. As a result only two journalists, selected from a cast of thousands, joined us. Unsurprisingly 'words' was the bearded, earnest and man-about-the-Outer-Office Kurt Schork of Reuters while 'pictures' (moving) were provided by an Australian freelancer working for ABC called Bartley Price.

We squeezed in as best we could. I took up my usual position behind the aircraft commander. General Rose and his wife sat starboard and forward with Goose and his gear opposite them. The journalists and the ADC sat where they could. Angela Rose was dressed simply – turquoise polo shirt, navy blue trousers and sensible brown walking shoes. Around her neck, on a long thin chain, hung her UNHCR accreditation card. It was refreshing for once to have a visitor whose ego did not appear to demand the usual accoutrements and symbols of a WZT (War Zone Tourist) – helmets, RBR body armour and other essential image-enhancing paraphernalia.

With a shudder the Sea King heaved itself out of the stadium and, dipping its nose, gathered ground speed and headed east over Bascarsija and scooted through the narrow and thickly wooded gorge leading to Pale. The hop was almost identical to the one flown with Douglas Hurd and Alain Juppé the previous month. Within ten minutes the scattered white houses of Pale gleamed enticingly in the distance. Shortly the football pitch became visible. Parked along one side was a row of police cars, Mercedes saloons and minibuses: the reception committee. Quite what would happen once we'd landed was anyone's guess and we were equally ignorant as to who would meet us and how the Serbs would play it. As the helicopter settled I peered anxiously through the Perspex but couldn't recognise anyone; Jovan Zametica's shining pate was not visible, and there was certainly no sign of Dr Karadzic's wind-blown locks. Nothing so grand – just a bunch of policemen, hospital workers in white coats and a gaggle of local press.

I glanced over at Angela Rose: ice cool and not a hint of stress or apprehension, not bad considering she'd just dropped into the pit of the 'Bosnian Serbs' Mountain Stronghold'. I leapt from the aircraft, scuttled up to one of the white coats and asked what he wanted doing with the boxes and with us. They'd already worked it out. Before he could answer, the minibus had reversed up to the heli. Angela Rose quickly seized control and under her direction Baggers, the white coat and I manhandled the two heavy boxes marked 'Pale' into the van. They were surprisingly heavy and the local press, who were unhelpfully shoving their lenses in our faces, caught it all on film.

Once the boxes had been loaded on we were ushered into the vehicles and, with sirens wailing and lights flashing, the cavalcade roared off up the hill in a cloud of dust, which smothered bemused bystanders hitching lifts on the roadside. Within minutes we'd come to a halt in front of the Koran hospital entrance. The hospital's director and Professor Sosic, in charge of all hospitals in the area, were waiting to greet us.

I sprinted from my vehicle up the line and just managed to catch up with the Roses in time to translate the first words of greeting. We were ushered into a small room, just the General, his wife, Baggers, the director, Professor Sosic, their interpreter and me. Goose remained outside where he kept at bay the glowering gaggle of journos and hangers on. While sweet Turkish coffee was poured Professor Sosic explained that the 'hospital' was in fact a converted hotel and suggested that we might like a guided tour while the boxes were moved up to the post-natal room. The General took a back seat and allowed his wife to do all the talking, only right and proper as it was her day and her mission on behalf of the British Red Cross.

'Just stick on the Boss's shoulder. Don't worry about these people,' grunted Goose out of the corner of his mouth as he elbowed a journo into the wall. In a similar manner we careered chaotically around the hospital, channelled like a surging wave through narrow, darkened passageways. Backlit by the bright halogen lamps of cameras bouncing menacingly on their owners' shoulders, grotesquely distorted shadows of heads and necks skipped and danced devilishly over the walls and ceiling. The scuffling and shuffling of the mob's feet and its general grunting and huffing was punctuated occasionally by a pained yelp as yet another journo found his foot crushed or fell victim to Goose's or my elbow in the ribs. Fair game. Good sport. In this manner we stayed right on top of Rose.

After a brief tour of the wards, we squeezed ourselves up a flight of stairs and along yet another narrow, gloomy corridor. Half way along we turned abruptly left into what was obviously the natal area. Two small rooms; to the left the delivery chamber, to the right some sort of post-natal recovery room. A glance into that chamber of horrors sent shivers down my spine. The centrepiece was a high couch complete with leather restraining straps and two high-mounted and widely-spaced leg clamps. Scattered about the chamber sullen instruments for prodding, gripping, gouging and prising – one resembling a bolt cutter particularly caught my eye – idly awaited use. We swung into another room. A small cot, various oxygen bottles and an incubator confirmed it was definitely post-natal.

Those who mattered had somehow squeezed themselves in and were roughly grouped around our two brown boxes, which were on the floor. Those who didn't crammed into the room as best they could. I was standing next to Rose and he next to his wife. The heat from a camera halogen lamp beat fiercely on my neck. I started to sweat.

A hush of anticipation settled upon us. Expectant eyes greedily followed the director's hands as he tore off strips of masking tape and opened first one, then the other box. The first revealed a rectangular trolley-type device with four small wheels. Creamy coloured, it sported various switches (large, black and clunky), dials, cables and a metal bracket. The other offered up an equally mysterious lump, L-shaped with a vertical arm (to be inserted into bracket) and an overhanging cluster of lamps affair. It looked nothing like the plastic box standing idle in the corner. Indeed, if it were a piece of post-natal gear its exact nature was further confused by the absence of anything into or onto which to place an infant. Nor was there an instruction manual or pamphlet. What words there were, stamped about the various dials and switches, looked suspiciously German – long, incomprehensible and convoluted directives. Smooth rounded corners and the sullen, sickly paint scheme screamed late Fifties/early Sixties tech! Foreheads furrowed in concentration, minds raced to identify the contraption.

'Michael! What is it?' Angela Rose's voice was shockingly loud.

Rose paused. I detected hesitation. Smelt rising panic.

Deftly the General tossed the potato at me – red hot. 'Mike! Ask them what it is!'

Suddenly the halogen lamp was oppressively hot. Eyeing Professor Sosic, whose vacant eyes promised no answers, I sought help.

He paused for an eternity. His gaze drifted over the boxes and their mysterious contents. Raising a bushy eyebrow and rubbing his chin he mumbled, *'Ma, bas nisam siguran.'*

'He's not really sure, sir.' This was of course of no use to Rose. By now the two bits had been mated. It looked even less like an incubator than ever.

'Looks to me like a sunbed,' said a voice behind me. I think it was Kurt Schork trying to be helpful. But the cat was out of the bag. The fateful words spoken, carved for eternity in press truth. *'SUNBED SCANDAL – Lady*

Rose Delivers Ultimate Rebuke To Bosnian Serbs.' Word that Lady Rose had presented the Serbs with a sunbed was to sweep the country like a bush fire, and was thus reported that evening on Serb TV.

Not a second could be lost. The initiative had to be regained. Decisively the General gripped the situation. Striding forward and flicking the switches and turning the dials purposefully he stated authoritatively, 'Rubbish! Of course it's an incubator . . . perfectly bloody obvious what it is . . . only there's a bit missing!'

I cast a sly look at Goose. He looked away quickly, knowing that if our eyes met the inevitable would happen. I could see him biting his lip.

'ADC!' barked the Boss.

'Yessir. Here,' came a voice from somewhere in the mob.

'Find out where the missing bit is, and the instruction manual. Get them here as soon as possible.'

'Right, sir!' bellowed Baggers.

The orders continued. 'Mike! Tell the Professor that the missing bit's on its way.'

I relayed this to the Professor. He in turn tried to come to terms with the situation. Earnestly and somewhat apologetically he thanked Lady Rose and the British Red Cross for their kind gift.

Then, miraculously and unexpectedly, the hospital director sallied forth and rescued us. He'd solved the riddle of the boxes: 'It's a computerised heater for babies born jaundiced or premature. We've got an incubator, but not one of these . . . and we need one desperately . . .'

We were delighted. They were delighted. Victory snatched from the jaws of defeat. Big, satisfied grins all round. Lots of handshaking, a glance at the watch – good heavens, is that the time? With that we swept out of the hospital and roared off, sirens blaring, dust flying and hitchhikers scattering, back to our waiting Sea King.

During the short fifteen-minute hop to Gorazde the helicopter's radio was used to pass back urgent instructions to get the missing part and the instruction book up to Sarajevo as soon as possible. In fact they were sitting at RAF Brize Norton in Oxfordshire, forgotten by the RAF. No doubt phones at JHQ, High Wycombe and in the MoD burned red hot and some hapless Crab was skewered for this oversight. As we flew on I eyed the remaining two boxes with suspicion and mounting anxiety, wondering what nasty little surprises lurked within, waiting to spring out and spoil our day again.

Legend has it that when the gods had finished the mountain ranges of the world what rubble was left they carelessly tossed out to create Montenegro. With no thought to aesthetics or to the ant-like humans who would later attempt to eke out an existence there the gods created an inhospitable world of grey rock and towering peaks. Somewhere far to the south on the horizon, beyond the Drina, these jagged peaks pointed accusingly at the heavens.

Two thousand feet below us eastern Bosnia stretched away in a seemingly endless vista of wooded hills and mountains riven with darkened gorges and valleys. The only evidence of man's existence on that wild landscape were the marks of his rural toil: a network of tightly winding, narrow, dusty tracks, which snaked, twisted and meandered around the hills like veins linking isolated hamlets and high, alpine, apple-green meadows. Occasionally, in the gloomy depths of some valley the thin sliver of an asphalt road mimicked the course of a river. From one horizon to another the earth wore a mantle of deep blue. It was scarcely believable that somewhere below us humans, invisible in the thick and ancient forest, were stalking and killing each other with fanatical determination.

'Red smoke on the nose.' The pilot's voice crackled through the headphones. In the middle distance a faint wisp of red smudged the crown of a dusty hilltop, which was noticeably devoid of trees. I was surprised that this was the designated HLS, having assumed that we'd be landing on the town's football pitch adjacent to the UN base. We began our descent on finals. The blades pitched, the aircraft slowed and for the last few feet the world outside and our reception party, which was grouped around a cluster of white vehicles including the Range and the snatch, was obliterated by a vortex of dust and red smoke.

Engines running we quickly de-planed and scurried through the blown dust. Once we were clear the aircraft lifted, turned and dropped down into the Drina valley below, presumably to drop off the hideous boxes. Lt Col. David Santa Ollala, the CO of the Duke of Wellington's Regiment ('Dukes' or 'Duke of Boots' as they're known in Army slang), stepped forward, saluted and welcomed the General and Lady Rose to Gorazde. He and the bulk of his battalion (BRITBAT 2) with a company of Ukrainians under command, had been sent to Gorazde by Rose in April following the BSA attack on the enclave. Gorazde Force's mission had been to demilitarise a three-kilometre radius Weapon Exclusion Zone, centred around the town itself, and to interpose itself between the Serbs and Muslims where the line of confrontation was most critical. Santa Ollala, later awarded the DSO for his efforts, was Commander Gorazde Force.

While he briefed the General and his wife with the aid of a map board I wandered off for a quiet cigarette. Goose was chatting to Frank Cannon and UJ who'd had no problems getting the vehicles to Gorazde. Baggers had wandered off a little way and was staring out across the Drina valley. While enjoying my first smoke for some hours my attention was drawn to voices rattling away in Serbo-Croat a little way down the slope. I went to investigate and encountered two young boys, one brandishing a huge axe, the other a bow saw. They were ambling up a narrow goat track to the top, then they saw me and stopped dead. Both looked like escapees, urchins from a Dickensian novel, with smudged and grubby faces, matted, dusty, dishevelled mops of hair, colourless rags for clothes and no shoes. They eyed me suspiciously.

'What're you up to?' *Silly question really.*

'Wood,' one of them replied blandly and then, 'who's that?' pointing with the haft of his axe, which was balanced on his right shoulder.

'General Rose and his wife. She's brought an incubator for your hospital.'

The boy grunted, then he spied my cigarette and perked up, eyes pleading, asking the eternal question to which one can never say no. I tossed them one each. Even if they didn't smoke at least it was currency.

'Don't go any further up there,' I cautioned, not merely to prevent disruption to the briefing, but more to avoid the axe and saw-wielding assassins from being drilled full of holes by Goose and Frank in front of Reuters and ABC – 'GORAZDE MASSACRE – *Teenage Refugees Cut Down In Hail of Bullets By Rose Bodyguard.'* They weren't fussed though and retreated a little way, sat down and lit up.

I lit a second cigarette and surveyed the scene before me. The dusty hill was almost completely treeless. In their never-ending search for firewood every tree had been hacked down by locals over the past two and a half years, leaving an untidy, blasted landscape of ragged stumps reminiscent of some Flanders battlefield. It was all so depressingly similar to the mass deforestation encountered around the town of Srebrenica to the north. Week by week, month by month and now year by year the blemishes had spread like some monstrous and unstoppable tide, loosening the soil and destabilising the precipitous hillsides.

With no trees to obscure the view, the immense panorama of the Drina valley fell away before me. Far below flowed the Drina, a huge, dark-green, glassy-smooth serpent, thousands of tons of water gliding effortlessly northwards past the two halves of the town of Gorazde, which was perched on the east and west banks.

The town was built in the bend of the river where the valley bottom flattened out. The centre was a tatty jumble of high-rise tower blocks on both sides. Beyond these were scattered red-roofed houses stretching up to the base of wooded hills to the east, now held by the Bosnian Serb Army. Two concrete bridges linked east to west. Immediately below us some 100 metres away stood forlorn clusters of red-brick houses without roofs or windows. At first glance they looked like casualties of war. Closer inspection revealed them to be the shells of unfinished projects, the objects of somebody's lifelong savings destroyed by war.

The briefing over, we were off by vehicle, bumping our way down a track and engulfed in clouds of choking dust thrown up by the General's Range.

After five minutes the gradient slackened and eventually merged with asphalt, leading us into town. Narrow streets, enveloped by shrapnel-scarred, flaking yellow buildings, were choked with ragged looking people, soldiers and civilians alike, most of whom seemed to be milling around aimlessly or hawking cigarettes and other trinkets by the roadside. Our convoy ground on slowly through this morass. We forced our way through a large crowd, which had gathered outside the hospital, and stopped and de-bussed at the entrance.

The long and short of it is that the Muslims of Gorazde got their incubator. There were no hiccups on this occasion. General Rose and his wife were warmly welcomed. Despite the official propaganda line of the Sarajevo government, which was beginning to attack Rose for not doing enough, it was obvious that these wretched people were extremely pleased to see him and delighted that his wife was donating an incubator to the hospital. These were important indications that they had not been forgotten or abandoned.

After the presentation we found ourselves ushered into a large, crowded conference room. This was dominated by a long table along one side of which, with their backs to the windows, sat the entire line-up of Gorazde's top people: President of the Opstina (a sort of local council), Mr Rasic, various military commanders, local dignitaries, Dr Begovic and his hospital staff – a veritable *Who's Who* of Gorazde. We took our places opposite them with Lady Rose and the General roughly in the centre flanked by me to her left and David Santa Ollala's interpreter to Rose's right. Yet more locals including press filed in and filled seats behind us along the wall. There must have been fifty or sixty people in there. The temperature (and smell) began to rise.

In true Communist style everyone had a little speech to make and something to say following the formula of 'greetings, thanks, complaints'. The General listened but said little, choosing to defer to his wife. Some of the speakers, including Dr Begovic, spoke excellent English. Throughout, sweet Turkish coffee, fruit juice and walnut cakes were served. Above the heads of the assembled group a TV played, on a continuous loop, a homemade horror video, minus sound effects, of street scenes from April's fighting: decapitated bodies, squashed corpses and, unbelievably, a dead baby, severed at the waist, entrails hanging out, being dragged along the street by one of its arms. While someone from across the table droned on I stared, mesmerised by this horrific snuff movie. I wondered if Lady Rose had spotted what had been prepared for her benefit. A sly glance from the corner of my eye revealed that she was intently *not* looking at the TV. She later admitted that she'd seen it. It was impossible to miss. '*GORAZDE HORROR. Lady Rose Gets Eyeful.*' I suddenly felt detached from the surroundings, a weightless voyeur of people stuffing walnut cakes into their mouths, sipping coffee and watching dismembered limbs and torn corpses being shovelled into plastic bags. *Perhaps I'll wake up from this shit.* But I didn't. It was real.

'Fucking hell. Did you see the video they had?' Baggers was seething as we piled into the snatch, the waffle at last at an end. '. . . Outrageous, I mean, can you believe the neck of it! Give 'em an incubator and they give you a snuff movie.'

Led by David Santa Ollala and pursued by haunting images of dead babies, we beat a hasty path out of Gorazde and through the last UN Ukrainian-manned checkpoint. After a brief stop there we pushed on down the road to Ustipraca and were waved through a Serb checkpoint towards Visegrad, a small town some twenty kilometres downriver. The plan was to stop and have a look at the famous sixteenth-century Ottoman bridge linking east to west, which is also the centrepiece of Ivo Andric's novel published in 1945, *Na Drini Cuprija*, published in English as *The Bridge Over The Drina*.

Not far from the checkpoint at Donja Suputnica, on the left of the road, stood the wrecked shell of a fifteenth-century Orthodox church. Its fate was frequently raised in meetings by the Serbs, and both General Mladic and Professor Koljevic (one of Dr Karadzic's two vice-presidents) had a special interest in the church. They claimed that during the Muslims' summer uprising of 1992 along the Drina valley the Muslims of Gorazde had sacked the church and desecrated the graves, disinterring bones and scattering them. Staring at the tiny church as we passed by reminded me of Brigadier Robin Searby's dismay and anger in August 1993 after a trip to Vukovar. Standing in his Split office showing me photos of Vukovar's destruction he became quite animated about a pair of pictures he'd taken of the shattered interior of Vukovar's Catholic cathedral. He was appalled that the top of a huge sar-cophagus had been prised off by the Serbs and the centuries-old remains of a bishop tossed carelessly onto the floor.

Two thoughts struck me. First, how little difference there was between the peoples of former Yugoslavia, particularly with regard to behavioural pat-terns, furiously deny it though they might. Secondly, the wars seemed less to do with grand strategic power struggles and much more to do with local perceptions, founded in the myths and mists of history, of who thought which bit of land belonged to whom based on who was buried where. A sort of necrowar.

Twenty kilometres further along a well-tarmaced road which hung precipi-tously over the Drina, and which wound its way through a series of blissfully cool tunnels, we came to Visegrad and its famous bridge. Twelve evenly spaced arches of white stone curved gracefully over the Drina. In the centre crown stood a stone buttress, raised such that both halves of the bridge sloped away gently to either bank. It was a timeless view, complemented by the only visible traffic on the bridge, a cart piled impossibly high with hay and shrieking children. To complete the scene, two large brown horses pulled the cart, lazily clip-clopping towards Visegrad on the east bank. Clinging to a spit of land

Visegrad was a medieval jumble of tight alleys and red roofs crowding around a white church.

We dismounted and began to walk across the bridge. We'd been joined by a Serbian colonel called Masal and a young female interpreter. As we walked my mind flashed back to Bianca Jagger's suggestion at Tuzla airfield in April 1993, that she would recommend to President Clinton the destruction of all the bridges over the Drina. Had Ivo Andric been a fly on the wall at that meeting he'd have been flabbergasted. To him bridges had a special philosophical and moral significance:

> 'Of all that a man is impelled to build in his life, nothing is in my eyes finer or more precious than a bridge. Bridges are more important than houses. Everywhere there is something to overcome or to bridge: disorder, death, meaninglessness. Everything is a transition, a bridge whose ends are lost in infinity, besides which all bridges of this earth are only children's toys, pale symbols.
> And all our hope lies on the other side.'

After halting in the alcove at the centre of the bridge for photographs, we proceeded to the east bank for an al fresco coffee overlooking the bridge. Half an hour later we were off leaving Colonel Santa Ollala and Colonel Masal at the café. It was time to find somewhere for phase two of the operation – the picnic.

We ground our way up tight hair-pin bends climbing slowly out of the Drina valley eventually popping out onto a plateau of lush fields and woods. Presently the Range pulled off the road and disappeared down a small track, which led to one of these meadows. Out hopped the General, his wife and Goose who summoned Frank and UJ to help him manhandle a huge cool-box over the fence. Blankets were spread out and the box delved into.

I was dispatched to a group of peasants who had emerged from a farmstead at the bottom of the field. Of various ages and sizes they brandished ancient-looking pitchforks and were headed for a field of freshly mown grass. I managed to intercept them before they got any closer to the picnic. More potential assassins. They were peasants to the last; headscarves, billowing black ankle-length dresses, tatty trousers held up with twine, deeply-tanned wrinkled old faces and not the foggiest idea who General Rose was, what an incubator did, or if pressed, who Dr Karadzic was. As timeless as the bridge, their sole concerns seemed to revolve around their cattle and the seasons. They didn't seem at all bothered by us. As they passed by an old crone uttered something uninteligible as she waved a bony hand in greeting, to which we all shouted back 'Dobar dan'; it did the trick.

Sarajevo was still some three hours drive away. As soon as the BH Command sandwiches had been consumed we pushed on. At the infamous 'mountain checkpoint' (a rusty ISO container at the Y-junction above Rogatica) we were held up by two teenage conscripts who knew nothing of our passage and had to radio down to Rogatica for instructions. General Rose wasn't bothered. Fortunately neither of the Roses ventured into the ISO container which was indescribably filthy. The guards spent a week at a time up there, which accounted for the fact that their girlfriends were cowering in the bushes beyond. We'd obviously caught them at it and they'd legged it, giggling and tittering. Fortunately no one else noticed. Just as well too that we'd ditched Kurt Schork and Bartley Price in Gorazde. *'CHECKPOINT CHICKS – Red Cross Rep In Serbian Sex Scandal.'*

In Rogatica itself we were delayed yet again, this time at the General's choosing. Rogatica was infamous for its brigands and pirates, who systematically delayed, worked over and pilfered from each UN convoy bound for Gorazde. They were a pain and the cause of much drama and angst at BH Command. Rogatica also boasted a sawmill, the band saws of which were reputedly used to chop up the town's Muslims. The Brigade Commander (chief pirate) and his sly and shifty sidekick, the infamous Captain Zoran, who had on a number of occasions been subjected to a Rose bollocking, ran the town. As we passed, Rose spotted Captain Zoran skulking about. The Range screeched to a halt and out leapt Rose, much to Zoran's consternation. Inevitably, this led to a meeting with the chief pirate in his office on an industrial estate. There wasn't much substance to the meeting other than to confirm that not only was he a pirate but he dressed like one too; black beard, outrageously flamboyant beret capping thick, greasy, dark ringlets of hair, sly but bright black eyes.

We passed through the town unmolested by a gang, which was working over a convoy going in the opposite direction. The general stopped briefly to check that the convoy commander, a Brit, was okay. A little way on we passed through Podromanija. Once a small town, virtually every house had either been flattened with explosives or burned to the ground, the inhabitants must have either fled or been fed to the voracious band saws in Rogatica. Magnificently in keeping with the times, the only edifice left standing was a huge pre-war billboard at the exit to the town advertising building materials: BUILD FOR A BETTER FUTURE.

We arrived back at the Residency in time to drop off Lady Rose and Baggers and to scoop up Simon Shadbolt and his replacement Jamie Daniell, who'd both remained in the city to conduct the hand-over–take-over. Then, to finish the day, straight down to the Presidency for a meeting with President Izetbegovic.

A few beers in the manic *Star Wars* bar completed my day. I felt faintly smug, both satisfied and relieved that the potential for disaster had remained unrealised, barring the sunbed drama, of course. But one could always blame the RAF for that. All that remained for the following day was to get Lady Rose through the Sierras to Kiseljak in time to catch a helicopter to Split. Potential for drama: v. v. low.

Friday 29 July 1994 – BH Command, Sarajevo

'That's us cleared through the Sierras,' I shouted across the bustling Outer Office at Baggers, having just put the phone down on Major Indjic.

'Y'sure?' He ran a troubled hand through his hair, back in mad professor mode, wrestling with the next visit or fixture.

'No probs. Indjic knew about it anyway. The Range, the snatch and Victor Andreyev's GMC, there and back by lunchtime.'

Just then Simon Shadbolt came scuttling out of the General's office followed by a bemused Jamie Daniell.

'The barber, Mike! Wasisname . . . ?'

'Mohamed.' *Oh yeah, here we go!*

'How quick can you get him?'

'Well, now I suppose. Why?'

'I think she's had a go at him about his hair. Demanding he sorts it out.'

'Righto. I'll get Goran to nip over the road and get him. Be about twenty minutes.'

None of this particularly surprised me. Haircuts were the least important things on our minds. In fact they never occurred to us. But, on a number of occasions, usually late at night, the general would emerge from his office looking twitchy. Sometimes it was the MA – 'Mike, get the barber in tomorrow.' She'd have seen him on the news, rung up and ticked him off about his hair. Sometimes she'd go further. I'd know because sometimes he'd tell me my hair was looking scruffy. She'd have spotted me on TV lurking behind the General. I'd quickly get Mohamed over from his little barber's shop on the other side of the park and sort the problem out before the cameras caught us again. I'd inherited this unusual duty from Nick Costello.

Getting the General's hair cut seemed to have been a thread that ran consistently throughout my time in the Balkans. If you're not armed with the lingo, getting your hair cut by one of the locals can lead to unfortunate results. Both Cumming and Searby had used me to this end, virtually under threat of sacking if I got it wrong. These performances were fraught with danger and were not to be undertaken lightly.

I hurried off to look for Goran, the waiter, and found him hidden away with Nada and Goca (Residency staff), who were smoking and drinking coffee behind the reception desk curtains.

'Goran. Get Mohamed up to the office as quick as you can.' He shot off towards the main gate while I went in search of the long extension cable. All part of the procedure for setting Mohamed and his gear up in Rose's bathroom, a lavish room with a huge mirror and cool tiles.

Within ten minutes Goran and Mohamed had presented themselves at the Outer Office. As usual the barber appeared immaculate in his white coat, clutching a large, black leather case stuffed with the tools of his trade. The MA dashed into the General's office and emerged a moment later.

'Set up in the usual place. Back way though. Not through the office.' The 'back way' meant nothing more than following the corridor outside the Outer Office to a door at the end, which led in behind the General's office to his bathroom and bedroom.

Lady Rose was already waiting for us. I introduced her to Mohamed, who was, as usual, charming. Quickly he set up his bits and pieces and connected his electric clippers to the extension cable. The General appeared, sat in the chair and was immediately enveloped in a maroon sheet from the neck downwards. Mohamed had no English so, rather than fuss over what the General wanted, which was only a trim anyway, I mainly interpreted the chit-chat. Mohamed was a good source of city and grass-roots' gossip. In his day he'd cut Karadzic's hair when the latter had lived a stone's throw away from the Residency opposite the secondary school (now refugee centre) in his former guise as chief psychiatrist to the Sarajevo football club. On this occasion chit-chat would not be possible so we deferred to Angela Rose.

'Off the ears . . . fringe needs trimming . . . and the back is far too long!'
'GOTCHA! – Bosnia Commander Scalped By Wife.'

'The usual, Mohamed,' I mumbled.

As he clipped away, Lady Rose slipped away. *Odd! I'd have thought she'd hang around to supervise.* However, within minutes Baggers appeared at the door with Angela standing behind. He grinned sheepishly, shrugged his shoulders and muttered something about being 'captured'. She'd penned him in behind his desk. Canny buggers that they were, the bodyguards had already legged it. Insufficiently forewarned and unable to bolt, Baggers had been blasted, 'You'd better have one too, Jeremy. Your hair's scruffy.' The General was finished and Mohamed looked delighted at the prospect of another 5 Deutschmarks easy pickings. *I wonder if he and Angela are in cahoots.*

'What's it gonna be then, Baggers?' A cruel and sadistic catch in my voice alerted the ADC as he eased into the chair.

'As little as possible . . . and no funny stuff, Mike!' He was acutely aware that I held the interpreter's trump card in these matters.

'*Skini mu sve!* – Off with it all!' I hissed at Mohamed who laughed loudly. This panicked the ADC who'd caught the tone if not the meaning.

'No, Mike! Just a trim.'

I relented, '*Dobro onda, skini mu samo malo* – All right then, just a trim.'
So, the BGs have legged it, have they! It nagged at me as Mohamed's

271

clippers attacked the ADC's mop. A horrible thought came into my mind. I cast a sly glance at Angela. She wasn't looking at me. *Fuuuck! I'm next!* Lamely muttering something about 'going to check the cable' I sidled out into the corridor. I'd almost made good my escape, almost turned the corner and was about to race down the stairs and go and hide with Goca, Nada and Goran behind the curtain. A shrill voice shot arrow-like down the corridor and hit me square between the shoulder blades.

'Mike Stanley! Where do you think you're going? Get back here at once! You're next!' *'BOSNIA INTERPRETER SAVAGED.'*

EIGHTEEN

Operation Bretton

November 1997 – Ian, UK

'Sounds as though she was quite fearsome.' Ian has been laughing about the incubators and haircuts.

'Lady Rose? She was fine. Kept us in our places. Looked after her boys. No, that story's not really about her. It could have been anyone delivering those incubators and the twist or moral in it would have been exactly the same. It's a story about the nature of the locals, and as far as I'm concerned it illustrates the point that well-meaning gestures by Westerners were either wasted on or perverted by the end-user.'

There's a sequel to that incubator escapade. The day Lady Rose departed a parcel appeared at my desk. A huge bloody great big Perspex 'tray'. It was the 'bit' that was missing from the baby-warmer-upper, the 'sunbed', we'd given to the Serbs. Those urgent messages buzzed from the helicopter must have got someone flapping back in the UK. The following day there wasn't much going on so Nick Magnall, the G3 Ops Lieutenant Colonel, Martin, the new JCO commander, and I jumped into a vehicle and took it up to the Koran hospital in Pale. There was also an instruction manual, in German, which none of us could decipher.

When we got up there the hospital director was delighted to see us and took us up to the post-natal room. The 'thing' was sitting in the corner next to the redundant incubator. The tray fitted perfectly. Angela Rose had asked me to get some pictures of the machine in use for the British Red Cross magazine, so a nurse was dispatched to fetch a baby. It came wrapped up like a cocoon in a towel and was placed in the tray of this machine (which wasn't working) while I snapped off a couple of shots. That was it really. I doubt that machine was ever used again.

It gets even worse. About three months later, in October, we're off to Gorazde for a visit. Lady Rose rings up and tells the General to go to the hospital and check up on the incubator and if possible get some photographs. A few changes have taken place: the 'Duke of Boots' have been replaced in Gorazde by the 'M4s', the RGBW (Royal Gloucestershire Berkshire and

Wiltshire Regiment). They had a really bad start in Gorazde. Within a week of arriving in the enclave in September one of their Land Rovers had rolled down a hill; a week later one of their Saxon wheeled APCs also rolls down a hill. Altogether, five soldiers are injured and four killed. Terrible start to a tour.

We arrive in Gorazde and the General gets a formal briefing in a Portakabin from the CO, Lt Col. Davidson-Houston. We're due to spend the night there, so the CO, or maybe it was the Ops Officer, goes through the visit programme. Visit to the mayor, visit to this commander etc, etc. But Rose has obviously got something on his mind and just ups and says he wants to go to the hospital to visit the incubator. Well, at this the CO blanches and looks incredibly concerned. He doesn't say anything though. As the briefing breaks up he grabs me by the arm, he's very perturbed, and says something like, 'You've gotta stop him going anywhere near the hospital. He can't go in there. Not to the incubator.'

I ask him why. When he tells me I nearly kill myself laughing. In fact, this is serious stuff: all our necks are on the line here. As we're walking away from the briefing room I grab Goose and tell him that we've got to keep the General away from the hospital, especially the incubator. When I tell Goose why he too laughs, but he recognises the seriousness of the situation. That's what we did for the next twenty-four hours: kept deflecting the General from the hospital, inventing extra meetings and so on. Whether he knew what we were up to I've no idea, but we kept him away from the place.

None of us knew at the time that incubators need to run off a purified air ventilation system. It seems this hospital was either built without one or if it had one, it wasn't working. The incubator couldn't be used, not as an incubator at any rate. But, unlike the Serbs in Pale who weren't using their machine at all, Dr Begovic and gang in Gorazde had, rather enterprisingly, found an alternative use for their incubator.

They were cultivating 'grass', marijuana, in the British Red Cross incubator. It's scarcely believable, but I've double-checked this. The RGBW's Ops Officer, David Brown, was at Staff College with me. I reminded him recently of the visit and the incident and he confirmed that it was exactly as I've just told you. Marijuana! That whole tale of the incubators just sums up again what Justin Webb of the BBC said of our first aborted heli op into Srebrenica on 24 March 1993 . . . 'Good intentions cruelly dashed.' That's Bosnia for you.

We've switched subjects. Ian has brought me back to something I had mentioned after we left Gorazde, the desecration of churches, the scattering of the bones of the dead. I'd called it necrowar. Just look at the British attitude to death and burial. You can virtually map out the history of the Empire simply by wandering from one graveyard or military cemetery to another anywhere in the world. The British have never cared too much about where someone's buried. What seems to be important is a person's *memory*, i.e. *in memoriam*, not where the bones actually are. Only very recently have we started to bring our fallen home. It started with the Falklands War and that's what we did in Bosnia. It's very American, bringing bodies home and not leaving them abroad, but by and large the Brits don't seem to care where the fallen lie, so long as the *in memoriam* bit is okay. That's why it can be hard for people to understand the necrowar bit.

The first thing you've got to understand about the Balkans is that the dead are more important than the living. To the living, that is. That's the basis of that particular side to their mentality. They're obsessed with their dead. The logic seems to be that territory belongs to he who is buried there. You'd often hear Mladic or Karadzic banging on about Serb territory and then justifying it by quoting some church and who was buried there. You'd hear it from the Croats too. You never heard it from the Muslims, not that I can recall anyway. But, that's not to let anyone off the hook for all the desecration that went on. They were all torching each other's churches or mosques. In Banja Luka the Serbs dynamited every single mosque, *disappeared* them, no mosques ergo Banja Luka must be Serb territory.

That's one part of the logic. The other is deliberately generated vindictiveness. Dig up the bodies and scatter the remains about. It was a kind of primitive rape of the dead; to the victor the bones. So, it wasn't enough to make people's lives a misery when they were living. You compounded that by ensuring that they didn't rest in peace either. The bonus of course was that once the bodies were 'up' the other side couldn't claim it was their territory.

That's just the beginning of it. None of this is new either. It's at the extreme end of this sort of pathological behaviour, but it's not new. Under Tito, where the mechanics of one-party control kept everyone living in blissful 'brotherhood and unity', these characters would find other ways of displaying their national tribalism. So, for example, in the JNA the rule was that conscripts had to be stationed anywhere but in their home region in Yugoslavia. Young Croats found themselves in Serb areas, young Serbs in Croat areas and so on. Extramural activities included smashing up and defacing each other's graveyards. It became a national sport. In war they just went that one step further and dug up the bodies for good measure.

They were deadly serious about the importance of their dead. Just look at those bizarre TV pictures after Dayton. When Ilidza and Grbavica were ceded to the Muslims. The Serbs just packed up and left, but not before they'd got the heavy plant and cranes in and dug up their nearest and dearest, whom they took with them. That's what I mean about obsession with the dead.

Not everyone out there is a shovel-wielding ghoul just waiting to dig up someone's grave. They didn't do it in Sarajevo where Serbs and Muslims were buried virtually side by side in Kosevo Cemetery. Not everyone has this extreme vampire-like instinct. But there's definitely something quite peculiar in their attitudes towards the dead.

We've got direct experience of this necrosyndrome in our own family. My father's lot came from this small village of Mrcajevci in Sumadija, in Serbia. Nothing special. All a bit dusty and provincial. My father's mother died when he was young and he was raised by his eldest sister, Nada. She was killed in an Allied bombing raid in 1943 and she and her husband and the unborn boy were buried in the graveyard at Mrcajevci. This left the youngest sister, Bisenija, alive, along with his father. When my father and his Royalist chums escaped from Yugoslavia with the Commies hot on their heels, his father and sister were left behind. Dad never went back and his father died in 1957 in Nis but was buried in the same plot as his wife and daughter. Bisa continued to live in the 'ancestral home' in Mrcajevci and tended the grave. Normal practice out there.

Bisa spent the rest of her life ranting and raving against the Communists, so much so that they cut off her pension and declared her mad. For that reason, she wasn't imprisoned. Her only income came from us in England. My father supported her to the end of her life, which came in January 1992 when I was in Kuwait. Over the years we sent her TVs and thousands of pounds. Mum used to go out with the money.

She took my sister and me out one year. I think it was 1967. I was four so have only a distant memory of the house in Mrcajevci. What I do recall was that it was a disgusting hovel: a shack with no electricity, no running water (that was got from a deep well in the 'garden', which was full of rubbish). My aunt slept on a dirty old mattress surrounded by piles and piles of ancient old newspapers, all eaten through by rats and other rodents. She cooked on a wood fire so the whole place was blackened including the odd photograph pinned to the wall. We were bathed in an iron tub in cold water from the well.

One day we all went to the graveyard. There was an old woman placing flowers on a nearby grave. As we approached, she flipped: started howling, wailing, screeching and crying. Then she flung herself onto the grave. We were terrified and my mother was shocked. I remember her shouting at the woman, 'Stop it this instant! You're scaring the children!' And she did. Just like that. Stood up totally composed having turned off the grief just as fast as she'd turned it on. That's what they're like.

That was 1967. And what happened to all the money, the thousands we'd sent out? When Bisa got so old, sick and infirm as to be incapable my mum would go out more frequently. One year, I think it was 1991, Mum went out. The house looked as it always had. She went up to the graveyard to put some flowers on the plot and discovered this huge, and I mean *giant*, black marble gravestone inscribed with gold lettering. That was it. Bisa had hoarded every penny of what we'd sent her and had spent it all on this piece of marble. She'd preferred to do that than get water into her place, or electricity. To her the dead were more important than the living.

After Bisa's death, we sold off the house. It was totally uninhabitable. The rest of the town was concrete with nice red roofs and slap bang in the middle was this wonky, decrepit, wooden shack which was infested with all sorts, and a garden strewn with empty bottles. My dad offered the house to me, said something to the effect that I could build a café there and run it. I ask you! So we sold it, got ripped off because there was a war on, and what little we got paid for Dad's funeral here in England. Weird thing was, though, that having alienated everyone around her when she was alive, after her death she lay in state in the church for three days. The whole town turned out to her funeral and she was buried in the plot. Well before her death she'd already got her name engraved on that outrageous piece of black marble. That's all that mattered to her.

Let me tell you about Balkan extremes, about what these buggers were capable of doing to the living, too. It couldn't be blacker. The most twisted and perverted mind couldn't have dreamt up some of the things that went on out there. Everyone has a pet horror story which confirms the particular nature of Balkan savagery. Lt Col. Patrick Davidson-Houston, the CO of the 'M4s' in Gorazde, tells of one. It defies belief. I got it second hand from Colonel Aldwin Wight but neither has any reason to lie or to embellish. Body exchanges were part and parcel of the war out there: each side wanted its bodies back for burial. The UN frequently acted as intermediaries. Usually it was done on a pro rata basis, ten bodies for ten bodies, as happened in Gorazde. The UN set up a tent on the front line in which the Muslim and Serb representatives met. They agreed on numbers and names. When the Serbs produced seven or so Muslim bodies the Muslims rejected the corpses, which had been horribly hacked up. They didn't reject them because they'd been horribly hacked up but because they disagreed with the manner in which they'd been hacked up. The Serbs had that sawmill in Rogatica. These bodies were victims of the band saws. But the Muslims weren't having any of it and countered with a, 'Oh, no no no. You've said these were killed in the sawmill, but it's quite clear to us that you've actually killed them with a chainsaw! The deal is off!' To which the Serbs emphatically replied something like, 'No, honest, it was the sawmill not chainsaws.' All this with the UN looking on speechless while the two parties bickered away as to the manner of death . . . just to be difficult.

There are other examples of this elsewhere, of unknown corpses being dug up just to make up the numbers. On another occasion, in the west, the Serbs were handed over a number of bodies and recognised one as having been a live prisoner, 'But he was alive yesterday!' to which the reply came, 'But you didn't specify dead or alive' which mollified the Serbs who shrugged their shoulders with an 'Oh, okay, fair one.'

The one that really sticks in my mind was told to me by a Serb soldier. I used to call him the *Gusle* Player. He'd been a historian before the war in Tuzla, and was also, according to him, a *gusle* player of some note. A *gusle* is a traditional Serbian instrument, a bit like a mandolin, which produces a screeching sound like a thousand scalded cats – torture really.

Whenever I drove up to Pale on some errand or other I'd always stop and pick up a hitchhiker. One day I spied the *gusle* player thumbing a lift and stopped to pick him up. This bloke was intelligent and had lots to talk about – history mainly. We chatted away about the course of the war and its origins and suddenly he just said, 'You Westerners are never going to understand the mentality here. You've no idea what really drives behaviour. All of it is history.' He told me this story which made my toes curl.

In his unit there was a soldier who was in his mid-fifties. He'd been born in Foca, on the Drina south of Sarajevo, and had grown up without a father. His family had lived next to a Muslim family. During the Second World War, when he was still an infant, the Muslim next door had killed his father, slashed his throat in a glade in a nearby wood. After the war the two families had continued living as neighbours, reconciled under Tito's all-embracing 'brother-hood and unity'. The Muslim had a son of similar age and the two boys grew up together, went to the same school, worked in the same factory, shared girlfriends, both got married and had families of their own. When the Bosnian war broke out, what do you think the Serb did? He flipped and dragged his Muslim neighbour and friend of fifty years to the exact same glade in the same wood and slashed his throat.

It was revenge. 'Brotherhood and unity' was really nothing but a shallow illusion. Until I heard this story I hadn't really appreciated what we were dealing with. In a nutshell it's pathological behaviour driven by deep-seated perceptions or misconceptions of past injustices. So, in a way, truth, whatever that may be, simply wasn't important. All that really mattered were percep-tions. People based their analysis and actions on these perceptions. And that was the basis of all our problems in dealing with these people.

You'd be sitting at a meeting with Mladic or someone banging on about something, almost always quoting some historical injustice. Or he'd write a diatribe and send it either to us or up to the Zagreb HQ. Quite often our side would comment, amongst ourselves, 'He's mad' or 'He's off his head' or 'That's simply not true.' But our perceptions or understanding of 'truth' were based on contemporary views and influences such as up-to-date intelligence, satellite imagery, policy, views and *Realpolitik* emanating from various capi-tals. The press too had a major impact on formulating our perceptions. Of critical importance here is that few if any of our perceptions were tailored by history. But theirs were. We were staring at each other over a table and our start-points for negotiation began at opposite ends of a spectrum of perception – theirs historical, ours contemporary. We were virtually communicating in two completely different languages and with almost no common ground.

In that sense 'truth', i.e. a common understanding of fact, was nowhere to be seen and was largely irrelevant. They *believed* they were right, and we thought they were liars for it. We *believed* in our monopoly of 'truth', and they saw us as liars. The bottom line is this: if Mladic *believed* something to be so, regardless of the fact that we knew it not to be that way, the fact that it wasn't so was totally irrelevant. He was always going to base his analysis and hence his actions on what he *believed* to be the case, conditioned as his perceptions were by history and upbringing. Perceptions based on *belief* were everything. 'Truth' had nothing to do with it. In a way it was our failing not to recognise this, and theirs too. In a sense it was translating one perception to another which became my job, albeit by accident and by blundering around in this grey middle world of 'truths' and 'perceptions' – a foot in both camps if you like. Nightmarish.

That was the saga of the incubators. It came and went just as fast as the Galvin visit and we just moved on, dealing with a deteriorating security situation around Sarajevo. Karadzic had closed down the Blue Routes, stifling the city once more. The Muslims' only source of resupply was over Mount Igman, down into Hrasnica and Butmir and thence through the tunnel under the airport into Dobrinja. The Serbs attempted to thwart this by firing at their convoys with their 30mm cannon in Ilidza, a clear violation of the Sarajevo Total (heavy weapons) Exclusion Zone.

All this was really HQ Sector Sarajevo's headache, but it also affected us, being located in the city. Sniping incidents too were on the increase. When we weren't on the road, i.e. when Rose was in the office, I spent quite a lot of time on the Serb side at Lukavica barracks trying to get a feel for the way they were going to vote in the referendum as to how the Contact Group Plan would settle the war. The mood seemed to indicate that the vast majority of Serbs were going to vote 'no' to the CG Plan. For their part Western governments, via their representatives on the Contact Group, had made it quite plain that it was a case of take it or leave it. No more room for negotiation or for manoeuvre. It looked as though we were all heading for an impasse.

It all became hugely Byzantine. The Serbs complained about the existence of the tunnel at the airport. They demanded that the UN dismantle it as it was a clear violation of the June 1992 Sarajevo Airport Agreement, in which the Serbs (JNA) had ceded the airport to the UN, on condition that the latter prevented the Muslims from transiting across the runway. Thus the UN had effectively been put into the position of acting as prison guards. In response the Muslims dug their way under the runway and completed their tunnel in about June 1993. Other than the Mafia trading across the front line (mafia activities stopped for no war) the tunnel was their lifeline. The UN turned a blind eye to its existence and the Sector Sarajevo commander told Major Indjic that it was a 'mirage'. The Serbs shot at Muslim convoys with their 30mm. The Muslims blamed the UN for not doing anything about the cannon. The Serbs blamed the UN for allowing Muslim convoys to transit the Bijelasnica and Igman DMZ. The French tried to hunt down the Ilidza cannon and actually found a firing pit full of empty cases, but the elusive cannon had disappeared and Major Indjic smugly informed them that the cannon too was a 'mirage'. And on it went. Serbs threatening to cut off the electricity, gas and water to the city. Tensions were rising and the situation nose-diving.

In and amongst all this I was increasingly being pestered by Jasna Pandure-vic, the Muslim woman working for the 'Flowers of Love' to whom Nick had introduced me during our hand-over. Nick had promised to get her husband and their young daughter out of the city. I'd inherited that promise and since then had done my best to forget it. I wasn't interested in Schindler's List. I'd scared myself to death getting Una's folks out with Matt Brey and didn't want to go through all that drama again. Besides, the situation had deteriorated: the Blue Routes were closed and it was no longer a case of bundling folk willy-nilly into a vehicle and just driving them out. With the closure of the Blue Routes the Muslims and Serbs had activated their checkpoints again and the risk of discovery was that much greater. By 'risk', I mean it in a two-fold sense. The risk of beneficiaries being lifted at a Bosnian checkpoint was unthinkable – they'd probably be made to 'disappear'. The risk of compromise to General Rose was also huge and just not worth the hassle. The other thing was that, although Nick had told me that Rose was briefed every time one of these Schindlers went down, exactly who briefed him was still unknown to me.

All this and a natural sense of cowardice caused me to keep putting Jasna off. She'd ring me, sometimes she'd write a note and on one occasion she even came to the Residency. She was desperate, not so much for herself, since she could still quite freely get to the Serb side by crossing the Bridge of Brotherhood and Unity over to Grbavica. What she couldn't do was take her four-year-old daughter and certainly not her Serb husband. As well as all his other problems, he had cancer and needed treatment abroad. All of this con-spired to create a mini human tragedy.

I'd pretend Jasna's problem didn't exist. Whenever she approached me saying that there was a window of opportunity I'd come up with some excuse. Secretly, I hoped she'd just give up and leave me alone, but life's not like that. She just kept on and eventually there was nowhere for me to hide. A promise was a promise.

She'd just phoned me. Her husband was out of hospital for a short period and the family was together. I told her it was too dangerous and I'd get back to her. I could hear her crying on the phone as I put it down. At the time my overriding emotion was not pity or sympathy. Rather selfishly, it was anger, anger at having been put into this position. I just wanted rid of the problem. I must have just flipped, blew a fuse, rang her back and snapped, 'OK. Be ready in half an hour. And no suitcases, nothing except passports and documents!' Suitcases were a terrible hassle: they took up room and could be seen. Moreover, if anyone observed them getting into a UN vehicle with suitcases it would have been bloody obvious what was going on. When you think about it, what an unreasonable demand. These people were going to leave this city for ever, to start a new life somewhere, and here was I telling them 'no suitcases'.

I grabbed Goose and explained the problem. He'd known that something was afoot. I half expected him to refuse to help but he agreed at once and went off to get the vehicle started. Within twenty minutes we'd driven to where the Pandurevics lived. Ominously, their road was a dead end, while they themselves lived on the fourth floor of an apartment block. It didn't look good at all. It got even worse when they answered the door and started lugging out one suitcase after another. I was cursing and swearing under my breath. What if some nosy neighbour poked his head out of a flat and saw us lugging this lot down the stairs? We looked as though we were off on holiday. Just about everything went bar the kitchen sink. The husband was nervous as hell, pale and sweating. The little girl looked ill too, almost feverish. I was fuming about the suitcases and really quite panicky. Their nervousness infected me, mine them, and by the time we emerged onto the street we were a bundle of sweating, swearing nerves.

Then disaster struck. Goose had turned the vehicle round ready for a quick getaway. As we struggled to stuff the cases and their owners into the vehicle a Bosnian policeman rounded the corner. He took one look at what was going on and, hackles up, marched straight up to Jasna. 'ID card!' he snapped. Stupidly she produced it and gave it to him. Goose looked horrified, his face a black mask of anger. 'Fuck!' he spat jumping into the driver's seat and gunning the engine. We'd botched it badly. There was no going back. 'Fuck this!' I was angry and scared. The policeman was starting to say something to Jasna. I didn't give him the chance and just pushed her into the vehicle and jumped in behind as Goose roared off. In the rear-view mirror we could see the policeman still holding the ID card and talking urgently into his radio.

It couldn't have been worse. Caught red-handed. What could we do now? They couldn't go back there. They'd be arrested. If we went straight into the Residency we couldn't harbour these people for ever. They'd probably plastered the vehicle's make and number plate all over the city. Basically, we'd screwed up the whole show. Goose was fuming. I was fuming. What to do?

For want of nothing better we raced into the Residency. 'Get 'em into the other vehicles,' someone hissed, Goose probably. Some of the other blokes were on hand and we stuffed the family and their gear into Victor Andreyev's pimp-mobile, a huge American GMC with black-tinted windows and violet, carpeted upholstery. With that and the snatch we tore out of the Residency and sped west along Sniper's Alley. There was an outside chance that, in different vehicles, we might just bluff our way through the BiH checkpoint at Stup if, and only if, they hadn't raised the chain. If we were stopped there, if they demanded to check the vehicles, the game would be up. I didn't even want to think about what would happen then. As we sped through the city we could see policemen eyeing every UN vehicle and reporting into their radios. They were alert and clearly looking for us. The only thing they didn't know was which vehicle to look for. Sweat was pouring down my face and soaking my shirt. Nobody said a word.

The snatch raced through the barriers at the Stup checkpoint just as the guards came running out trying to grab the girder bollards, one tug of which would have raised the chain suspended between the two. We shot across the chain just as it started to rise. I don't think Goose had any intention of stopping anyway. We were through, just. A little further on, right under the flyover, was another BiH checkpoint but having no physical barrier they could do nothing except stare at us as we swept past.

Those were the worst two. I don't think Jasna and her family realised that. They were probably flapping about the Serb one at Sierra 4 on the other side of the dash across no-man's-land. This really wasn't a problem. I knew the crew there and just got out and chatted briefly with them. Told them we were off to Lukavica for a meeting with Major Indjic. They didn't even bother to come close to the vehicle. We were through the worst of it and got through the two French checkpoints at the airport and a final Serb one near Lukavica with no mishaps or drama.

By the time we'd pulled up at Indjic's office we'd calmed down a bit and managed to reassure Jasna and her husband that they were safe. We pulled the little girl out of the boot where we'd hidden her. I don't think she had a clue of what had happened, but she looked dreadfully ill. The suitcases were unloaded and Indjic ushered us into his office. Fortunately, there were no other UN LOs about. Indjic produced a bottle of something, but we were too hyped up really to care what happened next.

Jasna started crying. Ranko started crying. Maja started crying. We damn nearly burst into tears as they thanked us for saving their lives. It's hard to describe the emotion. They were thanking us, but in reality we'd so nearly got them all killed and at the same time all this stress is washing off you. Made you feel weak. At the time we didn't really register what we'd done.

There was no feeling of having saved anyone's life, just immense relief that we hadn't actually killed them.

They were asked where they were off to. They said they had a plan to go to Canada but had very little money. We dug around in our pockets and pooled as much as we could find to see them on their way. Somehow I doubted they'd ever get abroad, I mean right through Serb-held territory, to Belgrade, and then there were visas and so on. But that was their problem. Ours was to get back and face the music. So we just jumped back in the vehicles and shot off again. Amazingly, there were no repercussions. No one said a word. No complaints were made. Nothing. Just as though it had never happened. I never saw those people again. To be honest, I banished the whole thing from my mind, just thankful that we'd got away with it, relieved that I wouldn't be pestered again and in a way secretly pleased that Nick's promise had been fulfilled. But that was it. As far as I was concerned it was too risky to do again.

Of course, we did loads more. Lots of blokes involved, including our American communicators and a couple of Canadians. I can't adequately explain why. I suppose we got hooked on it. It had a tangible result. Someone's lives were being affected for the better. That environment was so utterly without hope, the negotiations so absurdly unproductive, the lives of the 'Little People', the no-hopers, so beyond their own control that anything went. I suppose we believed we could make a difference to someone at any rate. Besides, the propaganda line coming out of the Bosnians was that the UN, by virtue of controlling the airport, was acting as camp guards in the world's largest concentration camp. So, in a way, it was two fingers up at them too. There's no point in trying to justify Schindler's List: we don't have to do that, those of us who took part in it. Strangely enough, you calmed down from the whole thing pretty quickly and moved on to other things.

At the time it was easy to forget about it; we just shot off to face another drama. Things had been happening in Bihac, an isolated enclave in north-west Bosnia. The situation there was even more complicated than anywhere else in Bosnia. Until about October 1993 the BiH 5th Corps under Atif Dudakovic had held out under pressure from the Bosnian Serbs to the south and east of the river Una and against the Krajina Serbs from the north and west. Distanced from Sarajevo by geography and by a succession of front lines between the Muslims and Croats, and Serbs, in Central Bosnia, Bihac was in almost all respects more isolated and beleaguered than Srebrenica, Zepa and Gorazde in the east. In addition, Fikret Abdic had established himself in Bihac. Thus more front lines were established within the enclave, further isolating the people of Bihac. Now you had Muslims versus Muslims in Bihac. Mad. At the beginning of July 1994, I think it was round about the 8th, 5th Corps engineered a massive defection from Abdic's forces and began to gain the upper hand. General Rose figured it was time for a visit to the French battalion based at Coralici, just north of Bihac.

We flew up to Zagreb first. At Pleso airport we were whisked off to HQ UNPROFOR in a fleet of sleek white Ford Caprices, the ubiquitous Zagreb UN staff car. The HQ complex sprawled across a JNA barracks in the centre of town. It was home to just about every UN agency under the sun, not just the military, and to others such as ICFY. SRSG, Mr Yasushi Akashi, the Big Boss, worked there as did the big military Boss, the Force Commander, General Bertrand de Lapresle, and all their staffs. The whole gang was there; HQ UNMOs, UN PInfo, UNTV, UN Civil Affairs and so on, all supported by well-appointed canteens and a well-stocked PX. The helmeted Swedish gate guards looked somewhat out of place considering we were in the middle of a relatively modern and unscathed city hundreds of miles from the chaos of Sarajevo. It was always a bit of a culture shock going up there.

After a quick meeting between bosses we tore back to Pleso and boarded a UN Huey and flew down to a UN Polish base at Maljevac in Sector North, still in the Krajina, but very close to the Bosnian border with the enclave of Bihac. A French convoy picked us up and for what seemed like hours we tramped south down Bihac's dusty roads. Goose and the General were in one vehicle, Jim Lenski and me in another jeep, just covered in thick red dust. I don't even remember passing through the Muslim-Muslim front line. Can't have been any fighting that day. The only thing that really struck me, apart from the dust, was how backward and underdeveloped the region was. It had the feel of a time warp.

The French were good hosts. We'd arrived at dusk so there wasn't much to do except clean up, eat, drink and sleep. The following day the Boss was going to meet Atif Dudakovic in Bihac, but in the end he never did get to see him. Something blew up out of nowhere the next morning. We began to get garbled messages that the situation in Sarajevo had gone pear-shaped. The Serbs had grabbed their heavy weapons from one of the Weapon Collection Sites in violation of the February agreement. We tore off north with Rose muttering something about winding up a BLUE SWORD Close Air Support strike (a UN-initiated air strike against a specific target, as in Gorazde in April, as opposed to 'air strikes' generally, which meant unrestrained, massive bombing campaigns by NATO). As we passed through Velika Kladusa on the way to Maljevac we swung off the road and drove straight up to a huge medieval castle – Fikret Abdic's HQ. He was exactly as I'd expected him to be, a corpulent businessman with a jowly and slightly jolly face, which gave no indication that he was a determined fighter of any sort. We couldn't hang around long and after about fifteen minutes were on the road again.

As we waited at Maljevac for the Huey to appear Rose got impatient. He was starved of information. I think he'd already ordered an air strike to be initiated against Serb targets in the Sarajevo TEZ. Jim Lenski set up the TACSAT in the middle of the car park. Rose spoke to Admiral Leighton Smith in Naples and then to BH Command. There was no doubt about it, a BLUE SWORD air strike was on the cards, fighting had broken out around Ilijas and across the airport. Our biggest concern now was to get back into Sarajevo, before the air strike went in. If we missed the opportunity, the Serbs would close down the airport, with fire, and all their checkpoints, and there'd be no way in. This was a constant problem, having one's HQ inside a besieged city, where the besiegers were the ones who'd do their best to keep you out. It became a recurring nightmare.

As the Huey settled on the pan at Pleso we leapt out and rushed towards a waiting Yak 40, a medium-sized ex-Soviet military exec jet which had been laid on to try and get us back into Sarajevo as soon as possible. We scurried behind a huge white UN Ukrainian Ilyushin 76, a massive ex-Soviet four-engined beast used for ferrying food and people into Sarajevo. It had just taxied to a halt, engines still blasting hot gasses. Lt Col. Gordon Rudd, our NATO LO, stepped off the ramp. 'What're you doing here?' barked Rose. 'Trying to get back to Sarajevo. Airport went red, lots of firing, just as we were on finals. Crew aborted back here,' replied Rudd with a shrug. 'Well, you'd better come with us. We're off to Sarajevo!' Rose hurled over his shoulder as he disappeared off towards the Yak. So we scooped up Gordon Rudd as well.

I had this horrid feeling that we were being pulled along by a mad irresistible force. The airport had gone to red. They were firing over it. This Il 76 had just aborted, which means the crew must have known how dangerous it was . . . and this lunatic wants us to fly into the same place! All this goes through your head. But he just pulled us along. I reckon he was fearless, not in the bravado sense of the word. I think fear was an emotion, a feeling that he just blotted out, didn't even occur to him I don't suppose. Well it occurred to me all right.

Off we fly, down the Croatian coast, turn left over Split, scoot across to Kiseljak, turn right and then start descending on finals. Whole thing took about an hour. The closer we got to Kiseljak the worse the feeling of impotence became. I had visions of skipping over the flats in Ilidza with lunatic gunmen pumping round after round into the aircraft and us ending up as a giant fireball on the threshold of the runway. Gordon Rudd looked pale. I don't think he appreciated doing this for a second time.

Rose was sitting a third of the way down the Yak, Goose, Rudd, Lenski and me in the small compartment at the back. The aircraft descends rapidly. We're minutes from the fireball. Goose suddenly grabs a French flak jacket, one of those with the huge ceramic plates, and slips it under Rose's seat, so that he doesn't take a round up the arse. Then Goose turns to us and in a dead serious voice says, 'Right we are going to get hit. We are going to take casualties ... okay?' Then he grabs his MP5 and all but takes up a firing position at the small door. I had this mental picture of him kicking it out and squirting rounds at likely firing points. Rudd goes even whiter and has a sort of sickly half-smile on his face. Can't say I was too happy with Goose's assessment either. There's sod all we can do about it so we just start giggling like girls and cocking around. We thought we were heading for certain death, being led into the fireball by Rose, who is reading a paper or something – he doesn't care – and there's us capering about in the back stuffing those little white head-rest slips on our heads as though they were anti-flash masks. I remember Rose looking round and grinning like mad ...

Nothing happened, of course. We landed quite normally, shot down the runway and turned onto the pan. Not a shot. Nothing. Interesting, though, how your imagination can get the better of you and how a couple of choice words can affect everyone. At that precise moment in time we'd convinced ourselves of our own deaths. But, truth is, your worst fears are never realised.

The air strike went ahead, after a fashion. After all the drama of getting back quickly it took the NATO aircraft another hour and a half to acquire, identify and drop a bomb or whatever on some tank out in the DMZ. It was on their bloody targeting list and they were forever bragging about the utility of air strikes. When it came to the crunch they faffed around for hours to strike some old hulk which had probably been left in the TEZ because the Serbs hadn't bothered to move it. Probably did them a favour by striking it. Rose was fuming. He just sat in the AOCC like a cat on a hot tin roof, 'Well, when's it going to happen? This week perhaps?' All a bit of an embarrassing damp squib.

In a curious sort of way this ineffectual bombing did have an effect. I spent the next day on the Serb side sniffing around Indjic trying to find out what had happened. The Serbs had put their heavy weapons back into the Ilidza WCP. It seems that the Serbs had thought that the Muslims were about to attack and take Ilijas. There'd been quite a lot of shelling of that town anyway. Basically, they'd panicked and gone for their guns without authority from the UN and without authority from General Mladic either. I know this because I asked Indjic what Major General Galic thought he was doing grabbing the weapons. Indjic simply replied that the Sarajevo-Romanija Corps Commander was called Major General Milosevic, not General Galic. Well, he'd been Galic before we'd gone to Bihac. I pressed him on what had happened to him and Indjic replied that he'd retired and 'gone into pension'. That was nonsense. No one retires that suddenly, in the middle of a war. Likeliest explanation was that Galic had done it off his own bat, an error in judgement, and, following the 'air strike', Mladic had sacked him. Simple as that.

Towards the end of the month I had a nasty brush with the past, which in many ways was a foretaste of things to come. We went to Srebrenica by vehicle, a long drive in the Range and snatch. It was Rose's first visit to the enclave and he wanted to visit the Dutch battalion there. I wasn't too keen to go back there, but it seemed all Rose wanted to do was visit the Dutch. Off we went on a long drive through Pale, Han Pijesak, Vlasenica, hooked through Zvornik and down the Konjevic Polje valley where Nick had nearly been killed. As we drove around that area memories of 1993 flooded back. I really didn't feel too good about going back into Srebrenica.

The Dutch had set themselves up in the warehouse complex at Potocari not far from the Serb front line. They'd made themselves quite comfortable and had a fully functioning hospital. We got the usual tour and briefing. The situation was discussed at length and Naser Oric's name kept cropping up. He was the BiH commander in the pocket, no great mate of mine and Nick's. The more his name was mentioned the more I got this sneaking suspicion that things would not go well for me. It was also hugely naive of me to think that Rose would drive all the way to Srebrenica and not have a good sniff around when he got there. "Well, I'd better meet this Naser Oric,' announced Rose suddenly. My heart sank and I started panicking. I knew that Oric had marked me in 1993: he knew exactly who I was and what my real name was. If I appeared standing next to Rose, interpreting for him, it wouldn't take Oric long to get onto his masters in Sarajevo and bubble me away. It would have been another weapon for them to use against him. There was no time to explain anything. Rose had never asked me what I'd done in Bosnia before, hadn't a clue. Probably didn't even know I'd been to Srebrenica before. As we broke up to go and find Oric I grabbed Jamie Daniel and just told him that I couldn't be seen by Oric and they'd have to find another interpreter. And that was it. I rushed off and hid in a vehicle with Jim Lenski and they just got on with it.

When we got back to the Residency that evening, having crashed on the way back, Jamie Daniel grabbed me and took me upstairs to his bedroom for a verbal bollocking. He banged on about Rose being disappointed that I'd deserted him etc, etc, so I explained why, told him what had happened to me in that place in April 1993. From the look in his eyes I could tell that it was all completely beyond his experience and understanding. It was hard to blame him in a way but at the time I was irritated, to put it mildly. People like him didn't really have an 'in' on the mentality. They had no idea what these people were capable of. They'd stitch you up like a kipper and you wouldn't even know you'd been stitched up, until it was too late. They stitched up just about everyone – got me in the end. They were masters at it. After football and digging up each other's graves, stitching people up was their favourite pastime. And they were bloody good at it. You'd never see it coming, but your nemesis would be silently homing in and you'd get whacked hard.

They had an unbelievable knack of finding a gap, a weakness, and ruthlessly exploiting it in the least expected way. Here's an example. Round about the end of August we had another visit, a high-powered one from an American general, another of Clinton's reps. He was stitched up like a kipper and none of us saw it coming.

NINETEEN

Operation Grapple, Bosnia-Hercegovina

Friday 26 August 1994 – BH Command, Sarajevo
'So, who's this bloke Wesley Clark, Lieutenant General Wesley, US Army?' Baggers was mumbling away to himself again, head bent over the General's rolling programme for the day. 'Any ideas, Mike?' He looked up, scratching his head.

I was engrossed in a computer game on my laptop and didn't bother looking up. 'Nope. No idea, mate.' I was still feeling very brittle from the previous day's adventure in Srebrenica and the crash on the way back. General Rose, Jamie Daniell, Baggers and Goose were due to fly to Vicenza in Italy for the long-awaited and much-postponed visit to 5 ATAF. I wasn't going, but was looking forward to a relaxing day off.

Colonel Daniell appeared from the General's office. 'Jeremy, the General's not desperately keen for this office call to happen. We don't even know who he is or what he's doing here. Have we heard anything from the American Embassy?'

We all shook our heads. General Clark's office call had been on the programme for about ten days. No one knew how it had got there and, like all these office calls, it had been ignored until the last minute. The Americans next door hadn't elaborated; with an afternoon hop to Italy planned, no one, least of all Rose, felt much like entertaining.

The MA was playing it safe though. 'Just before we make a boo-boo, ring up the Embassy and find out who he is.'

Baggers made the call and scribbled away furiously. I was too engrossed in trying to creep up behind an enemy jet to be too bothered with what was going on, but kept an ear cocked, more out of habit than anything else.

'General Wesley Clark. Three-star. Director Strategy, Plans and Policy in the Pentagon. Accompanied by a one-star, Brigadier General Hanlon, a Lieutenant Colonel Oaksmith and a Major Gerstein. Apparently, he's an adviser to and friend of Clinton . . . over here fact-finding . . . in town for only four hours . . . oh, and can we provide some vehicles?' Jeremy droned on impassively.

'Director Strategy, Plans and Policy! Friend of Clinton! Fact-finding!' The MA darted breathlessly back into Rose's office. Instantly he'd grasped the significance of Wes Clark.

I'd just about got the bugger in my sights. My finger jabbed down on the 'Enter' key, sending an air-to-air missile streaking towards the enemy aircraft piloted by Jennifer Brush. It exploded in a burst of yellow and red. *Ha! Gotcha!*

It was Rose's turn to be impressed: not with my flying abilities but with the Clark thing. He poked his head round the door and fixed Baggers with those laser eyes of his. 'Get back to 'em. Vehicles no problem. Quick office call, then we'll whip 'em round the city . . . Jewish Cemetery I think.'

Baggers was back on the phone again and an office call which had almost been dumped through ignorance and indifference was now being enthusiastically confirmed to the Americans. That done, he rang FREBAT 4 at Skenderija to warn the French CO that we'd be popping up with some guests to the Jewish Cemetery, which was part of his patch. Goose set about sorting the vehicles. Three would be needed for this gaggle; the Range, the snatch and an armoured Toyota Land Cruiser.

Ten-thirty came, and so did the Americans. They appeared at the door of the Outer Office dressed head to toe in woodland camouflage BDUs and surrounded by Ray-Ban-wearing BGs in lumberjack shirts, jeans and Timberland boots, all 'carrying' hardware. The soldiers all looked the same: clone-like and smart. We already knew Brigadier Hanlon, a US Marine on Admiral Leighton Smith's staff in Naples. The remaining three were all Army, all youthful-looking. Not one of them had the haggard, craggy look of an over-worked Pentagon three-star. 'CLARK' above the right pocket, 'US Army' above the left, three small black metal stars on each collar, and three silver ones across the top of his camouflaged fatigue cap, identified a youthful, steel-haired and tanned officer as the star of the show.

Clark was quickly ushered into Rose's office. The door was shut and we set about plying Hanlon, Oaksmith and Gerstein with coffee and biscuits. Hanlon, who had been to Sarajevo several times, was relaxed and chatted easily. The other two, Clark's MA and ADC, Pentagon staff officers with field satchels hanging properly from their shoulders, were stiff and subdued, probably shocked by their peculiar surroundings. Jon Ellis (Victor Andreyev's MA) was bellowing down the telephone to someone in Muratovic's office, 'This isn't a fucking taxi service!' Carmella (another of Andreyev's staff) was calmly filing (nails not papers), Jean quietly swearing at her computer, Baggers fighting three phones at once, my desk surrounded by parcels awaiting delivery, all presided over by the passably seductive nude over Colonel Daniell's desk. A perfect nuthouse.

A somewhat stilted ten minutes passed. The expressions of mild dismay and revulsion on the Americans' faces betrayed their secret thoughts. Then Rose's door flew open. The two generals emerged, Rose slapping his thigh with his beret. We were off. Rose was barking cryptically at Clark, '. . . French have done a superb job up there. CO's a good man . . . kept the two sides apart . . . Jewish Cemetery's problematic. They're literally tens of metres apart . . . good place to see the city from though . . .'

We scuttled off, thumping down the wooden stairs after them to where Goose was waiting with the vehicles. Bodyguards and drivers sprang into action, doors slammed, engines revved and off we swept; right, out of the Residency, down Djure Djakovic, straight on at the lights, over the river and past the FREBAT 4 HQ at Skenderija. After much weaving through Bistrik's tight *mahale* and labouring up steep gradients, we levelled out and stopped at the French OP at the eastern side of the Jewish Cemetery. The French CO was there to meet us.

We made our way forward on foot to the edge of the cemetery, a no-man's-land of weeds, fallen, battered and broken headstones clustered around a dilapidated pagoda-style mausoleum all of which clung precariously to a steep hill. It was a depressing place, heavy with irony: *Orthodox Serbs and Bosnian Muslims fighting, bickering and squabbling over a Jewish cemetery. That's it in a nutshell; fucked-up necrowar.* Below us Sarajevo, hot, hazy and tatty-looking, stretched away westwards towards Stup, eastwards towards Bascarsija and the Turkish fort above, and northwards past the Residency towards Zetra.

'Serbs over there and there, Muslims here and here . . .' Rose, hands flying, quickly (dis)orientated the American general before allowing the French CO to carry on the briefing. In excellent English he succinctly outlined his mission, explained how he had set about achieving it and touched on problems encountered. Clark was attentive. Suddenly, out of the blue, he shot a probing question.

'Let's just suppose the rules changed,' drawled Clark, '. . . and your mission was to clear and hold the Cemetery. How would you do it?' *Oh, that's a bit low. But typical. Fighting's all they know.*

This had nothing to do with peacekeeping and put the French colonel firmly on the spot: asked to produce a TEWT (Tactical Exercise Without Troops) solution without benefit of preparation or thinking time. But, the CO was not thrown and, with considerable dash and a lot of gesticulating, launched into his Concept of Ops.

'First, I would seize the high ground . . .' big sweep of left hand towards the Serb positions at the southern end of the Cemetery, '. . . then, using my 120mm mortars for indirect fire support, and a company on the high ground for direct fire support, I would sweep through from east to west.'

Rubbing chins, knowledgeably nodding their collective approval, these military sages were all back at Camberley or Fort Leavenworth DS-ing their 'student'. *What balls! Not bad though. I'd give you a C+ for that one. But you've forgotten to mention sappers. So, let's say C-, shall we.* The Jewish Cemetery was littered with anti-tank and anti-personnel mines.

'Well, let's hope you'll be ready should you have to do it,' Clark finished with a kind smile, too diplomatic to criticise the plan and award a mark. *Oh yeah, fat chance. Hell'll freeze over before the UN passes a Resolution to permit that.*

Although his was a somewhat inappropriate question, at least Clark was making an effort and looked genuinely interested. It was not difficult to warm to him. He was keen to learn, and moreover, had a winning, common touch, quite different from SACEUR, General George Joulwan, who some months earlier had been standing somewhat uncomfortably on the same spot. Deciding that discretion was the better part of valour, he'd sought refuge in the French OP, declaring, 'I wanna talk to a real soldier.' Presumably he'd not seen one for ages. Sadly for him the dramatic effect of this had dissolved rapidly when the black African-French conscript, to whom Joulwan was addressing himself, stared back uncomprehendingly with big, round, white eyes. Neither could understand what the other was saying. Others were less kind about Joulwan after he'd left and terms such as 'windy', and 'yellow streak' echoed about the Residency (all presumably taped by the Americans). No, Clark was definitely different.

Test over, it was time to depart. Clark was in Sarajevo and had to get on with his real task: a meeting with General Rasim Delic (ABiH supremo) and a quick check on Washington's new baby, the Federation. As our cavalcade pulled up at the Residency the offside rear door of Rose's Range sprang open. Out leapt the agitated figure of Colonel Daniell. Scuttling towards the backing vehicle he waved his notepad at me, beckoning me out.

'Quick! Mike! What're our chances of a meeting with Mladic?'

Rose had obviously cast a fly at Clark on the way back. Clark, it seemed, had bitten. It was peculiar how everyone wanted to meet 'the man the whole world loves to hate'. In Sarajevo it was 'murderer', 'thug', 'butcher', 'war criminal', but the moment we took these same people up the hill they'd be mesmerised by him: 'Mike, Mike, ask him if he wouldn't mind me taking his picture . . . take one with me and him in it!'

'I'd imagine it's zero,' I replied unhelpfully. 'He's in Banja Luka for that big conference.' I knew he was in Banja Luka, and had been there for a week or so. Karadzic had not heeded (not understood) Douglas Hurd's advice on semantics. The great 'vote-NO-to-the-Contact-Group-Plan-referendum' in Republika Srpska was due the following week and Mladic had made himself inaccessible.

'Well, could you at least try? The General's very keen for Clark to see

Mladic, and Clark's on for it.' I detected a note of pleading in the MA's voice.

'Sure. I'll give General Tolimir a ring . . .' *He's sure to fuck me off at the high port,* '. . . but don't hold your breath.' With that I shot upstairs, into the Outer Office and grabbed the INMARSAT.

I got straight through to the Han Pijesak switchboard. Rajko's laconic *'da'* was instantly recognisable.

'Rajko! Mike Stanley here.'

'Go ahead, Michael.'

'Can I speak to General Mladic?'

'No. He's not here.' Bored voice.

'Where is he then?'

'He's not here. He's *in the field.*'

'Well, is General Tolimir there?'

'Yes, he's around.'

'Could I speak to him?'

'I'll see if he's available.'

'Tell him it's urgent!' The ritual was always frustrating. After a few minutes of empty hissing and crackling static Tolimir was on.

'Michael. What is it?' *I wish they'd stop calling me Michael.*

'I need to speak to Mladic urgently.'

'He's not here.'

'I know, I know, he's in Banja Luka.'

'No! He's *in the field.*' *Cunning bugger. You're giving nothing away, are you?*

'Look. It's really important. We've got a very important visitor. Rose is keen for him to meet Mladic . . .'

'Who is it?' Tolimir's interest was up.

'An American general, from the Pentagon . . .'

'Which one?'

'Clark, Wesley Clark, *general-pukovnik*, same rank as Mladic and Rose.'

'What does he do? Why is he important to us?' *Wise up for once. They're all important.*

'Look, never mind that. He's a personal friend of Clinton's . . . his adviser . . . same as General Galvin. It's in *your* interests to meet him.' Colonel Daniell was hopping about in front of me, notebook at the ready. Long pause. The line was hissing again.

'General, are you there?'

'Yes, yes, Michael, I'm here.' Irritated. 'Ring me back in twenty minutes.' The line went dead.

'Ring him back in twenty minutes is what he said,' I said with a shrug. The MA scurried away to tell Rose, who was still chatting to Wes Clark downstairs. At least it was better than a flat *No.*

Within five minutes the MA was back. The generals and hangers-on had gone to lunch. Another ten minutes dragged by. The MA was getting impatient.

'Sod it, Colonel, I'll try now.' I dialled out and connected. 'Rajko?'

'Yes, Michael, just a moment, Tolimir's here.'

'Michael?'

'General.'

'Michael, General Mladic will meet with General Clark tomorrow at eleven . . .'

'Just a second, General . . .' I cupped the mouthpiece in my hand and winked at the MA mouthing, *'It's on. Tomorrow at eleven.'* His face lit up and he whispered back, *'Lukavica barracks?'* Fat chance!

'I presume Lukavica, as we did for Galvin, General?'

'No, Michael, not Lukavica.' *Not good.* I shook my head and soured my mouth for the MA's benefit.

'Where then? Pale? Jahorina?'

'No, Michael, Banja Luka.' *Ha. Gotcha!*

'Banja Luka!' I shouted, startling the MA, 'Banja Luka, General! How are we supposed to get there, all the way from Sarajevo by vehicle, by eleven?'

There was a slight pause, which seemed like hours, before Tolimir smugly replied, 'In your pretty little white helicopters, how else? Fax through the flight plan, usual details, numbers, timings etc, in the normal way through the UNMOs at Pale. We'll authorise the trip at our end. Any problems, ring me,' Tolimir finished curtly and put the phone down.

'Looks like it's helicopters to Banja Luka tomorrow morning, meeting with Mladic . . . somewhere (?) . . . at eleven.' I felt slightly drained.

The MA looked relieved, delighted even. I couldn't quite believe it myself. Helicopters to Banja Luka! *That's on the other side of the country across two confrontation lines. So, he is there. Typical.* Attempts to fly into any of the enclaves to visit troops had always been flatly rejected by the BSA HQ and we'd consistently been made to drive. But, as soon as they sniffed an advantage for themselves, anything was possible. Banja Luka! No one had ever been there except for UNHCR and ICRC, and they'd all been buggered around. No one had ever flown in there. This was rapidly turning into *the* trip to be on. We raced downstairs to brief Rose and Clark, who were seated around the General's table and well into lunch. Rose was delighted; Clark couldn't believe it. The 'magic wand' had worked again.

'We'll take Rudd and Schroeder, Goose and the comms, the MA, Mike, you'd better come along too . . . reckon we can still fit in the Vicenza trip, can't miss that. Put it off for too long . . .' Rose was rattling off a skeleton plan. The Americans enthusiastically agreed that they could reschedule their trip; stay a night in Sarajevo, Embassy to fix that, eat at the Residency . . . more time to hob-nob with the Muslims and the Federation. '. . . Yak into

Sarajevo from Vicenza, say 1000 hours, all meet at the airport for a quick strategy confab, into the helicopters to Banja Luka, meeting with Mladic, and then General Clark's party down to Split by helicopter . . .'

Americans: 'No can do. Got to meet a connecting flight early evening.'

Rose: 'Okay then. On the return leg your helicopter peels off direct to Split. Means two helicopters.'

I was scribbling notes furiously, knowing that once they'd all departed for Vicenza I'd be left to fix all this.

MA: 'Timings don't fit. Yak into Sarajevo and flight time to Banja Luka . . . Mike?' Colonel Daniell stared at me expectantly.

Why me? I'm not a pilot! 'An hour – ish,' I snapped back with a wild, decisive guess. You don't umm and aahhh in front of two three-stars.

'Can we slip the meeting by an hour?' *Meaning fix it.* I nodded and scribbled on, hoping the 'magic wand' had something left in it.

'Mike, you and Nick Magnall stick the package together and we'll all meet at the airport at ten o'clock tomorrow. Right! We're off!' With that Rose was on his feet and away, pursued by the MA and Baggers. The Americans also pushed off leaving me staring at my hastily scribbled notes.

'Banja Luka, eh?' Nick Magnall chuckled, blowing a plume of blue smoke through a huge gap in his front teeth. 'Should be an interesting one!' he concluded, with a sardonic leer.

We were sat at the little wooden table outside his G3 Ops cabin. I'd given him as much as I knew, including a list of all those going. His job was to drum up the helicopters and fax the flight plan and details to the UNMOs in Pale. There the whole lot would be translated by their interpreter, re-typed and re-faxed to the BSA HQ in Han Pijesak. Tolimir would then scrutinise the request, approve it and the entire process would be repeated in reverse. Painful! Like watching paint dry. Lead time for heli requests (to overfly Serb territory) was usually forty-eight hours. In this case I knew the inflexible Tolimir would bend slightly.

'But where in Banja Luka? Where exactly is this meeting to be held? Where do we land?' These were the real issues that were now vexing Nick Magnall.

'Dunno.'

'Where's the HLS?'

'Dunno that either.' Helpful.

It was time to pester Tolimir again.

'At the airfield, Michael. Land at the airfield,' Tolimir slammed down the phone.

'But they've got two airfields there,' Nick Magnall wailed. We were staring at the Banja Luka bit of the Ops map on his wall. Sure enough, two airfields. There they were, two purple strips, one just north of Banja Luka and one some twenty kilometres further north.

'They must mean the nearest one,' I muttered. *Perfectly bloody obvious. But, worth checking.*

'Michael! Michael! There is only one airstrip!' Tolimir was insisting.

'Well, we've got two on our maps, General.'

'There's only one so land on it!' he snapped back. He was furiously denying all knowledge of a second airfield. *JNA mentality. Secretive bastards. Forget we've got satellites, recce aircraft, technogadgets looking at the* whole *of FRY* all *the time. Head in the sand and deny everything. Try another tack.*

'So, it's about twenty kilometres north of Banja Luka? That's correct, isn't it, General?'

'There! You see! You knew all along. Now stop wasting my time.' I could hear him laughing.

'Er, just one other thing, General . . .'

'What now!'

'Any chance of slipping the meeting by an hour? Y'see Rose is away and his aircraft doesn't . . .'

By five o'clock that evening, after much frustration and a lot of wrangling with the irascible Tolimir, the plan had firmed up and the American Embassy had been informed.

'*Magnall-Stanley Tours* is what we should be called,' quipped Nick Magnall, drawing on another cigarette. We were sat at the wooden table sipping whisky. Tolimir had finally faxed us back. It was a 'go' for tomorrow.

Saturday 27 August 1994 – BH Command, Sarajevo

I was in Rose's office ferreting around. Someone, either Baggers or the MA, had rung late the night before from Vicenza – 'get the General's Gore-Tex waterproof jacket!' We'd all be meeting at the airport and he hadn't taken it with him to Italy. *There it is. Now, breakfast.*

Oaksmith, Gerstein, Rudd and Schroeder were all eating together. Lt Colonels Rudd and Schroeder both worked on Rose's staff, and Rudd was in the process of handing over to Schroeder. Having been taken up to Pale, following the TEZ air strike, to pump some sense into Karadzic by showing him part of the secret NATO targeting plan, Rudd had fallen from grace. Leighton Smith had had a fit. Rudd was declared to have gone 'native', i.e. too much in the Rose camp, which really meant that he understood what was going on. He was soon to be banished back to obscurity in Incirlik, in Turkey, where he'd previously been with the US Army, his career effectively in tatters thanks to the State Department.

'Michael, we need more information on this Clark general. It's unreasonable for Mladic to meet with a complete unknown.' Tolimir had been most insistent.

'He's quite young looking isn't he, General Clark?' I cast a fly at the munching Americans.

Gerstein bit. 'Yep. Youngest three-star in the Pentagon since Vietnam.'

'Gosh! How old is that then?' *Innocence.*

'Forty-seven I guess.' *Forty-seven! That is young. Rose is what? Fifty-five! What else?*

Gradually it emerged. Nothing desperately sensitive, a lot of it impressive. Wesley Clark, Vietnam record, unbelievably young and fast up the greasy pole, commanded 1 AD (1st US Armoured Division in Germany – the most potent fighting division in the world), tipped for four-star *soon*, the youngest of course. *Of course!* Some sort of patronage from the Clintons, very well connected and going places *fast*.

We arrived at Sarajevo airport ahead of Rose and gang. Wes Clark had driven direct from the Embassy, along with Hanlon, Oaksmith and Gerstein. They joined us at ten on the pan where our two helicopters – a NORAIR Arapaho and an 845 NAS Sea King from Split – sat closed down and off to one side. Odd combination, but the best that Nick Magnall could do at short notice. A few minutes later a greasy black smudge, the telltale signature of inefficient old Soviet engines, appeared on the western horizon somewhere over Kiseljak.

'Here they come,' I announced.

Eyes squinted westwards. Moments later a white speck connected itself to the greasy plume, grew in size, skipped over Ilidza and howling down the runway turned smartly off onto the pan coming to a halt next to the helicopters, engines still moaning softly. The Yak 40 stopped just long enough to spew out Rose, MA, Goose and Baggers, before disappearing off down the runway again. The pilots were all mad Ukrainians, veterans of many a landing and take-off at Kabul, and only too aware of the hazards of hanging around the pan at Sarajevo airport.

Rose greeted Clark, nodded in our direction and then out of the blue, 'Who's got my waterproof then?'

'It's here, General.' I patted my daysack. It was baking hot. Not a cloud in the sky.

With that Rose was off with Clark, striding towards the terminal with the rest of us traipsing behind. The tactics confab lasted thirty minutes. Apart from telling Clark that it was his show Rose uttered a dire warning about Mladic: 'Very slippery. Cunning. Clever. Whatever you do, play it absolutely straight. No emotions, smiling, nothing, particularly in front of the press. And the press will be there. It always is. This is a big scene for them.'

At eleven we lifted off, the important people in the smaller, more agile Arapaho, and Oaksmith, Gerstein, Schroeder, Rudd and me in the Sea King.

I grabbed a headset and took post behind the aircraft commander whom I recognised.

'Do you mind if I get one of the Yanks up here with a headset, give him an idea of the ground?'

'Fill your boots.'

As we headed west over Ilidza I waved frantically back down the aircraft until I'd got Colonel Oaksmith's attention. He pointed to himself and looked surprised. I nodded and waved a spare headset at him. With a big grin he was up in a flash and stuffing the headset over his ears.

'That's Ilidza below us, Serb-held suburb, a real hornet's nest.' We continued west. 'Still Serb territory. That's Sierra 1, Serb checkpoint, and the front line ahead. Croat town of Kiseljak on the nose, so we're now over Federation territory . . .'

We flew on in loose formation, the Arapaho about 100 metres out to port, both aircraft at 2,000 feet following the Busovaca valley. '. . . alternate Croat, Muslim, Croat, Muslim villages right along the road . . . did themselves enormous damage during the 1993 Croat-Muslim war . . .' From our vantage point burnt and trashed villages littered the valley floor and its slopes. '. . . now in the Lasva valley. That's Vitez, where we established the first British battalion base in 1992 . . .' As we swept over Vitez I could make out the school house at Stara Bila, the Portakabin City on the playing field and the Warrior tank-park, all gleaming white. I brushed aside memories of the captains' house, of Dobrila Kalaba, of the crazy Officers' Mess-cum-disco, of the mad old Muslim woman, whom Jules Amos and I had ineptly rescued, lying wounded by a sniper – all these memories seemed to belong to another life.

'. . . That's Travnik ahead, HQ of the BiH's 3rd Corps. Boss is Mehmet Alagic, whom your General Galvin met about a month ago. That huge feature ahead is called Vlasic. Serb-held. Dominates both valleys. Front line slips left off it and dips down into that valley ahead . . .' *Fuuuck!!* '. . . Hey! Hey, hey!' I tapped madly on the aircraft commander's shoulder. See that big green wood, on the nose?' We were headed straight for it.

'Got it. So what?'

'Avoid it! They've got sodding great 20mm and 30mm cannons under nets down there. We'll fly through their arcs . . . go right.'

'How the hell do you know that?' The commander was surprised.

'Trust me. We were down in that wood with General Galvin and Mehmet Alegic a little over a month ago. Got a guided tour of the unit in there.' I didn't bother to describe the absurd request for rock-climbing gear or the preposterous goose-stepping that had gone on in the wood. '. . . badly sited guns, we're flying into their arcs and . . .' ghastly thought, '. . . I doubt anyone's bothered telling them about our trip!' *Be even worse on the way back!*

'Thanks!' The pilot immediately banked right, while the commander radioed the message to the Arapaho, which conformed. We passed the wood on our port side. With a pang of nostalgia, I realised that, for a brief few moments, it had been like the bad old days of 1993 and the hairy heli ops into the eastern pockets with George Wallace, David Lord and Tim Kelly, when the RWRs had gone haywire telling us that we were being 'locked up' by all manner of ground-to-air systems, including 'unknown gun'.

As we crossed from Federation to Serb-held territory my patter to Oaksmith dried up. This was as far west as I'd ever been, as far west as anyone had been, except the heroes of Op DENY FLIGHT zipping about above 5,000 feet. The terrain below was completely unfamiliar to me and I lapsed into silence and was as visually on receive as Oaksmith.

Beyond Vlasic I'd expected to see the same mountainous ground as we'd become accustomed to seeing in Central Bosnia. Not a bit of it. By and large it was rolling pastures and woods. Slightly to the south the ground was more dramatic – high mountains and steep gorges where the river Vrbas flowed past Jajce. This had been Tito's wartime HQ, supposedly inaccessible until German mountain troops had rooted him out. Further west the ground flattened out even more and was littered with the confetti of smashed and broken villages. There wasn't a living soul below us.

'That's got to be Banja Luka,' the headset crackled. On the horizon a white smudge grew larger and larger and very shortly we were overhead a big, modern and, by the look of it, completely unscathed town.

'Don't know why they don't just let us land in the football stadium. Seems to be standard form everywhere else.' The commander had a point.

'Dunno. I suppose the meeting won't actually be in Banja Luka itself. Probably be at the airfield. Guess Mladic doesn't want us in the town.'

'That one?' queried the commander, pointing to an airfield just to the north, the one Tolimir had denied all knowledge of. We passed it by, hardened aircraft shelters clustered like petals on stalks, which led to a triangle of three runways, drab grey buildings and batteries of AAA.

'Definitely not that one! Try twenty kilometres to the north.'

Sure enough the other airfield was quite different. One long straight runway, more or less north-south, a terminal building to the east and not much else. In fact this was Banja Luka's new civilian airport, completed just before the war started and now devoid of aircraft. It was totally deserted – no cars, no people, nothing. Panic gripped me. Perhaps it had been the other one and Tolimir and I had thoroughly confused ourselves and buggered it up. As we approached on finals and the airport rose to meet us filling the cockpit I could see nothing to allay my fears.

'Where do you reckon we should put down?' The aircraft commander was as unsure as I felt.

'Just stick it on the pan in front of the terminal. I'll try and find someone.'

As we touched ground I ripped off the headset, grabbed my daysack and leapt out of the door just as soon as the aircraft had settled. As I darted across the pan, I noticed for the first time a man in uniform, a major. In my mind's eye I'd expected Mladic himself, surrounded by a coven of staff officers, to be standing there waiting for us.

'General Mladic?'

'No. He's in Banja Luka.'

'So, where's the meeting to be held?'

He looked at me strangely. 'In Banja Luka, of course . . .' cocking a thumb over his shoulder, '. . . vehicles are on their way. I'm your escort.'

By now Rose and Clark weren't far behind me and just as I'd started to brief them a convoy of two cars, a minibus and two motorcycle outriders appeared at speed from around the terminal building and stopped in front of the major.

Being a biker myself, my eye was immediately drawn to the two outriders. No swish BMWs for them: they were mounted on two very old East German two-stroke MZs fitted with sirens and two large round flashing lights, one red, one blue, mounted either side of the headlamp. The riders were even more extraordinary than their steeds. Drab camouflage uniforms clashed dramatically with huge white leather gauntlets, belts and cross straps. No conventional helmets either! Instead they wore those 1950s hard-top Norman Wisdom-types with leather ear protectors and slab-sided Biggles goggles. Clouds of acrid, blue, two-stroke engine smoke belched over the convoy choking us in the minibus.

Somewhere beyond this smokescreen sirens wailed. Our gallant outriders cleared the road, scattering hay carts, forcing slow-moving traffic off the road and generally panicking the public as we hurtled south towards Banja Luka. Flat, dull fields gave way to suburbs. In stark contrast to every other town or city I'd ever seen in Bosnia, this one bore none of the scars of war – no shell craters, no pitted and gouged walls, no boarded-up shop fronts, no fire-gutted houses. Even the people lacked that gaunt, hunted look which goes with living permanently on the edge. These people really had got off lightly, those that hadn't been cleansed out that is.

After a further fifteen minutes we pulled up in front of a large, glass-fronted hotel. De-bussing quickly, we were led up the steps, through two huge glass doors into a red-carpeted foyer, smartly up yet another set of stairs to the first floor, and then round a walkway which led round four sides of a central, hollow well. On the opposite side we dived back into the building and into a huge blue-carpeted but gloomy conference room with a long wide oak table. Beyond the table the blinds had been drawn over four large windows.

One or two Serbian officers were sitting along the far length of the table. The majority were standing at the far end of the room, deep in conversation with General Mladic. As we entered the group stiffened. Mladic strode forward, hand outstretched, greeting Rose, who in turn introduced Wes Clark.

'Welcome to Banja Luka and Republika Srpska,' boomed Mladic. With a sweep of his arm he bade us be seated along the opposite side of the table. Before turning away he winked at me, '*Kako si, mali? Jel' si mi doneo te podatke? – How are you, boy? Have you brought me those details?*' He was referring to Tolimir's request for some biographical notes on Clark. *I wish the sod wouldn't keep calling me 'boy', almost as bad as Michael.* I gave him a brand new note pad, on the first page of which I'd scribbled down as much as I'd gleaned from Gerstein at breakfast.

Since Mladic, was seated in the middle, it followed that Clark should sit opposite him. His staff slotted in to his right, while on his left sat the MA, Rose and finally me. Goose was outside ready to slot would-be assassins.

Apart from Mladic, all the other Serb officers were unknown to me, a mixed bunch of varying demeanours and looks, one of whom was a Major Kralj, Mladic's interpreter.

The meeting was, in any case, exclusively a Mladic-Clark affair. As Major Kralj was clearly determined to do all the interpreting, General Rose and I had the luxury of sitting back and taking in all that was being said, as Jamie Daniell scribbled away.

Introductions completed, Mladic invited Clark to kick off. He went straight to the point. As representative of General John Shalikashvili, the Chairman of the Joint Chiefs of Staff, he implored Mladic to exert some influence on the following day's referendum, suggesting that an outright 'no' to the CG Plan would be disastrous to all parties. All responsible leaders, Mladic included, had a duty to guide their people's decision wisely. Clark was wasting his time, just as surely as Douglas Hurd and Alain Juppé had up at Pale on 13 July and I doubted whether Mladic would be any better at understanding diplomatic wordsmithing than Karadzic had been. I doubt he even cared.

Throughout Clark's impassioned soliloquy, Mladic had been studying the bio notes in his new notebook. Suddenly, he let out a snort, a dramatic sigh of exasperation, and snapped back at Clark with a proverb (his, not biblical): 'Woe to the side that relies on the protection of a stronger power!' No sooner had Major Kralj wrestled out a twisted translation than Mladic was away, leaning forward and stabbing the table for emphasis with a thick index finger.

'You won't have anyone to give arms to . . . Shalikashvili should take his finger off the NATO trigger . . . Shalikashvili should compare the casualties and victims on both sides before . . .' On it went. Clark was silent while Kralj forced out one tortured translation after another. It became so painful that at one stage I interjected helpfully as Kralj ransacked his brain for the right word. Wasted effort. He merely glared back at me, eyes blazing with resentment.

'He looks ill to me,' whispered Rose out of the corner of his mouth, inclining his head slightly towards me. He was right. Mladic looked dreadful – flushed face, puffy red watery eyes.

'Think he's hung over, sir,' I whispered. Nick had warned me about this on the hand-over. 'Sometimes he just disappears for weeks at a time, just can't get hold of him . . . *na terenu* . . . and then he'll reappear for a meeting looking terrible having been on the piss for a week with his mates!'

'. . . It's not just arms that you give them. Look!' he waved a paw at the Americans, '. . . the Muslims are even wearing the same uniforms, even down to those little camouflage caps that you're wearing.' He stabbed a finger in the direction of Clark's, parked on the table. Mladic was working himself into a real froth, and then suddenly, just as quickly, he relaxed and spread his arms wide, smiling benevolently.

'Look,' suddenly he was reason itself, 'the only way this thing is going to end is if all the weapons are silenced, commanders on all sides sit down and work out a peace, and the politicians find a solution. I'm prepared to do this tomorrow. Let's have them all at the meeting . . .' He reeled off a military *Who's Who* of Bosnia, '. . . Bobetko, Delic, Rosso, Alispahic, Petkovic, Dudakovic . . .' We'd heard this one before, but Clark hadn't. It was his turn to lean forward, earnest and enthused.

'Good idea. If it'll work I'll even get General Shalikashvili to come out . . .' *He really means it. Pigs'll fly before this lot seriously get round a table.*

'Exactly!' Mladic was off again, reeling in his line with Clark on the end of it. 'Exactly that! Look! This Contact Group Plan is completely unworkable. We've done our own study.' With that he whipped out a map of Bosnia-Hercegovina, which was covered in a grid of tiny squares – shaded, coloured and with arrows pointing at various towns.

'Of course, you're aware of the such-and-such method of calculating percentage areas?' He didn't wait for a reply from Clark. 'Look, 67 per cent of the land is privately owned by Serbs and we hold 68.8 per cent, which is 1.2 per cent more than is privately owned. The Muslims and Croats have 34.2 per cent, but under the Contact Group Plan, in reality, we only get 43.27 per cent while they get 56.73 per cent which is not the 49–51 per cent split under the Plan . . .' His pen was racing all over the map, faster than the eye could follow, '. . . and look, thirty-six towns represents 49.32 per cent of all towns, while thirty-seven towns is 50.68 per cent. But under the Plan, we'll be forced to hand over sixteen towns leaving us with only twenty, whereas we should have thirty-six . . .'

'Mike, are you getting all this?' The MA looked harassed.

'Yeah, just.' I was scribbling like fury, but following Mladic's Serbo-Croat far faster than they were following Kralj's translation.

'And, then you have to consider that the Muslims have the three largest cities, Sarajevo, Tuzla and Zenica!' Then he banged on about what percentages of infrastructure fell to whom; bridges, power stations, even kilometres of high tension electricity lines etc. etc . . . 'So! You see, the Contact Group Plan, cooked up by your State Department and your Ambassador Redman, is designed to make the Serbs live in three worthless enclaves fit only for snakes!' With a flourish he flung his pen onto the map, sank back in his chair and, parting his hands in a gesture of supplication, eyebrows raised expectantly, finished sotto voce, '. . . how then can you expect the people to say anything but "no" to this Plan?'

It was a classic tactic: batter the opposition with facts and figures, which can neither be immediately verified nor countered. All sides were past masters at the game, extended versions of which could last tens of hours, turning negotiators' brains into jelly.

There was a long pause while Clark gathered himself. He looked shell-shocked and I doubted that he'd really followed very much of what Mladic had been saying. Why should he have? He wouldn't have been read into 'maps' or be used to their devilish detail in quite the same way we were. Wisely, he steered away from answering directly, bringing the conversation round full circle.

'Well, maps are for politicians to sort out. I'm just a soldier, one who is interested in peace . . .'

'If that's the case, why are you bombing our people? What exactly is America's strategic interest in the Balkans?' snapped back Mladic.

Clark was utterly honest. 'There are three: to prevent a widening of the war, to ensure that NATO remains strong, and to ensure that the United States and Russia keep working together.' He couldn't have stated it more simply or in a more soldierly manner. No hand-wringing, no bleeding heart references to genocide, victims, aggressors and all the rest of the guff that the media was endlessly bleating about. Just hard-nosed *Realpolitik*. It threw Mladic. Clark continued, 'But, I get back to my earlier point. You, as a responsible military leader, have a duty to guide your people along the path of peace . . . what's now required from you is a gesture . . .'

Kralj either didn't hear Clark correctly or had no idea how to translate 'gesture' (*'gest'*) so went for something that sounded similar *'sugestija'* ('suggestion'). I winced. *He's fucking this up big time.*

'I'll give you a suggestion,' barked Mladic. 'I suggest that you Americans stop meddling in the Balkans. Stop arming the Muslims and aiding our enemies. You don't know what you're playing with. One world war started here and there's no reason why another one shouldn't . . . and that's in none of our interests, not even yours.' He was now wagging his finger from side to side, admonishing his pupil, 'We Serbian officers and colleagues are duty bound to defend our dead from those who attacked us in 1992 . . .' this oblique reference to necrowar and the practice of disinterring the corpses of one's enemies and desecrating graves was totally lost on the Americans and sounded a bit odd in translation, '. . . but, here's another suggestion. A total and permanent cease-fire. I'm offering it to all the generals of all the sides . . .' This was much more up Clark's street and again he stated that he'd get General Shalikashvili to support such an initiative, but first Mladic would have to show willing and leadership . . .' Round and round we went in neverending circles of meaningless dialogue. Leaning back in his chair, Rose looked bored. He was probably quite thankful that, for once, it was not he who was having to fence with Mladic.

Mladic had changed tack again. Again a familiar subject. 'Look, we're all professional soldiers here, experienced in war, you in Vietnam, General Rose in the Falklands. We've all studied our professions. I finished top in every single career school, you must have too – "the youngest lieutenant general in the Pentagon since the Vietnam war . . ." Mladic threw me an amused look, '. . . three stars at forty-seven! I was only a colonel at your age!' He winked at me. I cringed. *You bastard!* '. . . I've studied my profession well. I've studied every army in the world. I've always had nothing but admiration for the American Army, so potent, so powerful . . .' the adulation continued in a similar vein. Clark was lapping it up.

Beside me Rose suddenly stiffened, imaginary antennae sensitive to something. 'Mike! He's up to something!' he hissed. He was right. Mladic loathed Americans.

'You're right. He *is* up to something,' I whispered back. *But, what? What have you cooked up this time?* We were both listening attentively now. On guard.

Mladic was still gushing, 'All that power! And now with the new world order you find yourselves as world policemen.' Clark seemed to be enjoying all this. I had a horrid, sinking feeling that we were perched on the edge of a bottomless pit and were about to be sucked down. 'And, with such a weighty responsibility, with such influence and power, you have to exercise great caution and wisdom . . . but, let me tell you something. The Balkans is not the rest of the world. The Balkans is the Balkans. For hundreds of years wars have been fought here. Powerful, well-trained armies, great generals have all come here, but in the end they have floundered . . .' His voice had lowered by an octave. He was speaking more slowly, deliberately enunciating each word, patronisingly, like a school teacher. Beside him his officers were grinning and exchanging conspiratorial glances. Thick as thieves.

'. . . but this is the Balkans, and always, always, they've floundered, been tripped up by a little unforeseen something, for which all their experience, their training, their colleges could not have prepared them. Always, there's a little something here in the Balkans. You go and tell that to Shalikashvili!' The Serbian officers all nodded their assent.

Rose was positively twitching. 'What's he up to, Mike?'

'Dunno, sir. Something, though.'

And then just as quickly we were back onto another tired old subject, hacking away at the Plan, or leadership, or the referendum. Towards the end we even got back onto the arms embargo and blasted uniforms. 'Those uniforms of yours. They're the same ones the Muslims are wearing . . .' Eventually the meeting just ground to a halt. Clark said he'd take Mladic's views back to the Pentagon. Mladic thanked Clark for his time and for being so forthright. Meeting over. Nothing achieved. *Another Groundhog Day in the Balkans really.*

'*Rucak!!* Lunch!!' cried Mladic, shoving his chair aside and rising. As we all rose the narcotic, almost hypnotic, gloomy veil that hangs over formal meetings dropped away. We all became human beings again. Mladic snatched up his hat and stuffed it on his head. 'I'll treat you to a real Serbian dish – *vojni pasulj.*'

'What's that, Mike?'

'Sounds like cookhouse bean broth to me.' I hated *pasulj.*

Mladic and his officers had come over to our side. Everyone was relaxed. Mladic tweaked the cloth of Clark's uniform between thumb and forefinger. 'Muslim uniform!' he cried. Everyone laughed, including Clark. Then he feigned surprise, pointed at Clark's fatigue cap with its three silver stars, which the latter was about to place on his head. Mladic intercepted it and holding it aloft roared, 'Muslim hat!' Whipping off his own he asked, 'Mind if I try it on?' Clark looked amused and nodded. Mladic pulled his off and handed it to Clark with a 'here's mine . . .' but then he withdrew it and, producing a biro, signed the inside of it with a flourish of Cyrillic, *R Mladic,* and then handed it to Clark, 'Here, have it as a souvenir of this meeting.' He then stuffed Clark's on his head and hooted, 'Do I look like a Muslim?' His officers roared with laughter. 'Can I keep it . . . three silver stars . . . and I am a three-star as well?'

Clark laughed, shook his head and smiled, 'Nooo.'

Mladic spotted that I had my camera out. A number of us did. 'Well, if I can't keep it, let's at least get some photographs, outside where there's more light.' He clapped a huge paw on Clark's shoulder and deftly steered him out onto the walkway. I snapped off a couple of photos, one with Rose looking concerned. The others, though, were grinning broadly, caught up in the bonhomie and absurdity of it all. Mladic was beaming, Clark grinning, while behind them the Serb officers were rocking with laughter.

'Lunch!' shouted Mladic again, spinning Clark around. As we made our way along the walkway, from the opposite direction came a phalanx of press, shoulder to shoulder, advancing swiftly – photographers, cameramen and reporters all wielding microphones and dictaphones. They blocked our further progress along the walkway.

'I smell a rat!' hissed Rose, and he, fleet of foot, closely followed by the MA, neatly sidestepped the ambush.

I was left trapped directly behind and between Clark and Mladic, my escape to the rear blocked by Mladic's officers pressing forward. Both generals were still wearing each other's hats. The press jostled and shouted questions. Seconds later Clark must have realised he was still wearing Mladic's hat and smartly tore it off. Mladic did likewise and both carried on the interview bareheaded. Yes, yes. Useful meeting. Frank exchange of views. Progress. Blah, blah, blah.

Eventually Mladic shooed the press away and we continued on our way down the walkway, back into the hotel and into a spacious, well-lit dining-room. The tables had been arranged into a three-sides-of-a-square affair and garlanded with crisp white tablecloths.

As we sat down, Clark next to Mladic, Rose turned to me, 'Mike, I think you should do the interpreting. Give wasisface a break.' *Which really means 'the other bloke was rubbish', now start earning your keep.* I placed myself in front of Clark and Mladic on the inside of the table-well. Determined not to fall from grace, Kralj joined me.

As so often happens during such post-meeting banquets, we revisited all the failed topics. But this was no banquet. *Vojni pasulj* turned out to be a large bowl of thick bean broth with a stout hamburger thrown in, accompanied by mixed salads, bread and white wine. This 'meeting' went much better. The atmosphere was more congenial, cosier somehow, and, knowing the topics, I found the interpreting easy. Proximity to both generals also helped a lot. Major Kralj was smouldering away beside me. He listened intently and pounced on my every little mistake.

Mladic's eyebrows knitted together while his eyes scoured the table for something. Unable to locate whatever it was, he snapped his fingers and barked out an order at one of the obsequious waiters, who scuttled off. Moments later he was back with a dish heaped high with large green chillies.

'*Dobro!*' grunted Mladic, popping a whole one into his mouth. Chewing vigorously, he proffered the plate to Clark, a mocking eyebrow raised, 'Want one?'

'What are they?' Clark asked me.

'Green chillies I think, sir.'

Clark winced and holding his hands up politely shook his head.

'Too hot for you, eh?' crowed Mladic, stuffing another into his mouth, hugely pleased that his guest had failed this test of virility.

'You'll have one, won't you Stanley?' *Is that a question or an order?* Mladic sniggered and tossed me one. Gingerly I nipped off the end. Blistering hot. Mladic read my face and erupted into laughter. By the end of the course he'd crunched his way through the whole plateful. Not a single one was left. All this without any external symptoms – not a single bead of sweat.

By pudding Rose was glancing at his watch. It was almost three in the afternoon and we had to be on our way if the Americans were to catch their plane in Split.

'Before you go . . .' Mladic snapped his fingers, '. . . a token of my respect. A memento of this historic meeting!'

On cue a waiter scurried in and handed him a brand new leather belt and pistol holster. Snapping open the clasp he produced an equally brand new Red Star pistol.

'See! It's engraved. Stanley, translate.' He handed me the 'short'. Engraved into its gunmetal blue slide in big shiny Cyrillic letters were four words: *From General Ratko Mladic.* I translated.

Mladic handed Clark the weapon and the holster. He examined the engraving, looked pleased as punch and thanked Mladic. *Wild West syndrome. Don't they just love their guns.* Holstering the pistol he handed the bundle over to Gerstein. Mladic was pleased that Clark was pleased. A good note to end on. Time to go.

As we thumped our way down the stairs Kralj sidled up to me. 'Where you learn Serbian?' he asked thickly.

'At home. Where else?' I twisted the knife.

For a moment he was floored but was quickly back on the attack. 'Then shame on you. You should speak it better.'

'And where did you learn such excellent English?'

The sarcasm was wasted. 'I am teacher of English language,' he announced proudly.

'You don't say!'

'Is true!' *Woooosh. Straight over your head.*

Sirens blaring, lights flashing, clouds of blue smoke and off we went through Banja Luka, leaving Mladic and gang waving, laughing and smiling on the hotel steps. It nagged at me. *Why so jolly?*

In the minibus Brigadier Hanlon and Colonel Oaksmith were comparing notes. Major Gerstein sat quietly clutching the pistol and Mladic's hat. From the banter it was obvious they considered the whole thing a success.

'How do you reckon it went then?' I asked.

'Brilliant, useful, outstanding . . . hey, where'd'ya learn the lingo so well?'

'Oh, university, then out here. This is my second year out here.' First part blatant lie. Second part calculated to stir.

'Two years! Holy shit! Howd'ya find it?'

Shite! 'Oh, very interesting.'

We fell silent. I was exhausted. The old interpreter's headache was upon me. To our front I could see one of the outriders out beyond the lead car. We were careering along at quite some speed. One of the bikes hit a pothole or something in the road. The headlamp unit fell off and was crushed under the wheels of the following car. I burst out laughing. The others, having missed the incident, looked at me as though I were the resident village idiot. I giggled even more. It wasn't just the headlamp ... it was everything. Hanlon and gang politely ignored me, convinced, no doubt, that my time out here had done me in.

We lifted from the airfield at about quarter past three. The Americans, less Rudd and Schroeder, were crammed into the Arapaho for the hop down to Split, while the rest of us, Sarajevo-bound, were in the Sea King. We flew in formation until we re-crossed the confrontation line at Turbe. Mercifully, Alagic's woodland goose-steppers didn't blast away at us with their cannons. Over Travnik the Arapaho peeled off right and disappeared south towards Split. We maintained course and height for Sarajevo where we landed some twenty minutes later. The vehicles were there to meet us and whisk us off to the Residency.

'Mike! How many pictures did you take of Mladic and Clark with the hats?' We'd barely arrived at the Residency before the MA was upon me.

'Dunno. Two or three I guess. Why?' *What's suddenly gripped you?*

'Any of Rose ... in that group, I mean?'

'Yeah. One I think. He was next to Clark. Why?'

The MA looked extremely worried. 'Be very careful what you do with those pictures!'

'Don't worry. They're slides. Won't get developed till I'm finished here ... anyway there were plenty of other cameras out, so what's the big deal?' *What has got into you?*

He eyed me carefully, 'I think we've just been had!' The penny dropped. *Shit! We've been had!*

An hour later Colonel Schroeder approached me. He wasn't just concerned, he was deeply worried. 'Mike, d'ya reckon they'll show it on TV ... the *hat?*' He winced as he said the word.

'They could but I doubt it. Why should they? Not Mladic's style.' I thought for a moment. 'Look we don't get their TV here, but I'll find a way of watching their news tonight. If they're going to use it they'll do it now.' He was grateful, though still worried. I went in search of Darko and found him in the Civil Affairs Portakabin. Could he help?

'The only place I know of that gets their TV is the Croatian Ambassador's house.'

'Can we go there, Darko?'

'He's not there, but I know the others well. Shouldn't be a problem. Six o'clock news. Still got an hour.'

The Croatian Ambassador's house, a sumptuous pad, wasn't far away, just across the park and up one of the steep café-lined alleys. By five to six we were sitting comfortably in deep leather armchairs. RST news came on. We craned forward. Nothing! Just lots of reports and interviews from around Republika Srpska asking folk how they were going to vote in tomorrow's referendum. *NO!* was the predictable answer. Twenty-five minutes of this and still nothing about us.

'I can't believe it, Darko!'

'Wait. Look!'

'Today in Banja Luka General Mladic met with General Clark . . .' The picture on the screen was a close-up of the interviews. Mladic and Clark without hats.

'Look at you, Mike! Chewing gum. What're you like!' Sure enough there I was penned in and chewing.

'Looks a bit slack. Bit sloppy,' I conceded. Anyway, no hats!

'No hats, Colonel! Definitely no hats. Not a hint of it. Footage is all bare-headed. He's off the hook.'

Schroeder still looked deeply worried and unconvinced, 'Y'sure?'

'Positive. No hats.'

'Wreck his career for sure if it ever gets out. No hats you say? Funny. State Department's gone crazy. The Embassy in Zagreb is denying all knowledge, "Clark had no authority to meet with Mladic" . . . somehow it's out.'

'Well, it's a mystery to me. It wasn't on the box.'

Tuesday 30 August 1994 – Trogir, Croatia

'I warned him, that morning at the airport, "he's cunning and clever . . . play it absolutely straight . . . no smiling, no emotions" . . . , I warned him! We briefed him!' Rose was emphatic, chopping the air with his hand, a word at a time, '. . . Mike, what's that?'

I leant across and studied the part of the menu at which he was pointing. 'Plaice, General.'

'Mmmm, a nice fresh plaice for me, I think. What's everyone else having?'

There hadn't been much time to dwell on the Banja Luka affair. As ever, there was always a new crisis looming to keep our minds focused on the present and future.

As Darko and I had been sitting watching RSTV that night in the Croatian

Ambassador's pad, two J5 officers, Michelle Stinton and a Canadian naval lieutenant commander called Wilcox, had been stopped and 'taken prisoner' in Ilidza while en route from Kiseljak to Sarajevo. The word hostage always made people break out in a cold sweat and caused emotions to run high, particularly amongst the Americans. Nothing was guaranteed to reach the ears of a Prime Minister or President faster than the news that one of his citizens had been 'taken hostage' (press speak) by the Serbs in Bosnia.

By the following morning, Sunday, Wilcox and Stinton were still 'guests' of the Ilidza police. Rose had been due to go to Hadzici with Fred Price, an RN lieutenant commander, for a trout lunch with the mayor, Ratko Radic. This fixture had already been cancelled several times. This was an important social visit. Fred, the 'utilities' man in the HQ had slaved away for months with various NGOs repairing the wells and water pumps in Hadzici, which ultimately fed Sarajevo. In terms of glamour, J5 was almost at the bottom of the pile. The world was only interested in the war and the politics of it all – the sexy bits. Those who slaved away behind the scenes restoring utilities and feeding folk really were the unsung, unrecognised heroes of the international effort. However, their work was very much part of Rose's campaign plan and he set much store by their efforts. For this reason the lunch at Hadzici was important.

The daily 0830 hours brief had not only highlighted the plight of the hostages but also revealed that the Serbs had turned off the gas supply into the city. The mood in Sarajevo was not good. Thus, the General decided that it would now be improper to have lunch with the mayor of Hadzici.

'Get off to Hadzici and explain why!' He was furious about the detention of Wilcox and Stinton, '. . . and while you're at it get onto that lot in Ilidza and get those two released!'

Being a Sunday it was impossible to find anyone with any authority in Ilidza. The mayor was away and various commanders became strangely elusive. We were allowed to view the 'captives', who seemed quite perky, even defiant. They hadn't been 'tortured' (as reported), had been fed and had basically spent a boring night in the police station. Eventually the deputy mayor turned up with the police chief. The latter claimed that Stinton and Wilcox had been rude to the checkpoint soldiers in Ilidza and were being taught a lesson in manners. Be that as it may it was a mistake to hold them and could only damage the Serbs further. After much wrangling they were persuaded to release them, but only if they were escorted back to Sierra 1 from where they could 'resume' their journey, come through Ilidza and try again, this time being *polite*. We acted out this pathetic and absurd charade and the pair arrived back at the Residency to heroes' welcomes. No doubt the Pentagon gave Stinton a gong for being 'captured'.

The real reason for their detention had been Michelle Stinton's American uniform, which had inflamed the checkpoint guards. With the referendum due the next day feelings throughout Republika Srpska were running high, particularly in hard-core areas such as Ilidza. They all blamed Ambassador Redman (the US rep on the Contact group) for tweaking the Contact Group Plan in such a way as to ensure that the Serbs were left not only with 'three enclaves fit only for snakes', but also with no choice other than to say 'no' to the Plan. The Great Conspiracy theory. *Fuck Clinton* was not an uncommon example of Ilidza graffiti during the run-up to the referendum. The Yanks, what few of them there were in theatre, were simply not welcome on the Dark Side. That evening Jon Ellis, Baggers and I were treated to supper by Mark Laity, the BBC's Defence and Foreign Affairs correspondent, at the Bazeni restaurant beyond Bascarsija. The topic of conversation had been the 'hostages'. In the madness of the day the Banja Luka episode and Clark's *faux pas* had slipped from our minds. History.

Forty-eight hours later we were sitting al fresco in a charming Trogir fish restaurant. Relaxed, and dressed in civvies, we were all looking forward to a week's R&R on the Dalmatian coast. The MA had remained in Sarajevo to hold the fort and to keep an eye on the Chief of Staff. Baggers had shot off to Rome for his week, which left the Boss, Goose, Jim Lenski, Lance Corporal Glenn Burton (Rose's new batman) and me to fly down to Split and await the next morning's arrival of Angela Rose and the Roses' two sons.

They'd driven down from Germany in the new tax-free Merc estate; registered with Commie Sarajevo number plates of which the General was immensely proud. Its organisation had plagued Baggers as he'd had to sort it out with Hasan Muratovic, the minister for co-operation with UNPROFOR. They'd been met at the Austro-Slovenian border by Mick Proud and Clive Davies and been escorted down to Rijeka in Croatia and onto the Split-bound ferry. We were due to meet them off the ferry at six the next morning. The Roses, Goose and Jim Lenski would motor down the coast to Korcula and stay a week in Sir Fitzroy Maclean's house. The General had known Fitzroy Maclean for a number of years and they had served in the same regiment. The rest of us could do what we wanted. I'd planned to spend the seven days in Bol on the island of Brac; I hadn't been there since Una and I had spent four days there in late April 1993 after my escape from Srebrenica.

The day had been fraught. General Rose had spent the morning wandering around the market under the flyover pricing its wares. Peasants with their worldly possessions spread out on blankets in front of them sold anything they could to raise a few Deutschmarks, the only currency worth trading in, even to them – mirrors, pipes, old taps, books, anything. Rose's eye had been drawn to a large adjustable spanner.

'What do you reckon, Goose?' A toothless old man looked on hopefully.
'Not bad, Boss.'

'Reckon it would be useful for the Range Rover. Ask him how much, Mike!'

We got it for a bargain – 10 Deutschmarks. Rose had beaten the old man down. I never saw that spanner again. It's probably still in the boot of the Range, wherever that is now.

Then mild panic and consternation set in. Angela Rose was less than twenty-four hours away. 'Mike! Get the barber in!'

By five-thirty we'd arrived in BHC Rear at Divulje barracks, Split. Jim Lenski and I had been dispatched to the port to make sure we knew exactly when and where Lady Rose's ferry would berth. Meanwhile, Rose and Goose had popped into the HQ where the true horror of what had befallen Wes Clark after his departure became apparent. We'd all met up at COMBRITFOR's villa on the south side of Ciovo island where the General had suggested that he might treat us all to supper.

'I warned him. I bloody well told him to watch Mladic like a hawk!' He was karate chopping the air again. I was astounded by the tale: it explained everything that had gone on and why Clifford Schroeder had been so anxious.

Having arrived at Split airport in the Arapaho, Clark and entourage had promptly been arrested by Croatian customs officials and detained for four hours. Spotting a Serbian general's hat being carried quite openly and innocently, the Croats had thrown an epi when they'd discovered that not only was it Mladic's, but that he'd signed it personally. When they discovered the engraved pistol their reaction had turned into near hysteria. Considering that the Americans had been and were still using Pleso airport at Zagreb, particularly the MASH there, as a base for planning and mounting covert 'black' operations, the Croats no doubt felt that Clark's trophies were evidence of double-dealing. Whatever the case, the State Department furiously back-pedalled and disassociated itself from the unfortunate Clark.

'Oh, well. It's their fault. So the Serbs didn't leak any of it.'

'Not true! Reuters have *the picture* on the wire already!' This was getting worse by the minute.

A week later an American magazine was to have the infamous picture on its front cover. Wes Clark had to face probably the worst press conference in his life in which he was asked whether it would have been appropriate for a Second World War US General to have been seen standing next to Hermann Goering and wearing his hat!

'He's finished, finished. No one can survive that. The poor sod. He'll never make four-star!'

Curiously, Clark wasn't finished. He went on to command the US Southern Command in Panama and thereafter succeeded General Joulwan as the Supreme Allied Commander in Europe . . . as a four-star.

'Mladic planned the whole thing, didn't he, Mike?' Rose was emphatic.

I thought for a moment. 'I suppose there are two possibilities. First, that it was unplanned, an unhappy coincidence, and that someone from the Serbian press had decided to make a fast buck . . .'

This was not an unreasonable explanation. Mladic himself had fallen victim to just that during April's fiasco in Gorazde. Major Indjic had shown me a French magazine, *Le Monde* or something, the front cover of which had a huge picture of Mladic and a caption screaming *'Chien de Guerre!'* The article and pictures inside were even more shocking – a selection of snaps of the *chien* swigging from a bottle of whisky while directing operations in the field. 'How on earth did you allow these pictures to get out?' I'd asked. 'One of our photographers, not army, but a Serb, couldn't resist selling them,' Indjic had replied. His eyes had flashed menacingly as he'd added, 'Mind you, he won't be taking pictures again in a hurry.' So that was one possibility.

'. . . or the second is . . .' I could see the images of grinning officers, of conspiratorial looks, laughing on the steps of the hotel as they waved us off . . . the little something, *he's up to something Mike!* . . . feint and absurdly grovelling praise of the detested American war machine . . . little *something* tripping up big powers . . .

'. . . or, General, it really was a fix, a *sting*, and they cooked the whole thing up. Look at the meeting. Nothing was achieved, no compromise, nothing but hot air, waffle, belligerence and aggression. They weren't going to compromise on anything. Simply weren't in the mood . . .' It was all falling into place. '. . . what's the most important thing Mladic had to say? Huge powers being tripped up by a little unforeseen Balkan *something*. He banged on and on about uniforms . . .' the veil lifted, '. . . that's it! A message for Shalikashvili, *you can bomb the shit out of us, we know that, but I can stitch you up and you won't even see it coming, so don't fuck around with us!* Stitched up like a kipper!'

'Do you think so?' Secretly we all wanted it to be so. So much more interesting than something boring like an avaricious little press leak.

'Yeah. Yeah, I do.' I was sure. 'Look, there's an expression in the language. *Seljacka lukavost*. Means sort of 'peasant cunning' or 'native cunning'. Mladic has it by the bucketful. We know that. Slippery customer.'

We lapsed into silence.

An absurd mental picture came to me. 'You know, you can just picture it, can't you?'

'What?'

'Tolimir's rung them up in Banja Luka. Mladic decides to see Clark. But they know there's no real value in it. The referendum's already been decided. So they decide to get him. So, they're all sitting there pissed up on slivo the night before, plotting, laughing and browsing through the *JNA Book of Nasty Tricks to Play on Unsuspecting Foreigners*. And, there it is! *'Trick No 276, HAT-SWAPPING*. That's the one. We'll get him with the hat trick!'

TWENTY

Operation Bretton

December 1997 – Ian, UK

There's something particularly grim about British winters. I'm into yet another session with Ian. As ever it's an afternoon job and already it's getting dark. Through the window the sea seems not to have changed in the past two and a half months – still heavy, malevolent and stormy. It seems to be worse this time, with strong south-westerlies whipping across an ebbing tide promising a wintry gale, just to keep everyone's spirits up. It's always stormy out there and it depresses me. Dark and bloody stormy – a million miles and a time warp away from the blazing heat of an Adriatic island.

I did next to nothing for eight whole days except sit on the beach at Bol watching the waves and thinking about . . . nothing. I was quite thankful that the Roses' holiday on Korcula was a purely private affair. The moment their backs were turned I hopped onto the ferry to Brac, caught a taxi over the island to Bol and got myself into a cheap room and just sat on the beach.

It's the strangest feeling. You rush around at Mach seven – generals everywhere, UN, American, Serb – hats, pistols, the State Department getting its knickers in a twist, and then suddenly you're sitting on a beach on your own doing zero. I kept an eye on things through reading various Croatian newspapers: the headlines were dominated by the Pope's forthcoming visit to Croatia and Bosnia. That would be the first thing on our agenda when we returned to Sarajevo. As I sat on the beach I wondered what dramas would unfold and had quite a bad feeling about it, wondering whether Mladic was plotting to swap his hat with the Pope. I wouldn't put it past him, but I think even he would have drawn a line at giving the Pope an engraved pistol. Anything's possible in Bosnia.

After a week of loafing around on the beach we all met up at Divulje barracks for the hop back to Sarajevo. General Rose looked refreshed but was wittering on about his 'deck shoes'. Goose had covered himself in glory by swimming from Korcula to the mainland and back again, a total of eight miles, in some absurdly short time. The locals had claimed that it hadn't been done since the Second World War. Fitzroy MacLean would have been proud of Goose, though I don't suppose anyone bothered to tell him . . .

The job out there went from the sublime to the ridiculous: fixing this or that with the Serbs; sorting out haircuts; and then getting the General's deck shoes fixed. He came back with a bee in his bonnet about them. Lady Rose had had a go at him about them looking tatty and needing replacing. When we got back to the office, in and amongst the drama surrounding the Pope he'd slung these scruffy old leather deck shoes at me saying that he'd got them in India in 1968, and that they were perfectly okay, only needed a decent cobbler to look at them. A good Sarajevo cobbler he'd said. So, while Karadzic was writing letters saying that the Pope shouldn't come to Sarajevo because the Serbs couldn't 'guarantee his safety', I was rushing around the city haggling with cobblers to get these things fixed. Of course they all turned their noses up at them saying they couldn't be mended. They were right. Lady Rose was right. They were falling to bits. No one would touch them. In the end I just hid them under my desk and hoped he'd forget about them, which he did. And so did I, until I found them again after Rose had left and quietly slung them in the bin. That wasn't the end of it by any means. If it wasn't haircuts and deck shoes then it was parasols and fishing.

Wheeling and dealing with the Serbs was kid's stuff compared to the others. The General's eye was taken by these rather smart large wooden and coloured cotton parasols which every café seemed to sport. And he was right: they would look smart in any garden. I was dispatched around the city to price them up and haggle for one. None of the cafés was prepared to sell, but all told me that they were in fact made in Italy. I thought that would be enough to put the General off, that Baggers would be palmed off with getting one from Italy. But, oh no! He wanted one from Sarajevo. Sarajevo was 'special', you see.

After more scampering around I ended up in a dark, smoky subterranean den of a café haggling with the only people who controlled parasols: the Mafia. The whole place was sown up. Forget Karadzic, Mladic or Indjic. They were small fry compared to parasols. The Mafia had one, a 'good second-hand one', which the General could buy for 180 Deutschmarks. Triumphantly, I returned to the Residency with the good news only to be told by the General that he reckoned they were only worth 100 Deutschmarks and to get back and haggle with the supplier. You don't haggle with these people. They told me to fuck off and tell the General that they weren't going to be ripped off, which is rich coming from the Mafia. So, that was it. The deal fell through and the General didn't get his parasol.

There was other stuff too, such as hand-made, brass coffee grinders. Market price 80 Deutschmarks apiece. Minka managed to get me two for 40 Deutschmarks but the General figured that was too steep, so I ended up keeping them and gave one to Brigadier Andrew Cumming.

The fishing was a drama all of its own. I blame Nick Costello entirely for failing to hand that one over to me. He never mentioned that Rose was a keen fly-fisherman and had all his gear in theatre. More importantly, what did I know about bloody fly-fishing? If you don't do something then you don't even know the words for it in English, let alone Serbo-Croat. I know what a 'trout' and a 'salmon' are in English but I'm buggered if I know their equivalents in Serbo-Croat. Nick had accompanied the General on his various fishing exploits around Bosnia when they'd been on the road but had failed entirely to pass on the critical vocab list. So I got badly caught out.

Early on, during Simon Shadbolt's time, we were on the road visiting; first stop the Turkish battalion in the Zenica steel works and then up the road to Zepce to chinwag with the BiH commander there. Every so often the General's vehicle would screech to a halt. Out he'd leap and inspect a stretch of river. If it met with his approval we'd note it. In fact I kept an Ops fishing map marked up with likely trout-bearing stretches of river. I'd even get about town and canvass my 'contacts', experts such as Minka and Tomo. So, gradually, my map of good fishing spots grew. MoD Plod have probably got it now and are reading something sinister into all the markings on it. I mean it *is* an Int map of sorts – best kept secret trout locations of Bosnia – but it's hardly a breach of the Official Secrets Act.

We are at this meeting in Zepce and Rose starts asking about local trout fishing. The BiH chap's eyes light up and to my horror we discover that he too is a keen fisherman. Before I know it he's produced an 'expert' local guide, we've piled into the vehicles and driven a little way to a river where we've parked up. We're tramping along this path with the General, clutching his waders, rod and bag of whatever fishermen have. He's interrogating this bloke about the local fish. Rose assumes that I know fishing terminology, which I don't. I've guessed that *'pastrmka'* is a 'trout' which is all well and good but then he wants to know what else is in the river. I ask the guide and he mentions some bloody fish I've never heard of in the local language and certainly wouldn't know what it was in English anyway. So, in a mild panic I say, 'just describe what it is' to which he replies, 'it's the younger cousin of the trout, only smaller bones and with black dots'. That's exactly what I tell Rose who just says, 'Oh yes, grayling.'

We get to this river, which is broad, flat and looks quite shallow. There are loads of other people fishing and bathing. Rose mutters something about them scaring off the fish and casts about for a spot. He climbs into his waders, checks his gear and then just wades off into the middle of the river. Goose and I just look at each other. What are we supposed to do? Go out there with him, get soaking wet because we've got no waders and stand beside him while he casts away? That's all a bit beyond the call of duty so the three of us, Simon, Goose and myself, sit ourselves down on the bank. The MA falls asleep. Goose is maintaining 'watch' over the Boss who is about 100 metres away and I chat to some blokes who are smoking grayling and swigging Slivo.

You've got to imagine this unwarlike, almost idyllic scene of blue skies, sparkling clear river and folk frolicking about. Suddenly there's this almighty long burst of automatic fire from the opposite bank. It's followed by more and more. We can't hear any 'crack' which means nothing's coming towards us, but the noise of gunfire is quite deafening. Goose stiffens up, clutching his MP5, and is staring at the Boss who isn't bothered in the least about the firing and is casting away merrily, totally oblivious. Goose goes white and just hangs his head in his hands shaking it from side to side. 'Bet that got you going, eh Goose?' says Rose with a laugh when he eventually wades ashore. 'Yes, Boss. I was just wondering what I was going to tell Angela when your body's brought off the plane!'

Turns out there was a wedding somewhere on the opposite bank and all the guests were 'letting off', as they do in the Balkans. Confetti in England, bullets in Bosnia! The next time we did it I was better prepared. The 'map' was well marked up with secret trout havens, the fruit of many hours of interrogating my contacts and wheedling the info out of them. It's several months later. Daniel has replaced Shadbolt as MA, we've had the hat affair with Mladic and Clark and we've done our week on the coast. As frequently happened, the General's 'rolling programme' has gone awry, someone's visit was cancelled, so we've got a day and a night to fill. Daniel is mad keen to get the General out of the office for a break and suggests a day of fishing and a night 'camping out'. The General is persuaded, so off we go with fishing gear, rations and sleeping bags. He virtually came charging out of his office clutching waders, rods and nets saying, 'Right! We're off. Mike, where do you reckon?'

I've got the map all ready and he just takes one look at it and ignores all my hard-earned trout intelligence and stabs his finger on a ribbon of blue right on the BiH-Serb front line near Zepce: 'That's where we're going. Looks like a good stretch for trout!' My heart sinks. It's right on the front line. And anyway, how can he tell what's going to be in a tiny strand of blue on a 1:100,000 scale map?

Off we go and two hours later turn off the main Zenica–Zepce drag onto a minor road that leads some five kilometres to this 'trout haven'. As we turn off we hit a BiH checkpoint manned by soldiers who tell us we can't go any further because of combat activities in that area. They're exercising or preparing for an attack on the Serbs and don't want anyone snooping in the area, least of all the UN and least of all Rose. Fair one really, but Rose isn't having it and demands to exercise his freedom of movement. They refuse and ask what business we have in the area and when we tell them they just laugh and say, 'You're wasting your time. The river's too shallow there and there are no fish.' But Rose won't have that either. 'Rubbish. Of course there are fish there. Perfectly obvious!'

Eventually the guards are so fed up with this that they tell us to go into Zepce and get permission from the local commander. If we can do that then we can pass with an escort. That's what we do. We get to the HQ in Zepce and I'm sent in to haggle with the commander. None of them comes with me. They just sit in the vehicles impatient to get on with fishing. Jamie Daniel in particular is getting stressed as the whole fishing plan is about to go down the tubes; it's already three in the afternoon and the General has yet to cast a fly. At first the commander won't hear of it. I'm virtually on my knees begging him. Failure really wasn't worth contemplating, not where fishing's involved. Parasols, deck shoes and coffee grinders are one thing, but fishing's a different ball game altogether!

The BiH commander finally relents and we get our military escort. We rattle down this track for five kilometres to the exact spot. I'm feeling quite pleased with myself by this stage. Out we hop. Rose strides down to the river, takes one look at it and says, 'That's no bloody good. Far too shallow. Let's find somewhere else!' The escorting soldiers are smirking like mad. You couldn't even call it a river. Couldn't even get your toe wet.

Rose was wrong about the fish, but that wasn't the point. He didn't care whether there were fish or not. He didn't want to be told he couldn't go down a track. He was just making his point and exercising his right to free movement. But that didn't help the MA who by now was in a panic and desperate to save what little was left of the day. We went for a safe option, to drive all the way back, virtually to Kiseljak then down the Fojnica valley, through that town and then straight up a steep wooded mountain track. This eventually escaped from the tree line into a peak of high alpine grass and boulders. At the very top was a lake, a small tarn set in what looked like a little volcanic crater. Dotted around the lake were old wooden huts. The mountain area is called Travnicka Vrata and is one of the highest peaks in Bosnia, but with a lake. All very remote and otherworldly.

It was close to eight by the time we'd parked up. Rose didn't lose a moment and rushed off down to the water with his gear. Goose and I went with him and sat beside the lake watching the General casting away. It was quite magical: wild horses champing in the bulrushes, smoke twisting from the wooden huts. The sun had gone but there was still a pinkish warmth to the dusk.

After about ten minutes a Croat soldier appeared and asked us who was fishing. When I told him he immediately asked whether we'd stopped in Fojnica and asked permission from the Croat commander to come up here. I just lied and said 'yes'. The soldier became curious and started asking about

Rose's gear: 'What kind of bait is he using?' Instantly I replied 'wet fly' because by then I'd bothered to find out and learn the fishing vocab. 'Wet fly, eh? No way is he going to catch anything with that!' said the soldier before ambling off.

Goose was sipping from a can of Coke. When I voiced my concern at what the soldier had told me, he didn't even bother to look at me or to lower the can, but just said in a tired but wise voice, 'It doesn't matter, Mike. He's never caught a thing out here. So long as he's made that first cast he'll be happy.' He was right. Goose knew the Boss better than any of us.

We had a bit of a camp fire that night and ate German rations which Rose thought were brilliant. Early the next morning there was a bit more fishing. Jamie Daniell had brought his telescopic rod and was casting away on a rock until some jealous Croat caught him in 'his' spot and sat in the woods throwing stones at the MA until Jamie was driven off. Then we packed up and drove back to the mayhem of war in Sarajevo.

There were a lot more of these weird trips. If you think the fishing was bad just wait till you hear of the Boss's attempts to kill his entire staff by leading them down the Mount Bijelasnica Olympic men's downhill run, un-pisted and covered in land mines! Goose loved that one, being a non-skier.

Back in Sarajevo, the Pope's impending visit was definitely off. By this stage just about every airlift transport aircraft was being shot at by small arms and occasionally cannon. No aircraft were ever shot down or grounded because, if you think about it, these multi-engined aircraft are giant flying boxes of empty space so it's hard to take one down with small arms unless you're particularly lucky. But it was still dangerous. Virtually all would get back to Ancona or wherever and find tiny bullet holes in the fuselage, tail or wings. Occasionally passengers were hit. An American aid worker, outbound from Sarajevo, was hit in the leg by a round coming through the skin of the aircraft as it was taking off. He died three weeks later of complications. On another occasion a whole Ukrainian battalion was being rotated out and a .50 inch round smashed through the skin of an Il 76 and hit a Ukrainian conscript in the stomach. When they landed in Kiev the bloke was dead. Flying into or out of Sarajevo had its risks.

Most of the firing came from the Serbs in Ilidza, either from apartments or from the roofs of buildings. It was their way of exerting pressure on the airlift by closing down the airport. The problem was that they weren't the only ones. Sometimes the Bosnians would do it in order to have it blamed on the Serbs. At other times the Serbs would do it in order to claim it was the Bosnians who were doing it in order to blame it on the Serbs. Horrible treble thinking. So when Dr Karadzic says they can't 'guarantee the safety of the Pope', he's saying 'the Muslims will shoot at the aircraft to blame us', which in turn can mean 'we'll shoot at the aircraft to blame it on the Muslims who've done it to blame it on us'.

Well, it's outrageous that anyone was shooting at aircraft which, at the end of the day, were bringing in food for both sides, but they didn't care. The airlift became a pawn in this Balkan game. Rose was furious whenever it happened, as was Admiral Leighton Smith in Naples. A lot of effort went into trying to locate firing points and in negotiating with the heads of all sides, but it was virtually useless. As we know from Northern Ireland, you can fire from any bloody room in an urban environment and it's very hard to locate the firing point. Equally, each side blamed it on the other. But, threats of 'non guarantee of safety', whether genuine, bluff, double bluff or triple bluff, had to be taken seriously which was why the UN recommended that it was too dangerous for the Pope to fly in.

That decision was made in Zagreb, but the world and its press blamed Rose. The way they were banging on about it, it was as if Mike Rose had personally threatened the Pope. That was the point when the press, the Bosnians and Washington turned against Rose. From then on he couldn't win. If the Pope had come and been shot at, Rose would have been blamed for that. By him not coming he was equally blamed for kowtowing to the Serbs and not doing anything about Karadzic's threats. So Rose was the loser. The Serbs were ambivalent: the Pope wasn't going to be visiting them anyway, so they didn't care. The only winners in all this nonsense were the Bosnian government who could use the Pope's non-appearance to attack Rose and the UN for not doing enough.

Into this mess came new arrivals to the HQ. Rose had decided that he no longer wanted UN civilians representing him in front of the press at eleven each morning in the PTT building. He wanted a military man who could express military views and that job fell to Lieutenant Colonel Tim Spicer. He actually had a staff job in the School of Infantry in Warminster where, having finished commanding a Scots Guards battalion, he was working out his last three months in the Army prior to getting out. Rose had requested him by name, so out he came on 15 September and was charged with presenting the Boss's policy line to the press.

The following day yet another new JCO commander appeared. The current OC, Martin, was at the end of his tour and the Army wanted him back. Again, Rose nominated his replacement by name, a major from the Irish Guards called Jamie Lowther-Pinkerton. So, out came L-P. I felt sure I wouldn't like him: double-barrelled name means chinless wonder from the Brigade of Guards, enough said. I'd liked Martin and had taken him up to Pale recently when I'd been dispatched on some errand. We'd been standing outside the UNMO's house, which was about 300 metres from Karadzic's 'Presidency', that annex building of the Hotel Panorama. Martin's eye had been drawn to a flat concrete-roofed shed built into the side of a hill next to a barn. 'You know that's down on the NATO targeting list as a bunker?' he'd said. I'd just laughed, 'You know what's in there don't you? It's stuffed full of skis and thousands and thousands of mushrooms!' The 'bunker' belonged to Dani Savic who rented out part of his house to the UNMOs. Dani was a skiing instructor and had 'liberated' for safe keeping all the skis from the various resort hotels on Mount Jahorina just as the war broke out. He was also something of an entrepreneur and had grown mushrooms in the 'bunker' which he'd sold all over Yugoslavia.

It's just typical of that gang in Italy and in NATO. You find something that looks like a bunker on a satellite photo and it's immediately put on the targeting list. The reality on the ground is that a bomb into it would have done nothing but blow up a load of skis and mushrooms. But NATO just weren't going to be told a thing. They were right and we were all wrong. The Americans, through Leighton Smith, had this view that peace could be achieved by bombing from the air – showing the usual Western penchant for zero-risk, high-tech, quick-fix solutions. That policy failed in Somalia, where the Americans were dragged over the 'Mogadishu Line', as Rose called it, and got the biggest kicking of their lives since Vietnam, and it wasn't going to work in Bosnia, where you had a low-tech, internal security or guerrilla-type war on the ground.

But in Naples and elsewhere they were wedded to bombing the war to an end. In the end they did just that but look what happened. The war ended. The Serbs were dragged to the table, but it didn't really achieve much. Bosnia is now divided into three mini states. Refugees still haven't gone home. Everyone's re-armed themselves. Inter-ethnic hatreds are still smouldering and the Serbs got 49 per cent of the land anyway. That's no great achievement. All that quick-fix bombing and Dayton stuff has done is to chuck the entire problem into the deep freezer. It'll come out again though and when it thaws they'll be at it again hammer and tongs, sorting out all those unresolved issues. High-tech short-termism. But they've all proved the humanitarian qualities of their fast jets so it must have been worth it, eh?

Those jets really pissed us off. Zipping around making pretty patterns in the sky and then back to Italy and their five-star hotels to slap each other on the back for a job well done protecting the UN on the ground. Hardly the case. When we called on them for a bit of Close Air Support, i.e. hitting a specific target like a tank or whatever was violating the Total Exclusion Zones, either they couldn't acquire the target, or when they did they missed. The problem was that, without risking troops in combat on the ground, air power was seen by NATO as the only tool available to express force. Convinced by the efficacy of so-called pin-point, surgical strikes in the Gulf War, NATO failed to see how desperately inappropriate they were in Bosnia. Imagine suggesting that the RAF conduct air strikes against the IRA in Northern Ireland. You'd be declared insane and chucked into a loony bin within minutes and left there to rot.

NATO's frustration at not being allowed to indulge in unbridled air strikes must have been acute because it led to some harsh words between Leighton Smith and Rose. The former ranted, 'Plinking tanks is not warfighting!' to which Rose replied, 'No, Admiral, we're asking you to do this the hard way.'

That really summed up Rose's philosophy – the hard way. Frequently he'd quote JFK, saying that the road to peace was long and tortuous, pitted and difficult. That is, no quick fix. But they couldn't see it, and, my God were they precious! At one stage one of their jets got illuminated by some Serb tracking radar. That had them scuttling for cover and DENY FLIGHT operations, i.e. flying over Bosnia, were suspended for three weeks. Too dangerous to fly below 5,000 feet they'd claimed. When the General heard that one he flipped his lid: 'Too dangerous to fly under five thousand feet!' he raged. 'We fucking well live below five thousand feet!'

All in all, relations with NATO were strained. Despite the fact that both they and the UN claimed to have the same goal, peace, in reality their agendas were quite divergent, their methods poles apart. They also forgot that they were in support of us, but a backseat role wasn't good enough for them and they frequently frustrated peacekeeping operations on the ground instead of complementing them.

It couldn't be simpler. You've got these two global organisations which are both pretending to be working towards the same aim. But really they can't because their methods are not complementary and, more importantly, the ethos of each is wildly different. NATO is a warfighting machine. At the military level its aim is the defeat of an enemy in order to satisfy some collective political goal. Its ethos is warfighting and its doctrine is unashamedly an American one – the application of serious firepower. At Staff College we were forever being told about Find, Fix and Strike. And when it strikes it does so absolutely, with overwhelming ferocity and, where possible, indirectly using aircraft, missiles and shells. Today's generation of US generals grew up with Vietnam, with the image of tens of thousands of young American conscripts being annihilated by Vietnamese guerrillas in black pyjamas. So, firepower is their god, which is exactly what they brought to bear against the Iraqis for so few casualties. The perfect American war.

The UN's ethos is quite the opposite. It's all driven by peace. Military activities are proscribed by ludicrously complicated rules of engagement which effectively neuter any soldier on the ground. Because the various UN Resolutions which create UN operations are driven by the peace ethos, the force structures of UN military commands are necessarily minimalist in the firepower department. They're given just enough by the mandates coming out of

New York to exercise the application of minuscule amounts of firepower, usually in the protection of aid agencies. Inevitably, when surrounded by belligerents who are far better armed, who have no rules of engagement and are not shackled by mandates, the mentality becomes defensive and self-protective. It stands to reason then that if the mandates don't structure the UN ground forces for anything more than protection operations, it is totally absurd for the international community, which incidentally *is* the UN, to expect them to engage in combat operations. But that's what the press and everyone expected and instead of blaming themselves for not 'doing enough' they focused their frustrations on one man – Rose.

Goose got it absolutely right, in his no-nonsense way. He told Rose, 'That's right, Boss. You can't fight wars in white vehicles!' This has since been much quoted by Rose, but it was Goose who said it. Funny how it takes someone such as Goose to cut through the bullshit handwringing and academic mastur-bation and state the blindingly obvious. If the international community had wanted us to fight they should have equipped us with the requisite mandates and force structures instead of a whole lot of guff, hot air and fancy words, which helped nobody and frankly either confused or misled the locals on the ground.

That was the essence of the problem. Bosnia really was little more than a mad professor's laboratory in which a very unpleasant war was used as a proving ground to define the set of the New World Disorder. NATO and the UN were like two stags whose horns were locked in a conflict to see whose ethos would triumph. NATO was out to prove it could outlast the Cold War, but having US hegemony was manipulated, or rather, bullied, into prosecuting Washington's foreign policy. That was all wrapped up in American policy elsewhere, notably in the Middle East where in 1991–2 they were trying to broker a peace between the Arabs and Israelis. Don't forget also the multi-billion dollar defence contracts with the Saudis and Kuwaitis that fell out of the Gulf War, all of which meant that the Yanks couldn't be seen not to be supporting 'European' Muslims.

Then you had America's other policy – withdrawal of her European army back to the US, which of course won't happen until she leaves behind a strong, trustworthy partner in Europe. It's not going to be the British. It's the Germans, which is why the US supported German foreign policy in recognising Slovenia, Croatia and Bosnia. Remember General Wes Clark's honest reply to Mladic when asked what America's interest in the Balkans was; to keep NATO strong, to prevent the war from spilling over and to keep the US-Russian relationship up. Nothing there at all about Bosnians per se.

That's just the simple part of it. Into the test tube you then chuck in all the little national agendas of the other troop-contributing nations. The French were in it virtually to shore up the post-war rebuild contracts. Brazenly, they brought in fourteen captains of industry who'd all been transformed into French Army full colonels. You can't imagine us doing that! We're so wrapped up in our anal little obsessions with uniforms and rank that we'd rather forgo any rebuild contracts than allow fourteen smelly low-life captains of industry to wear our precious outfits, and heaven forbid, not as colonels. Everyone had some agenda out there. We of course didn't have one but we had to be there because the French were there.

All this politicking, all these secret little agendas got chucked into the pot and stirred about by the press. All done in the pursuit of some personal national or sovereign aim and very little of it to do with love of Balkan people. Any benefits, scraps, that fell off the table were largely incidental. So where did that leave the locals? The Serbs were so paranoid and unimaginative that they lumped the UN in with NATO and viewed the whole ghastly blob as one giant, anti-Serb, Western conspiracy. They saw us on the ground as nothing more than NATO ground troops in blue berets. The Bosnians, on the other hand, were smarter: they immediately appreciated the difference and quickly identified the gaping weakness in the two organisations' mutual efforts to find peace and exploited it ruthlessly and cleverly. Quite rightly, being involved in a war of national survival, they chose to court NATO, i.e. the US. They barely concealed their hatred of the UN but tolerated it in so far as we were vaguely useful for getting them some food and for being used as whipping boys. The Croats didn't seem to give a damn about anything so long as Germany, and hence the US, was on their side. But for all of them it was frustrating. All they really wanted to do was win their war, but each in their own way was thwarted by Bosnia being peripheral and incidental to the big boys' stag fight. The Bosnia of today is a horribly deformed test tube baby conceived and reared in the mad professor's laboratory. Anyway, the stag fight is littered with examples of non-complementary and totally counterproductive behaviour.

The arrival of Tim Spicer and L-P heralded a new era. The honeymoon was about to come to an abrupt end and life for all of us started to become serious. It would not be an exaggeration to say that their tours began with a bang. The Serbs had a rough track supply route that ran north around Sarajevo which kept Ilidza, Rajlovac, Ilijas, Vogosca and Centar connected to Pale and beyond. Loss of this route to the BiH would have made their positions around the city totally untenable. At the north-eastern end of Sarajevo they dominated a high piece of ground called Spicasta Stena (Pointed Rock) from which they were able to fire into the city and behind which ran this track. Their occupation of this ground had become a hot topic for negotiations and moves were afoot for the UN to interpose itself on the hill to prevent further sniping. The Serbs resisted this idea claiming with some justification that the UN had failed to prevent BiH encroachments of the Igman and Bijelasnica DMZ to the south and that the UN's occupation of Spicasta Stena would merely be a precursor to the BiH cutting their supply route. This was not an unfounded worry and negotiations had not proceeded well.

At about 7 p.m. on Sunday 18 September the BiH launched a massive attack out of the city with the aim of capturing Spicasta Stena. Several hundred elite Black Swans, BiH Special Forces, had been drafted in, at considerable financial cost of course, from central Bosnia through the tunnel. At the time I was sitting in Vogosca with a Serb family Goose and I had met a month or so earlier while on the road with Rose. Theirs was an interesting case. They'd obviously been wealthy before the war and had a smart house in town not far from the Residency; they also had this flat in Vogosca. Their next door neighbours and friends were a Muslim family. When the war broke out this Serb family fled the town house, giving the keys to the Muslim family who had themselves fled from Vogosca into town. There'd been no contact between the two families until Goose and I appeared on the scene. Routinely we'd act as go-betweens. The Serbs would package up food, rations and letters for the Muslim family which we'd take in and we'd return with books and other personal effects which had been left behind. We even recovered 1,000 Deutschmarks which the Serbs had hidden in the cellar in Sarajevo and were instructed to give half the money to the Muslim family, which we did. It really did pose the question that if these two families could still care for each other in this way why on earth was this war being fought in the first place?

From the flat in Vogosca that evening, firing and thumping can be heard from the east. It gets louder and louder, to the point where the windows began to rattle. Something big was going on and Rose was in the Residency and I was on the 'wrong' side of the line. I grabbed the parcel, which they'd prepared for the Muslim family, and drove the long way back into town approaching from Ilidza. By the time I'd got into the old part of Sarajevo it was obvious that something serious was happening. The streets were all but deserted. Fresh mortar impacts peppered the roads and lines of tracer flicked across the city from one hill to another. When I reached them, the Muslim family was petrified and wailing that we'd just regressed to 1992–3. By the time I'd got back to the Residency I'd missed Rose's road show. He'd grabbed L-P, Tim Spicer and a few others and gone touring. Up at the Turkish fort they'd been engaged by a Serb heavy machine gun and had had to take cover. Mortar fire into and out of the city had been incredibly heavy. The attempt to capture Spicasta Stena failed but in all respects this was the most serious cease-fire breach since I'd arrived and since the February cease-fire. This was L-P's and Spicer's personal welcome to Sarajevo.

Naturally, each side blamed the other, so the next day off we went up to Pale where we met with Momcilo Krajisnik, the leader of the Bosnian Serb assembly. They were spitting with fury and blaming the Muslims and the UN for the attack. Worse still, they cut off the gas and electricity supply to the city as 'punishment'. Following that we shot back to Sarajevo and had a meeting with President Izetbegovic. He blamed the Serbs. Both parties of course blamed the UN for not doing enough. It made me sick, particularly when I thought of that poor, petrified Muslim family. At the end of the meeting I stuffed my notebooks away in my daysack and we departed. That was to come back and haunt me later.

A day or so later Rose was attacked from another quarter. We'd been hosting Admiral Leighton Smith, had whipped him around the city and had even taken him to the UNHCR distribution warehouse in Rajlovac. His major concern was that airlift aircraft were continually being shot at on landing and take-off. At the airport they were ambushed by the press, one of whom, Roger Cohen of *The New York Times,* personally attacked Rose for not doing enough, for promising electricity, gas and water and for not delivering the goods. This was not true. Cohen persisted with this line and Rose came close to losing his cool. It was the most virulent attack to date and was, it seemed, the precursor to a shift in the press line. Rose's response when we got back to the Residency was predictable: 'Get Cohen round for supper.' Sounds odd, but Rose didn't like sycophants and he'd now realised that seventy per cent of effort needed to be directed towards the media.

A day later, on Thursday 22 September, Rose departed for the UK. He was due to lecture to the Staff Course at Camberley and took Kurt Schork of Reuters with him. An unusual but interesting move. His departure filled me with complete dread.

Rose was jinxed. There was some sort of bad juju attached to him. Whenever he left theatre something would happen, some disaster which would make the Serbs close down their checkpoints and make it virtually impossible for him to get back into the city. The downside to all this was that I'd get left behind 'just in case' . . . just in case it happened and I had to leap over to the Serb side, and wave the magic wand and pull in whatever favour to get him back in. With him gone back to the UK I just knew that something ghastly was going to happen.

He'd only been gone about four hours when disaster struck. Following the BiH attack on Spicasta Stena the French Sector Sarajevo commander, General André Soubirou, ordered a French cavalry armoured car unit based in the Zetra stadium to interpose itself on the hillock. Whether they'd agreed this with the Serbs or not I don't know, but the latter retaliated by firing an RPG7 rocket at a Sagei armoured car which was probing up the hill. It was hit and knocked out. Mercifully there were no casualties. The French went berserk. Within moments Soubirou and a gaggle of French staff officers had invaded Rose's office and were on the phone direct to their Force Commander, General de Lapresle, up in Zagreb. The Dutch BHC Chief of Staff, General Van Baal, whom Rose had nominally left in charge, was completely side-lined. He spent his time on the phone to Mladic's Chief of Staff, General Manojlo Milovanovic, trying to sort the problem out and went as far as to assure Milovanovic that there'd be no air strikes.

It was absurd. You could see this debacle happening before your very eyes. While Van Baal was talking to Milovanovic, Soubirou and gang were in Rose's office gabbling away in French to de Lapresle frequently mentioning *'frappes de l'air'*, air strikes. To be more precise, they were cooking up a BLUE SWORD strike against a specific target. Rose of course couldn't be contacted as he was airborne somewhere over Europe. By the time he'd landed at Boscombe Down in Wiltshire he was virtually presented with a *fait accompli*, and had no choice other than to take the advice of those on the ground, which was all French. So, the BLUE SWORD went in in the early evening. The target chosen was a Serb tank known to be in violation of the TEZ and lurking somewhere to the west of Sarajevo in the village of Dobrosevici. The first pair of French Mirages failed to acquire the tank and had to fly back to Italy. Next on the scene was an A10 which conducted a strafing run and, finally, a pair of British Jaguars dropped a 1,000 lb free-fall bomb. From the eastern end of the city we watched a huge black cloud drift up into the evening air.

It's uncertain whether the tank was ever hit. What is certain was that General Soubirou had delivered his farewell present to the Serbs, who had made his life a misery for a year. Moreover, it escaped no one's attention that General de Lapresle's young son, a captain, had been commanding the armoured unit in Zetra. Some said he'd even been in the Sagei when it had been hit. The extent to which this had been a French affair became obvious that evening. Tim Spicer had prepared a detailed press release. The draft of this was snatched from him by Soubirou who inserted his name where he could and delivered the release personally. Not only had he recovered the good name of Captain de Lapresle, but he'd also stuck two fingers up at the Serbs to boot. Both his standing as national hero and his career were now assured.

All this left us in a lousy position. Regardless of whether or not a strike had been justified, we'd sent quite contrary and conflicting signals to the Serbs. Van Baal had told Milovanovic one thing and we'd done the other. From the Serb perspective we, the UN, had lied. Mladic went ballistic and condemned NATO as a bunch of 'criminals' claiming that the tank had not been hit and that the bombs had knocked the windows out of Dobrosevici's school house. True or not I don't know, but that's the way he saw it. A couple of weeks later we were visited by the Minister for the Armed Forces, Nicholas Soames, and the CinC Land, General Sir John Wilsey. Rose was busy at a meeting so I was dispatched to pick them up from Kiseljak and act as driver/guide. On the drive through the Sierras, Soames questioned me about the air strike and asked me directly whether Rose would have conducted it had he been around. I told him that I thought it had been an entirely French affair and that Rose probably wouldn't have reacted in that way, knowing that it would have set us back on the road to peace. It was way above my pay grade to make a comment like that but, since he asked, I told him.

I wasn't that wrong. Milovanovic blew his stop. So did Mladic. They closed down the airport and threatened to shoot down everything 'south of Paris'. Convoys to Gorazde and Srebrenica were frozen as were the checkpoints. Mladic threatened that the airport would remain closed until he'd received a formal apology from the 'criminals in NATO'. So, all in all, no food into Sarajevo, no fuel or resupply of rations to the UN in the enclaves and a lot of misery ahead for those living under 5,000 feet. Who were the losers in this egotistical stag fight? The Little People of course, as ever.

The day after the French air strike I was approached by L-P. Perhaps confronted is a better word. He'd been in theatre less than a week and had already made his mind up about me. There had been 'mutterings at court' and he'd decided to tell me about them. I hardly knew him and we hadn't talked much at all. What the JCOs did was their business. They were directly tasked by Rose and as far as I was concerned were nothing to do with me or what I did, or so I rather naively thought. The 'mutterings at court' were mainly inspired by the MA and on this occasion centred on the fact that, when we'd broken up from the meeting with Izetbegovic (after the Spicasta Stena affair) I hadn't shaken his hand. Earlier in the day, I'd been spied by Goose showing one of the Serb bodyguards a photograph of my father in wartime uniform. On the basis of that Stanley was 'pro-Serb'. I was furious when LP told me that: it had come from someone who'd been in the Balkans a bare week. Of course, nobody bothered to notice that when we'd broken up from the meeting with the Serbs I hadn't bothered to shake their hands either. They only saw what they wanted to see in order to confirm a stereotypical picture of me. They didn't know, for example, that the folk I knew best in the Balkans were Minka and Munir Pijalovic, the Muslim family in Bascarsija I'd been looking after on behalf of General Jackson's au pair, Aida, for almost a year and a half. They didn't know about Tomo, Vera and Nada, all old age pensioners, nor did they know about the Serb family in Vogosca and their Muslim friends in the city. They didn't know because I didn't tell them about it. I didn't scream and shout about it simply because that was private. But because I didn't reveal the whole picture I was vulnerable to such accusations.

I had no choice but to sit L-P down and explain the whole saga to him. I told him everything: about my past, about how I'd ended up in the Balkans, what had happened during the first tour and the fact that I had now found myself, largely because I loathed interpreting, acting as a go-between and prostituting my family's history and background in order to get closer to and gain the confidence of the most difficult and impenetrable bunch of suspicious paranoids in the world – the Pale cabal. Unorthodox though the methods were it was all in pursuit of the General's campaign plan, and, of course, it was inevitably going to leave me vulnerable to accusations.

I didn't carry that photograph of my father around for fun. There was a purpose to that too. It was a key, a passport if you like, which unlocked people's suspicion and paranoia. A lot earlier, must have been about July, we were up touring the Serb front line at Ilijas and visiting a Canadian OP there. We were walking back to the vehicles when we were stopped by a local Serb commander. He was suspicious as hell and took one look at Frank Cannon and announced that he recognised Frank from Visoko before the war, and that Frank was a Muslim spy. The fact that Frank was a sergeant in the RMP and couldn't speak a word of Serbo-Croat meant nothing to this fellow. As far as he was concerned Frank was a spy and we weren't going anywhere until his commander arrived. I was able to sweet-talk this ruffian and whip out the photograph and convince him that poor Frank was actually a Brit and not a spy. It did the trick and we parted company with this fellow after handshakes, big grins and invitations to drinks. The point is, on that occasion the key worked and it got us out of a spot of bother. Rose didn't bat an eyelid and the photograph was never mentioned. It suited the situation and it worked. People only remember and see things which suit their preconceptions and fit their stereotypes. Their view is therefore incomplete and unbalanced. But that's not to say that it wasn't going to be a problem for me. Clearly it was, and L-P's words were the first inkling of that.

As for diplomatic *faux pas* concerning handshakes, if we're going to play that game, my worst gaffe, if anything, was not with the Muslims or Croats. It was with the Serbs. We'd just broken up from a meeting with Karadzic and gang. Before we departed drinks were served and people split up into groups. I found myself deep in conversation with Professor Nikola Koljevic, one of Karadzic's vice presidents (he was a professor of English who specialised in Shakespeare). He was wittering on about the virtues of Serbs and their culture. The more he banged on the more irritated I became. Eventually I stuck the knife in and told him that anything that was good about Serbdom was being safeguarded by the likes of my father whom the Communists had forced out. I pointed out that Koljevic and the rest had profited from their years of compromising with Communism while 'our lot' had been forced to live in exile for half a century. I rounded it off by informing the professor that they'd hijacked Serbian culture, resurrected it and twisted it to their own ends.

Koljevic lost his temper. His face went purple. The vein in his neck stood out like a hawser and his spittle was splattering my face. Apoplectic is the word. The room fell silent as the professor ranted on in Serbo-Croat. Rose gave me a withering look. It took me ages to calm Koljevic down. Obviously, I'd hit a nerve. Not shaking hands with Izetbegovic is neither here nor there. They remember that but conveniently forget that I tried to give Koljevic a heart attack.

I'd never done it before with anyone. I'd deliberately tried to keep my work completely separate from Minka and my 'charges'. But on this occasion, after my chat with L-P, I took him up to see Minka. She was all over us and told LP that she considered me to be her son, that her home was my home. Of more interest, after we'd drunk a number of cups of thick coffee, she sprang into soothsayer mode and read his past, present and future. I barely knew L-P, knew nothing of his past, let alone his personal life, and therefore Minka couldn't possibly have known either. What she saw staggered L-P. As I translated I watched him go whiter and whiter with each revelation. Everything she saw had happened; everything she predicted has since happened to him. More soberingly, she told me that I had enemies at work and that someone unfriendly to me was plotting against me and that I should take care. She merely confirmed what I'd suspected for a while. In the Outer Office there were elements hostile to me and working against me. I heeded her warning, though I have to say it made me sick to hear it. I knew who they were.

Momentarily, all that was forgotten. Rose was still away and Tim Spicer, acting on Rose's orders, had invited a number of the press around for drinks and dinner. L-P, Spicer and I sat in the General's office watching the BBC's Bob Simpson, Robert Fox (of the *Daily Telegraph*) and Roger Cohen, who arrived expecting an ambush, guzzling Rose's whisky. Roger Cohen used the opportunity to stab Rose in the back still further. I remember explaining the Serb perspective of the Contact Group plan. As far as the Serbs were concerned it was ridiculous and stupid and designed only to make them say 'no'. That was their perception and that's the perception I explained. That inevitably got twisted and ascribed directly to me. I learnt a salutary lesson. There are no confidences where the press are concerned. You open your mouth at your peril.

That wasn't the only thing that got twisted. Rose had a mounted photograph on his wall to which Cohen's eye was drawn, a Serb ambulance riddled with holes. The Serbs had presented it to him after the bombing of Gorazde in April as 'evidence' that the air strikes had targeted an ambulance. It was a fake. If you looked carefully at it the tyres were still inflated – they're the first to go when shrapnel's flying about – and a neat little ladder was propped up at the rear. In the foreground was a bomb crater. The vehicle had clearly been driven up to the crater after the event and the whole thing posed. The caption underneath read 'NICE ONE NATO!' Rose had actually sent the 5 ATAF commander a copy as a joke, and that's how it had been received. But to Roger Cohen it was firm 'evidence' of Rose's disaffection with NATO and that's how he reported it. We were naïve and unused to the machinations of the media. To us the dinner resulted in nothing more than headaches the next day. The real repercussions were only felt later.

I smouldered the whole weekend over what L-P had told me about mutterings at court. Inevitably, this erupted into a full-blown fire. The storm came on the Sunday night in the most unexpected of places. It was Martin's last night. Effectively he'd finished his hand-over to L-P and was off the next day. The three of us decided to go out for a drink. When I'd worked for UNHCR in 1993 we'd had a driver called Rajko, whose brother owned a café-bar called *Piramida* (Pyramids), a short drive away and concealed at the bottom of a steep, tight and battle-scarred *mahala*, or alley. The atmosphere inside was definitely wartime-Sarajevo; thick with smoke, laughter and guitar music and packed out with stunning girls. It was underground Paris or Berlin of the early 1940s.

So, we're in this place at the bar. You've got to picture the scene. Air thick with smoke. In one corner a young Sarajevan girl strumming and singing, surrounded by friends who are clapping and drinking. In another corner two BiH soldiers drinking beer. They're still in uniform! are unshaven and ingrained with dirt. They've got these haunted, thousand-yard stares. They look as though they've just come down from the front line after weeks in combat. And then there's the three of us at the bar. The wailing and strumming is loud and the atmosphere alone is enough to alter your mood. It's frenzied. We're drinking and chatting. Suddenly we're arguing.

L-P's said something, a comment has ignited me. I flash up instantly and we both take a step back. 'Who the fuck do you think you are coming here armed with a week's experience telling me about my own fucking people!' L-P's gone white. His pale blue eyes are pinpoints of fire. 'What do you mean?' he snaps back. 'You're Irish aren't you? What makes you so grand that you can come here and fucking well tell me all about these people and how to solve their problems when you can't even sort your own fucking country out!' He doesn't even bother to reply. We've squared off and I'm fucked if I'm going to let him throw the first punch. The music has stopped. The two soldiers are staring at us, as is everyone else. *Fuck it! I'm going to let him have it first!* But before I can get my first blow in the barman's intervened. His hands are stretched out over the bar with two cans of beer. 'Please! We don't want any trouble here!' The blows are never delivered. We accept the beers, though we're still glowering at each other. Eventually the music starts again, the soldiers go back to staring and drinking and L-P and I are left sipping furiously and hurling daggers at each other. I tell you Ian, his diary entry is fascinating: *'Mike and I got into a furious argument about something or other, which almost came to blows. We were screaming at each other so loud that the banshees in the corner almost lost their thread. It obviously impressed everyone as highly Balkanite; the barman even brought us a free round of drinks. The Serbo-Irish mix of Mike and I is explosive, particularly when shaken and stirred by alcohol. I like him more and more.'*

It makes me laugh. In a way it sums up that place in a nutshell. That bar was a microcosm of the war. Here we were, two members of the UN, who'd come to these people's 'rescue' and we were about to punch each other's lights out so much so that one of the locals had to intervene and stop it.

That night I could barely sleep. I mulled everything over, examined each angle and the pros and cons of staying on. In the early morning I reached my decision: I was going to seek an interview with the General and tell him that, in view of the rising suspicion and the unpleasant atmosphere in the Outer Office, I wished to return to the UK and leave his service. You don't do something like that lightly. Asking to be removed from an operational theatre, particularly when you're working for a three-star, is the kiss of death career-wise. But I didn't care. I wasn't prepared to suffer that type of suspicion and racial stereotyping any longer.

In many ways that morning was a watershed. Before going to see the General I sought out L-P's opinion. Had I got it right? Was I acting in a fit of pique? When I finished explaining to him there was a long silence. He spoke deliberately, earnestly: 'No. Don't do that. He needs you.'

We spent hours discussing how best to proceed and how we could mutually support each other. It was patently obvious that, if I was to continue providing Rose with a window on the Serbs' mentality, if I was to continue burrowing deeper into their confidences (which I could only do by compromising myself further and deploying a range of unorthodox tactics, which would leave me even more vulnerable to suspicion), then I'd need a backstop. What I needed was top cover, people who would vouch for me when the going got particularly tough and unpleasant 'at court' and who, God forbid, would support me if the thing ever got out of hand. It has got tough, and it is out of control, and those boys are still there right behind me. I haven't got many supporters now. Most have scuttled off now that it's blown up in their faces, but I don't care because those boys, my top cover or insurance policy, are still there. They're the only ones who really know what went on out there.

Inevitably, there was a quid pro quo in all this that I was more than happy to go along with. The truth is that Rose had all but decided to sack the JCO organisation. L-P had been summoned to save it and he had an uphill struggle ahead of him. I promised him that I'd exert as much influence on the Serbs as I could, introduce him and his Ops Officer, Geordie, to the likes of Indjic with the aim of expanding the JCO role and of getting JCO patrols working on the Serb side. After they'd been identified by Mladic as being the unit in Gorazde which had called in the air strikes in April, their status with him had been not much better than NATO's – 'criminal'. Turning that around was going to require some delicate handling. I warned L-P of the dangers of dealing with Indjic, of his ability to drive a wedge between us if he could identify even the tiniest flaw. We agreed that any dealings we had with him had to be carefully considered and coordinated, to prevent us being manipulated by him. After much discussion we agreed on how to proceed. I felt at last that I had allies 'at court' as well as enemies.

There was something else about L-P. He gave me a new lease of life, a new sense of purpose. I'd become stale and over-tired and was lacking any real direction. Much of my access to Pale was accidental. It was also having unforeseen consequences. Unwittingly I'd moved a step or two closer to opening the window on the Pale mentality. The man with whom I had the most frequent contact up there was Jovan Zametica, their press spokesman. He appeared to have Karadzic's ear, but even his access was limited. The bottom line is that they didn't trust him much either. When he'd arrived in late 1993 Karadzic's daughter, Sonja, who ran the Bosnian Serb press disaster, had denounced him as an MI6 agent and suspicion had been heaped on him too. He was clearly useful to them as their window on the West's mentality, but they kept him at arm's length. He was marooned in a room in the Hotel Bistrica right on top of Mount Jahorina and depended on them for a driver and a car to pick him up each day for the hop down the mountain to work. After a year of being kept at arm's length the rift between him and Sonja healed a little, though not completely. I also discovered that the army – Mladic down to Indjic – loathed Zametica and still believed he was an MI6 spy. It became blatantly obvious to me that Mladic and the army viewed Karadzic and his politicians with great suspicion. Both were on different agendas; any belief that they were working hand in glove towards some common purpose was nonsense. They weren't clever or co-ordinated enough for that and the army loathed Karadzic's secret policemen.

So things weren't as simple as folk down in BHC assumed. In public, i.e. during meetings with UNPROFOR, they put on a united front. Behind the scenes, though, chaotic mistrust and mutual suspicion ruled. By peeking behind the curtains I was getting my first sight of all this. It was no longer a case of straightforward dealing with the Serbs. Increasingly, I'd find myself having to consider whose button to push in order to get the best result: politicians or the military. If I dealt with Zametica, Indjic became suspicious; with Indjic and, occasionally, Mladic, the politicians became suspicious. I still needed Indjic in order to help the JCOs, but equally I found myself on errands where only Zametica's, and hence Karadzic's, ear would do. It was bloody difficult because I was bridging the chasm between the UN's and Western mentality and the Serbs' Machiavellian Balkan mentality, while at the same time walking a tightrope between the Serb politicians and Serb military.

It was all very strange. Any military manual will explain the duties of an

LO and the principles of liaising, but nowhere will it actually tell you what to do, how to speak, talk, whose button to push. That was all trial and error, but what is certain is that it's all about human relationships, how you interact with an individual. You'd say things one way to Indjic and a completely different way to Zametica. Sometimes you'd have to play off one against the other and hope neither would find out. What barriers do you throw up to protect yourself? How close do you get in order to achieve a task or end-state and what are the repercussions of doing so? What is the long-term damage? No one tells you about these things because no one knows. You're on your own and it's left to you to find out the hard way.

All this is relevant because I was starting to flounder and I was unsure how much further to go. L-P put me straight and breathed new vigour into my life. His sense of history and his knowledge of European history and Empire are amazing. He told me that I wasn't up against anything new, that it had, for example, been going on in the last century between Russia and Britain. The military tradition of Great Game-ism. He also made the parallel with the SOE agents of the Second World War, many of whom had an ethnic or linguistic background from the countries in which they operated. The problem was that these unorthodox methods of operating had been forgotten in the forty-five years of Cold War stagnation and military orthodoxy and the current generation of senior officers simply couldn't tolerate it or understand it.

Rose was one of those who did, but the rest became hugely suspicious and hostile. Envy and jealousy came into it, too. Rose gave me, a mere captain, a long leash and very broad directives and left me to get on with it. All he was interested in was results. That's what he got. But others didn't see it that way. If you consider that the military structure is necessarily defined by a hierarchical chain of command in which everyone by rank knows his place and reports upwards to his next superior, one can be said to be trapped somewhere in that food chain. In my case those norms had been obliterated by the way in which Rose chose to operate. Frequently I'd return from some foray onto the Dark Side and Rose would grab me, give me a whisky and sit me down in his office and say something like, 'It's war, isn't it?' and I'd sit there telling him what I'd got while the MA would trot in with his notebook. Imagine if you were a lieutenant colonel and some captain bypassed the normal chain and was briefing the General himself, how would you feel? Your nose would be put out of joint particularly because your perception of your control and influence had been weakened and usurped. I suspect that the MA resented my apparent freedom and my access to Rose. He'd have wanted things to go right up the chain, through him, but that's not the way it worked and that's not my fault. The MA and others had to tolerate it because that's the way Rose operated. It made me no friends 'at court', only enemies. Boils down to human relationships again. They might have convinced themselves that I was free, but I wasn't. I was trapped elsewhere in a cultural divide, in that weird zone between the West and the East.

LP and I embarked on a pact of mutual co-operation. It was defined in principle, though the details themselves would have to be worked out as and when we came to each hurdle. Largely because of him and Geordie I stayed.

An example of just how weird and beyond my pay grade the job had become: one day we received a call from Zametica asking me to go to Pale to pick up some information for the General which was too important to pass over the telephone. When I reached Pale I learnt that Karadzic had got wind of the fact that Rose was planning to replace the French battalion in Bihac with a Bangladeshi battalion. Karadzic felt that this was not on; the Bangladeshis were Muslims and would help Dudakovic's 5th Corps. Furthermore, Karadzic felt it would be better if Rose sent in the British Cavalry Battalion which was at Zepce. I knew that neither Rose nor John Major would wear that one and that Rose in particular was not going to be told by anyone what he should do with his units.

I told them straightaway that this wasn't going to happen, and reminded them that since they'd messed up our convoys to Gorazde no one in their right mind was going to willingly abandon yet another British unit in an enclave where it couldn't be supported. As messenger boy I should have taken the message to Rose and traipsed back up the hill to Pale with the response. But I knew what Rose's answer would be. I said 'no' and told Rose what I'd done. He didn't give it a moment's thought, but you could see what was going through the others' minds: 'Hurrumph, hurrumph, what's a lowly little captain doing making policy all on his own?'

Another example: two weeks after Soubirou's parting shot at Mladic the airport is still closed. No aid flights are getting in, so no food. The Serbs' checkpoints are still frozen over and we're only managing to get Rose through with some difficulty. In essence the UN is isolated in the city and in the eastern enclaves. There's been no contact whatsoever with Mladic who is still furious about the 'NATO criminals'. He's still not had the apology he's been demanding. The situation reaches crisis point. The fate of the airlift is discussed in various capitals and yet again we're approaching the eleventh hour and fifty-ninth minute. Again there's much talk of 'lift and strike', i.e. lift the arms embargo, pull out the UN and strike the Serbs. It's Wednesday 5 October. In a last-ditch attempt to talk some sense into the Serbs a large delegation including Sergio Vieira de Mello, the brilliant Brazilian head of Civil Affairs for the whole of FRY, and a number of Mr Akashi's UN staff come down from Zagreb. We all head off up to Pale for this big powwow with the Serbs. Their 1st XI is there including Generals Mladic and Tolimir and Dr Karadzic. The conference room in the annex is crammed to capacity. Rose and his team, de Mello and his have occupied every seat opposite the Serbs.

As usual during such 'events' I take up a seat directly behind Karadzic and Mladic. Since Darko's doing the interpreting I've resorted to my other function as 'snoop'. The advantage of positioning myself behind those two, however odd that may have appeared to the various hangers-on from Zagreb, was that Karadzic and Mladic would soon forget I was there and I'd be privy to their whisperings and could thus pass on information to Rose. The meeting grinds on for hours. The topic is, of course, the airport, but the Serbs manage to lead everyone up various blind alleys and confuse the issue by linking the re-opening of the airport to their own concerns, such as BiH infringements of the DMZ. We've been at it nearly ten hours and we're still getting nowhere.

Suddenly, Mladic turns round to me, digs me in the ribs and whispers, 'Boy. How much longer can we spin this one out for?' At first I think he's joking so I just look at my watch and say, 'Oh, about another half an hour and then you'll have to open the airport.' It was a throwaway remark. When he started whispering to Karadzic I realised that he'd canvassed my opinion in earnest. Somewhat alarmed, I scribbled a note to Rose to let him know what Mladic had said and how I'd replied. He scribbled one to de Mello and before we knew it de Mello and Karadzic had disappeared into the latter's office for a private chat. Twenty minutes later they emerged and announced that the airport would open the next day. That's how we did that. Pure bluff, a wing and a prayer. Nothing more. Nothing was ever achieved normally 'across' the table. All the real results happened 'under' it. That's the only way to do business out there.

The next day everything went to ape again. Surprise, surprise. At dawn a BiH fighting patrol transited the DMZ, penetrated Serb lines and attacked a hut that served as a rudimentary dressing station. They caught everyone napping, quite literally, and killed all twenty Serbs in their sleeping bags and then burnt down the shack. The casualties included four female nurses who had their throats cut. The French found charred bodies, and some of the victims had been killed with knives. Rose, Goose and the MA were en route to Kiseljak to catch a helicopter up to Tuzla. I'd stayed behind to act as Mr Akashi's interpreter at an airport meeting which never took place because rumours filtered down from Igman via the French net that a massacre had taken place. It was quickly elevated to a 'war crime' and, before anyone could say anything, Mr Akashi had marched off to confront President Izetbegovic, who probably didn't know anything about it anyway. I got on the radio and managed to get hold of Rose and his team just in time to bring them hurtling back into Sarajevo.

All this was is in response to a rumour and everyone had got themselves into a mindset where they believed in this 'war crime'. But no one had received a proper sitrep. Indjic, of course, was livid and invited us over to view the victims in the mortuary at Lukavica. Mr Akashi jumped the gun and went public with the press outside the Bosnian Presidency and uttered the word 'mutilations', which of course did for him. Rose dispatched a joint UK-French JCO team up to Igman, commanded by L-P, to find out what had gone on and to select targets, BiH, for likely strikes. The balanced report L-P sent back painted a very different picture. It hadn't been a 'war crime', but it had been a good commando-style hit. However distasteful the sight of dead women with their throats cut, they were still dead military women. The real issue here was not the result of that action but more that a BiH fighting patrol had crossed the DMZ in violation of the agreement. The tasking was changed to one of dominating the ground as opposed to selecting BiH targets.

That report was in fact the first real information anyone received in the city, Rose included, and it came well over twelve hours after the event and the first rumours. Of course, none of that placated the Serbs: they were still furious that the UN had 'allowed' this to happen and, worse still, had down-graded the 'war crime' category and not struck back at the BiH. So, if anything my job was going to be even harder, though the affair proved the utility of the JCOs and their ability not only to co-operate with the French but also to paint a true picture of what was going on for the General. On this occasion it worked for the BiH and against the Serbs.

If that wasn't bad enough it seemed that one event was followed by yet another disaster. The next day we went to see General Rasim Delic the BiH supremo at his HQ downtown. He wasn't there but General 'Taljan' Hajrula-hovic, head of BiH intelligence, was. The issue was not the raid, rather the infringement of the DMZ. He made some caustic remark about Rose, which Darko caught: '*Ovde Cetnik delux pun suplje price* – Here's a delux Chetnik full of empty words.' Rose was amused when we told him about it afterwards and made me repeat it until he'd got it off pat for the next meeting which was scheduled with Delic himself the next day, Saturday.

'Well, here I am Chetnik delux full of empty words,' Rose roared, laughing, at the meeting. Delic looked bemused and 'Taljan' mortified. He started blathering something about having been misheard and things being lost in translation and threw me a dark look. '*Wasn't me it was fucking Darko. Cut his throat!*' I felt like saying in my cowardly way but didn't. Rasim Delic said he'd look into the DMZ infringement and try to keep his overzealous troops at bay. We left the meeting slightly early. As we were piling into the vehicles in the courtyard below, Delic leant out of his window and started screaming something about a massacre and a tram. We raced upstairs to learn that a tram had just been shot up on Sniper's Alley and lots of people killed.

We roared straight off to the site, only to be ambushed by the press as we arrived. Rose looked grim as he surveyed the tram which was full of bullet holes, broken glass, and was dripping with blood. The burst of fire had clearly come from the notorious gap between two buildings and from over the river

Miljacka, which meant Serbs. To make matters worse, Rose banged on the French APC which was supposed to house an anti-sniping team. They were virtually asleep and hadn't seen where the bursts had come from. This was by far the most serious incident yet, but it was one which was to have unforeseen consequences.

Back at the Outer Office the phone was red hot – it was Major Indjic in Lukavica barracks furiously denying that the Serbs were responsible and pleading for us to conduct a thorough investigation of all possible firing points on the Serb side. The speed of denial was unusual. Normally it was left to us to make the accusation before any denial was proffered. The open invitation to examine a part of their front line to which the UN had always been denied access was unprecedented. Rose dispatched L-P and me immediately.

Indjic wasted no time whatsoever in taking us down into Grbavica. The part of the front line in question was a long, six-storey, red-painted block of flats. Further resemblance to domestic accommodation ended there. Some of the upper floors had been sealed off and mined to prevent the enemy from outflanking the defenders from above in the event of the building being penetrated. The floors that were occupied had ceased to resemble the original architect's plans. Corridors were mined and filled with barbed wire while access through the building involved scrambling through 'mouse holes' knocked through from one room to the other. For the most part we stumbled over rubble, empty ammunition boxes and rubbish in darkened rooms. Here and there a naked yellow bulb cast a dull glow over a sleeping soldier. The occupants were a mixed bag. They lived in squalor and looked filthy. In one room we came across an old man in his seventies. Craggy-faced and dressed from head to toe in Partisan gear from the last war he sprang to attention as we entered and spying L-P's rank gave him a quivering salute. I nearly fell over. The last British major this bloke had probably seen had been fifty years earlier, no doubt one of the British Military Liaison Officers with the Partisans.

After crawling through more holes and keeping our heads down for fear of snipers, we made it to the eastern end of the building. The rooms facing the Miljacka and the Holiday Inn beyond Sniper's Alley were gutted and unoccupied, the windows blown out. The second set of rooms back was where business was done. Observation and firing took place through tiny holes knocked in the walls. Here only whispering was permitted. There was no doubt about it. The gunfire could easily have come from the end rooms which had a good angle through the buildings to the left and right. Beyond them, in a narrow gap, could be seen the tram and the French anti-sniper APC. L-P set about measuring angles and trying to sniff out evidence of recent firing. In all of this the Serbs were totally cooperative.

Eventually, we ran out of time. By the time we got back to Lukavica Indjic was virtually in a state of nervous exhaustion. I think it had been his first foray to the 'front' for several years. It didn't end there. There was more sniffing around to be done both in the building and elsewhere, one problem being that there was also a slight line through the gap from a part of the Jewish Cemetery occupied by the BiH. The next day L-P and Geordie carried on the investigation and ran into trouble from the French whose noses had been put out of joint by Rose tasking his own people instead of Sector Sarajevo. Fortunately I wasn't around for that as Rose had whisked us off to Vares for the day to visit the Pakistani battalion . . . and to have a good curry. L-P and Geordie got on with it: by the end of the day they'd scoured the building and other likely firing points, examined the angle of the bullet holes in the tram and the strike marks on the tarmac. L-P produced a map with angles of view and fire and so on. The conclusion? Either side could have done it.

That's the bottom line. But then you've got the politics of the whole thing. The likeliest explanation is that the Serbs did it in revenge for the commando raid on the dressing station. That fits with the mood of the moment. Their eagerness to show us around the building might have been a ruse to make us think that they were blameless. The BiH may have done it knowing that, in the mood of the moment, the Serbs would automatically get the blame. As with the aircraft, there was a lot of double and treble thinking; you could have tied yourself up in knots with one theory or another. All L-P could do was submit a report stating quite correctly that the burst of fire could have come from any number of firing points, Serb or BiH. That's what he told Rose and Indjic, which satisfied the latter. The following day Tim Spicer informed the press of Rose's conclusion. The Serbs had done it. End of story.

The politics and mood of the moment, particularly with the way the press were banking up against Rose, meant suggesting that either side might have been responsible was as good as blaming the Muslims. Rose might well have been privy to other information which we didn't know about. Maybe he knew all along and all that scrambling about the building was doing nothing more than tying up loose ends. That's what he told the press and later that day he also told General Mladic. We went up to Jahorina for a meeting. I can't remember much of what was said because Darko and I shared the interpreting. He sat next to Rose and translated English to Serbo-Croat and I sat next to Mladic doing it in reverse, a good scheme which halved the workload. Indjic was on my right. He point-blank refused to help in the interpreting, scowled at me and glared in Balkan style at L-P. At the end of the meeting he refused to shake L-P's hand and flounced off in a huff. I grabbed Indjic a few minutes later and asked for an explanation. He was seething. It transpired that he'd told Mladic that Rose was going to tell the press that blame for the tram shooting couldn't be attributed with any accuracy. In fact Rose did the opposite and laid the blame on the Serbs. Indjic, of course, thought he'd got the whole thing taped up and jumped the gun. He'd been caught out and was now blaming L-P for deceiving him.

L-P was mortified. Indjic held the key to the checkpoints and without his cooperation the JCOs wouldn't be going anywhere meaningful. A vital task was on: Rose had ordered that the Sarajevo front lines be mapped. It was a classic JCO task and one which required access and unrestricted freedom of movement on both sides of the front line. With Indjic's feathers ruffled by the tram incident we weren't going to get anywhere. It was time for a bit of damage limitation.

That evening L-P, Geordie and I drove over to Lukavica to try and calm Indjic. He was still angry, would barely speak to L-P, and ranted about the risk he had taken in that building and how he'd nearly given himself a heart attack in the process. L-P produced his report and made Indjic read it. As if by magic the man was calmed. He broke into a huge, toothy smile and produced a bottle of Slivovica. The tram incident was forgotten; there was more intrigue to be getting on with as far as Indjic was concerned. The speed with which his 'injured pride' was restored really made me suspicious that perhaps the Serbs had done it all along and had tried to dupe us with their over-zealous cooperation.

I got into an argument with Indjic. He tackled me in Serbo-Croat over an issue he wanted to keep from L-P and the others. He'd been hounding me for several months to get a man out of Sarajevo. The man's wife had fled at the start of the war and hadn't seen her husband, who was stuck in the city. No one knew if he was still alive. Indjic had promised the woman he'd do something. The more he hounded me the more suspicious I became. The beneficiaries of Schindler's List were all carefully screened: names popped up from all over the place; in letters from abroad, from folk in the city and from separated parties on the Serb side. All of them had to be verified and checked out as to whether they fell into the 'endangered to no-hoper' category. We couldn't allow someone like Indjic to hijack the operation for his own purposes and the more he pestered me the more I'd convinced myself that he was trying to get one of his 'agents' out. When I refused to help, Indjic flashed up in an instant. I hadn't told Geordie or L-P about this, which was my mistake.

As we rose to leave I leapt off down the corridor to the lavatory. Glancing back down the corridor I saw Indjic deep in conversation with L-P and Geordie who were nodding their heads while the canny Serb shot furtive glances down the corridor towards me. I caught this in a split second before entering the loo. As I stood there holding my breath (the place stank) I thought, *I know exactly what you're up to you little shit.*

We were about fifty metres down the hill from Lukavica before I exploded. 'So, what was Indjic telling you as I was having a pee?' L-P and Geordie didn't have a clue where this was leading: 'Oh, he was asking us to get someone out . . .' I didn't let him finish. 'Yeah, and I'll bet it was so-and-so, wasn't it?' L-P gave me one of those looks, which did for me. 'Stop the fucking vehicle this instant! Stop this instant!'

The wheels had barely stopped turning before I was out and storming back up the hill in the dark, leaving an astonished L-P and Geordie gaping in horror and reversing the vehicle level with me. 'Mike! For fuck's sake, get back in the vehicle. Where are you going? Get back in!' I was beside myself with fury that Indjic had already tried to drive a wedge between us in such a blatant way. I was puffing furiously. The Land Rover was still reversing, weaving in the darkness. 'Mike. What are you doing?' *Stupid question. Perfectly bloody obvious what I'm doing.* The night air was split. 'I'M GONNA KILL THAT STUPID BASTARD.'

TWENTY-ONE

Operation Bretton

December 1997 – Ian, UK

'Do you remember your childhood, Ian? Do you remember what it was like when you were supposed to be in bed while your parents entertained guests for dinner? That feeling of curiosity, wondering what the grown-ups were saying, what was happening in that downstairs world of clinking cutlery and glasses and laughter from which you'd been unfairly excluded? Perhaps you sat on the landing listening or, a little bolder, you crept downstairs and peeped through the keyhole. And, can you remember what you saw or heard? Not much really. Someone's elbow, perhaps, or indistinct shadows and muffled conversation, none of which was discernible as a whole. But, God, wasn't it intriguing and fascinating particularly with the ever-present fear of the door being flung open and inevitable capture and retribution!'

'Where's this going, Milos?'

'Or perhaps you've been taken to some grand country house, an enormous one, because they all look enormous when you're that age. And you're off exploring. You open one door and you're in a room but it has a second door and very quickly you forget the room you're in and all that matters is seeing what's beyond the next door. And on it goes, the Game.'

'I'm not sure I follow you.' Ian's amused but a bit hesitant.

That's what it was like out there. It became a game. What lay beyond the next door? You've peeped into this secret little world of chaos and paranoia and it's not enough to leave it there. Curiosity drives you to open the next door. Once you have access you want more, just to see how far you can go. Just how far could you go before all the doors shut in your face? It was compulsive and dangerous. But that was the charm and grip of the Game.

Not for the first time I can see he still hasn't got it. One morning in October I was rung up by Zametica. He insisted that I come up to Pale as they had something vital to say . . . again. He sounded more earnest than usual so up I went, straight into Karadzic's office. It was the first time I'd been allowed in there, which gave me more than an inkling that something was up. Jovan was not his usual self. He was serious, business-like, and ordered me to get my notebook out and to listen carefully. We sat at a big oak table on which lay a shaded map of all of Yugoslavia showing the front lines in Bosnia and Croatia. Karadzic was absent, so it was just the two of us.

'I have been authorised by the President to pass on to you a proposal for ending the war quickly. You are to pin your ears back, take notes, pass this information to Rose and urge him to pass it on to the Contact Group.' He rattled off a scarcely believable proposal while I scribbled away furiously. In essence, it was a global solution which involved massive land-swapping. In exchange for the Croats giving up the last twenty kilometres of the Croatian coast from Cavtat south of Dubrovnik to the Montenegrin border the Serbs would cede to Croatia virtually all of Sector West, Sector North and most of Sector South in the Croatian Krajinas, which was almost all of the self-styled Republika Srpska Krajina. That was the Serb-Croat bit.

Next, the Muslims would give up Srebrenica, Zepa and Gorazde in the east in exchange for a large, wide corridor linking Sarajevo to central Bosnia. Bihac would be ceded back to the Serbs. All of this seemed to favour the Serbs and the Croats but left nothing for the Muslims. 'So, what do they get, Jovan? How're you going to convince them that there's anything in this for them? All you've given them is a corridor and not much else.' You didn't need to be a rocket scientist to work that one out. He just looked at me and said, 'We're prepared to go down to 31 per cent in Bosnia. I repeat, 31 per cent but it has to be the right 31 per cent. We're prepared to be very generous in Bosnia.'

There was a bit more to it than that, but, in essence, it appeared that they were prepared to give up over half of what they'd captured in order to settle this globally. Remember, Dayton gave them 49 per cent and we're talking here of 31 per cent in October 1994.

Whether or not I believed him was beside the point. On this occasion I really was just a messenger boy and took notes. But you don't drag someone up to Pale and put them through that for no reason. I knew Jovan quite well by this stage and I'd never seen him so serious. It all made sense, depending on the 31 per cent concession. I took it all back down the hill and typed it up in one of those reports for the General and threw in a 'global' map for clarification. If nothing else, it was a basis for further negotiation. I was itching to get it in front of Rose but for some reason the MA kept it sitting in his in tray. Eventually Rose got sight of it and immediately saw its significance. He asked me to reword the part of the report describing how we'd come by this proposal: once that was done it was fired off as quickly as possible to the FCO with instructions that it be forwarded to Pauline Neville-Jones, the UK's rep on the Contact Group. In doing this we missed our best opportunity for resolving that conflict fifteen months earlier than it eventually ended. The Contact Group weren't interested and nothing came of it.

I didn't understand at the time, but it became clearer as one analysed it. The CG put forward a plan and told the Serbs this was their last chance. A line in the sand has been drawn rather publicly. Rather stupidly Dr Karadzic cooks up a referendum in which the Serbs all say 'no' to the CG plan: this they do, calling the CG's bluff. And therein lies the problem. The CG can't move because they've told the world that's their final offer. Karadzic is trapped by the result of his referendum. Referendums are extremely dangerous in democracies or quasi-democracies in that the people are given the executive power. Once the people decide one way or another their 'elected' leaders can't revoke the result of a referendum without exploding the illusion of 'democracy'. Had Dr Karadzic not gone to the people for a decision but had said 'no' on his own, he might easily have been able to reverse that 'no'. But since the people had said 'no' he couldn't overrule that decision. Hence, he's trapped by the result of the referendum just as surely as the CG's trapped by its own rhetoric. Therefore, no ability to move on either side, no options are left open and no scope for compromise. Pride seems to have been a bigger driver here than anything else. Not exactly diplomacy.

The next thing that comes into the equation is Karadzic's realisation that they've made a bad mistake in not heeding Douglas Hurd's 'say *yes and* and not *no but*' advice on 13 July. Moreover, the war is unwinnable in the sense that the BSA is overstretched, manning a ridiculously long front line. Manpower is a scarce resource. Sanctions imposed by Milosevic in Belgrade in August, in response to Bosnian Serbs saying 'no' to the CG Plan, are biting and Mladic can't pay his soldiers. Desertion is increasing. Biljana Plavsic calls for summary execution of deserters, which Karadzic rejects. Meanwhile, the Federation brokered by Washington is getting stronger by the day. In summary, the Serbs reached their 'culminating point' in August 1993 and thereafter they've stagnated and gradually weakened as the Federation has strengthened. The eventual outcome is obvious – defeat. Hence the under-the-counter global land-swap plan suggested to me by Zametica. What I didn't know at the time is that all this had been cooked up by Karadzic and others without telling Mladic.

Although the proposal came to nothing there is one other thing that is vital to note here. If you look at the timing of the proposal, Karadzic and gang had already got themselves into a mindset as early as October 1994 that the Serb-held Krajinas were expendable and could be bargained away. I'm sure they didn't tell them that, but in reality the Krajinas were untenable without Republika Srpska. As early as October 1994 they were quite prepared to shaft their own people in Krajina and when the Croats finally attacked on 4 August 1995 the region crumbled within twenty-four hours – no resistance, nothing except headlong flight. They'd been sold out almost a year earlier, mentally at least. It's only my opinion, I'm sure academics and other Balkan gurus the world over will disagree, but from my perspective and experience on the ground we missed an opportunity to find a solution to the war before the winter of 1994. That's what I discovered in one of the rooms.

Just before Rose left in January 1995, he was visited by Richard Holbrooke and his team of US negotiators, including David Frasure, who was killed later that year. They were in the General's office. Suddenly, the door was flung open and Rose ordered me, without warning, to come in and brief Holbrooke on what Karadzic had told me. Talk about a cold start! I went through the land-swap deal on the map. Inevitably, he asked what concessions were to be made to the Muslims. When I told him that the Serbs had been prepared to go down to 31 per cent, Holbrooke just looked at me as though I was crazy and said, 'I don't believe it.' Didn't want to believe it more like. The Serbs have now got 49 per cent of Bosnia.

After that, the contents of that room were left behind as the whole region fell back to a state of war and of broken cease-fire agreements. After the tram-shooting incident things just seemed to get worse in an exponential way. There didn't seem to be any part of Bosnia which wasn't prone to some form of cease-fire violation. We're in mid October 1994 now, about the 15th. The BSA and BiH are at it hammer and tongs, fighting over high ground just north of Sarajevo called Cemerska Planina. Three days later the Serbs hijack medical aid trucks on their way to Gorazde and seize three Muslim doctors whom they imprison in Kula near Lukavica barracks. On 18 October the Bangladeshi battalion enters Bihac to replace the French. Mysteriously, they deploy with no personal weapons whatsoever, which is about as much good as tits on a bull.

That was a busy day. At the same time fifteen US military advisers arrive in Sarajevo to begin the process of welding the Federation forces together into some sort of coherent fighting force. Elsewhere, in Gorazde, the Serbs fire on a local aid convoy killing the driver of a truck and wounding one other. We were in the office at the time and when this was reported Rose went mad and ordered me to ring the Serbs and tell them we were going to hit them.

You've got to understand, what the pressure was like. He came running out of his office and barked, 'Mike! Ring 'em up and tell them we're going to hit them!' He hung on my shoulder like a monkey while I rang Pale. Dr Karadzic wasn't available but Professor Koljevic was. I didn't really stop to think what I was saying, and in any case 'we're going to hit 'em' is pretty loose. But, there's a massive difference between Close Air Support/BLUE SWORD and Air Strike. The problem is that in translation the former is 'bliska vazdusna podrska', a hideous tongue-twister if ever there was one, while the latter is a much more manageable 'vazdusni udar'. So, under pressure, that's what I used.

Koljevic went completely insane. I could picture his reaction. At my end the earpiece started to melt against my ear as he threatened to burn Sarajevo's Bascarsija to the ground. I was quietly appalled to say the least and quickly put the phone down. I had a sneaking suspicion that I'd got it wrong but didn't tell Rose. In fact I was still so worried that I rang Koljevic again a few minutes later. He was still spitting, saying that Republika Srpska had been put on Red Alert, that they were expecting NATO air strikes and that it was now war with the UN. My guts nearly hit the floor. It took me a while to calm Koljevic and assure him that we hadn't meant widespread air strikes, merely a retaliatory swipe at those who had attacked the convoy. Eventually, he was mollified and RS came off Red Alert.

Can you believe how a mis-translation and slight change of meaning could so dramatically alter events out there? It was a sobering lesson in the need for accuracy. A couple of days later we were on our way to Gorazde or somewhere and popped in to see Koljevic. He raised the subject and I started sweating like mad as I knew it had been my fault. But then he said something like, 'Thank God there are reasonable people like young Mike Stanley here who are able to keep their cool.' I almost choked when he said that and cast a sly look at Rose who seemed to agree. I'd survived to bluff another day.

If it wasn't that, then mice and Marmite were guaranteed to spoil your day . . .

I can't remember exactly why but one day Clive Davies, Goose's number two, and I were driving through the Sierras to pick up Rose and Goose from Kiseljak. We were in the General's Range Rover about a mile short of Sierra 1, nice hot day, driving along without a care in the world. There's an irritating squeaking coming from somewhere behind the dashboard; it's been there for ages and is a real pain. Clive starts thumping the dash and before we know it this brown streak – a mouse – comes shooting out of the ventilator duct and scurries up his arm. The Range screeches to a halt and we leap out screaming like girls, running around the vehicle waving our arms in blind panic. All this capering about going on while Serbian soldiers ride past us on their bicycles giving us strange looks.

It took us ages to summon up the courage to get back in the Range. We still hadn't located the mouse and the squeaking was still there. 'Shall we tell the Boss there's a mouse living in his car?' Big decision. We decide to tell Goose and see what he reckons. Anyway, Goose tasks Clive with ethnically cleansing the rodent from the vehicle.

A few weeks later we're off up to Pale for yet another meeting. I'm in the snatch. Mick is driving and Clive's in the back. 'By the way, Clive, how've you got on with killing the mouse?' Mick just sniggers as Clive launches into this sorry sob story. 'Oh, Mike. It's a nightmare. I've tried everything. Set mouse traps all over the car each evening. Nothing seems to work.' Well it all sounds a bit strange to me, so we ask him what he's been using as bait.

'Oh, first of all I tried boiled sweets, but they didn't work . . .' Mick nearly drove us off the road, '. . . and then I've tried Mars Bars . . .' Now we really are in danger of crashing. Tears are streaming down Mick's face. 'For fuck's sake, Clive! When I grew up Mummy told me that mice like cheese. Tried that yet? I mean, I could be wrong, but cheese might just work.' And this was a sergeant in the Royal Military Police charged with protecting the General's life.

We never caught the mouse. It wasn't coming out of that vehicle for anything. That Range had been given to Peter Jones in the early days. It had been the British Ambassador's vehicle in Athens before being snaffled by Glynne Evans for duty in Sarajevo. I reckon that mouse had stowed away in Athens and when it had got to Sarajevo was so appalled at what was going on that it decided to stay in the vehicle. So, Rupert Smith not only inherited the poisoned chalice of UNPROFOR from Rose, he also got the mouse as well.

The Marmite story is a tale of international disinformation. The food at the Residency was pretty grotty and we always needed little extras that weren't on the menu. Most of us had our own secret hoard of goodies sent out from the UK and which we jealously guarded; they appeared at mealtimes but otherwise were kept under lock and key. Stuff like Coleman's English mustard, bottles of Tabasco sauce and jars of Marmite. We were forever getting newcomers in the HQ and one breakfast I'm sitting next to a Russian major called Volkov. He's just arrived and is quiet as a mouse. To break the ice, I ask him where he's from. 'Russia,' he replies cryptically. 'Oh yes, but where in Russia?' He gives me this very suspicious look and says with an enigmatic flash of a solid gold front tooth, 'Russia is a very big place.' Which is code for 'Fuck off. I'm not telling you.'

Sometime later I find myself sitting next to him again. I've got my pot of Marmite out and I'm eating a slice of bread, Marmite spread thinly of course. Volkov, who has relaxed a bit, is staring at the pot and the bread. He asks what's in the pot . . . 'It's Marmite. Want to try some?' His eyes light up. 'Just slap it on,' I say rather cruelly. He covers a piece of bread with a thick layer of Marmite. I'm watching this with anticipation. It's in his mouth for a nanosecond before he spits it out onto his side plate. His eyes are watering as he rubs his lips furiously with his napkin. 'Disgusting!!' he splutters.

I fall about laughing. 'You're not as tough as you thought, Major Volkov.' And then I give him a line about the virtues of Marmite. 'All British kids are raised on the stuff. Have been for centuries. It's part of our basic education. The Empire was built by men hardened on Marmite. It's incredibly useful stuff – you can grease the breach of an artillery gun with it, or lubricate tank tracks. You've got to understand, you lost the Cold War for lack of Marmite. That's why the Soviet Army never washed its boots in the Indian Ocean.' Imagine what went into his little intelligence report back to Moscow! Marmite

– British secret weapon. I wonder if that qualifies as a breach of the Official Secrets Act.

Meanwhile, back at the war Bosnians are refusing point-blank to move some 500 troops out of the Igman DMZ. Worse still they begin an offensive southwards with the aim of severing the BSA's supply route through Trnovo. Karadzic is told by the Contact Group 'no change to the map'. Haris Silajdzic is complaining that nearly 2,500 Russian troops have been fighting for the Serbs for the past two years. But then, on 22 October, they agree to troop withdrawals from Igman. The next day the UN accuses the Bosnian government of expanding its front lines in violation of the 8 June cease-fire agreement. All in all it's a mess.

More significantly, the Bangladeshi deployment is giving Rose food for thought. Not only have they deployed into the pocket with no weapons but, it would seem, no real communications either. The only contact with them is via an insecure VSAT telephone which the whole world can listen to. Fighting is on the up in the pocket and we're being starved of accurate information as to what's going on. Quite sensibly, the only option is to deploy a JCO patrol of four men into the pocket. L-P gets onto this immediately and a JCO officer and three others are diverted from central Bosnia up to Bihac taking with them a secure TACSAT radio. Just as well that happened otherwise we'd have been well and truly stuffed. A couple of days later Dudakovic's 5th Corps attacks south of the river Una and overruns a Serb barracks on the Grabez plateau. Thus began the battle of Bihac. At the time its 'global' significance was not apparent.

This somewhat passed us by; on the day before, the 24th, we were on the road again visiting the British Sector South-West HQ in Gornji Vakuf where we were due to spend the night. In the north you've got the BiH attacking out of Bihac. In the east they're attempting to take Trnovo and in central Bosnia they and the HVO are gearing up to attack and take Kupres. All in all the Serbs are on the back foot attempting to put out fires which are springing up all over the place. And we're in Gornji Vakuf visiting Brigadier Gordon, commander of UN Sector South-West, B-H.

It's about 10.30 p.m. on 24 October. We've had a guided tour of the destruction of GV and are sitting around Brigadier Gordon's table in the canteen having a late supper. Jamie Daniel is called away to the Ops Room as some drama has blown up. Our relationship had hit a new low that day. During the walk round GV he'd announced his intention of having me removed from theatre. This was to become a personal struggle of wills over the coming months. Needless to say I was smouldering inside again.

Suddenly, Jamie's back at the table tapping me on the shoulder. Uh oh, drama! He's pretty agitated, 'Mike. Ring up whoever you can in Pale and get the situation sorted out before it becomes a headache.' Apparently Brigadier

Gordon had issued some directive to his UKLOs stressing the need to create closer ties with the local Serb commanders on the other side of the line in his AOR. Nothing wrong with that since the intention is to defuse tensions. But, and this is a big 'but', earlier in the day an UKLO team in the local area had decided to interpret his directive in rather an unusual way. Three of them, the UKLO himself, a RAF flight lieutenant, his Royal Marines driver and their local female Muslim interpreter, had parked up their Land Rover on the Federation side of the line and had gone on foot, skirting around land mines on the road, onto the Serb side.

Unfortunately for them, and unbeknown to them, this well-intentioned act had coincided with a co-ordinated BiH-HVO attack elsewhere in the area undertaken with the aim of taking Kupres. The Serbs had found these three wandering about and had put two and two together and come up with seven – UN spies conducting a recce for the Muslim attack. They'd been grabbed and held in a barracks in Kupres. That was Jamie's message in the canteen.

I tried to ring Dr Karadzic's annex presidency at Pale on the INMARSAT but, predictably enough, no one was there. I then rang Jovan Zametica in his hotel on Mount Jahorina, explained the misunderstanding and asked if he could get hold of Karadzic and explain the circumstances before the situation got out of hand. His reply was curt: 'Don't be so stupid. It's eleven o'clock at night and it's impossible to get hold of anyone.' There was no point asking him to get hold of Mladic, first because there was no answer from the Han Pijesak switchboard, and secondly, because Mladic hated Zametica. I'd done my best that night but we'd got nowhere other than to register our concern and elicit a 'come up and see me' from Zametica. It didn't seem like a huge drama anyway.

The next day we were still on the road visiting a beleaguered British company in Bugojnjo. By the time we'd got back to Sarajevo it was too late to go all the way up to Pale so I popped across to Lukavica to see if I could get any sense from Indjic. Fat chance – 'They were caught spying for the Muslims. Mladic is holding them until a full investigation is carried out.' The Serb line was hardening on this one at a frightening rate and the alarm bells were beginning to ring. This was turning into something quite serious, particularly with the capture of the Serb barracks by Dudakovic's 5th Corps fighters. The Serbs weren't in any mood to negotiate with the UN. That same day all eight parties in the Bosnian government's parliament voted and demanded that General Rose be removed. All in all, a nice little screw-up and the chances of seeing our UKLOs soon were slipping away quickly.

The following day I went up to Jahorina for a long chat with Zametica in his hotel. It was pointless trying to deal with the Serb military. As far as they were concerned the UKLOs were spies. More than anything people were concerned for the fate of the female interpreter. Rumours abounded that even if the Brits were freed the Serbs would hang onto her. Jovan wasn't much use either. He'd spoken to Karadzic who was following Mladic's line: they were spies and a full investigation had to be conducted. Jovan could see that it was nothing but a misunderstanding but was completely unable to turn anyone around. So, I took back a zero result to Rose that day, too.

This went on for almost a week. In the UK the fate of the UKLOs had been elevated to high drama. The word 'hostages' was being bandied about more and more frequently and was occupying the attentions not only of the 'brass' but increasingly the press and ministers. HOSTAGES. You can just imagine the panic that was causing back home. I'd done my best, but all I'd hit was a brick wall.

One morning, while I was fiddling around on my laptop, Rose came rushing out of his office, as he was wont to do more and more during those days. I think the PM had just been pestering him on the phone about the hostages. 'Stanley! Get up to Pale now and get those hostages released!' with the unstated message 'And don't come back until you've done it' clear in his address. He looked sick to death of the saga; there was enough going on without having to be pestered by the PM about three UKLOs. His response was a typical one, and there was no point whatsoever trying to reason with him. As I drove up to Pale I wondered what on earth I was going to do.

Before I left I rang Jovan. We agreed to meet for lunch at the Hotel Panorama but when I told him what it was about he just laughed down the phone. 'You're wasting your time. But come up for lunch anyway.' So, up I went, not feeling terribly happy about any of it, but driven on by my fear of Rose and his dreadful look.

Jovan spent lunch smirking about the whole situation. He was delighted when I told him that John Major was getting so worked up about the whole episode, particularly as he knew that the drama was as much to do with Dr Karadzic's and General Mladic's paranoia as it was to do with three minions and their error in map reading. 'I know there's nothing in it. You know there's nothing in it. But you can't tell Karadzic or Mladic. They're convinced they're spies and are hanging onto them. They won't come to any harm, but there's nothing I can do about it,' he finished with relish.

There was nothing for it but to point out a few home truths and then lie through my teeth. 'Jovan, you've lived in the UK for eighteen years and you're well aware how panicky people become in the West about hostages. To you it might be nothing but to the likes of the PM and others it's a big deal. It's taken very seriously. I mean, the PM doesn't ring up Rose for no reason.' He was listening but still smirking. It was time for the big lie. 'You've got to understand, we know exactly where you're holding them . . . the exact building. Got satellites looking at it all the time. I've seen the pictures myself . . .' The truth is that I hadn't got a clue what the actual truth was, but Jovan wasn't to know that, '. . . and I'm telling you now, Jovan, hostage situations in the West resolve themselves in one of two ways. Negotiated settlement or . . . through the use of force!' I let that one hang in the air.

'Are you threatening us with an SAS raid?' Jovan spat back at me, eyes flashing behind his round glasses. 'No, Jovan, those are your words not mine . . .' and before he could say something smart in reply, '. . . but, hypothetically speaking, were that to be the case then all you lot would know about it would be waking up to a smoking barracks, lots of dead guards and no hostages . . .'

Zametica could barely control himself and snapped back, 'Oh yes. Indeed. But wouldn't it be enormously embarrassing to the British if such a raid were to fail. Very embarrassing.' He had a point, of course, so another lie was in order, 'You're right, Jovan. It would be embarrassing, but remember the Iranian Embassy in London. A much tougher nut than your poxy barracks . . . and besides, you're a historian, you tell me when an SAS raid has ever failed!' I just sat there fingers crossed praying he hadn't read *Bravo Two Zero*.

Clearly he hadn't. His jaw just dropped and he stared at me in silence, so I rammed it home trying to sound menacing, 'hypothetically speaking, of course, Jovan'. After a moment or two's silence, he wiped his mouth with his napkin, slung it down on his plate and announced in a very business-like and clipped tone, 'You wait here. I'm off to brief Karadzic!'

An hour later he was back looking very pleased with himself. 'Go and tell Rose to tell John Major to stop panicking. The hostages will be released tomorrow!' I couldn't believe it. All I'd done was bluff and lie. 'You sure, Jovan? I mean, I am going to tell Rose just that and he is going to tell the PM this evening. You absolutely sure we're on for tomorrow?' Jovan was adamant and then proceeded to tell me that there was a lot of face-saving to be done. 'You just get back down to Sarajevo and tell Rose. But, you've got to ring us up and request a meeting here tomorrow on something spurious like convoys to Gorazde. Make sure he raises the hostages as a side issue at the end of the meeting and all will be okay. Trust me.'

I wasn't too sure about all this but had no option. I was about to go down the hill and tell Rose something that could blow up in our faces and I only had Zametica's word to go on. But, that was the best deal we'd got so far. On the way down I popped into Lukavica to sniff around. Major Indjic pulled me to one side and said, 'I think your hostage problem will resolve itself very soon.' I was staggered that word had got round so quickly but returned to the Residency slightly more confident. Rose dragged me into his office and plied me with whisky. The MA trotted in to take notes. I didn't bother telling Rose the whole saga but assured him that if we went up the next day for a 'spurious' meeting and if he raised the issue in passing at the end then all would be fine.

It all went like clockwork. Up we went for this meeting with Karadzic and Mladic. It was the first time we'd seen Mladic for ages. While convoys or whatever were argued over, Zametica and I exchanged conspiratorial glances. When the meeting was over Rose stood up and as he was putting his pen away, said something like, 'Oh, yes, there is one other minor issue, a misunderstanding. Some of our people inadvertently crossed the front line . . .' Bloody good role-playing, good timing from the General, if you ask me. This allowed Mladic to bash the table and bellow about spies and Muslim attacks and UNPROFOR's disgraceful behaviour and the need for a full investigation. And then, suddenly, he broke out into a big grin and said, 'But, on this occasion, in the interests of fostering better relationships with UNPROFOR we'll forgo the investigation and release them.'

Things happened so fast after that you couldn't blink. A telephone call was made by Tolimir and Mladic announced that the hostages were being released *now*. That sent us into a panic because we had no troops on our side to nab our people as they re-crossed the line. A JCO patrol was tasked immediately to get down to the crossing point at a rapid rate of knots. They got there just in time to find the Croats waiting to grab our unfortunate UKLOs and conduct their own interrogation to find out what they'd seen in Kupres. That's how fast it all happened. We got the lot back including the Muslim interpreter who hadn't been molested. The two Brits were immediately flown out of theatre. A day or so later Kupres fell to the Federation and the Serbs lost the town. And that is how we did that – pure bluff, cuff and lies.

I'm amazed we got away with it at all considering what was going on at the time. Without Zametica's ability to get in and button-hole Dr Karadzic those hostages wouldn't have been released. If anything, their release is as much down to him as it was to me. We got on well. I found him a lot easier to deal with than the likes of Indjic. Having drifted around various academic institutions in the UK for eighteen years helped a lot; he understood our mentality. The job was all about human relationships and mine with Jovan was probably the most important.

In a way we were virtually mirror images of each other. He was born and raised in the Balkans but had lived in the UK and was almost completely Anglicised; he offered his masters a window on the Western mentality. I was born, raised and educated in the West but had an insight into Balkan mentality; I in turn offered our window on the Eastern mentality. Somewhere in the middle of this mess we both met. We had something else in common: both the sides we worked for distrusted us. In that sense we were alone and together.

Once you get under the skin of someone like Zametica you realise that all is not what it first seems. In the West he was seen as something of a Lord Haw Haw, whose high-pitched, Cambridge accent was frequently heard ranting on BBC Radio 4's *Today* programme. Any preconceptions derived from that or from brief meetings with the dapper and donnish Jermyn Street-shirt wearing Zametica are bound to be false. To me he was one of the most enigmatic characters of the whole war.

The real question is, whose man was Jovan Zametica? At face value he appeared to be Dr Karadzic's. Karadzic's lot thought he was an MI6 spy. Others thought he was Milosevic's mole in Pale. But no one lives in the UK, becomes part of the academic establishment for nearly twenty years and then just ups and changes his name, his religion, gives up paid, secure employment and throws his lot in with a gang of people who are proscribed across the globe and who are on a losing wicket – all this to be virtually unpaid, treated as a leper and marooned up on mount Jahorina. It doesn't fit any logical pattern.

There is no simple answer about Zametica. We had long conversations about the causes of the war and its direction. His perspective on the Pale mentality was fascinating. He was the closest to them by far and, because he could articulate himself intelligently, he offered a view through the impenetrable cloud of chaotic paranoia and suspicion. He was bright enough to realise that the Bosnian Serbs were going to lose the war. I pointed out that they'd lost it in 1992 by losing the propaganda war and shunning the international media. He agreed and entirely blamed Sonja Karadzic, who ran their pitiful media effort. On another occasion over lunch I pointed out that, despite the unbalanced view of the rights and wrongs of the war which was the vogue in the West, no one was ever going to forget or to forgive them for shelling a modern city and killing tens of thousands of innocent civilians. I challenged him to justify that, expecting a diatribe of denial and tit-for-tat excuses. Instead he just looked at me and said, 'You won't understand it. But it's passion. Passion drives men beyond reason. It's the passion.' An honest opinion, but not one that would stand up in any court.

In private he was quite happy to heap criticism on Karadzic and others. On one occasion I was standing outside the annex presidency. He was pestering Karadzic on my behalf over some errand for Rose. As I waited for him to emerge I noticed some quite peculiar behaviour going on amongst the staff. As I drove him home I couldn't contain myself any longer, 'You've got it all wrong, Jovan. I mean, just unbelievable. While you were in with Karadzic I watched your Chef de Cabinet passing several cartons of cigarettes out of the toilet window to a soldier. Down in Sarajevo when we go to visit President Izetbegovic we're met by a smart and well-dressed young man who smiles profusely and, regardless of what he personally thinks of us, he's faultlessly polite – please follow me, gentlemen. It's called protocol. But here, your Chef de Cabinet is a vulgar, fat, greasy ruffian who scowls at everyone as he scratches his belly. And I've just seen him passing cartons of cigarettes out of the toilet window. You'd never see that in Sarajevo!' Jovan was silent for a moment and then he just threw his head back and howled with laughter, tears streaming down his face as he thumped the dash. 'You're right. It's a fucking disaster!' he shrieked.

Forget all these fanciful theories about Zametica being an MI6 spy. The truth is much simpler. You have to understand human nature to get to the bottom of it. When I asked him why he was doing it, he told me direct. None of it surprised me in the least. First of all, like anyone who has broken the fetters of a humdrum life he was suddenly at the epicentre of world events. Rather like me. It's intoxicating. But, that goes for a lot of people if they're honest enough to admit it.

Look at what Zametica has been in his life. An academic, pure and simple. 'I get access to all Karadzic's secret papers, unparalleled access. One day I'm going to write the definitive book about the war.' That was it in a nutshell. He'd wormed his way in there to get access to their most secret thoughts and in a sense was driven by nothing more than academic fervour. When he told me that I was appalled. I knew that, if they ever found out, he ran the risk of getting his throat cut. He was playing an extraordinarily dangerous game to satisfy an insatiable academic appetite. He didn't really believe in their cause and his whole persona was a bluff. He was operating, for himself, on a much higher mental plane than the buffoons for whom he worked. It's strange what makes people tick, but there's no doubt that one day he'll write quite an explosive book about the whole thing.

The problem was that he took himself far too seriously. He believed the bluff. Quite often I'd take people up to his hotel room, those who wanted a break from the tedium of Sarajevo. Geordie usually accompanied me on these forays. Remember what Jovan looked like. He was dapper, almost always dressed in expensive suits which the Serbs found both effete and distasteful. To complete the 'cover', he'd frequently wear a long fawn 'flasher's' mackintosh and a brown trilby. Add a pair of gold-rimmed glasses and you could understand why Geordie instantly christened him Herr Flick, after that obnoxious Gestapo officer in 'Allo 'Allo! From then on it was, 'Let's get up the hill and see Herr Flick!' It was so much easier than Jovan Zametica. Stupidly, in a more relaxed moment, I once told Jovan about Herr Flick. He didn't get the joke at all: 'I don't think that's very funny at all. You will never refer to me as Herr Flick again!', which of course we ignored.

You had to find something to laugh about in all that mess, otherwise you'd go mad trying to figure out what was going on. In many respects the fate of the UKLOs in Kupres was very much a side issue, quite peripheral to Bosnia's alarming slide back into anarchy and war. The situation seemed to be deteriorating around us, encouraged not only by the exertions of the warring factions but also by significant shifts in policy by the warring international community. The stag fight between NATO and the UN continued, with NATO on top.

On 26 October NATO secured from the UN greater freedom in conducting air strikes. Henceforth NATO would be allowed to launch unannounced strikes, hitting from three to four Serb targets where no civilian collateral damage would be incurred and where it was appropriate and proportional to Serb provocation. All this is a fancy way of saying that control was slowly being wrested from Rose and the UN.

If that wasn't bad enough, the antics of the warring factions added colour to this chaotic picture. What began as a limited attack out of Bihac by the BiH 5th Corps, during which the Serb barracks on the Grabez plateau was seized, turned into a full-scale rout of the BSA 2nd Krajina Corps which fled in the face of determined pursuit and lost, in just over a week, some 200 square kilometres of territory south of Bihac and the River Una. In truth they'd been caught napping, having done little more during the war than shell Bihac. The Corps had become rusty, complacent and lacking in combat effectiveness. They fell back in tatters.

To the south of Sarajevo the BiH were making significant gains towards Trnovo. The BSA Sarajevo-Romanija Corps Commander, Dragomir Milosevic, threatened to renew attacks on Sarajevo, which caused the UN to threaten air strikes. The deteriorating situation caused Karadzic to call for a counter-offensive against Dudakovic's 5 Corps to recapture lost ground around Bihac and to retake Kupres. This coincided with the US asking the Security Council to lift the arms embargo (28 October), which the latter failed to do causing the US to withdraw unilaterally from the naval blockade of FRY and to sign a Memorandum of Understanding with Croatia for closer military co-operation (8 November).

In and amongst all this, any semblance that the peace of 8 June was anything more than words on a piece of paper, long since cast into the dustbin of history, was evidenced by nightly battles up and down the Sarajevo confrontation line. On 7 November alone 175 artillery rounds were exchanged by both sides in the city. The Boss was busy warning both sides to stop fighting, whilst NATO jets buzzed Sarajevo with greater frequency in the hope that this would intimidate the locals into good behaviour. Fat chance.

The following day, on 8 November, there were two nasty incidents in Sarajevo, in which indirect fire, rounds landing twice within fifteen minutes in the same spot, killed three little girls and wounded five others in a school playground. Investigations into the first hit determined that the round had been fired from the area of the confrontation line and was ascribed to the Serbs. The real drama came the next day when Lt Col. Jacques Lechevallier, the French Sector Sarajevo Operations Officer, presented to the press scientific ballistic evidence that the second round, which had killed the girls, could not have come from the Serbs.

The press refused to believe it and didn't bother to report it, and that

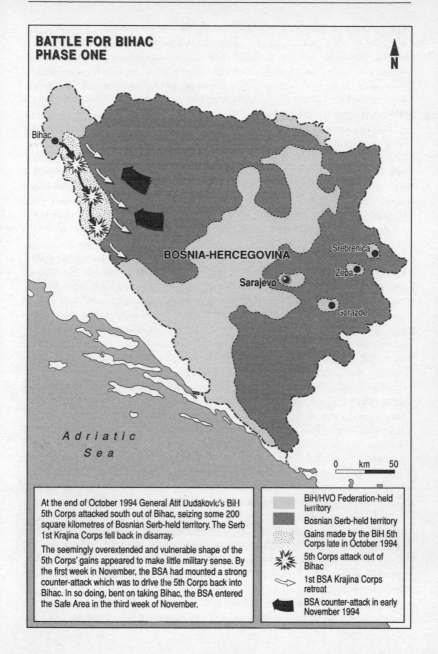

BATTLE FOR BIHAC PHASE ONE

N

Bihac

BOSNIA-HERCEGOVINA

Srebrenica

Zepa

Sarajevo

Gorazde

Adriatic Sea

0   km   50

At the end of October 1994 General Atif Dudakovic's BiH 5th Corps attacked south out of Bihac, seizing some 200 square kilometres of Bosnian Serb-held territory. The Serb 1st Krajina Corps fell back in disarray.

The seemingly overextended and vulnerable shape of the 5th Corps' gains appeared to make little military sense. By the first week in November, the BSA had mounted a strong counter-attack which was to drive the 5th Corps back into Bihac. In so doing, bent on taking Bihac, the BSA entered the Safe Area in the third week of November.

BiH/HVO Federation-held territory

Bosnian Serb-held territory

Gains made by the BiH 5th Corps late in October 1994

5th Corps attack out of Bihac

1st BSA Krajina Corps retreat

BSA counter-attack in early November 1994

caused more ill-feeling between the UN, the press and the Bosnian government. Up the hill other dramas were unfolding. Karadzic was persuading his parliament to impose martial law across Republika Srpska and to 'declare war' on Bosnian and Croatian forces . . . as if that wasn't the case already. Curiously, the Bosnian Serbs had, having grabbed seventy per cent of the land, consistently claimed that they were not at war but were, rather, 'defending their borders'. This was nothing more than technical wordsmithing.

The most curious result of all this hot air in the Bosnian Serb parliament was that martial law was imposed, which, ludicrously, propelled Karadzic into the field in full fighting gear, all seen on TV. Not to be outdone, the next thing we saw on Bosnian TV were pictures of President Izetbegovic also in uniform inspecting troops on Igman. Picture Karadzic bursting out of his flak jacket, hair all over the place; then imagine Izetbegovic in a huge trench coat and helicopter-landing-pad beret; and us in fits of laughter trying to work out who'd won this military fashion parade. Clearly, the situation had got way out of hand.

Mladic had disappeared off the face of the earth. He'd gone to ground as he always did during times of crisis and was apparently over in the Banja Luka area co-ordinating the counter-attack against 5 Corps. Rumours filtered back that he'd involved himself in the fighting around Bihac and had been wounded during the withdrawal. Sometime later I got confirmation from one of his bodyguards that he'd been hit in the neck whilst firing a heavy machine gun from a disabled tank. Whatever the case, the fact that he was up there was a clear indication of how seriously the Serbs viewed the situation. It also indicated that his counter-attack was inevitable.

Astonishingly, there was no Safe Area map for Bihac. There was nothing delineated on any map showing what actually constituted the Bihac Safe Area. One was produced, however, at BHC and I was dispatched up to Pale to pass it on to Karadzic via Zametica and to warn them not to enter the Safe Area. Zametica turned his nose up at it as did Dr Karadzic, claiming that it was 'unofficial'. I couldn't resist it and mentioned to Zametica that we'd seen Dr Karadzic on TV in his war gear. 'Very fetching, Jovan. Nice cut, but the flak jacket was a bit tight.' He didn't see the funny side of it and took my comments as gross irreverence. Jovan had a brand new American uniform hanging up behind his door, 'Watch it, Jovan. They'll have you wearing that before long!' He never tired of telling me that he held reserve officer rank and that he was quite prepared to fight. The thought of Zametica in US combat gear brandishing an AK and sallying forth, glasses glinting, amused me endlessly. He was quite defensive. 'I wore it once! On Igman, when I was doing some interpreting!'

At the same time that Karadzic was blathering about imposing martial law a Krajina Serb jet fired a missile into Bihac wounding ten civilians. NATO was unable to do anything about this as the rocket had been fired from outside Bosnian territory and technically the aircraft hadn't breached the DENY FIGHT rules.

Worse was to come on 11 November. The JCO patrol of four which Rose and L-P had sent up into Bihac started to produce the goods. The officer was a Life Guard called Charles who had what I always thought was a slightly deliberate and plummy voice. The radio in the JCO office crackled into life, most of it relaying the shrieking of shells. The patrol was south of Bangladeshi battalion OP 30 and was being engaged by a sustained artillery barrage fired by Krajina Serbs from over the border. They'd taken shelter in the crypt of a church but couldn't communicate from there so every so often Charles would poke his head up and give a live commentary in a completely calm voice, then seconds later, 'Oh, gosh, here come some more shells . . . back in a tick' voice. He'd disappear into the crypt '. . . that was a bit close . . .' A classic Englishman at war. In the Ops Room L-P was pulling his hair out telling Charles to keep his head down while a BLUE SWORD was being generated to hit the artillery. This caused much sucking of teeth from NATO who finally decided that it was too dangerous to come below 10,000 feet; the patrol was left unsupported and had to scurry to safety through gaps in the shelling. Good old NATO. The most important thing was that we were getting accurate information as to what was actually happening around Bihac.

That afternoon we all went up to Pale with Mr Yasushi Akashi and his staff. I suppose the meeting was about Bihac and the intention was to persuade Karadzic not to enter the Safe Area. I say 'suppose' because there were so many people in the meeting, most of them Akashi's staff on a foray down from Zagreb, that there was no room for minions like me. I sat out the meeting in Dr Karadzic's secretary's office chatting to a small, middle-aged, dark-haired woman wearing an outrageous pink suit. She spent hours telling me how she and her family had been ethnically cleansed out of their house in Sarajevo, how they'd lost their flat in Split etc. etc. At the end of the meeting I asked one of the bodyguards who the woman was. She turned out to be Karadzic's wife.

There was a huge meal after the meeting. I squeezed myself onto the table next to Izumi Nakamitzu, one of Akashi's staff, but couldn't eat. I had terrible flu and could scarcely speak. The meeting can't have gone well as conversation was stilted and awkward. Dr Karadzic told Akashi a joke while we listened without interest. Mr Akashi replied with one of his own, one so disgustingly explicit that it left us stunned. So, in and amongst dirty jokes, nothing much was achieved.

The fate of Bihac must have been uppermost in Rose's mind. When we returned to Sarajevo that evening he dispatched me over to Lukavica with L-P to give Major Indjic a copy of the Bihac Safe Area map with instructions to persuade the Serb military of the folly of entering the Bihac Safe Area. Indjic was equally sniffy about it though he took the map and said he'd pass it on to Mladic.

While all this was happening, my bags were packed. Rose was departing the next day for a week's break in the UK and I'd managed to worm my way onto the trip and had avoided being left behind 'just in case'. I was desperate for a break as I'd been at it for five months without a rest from the Balkans. I was exhausted and quite run down. The flu had got to me badly as had the endless wheeling and dealing with Zametica and others.

Despite the deteriorating security situation we'd managed to forge ahead with the Schindler's List operation. If anything, the situation gave it more impetus and urgency. Just about everybody got involved and the thing developed into a slick, well-practised event which minimised the risks to the beneficiaries; nothing like the cack-handed affair with Jasna Pandurevic.

I'd even managed to see Minka, Tomo, Vera and Nada regularly. They became a vital check in my life. It was all very well gallivanting about with the various officials this war had thrown up, but there was a danger of losing perspective on what we were really all about. In the evenings I'd sneak off and visit Tomo and Vera or Minka. Great levellers, they offered a constant reminder that the focus was the Little People. Tomo and Vera in particular worried me most. It was already bitterly cold. Their flat was unheated and, being in their eighties, I doubted they'd see another winter out. L-P's mother helped a lot by sending warm clothing and food out from Suffolk and it was largely because of that that they were still alive.

On Sunday 13 November we leapt into the vehicles and drove out of a Sarajevo echoing to gunfire and explosions. First stop was Gornji Vakuf where we attended a Remembrance Day service organised by the British. Then it was off to Split down Route Triangle and Circle. I hadn't been that way by road since 1993 and was amazed that the Royal Engineers had managed to widen the mountain route at Fort Redoubt into a highway. Towards dusk we approached the drop down from the Dinaric Alps to Split and the Adriatic. You could never escape the situation in Sarajevo, however. It followed you around like a bad smell.

On the radio in the backing vehicle I could hear excited babbling from Sarajevo. L-P's callsign came through; it sounded as though he, Tim Spicer and others were mounting up and charging off to the Holiday Inn where something had happened. I asked Mick to radio Goose and get him to switch on their radio and follow the commentary. None of this surprised me. As I said, Rose was jinxed. Bad juju. He'd barely turned his back on the city when another drama was unfolding.

In Split, Rose ordered me to get onto Mladic and find out what was going on. He couldn't be contacted so I spoke to Indjic and got his version. They were responding to provocation . . . of course! It transpired that the Serbs had rocketed the south side of the Holiday Inn from over the Miljacka. An enormous fire-fight had ensued and the press in the hotel were in a state of panic. L-P, Spicer and one or two others had deployed to see what could be done and had got themselves pinned down by fire in one of the gutted south-facing rooms. According to L-P the resolute and heroic press folk were capering about the hotel like headless chickens.

My heart sank at one stage when General Rose whacked me with a 'You'd better stay behind, just in case.' I couldn't believe it. So near yet so far. I was in danger of losing my first break in five months because the General wanted me to stay behind just in case he couldn't get back into Sarajevo. Fortunately, the situation seemed to die down as quickly as it had arisen and Rose relented. It left me wondering whether I'd ever escape the Balkans!

The following day one of those little RAF HS125s zipped into Split from RAF Northolt with Angela Rose on board. Goose, the General and I crammed ourselves in and within minutes we were airborne and heading to Rheindhalen in Germany where Rose was going to see the Commander of the Allied Rapid Reaction Corps. It was strange. High above Europe's cloud base the trials of Sarajevo washed off us as we were served tea from a silver service.

We overnighted in Germany and the next day landed at Boscombe Down. Staff cars from the pool at Wilton whisked us off to our various destinations and by midday I was in the Nelson Arms supping a pint of Guinness, wondering what was going on back in Sarajevo and totally oblivious to the usual crowd welded to the bar and still bitching about their MOTs, mortgages and who was doing what in the Premier League.

The shock wasn't as bad as the time Searby had given me six weeks off in 1993. I wasn't left wondering what to do as we were only in the UK for five days until the following Monday. I managed to extricate the bike from its hiding place in a mate's garden shed. It seemed to work and I was even spared the toil of having to bike down to Cornwall. My parents were coming up to see me on Friday and they'd be staying the weekend. The cause of all this was Slava.

Slava – Glory – is a big day in every Serb household, in a way bigger than Christmas. It goes back to pagan times when we all prayed to various gods. The South Slavs were a wild bunch from Russia and took some taming by the Church in Constantinople. Gradually they were converted to Christianity, an event usually marked by a saint's day, and each family celebrates each year on the day they were converted to Christianity. For us it's St Michael the Archangel, 21 November. You fast the day before and celebrate on the actual day. We're the only Slavs who do it. The Russians have nothing like it. The folks were coming up on Friday. Slava would be celebrated on Sunday 20th as I was due to leave on the Monday.

I was careful to avoid any mention of the Serbs' wrongdoing for fear of causing a drama with my father. We kept it all nice and cordial, anything to avoid fighting and bickering about Muslims and Serbs.

On Saturday night I left my parents at home, leapt onto the bike and shot off to London. One of the JCO officers, Jack, another Para, was also taking a break from Sarajevo and we'd agreed to meet in London on Saturday night for a drink. He had a house in Putney; it was convenient to park there and wander over to a bar in Fulham. I wasn't drinking because I'd promised my parents I'd be back late on Saturday evening or very early on Sunday morning, ready for Slava. Tempting though it was to drink and kip down at Jack's place, I resisted it and stuck to soft drinks and coffee. Something had been nagging me all evening, more than just the commitment to be home in a fit state to observe Slava. It is strange how the tentacles of that Bosnian war can stretch out and envelop you even in a bar in London.

I resisted the offer of a bed and finally left Jack's at two in the morning after umpteen cups of coffee. I arrived back at Farnham at three intending to steal in quietly but as I walked up the path the front door was flung open. My mother stood there looking quite wild and distraught. She had a blanket round her shoulders and was almost jumping up and down on the spot, shouting, *'Quick, quick, Milos! They're coming to get you! They're coming to get you!'*

TWENTY-TWO

Operation 'Bluetit 1'

Sunday 20 November 1994 – Farnham, Surrey, UK

'We had no way of contacting you. They're coming to get you. Quick, quick, there's no time to lose!' Mum was still jumping around. *What the hell has got into you?* Nasty pictures of ambulances with doctors in white coats wielding straitjackets flashed through my mind.

I managed to calm her down enough to get some semblance of sense out of her. Ten minutes after I'd left for London some staff officer in Wilton had rung up and said that a disaster had blown up in the Balkans. Rose was returning to theatre at six in the morning from RAF Brize Norton. Staff cars had been dispatched to scoop up his staff and mine was arriving at four, within an hour. My parents hadn't been able to get hold of me. Dad had gone to bed and poor Mum had stayed up fretting. She was right. There wasn't a moment to lose.

The most pressing problem was the motorbike. It couldn't be left on the street for fear of being stolen and there was nowhere to garage it. At half past three on Sunday morning a curious observer would have seen a seventy-two-year old woman and her cursing son manhandling a Suzuki down a narrow garden path and into the front room of a two-up two-down terraced house. Our exertions left me quite weak and flustered since there was only a quarter of an hour to go before my lift arrived. I threw off my jeans and climbed into uniform while Mum waited in the street to flag down the staff car.

I'd just laced up my boots when a young girl appeared at the front door chaperoned by Mum. 'Yes, that's right, Major Stankovic, this way my dear,' I could hear Mum cooing at the girl who turned out to be a very lost, and now mightily relieved, lance corporal. We gave her a cup of tea and with a peck on Mum's cheek we were off. There hadn't even been time to say goodbye to Dad. I was still in a state of shock as we sped out of Farnham. The only thing I knew for sure was that Rose really was jinxed.

The driver knew nothing of all this. In fact it had been her birthday and some bloke in Wilton had put her on duty. She'd been drinking Coke when she was suddenly tasked to Farnham. We sped quickly through the darkness, down the M4, up to Oxford and across to Brize Norton where she dropped me off at the departures terminal.

The first person I spotted was Goose looking red-eyed and really grumpy. Next to him sat an equally ruffled Glenn, the batman.

'What's this all about, Goose?'

He just shook his head, 'Dunno. Got a call at six yesterday evening and I've been travelling down from the North ever since.'

There was no sign of Rose and there was no one to tell us what to do. I went over to the counter and collared an RAF type and explained that we were Rose's personal staff and would be flying back with him. This did the trick. We scooped up our bags and were led off to the VIP lounge where Rose was pacing up and down in full camouflage gear, looking more manic than I'd ever seen him. Some senior Crab sycophant was standing next to him wringing his hands, clearly unable to engage the General in mindless small talk.

Rose spied me and barked, 'It's war, Mike! It's fucking war!'

There was no time to try to get any sense out of him as the HS125 had arrived and we piled in and took off immediately. During the two-hour hop to Zagreb the General rattled off something about Serb aircraft and NATO. Goose looked bored. Glenn was asleep. The General spent the flight squirming in his seat. By the time we reached Pleso and had been whisked off to HQ UNPROFOR I was still none the wiser. Whatever it was must be bad to have us scuttling back so fast.

The base was in pandemonium. Squads of UN guards were scurrying about in helmets and flak jackets. The UN right across the Former Republics of Yugoslavia had been put on Red Alert. The tension and air of panic across the HQ was enough to tell us that this was serious. Up in the Chief of Staff's office it all became clear.

The situation around Bihac had deteriorated dramatically. The Serbs had not only regained lost ground but were hard up against the River Una and very close to entering the Bihac Safe Area. The Krajina Serbs had been flying jet sorties from their airbase at Udbina in support of the BSA. NATO had flipped and was going to strike Udbina with a multi-aircraft attack at half past twelve. This left us with barely two hours to get back into Sarajevo before the strike went in and before the Serbs closed down all their checkpoints and the airport. Time was against us.

Being a Sunday there were no airlift flights into Sarajevo. A crew of sleepy and hung-over Ukrainians were prised reluctantly from their beds and ordered to fire up their ancient looking twin-prop AN26, an old flying box originally designed to drop a company of paratroopers. None of us had any faith in the aircraft: Rose, L-P and Spicer had recently flown down from Zagreb in one, piloted by a crew who couldn't map read and who had flown around the city for half an hour while they tried to lower the landing gear with a hammer. As the four of us sat in this droning heap I kept glancing at my watch trying to calculate the timings and managed to convince myself that we weren't going to make it in time. If Serb fire from the Ilidza flats didn't bring us down, then the faulty landing gear was going to kill us. I felt sick.

We banged down on the threshold at Sarajevo at exactly half past twelve. Instead of a hail of bullets and the expected fireball we were met by the vehicles and taken to the Residency. There the bubble burst. The NATO air strike had encountered bad weather and was being postponed by twenty-four hours until midday the next day. Less than twelve hours earlier I'd been in a bar in Fulham.

The Residency was alive with rumour and speculation as to how the Serbs would react once Udbina had been struck. Consensus suggested that at the very least they'd freeze any UN movement over their territory, close down the airport and generally make life thoroughly miserable for all of us. Some even speculated that they'd go further and embark on a sustained shelling of the city. Whatever the reaction, there was only one place to find out – Lukavica barracks.

Monday 21 November 1994 – Sarajevo

Geordie and I drove over to Lukavica to take coffee with Indjic. There were a couple of hours left to go before the strike. Indjic had no idea what was cooking and it was business as usual in his office – clearance for vehicles transiting the Sierras, a bit of lying down the phone to various UN LOs ringing up on whatever business, and coffee.

Geordie was exactly the right bloke to be with. Although a captain, he'd been an RSM and was older, wiser, more experienced and definitely smellier than me. He went with me just about everywhere on the Dark Side as the top cover that L-P had agreed to give me. He had a good sense of humour and was unflappable.

With fifteen minutes to go to the deadline my radio started squawking. It was the MA in the Outer Office. He was trying to find out, indirectly, if we were 'on the right side', which meant that he'd started flapping about the strike and probably thought Geordie and I would be slung into Kula prison the moment the first bomb fell. I assured him we were all right before switching off the annoying radio. Indjic gave me a dark look.

Half past twelve came and went. No telephones rang. More coffee was dished out. More mindless chitchat. An hour later we got bored and returned to the Residency for lunch. Geordie had heard on his secure PR radio that the strike had gone in but the MA's worst fears of a backlash had, mysteriously, been unfounded.

Curious at this lack of response we returned to Lukavica later that afternoon. Still nothing from Indjic. Eventually I couldn't bear this cat and mouse game any longer.

'I hear your airbase at Udbina was attacked today.' I cast a fly at him.

Indjic gave his moustache a furtive stroke. His black eyes glittered and he rasped, 'Errrr, that's nothing to do with us. Republika Srpska Krajina is a foreign country.'

'So, you're not bothered?'

'No. Why should we be?' he asked slowly.

His reaction astonished me. We returned to the Residency to report our findings. Damp squib, the whole thing. All our fears were unfounded. All that rushing back from the UK for nothing. Drama over. Time to head to the bar.

Tuesday 22 November 1994 – Sarajevo

The BSA attack towards Bihac wasn't slowing down and General Rose dispatched me up to Pale. I met Zametica at the annex Presidency and thrust more maps of the Bihac Safe Area under his nose. The task was a simple one: give them the maps and convince them of the folly of attacking Bihac. Zametica assured me that they wouldn't be crossing the Una and were only interested in recovering lost territory. It was also quite clear that, whatever folk in Pale were saying, the reality on the ground was quite different. Mladic was the only person controlling events around Bihac and it was highly doubtful whether any of the politicians were in a position to restrain him. Whatever the case, events were spiralling out of control.

At about seven in the evening we were rudely interrupted by Zametica ringing from Pale. Indjic's feathers hadn't been ruffled but clearly someone's had. I barely recognised his voice. He was screaming down the phone.

'Michael? Is that you?'

'Yes. It's me.'

'I have a message for your General. If you hit us it means war. If you hit us it means all-out war. Don't fuck around with us.' The Safe Area map had spooked them.

The phone was getting too hot to handle. Rose was standing next to me.

'Is your General there, Michael?'

I seized the moment. This was well beyond my pay grade. 'Yes, he's right next to me . . . just a moment.' I gave the Boss the handset that was glowing red hot with invective and abuse.

I only caught half the conversation, which seemed to have drifted onto 'hot pursuit across the border in Northern Ireland'. It seemed that Zametica was justifying the BSA's encroachment into the Bihac Safe Area in those terms. Rose, a man of considerable Northern Ireland experience, was disabusing Herr Flick of any such similarities. Eventually he just gave up and slung the telephone back to me. Zametica was still screaming about 'all-out war' and 'don't fuck about with us'. I got bored with this, hung up on him and went to the bar. The Udbina strike had really rattled them badly.

Zametica had made an extremely irritating comment, that the Bihac Safe Area maps were not official because they hadn't been delivered officially by a high representative of any kind. My passing them maps wasn't enough for the Serbs to take notice of them. And yet, when it suited their purposes to pass information which was in their interests, such as the global land-swapping plan, they were quite happy to use a more discreet conduit. They couldn't have it both ways.

A manic atmosphere had gripped the Outer Office. Everything Rose had worked for was slipping away fast and the chances of a real peace, that is, one reached through negotiation with the willing cooperation of the locals, seemed more remote than ever. The UN had all but lost the stag fight with NATO and it seemed that control of events had been wrested from the General.

General Rose might well have been momentarily depressed about events, but the mania within him soon surfaced. He dragged a tatty old A-frame bergen out of his bedroom and dumped it in his office.

'It's war! That's me packed and ready to go!' he quipped, eyes blazing.

He was wearing his Arctic windproof jacket to the zip of which was always fastened a small compass. Even more bizarrely he hoiked out of the top right hand pocket a bent and twisted Mars Bar which had been there since he'd first deployed to Sarajevo ten months ago.

'There you go. Got my survival rations. Right! Goose. Whatd'ya reckon? Quick exfil over the mountains. Over Igman, through the passes. I reckon four days! Whatd'ya think? Last one to the coast's a sissy!!'

He was grinning his head off and rattling off at high speed his escape and evasion plan to lots of 'yes Boss . . . that's right Boss' from Goose. The MA looked little and lost. I don't think the prospect of a 200-mile hike over the mountains appealed to him.

Although funny, half of me really believed that the General had had enough of this shit and wasn't bluffing about legging it to the coast.

Wednesday 23 November 1994 – Sarajevo

'It's on the wire already!' someone in the Outer Office said. The previous night's conversation had been intercepted, taped and passed to the Bosnian government. They wasted no time in leaking it to the press and Reuters already had it on the wire. Even more bizarrely, copies of the conversation were dispatched to New York where the Bosnian Ambassador, Muhamed Sacirbey, rushed about furnishing anyone he could get hold of with copies of the tape.

It didn't bother me in the least, particularly as Rose had made it clear that infringements of the Safe Area would result in air strikes. Of much greater concern was that this incident confirmed once and for all that everything that was said in the office, everything said on the phone, was taped and passed to the Bosnians. This weakened any attempts to negotiate by phone as one party was always going to be forewarned of any negotiating gambit. In this respect the Bosnians always had the upper hand and would be able to erode any privileged middle ground that the UN held.

That morning NATO aircraft attacked two Serb SAM sites at Otoka and Bosanska Krupa. The Serbs had turned on their tracking radar and had illuminated but not fired at NATO jets. Although Rose opposed the strikes, NATO saw it differently and viewed the 'illumination' of its aircraft as a hostile act. The attack on the SAM sites was bound to provoke the Serbs still further. Indjic could no longer claim that it had happened in 'a foreign country'.

Geordie and I leapt off to Lukavica to see what effect this latest strike would have. We got there just in time to be confronted by a furious Major Indjic threatening all-out war. A totally different atmosphere from Monday's genteel 'it's a foreign country' over coffee. Before our very eyes Indjic started closing down Sarajevo. Checkpoints were frozen. UN troops in the nine Weapon Collection Points were surrounded. In Ilijas fifty Canadians were disarmed and held hostage. The mood was so ugly that I was convinced we'd be next so we beat a hasty retreat.

As we swung out of Lukavica barracks we were faced with a dilemma. If we tried to cross the airport it was highly likely we'd be held up at Sierra 4. Even if we got back into the city we'd be trapped there along with all the others, where we'd be of no use to anyone.

'Fuck, it Geordie! Turn right. Let's get up to the UNMOs in Pale before the road is blocked.'

Geordie didn't bat an eyelid and off we went. At least up at Pale we'd be able to get a better feel for what was going on. Fortunately, Geordie had brought an SMT secure radio which had a range of about twenty kilometres. With that we'd be able to communicate direct back to L-P in Sarajevo without the press, the Bosnians and every other snoop listening in. It seemed the most sensible thing to do at the time.

We reached Pale unscathed. In contrast to the drama unfolding around Sarajevo and Bihac, Pale was, as ever, a sleepy hollow. The UNMOs seemed unperturbed when we turned up and announced we were staying. The boss there was a Royal Naval lieutenant commander called Rob Lowe. His number two was a Belgian captain called Luc Willems. There was no telling how long we'd be staying. We had no gear with us, not even a toothbrush. Worse still we had no money with which to pay for our board with the Savic family. Nevertheless, we were shown into a spare room in the attic where the other UNMOs also had rooms.

As soon as we could we tried to establish comms with the JCO office in Sarajevo. The signal was scratchy and weak. The set operated by bouncing its signal off a repeater antenna or talk-through. The one for the Sarajevo area was on top of Mount Bijelasnica, some twenty kilometres away, so the set was operating at its limit. Despite these minor problems we got through to L-P.

'Where are you?'

'Pale.'

'What! What're you doing there?'

'We're with the UNMOs. We're okay. What does the General want us to do?'

The line had been opened. Rose wasted no time in exploiting it and issued a stream of instructions which involved making contact with the Serbs in order to attempt to resolve the situation. We also discovered that the situation was far worse than we feared. Not only were the peacekeepers in Ilijas and the WCPs effectively held hostage, so too were two convoys, which had been caught in transit to Srebrenica and from Gorazde. The Gorazde convoy was British.

Jovan Zametica was in no mood to talk but graciously granted us an audience up at the annex presidency where we braved the hostile stares of Karadzic's bodyguards. Herr Flick was in good humour.

'I told you it would be war,' he announced smugly.

Geordie and I launched into him and informed him that it hadn't been the UN who had fired the missiles at Otoka and that the Serbs' knee-jerk reaction in grabbing hostages would be totally counter-productive. We made little impression on him and it became obvious that events had eclipsed him too. He made it abundantly clear that they no longer wanted to talk to General Rose. On the way out one of Karadzic's massive bodyguards stopped me. He unzipped his blue one-piece cammo romper suit.

'See this?' he said with pride. He was fingering a folded Serb flag. 'I'm the one who's been selected to raise it above the town hall in Bihac just as soon as we've taken the town, which will be very soon,' he added menacingly.

He left me in no doubt that this was no longer a 'hot pursuit' operation and that the agenda was quite different. They had every intention of taking Bihac and forcing the surrender of 5th Corps. This was all gloomy news to report back on the radio. The General urged us to keep plugging away at the problem.

If that wasn't enough to be getting on with, our other concerns centred around our lack of money and, more importantly, that the SMT's battery was starting to give out. Without a replacement our being in Pale would be nothing but a waste of time.

The next day Geordie drove back to Sarajevo to sort out these administrative details. We'd managed to persuade Zametica about the point of having us up there, and he made Karadzic see the sense in keeping this unofficial channel of communication open. Pressure was put on a very reluctant Indjic to allow Geordie and his vehicle to pass down into the city and back again. By late afternoon he was back with the goodies, including a new battery and some toothbrushes.

In Geordie's absence Zametica had popped into the UNMOs' house and together we hatched a plan to try and bring the two sides to the table. This was passed down to Rose whose team tried to cajole the Bosnians into a meeting. At the same time Zametica was ear-bending Karadzic over the proposal. By early evening it seemed to be coming together. Sarajevo reported that the Bosnian government was prepared to meet the Serbs at the airport the following day.

Geordie and I wasted no time in driving up to the annex presidency to tie up the loose ends. Karadzic was absent and on the road somewhere. Zametica had already gone home up the mountain so we were left to deal with Professor Koljevic who'd been empowered by Karadzic to conduct negotiations.

As we entered the building one of the guards insisted that I surrender my pistol and magazines, just in case I took it into my head to assassinate Koljevic. We were led up two flights of stairs to the professor's office. He was working late, as was his frosty, sour-faced secretary. He seemed to be in something of a dither now that the spotlight was on him, and he wouldn't make a decision about timings for the meeting without referring to Karadzic by mobile phone. At times Geordie and I were left on our own in his office the door of which was slammed shut by his secretary.

Curious to hear what was being said on the phone in her office I stuck my ear to the keyhole. She wasn't stupid though, and flung the door open and caught me red-handed. As she berated me for spying, it looked as though we'd blown it.

Eventually, Koljevic made a decision. All that remained was for him to speak directly with Rose in Sarajevo. Geordie stuck the antenna out of the window into the night air but the signal couldn't hit the Bijelasnica talk-through.

'We can't hit the talk through, professor.'

'The what, Michael?'

'Never mind. Can we go higher to get a better signal?'

Koljevic quickly entered into the spirit of things. We spent half an hour capering about the building sticking the antenna out of every conceivable window and hole, trying to resolve the comms problem, while Rose champed at the bit back in Sarajevo, waiting for the final word.

After much rushing about the building, we found that the best spot was in fact in the car park, in the freezing wind and snow, with Geordie standing there holding the SMT high above his head while Koljevic was coached in the intricacies of pressing buttons, saying 'over' and 'roger' and 'roger so far, over'. Eventually we got there. Rose and Koljevic had spoken and fixed the airport meeting for ten thirty the next day. Frozen but satisfied, Geordie and I drove the 300 metres back down to the UNMOs' house. It was well after midnight.

Friday 25 November 1994 – Pale

The day started badly. Geordie and I got up to the annex to discover that no one had bothered to show up. I was fuming with impatience.

'There's a meeting supposed to take place in an hour and a half's time at the airport and they're still not out of bed.' The lack of urgency and the manner in which the Pale bunch approached problems, coupled with an unbelievably lackadaisical attitude, did nothing but reinforce Zametica's assessment of the management of Republika Srpska as 'a fucking disaster!'

We raced back to the UNMOs and got on the phone to Zametica. He was still in bed.

'Don't worry, Michael. We'll be there. Don't worry.'

They left it till virtually the last minute. We tagged onto a Wacky Races convoy of VW Golfs which careered along the narrow Trebevic road at breakneck speed with sirens blaring. At Lukavica there was a slight delay as the Serb delegation waited for the French to provide an APC for the hop across the runway to the airport complex.

During the wait I discovered that half my rounds had been stolen by the guard to whom I surrendered my weapon and magazines the night before. I hit the roof and grabbed Peggy, one of the more oddly named but reasonable bodyguards who'd lived in New York for years but had returned when war broke out. He promised to get the rounds back.

The meeting at the airport achieved almost nothing and broke up quickly with neither side finding common ground. Haris Silajdzic represented President Izetbegovic and Nikola Koljevic the Serbs. However, the very fact that we'd managed to drag the Serbs from a position of isolation in their 'mountain stronghold' from where they spat war rhetoric to the negotiating table was achievement enough. As was maintaining and establishing a fragile link with them.

Others didn't see it that way. Despite Muhamed Sacirbey's best efforts to blacken Rose and me in New York by distributing the tapes, the Secretary General merely passed comment on the phone that he was quite satisfied with the way his peacekeepers had behaved. That problem didn't really concern me. More worrying were recent newspaper articles. Roger Cohen had launched a blistering attack on Rose in *The New York Times*, accusing him of failing the people of Sarajevo. He used the 'Nice one NATO!' photograph as evidence of Rose's antagonism to NATO. And he accused the General's staff of having a skewed view and made heavy reference to the General's interpreter, Mike

371

Stanley, a man of Serb origin who pooh-poohed the CG Plan and wielded an unholy influence over Rose.

The British press had known about Abbott, Costello and Stanley almost from the outset. They'd kept quiet about it, recognising the difficult position we were in, and by and large Costello and I had survived any major dramas. That all changed with Roger Cohen, who simply couldn't resist the temptation to use it as ammunition against Rose. It didn't take long for the Bosnians to pick up on this. After the airport meeting the front page of *Ljiljan*, the SDA rag, carried a photograph of a peacekeeper, not me, talking into a satellite radio. The caption read: Mike Stanley, Rose's Adjutant, is really Mihajlo Stefanovic, Chetnik Spy in HQ UNPROFOR.

It was a cheap trick. The use of secure comms which they couldn't intercept and which had dragged them quickly to the negotiation table must really have been an irritation. The caption infuriated me for no other reason than my exposure meter had just tripped out. It was bound to happen eventually. What really surprised me was that they'd got the name wrong and were clearly trying to build 'Mike Stanley' into a Balkan equivalent. In a way it was heartening because many of the Muslims in the city to whom I was close and who knew my real name clearly hadn't blabbed.

There wasn't much time to dwell on all this. There was much to do. Geordie and I figured that we couldn't survive up in Pale with a scratchy old SMT and a toothbrush. We'd need more gear if we were to establish ourselves up there for the duration of the crisis. Most importantly we needed a more substantial secure radio, preferably a TACSAT, such as the one being used by Charles's patrol in Bihac. We decided to stay the night in the Residency and prepare more carefully. Before the Serbs shot off back up to Pale we screwed a promise out of them that we'd be given unmolested passage back up the hill.

'You just sort it out with Indjic,' were my last words to Zametica before he disappeared into the back of the French APC.

'Don't worry about a thing,' he grinned back, which meant there was a lot to worry about. Lackadaisical!

Saturday 26 November 1994 – Sarajevo

Sure enough, Zametica lived up to his reputation. Geordie and I, packed and ready to go, found ourselves trapped in the Residency. The problem was not so much Zametica as the mercurial Major Indjic. His nose had been severely knocked out of joint by Geordie's and my antics up in Pale. He bitterly resented, as any control freak would, having his position at the centre of the spider's web usurped. More than anything he was deeply suspicious of the fact that we were dealing directly with the Pale politicians, and worse still intimately with the 'MI6 spy Zametica'. For all these petty internecine reasons

Indjic did his best to frustrate our efforts in getting back up the hill. Regardless of what the politicians told him to do, he ultimately held the key in that it was army personnel who manned the checkpoints.

Most of the day was spent on the phone, with US and Bosnian snoops listening in, trying to put pressure on Zametica to force Indjic to relent. Absurdly, the decision had to be referred to Karadzic. By the time the problem was resolved it was too late to go up and we postponed our departure until Sunday.

That evening, Rose, the MA and Goose shot down to the Bosnian presidency for a meeting with President Izetbegovic. Topic – Bihac. I deliberately avoided going along for two reasons. First, no interpreter was needed and second, since the dealings with the Pale cabal were becoming deeper and publicly so in the press, by not having any contact whatsoever with the Bosnian side I couldn't be accused of passing 'secrets' to the Serbs.

It's just as well I didn't accompany the General. He returned half an hour later. As he strode back into the Outer Office his face was a mask of rage. 'Bollocks to the lot of them, that's what I say!' he snarled.

They hadn't got as far as Izetbegovic. On the first floor the party was ambushed by Haris Silajdzic and the entire press corps in Sarajevo. It was a cheap set-up. Their further progress was blocked while the maestro of the sound-bite harangued Rose and directly accused him of being responsible for the deaths of 70,000 Muslims in Bihac. The General should have got out of the 'killing zone' as quickly as possible. Instead he stayed and soaked up this abuse and in so doing provided the media with the pictures they wanted. 'YELLOW ROSE' trumpeted the US media. Toads!

From my point of view all this was intriguing. The Bosnians were irritated that secure comms reports were coming out to Bihac and Pale which enabled Rose to manoeuvre and to refute grossly over-exaggerated reports of the situation there, which were designed further to pull the rug from under the UN and to entice NATO into crushing the Serbs. Something else was beginning to take shape; Bihac was more than just about Bihac. It was much bigger than that and the stakes much higher. Just how high I was soon to discover from Jovan Zametica.

Sunday 27 November – Thursday 8 December 1994 – Pale

Reluctantly, Indjic allowed us to pass up the Trebevic road without being molested. By mid-afternoon Geordie and I were safely ensconced in the attic of the Savic house. Rob and Luke seemed pleased to see us and the goodies and mail that we'd brought them from Sarajevo. They were polite enough not to ask too much about our task. In truth, we wouldn't have been able to give them a straight answer anyway. The task was, in essence, to remain on station and provide a secure comms link between Rose and the Bosnian Serbs. Quite how events would pan out was largely left to cuffing and bluffing. There was no rule book for this one.

The first task was to establish comms. The invaluable TACSAT comes in three parts: the radio unit, a rectangular black box, the battery, another equally hefty rectangular box, and the antenna. The antenna was rather like a little telescoping umbrella with 'feet'. Connected to the radio by a coax cable, it had to be pointed in bearing and elevation at an appropriate satellite. In fact all you need are the bearing and elevation. Relatively low wattages of power send the signal in an ever-expanding 'cone' up to the satellite. As long as part of that cone hits the satellite the signal will be processed and redirected earthwards to any other TACSAT or ground station whose antenna is pointing at the satellite. Thus anyone could hear the signal, but they needed the appropriate codes to decipher it. In a sense the system is insecure in that the very act of 'radiating' a signal from a fixed spot gives away the fact that you're there. Since the whole world knew we were in Pale, that didn't matter anyway. What was vital was that Rose's instructions to us and our reports back to him were privileged and for his ears only.

Rooting about in the attic revealed that, with the only aspect on the satellite, Luc Willem's bedroom was the best place to set up. A skylight allowed us to set the antenna up on the roof in the snow and draw the cable back into the room. Limited by cable length, all transmissions had to be carried out at the foot of Luc's bed, usually with him snoring in it. The TACSAT had no headset. Limited to a telephone handset Geordie and I would sit hunched over, each with an ear glued to it, while Rose barked out his instructions. It all looked highly furtive.

Operating the machine was easy. A press of the bar on the handset was followed by two 'beeps', indicating that the signal had hit the satellite. Thereafter one could speak freely. To conserve battery life we closed down the set and only came up on regular morning and evening schedules. If Rose or anyone wanted to get hold of us and speak 'secure' they'd ring up on the insecure INMARSAT and simply say 'switch to your other means'. This, more than anything, must have annoyed the snoops in Sarajevo.

Luc Willems seemed permanently asleep in his bed. The posting to UNMOs Pale was dull. The Savics' garage had been converted into a message switching centre. All faxes and CAPSATS came in to them in English. Two locally-hired Serb girls, Svetlana and Snezana, acted as translators, typing the texts into Serbo-Croat which would then be faxed either to Mladic or to Karadzic. Their responses would be translated into English and sent back. In many ways the sole function of the UNMOs there was to oversee this dull and boring process. It was hardly surprising, therefore, that Luke slept through most of his tour, for which Geordie christened him 'Captain of the Belgian Sleeping Team'.

In addition to the ever-present threat of bedsores, other dangers lurked in the Savic household. Dani Savic's wife, Mira, was a superb cook. A six-month stint as a Pale UNMO was guaranteed to result in the UNMO having to be hoiked out by a fork-lift truck. It amused me that some folk in Sarajevo thought that we were in mortal danger on the Dark Side. They were right in a way. The threat of piling on the pounds and hardening one's arteries was a serious one. The only thing that saved us from this fate was the constant messages of 'switch to your other means' which were received in the garage and which propelled Geordie and me at high speed up four flights of stairs and into the attic to turn on the 'other means'. This scampering was frequently cursed as being 'worse than P Company!' Luke slept through it all.

Rob Lowe was highly amused by all this. He was fiddling around upstairs and wandered into Luc's room as Geordie and I were crouched over the set taking notes from the General barely able to hear what he was saying over Luc's snoring. Rob took one look at this and fell about laughing.

'What's so fucking funny, Rob? This is serious stuff!' His irreverence was irritating.

Rob was gasping for breath, pointing at us and then at Luke and barely able to force out the words. 'Bluetit . . . it's Bluetit . . .' he stammered.

'What? What're you on about?' *You've been up here too long, that's what it is.*

'Bluetit. You know, as in *'Allo 'Allo!* . . . when René communicates with the British using the radio concealed under his mad old mother-in-law's bed . . . with her in it . . . you know, "*'allo, Nighthawk, Nighthawk, this is Bluetit over!*"' he mimicked before dissolving in another fit of giggles.

Geordie and I looked at the snoring Luc, down at the TACSAT at our feet and saw the joke. What with Herr Flick up the road, Luke snoring away, a mad General in Sarajevo barking out instructions, us scampering to the 'other means' and the Bosnian war spiralling out of control, Rob had a point. We became Bluetit.

The job, though, wasn't quite that funny. The stakes were extremely high. The fate of some 200 peacekeepers trapped as 'hostages' on the Dark Side, the complete lack of freedom of movement of the UN and the suspension of the airlift into the city really were side issues which could be resolved in slow time. The most critical task in hand was somehow to prevent the BSA from entering and taking Bihac. Just how critical this was Zametica revealed to us.

We saw him not long after establishing ourselves in the UNMOs' house. I was furious about Indjic messing us about and suggested to Zametica that Mladic and the BSA really were beyond the control of Karadzic. He wouldn't be drawn though, and merely mentioned that it was particularly difficult dealing with Indjic.

Despite that, he was quite chirpy. 'Are you aware that you and I made history on Friday?' He looked smug and self-satisfied.

'Sorry?'

'The meeting at the airport. You and I cooked it up ourselves. Convinced Karadzic and Rose, didn't we?'

'Jovan, it was a disaster. It achieved nothing, which is why we're still up here fiddling about with Bihac.'

Zametica's comment was interesting. He wasn't in the least bit fussed that our cooked-up meeting had been a disaster. What was important to him was that he'd manipulated Karadzic. To him the whole affair had been an academic exercise in exerting his influence and massaging his ego. He did have a point, though. If we could manipulate Karadzic through him then we had a chance of getting somewhere with the Bihac debacle.

To the Serbs, Bihac was everything. The winning or losing of the war would be decided by the side that gained or held onto Bihac. The intelligence which Zametica shared with us indicated that, if the Serbs took Bihac and Dudakovic's 5th Corps surrendered, the whole house of cards would come tumbling down. The BiH commanders in Gorazde and Srebrenica had indicated that if Bihac fell then they'd surrender the pockets. Without those the Bosnian government's position would be untenable and capitulation would follow. It's hardly surprising then that the Bosnians were desperate to cajole NATO into systematically bombing the BSA around Bihac. If Bihac held, the pockets would hold, and the government would stand steadfast. As the Federation strengthened and the Serb position weakened, in time the roles would be reversed. In that sense Bihac was everything to both sides.

The Serbs had by this stage encroached well into the Safe Area and had virtually, but not quite, surrounded the town. They'd left a corridor to the north.

'It's quite simple,' snapped Zametica. 'We're leaving them a corridor out. They can withdraw without fighting if they want to.'

'There's no way they're going to do that. They've as good as lost if they hand Bihac over to you on a plate.'

'Then we'll fight our way into the town and take it anyway! Either way they'll lose.'

'If you enter the town then the whole thing's out of Rose's hands. You'll have NATO to deal with.'

In all of this, bluff and cuff were the only things with which we could bargain. The only unknown factor to the Serbs was the extent to which NATO would dismantle their war machine. It was an unknown factor to us, too. Given the inaccuracies of pinpoint bombing experienced in the Gulf War and in Bosnia so far, it remained doubtful whether NATO could really achieve anything in the time it would take the BSA to commence serious street fighting in the town. Once the Serbs engaged in fighting in built-up areas, NATO would be unable to strike directly for fear of civilian collateral damage in Bihac. It would then be a case of whose nerves held out the longest.

Zametica and others didn't know this. Widespread air strikes still posed a considerable perceived threat, and it was that perception that Geordie and I worked on. He was better than me at graphically detailing just what would happen if the Serbs set foot in Bihac. He was wasted: his imagination could have been put to better use working for Steven Spielberg. He almost convinced me, too.

Not all of this badgering and bluffing happened during one meeting. The same subject would crop up time and time again and off we'd go, grinding away with the same old threats. Each day was standard. Morning schedule and instructions from Rose. Fix up a meeting with Zametica either in the annex, his hotel room or even in the UNMOs' house. Pester him to exert pressure on Karadzic and then wait for the answer and report back to Sarajevo. A painfully slow process. Sometimes whole frustrating days would pass with nothing achieved. On others we'd glean a gem of information and scuttle back to the attic to pass it on. But always the focus was on threatening dire retribution if they set foot in Bihac.

Days rolled into each other. Snow was thick on the ground and our bellies were getting fatter on Mira's cooking.

'Don't worry about us up here, L-P. We're on beans and stale bread but we'll be all right.' Sarajevo had to be kept informed of our hardships. And Mira's cooking had to be kept Top Secret, just in case someone decided to replace us.

Suddenly, on 29 November, the emphasis of our effort was diverted from that of threatening Zametica with air strikes to that of trying to persuade Karadzic to meet with the Secretary General of the United Nations. Boutros Boutros-Ghali, the SG, would be appearing in Bosnia the following day intent on talking some sense into whoever needed it. If things went well we were in with a real chance of sorting the problem out.

Nothing was that simple. The Bosnians were quite happy to meet the SG on 'neutral ground' at the airport. The Serbs weren't. Karadzic insisted that the SG come up to Pale. Boutros-Ghali was having none of that, claiming that his presence there would lend legitimacy to the Bosnian Serbs' territorial claims, which was precisely what Karadzic had in mind. It fell to Geordie and me to persuade him that regardless of where he met the SG, it would ultimately be in all parties' interests. Karadzic relented, but only so far, and agreed to meet the SG in Grbavica in Sarajevo. It was a step down for him and the best compromise we could screw out of Pale. Boutros-Ghali wouldn't meet them half way and insisted it was the airport or nothing.

In the end egos interfered with everything. The SG met the Bosnians in the

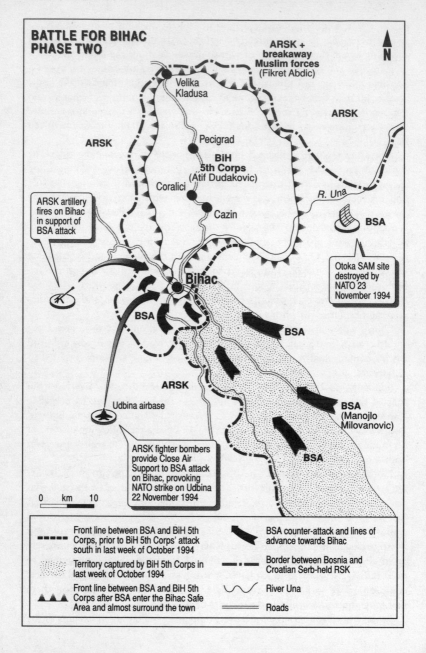

Presidency and departed Sarajevo without meeting the Serbs. It must have escaped SG's notice that his Special Representative, Mr Akashi, regularly tripped up to Pale. Technically speaking, in so doing, Akashi was lending the Serbs legitimacy. But that wasn't the case and SG failed to appreciate that by stepping into Grbavica he was no more lending legitimacy to the Serbs than his Special Representative did by telling Dr Karadzic dirty jokes over dinner. A lost opportunity.

By 3 December the Serbs' huffing and puffing had subsided enough for them to allow Rose to visit. 5 Corps was still holding firm in Bihac. The Serbs hadn't entered the place. We'd reached an impasse. However, there were still the hostages to think about, so no one was out of the woods. The General's visit was not without mishap. On the Trebevic road Goose narrowly missed mowing down a stationary cow. The backing vehicle containing L-P slid into the back of the Range. Almost without pausing Goose leapt out and physically manhandled the cow off the road. L-P was left stranded with the broken backing vehicle while Rose and gang careered on to Pale. The meeting seemed to pass cordially enough with Karadzic smirking about the cow incident and commenting that Serbian cows were the most stubborn in the world.

Geordie was needed back in Sarajevo so his replacement, Dave, drove up with the convoy in his own vehicle. Geordie stayed on that night packing his gear while Dave and I sat in the annex conference room drinking a bottle of whisky with Professor Koljevic. Over a period of several hours we got from him a rather sozzled version of how the war had started. The most startling revelation, unknown to all but us, was that once the Serbs had scuttled off up to Pale at the start, there had followed a long and tortured bickering session as to who would be 'president'. It had been offered to Koljevic, but he'd declined. Biljana Plavsic had refused also, which had left Karadzic saying that he might as well do it. The entire mismanagement of Republika Srpska actually began in typical Serbian style – with bickering and feuding.

The divisions between Pale and the BSA had become more than apparent to Geordie and me. In many respects, engineering a meeting between Rose and Karadzic had been easily achieved. To get Mladic to the table was much harder. He still hadn't surfaced and contact with Han Pijesak had been intermittent. Predictably enough, the BSA, no doubt encouraged by Indjic, had become sniffy towards Geordie and me, largely because they didn't trust Zametica. The key to unlocking the hostages, freeing the convoys and opening the airport again lay firmly with the military.

With a lot of cajoling Dave and I managed to persuade the BSA to meet with General Rose. The meeting was fixed for the evening of Monday 5 December up at the hotel Rajska Dolina on Jahorina. We were optimistic that Mladic would show up. Anything less and there'd be no real progress.

Mladic, however, declined to appear. Instead he sent his deputy, General

Milan Gvero, whose perfect straight, white false teeth gave him the appearance of a country vicar rather than a warlord. The meeting achieved very little. Gvero would refer everything to Mladic by phone. Mladic was still in a huff with Rose over the destruction of the SAM sites. His mood probably hadn't been improved by being bluffed into not taking Bihac. Nevertheless, it was the first contact with them since the crisis had begun and that alone was an encouraging sign that the hostage issue would resolve itself. It was rather like extracting teeth – painful, bloody and delicate.

On this occasion L-P had made it up to the meeting, bringing with him some mail. His perspective on what had gone on was fascinating. His chief concern, despite our protests about 'cold beans and stale bread', had been Charles's patrol in Bihac. They'd been vital in supplying General Rose with an accurate picture of what was happening on the ground. He'd been able to use much of their information to defuse the grossly over-exaggerated war propaganda of both the Bosnians and the Serbs. Unlike us, who were virtually untouchable in Pale, Charles's group had become the targets of 5 Corps once they realised the source of the accurate reporting. The constant dangers that they faced should never be understated. They were a critical element in the battle for Bihac.

The meeting wound up late. Dave and I didn't arrive back at the UNMOs' until two in the morning. It was biting cold and everyone had gone to bed, leaving us locked out. We spent half an hour capering about banging on windows and doors to no avail. We were saved only by a frozen Mars Bar which Dave found in his pocket. We threw this repeatedly at Luc's fourth-storey window until we awoke the captain of the Belgian sleeping team and were let in.

Over the next few days the situation seemed to improve. The thaw had begun; gradually convoys were unblocked and hostages released. There seemed no point in staying up in Pale any longer. A radio call from the MA had us packing up our TACSAT and bags and bidding farewell to Rob, Luc and the Savic family.

Operation Bretton, December 1997 – Ian, UK

The relief of getting back to Sarajevo and seeing familiar faces was short-lived. Two things spoilt that. In my absence the Bosnian press had had a field day with the 'Stanley's a Chetnik spy' story. More dirt had been thrown, which was more than a little disconcerting. I couldn't work out quite how we'd become so over-exposed, given that we'd been using a secure TACSAT. Darko put me straight. 'Mike, you're name's been mentioned frequently by the General at the morning conferences – Stanley's up there, he'll sort it out!' That may have been the case but that morning conference was always stuffed full of all sorts of odds and sods, some of whom were quite hostile to Rose and would think nothing of running to the press or to the Bosnians. There were no secrets in the Residency.

If that wasn't bad enough, the very morning Dave and I returned I learnt that the folk hostile to me within BH Command had been working behind my back to get me removed from theatre. That upset me. There was I stuck up in Pale doing the General's bidding, dealing with those suspicious monsters, which resulted in over-exposure and hounding in the Bosnian and US presses, only to return and discover that my own people had been busy stabbing me in the back.

I still had one or two allies left and L-P soon cheered me up with a story of another Rose caper. This happened just after Geordie got back to Sarajevo. Charles's patrol in Bihac had been running short of battery power. Without a resupply of batteries their presence there would have been of no use to the General. Rose was still frustrated at his inability to get into Bihac. Up in Pale Geordie and I had pulled out the stops trying to get him in but Mladic had put his foot down.

In a last-ditch effort Rose stormed into the JCO's office. 'J-P!' he could never remember L-P's name, 'I want you to get us into Bihac covertly. It may seem a bit Mickey Mouse, but we could all free-fall into the pocket by night!' According to L-P, at this point the MA started to look a little ill. Rose was deadly serious about leaping out of an aircraft five miles up to deliver some batteries and get one over Mladic. L-P back-tracked furiously, 'Of course we could, sir, but it does seem a bit Mickey Mouse.' This was enough to put him off and the MA at ease. But that wasn't the end of it as far as Rose was concerned: 'Oh well, let's go and have some fun with Victor!'

Victor Andreyev was not only Rose's superior but he was also somewhat overweight. He'd been around for years and had known Mladic when he had been a mere colonel in Knin. Victor prided himself on his influence over the Serbs, but even he'd failed to get Rose into Bihac.

Into his office march Rose, L-P and Geordie. 'Victor! We're going to Bihac!' Andreyev was unflustered. 'Absolute, absolute, Michael. We ask for diplomatic and political clearances and then we go.' Rose wasn't having that. 'No, Victor, we've got to do this soon. We're going to do it my way – covertly!' Rose then glared at L-P and Geordie. The latter asked Andreyev how much he weighed, to which the bemused Russian replied, 'About 80 kilos, why?' Geordie turned to Rose and said, 'No problem, sir, we can take him in on tandem.' Rose barked at Andreyev, 'Free-fall, Victor. Free-fall! We're going to jump in by night from 25,000 feet. You'll be strapped to the front of Geordie!' A wild look spread across Victor's face. His diplomatic polish disappeared for a second or two before he bounced back with a sickly smile. 'Michael, I love adventure, but I really think diplomacy is best in this case!' L-P, Rose and

Geordie couldn't keep this up any longer and gave the game away, much to the nervous Andreyev's relief.

L-P was leaving in a week's time. He was to attend Staff College, a prospect which did not please him greatly. His replacement, David, a Grenadier Guards major, had arrived and the two had begun their hand-over. On the night I got back from Pale we put together a Schindler's List. Despite our differences and Indjic's growing suspicion of my dealings with Zametica, we were still able to use Indjic to get people out. Nothing had changed there.

Rose still wasn't willing to be kept out of Bihac so he decided to brazen it out. On 9 December we all flew up to Zagreb in a Yak 40: Rose, L-P, David, Goose and myself. Something was niggling the General. In mid-flight he turned to me and simply said, 'I want you to suspend Schindler's List until further notice.' I had no idea what was behind this but he was the boss and had his reasons. I cheered inwardly. The pressure was off for the time being.

The next day we tried to drive through to Bihac, approaching overland through Serb-held Krajina, only to be stopped by their border guards and denied further access. It was bitterly cold. The General refused to budge until someone senior appeared, and five hours later a lame colonel from the ARSK turned up and told Rose he was under orders, Mladic's of course, not to let anyone pass. Rose let fly at this fellow and threatened to expose his unsuitability as an officer. After giving the officer a tongue-lashing to end them all, we returned to Zagreb's Hotel Intercontinental.

The following afternoon, back in Sarajevo, I took great pleasure in telling Indjic that Schindler's List had been suspended and he was not to pester us again until we decided it was all right to carry on. His reaction was predictable. His eyes betrayed his annoyance and you could see him already planning his revenge.

We didn't have long to wait for that one either. His revenge came on the day the General had planned to hold a meeting of his Sector Commanders at the Residency. Those travelling by road were mysteriously barred further access at Sierra 1. I was dispatched to sort out Indjic. Truculently, he informed me that he'd barred further passage for Rose's subordinates because Rose had ordered an end to Schindler's List. I'd never seen Rose so angry. 'I will not be blackmailed by some cheap and nasty little Commie major!' he ranted.

I was sick to death of Indjic, too. He'd got too big for his boots and needed chopping down to size. I felt sure he was still suffering control-freak-withdrawal-symptoms as a result of our Bluetit deployment and was now trying to reassert his authority. While Rose fumed and plotted his own revenge on the mad major, I resolved to speak to Mladic about Indjic's behaviour. We got him in the end.

We were off again for a week's leave. The Roses would be skiing in Italy, L-P would be going home for good and I decided to make the most of this exodus from Sarajevo and try and get a break myself. Predictably, our departure was fraught with drama as we drove out of Sarajevo on 15 December.

For a week the city had suffered pressure inversion with dirty, thick, low cloud clogging the airport. No flights in or out. Above the cloud Igman and Bijelasnica were clear and the French had been resupplying themselves by flying helicopters onto the mountains. The ADC's plan for our travel was very simple – drive up to the Babin Dol ski-jump on Igman and pick up a Sea King for a hop to Split. There we'd all cross-over to a Yak for the trip over to Vicenza where we'd drop off Rose and Goose before flying on to Ancona to overnight before catching a Herc back to the UK. Easy. Except for one thing. The weather.

When we woke, the cloud base had lifted and it was snowing heavily. We wouldn't be flying off Igman in a Sea King. Despite this, Baggers persisted with the original plan and we drove up to a foggy and snow-bound Babin Dol. Rose was already fretting. We could hear the Sea King battering its way slowly towards us in zero visibility. Suddenly, a heavy machine gun opened up from somewhere and the helicopter disappeared instantly. We were stranded. The General was now in a real temper; he snatched Baggers' radio and barked instructions down to the Ops Room in Sarajevo. Feverishly, the staff there cobbled together Plan B.

Plan B necessitated us bumping our way over Igman and down to Konjic where a French Puma plucked us up and flew back to Kiseljak to refuel. Ironically, we parked up next to the Sea King whose tail section was riddled with .50 bullet holes. As the fuel was fed into the Puma the General whipped out his notebook and scribbled a furious note which I passed to a chastened Baggers: 'Well done, ADC. This is where we should have been two hours ago!' He took no prisoners when he was angry, and Indjic had yet to find this out.

The rest of the hop went pretty smoothly until we landed at Vicenza. As we taxied off the runway Rose peered out of the window and at the sight of something blew his top again.

Through the portholes we could see a very large Italian guard of honour and a band playing. 'It's a guard of honour, sir.' The general was flustered. He detested pomp and circumstance. 'A fucking guard of honour! What for? I've fucking well come here to go skiing, not to inspect some guard! ADC! What do I do?' The General was almost in a blind panic at the thought of confronting a sword-wielding Italian. Baggers tried to calm him down. As the plane taxied and slowed both the ADC and the General were on their feet with Baggers giving Rose a quick lesson in saluting. 'What! Like this?' snapped Rose as he practised in front of the ADC, much to Goose's amusement.

This performance was all too much for me, too. 'General, why don't you give Goose your beret and grab his Softie jacket. He can take the parade and you can be his BG!' Rose looked at Goose. 'Good idea! Goose!' Goose turned to me and hissed, 'You bastard. You know he'd do it as well.' In the end Rose took the salute and inspected the guard while we skulked behind the Yak. That was our last sight of Rose for a week.

The Yak deposited us in Ancona, from where we were driven up the coast to Senegalia for a night in the RAF hotel. In mid-winter the place was no better than Bognor Regis out of season – dreary, devoid of life. L-P and I walked along the beach. He was melancholy, clearly sad that it was all over for him. 'I think I'm going to ask Suzie to marry me,' he said finally. 'Well, that doesn't surprise me, mate, it's been on the cards for months now.' He didn't quite follow what I was saying. 'Minka. She told you it would happen, so it'll happen. End of story.' And it did.

A week's leave was okay, but, wandering along that boring, deserted beach at Senegalia I had another awful feeling of dread. Suddenly, I envied L-P his freedom to plan a future. I knew from experience that, as soon as Rose turned his back on Bosnia, there'd be a disaster. I could put money on it that I'd be dragged back before the week was out.

TWENTY-THREE

Operation Bretton

December 1997 – Ian, UK

'I was wrong on that one, Ian. For once there was no mad dash back to the Balkans. The MA had been left behind to hold the fort. He'd be taking leave over Christmas when we were back. Of course, we'd be back in Sarajevo for Christmas as that's where Rose had to be, with the troops, so we got a week early in lieu. He was skiing with Angela in Italy, while I struggled with my next door neighbour to get the Suzuki out of the living room, no mean feat.'

I didn't have any plans so shot off to the country to stay with L-P and Suzie. He was still feeling a little deflated about leaving Bosnia and at the prospect of climbing into those ghastly green plastic trousers and brown leather shoes that are standard dress at Staff College. We were cheered up by Geordie, who was back for a short break, too. It was odd to say the least to be drinking with these people in a quaint country pub where the most dangerous person for miles around was an over-zealous landlord. Equally strange was the fact that I'd only known them in Sarajevo, careering up and down the stairs of the Bosnian Serb presidency with a puffing Professor Koljevic in tow was a world away from a crackling log fire and pints of Guinness. Geordie was going back to Sarajevo so I'd be seeing him again.

All too quickly it was over. A few days before Christmas I returned to Split by Herc and met up with Rose and Goose. We crossed with the MA in the VIP lounge at Split airport: for about an hour where he briefed the General on events that had taken place in our absence. The most significant of these was the visit of ex-US President Jimmy Carter on a peace mission in the wake of the battle for Bihac. He'd spent some time up in Pale with Karadzic and the Bosnian Serbs persuading them about the benefits of peace. The upshot of all this was that efforts to find a peace settlement had been given a shot in the arm.

The most important thing to remember is that, having failed to take Bihac and thus to force the capitulation of the Bosnian government, the Serbs were now in a mood to talk seriously. The integrity and thus future of the self-styled Republika Srpska Krajina, particularly the Knin area, was wholly dependent on the BSA taking Bihac and establishing a strong supply route to RSK. This they'd failed to do; therefore, not only had that aspiration evaporated but also the BSA was exhausted and on its back foot. For them the war could not be won by military means and their only hope now lay in the impetus that Jimmy Carter's visit had given to the peace process.

This gave rise to a series of shuttle negotiations between Pale and the Bosnian Presidency in the hope of securing a Cessation of Hostilities Agreement (COHA) as a precursor to the diplomats and negotiators stepping in and coming up with something agreeable to all parties. The Contact Group was still telling Karadzic and the world that 'the map was the map' and there'd be no movement on that. That said, if they'd hoisted on board the 'global' solution in which Karadzic had indicated that they'd be willing to go down to 31 per cent in Bosnia, there'd still be some basis for negotiation without anyone losing face. In the hope of securing the first step, the COHA, we spent virtually every day scurrying between Pale and the Bosnians trying to secure the wording of an agreement that they'd all be able to live with.

There were constant interruptions, not least of which was Christmas. On Christmas Eve, General Rose dragged us off to Midnight Mass in St Joseph's, the huge Catholic cathedral close to Bascarsija. It was bitterly cold despite the tracksuit I was wearing underneath my suit, the only occasion I ever wore it. Nothing in Bosnia ever went as it should. St. Joseph's was crammed to capacity. Every seat was taken and as many people again crowded into the aisles and wings. Rose and I managed to get a seat in the second row where we were flanked by nuns. In front of us were Croat representatives in the Bosnian government. Goose and Baggers had to stand to one side, but there was little danger, particularly as we were safely buried amongst all those nuns.

The service was extraordinarily moving, and all conducted in Latin and Serbo-Croat. I gave the General a running commentary of the Serbo-Croat, but, for the most part, we were content to listen to the amazing singing of the choir. Half way through the service I became aware of something other than the singing. Outside the entrance to the cathedral a mob of several hundred had gathered; those who'd failed to get in but were outside in the cold listening. As the service progressed the noise from the crowd grew louder and louder. It wasn't singing though. After a while the sound of smashing bottles, drunken curses, yelling and fighting eclipsed the angelic voices of the choir. In contrast to the religious gravitas inside, drunken Balkan pandemonium reigned outside. Eventually, the drunks won the singing contest.

Back in the Outer Office we cracked a few bottles of champagne before going to bed. On Christmas Day the General followed tradition and visited every single UN outpost and OP along the Sarajevo confrontation line, wishing his troops a happy Christmas. Christmas lunch in the Residency was also an event, given over to our local staff who'd remained in the Residency and served by all the Commanders BHC from General Morillon onwards. While they sat with their families and children we, including the General, rushed to and fro dishing out turkey, stuffing, Christmas pudding and mince pies. The few American officers in the HQ threw themselves into this with gusto and wheeled in a huge catering trolley stuffed with presents for the children. It was the least we could do for our staff. Lunch ended with a huge snowball fight outside between the officers of UNPROFOR and the children of Sarajevo. We lost.

Late afternoon marked another first in Sarajevo's history. The officers in the Air Operations Co-ordination Cell, led by Wing Commander Pete Rycroft and an American colonel, Vic Dutil, organised the inaugural run of the Sarajevo Hash House Harriers. Rose had to be cajoled into it: 'What the fuck is hashing?' he snapped. Coerced into it, he loved it, particularly as it involved running. The war-weary citizens of Sarajevo were treated to the spectacle of forty lunatics charging up and down snow-filled streets following trails of sawdust and screaming 'On! On!' before darting down various alleys. The details of the Hash were sent to whichever body regulates world-wide Hashing and officially entered into the Book of Hashing.

With Christmas over it was back to endless shuttle negotiations: up to Pale, back to Sarajevo. As ever, both sides were chewing over the specific wording, trying to ensure the best deal for themselves. The entire process was best described to Karadzic by one of our negotiators, Colm Murphy, as similar to going to the dentist. Extracting consensus was like extracting teeth, bloody and painful, particularly for the negotiators.

By 30 December we were still at it, rushing up hill and down dale in the hope of getting this COHA boxed off before the New Year. There seemed to be a slim chance. Both sides were still deliberating over the wording. We'd spent the afternoon in Pale. Colm Murphy, standing in for Victor Andreyev who was on leave, and Matt Hodes, an ex-82nd Airborne Division paratrooper and now a UN negotiator, were leading the negotiations. Karadzic was holding out on wording. Mladic looked bored to bits and totally uninterested in the proceedings.

Some of the things that happened there defied belief. To an outsider, to an interested observer scanning the newspapers or watching TV, it would appear that these high-level discussions were conducted in a tense and earnest atmosphere. Not so. Mladic was so bored by all this that he said almost nothing during the meeting. Instead he indulged in another crime against humanity which had us all gagging. He had an enormous boil on the end of his nose that he picked and squeezed, attacking it from all directions. Every so often he'd whip out a small, rectangular vanity mirror from his pocket and, staring and straining, would squeeze away at the boil, totally oblivious to the silent horror of the negotiators. Failing to cleanse the wretched boil, Mladic would glare balefully at us, at which point all heads would drop to their note pads pretending they hadn't seen anything. This performance amused me for hours, much more than that teeth-pulling.

We returned to Sarajevo that evening feeling as if we were getting nowhere. More importantly, we were gearing up for a massive New Year's Eve party in the *Star Wars* bar. Prior to this the French in the Residency had kindly thrown a Beaujolais evening on the 30th at which we did our best to polish off every bottle. That done, Geordie and I repaired to the bar and were tucking into cans of beer. The place was packed, smoky, jostling with Residency staff making the most of the seasonal bar extension.

Weird and unpredictable as I always knew the job to be, what happened next came out of nowhere and smacked us straight in the chops. It was close to midnight. Geordie and I were well away. We had an inkling something was up when we spied Baggers pushing through the crowd, looking a bit hassled. 'Mike! The General wants you in the office now!!' I just looked at Geordie; he smirked and promised to look after my beer.

Operation 'Bluetit 2'

30 December 1994 – BH Command, Sarajevo

'Mike! Ring Karadzic now. We have to talk to him about the COHA. There have been some changes and it's their last chance to sign.' Rose was standing in the middle of the office, eyes blazing, surrounded by his negotiators. Also skulking about was John Menzies, the number two in the US Embassy next door. A man whose only vice was Diet Coke, Menzies was something of a fanatic State Department apostle and an advocate of the wider bombing of the Serbs. I wondered what he was doing there and why we were telephoning Karadzic at midnight. My head was thumping from all the Beaujolais.

The INMARSAT phone failed to perform. The signal couldn't hit the satellite and make a connection. Too bad. It happened regularly enough, but that wasn't good enough for the General. 'Well, you're just going to have to go next door with John Menzies and try their phone. And if that doesn't work, you'll have to get up there and find them.' *Tonight! At midnight! To find Karadzic!*

As Menzies and I tore down the wooden stairs I shot off to the bar and grabbed Geordie who was tucking into another beer.

'Geordie. Get the TACSAT sorted, kit and vehicle. I think we're off up there now. Going to try the INMARSAT in the Yank embassy and if that doesn't work we're off . . . okay?'

He gave me one of those looks and said, 'Right . . . but what's it all about?'

'Dunno. Something to do with the agreement . . . Jimmy Carter. Anyway, it's a Bluetit. Tonight!' I scuttled off leaving Geordie looking black, his beer frozen half way to his lips.

I was surprised at what I found in the US Embassy, which was precisely nothing, except a few camp beds and a telephone. It may have had a flag fluttering above it, but to all intents and purposes it was a shell within. Worse still, their phone wasn't hitting the spot either. The slide into New Year's Eve festivities had taken a dramatic U-turn and this was becoming something of a nightmare. It was obvious that the General wanted us to hit the road tonight, but how we were going to bluff our way through all the BiH and then Serb checkpoints, unannounced and at night, was a concern.

Typically, Geordie had everything sorted. The ancient, canvas-topped Land Rover was rattling away. As I grabbed my daysack from the office Rose hurled a few more cryptic instructions at me: 'We'll CAPSAT you instructions in the morning.'

In the hope of shortening the journey by half an hour we tried to cross the Bridge of Brotherhood and Unity but the BiH guards refused to let us cross as we were in violation of the curfew and had no clearance. We were therefore forced to go the long way round via Stup, Sierra 4, the French at the airport, the Serbs again at Gornji Kotorac, at any one of which we could have been turned back. At Stup we crashed the checkpoint and left an enraged Muslim soldier waving, but not firing, his rifle at us. At Sierra 4 the Serbs were asleep. The French graciously allowed us to transit across 'their' airport. We were out and running, climbing the narrow road past Lukavica and Grbavica and on up Mount Trebevic's ice- and snow-bound road. Fortunately, our tyres dropped neatly into a track of deep but icy grooves. Given that all ruts eventually led to Pale, Geordie didn't really have to drive so much as control a wildly bucking steering wheel. It was a hellish journey. We barely spoke, both nursing those hideous headaches that come with sobering up too quickly. General Rose had dispatched us on a mission from hell. Just getting to Pale in one piece would be an accomplishment in itself.

An hour and a half later we thankfully rattled to a stop outside the UNMOs' house in Pale. It was past two in the morning. Much to our surprise Luc Willems, captain of the Belgian sleeping team, had stayed up to greet us. It concerned me slightly that they had prior knowledge of our arrival. Someone in BHC must have radioed them, which meant the whole world knew we were up there, but it didn't matter that much as John Menzies was bound to to have told his mates in the Bosnian Presidency anyway.

'Back again? How long for this time?'

'Don't know, Luc. Find out tomorrow.' We were past caring.

Luc and Rob had prepared two beds for us in the attic. We collapsed into them and were out in an instant.

Saturday 31 December 1994 – Pale

At eight-thirty, Luc burst into my room and thrust almost three feet of CAP-SAT fax paper in my face. 'General Rose wants to speak to you on the other means,' he added breathlessly, having rushed up four flights from the garage.

'What, no coffee, Luc?' But he'd gone.

I woke Geordie who busied himself setting up the TACSAT while I blearily tried to make sense of the fax. It was the latest draft version of the Cessation of Hostilities Agreement. They'd obviously been working on it during the night in Sarajevo. It contained eleven paragraphs obligating both parties to various conditions, and the UN to fulfilling certain tasks. To me it was just an agreement couched in legal jargon. At the bottom of the fax were some instructions from Rose to me:

- Para 9: No change as 'processes' refers to what is at start of para i.e.:- early release and cross-checking of all available info etc.
- Para 10: This is better, i.e. no mention of 'borders' or BiH.
- Para 7: Still discussing at 0930 hrs. Stand by . . . Akashi en route.

Pure mumbo-jumbo. At that time in the morning it meant nothing to me. Geordie had established comms with Sarajevo and slung me the handset, 'General's on the line for you.'

The nice thing about General Rose was that he didn't indulge in time-wasting pleasantries. His voice barked out of the handset.

'Mike! Are you there?'

'Yessir.'

'Have you got the CAPSAT and the instructions?'

'Yessir.'

'Right. Get hold of Karadzic. Show him the agreement, but not the notes. Explain them if necessary. Get an answer from him. Stand by for another amendment. That's it. Speak to you soon. Out.'

I looked at Geordie. He'd heard it all. 'Geordie, it's eight-thirty in the morning on New Year's Eve. No prizes for guessing where Karadzic is at present.'

'In bed?' he laughed. Geordie had the measure of the place. The Pale lot, as we'd discovered in November, had a peculiar habit of working until the small hours and then not emerging until eleven or twelve the next day. The chances of raising anyone, let alone Karadzic, at this time in the morning would be difficult if not impossible. And Rose was itching for an answer . . . NOW. This was going to be difficult. I left Geordie to man the radio and made my way down to the UNMOs' garage to use the phone. Up at the annex presidency, Karadzic's secretary, Milijana, answered the phone.

'Could I speak to Dr Karadzic please, Milijana?'

'No!'

'Why not?'

'Because he's not here.'

'He's in bed at home, isn't he? When's he due in to work?'

'Oh, usual time I suppose.'

At least it meant that he was still in Pale and hadn't flitted off to Banja Luka or somewhere. Milijana promised to phone me back just as soon as he arrived at work. Rose wouldn't be happy about this. An hour went by and Milijana had still not phoned. This was just as well as a second CAPSAT came through from Sarajevo with a much changed COHA text and some very explicit instructions from the General:

Notes by General Rose, not part of text (for Stanley eyes only until authority given for wider exposure).

1. BiH still insist on insertion of 'starting with Sarajevo' early in text of para 7. However they are willing to insert new para 7 (see text) which encapsulates all elements required by Pale, in return for giving up para 12 from BiH earlier drafts which made reference to the Contact Group Plan.

2. Strongly urge Dr Karadzic to accept this compromise which makes implied reference to the process of demilitarisation and Safe Areas through mention of relevant Security Council Resolutions.

3. Emphasise that none of this concerns matters of substance, only wordsmithing exclam. This is as good as they're going to get. ENDALL.

More gibberish. Within moments Rose was on the TACSAT. 'Have you got the latest draft?'

'Yes, General.'

'Have you got hold of Karadzic yet?'

'No sir, he's not come to work yet. In fact, I'm sure he's still in bed . . . you know what they're like up here.'

'Well, you've got to get him up!' the General barked. 'There's no time to waste. Keep trying. Speak to you soon. Out.'

'Fucking hell, Geordie!' I slung down the handset. The pressure was mounting. We'd get nothing achieved by hanging around waiting for Dr Karadzic to come into work and then hope that Milijana would remember to call us.

'Right. Let's get up there and start applying a little pressure of our own.'

Geordie quickly dismantled the TACSAT and we hoofed it with our kit into the Land Rover. With a wave from me and a 'don't sleep too much now Luc!' from Geordie we shot off up the road to the Serbs' Presidency. The first obstacle was the sentry.

'Of course we've got permission. Karadzic knows all about it. He's well aware of the meeting!' Lies always worked a treat in the Balkans, especially brazen, barefaced ones. The better and bigger the lie the more they respected you. It got us through. We parked up outside the annex building. I sprinted through driving icy rain while Geordie set up the TACSAT on the bonnet of the vehicle. The Land Rover's cab leaked like mad and within moments a very unhappy Geordie was slumped in the front seat, ice-cold water dripping down his neck, waiting for the next blast from Rose.

Milijana was at her desk. Apart from her and the duty policeman the place was deserted. I waved the fax in her face.

'This, Milijana, is the draft of the COHA. Karadzic has got to see it now. It might just mean the end to the war.' I was trying to be as dramatic as possible. They responded well to dramatics as well as to lies.

'I'll make a phone call.' She waved me from her office. A minute later I was summoned back. 'You're to give the draft to one of the bodyguards who will deliver it to the President.'

'Look, Milijana. I've been given specific instructions to present the document myself and to explain some of the points in it. It's me and the draft together.'

Again, I was banished from the office while she rang Karadzic. I popped outside to see how Geordie was getting on. He looked flustered.

'It's Rose! I can't keep stalling him. He wants to know Karadzic's answer!'

'Karadzic's fucking answer! Geordie, the man's still in bed! There is no answer. Keep stalling Rose. Tell him we're doing our best!' I escaped back into the building leaving Geordie to fend off the impatient general.

Milijana's reply from Karadzic didn't improve matters either. 'Karadzic says you can go to his house with the draft. Of course, you'll have to be blindfolded and driven there by one of the bodyguards.'

'Blindfolded, Milijana! Blindfolded! Is that what you just said? Blindfolded?' I burst out laughing. 'This is a joke, isn't it?'

'No. It's not. Those were his instructions . . . it's a secret where he lives.' She was deadly serious.

'Milijana! I'm a member of the United Nations. I'm General Rose's liaison officer. We're not the enemy for God's sake! You can't go around blindfolding members of the UN. It's absurd! I refuse!'

'Well, you either get blindfolded or you wait!' she snapped back.

'I'll bloody wait then!' I hissed back and stalked out of her office in a huff. Either way this was a disaster. A feeling of failure swept over me as I headed for the exit and the icy rain.

Then Fate intervened: before I could get out of the building my exit was blocked by the hulking frame of General Mladic. Trotting behind him was his interpreter, Major Kralj, with whom I'd crossed swords in Banja Luka during General Clark's visit and the hat-swapping affair. Mladic fixed me with an amused stare.

'Stanley!' he bellowed, 'what are you doing here? Spying again, eh? We know all about you!' He winked at Kralj.

'That's right, General. A spy's work is never done. Not even on New Year's Eve.' Mladic smirked at this, a good sign, '. . . seriously though, General Rose has sent me up here with the latest draft of the COHA for you and Karadzic to sign.' I waved the flimsy in his face.

'Right. We'd better have a look at it then.' Suddenly, he'd become quite serious. We disappeared into the conference room where Kralj and I translated it for him. When we'd finished, Mladic bellowed, 'The Muslims and UNPRO-FOR are trying to trick us. Where's the President?'

I gave Mladic a sly look. 'He's still in bed, General. You know what these civilians are like . . . can't get up in the morning. I've been trying all morning to get him up, but he just won't!'

Mladic flew into a rage. 'Won't he! Toso!' he called out to General Tolimir who was lurking outside, 'Toso! Get the President up here . . . and the rest of them. This is important. We're being tricked!'

I suspected that Mladic, who'd spent almost the whole of the previous day's meeting squeezing his boil, really didn't know whether he was being tricked or not, but clearly he wasn't about to make any decisions until one of the politicians emerged from hibernation. Geordie must have seen Mladic and gang arriving. He appeared at the door.

'Quick, Geordie. Get on to Rose and tell him we've got Mladic here. Tell him he's seen the draft and we're expecting Karadzic here any minute. That should keep Sarajevo off our backs . . . and then get that TACSAT set up in here.'

Within minutes Geordie was back, arms full of satellite radio which he plonked on the table. As we assembled it, opening up the antenna which we dropped out of the window into the snow, and connecting its coax lead to the set, Mladic's eyes virtually popped out of his head.

'You can stop that right now! What is this?' He prodded the radio on the table.

'It's a satellite radio. So that you can talk direct to General Rose in Sarajevo.'

He wasn't impressed though. 'You can stop that this instant . . .' adding with a laugh, '. . . we might just have to take it off you.'

'Oh yes, General. There's no need for that. You've already got one of these. Your soldiers in Rogatica stole one off a convoy three months ago!'

'Even better!' he laughed. 'Then we'll have two. One can talk to the other. There's no point having just one radio now is there?' he finished, deadpan, before turning and winking again at Major Kralj.

We were saved by a commotion in the lobby as Karadzic swept in, dragging with him the entire political and military hierarchy of Republika Srpska. They were all there: the two vice presidents, Professor Nikola Koljevic and Biljana Plavsic, Aleksa Buha, the Foreign Minister, Jovan Zametica, glasses glinting, and in addition to Mladic and Tolimir there was a third general, Subotic. And then, of course, there was us – hurled up to Pale in the dead of night by Rose and blundering into this improbable cabal. Within moments we were all in Karadzic's office poring over the draft. Geordie and Major Kralj were left in the conference room. Geordie made good use of this opportunity and had finished setting up the radio by the time I was ejected from Dr Karadzic's office as they went into 'closed session'.

'The General's on the line for you, Mike.' He handed me the handset, thankful to get rid of it.

Rose was still barking and snapping, 'Mike! What's going on up there?'

'General, hang on a second. I've got Dr Karadzic here. He wants to speak to you. Wait one.'

I rushed out of the conference room and past a protesting Milijana, who was wittering on about me not being able to go into Karadzic's office, and burst in on the 'closed session'.

'Dr Karadzic. General Rose is on the line and wants to speak to you!'

They leapt to their feet and trooped after the doctor into the conference room. Geordie was waiting to give Karadzic a quick lesson in voice procedure.

'Right, sir.' He handed the set to Dr Karadzic who had sat down behind the radio. Everyone else crowded in around him, eager to hear what was being said. '. . . just press the bar on the handset, listen for the two bleeps and then speak. When you've finished say *"over"*.'

'Over?' Dr Karadzic was baffled.

'Yes. *Over.*'

Karadzic pressed the bar. The mob held its breath. The two bleeps could be heard as the signal hit the satellite. 'Hello, hello . . . General Rose? Can you hear me?'

'Say *'over'*.' hissed Geordie.

'What?'

'*Over*, remember? Say *"over"*!'

'Over,' said Karadzic unconvincingly.

'Now, release the pressle switch.' Geordie was losing his patience.

'The what?'

'The button, sir. The bar!'

Karadzic did as he was told. The handset crackled for a few seconds. Then two bleeps and Rose's voice boomed through.

'Doctor Karadzic, I can hear you perfectly. Have you studied the agreement?'

'Yes, General Rose we . . . ,' began Karadzic.

Geordie cut him short. 'Sir, you've got to press the bar, remember? Then pause, then speak . . . and remember *"over"* . . .'

Karadzic pressed, paused, and then spoke. 'Yes, General Rose, we have. We're not happy. In paragraph four you say . . .'

And that's how it all began. It was approximately eleven in the morning and just the beginning of a very long, tiring and, at times, frustrating day. The list of complaints and desired changes from the Serbs seemed endless. It appeared that our efforts to get up there were doomed to failure. Naïvely, I assumed that, having overcome the Herculean task of rounding up the Pale cabal, it would be a simple matter of Karadzic rubber-stamping the agreement and we could all go home. Not so.

Satisfied that they'd demanded as much as they thought they could squeeze from this agreement, Karadzic and mob retired again into 'closed session'. The conference room emptied leaving Geordie and me to the tender mercies of our 'minder', the enigmatic Major Kralj, who proceeded to practise his dreadfully broken English on us. General Rose also left us with a terse message – put as much pressure on Karadzic as possible, because he wouldn't get a better deal than this one.

Kralj was short and balding with black, slitty, unblinking eyes set deep into a puffy, dead-pan, Mongolian face. He seldom smiled. He had two irritating habits. First, he asked endless questions about England and the British Army. Second was an alarming habit of picking and scratching at a clutch of revolting open sores on his scalp. The combination of tortured English and ceaseless scratching drove us mad. I felt sure that Mladic had inflicted Kralj on us as a sick joke. His companionship belied his real task which was to keep his eyes and ears open.

Back in Sarajevo, Rose marshalled his negotiators and sent them off to the Bosnian Presidency to get on with the negotiations, based on any new responses from the Serbs. Somewhere between their two positions lay common ground and it was towards this that we were attempting to drag both sides. We could only wait, which left signallers Rose, Stanley and Geordie 'stagging on' on the radios. Unbelievably, this cycle would repeat itself some eleven times before the day was up.

Within an hour the handset crackled into life with a demand from Rose to speak to Karadzic. Duly I scuttled into Dr Karadzic's office interrupting their 'closed session' and returned Pied Piper-like with the mob in tow. Steeled for round two, they immediately huddled around the handset. As the General read out the latest amended text it became clear that some progress had been made. At least we were taking two steps forward and only one back. Periodically, they'd cut Rose short to translate for the non-English speakers. A brief discussion would ensue before Karadzic got back to Rose: 'Yes. We'll accept that. But, on the other point the Muslims are trying to trick us and we'll never accept it!' That was one step forward and two back.

Sometimes the proceedings went into complete free-fall: 'No! Never! There is no agreement!' and they'd all stalk back into Dr Karadzic's office leaving Geordie and me handling a red-hot handset. On these occasions it fell to me to go into Karadzic's office and bat on the General's behalf. Sometimes I was successful but more often than not I wasn't and was howled out of the wolves' lair. It all depended on how much mileage they were trying to screw out of a certain point. This was brinkmanship, three-dimensional Balkan chess, with high stakes; all three sides, UN included, trying to outmanoeuvre each other. Only Rose and his negotiators knew both sides' stratagems.

Sometimes Rose specifically did not want to speak to Karadzic. 'Right. Mike. This is the Bosnian government's line in the sand. But don't tell Karadzic that. Tell him this instead. Explain it like this, but don't mention that. See if they'll go this way.' I often feared that I'd get it all mixed up.

Mostly, though, there were great periods of boredom, of drinking sweet coffee and juice while the Sarajevo team haggled with the Bosnian government. For hours we'd be marooned on our desert island with our tormentor, Major Kralj.

'Vy whole vorld hate Serbs? Ve allies in two vors. Ve are Christians fighting to protect Europe from the Turks.' Inevitably, a painful history lesson would follow commencing with the battle of Kosovo and ending with today. Six hundred and five years of broken English!

Outside it was getting dark and snowing heavily. Progress had been made on a number of paragraphs. The room was packed again. Karadzic was arguing with Rose about paragraph 7. Six down, five to go. With only five rounds more, this looked encouraging. Suddenly, it all came to a grinding halt: 'No! Never, General Rose! We can't accept that. Please wait while I consult with my colleagues. Out.'

'Actually, it's *"wait out"*,' muttered Geordie, but no one took any notice because they were too busy debating the issue. They'd forgotten to repair to Karadzic's office and seemed content to conduct their business in front of us. The offending paragraph stated simply:

The parties commit themselves immediately to enhance the security of all Safe Areas, consistent with all Security Council Resolutions.

They weren't so much rejecting as debating the interpretation of the words 'consistent with all relevant Security Council Resolutions'. General Tolimir's camp was arguing that, since at least one UNSCR recognised Bosnia-Hercegovina as a sovereign state, to sign up to that paragraph would be tantamount to throwing away any constitutional settlement for Republika

Srpska. Karadzic was inclined to agree, but was open to persuasion by the other camp which was just not sure what it meant. I chimed in and said that it referred to UNSCRs which were relevant only to the question of the Safe Areas. Tolimir stuffed his officer's hat on his head, for extra effect presumably, and whipped himself up into a real froth. 'It's a trick. I won't allow it!' As the Intelligence Chief and self-styled legal guru of the cabal he felt he had every right to put his foot down. I kept my mouth shut. There was no point in crossing swords with Tolimir.

In an instant the spark had become a raging fire. A debate had become an open slanging match. Tolimir shouted down anyone who tried to say something. Koljevic managed a 'maybe Stanley is right' before Tolimir got to him. Biljana Plavsic was savaged the moment she opened her mouth. Karadzic, pale and drawn, slumped in his chair, was Tolimir's next victim. Throughout, Mladic said nothing. I took some photographs of this performance. Geordie, I noticed, was attempting to hide behind the radio. Although he didn't know what was being said he'd clearly got the gist of it. Saturation point was reached. Mladic fired a broadside at Tolimir.

'For God's sake, Toso! Shut up! Let others have their say!'

Tolimir fell silent for a moment. Plavsic sallied forth again, which was more than the furious Tolimir could bear. Promptly, he mauled her. Mladic was furious.

'Toso! Sit down! Shut up! Somebody go and get those wretched resolutions and we'll see what they say.' Aleksa Buha fled from the room. Mladic continued, 'This is ridiculous. We're arguing about something we know nothing about. None of us is even a lawyer. We should have hired ourselves proper lawyers.'

This wasn't the workings of a presidency. This was a circus, a playground squabble. And, they were all equals in it. Fascinating. A unique glimpse into the life and workings of the Presidency behind the scenes. For some reason they still hadn't twigged that we'd witnessed the whole thing.

It went on like this for hours.

Matters were made even worse when the TACSAT started to go on the blink; at a critical point in either Rose's or Karadzic's transmission the signal would cut out. We were frustrated. Rose was frustrated. Either we'd not get the bleeps, or the signal would die. 'Signal's slipping off the satellite,' Geordie would mutter.

'Sorry, General. The signal's slipping off the satellite. We'll have to work through it.' 'Working through it', we discovered, entailed Geordie leaning heavily on the radio as if applying direct pressure to a wound. This helped, though it meant Geordie maintaining this posture for some two hours. Months later, Geordie admitted that 'signals slipping off the satellite' had been pure invention to keep Rose at bay.

The original agreement had mutated into something quite different. Paragraph 7 changed completely – no mention of UNSCRs. Two paragraphs had somehow merged giving a total of ten. Given that the last one simply said, 'This agreement is to be without prejudice to the final political or territorial solution', a catch-all clause to allay any latent fears, we were left with paragraph 9 to resolve.

Again we found ourselves bogged down in devilish detail referring to a text relating to the withdrawal of foreign troops, less UNPROFOR, '. . . as demanded by relevant Security Council Resolutions and statements'. This set the Serbs off again. Having told Rose that the wording must be changed in such a way as to make it clear that the UNSCRs referred to UNPROFOR only, they disappeared in a huff for another 'closed session'.

General Rose didn't seem too confident that the Bosnians would buy that one. It was close to 5 p.m. For the next forty-five minutes or so Geordie and I sat in virtual silence. We were exhausted and wondering whether this psychological war of words and nerves would continue through the night. At a quarter to six the handset crackled into life.

'Mike. It's General Rose here. We've got the word change they wanted. It's over.' He sounded jubilant.

'Let me just get Karadzic. Wait out.'

I swept out of the room past Milijana and burst in on the 'closed session'. I expected to find them huddled over documents, drafts and maps, plotting and scheming their next move. I stopped short in amazement. They were all huddled all right, like witches over a cauldron, around Mladic and Karadzic who were locked into an altogether different sort of battle.

'Ha! Check mate in two,' roared Mladic.

When they looked up and saw me standing there with my thumbs up, their haste to get to the TACSAT was positively indecent. While Geordie applied 'first aid' to the set and with me sitting behind it, General Rose began dictating the last change of words, which I scribbled down on my pad. No sooner had I finished than Karadzic stiffened and snorted, 'That's no good. It's exactly the same.'

'What's the reaction, Mike?' I didn't know how to reply to Rose.

Cautiously, 'Well sir, they're not happy.'

'Why not?' he snapped back.

This was all too much. I thrust it at Karadzic. 'Here. It's your agreement. You explain it.'

'General Rose. This text is exactly the same as the last one. There's no change at all.'

We waited for the next two bleeps heralding Mike Rose's next blast. They never came. Silence. Almost a minute passed and then, 'I'm terribly sorry, Dr

Karadzic. I was reading from the last draft and not the latest one. Standby for text. Wait out.'

Geordie winced and we both imagined that a bare ten miles away a minor nuclear device called Mike Rose had reached critical mass and was detonating. With so many rewrites of the agreement floating about the JCO's office, some eleven in all, it was hardly surprising that this mistake had occurred. I was ready to copy again and glanced at my watch – 1800 hours local. Two bleeps and Rose was back.

'Mike, are you ready to copy?'

'Yessir.'

'UNPROFOR will perform this specific task on the basis of this agreement with the parties to the conflict and in accordance with its obligations towards the relevant Security Council Resolutions and statements. That's it. Read back. Over.'

I read the whole thing back to him. As I finished pandemonium broke out behind me. They were grinning, laughing and slapping each other on their backs. 'The war's over!' someone shouted. They really did believe it. The tension of the past seven hours evaporated. Even Major Kralj had a big smile on his face. Beers were produced and we began to relax. The Serbs departed the conference room. 'Come on, Mr President. Let me give you another thrashing!' Mladic bellowed.

Shortly after that we were informed by Sarajevo that we were to remain in place and await the arrival of the negotiators. General Rose, Mr Akashi and others would be coming to Pale for the signing ceremony just as soon as they'd stopped by the Bosnian Presidency to collect their signatures. The rush was to get it done by midnight as there remained only six hours of 1994. Their estimated time of arrival in Pale was half-eight which meant another two and a half hours of hanging around.

The sport of thrashing Karadzic at chess had clearly waned for Mladic. He wandered into the room looking bored and flung himself into a chair next to Geordie. For ten or twenty minutes he regaled us with sporting achievements from his days as a young army officer – best at everything, surprise, surprise. His braggadocio had a particular, almost child-like charm, as though seeking approval in some way. Eventually even that topic dried up. There was a long, pregnant pause.

'The British,' he announced, 'have done very well out here. They are the most professional by a long way. Why is that?' He seemed genuinely interested. I quickly translated for Geordie's benefit. He paused before replying and relegated Kralj and me to the role of interpreters.

'No conscripts. We're a professional army. Soldiers and officers join voluntarily on differing tour lengths and we've been doing this since the early 1960s.'

Swiftly Geordie summarised the differences between a professional volunteer army and the conscripted models in Europe and elsewhere. All this was new to Mladic. He grown up in an army based on mass conscription where his sole contact with other armies had been those of the Warsaw Pact. And so began a frank exchange of views which had nothing to do with the Balkans or its problems. He was fascinated to discover that a private soldier might lead a four-man patrol in Northern Ireland. Unlike the JNA, the British Army had an almost unbroken record of operational service since the end of the Second World War. As we talked his questions became more penetrating: what of the role of priests? What of ethnic minorities? Career structures and pensions. Housing and quartering. I couldn't help feeling that he was looking for a blueprint for a new model army once hostilities had ended and a political solution was in place. It was fascinating to hear the man talking not of the petty wranglings of the war and its blathering rhetoric and propaganda. The hours flew by.

Half-eight was upon us. The signing ceremony, we were told, would take place in the huge conference room in the Hotel Panorama. We packed up our TACSAT and drifted over to the hotel, crunching our way through thick, crisp snow. The night was freezing.

The conference room was a hive of activity. At one end bodyguards, pressmen, cameras on tripods all vied with each other for space. Karadzic and gang and other baggage such as his wife and daughter Sonja and others from the government were grouped at the other end. The atmosphere buzzed as we waited for Mr Akashi and General Rose to arrive.

In the hallway there was commotion. One of the BGs rushed in and announced, 'They're here.' Moments later Akashi and Rose strode in followed by Goose, Matt Hodes, Colm Murphy, Gary Coward, Jamie Daniell (obviously just back off leave), David, L-P's replacement, and a number of others who'd hitched a ride to Pale to witness the signing.

Geordie and I no longer had a role to play in the proceedings and in deference to the Big Boys we stood off to one side. Those signing the agreement were seated from left to right at the end of the table: Tolimir, Mladic, Karadzic, Akashi, Rose while the rest pressed in behind them. There were no speeches. The signing seemed to begin of its own accord. Copies of the agreements slid from one signatory to another while cameras flashed and whirred. Hands were shaken and it was over. As quickly as they'd entered the principals departed, easing past the baying press to a private reception room where drinks and snacks were served. Geordie and I joined them there.

The party broke up into small groups. Akashi with Karadzic. The military with the military. Dragan, the mad, drunk photographer who'd been with us for most of the day's traumas, careered around the room helping himself to whisky as he clicked away furiously. At one stage he was so overcome by the whole thing that he burst into tears and hugged Mladic, who roared with laughter.

The reception lasted no more than an hour. Before we knew it the Rose/ Akashi ensemble had disappeared into the freezing mountain air, a trace of red brake lights racing off into the darkness back to Sarajevo. The Serbs too beat a hasty retreat leaving Geordie, David and me to finish off a bottle of wine with Professor Koljevic. By a quarter to eleven we realised that if we didn't get going we'd miss the party in Sarajevo. We retreated back down to the annex, grabbed our gear and climbed into the Land Rover.

We'd cut it fine and probably weren't going to make it back in time. Geordie did his best to keep the vehicle bouncing along in the ruts. Nothing else seemed to matter other than getting back to the Residency before midnight. As we approached the Jahorina junction to turn right along the Trebevic road, our headlights picked up a lone figure: it was Peggy, Koljevic's BG. He was waving his arms frantically, indicating that we should follow him up the hill to Jahorina. Clearly they wanted us to see the New Year in with them. But that wasn't part of the plan and there was only one place to be – back with our own people in Sarajevo.

At twenty minutes to midnight we'd only reached Grbavica. Realising we would not make it if we went via the airport, we took the plunge and dropped down through Grbavica to the Bridge of Brotherhood and Unity. The Serbs waved us across and didn't even bother to stop us. Too drunk already. At the other end we were stopped by a Muslim guard.

'We're part of the Rose/Akashi team that passed earlier.'

'No problems,' he replied with a smile and added, 'so, you were up there, eh?'

'We were.'

'Well? Is it peace then?' There was an earnest catch in his voice.

I thought back to the Serbs' reaction to the final transmission from Rose. 'Yes. Yes, I really do believe it is.' I wasn't totally convinced though. We wished him a happy New Year and drove on. Five minutes later we were back at the Residency, a few minutes before midnight.

Geordie dropped off the TACSAT in his office and together we raced up the steps to the Outer Office where we met General Rose and his team on the way out. Someone said there was champagne downstairs.

At the bottom of the internal stairs leading to the foyer the entire population of the Residency, familiar faces, was heaving and swaying and hoofing down champagne. With a minute to go we grabbed a glass. As a hush descended, all heads turned to the top of the stairs where General Rose stood alone. He was never one for long, boring speeches.

'I'd just like to thank each and every one of you for your hard work today and throughout the year and to wish you a happy New Year. I hope that 1995 will bring peace to the people of Bosnia–Hercegovina . . .'

No sooner had he uttered the last syllable than the silence of the night was ripped by a shockingly loud, long burst of automatic fire very close to the Residency. We all looked at each other, amused by the irony of the moment, and roared with laughter. The divided city rocked with gunfire heralding the New Year. With that the party got going. The champagne was soon consumed and we were forced to retire to the place where it had all started twenty-four hours earlier – to the *Star Wars* bar.

And that is how we did that.

TWENTY-FOUR

Operation Bretton

December 1997 – Ian, UK

'That Bluetit 2 had been a good hit; had telescoped days if not weeks of shuttling backwards and forwards between the Serbs and Muslims into a matter of hours. By using secure comms and denying each side the ability to intercept insecure telephone conversations, thereby stealing a march on the opposition and developing a counter-tactic, we were able to tighten our decision-making loop relative to theirs. The result was signatures. But none of that did me any good at all.

'Within days of the COHA signing the Muslim propaganda machine swung into action. There was more "Stanley's a Chetnik Spy in UNPROFOR" stuff in *Liljan*. They even produced a doctored photograph of Rose kissing Karadzic. I don't mean pecks on the cheek: I'm talking of a full Hollywood kiss. Cheap. Bluetit 2 had screwed them into signing the COHA which if nothing else gave them a four-month break from fighting, but they didn't like it one bit. They were furious. More dirt appeared in *The New York Times* and the *International Herald Tribune* along the lines of Roger Cohen's original article. When I showed it to Rose he snapped back at me, "This is actionable. You should sue 'em!" So, that was our reward for producing a cessation of hostilities – more filth and propaganda from the Americans and the Bosnians.'

Rose only had three weeks to go before his tour was up. He was leaving on Monday 25 January 1995, after exactly a year in theatre. If you think that it was three weeks of sitting on our post-COHA laurels you'd be quite wrong. There was plenty of tidying up to be done. Signatures are one thing, but actions quite another.

On the morning of 1 January, nursing hideous hangovers, we drove to the airport for the first of many meetings between the UN, Serbs, Muslims and Croats. As we arrived Rose spied Major Indjic and gave him a filthy look. He was still angry about Indjic's petulant reaction to Schindler's List being suspended. Indjic looked sheepish and slunk off into the background.

The purpose of the meeting was to work out the mechanics of making the agreement work. To that end a Central Joint Commission comprising all four parties was created at the airport. Mirroring this, two Regional Joint Commissions (RJCs) were established at HQs Sector North-East and South-West. The COHA made provision for Serb liaison officers to be established under UN protection at Gornji Vakuf and Tuzla. Equally, UN liaison officers were to be based at Banja Luka and Foca on Serb-held territory.

In principle all this was fine. In practice it was hugely problematic. The Muslims simply did not want, nor would tolerate, the presence of Serb officers on their territory. If that wasn't bad enough, the Serbs refused to nominate LOs for central Bosnia unless the Muslims removed themselves from the Igman/Bijelasnica DMZ. More devilish Balkan linkage. Before the COHA had even begun to work it was in danger of grinding to a halt.

Putting this straight took Rose and Victor Andreyev hours of effort at the airport Central Joint Commission meetings. The first of the RJCs' meetings at GV and Tuzla was fast approaching and the Serbs still hadn't provided their representatives. The day before these took place, Rose and the MA shot off down to Mostar to get the Croats' signatures on the COHA. I was left in Sarajevo to apply pressure on the Serbs to provide LOs for the next day's meetings in Central Bosnia. They were refusing point-blank to co-operate. Rose was in constant touch with BHC by radio and, as the afternoon wore on, was becoming increasingly impatient with the Serbs.

In desperation that evening I rang Karadzic direct and informed him that the Serbs' failure, i.e. Mladic and Indjic's refusal, to nominate and provide LOs for the next day would signal the failure of the COHA and that the world would blame the Serbs. That did the trick. By eleven they'd rung back: their representative would be waiting at Lukavica barracks at seven-thirty the next morning ready to be picked up by us, taken to the airport and flown to GV by helicopter. They wouldn't tell us the name of the representative but we assumed it would be someone senior like Tolimir.

The original plan was to fly by helicopter from the airport to GV, to attend the meeting there between the UN, HVO and BiH, and then to fly up to Tuzla to do likewise before returning to Sarajevo. While discussing the details of this with Indjic on the phone he insisted that we fly rather than travel by road just in case the Muslims ambushed the vehicles and tried to kill the Serb LO. We agreed to go by road only as a last resort.

The next morning, because helicopters couldn't get into Sarajevo, we drove over to Lukavica to pick up the LO. Indjic was waiting for us outside his office. I asked him where General Tolimir was. Something was troubling Indjic. He looked deflated and lacking his usual bluff and bluster. He was oddly dressed too, wearing a satchel over his shoulder. 'All right, then, who's the LO?' Indjic gave me a rather pathetic, little-boy-lost look and said in a timorous, self-pitying voice, 'It's me.'

Rose had been hoping for Tolimir and had planned to allow him to travel in the Range Rover. When he discovered it was Indjic he snapped, 'I'm not having that little Commie blackmailer in my vehicle. He can go with you, Stanley, in the backing vehicle!' He refused even to acknowledge Indjic. We bundled him into the HMMWV and gave him a British Arctic windproof smock to slip over his uniform. He became agitated. 'Aren't we flying?' His hackles were up. 'No. We're driving to GV. Helicopters couldn't get in. Bad weather.' Indjic went pale and started babbling that it wasn't a good idea. Too late. We were already moving. For the first time ever his life was in our hands; he was totally dependent on us. He bundled himself up as best he could in the smock but he couldn't cover his legs which were clad in Serb camouflage, and started quietly fretting about the first Muslim checkpoint.

After months of being messed around by Indjic, it was a real pleasure to turn the tables on him. As we approached the first BiH checkpoint after Hadzici he started flapping and sweating, convinced that he'd be hoiked out and shot by the side of the road. As it happened we sailed through into Central Bosnia. As we drove through Konjic, Jablanica and Prozor he became almost wistful, recalling that he'd frequently driven this route before the war. The ground was blanketed in snow so there wasn't much to see. We climbed the S-bends up to Tito's war memorial above Prozor. We were on the road leading directly to GV some three miles away and had just passed an HVO checkpoint, when disaster struck. Rose's Range hit ice and careered off the road, slithered down a steep bank and came to rest on its side. It looked serious enough to have killed Rose, Goose and the MA. In an instant Mungo Brookes, the EUCOM communicator driving the Hummer, brought us to a standstill and we were out racing down the bank to the stricken Range.

It was on its side, and the armoured doors were incredibly heavy and almost impossible to pull open against gravity. The greatest risk was fire. Mungo managed to heave open one door. Both Rose and Goose were unhurt, but the MA had dislocated his shoulder. Getting him out was a struggle. Rose was completely unflustered and more interested in his beret, which we also had to rescue. He really had not an ounce of sympathy in him. Back at the Residency that evening he still was laughing like mad about it all and quipped to the MA, 'You're the only one to get hurt in that vehicle. That's because you're a "hat"!' The MA had no Airborne or Special Forces background and therefore qualified for the unkind accolade of being a 'hat' . . . a mere 'craphat'.

In all of this I'd forgotten Indjic. Glancing back at the Hummer, it became clear why he hadn't leapt out to help. Three HVO military policemen were standing by the vehicle watching our caperings. Beyond them, through the open door, I spied a very frightened Indjic, eyes as wide as saucers, desperately trying to cover up his legs and praying that the HVO blokes wouldn't see him, a Serb stowaway, hiding unprotected in the vehicle. 'You could have killed me!' he moaned as we roared off to GV with Rose and Goose. The

MA was left nursing his shoulder by the overturned Range, awaiting rescue by the British in GV. Rose didn't care. We had a meeting to get to.

Stripped of his Arctic smock, Major Indjic made his appearance at a packed RJC meeting headed up by Brigadier Gordon. The Croats and Muslims were dumbfounded at Indjic's appearance and watched him suspiciously throughout the meeting. 'They know I'm here now,' he whimpered after the meeting, convinced by now that his last day on earth would be spent with Rose's mad gang, culminating in his capture and death in Central Bosnia.

845 NAS managed to lay on a Sea King for the hop to Tuzla. The weather was marginal, the cloud base low and it was beginning to snow. Nevertheless, they reckoned that by flying low through the valleys they'd be able to get us over the mountains and into Tuzla. Indjic's relief at climbing into the helicopter and buckling up in a seat next to Rose didn't last long. The helicopter flew low, below the tree line. The crewman in the back had the door open and was checking the rotor clearance to the trees.

I was sitting opposite Rose. Suddenly, he looked at me, cocked a thumb at Indjic and made a sign to unbuckle the seatbelt. What he meant was for me to unbuckle Indjic and get him to stand behind the aircraft commander, standard practice for visitors. That's not what went through Indjic's mind. When I indicated to him to unbuckle he held onto the clasp until his knuckles went white and, wild-eyed and terrified, shook his head vigorously. As far as he was concerned Rose had decided to toss him out of the helicopter at 100 feet over Central Bosnia, revenge at last for Indjic's behaviour over Schindler's List.

His personal dramas didn't end there either. After the meeting at Tuzla the Sea King tried for an hour to fly up various valleys but the snow was so bad that we had to abort back to Tuzla. Indjic was terrified and by now quite tired. As darkness fell the weather deteriorated. There was nothing for it but to commandeer two vehicles and drive back south in that appalling weather and along unknown routes. For the first half hour we had Indjic in the front vehicle. After an hour of churning through snow we reached the first Muslim checkpoint which took some smart talking to get through.

Once through, Rose stopped the convoy. The gravity of Indjic's situation (word was out that he was on the loose somewhere in Central Bosnia) had finally dawned on him. He held a mini-O Group in the snow: 'Right. You and David are armed. You're now personally responsible for Major Indjic's life. The three of you, into the backing vehicle. He's not to be captured at any cost.' Indjic nearly fainted on the spot when Rose said this. Whether the General was role-playing or whether he was genuinely concerned I'll never know.

Solemnly David and I drew our pistols. Poor Major Indjic nearly wet himself. 'Let's have some fun here!' David whispered to me as we bundled

Indjic into the back of the following vehicle. We sat on either side of him, pistols still drawn. 'Don't worry, Major Indjic. We'll fight to the last bullet!' This only agitated him even more. We proceeded into the darkness. As each checkpoint loomed, Indjic would start sweating and shaking. 'Major Indjic! Your moustache! It's very Serbian. Cover it up as we pass through the checkpoint!' hissed David theatrically. Astonishingly, Indjic obeyed and we cruised through with him covering his mouth with his hand.

Occasionally we'd pass through a small town and under the glare of a rare street lamp we'd hiss, 'Christ! Major Indjic! Your knees can be seen!' Indjic's hands would fly to his knees to cover up the Serbian camouflage. 'No. For God's sake! Your moustache!' A hand would fly back up to his mouth. 'Now your knees aren't covered. They'll see you.' After four hours of David's cruel hissing and Indjic's flying hands, the poor man was a wreck. Once through Kiseljak we knew the danger was over but we didn't tell Indjic. He only began to calm down after we passed through Sierra 1. By the time we dropped him at Lukavica he'd all but recovered his composure and leapt out with a triumphant snarl, 'Now! I make my intelligence report to General Tolimir!' Pathetic really, but I'm sure he did too, with lots of self-glorifying embellishment and no mention of his frantic hands. Rose's revenge. I'll never forget that day.

Indjic wasn't the only one trying to avoid certain death. I'd managed to survive almost exactly seven months, despite being dragged from one near-disaster to another by Mike Rose. With only a couple of weeks of his tour left, my instincts for survival and self-preservation were heightened almost to fever pitch. Worryingly, Rose kept talking about skiing. He was determined to finish his tour with a final fling down the Bijelasnica men's Olympic downhill run. I was equally determined not to be part of such a caper. The more this was mentioned, the darker Goose's mood became.

When Goose gloomily told me all this I laughed but made a mental note, come the day, to be on vital business up in Pale. Within weeks of arriving in theatre the Boss had visited every UN contingent under his command. At the time the Swedes manned an outpost right at the top of Mount Bijelasnica which, coincidentally, was also the start of the downhill run. One look at the precipitous, un-pisted run and the General had decided that he and his team would try it out. The Swedes provided the 'planks' and one day off they went: Rose (expert skier), the old ADC, George Waters (expert skier), the MA, Simon Shadbolt (expert skier), Nick Costello (good skier) and Goose (complete novice – never strapped on a pair of skis in his life). To make matters worse, while the 'expert skiers' zipped about with no gear, Goose had to carry a rucksack and his MP5 slung around his neck.

The first thirty metres were a vertical drop, concrete slide, just to get the speed up. The rest was near-vertical hell. Down they went with gay abandon, happily swishing through an unmarked minefield, which no one had told them about. Last, of course, was Goose. He'd survived a couple of seconds before he became a very large and fast snowball – arms, poles and broken skis sticking out at all angles. By the time he'd reached the bottom his MP5 had smashed his face and nose. The 'experts' were crowing: 'What kept you then, Goose?' Goose's language, directed at the General as much as anyone else, could be heard by the Swedes at the top; they were in fits. When he told me that I just disappeared as quickly as I could up to Pale as soon as I heard that Rose had more plans to try to kill his staff. Schindler's List and similar risks were one thing, but committing suicide on Bijelasnica was quite another.

We hadn't done a Schindler's List since the Boss had put a temporary halt to them in early December. At the end of the day, he gave the orders. Then, however, a problem cropped up quite by accident. Shortly after the episode with Indjic, we flew up to Zagreb where Rose had a meeting with Akashi. He had dinner with him that evening which left me at a loose end. By this stage little Mica had escaped UNHCR Sarajevo and was working at head office in Zagreb. I rang her and discovered that Una was in town. She'd left UNHCR and was studying for a Master's Degree at the Soros University in Prague. That evening we met up for dinner. Una had some stuff, letters, food and so on, for me to take down to her grandparents, Vera and Tomo, in Sarajevo.

Now that Una had left the UN there was virtually no chance of her returning to Sarajevo and visiting her grandparents. More worryingly, though I didn't tell her this, there was no chance that they'd survive the winter. I'd visited them shortly after the COHA thing and had been horrified at their state. The flat was a fridge. Tomo and Vera were shuffling about in several overcoats and, absurd though it sounds, Tomo was wearing a pair of Vera's stockings on his head keep some heat in his body. They were both in their eighties. They were frail, undernourished and were slowly freezing to death.

Una told me that she'd frequently thought of evacuating them through UNHCR down to Trpanj in Croatia where they had a holiday cottage. The problem was that it was so isolated down there that they'd be miles from any medical aid and therefore the plan was unfeasible. They would also be subjected to a hellish journey through Central Bosnia and, even if they survived that, as Serbs there was no guarantee that they'd be well received in Croatia. It was a mess. In many ways, the problem went right back to the day Matt Brey and I had spirited Una's parents out of the city in August 1993. In so doing we set in train a series of events which had propelled Una out of Sarajevo and then to Prague. The upshot of all this was that her grandparents were now isolated and unlikely to survive the winter or the war.

The whole affair preyed on my mind. Inadvertently, we had managed to split up a whole family; thanks to the absurdities and misfortunes of war, they had little chance of seeing each other again. This nagged at me for days.

I dreaded leaving the Balkans without at least attempting to do something about it, but it looked virtually impossible. As a mission statement it would look something like this: mission – to evacuate two octogenarians from Sarajevo in midwinter and get them to Belgrade without killing them, while at the same time finding a way for Una to get to Belgrade . . . in order to tie up this loose end. Problems – Rose's block on Schindler's List; they'd never survive a bus journey from Pale to Belgrade; recovery of Una's passport etc, etc. Una was right. So impossible was it that I put it to the back of my mind.

But life's not that simple; you can't just ignore a problem. When we got back from Zagreb I went down to visit Tomo and Vera to give them Una's letter; I found them shivering in that filthy, freezing flat. Tomo was still wearing the stockings on his head. They never complained once, but the sight of two frail old folk breathing clouds of condensation every time they spoke was enough to convince me they weren't going to make it. I asked them about Trpanj; they said they were too old to live there. Who would look after them when they reached Belgrade? Friends and family. Did they want to leave Sarajevo? Their eyes lit up. My mind was made up. I spoke to Geordie and some of the others. They were up for it. We decided to do it the day after Rose's departure, before the arrival of his replacement, General Rupert Smith. That way, if anything went wrong neither general could be held responsible.

It was a difficult operation. Tomo and Vera were virtually immobile. They'd need picking up. In addition, the exit from their building was within full view of the crossroads permanently manned by BiH policemen. The consequences of their being spotted being bundled into a UN vehicle were unthinkable. Over the next ten days I came close to calling the whole thing off but Geordie stayed cool. It rubbed off on me. Another problem was that Tomo's and Vera's hopes were high. We could not now dash them.

On Friday 24 January Rose paid his last visit to the Dark Side, to say goodbye to the Serbs. There was quite a debate about that, too. Rose's name was mud with the Muslims; they believed he had done nothing during the battle of Bihac, but the truth was that he had actually stopped the Serbs from entering the town. Was there any point in Rose going to Pale? He dragged me into his office and sought my opinion. If the Muslims wanted to cold-shoulder him that was their choice. Rose's position as the UN boss had been predicated on his remaining impartial and neutral. While he had conducted four air strikes against the Serbs, some of which had caused fatalities, he had never conducted an air strike against the BiH. Therefore, how could he be pro-Serb? And, despite the difficulties of the past year, the Serbs still wanted to say goodbye to him. The next day we went over to the Dark Side.

First stop, Pale and Karadzic. We weren't there long, perhaps fifteen minutes. The conversation was somewhat stilted. They talked about the wider roles of the UN. Karadzic gave Rose some trinkets – a leather wallet and some other bits and pieces. Rose gave Karadzic nothing but a handshake. Next stop Jahorina, to see Mladic, where the atmosphere was carnival-like. We were pursued up the hill by a fleet of press cars. The conference room was full of press, too. It looked like an ambush. For about three weeks Mladic had been pestering me about what I thought he should give Rose: he'd even mentioned a portrait. 'A fucking portrait? I don't want a fucking portrait!' Rose had fumed. So, we settled on something more innocuous – a painted wooden icon of St George, the patron Saint of the Coldstream Guards. Fitting.

Rose had been as effectively ambushed by Mladic as General Wes Clark had been. As well as the little wooden icon there was, under a huge white sheet which Mladic tore off with a flourish, a piece of modern art the size of a door. It was dreadful. It showed Rose's head above the face of a woman with an open, bleeding heart. Her outstretched arms formed the shape of a cross; one arm was clothed in denim. There were also four bullet holes, one in her arm. Mladic rattled through the symbolism of it all. The only thing that stuck in my mind was that the bullet hole in her arm represented the air strike that had killed Serbs. Strangely enough Rose seemed to like it. Either way, it was bundled into one of the vehicles. Rose was too much of a gentleman to reject it out of hand. At least it wasn't a pistol or a hat. Once again, Rose did not give a present. After lunch and another rather stilted conversation during which Mladic pursued his latest obsession with the role of priests and ethnic minorities in the British Army, we went back to Sarajevo.

That evening Rose relaxed. His tour was over and he couldn't wait to get out of the place on Monday. He kept on about the portrait and ordered me to get Mladic to find out more about the symbolism. It is worth repeating that Rose gave no presents. I later saw more senior UN generals lavishing gifts on Mladic. I also know exactly which UN officers walked away with things like commemorative pistols. There's quite a list of British officers and UN officers who accepted the Muslims' Golden Lily, their VC equivalent, and Bosnian passports – honorary Bosnian citizens.

I wasn't going to allow some wrteched portrait to preoccupy me. The main concern was how to get Tomo and Vera out of Sarajevo and off to Belgrade in one piece. So much could go wrong. Geordie came to see me late on Friday night, with the good news that Rose had lifted the ban on Schindler's List. We could go for it whenever we wanted. It was almost irrelevant since we'd already gone firm on Monday.

On Sunday afternoon I popped over to Lukavica to tie up the last details. Fortunately, Indjic was nowhere to be seen and the much more reasonable Brane Luledzija was on duty. I continued to fret about the whole business, but Brane was quite cool. 'I'll drive them myself. Why don't you do it today? They can sleep here. We've got a nice heater and we'll feed them. They'll be refreshed and less stressed for the drive to Belgrade.' His point was a valid one. It all made sense and Rose had lifted the ban. On the way back to the Residency I decided there was no point in delaying the inevitable. I sought out Geordie who was asleep in his bunk, suffering with Sarajevo flu. I shook him awake; I expected him to tell me to piss off but instead he roused himself to get the team ready.

We turned on that Schindler's in half an hour from a cold start. It was the most complicated one we'd ever attempted, mainly because of the pick-up location and because of Tomo's and Vera's age. I left the mechanics to the ever-calm Geordie who dropped me off at Vera and Tomo's building. All the comms, including the PR radios, were secure so there'd be no chance of the Americans or the press snooping on us. Their flat was as freezing as ever. One look at Tomo and Vera in that joyless place was enough to calm my nerves. We were doing the right thing.

They were pretty much out of it; they hadn't a clue as to what day it was, nor about front lines and checkpoints or the risks involved. They were quite calm. As far as they were concerned they were going for a drive. We'd moved some of their gear a few days before so all we really had to do was walk out of the place. On the net I could hear the teams doing their thing and reporting back to a Zero callsign which repeated each message. Some were mobile checking the BiH checkpoints for their alertness; others were doing drive-by runs checking on the police in the area. Another callsign came up reporting that the caller was 'foxtrot' (on foot) in the area and that all was clear. I was amazed at what Geordie had thrown together. We had timed the run from the Residency to the doorway of the block of flats – thirty seconds. The trigger for Geordie to 'go mobile' to the pick-up was my call that we were leaving the flat. I figured thirty seconds to get down four flights of stairs was adequate.

One last 'foxtrot' just to make sure; Geordie came up to say he was set to 'go mobile'. Then Vera started flapping about the bloody canary. It was quite grey with dirt and had long since stopped singing. I promised to look after it and she calmed down. We were in the dingy hallway, all set to go. We extinguished the last candle and it was quite dark. I paused for a moment. Once we opened the door we were committed. I had the same feeling of dread that precedes a jump from an aircraft but there was a big team out there of very committed, professional soldiers. Without them none of this was possible. I came up on the net, 'Stand by, stand by. That's us out of the flat and towards the pickup.' Zero repeated the message, 'Stand by, stand by. That's Mike plus two foxtrot out of the flat.' The next call came immediately from Geordie, 'Roger. That's me mobile towards the pick-up.' We stepped out of the flat and I shut the door behind us. We had thirty seconds.

We thought we'd covered every angle, considered everything, every step and kink in the pipeline from the flat to Belgrade. And yet, within ten feet of the flat, we nearly blew it. Vera couldn't walk. For two years I'd watched her shuffling about the flat, but only when she took the first step did I realise she hadn't left the place in three years, hadn't used stairs for three years. Her muscles were wasted, her bones brittle. I started flapping like a good 'un. I scooped her up like a baby. Tomo clung to my arm to steady himself and together we shuffled down the stairs as quickly as he could manage it. I prayed no one would poke their head out of a flat on one of the lower landings. Just as we reached the darkened entrance and were crunching over broken glass and rubbish, Geordie's headlamps appeared. Perfect timing. We shuffled out of the doorway to the back of the snatch. The door was open. One of the female interpreters was in the back and pulled them in, first Vera then Tomo. The door slammed shut and I leapt into the passenger seat beside Geordie. He winked at me. 'Piece of cake, Mike.' I was spluttering, 'Piece of fucking cake! I had to carry her down the sodding stairs.' He just laughed.

The rest of it really was a piece of cake. It was freezing cold and pitch black out there and we had to crawl through a clinging, white mist. No one at any of the checkpoints, Muslim, Serb or French, was in the least bit interested in abandoning a glowing brazier to check our vehicles. It seemed to take hours to creep through the fog to reach Lukavica, but we did it. Phase 1 was over.

To our amazement no one was there: no Indjic, no Biljana, no Brane. It was the first time I could remember the place being deserted. We found a three-bar electric heater and got that working to heat up Tomo and Vera. This, and the light bulb dangling from the ceiling, was the first electricity they'd had for years. Gradually they warmed themselves by the fire.

Geordie and the others couldn't hang around much longer and departed leaving me a vehicle. The JCO interpreter stayed with me. She had done a wonderful job soothing Tomo and Vera and had spent the entire journey holding Vera's hand. Rather than just abandon them in an empty barrack block, we decided to stay until we could safely hand them over to Brane, who'd promised them food and a bed.

When Indjic arrived, it couldn't have been worse: he was as drunk as a skunk. He was slurring his words and in an evil mood. I'd never seen him like this before. He glared at the JCO interpreter, totally ignored Vera and Tomo, and grabbed my arm. 'Brane's a fucking Muslim spy! I know. I have information. He's a spy. Don't trust him.' He was talking about the man he'd worked with in that office for two years. Not long after that Brane too appeared, also drunk. My heart sank. We couldn't leave Tomo and Vera to the mercies of two drunkards and then trust them to see them safely on their way in the morning. I was furious.

Indjic managed to compose himself and even suggested that Tomo ring his son Bobo in Belgrade. For a moment his generosity floored me. We managed to get through and Tomo spoke to his son for the first time in eighteen months.

You could hear Bobo crying at the other end. Tomo had a tear in his eye, but Indjic even managed to spoil that. He grabbed the microphone and asked Bobo how old he was. On hearing that he was fifty-eight, Indjic began berating him for being a traitor, for scuttling away from Republika Srpska when he still had two years' military service left in him. Indjic was ranting. Tomo was shocked. I exploded and started swearing at Indjic. At that moment I loathed him.

Biljana Andjelkovic arrived and soon whipped Indjic into shape. He skulked off into a corner while she busied herself making up a bed and cooking Tomo and Vera a large plate of eggs and ham. I knew I couldn't leave them now. The JCO interpreter agreed. We were there for the night. With a plate of hot food inside him and his bones warmed, Tomo became perky for the first time. He told us tales of his days as a soldier in the Yugoslav brigade during the Spanish Civil War. It was impossible to get him to go to bed. Eventually, he talked himself to sleep.

In an adjoining office I noticed that Indjic had put a couple of bottles of cheap champagne and two fluted glasses on the table. The JCO interpreter was in there with him. He cast a conspiratorial glance my way, leapt to his feet, grabbed my arm and whispered in my ear that I wasn't welcome at the private party as he had designs on her. He was appalling. 'Errrr, as one man to another,' he slurred in my ear, 'you'll understand. I know the signs women make.' He gave me a lascivious wink. 'I'm going to fuck her tonight.' I told him he had no chance whatsoever. She didn't seem too bothered about drinking with him alone and assured me she could look after herself.

Indjic was so desperate to get rid of me that he offered me his own bed. I agreed and told him straight, 'If she agrees, fine. But if she screams once, I'm going to fucking shoot you dead. Do you understand?' I meant it, too, and brandished John Jordan's Beretta for good measure. He just sniggered and said that if he got nowhere with her he'd sleep on the floor in his room.

Well, that little lot got him nowhere with her. Two wasted bottles of champagne. Two hours later, true to his word, he slunk into the room. He had the cheek to ask me for his bed back. I just laughed and said, 'You lost! You're on the fucking floor!' And that's where he slept, fully clothed and snoring his head off until the sun came up. At half past seven a small black VW Golf arrived. Tomo and Vera climbed in with their suitcases. I was hugely relieved that the nominated driver was a quite sober and clean-shaven Brane Luledzija. With a wave we saw them on their way. And that is the last I ever saw of them.

We had to get back to the Residency after that. It was Rose's last morning and there was sure to be some sort of farewell to him. We couldn't miss that. We arrived back just in time for Rose's official photograph with his staff. It seemed like any old normal day. Rose and Goose shot off up to Zetra to visit the Danish bakery. There was no real sense of his imminent departure.

There was always something to make you laugh in the Residency. For example, I'm sitting chinwagging with Geordie and I spy a bottle of French champagne on the shelf. That office was more like a corner shop than anything else. The shelf was crammed with jars of jam, marmalade, boxes of curry powder, mustard, you name it. Round the edge of the room were about forty bottles of cheap, white wine that had been forced on us after some meeting with the Serbs. I'm staring at this bottle of champagne and idly ask, 'Where did the bubbly come from, Geordie?'

Geordie just starts giggling. 'The French gave the Boss a smart presentation pack of four of these bottles. Lovely presentation box. Rose, Goose and the ADC are going to be having a little end of tour piss-up in Zagreb tonight.' I automatically assumed that Rose had presented the JCOs with one of the bottles. Geordie just laughed at that one. 'No, Mike. You've got it wrong! He'd never do that. He popped his head in an hour ago and just said, right then you wankers I'm off, bye then. And then he spied these Serbian bottles of plonk and picked one up and said, ha! I'm never going to have to drink this muck again! And then he just buggered off.' Geordie loved telling me what he did next: 'I fucking grabbed Goose and told him to get me the General's presentation pack, which he did. Quick razor blade job on the bottom. One bottle of French bubbly out and one bottle of Serbian muck in. That'll fucking teach him. I'd love to be a fly on the wall of their little party tonight in Zagreb!'

General Rose, the MA and one or two others were having lunch downstairs. I couldn't be bothered to join them and it still didn't seem as if Rose was leaving anyway. After lunch Rose was still fiddling about in his office. I was at my desk on the laptop when he came striding out, as he always did. 'Right then. Let's go.' He was slapping his thigh with his beret. We could have been going anywhere – Pale, fishing, touring around Central Bosnia. It was all so normal. I jumped into the backing vehicle and we shot off to the airport.

The press were waiting for him. No great hoo-ha. He spoke to them briefly, mentioned the UN's successes and then strode off to the waiting Yak. I followed on behind. Two fire tenders fell in on either side of the group and sounded their sirens as a final salute to the General. Only then did it hit me that he was finally going.

In that instant everyone left for Zagreb – General Rose, the MA, Goose, the ADC and Mungo Brookes. Pete Schuster, the other communicator, and I were the only members of the team left standing on the pan watching the Yak taxi to the Lukavica end of the runway. It stopped, ran up its engines and then shot down the runway. Level with us it was steady at fifteen feet off the ground, a classic Kabul take-off. Then it lurched upwards and disappeared over the Ilidza flats trailing two filthy plumes of smoke. Pete and I stared after it in silence until we couldn't see it anymore. I felt empty. Pete turned to me. His face told the whole story. 'It's a real pisser, isn't it?' His voice was quiet and sad. I couldn't answer him. I didn't need to.

TWENTY-FIVE

Operation Bretton

And it is not my very own extremity I remember best – a vision of greyness without form filled with physical pain, and a careless contempt for the evanescence of all things – even of this pain itself. No! It is his extremity that I seemed to have lived through. True, he had made that last stride, he had stepped over the edge, while I had been permitted to draw back my hesitating foot. And perhaps in this is the whole difference; perhaps all the wisdom, and all truth, and all sincerity, are just compressed into that inappreciable moment of time in which we step over the threshold of the invisible.

Heart of Darkness, Joseph Conrad

December 1997 – Ian, UK

'The end of an era. When I look back on it, Ian, that's when it all ended.'

'What did?'

'My tour. Or rather, my time in the Balkans. It ended that day we got Tomo and Vera out and the day he left. It left us hollow, Rose's leaving. You'd got so used to him and his manic ways, of being whirled around on that insane merry-go-round. I should have gone with him. Easy to say in retrospect. It's not the way it happened, though.'

'How much longer did you stay?'

'Another three months. But it was dull really – more of the same, but without that mania. When General Rose left he took with him the madness and left behind a numbing desolation.'

'Why did you stay on then?'

'Lots of reasons. Much later I discovered that Rose and General Rupert Smith had crossed over in Zagreb. Rose told him that I'd basically "had it" out there and that he should keep me on for no more than a week.'

'So, it was Smith's fault you stayed for an extra three months?'

'Not entirely. It's a bit more complicated than that. When Rose left he took with him his entire team. With them went a year's worth of institutional knowledge. Worse still, a week after Rose left, Victor Andreyev, the real Bosnia and Balkan vet., also departed after nearly four years there. Smith was therefore coming in virtually cold. I stayed on for the short term, long enough to bed him in. There was a second reason for staying: the prospect of returning to Chilwell was too awful to contemplate.

'In fact, General Smith didn't arrive immediately. General Rose went out on the Monday and Smith arrived two days later. On the Tuesday I went to Lukavica to see whether Indjic had sobered up. I also rang Belgrade and learnt that Tomo and Vera had arrived safely and were being well looked after. That evening I told Nada what had happened and gave her the keys to the flat: a few days later a young Muslim doctor, his wife and children have moved in. It all worked out quite well in the end.

'At lunchtime on the Wednesday General Smith arrived. He spoke briefly to the press before being whisked off to the Residency by his new bodyguard, Ginge, who had been out before as Victor Andreyev's driver. Clive Davies' replacement RMP staff sergeant found it extremely difficult to accept the fact that Ginge was the General's principal. The RMP Close Protection bunch are a precious lot at the best of times and not a patch on real BGs. So there was that little domestic unhappiness to sour the atmosphere in the Outer Office. The new ADC was Guy Lavender with whom I'd been in Kuwait all those years ago and who had been sent to Croatia in early 1992 when I'd been left to fester in the desert. General Smith couldn't have picked a better man as his ADC.

'With the arrival of General Smith, it became clear that things were going to change. The Outer Office would become a more recognisable, military body. No more nicknames or first names: "Ginge" would become "Sergeant Major". A new broom was sweeping the dust of Rose's term from the Outer Office.

'The transitional period was not a particularly happy one, not least because the COHA which Rose had negotiated was beginning to get bogged down in detail. Victor Andreyev had suggested that the war would go another round before they finally stopped fighting and he was right. The locals viewed the four-month COHA as a brief respite from fighting and a chance to prepare for spring offensives. That's not to say that Rose hadn't fulfilled his obligations. His Campaign Plan had stressed the creation of the conditions for peace. That's exactly what he did with the COHA, but the international community lacked the determination to seize the opportunity to negotiate a final political territorial settlement.

'By this stage the Serbs had finally produced a permanent LO in Central Bosnia. His name, appropriately, was Colonel Guzvic and with him went a Serb interpreter. His surname was appropriate because it is based on the word "guzva", which means "a crowd", in the sense of pressing bodies. More loosely and colloquially it means a "palaver", or "drama". Well, Colonel "Drama" was just that. The moment he appeared in the UN HQ in Tuzla the BiH virtually surrounded the place and demanded his removal. This became too much for the Tuzla mob and Colonel Guzvic was spirited down to GV with his interpreter, where he was protected by the British. Even so he was still a marked man and was virtually in a state of benevolent open arrest.

'The response to Colonel Guzvic in GV was not the only indication that the COHA meant little to the Muslims and Croats. In February the covert landings of large, blacked-out transport aircraft touching down on Tuzla's secondary runways were observed and reported by UN personnel. This occurred twice and on both occasions two twin-tailed, twin-engined jets circled over Tuzla at about 3,000 feet with full nav lights and afterburners on. To observers they looked like decoys to draw eyes off the black transports landing at the airbase. NATO denied that any aircraft had been over Bosnia on either occasion and even sent an American-led 'investigation' team over to Bosnia whose line of questioning seemed determined to debunk anything observers had seen. It was a messy, shallow and shabby attempt to conceal what was widely believed to be the covert re-supplying of arms to the Muslims in defiance of the UN embargo.

'From the Dark Side came similar complaints where Serb observers on the Vis feature had also witnessed these nocturnal goings-on. NATO's eagle-eyed AWACs seemed to be suffering from temporary blindness. That myopia extended to the UN whose policy seemed to be one of silence, and reflected the unwillingness of anyone to step in and negotiate a political settlement. The COHA was withering on the vine. By mid-February, Bosnia seemed resigned to another round of war come spring.

'This climate did little to cheer me up. Two events convinced me that my time was nearly up. The first was a visit to General Smith by General "Taljan" Hajrulahovic, the BiH Intelligence guru. When I met him at the front gate to the Residency to take him up to see the General, he told me bluntly that I should have left with Rose, that I was no longer safe. When I gave him my Parachute Regiment Zippo lighter, he pulled it to pieces in a fit of paranoid suspicion, removing all the stuffing out of it as though he was looking for a bug of some sort.

'At about the same time I bumped into a French Warrant Officer of Slovene extraction, Sarnai. One of General Soubirou's original interpreters, he had recently returned for another tour as FREBAT 2's interpreter and LO. On his way from the airport into town he had been stopped at the BiH checkpoint at Stup and found himself staring down the barrel of a gun. The Muslims told him that he was "known", that if he ever tried to drive into town again he would be killed. He wasn't a Serb or anything like that, but it seemed immaterial. While he had been working for Soubirou, Muslim Intelligence had furnished Soubirou with a list of UN personnel of all nationalities known to have a Balkan background and had accused them of being spies. Nick Costello's and my name were on the list.

'The only person who was attuned to all this was Geordie. The newcomers hadn't a clue about the nature of the people we were dealing with and frankly couldn't have cared less. It soon became obvious that whenever I moved out of that Residency on an errand I was tracked. It was quite simple to do. Our faithful Residency manager, a Serb, had been intimidated and beaten up by the mafia; he was forced to resign, leaving the mysterious Suad in charge. Suad's daily trips down to the Bosnian Presidency didn't go unnoticed. Furthermore, each time we passed through a checkpoint they'd note our ID card details and our vehicle registration number. Someone would collate our daily movements and, over the weeks and months they built up quite a nice little picture of our movements. So Geordie and I simply concocted two extra UN ID cards with different names

'The only good thing to happen in late February was the appearance of General Mike Jackson in Sarajevo. He and his wife, Sarah, had looked after Aida Pijalovic and through me had managed to keep Minka and Munir supplied with parcels. General Jackson was by now the GOC of 3 UK Division and one of his units was currently in Gorazde. As a "mere" major general, he was way down on the pecking order of visitors to the Balkans. Despite having troops in Bosnia it seemed that the precious "war tourist" slots went to every senior Tom, Dick and Harry from the MoD and FCO who fancied clicking off a roll of film. In a rare moment of common sense someone allowed Jackson to visit his troops. So, out came General Mike, laden with a huge parcel for Minka and Munir.

'We gave him a whistle-stop tour of the city and then that evening the two of us went to see Minka and Munir.

For more than two years, General Jackson had been sending parcels to two people he had never met. Minka and Munir were beside themselves, their gratitude palpable. The emotional charge that evening was as you would expect.

'We returned to the Residency to find another problem. The Serbs had refused to give clearance for Jackson's helicopter flight into Gorazde, putting his visit in jeopardy . . . I rang Mladic direct and fixed that one. Mladic's only stipulation was that he wanted to meet this General Jackson on his way back from Gorazde, which is exactly what happened. Jackson met Mladic in Sokolac on his way back from visiting his troops, which was useful as he could complain about the Serbs screwing around with the re-supply convoys to Gorazde. Brigadier Gordon, the Commander of Sector South-West, was also present at the meeting.

'Shortly after that there was a shift in Mladic's behaviour. On Saturday 3

March we had a crisis on our hands. The Dutch battalion in Srebrenica had all but run out of supplies. Successive re-supply convoys had been thwarted by the Serbs and Smith had reached the end of his tether. His solution was simple, dramatic and extremely risky: load up a number of giant Russian Halo helicopters with supplies and bust into Srebrenica unilaterally at night. They'd almost certainly have attracted Serb fire from those besieging Srebrenica, who might well have thought it was the Muslims trying to fly into the pocket. That afternoon we threw Bluetit up the hill. A JCO and I went up with the TACSAT and in a matter of hours managed to persuade Karadzic to exert pressure on Mladic to let the convoy run. Amazingly, it ran that night, virtually without a hiccup. More than that, Mladic called for a meeting with Smith early the next day on mount Jahorina during which he not only graciously allowed Smith to travel to Srebrenica the following day but even suggested a further meeting in Vlasenica on our way back from the pocket.'

'So?'

'So? So, Ian! This was the first occasion during my time with either Rose or Smith that Mladic actually suggested two meetings. Normally, it was down to us to try and pin him down. This time he had taken the initiative.

'Srebrenica was an eye-opener. That was General Smith's first trip and my last into the pocket. We drove up there on Tuesday 6 March and stayed overnight as guests of the Dutch battalion at Potocari. Doom and gloom reigned. Morale amongst the Dutch seemed to be rock bottom and they didn't have a good word to say about any of the locals, either besieged Muslims or besieging Serbs. As we drove away the next day for the Vlasenica meeting with Mladic I was convinced there was going to be a disaster in Srebrenica.

'In Vlasenica, Smith pointed out to Mladic the military realities of his position. When he told him that his greatest problem was that of having to tie up some 4,000 troops investing Gorazde, Srebrenica and Zepa, Mladic went white and was, for the first time, left speechless. Smith's succinct assessment had rattled his cage. It didn't take long for him to bounce back with some outrageous threat to divert the course of the river Drina and flood out the Muslims. When people say those sorts of things, it's clear that they've run out of options. Mladic was on the back foot.

'As well as threatening to drown the Muslims, Mladic also complained bitterly that UN convoys into Gorazde were carrying pineapples to Gorazde Force. He had a real bee in his bonnet about pineapples. There were complaints about the covert resupply of arms in Tuzla, about Croat attacks up the Glamoc valley in Hercegovina, which guarded the back door to Knin, and about a whole host of COHA violations by the Muslims and Croats. In a nutshell, the meeting achieved nothing; it merely highlighted Mladic's obsession with pineapples.

'There were other indications, too, that things were breaking up. Banditry in Republika Srpska was increasing. The UNMOs in Pale had their vehicles hijacked several times. On the road through the Sierras from Ilidza to Kiseljak masked gunmen operated freely, hijacking and stealing lone UN vehicles transiting the route. They were probably in cahoots with Serb troops at the Ilidza checkpoint. To make matters worse, they started shooting at aircraft again.

'We took a trip up to Zagreb where Smith had supper with Mr Akashi to discuss the way ahead. The situation had deteriorated so much that Zagreb had decided it was time for another high-level powwow with the Serbs in Pale. The purpose of the Zagreb trip was to sort out the game plan before flying down to Sarajevo the next day. Prior to the meeting with Mr Akashi, Smith met with a British brigadier from the MoD who was out on a fact-finding tour. They skulked about the woods at Pleso airfield having a clandestine chinwag.

'While General Smith had supper with the SRSG we hung around the bar at the Intercontinental. Late in the evening the General's BG, Ginge, joined us. He'd just returned from the dinner and was preening himself in his smart suit. He'd come well equipped for the job. His suit was of an excellent cut, his shirts expensive double-cuffers and his shoes good quality black brogues. He looked every bit an officer and we teased him mercilessly for it. His tailoring bill must have cost him a small fortune.

'The following day every man and his dog flew down to Sarajevo for the meeting; Akashi with his advisers and BGs, the Force Commander with his BGs, the Sector Sarajevo Commander, General Hervé Gobillard, and his BGs and, of course, Smith and his team. There were so many personnel that two Yaks had to be laid on and Guy Lavender and I found ourselves bumped off the lead UN Yak and onto the second, which for some reason had on board members of President Izetbegovic's delegation who were returning from some trip abroad. It's absurd when you think about it, but just about every single UN VIP was crammed into that leading Yak – all the eggs in one basket.

'Our Yak took off some twenty minutes after the lead one and as we'd passed overhead Split I noticed that we were turning back. Somewhat alarmed I rushed up to the cockpit where the Ukrainians informed me that the VIP Yak had been hit by ground fire as it had landed. We'd been ordered back to Zagreb, not the place to be if there was a drama going on in Sarajevo. Reluctantly, the Ukrainians agreed to drop us in Split from where we'd have a fighting chance of getting back to Sarajevo by helicopter. That was just the beginning of an utter nonsense.

'From Split I phoned the MA, Jim Baxter, to find out what was going on. He confirmed that the VIP Yak had been hit but that there had been no casualties. But that seemed a side issue. He told me to get up to Kiseljak as soon as possible: a vehicle would meet me and I was to get myself over to Lukavica immediately and sort out another drama. From what I could gather the British brigadier, who'd been skulking about in the Pleso woods with Smith, and his MoD staff officers had been hijacked on the Ilidza road by bandits. Four of them had been transiting early in the morning in a single, unescorted vehicle. They had been held up and turfed out at gunpoint. The Brigadier had had his brief-case stolen and they'd all been deprived of their personal effects and been dumped on the side of the road to walk back into Sarajevo.

'845 NAS laid on a Sea King to Kiseljak. We managed to get through the Sierras without meeting the highwaymen and I rendezvoused with a fuming Geordie at Sierra 4. Together we shot over to Lukavica where a rather smug Indjic was almost throttled to death by Geordie. Miraculously the BSA war machine swung into action. We spent the day tracking down the stolen goods. We recovered the vehicle, which had been left abandoned in Vogosca. The brief-case and personal effects were never found.

'Back at the Residency I found the unfortunate brigadier, whom I knew well, puffing away furiously on a cigarette. Despite the personal dramas of the day he waved his cigarette in the direction of Smith's office and muttered, "What's going through his mind? I've just been in with Smith and can't understand what he's on about. Something about being a circus trick horseman." Smith had compared himself with a trick rider with one foot each on the backs of two galloping horses called War and Peace. The horses were diverging and soon he would be forced to choose one horse. War seemed to be the favourite.

'The saga of the brigadier and his staff officers ended with them having to buy cheap flared jeans with huge turn-ups and tacky lumberjack shirts in Split. Looking like the *Village People* they skulked through Italy's airports clutching black bin-liners containing their uniforms. As for the Yak, that had been hit by a high velocity .50 round. There was an almighty bang and lots of red smoke in the rear compartment. Pandemonium broke out in the cabin. Akashi had been hurled to the floor by his BGs and almost smothered by flak jackets. The French BGs reacted in the same way, hurling their bosses to the floor and leaping on them, gang-bang style. Smith and Ginge remained seated, tittering and sniggering away like mad, knowing that the BGs' response had come far too late to serve any useful purpose. When they got off the Yak and recovered their bags Ginge was laughing on the other side of his face. The only casualties were his smart clothes. The round had entered his suit-carrier and destroyed the jacket, trousers, shirt and both pairs of shoes before exiting and burying itself in a mail bag. The Danes later found the round and gave it to Ginge. Smith's only comment was to suggest that Ginge raise a bill and forward it to Mladic.

'The big meeting up at Pale the next day achieved nothing. It was conducted in the large conference room in the Hotel Panorama. The Serb 1st XI was lined up opposite the UN 1st XI. I was sitting behind Smith and next to David and dozed off. It was absolutely deadly. There was no middle ground whatsoever. The Serbs were vying with each other to see who could come out with the most outrageous anti-UN or anti-whoever accusation. Mladic spent almost half an hour banging on about the bones of some old woman which the Croats had violated. He then got onto pineapples. At their very mention Smith started laughing. He hadn't realised that pineapples were a luxury item in the Balkans. Mladic went berserk. I was awoken with a nudge in the ribs. David passed me a note from Smith which read "I know you've heard it all before but could you at least pretend to be taking an interest". I think it was at this point that the Peace horse was abandoned.

'This slanging match marked a turning-point. Shortly after it the Serbs announced that Mladic and his officers were to have no further contact with UNPROFOR. Henceforth all contact and business with the UN was to be conducted through Karadzic or Koljevic, the rationale being that Mladic should be concentrating on conducting defensive operations and not wasting his time chatting to the UN. The UN swallowed this but the truth was that the gulf of mistrust between the Serb politicians and their military was widening still further. I realised this when Indjic started questioning me closely about the global plan that Karadzic had passed to me in October. I was amazed that the military knew nothing about it. They were furious when they discovered the extent to which the Krajinas and other areas were to be sold out.

'Closer to home I had other problems. Although Jim Baxter had told me that Smith was angling to keep me out for the duration of his tour, a move which JHQ were taking a dim view of, pressure in Bosnia suggested that it was time to go. General Tolimir had told me that the Muslims wanted to kill me and that I should leave Bosnia and never return. Only when this was corroborated by Goran, our head waiter, who had links with the Sarajevo mafia, did I really begin to believe it.

I also learnt that John Menzies, from the US Embassy in Sarajevo, had been critical of me, saying that I should not be advising UN generals. And yet, this same man had not thought twice about using me to telephone Karadzic on both his and Jimmy Carter's behalf. Menzies was disliked even by his own people. When Admiral Leighton Smith was nominated for IFOR Commander after the war he refused to allow Menzies, by then US Ambassador to Bosnia, anywhere near his HQ in the Residency. Because the Admiral was not a nodding donkey willing to do the State Department's bidding without question he was removed from the theatre. So the Americans weren't beyond wrecking the careers of their own officers like Leighton Smith, Gordon Rudd and Marty Petross for daring to speak out, i.e. to speak the truth.

'I was more than a little disgruntled with the Americans. Not long after Geordie and I pulled off the COHA "telephone through the window" stunt, the US Embassy produced their own version of Mike Stanley. A US lieutenant colonel in a brand new uniform suddenly appeared in their embassy. He also appeared, uninvited, in our *Star Wars* bar, where he'd hoover up our conversations. His name was Chuck Vuckovic. The first time I met him I was appalled to see that he had his original name-tag on.

'When he told us that he was the son of Zvonomir Vuckovic, Draza Mihajlovic's right-hand man in the Chetnik movement of the last war – the very Vuckovic that Mihajlovic had sent to Italy in a final attempt to persuade the Allies to switch from Tito to him – I was horrified. It got worse when he passionately announced that he wouldn't hear a word said against the Chetniks or Mihajlovic. I told him to keep his mouth shut about all that; it wouldn't impress the Muslims or anyone else. The Yanks had been stupid to stick him in there so blatantly, and he'd been naïve in singing the praises of the Chetniks. Needless to say, no one trusted him. We didn't give a damn about him and his past but got thoroughly pissed off with his snooping around the bar. Eventually, he was thrown out and asked not to return. He wasn't Kosher US Army anyway, he'd retired from the Army years before. All this, and I later discovered that he was a very distant cousin of mine . . .

'Alarm bells started ringing for me when another Sarajevo rag, *Vecernje Novine*, ran a week-long exposé of the UN and its ills. Each day there'd be an article attacking some member of the UN. Monday's leader indicated who would be horse-whipped on which day. My own expose, *'What was the real role of Rose's adjutant, Mike Stanley'*, was billed as the last piece. They began with Boutros Boutros-Ghali. The next day it was Yasushi Akashi, then Victor Andreyev, then Rose. All very brave, considering their victims of this filth were all out of the country. Finally the last day of this campaign arrived: the headline to my piece read *"TRUSTED MOLE"*.

'Trusted Mole?'

'Yep. "*Krtica Od Poverenja* – Trusted Mole". The gist of it was that Rose had left his "Trusted Mole" behind to carry on spying for the British government.'

'But I thought they'd branded you the Chetnik spy in HQ UNPROFOR.'

'They had, them and the Americans. But obviously they got bored with that and turned me into a British spy. Pathetic! The real twist in all this is that now that the Brits have turned round and accused me of being a Serb spy against the British, I suppose that means I've been spying against everyone for everyone. First triple spy in history, Ian? Absurd bullshit.'

'What did you think of that then? The Trusted Mole article.'

'It was laughable. They couldn't even get their propaganda consistent, but bearing in mind what Menzies, Tolimir and Goran had said, it was all rather worrying. No one in the Outer Office paid it the slightest attention.

'As the day wore on I sought solace with friends in the BBC: Martin Bell,

Nigel Bateson and Anamarija, their gorgeous and faithful Croatian interpreter/producer. We had supper that evening in the Writers' Club. Martin was quite sanguine about the whole thing, "Looks as though the Muslims have just given you the title of your book. You should thank them!"

'While all this was going on, a little signal arrived from JHQ in the UK – "Stanley to be replaced by Captain T. Dibb LI as Commander BHC's LO to the BSA". The beginning of the end. Tom Dibb was coming out on 1 April and the plan was that I'd do a rolling hand-over to him. The good news was that we'd managed to turn the whole thing round.'

'Turn what round?'

'The job, Ian. Or rather the job description. Nick Costello went out there as the General's interpreter. That was my role when I took over from Nick. And yet, here was my replacement coming out not as interpreter but as LO to the BSA. Despite all the bleating about the role, someone somewhere considered our work important enough to change the job description. So, that was it – an end date had been chosen. I later learnt that Wilton had overruled Smith's wish to keep me on out there for the duration of his tour. They said that I'd had enough and it would be destructive to my career. It was probably Rose, who was back in his old job as Deputy Commander Land, who put an end to it. Did me a huge favour.

'I was still in touch with Rose. One day in April I was at my desk wading through all the Serbo-Croat letters that came into the office for the General. One was addressed to Mike Stanley; it bore a Canadian stamp. I thought it was more hate mail. When I opened it I got the shock of my life. It was a letter from Jasna Pandurevic, her husband, Ranko, and their daughter, Maja, now living in Toronto. It was hard to believe they were the first Schindler's List folk that Goose and I had moved after I took over from Nick. Miraculously, they made it to Toronto eight months after being hoiked out of Sarajevo and were writing to thank us all. Their letter was so touching, so uplifting that I immediately translated it and sent it to Rose who was moved enough to read it out in Sherborne Abbey to a packed congregation.

'Smith didn't really change my role. If anything, I was even busier shuffling up and down to Pale almost every day delivering letters to Dr Karadzic. Not only had we stopped CAPSATing them to the UNMOs in Pale, largely because the system was insecure, but we also translated them into Serbo-Croat at source. That meant that we controlled the translation as well.

'The major issue at the time revolved around General Smith's desire to get rid of Colonel Guzvic and his interpreter from GV. Their presence there was almost completely untenable. The RJCs had broken down. The Muslims and Croats were as insistent as ever that they be moved and Smith was getting concerned that the UN would not be able to guarantee their safety. Ironically, both Karadzic and Mladic wanted them to remain in place until such time as

the UN openly admitted that it could no longer protect them, thereby transfer-
ring the blame for the collapse of the COHA onto them and the UN. Colonel
Guzvic thus became a pawn in a game of words between Pale and the UN.

'Most of my time was spent trying to persuade the Serbs to remove Guzvic
from GV. Mladic was completely against it, and in any case wasn't "allowed"
to talk to the UN, which was most convenient for him. He had problems
elsewhere. General Alagic had finally managed to shove the Serbs off the top
of the Vlasic feature without the rock climbing gear he'd demanded from
Clinton via General Galvin, something that was achieved with little Serb
resistance. The Croats had managed to take and hold the Glamoc valley in
Hercegovina which threatened to kick in the back door to Knin. By the end
of March the COHA had disappeared in a puff of Balkan smoke and Smith
was desperate to be rid of Guzvic.

'At about the same time there was a complete changeover of JCOs. L-P's
and his successor, David's lot – out. Complete fresh bunch – in, with a new
major in charge. Geordie stayed on to maintain continuity but the rest were
all new.

'Fortunately, Tom Dibb arrived on 1 April. No greenhorn, he had already
completed one tour of Bosnia during which he'd been blown up in a landmine
incident that had killed another captain. For a non-native his Serbo-Croat
was extremely good and I considered him an ideal choice. In a sense he and
I were fellow countrymen in that I'd been born in Rhodesia and he was a
Zimbabwean. The only real concern in all this was whether the likes of Karadzic, Mladic, Indjic and Zametica would allow him the access that I had
been granted. We could only assume they would and so cracked on with a
rolling hand-over.

'The JCOs trained him up on the TACSAT and shortly after Tom's arrival
some crisis or other led to Smith deploying the two of us up to the UNMOs
in Pale for another Bluetit. Tom did all the TACSAT stuff himself and together
we went up to the Serbs to lock horns with Zametica. I'd already told Zametica
that back in the UK there was talk that I'd deliberately sabotage the hand-over
and to that end begged him to convince Karadzic and Mladic that Tom should
be treated exactly the same as I had been. He agreed, and we managed to
wheel Tom in front of Karadzic to make his introductions. That also went
well.

'The problem with Colonel Guzvic wouldn't go away and we had been
pestering the Serbs for days to get them in the right frame of mind to consider
removing him from GV. Karadzic firmly believed that there was no point in
talking to the UN, officially at least, but he was was aware of the need to
maintain some unofficial communication. I used to fix up "secret" meetings,
or "meetings between four eyes" (face to face), in which he and Smith would
meet in a small room with a scribe each and without the press knowing.

Usually, these required some deception on the General's part, if only to keep the press at bay.

'On the day of one of these meetings we'd put it about that the General would be visiting troops on Mount Igman. Instead he went to Pale and met with Karadzic in an obscure hotel. After an hour's discussion, the Colonel Guzvic issue was raised and Karadzic agreed that it was pointless and dangerous to keep him in GV any longer. He agreed that he should be returned to the Serb side. Guzvic, however, belonged to Mladic and, given their unsteady relationship, Karadzic had to clear the man's repatriation with the general. He didn't say so in as many words but he did say, "You'll get my answer." He agreed but to do it had to get Mladic's approval – more evidence of the dysfunction between the military and the politicians – which we'd have got if we'd waited a further twenty-four hours.

'After the meeting Tom and I went up to see Zametica and Karadzic to continue the hand-over. Smith and the new JCO commander returned to Sarajevo. We returned to the Residency that evening to an air of mild panic. A problem had arisen following the earlier meeting with Karadzic.

'Despite Karadzic's assurance that we'd get an answer, they couldn't wait to get rid of Guzvic and decided to do it that afternoon. Both Guzvic and his interpreter were bundled into a helicopter in GV, thus alerting the Muslims and Croats that he was on the move. Unaware of the flight plan, the Serbs refused landing permission, so they had to turn back to Kiseljak. They couldn't go back to GV because of the threat from the Muslims and Croats, so they went for Plan B which was to stuff the pair into an APC and drive them in through the Sierras. Plan B didn't go according to plan either. Colonel Guzvic smelt a rat while sitting in the helicopter and refused to budge until he'd received authorisation from Mladic.

'Modified Plan B then went into action: they disarmed Guzvic, hoiked both men out of the helicopter and handcuffed them. They were then bundled into the APC, taken through Kilo 1, on through no-man's-land, and dropped 100 metres short of Sierra 1 by the side of the road, still handcuffed. The APC then beat a hasty retreat back to Kiseljak, where these bungling fools discovered they still had Colonel Guzvic's pistol.

'It infuriated me. Days of delicate negotiations had led to Serbian agreement to the repatriation of Colonel Guzvic. But for the want of twenty-four hours we'd screwed up the whole thing.

'Damage limitation was now the name of the game. We had an emergency conference in Smith's office that night. In a report I had tried to put myself in Karadzic's position, but in fact it wasn't Karadzic who was the problem. He couldn't give a hoot about Guzvic and his pistol. Mladic was the real problem.

'Serb TV went bananas over the incident; they interviewed Guzvic ad nauseam. Mladic went spare and the chances of getting him to agree to convoys to Gorazde or anything else were fast receding.

'Some days later, when Tom and I were being deployed up to Pale on a Bluetit, fighting broke out in earnest around Dobrinja. At Sierra 4 the French and Serbs were engaged in a huge stand-off, as a result of the theft of 126 flak jackets from the French. Sarajevo was in chaos. Tom and I took a trip out to the airport to assess the situation and drove through a fire-fight to get there. To make matters worse, UK's Chief of Defence Staff, Field Marshal Sir Peter Inge, was out on yet another visit from the MoD and was due to transit through the Sierras into Sarajevo. His timing couldn't have been worse. In the Outer Office the MA, Jim Baxter, was grappling with a momentous and potentially career-damaging decision as to whether or not the Field Marshal's visit to Sarajevo should be cancelled. Jim Baxter asked me for a "balanced and unemotional" assessment.

'When you've just driven through the chaos at Dobrinja in an unarmoured vehicle and back again it is difficult to give such an assessment but it seemed sheer folly to allow the Chief of Defence Staff to try and drive through the Sierras. The Serbs would be itching to grab a British officer, handcuff him and dump him on the side of the road. Even if he got through the Sierras he'd never have got through Ilidza, a hornet's nest which had come alive. My decision led to the cancellation of Field Marshal Sir Peter Inge's trip into Sarajevo. I sometimes think that this little incident was the genesis of a decision which later heaped suspicion on Geordie, L-P and me for two years.'

'What?'

'Another altogether different story. Perhaps one day I'll tell you what it was all about.'

'But if it's something to do with your arrest why weren't the other two arrested?'

'That's a good question. I don't know why these other two majors, both decorated for gallantry on operations, one of whom had been equerry to the Queen Mother, came under suspicion but were subsequently not arrested.'

'The Chief of Defence Staff didn't get his trip into Sarajevo. That Guzvic episode – more than any racist vitriol in the press, more than any bleatings from Menzies and crew, more than warnings from Tolimir, threats from Hajrulahovic, affirmations of those threats from Goran and Sarnai – convinced me to get out. Geordie was packing to go, too. He left a week or so before me and his parting words were, "Mike. There's a new regime in place now. Their agenda's different and you've got no friends here. Get out."

'The hand-over to Tom went better than expected. We met most of the personalities involved in the job, except Mladic. In two weeks there was enough drama for us to go leaping up the hill on a regular basis. Towards the end of the two weeks we were driving back to Sarajevo and passed a fleet of military jeeps stuffed full of Russian officers in big hats going in the opposite direction. In the lead vehicle I spotted Tolimir. "I'll bet they've just had a big meeting at Lukavica. I'll bet also that Mladic was there,' I said to Tom. We decided to investigate and stopped off at Lukavica, where we found a jeep parked outside Indjic's office. Lurking in the doorway were Mladic's two bodyguards. This was a perfect opportunity to ambush him and get Tom introduced.

'We hung around in Indjic's waiting room until we heard Mladic and crew coming down the stairs. He was surprised to see me. "Boy. What're you doing here?" I told him I was off and that I had my replacement waiting to meet him. "Another spy, eh Stanley?" he said with a laugh. There was no mention of the Guzvic incident. When Tom and Mladic came face to face the General boomed at him, "Do you know who I am?" Tom was a bit taken aback but replied, "You're the general." Mladic was amused. "Ah, but which one?" "You're General Mladic!" The General burst out laughing, clapped Tom on the back and roared, "Well done! I can see that you and I are going to get on very well. Where are you from, boy?" Tom was getting into the stride of all this. "I'm from Zimbabwe." Mladic's eyes opened wide in surprise. "Zimbabwe, eh! Why aren't you black then? Lying already! I can see we're going to get on well."

'That's the last I ever saw of Mladic. He leapt into his jeep and roared off to join his Russian mates in Han Pijesak. With that done, I was able to tell Smith that night that Tom had met Mladic and that the hand-over had been completed. At 1600 hours on Monday 17 April I officially handed over the job to Tom. We went over to the spot where Gavrilo Princip had shot Archduke Ferdinand on 28 June 1914. We shook hands and I handed him a giant plastic blue and white UNPROFOR mug, the symbolic poisoned chalice. He was now in the hot seat.

'I was due to fly from Split on Saturday. Rather than fly by helicopter from Kiseljak, like Peter Jones before me, I wanted to drive back down the routes. The General lent me his Discovery and his ADC, Guy Lavender. We planned to leave on Thursday and spend two nights in Split. I had a couple of days left to kill and filled them by rushing about saying goodbye to people whom I knew I'd never meet again.

'First stop was the Pijalovic family. Minka wasn't there; she was out of the country and in the UK. General Mike Jackson had finally arranged it for her to visit the UK and to see her daughter, Aida, for the first time in three years. As I talked to Munir we were joined by their next door neighbour. I vaguely recognised her. "Do you remember me? You don't do you?" I'm afraid I didn't. "You came to my flat in January 1993 when you were looking for Minka and Munir and left the parcel for them. I remember you emptied your wallet for me. We've never forgotten that. It gave us hope, which allowed us to survive." With a jolt, I remembered Greta. In all those visits to the Pijalovics' I had completely forgotten her. She'd heard I'd come to bid farewell to Munir and came laden with a special bottle of Slivovica for me.

'Nada Miletic was a survivor. She'd quickly come to terms with the "removal" of Tomo and Vera. I'd offered to get her out as well since she had a brother in Birmingham. "No, dear. I've lived in this city for forty years and this is where I want to stay. I'm too old to be a refugee somewhere else." She asked after Goose and General Rose. I think she missed her afternoon teas with the Rose's hulking BG.

'I spent an afternoon with Indjic, Brane and Biljana in their tatty office in Lukavica, the scene of so much drama, angst, of so many mind games. I'd miss them, too. Theirs was the worst job of all; cooped up for years in that office, pressured by Mladic, pressured by a succession of UN LOs, pressure, pressure, pressure playing manipulative mind games which I'm sure addled them all. It was all right for me, I was getting out of it. They'd be staying for yet another round of violence.

'On Wednesday I went up to Pale for a final lunch with Jovan Zametica. He more than anyone had helped to make the job possible, the go-between who'd helped to get our hostages released, who'd been forced to go in and bat with Karadzic over whatever task Rose had set me. He'd be staying, trapped in the middle, trusted by no one. After lunch he wheeled me in to see Karadzic, who said something quite peculiar to me. It was, he said, time for me to go back to the UK and continue in a successful career and show that not all Serbs were bad. Without saying so in as many words he was indicating that they'd blown it.

'As a parting shot he gave me a few things. A book of their stamps: "I gave your Queen one of these." He gave me one of those wooden *gusle* musical instruments, whose screeching had so plagued us whenever we'd gone up to Pale: "We gave one of these to President Jimmy Carter." Finally, he gave me a sheet of A4 paper, the citation for a medal called the Humanitarian Cross. It read, "To Major Mike Stanley (Milos Stankovic), for extraordinary efforts in reducing the suffering of the civilian population of Bosnia-Hercegovina." "We've worded it that way because we know that you've helped Muslims, Croats and Serbs alike." I explained to him that Schindler's List was a combined effort that had involved many people, not just Brits, but Canadians, Americans and local Muslims in Sarajevo. The paper also said, "to be published in the Gazette of Republika Srpska". At that point I told him that we weren't allowed to accept foreign awards and begged him not to publish anything.'

'Why not?'

'It's bloody obvious, isn't it? That piece of paper was the only evidence linking my two names. The Muslims were still fiddling about with "Mihajlo

Staneslavljevic, Mihajlo Stefanovic". General Delic was convinced I was "Milan Something-or-Other". As far as I was concerned that's what they could continue thinking. Interestingly, the first time the two names were linked in print was three weeks after my arrest when *The Times* blew the gaff on Saturday 8 November 1997. More importantly, though, publication of that would have caused a witch hunt which would have required explaining Schindler's List and would have implicated Rose and Smith. Just wasn't worth the hassle. Fortunately, there were no medals. They were still being struck in St Petersburg in Russia. I showed the citation to Gary Coward and others that evening in Sarajevo. Really, though, it belonged to everyone who had participated in Schindler's List. It's all so dated and irrelevant and it doesn't matter a jot anymore.'

'How do you mean?'

'The Serbs gave Tony Blair exactly the same gong at the end of 1997 when he was visiting B-H, for his efforts in finding peace. Bizarre, when you consider that the war ended eighteen months before Blair got into power. The main difference is that by then their gongs had been minted and he walked away with the real thing. I'm sure Plod haven't made that connection yet.

'The next day Guy Lavender and I were all set to go. We were hanging around the Outer Office waiting to say goodbye to Smith. A drama had blown up in Gorazde: a couple of British troops had blown themselves up on a mine. Their situation was critical and we needed to get a helicopter into the place fast. Tom was on the phone to Han Pijesak. He was having trouble getting past Rajko on the switchboard and was struggling away like mad. It was frustrating and I shouldn't have interfered. The job was now Tom's and nothing to do with me, but British troops were injured and needing help. I grabbed the phone, told Rajko that I wanted to speak to Colonel Pandjic immediately. I'd known Pandjic, their air officer, for years. Within five minutes we'd fixed clearance for the helicopter to fly direct to Gorazde without needing a Serb inspection. Guy and I then left.

'We drove through the Hadzici checkpoint and on down the length of the Neretva to the coast before swinging north towards Split on that high, precipitous coast road, the very same one that Brigadier Cumming and I had driven in early January 1993 during my first trip out of Split. We spent a very uncomfortable night in the Palace Hotel, which was crawling with Pakistani troops intent on stopping Guy and me and demanding that we have our photo taken. I think we were the first Brits they'd ever seen. That was enough for me. I wasn't spending my last night in the Balkans in that hotel.

'The following morning I stormed into the office of the Split UN Accommodation Officer: "Edge, you little shit! You've stitched me up here!" Bob Edge looked as though he'd been in a fist-fight – two huge black eyes and a bruised and scabby face. Despite that he was smirking like mad: "First of all, Major

Stanley, it's Mr Edge to you. Secondly, you're a disgrace. You're boots haven't seen any polish for years. Call yourself an officer. You obviously need a good colour sergeant to look after you . . ." It was our age-old game, that bloke was still out in the Balkans wheeling and dealing with his mates up and down the coastal hotels. He hadn't changed a bit since we'd both flown out together on 29 December 1992. ". . . so on this occasion I'll let you stay in my flat tonight and if you behave yourself, I'll even take you to the airport tomorrow!"

'My last night in the Balkans was spent getting drunk with Bob Edge and reminiscing about old times. The next day he drove me to the airport and saw me off. The Herc banged down at Lyneham in pitch darkness and pouring rain. I hung around for an hour wondering if my lift would materialise. It did, eventually – a portly middle-aged lady, a civilian driver from the Aldershot motor pool, bustled into arrivals. It was still pouring with rain as we drove east; I remember we talked about the weather. My driver left me standing on the pavement, surrounded by my bags, still in uniform and getting soaking wet. And that, Ian, was it. End of tour.'

'What did you do next?'

'Put on some jeans and went to the pub. The locals were still there, banging on about the football and another new-fangled thing, the National Lottery. You come away from a country two hours away which is about to return to the Dark Ages and all these people were interested in was turning themselves into instant millionaires.'

'And that's it?'

'Yep, that's about it. There's more, but we'd be here for ever, wouldn't we?' I'm tired out by all this talking. We've been at it almost through the night.

'I *should* have left with Rose. It was painful watching the COHA fall apart. It was painful, too, watching the UN lose the stag fight with NATO. People had got bored and fed up with the lying ways of the locals out there and just wanted a quick fix. The long, rocky, twisting road to peace that had taxed us all was no longer an attractive option. It was too hard. "Plinking tanks is not warfighting," Admiral Leighton Smith had told Rose. So they stopped "plinking tanks" and went for the easy option of warfighting the thing to an end. NATO's ethos won out over the UN's. Sad.

'It was all so predictable. The Serbs had stuffed themselves up with their "no to the Contact Group Plan" vote. Realising that error they'd tried for a "global solution" involving the sell-out of the Krajinas and a reduction to 31 per cent of held territory in Bosnia. The international community wouldn't move on that, which resulted in the Serbs trying to win the war militarily with the attempt to take Bihac in order to precipitate a surrender of the eastern enclaves, and thus the capitulation of the Bosnian government. Rose prevented that tactic from succeeding. With no other option left to them the Serbs signed up to a four-month Cessation of Hostilities Agreement, again brokered by Rose, as a precursor to the international community moving to exploit it and secure a permanent political and territorial solution. That community failed to move at all, while at the same time the covert re-supplying of Muslims and Croats progressed apace in readiness for the inevitable spring offensives. Circumstances forced Rupert Smith to jump on the War horse. The Serbs took Srebrenica and Zepa, probably in order to free up the troops they needed for combat operations elsewhere and in preparation for "shaping" the inevitable territorial outcome. The joint Muslim-Croat offensives of early August 1995 swept the Croatian Serbs out of the Krajina without a fight, which confirms Karadzic's October 1994 "global solution" view that the Krajinas were expendable. Left with no option whatsoever, the Serbs were forced to fall back and conform to the lines and shape of the Contact Group Plan of June 1994. That by and large was set in concrete by the Dayton settlement. A year and a half of extra war for nothing.

'That's what happened – superficially at least. But if you really want to understand what happened you've got to apply even more analysis and look down at what went on at the deep level of operations. The starting point for this is a comment Mladic made to me some weeks before I left. I'd told him that they'd lost the war over Bihac. He'd agreed and then added, "We are better fighters than they are. But they're cleverer than we are." Those words have always stuck in my mind. So too has Bihac, which was everything. There's always been a missing piece of the jigsaw which has nagged at me, which has left unexplained what happened at the deep level. Not long ago I was chatting to a freelance journalist, Robert Adams, about Bihac. Unexpectedly, he provided the missing piece and knocked me dead. In fact it was quite a simple question: "Do you really think Dudakovic would have been stupid enough to attack that far south? It made absolutely no sense."

'He was right. At the time of Dudakovic's 5th Corps attack across the Una which sent the BSA reeling and forced them to give up a long, south-pointing finger of some 200 square kilometres, we in BHC merely assumed that the Serbs had run away so fast that Dudakovic's force had over-extended itself. Mladic himself had called that area a rocky barren wasteland, a place fit only for snakes. So why attack in that direction? We really didn't bother to consider this as part of a whole. We were still operating at the superficial level, mentally that is, knee-jerking to every new crisis, and not really taking the time to sit back and work out what was really going on. To understand what I'm saying you've got to remember all the other pieces of the jigsaw:

- Dudakovic attacks south out of the Bihac pocket and over-extends his force.
- The BSA gathers together a fire brigade force and counter-attacks to gain lost ground.

- 5th Corps is pushed back while ARSK artillery and jets pound Bihac town.
- NATO attacks the airbase at Udbina and we rush back from the UK (Sunday 20 November).
- BSA enters the Bihac Safe area and begins encroaching on Bihac town.
- NATO gathers itself for wider bombing of the Serbs and hits the SAM sites at Otoka.
- Serbs go mad and threaten an all-out war with the UN if NATO comes into the war.
- Geordie and I deploy, on the spur of the moment, up to Pale and begin the process of badgering the Serbs into drawing in their horns. This results in the inconclusive airport meeting on Friday 26 November.
- Rose is ambushed and publicly accused by Haris Silajdzic of being responsible for the deaths of 70,000 people in Bihac (Saturday 27 November). Geordie and I deploy again up to Pale to continue putting pressure on the Serbs.
- Serbs reveal to us that that intercepted intelligence from the BiH commanders in Srebrenica, Zepa and Gorazde convinces them that if Bihac falls to the Serbs, the eastern enclaves will surrender thus forcing the capitulation of the Bosnian government. This strengthens their resolve to take Bihac. Geordie and I lie through our teeth to prevent this happening.
- The Serbs stop short and create a horseshoe around Bihac in the hope that Dudakovic's forces will escape north and cede the town without fighting. Massive shelling of the town does not happen.
- Serbs do not take Bihac. Dudakovic's 5th Corps holds firm. The battle of Bihac is lost by the Serbs.
- Unable to win the war militarily the Serbs respond to Jimmy Carter's initiative which results in the Cessation of Hostilities Agreement of 31 December.
- COHA, predictably, breaks down after its four months expire. Hostilities resume in May 1995 and the war is finally brought to an end by wider NATO bombing of the Bosnian Serbs in September. The Dayton Agreement follows.

'The twist in all of this is that the Bosnian government also lost the battle of Bihac. If you piece together the jigsaw a different picture emerges. I'm convinced that from the Bosnian government side everything was part of a cleverly co-ordinated whole to draw NATO into the fray and end the war by Christmas 1994. Dudakovic's seemingly inexplicable and over-extended attack south into the land of rocks and snakes was deliberately planned to provoke a Serb counter attack and draw them into Bihac. At the same time the commanders in the eastern enclaves were pumping out disinformation that they'd surrender if Bihac fell. This further fuelled the Serbs' determination to take Bihac and

THE DAYTON AGREEMENT,
DECEMBER 1995

N

CROATIA

• Bihac

• Banja Luka

Brcko

Tuzla •

SERBIA

• Zenica

BOSNIA-HERCEGOVINA

Sarajevo

• Gorazde

CROATIA

F
R
Y

Mostar •

MONTENEGRO

Territorial Division of Bosnia-Hercegovina
Territory of the Bosnian Muslim and
Bosnian Croat Federation
Territory of Bosnian Serb-held
Republika Srpska

0   km   50

"end the war". In fact the eastern enclaves had no intention whatsoever
of "surrendering" and the government had no intention of "capitulating".
Co-ordinated with that was the propaganda attack on Rose by Haris Silajdzic
designed for an American audience. All of this was planned and co-ordinated.
Without doubt it was one of the cleverest deep operations of the war. A
perfect example of Soviet *Maskirovka* – deception. None of us saw it for what
it was at the time. The wool was firmly pulled over all our eyes. I'm sure that

the architect of this was General Atif Dudakovic, whose tactical handling of 5 Corps throughout the war was extraordinary. Dudakovic was probably the most accomplished general in that war. Perhaps that's what Mladic meant when he said, "But they're cleverer than we are."

'They were also cleverer than us. While Geordie and I sat up there in Pale bashing the Serbs over the head with threats of air strikes and convincing them to put the brakes on the attack, we were only operating at the superficial level. All we were doing was working in support of the Campaign Plan and the UN mandates. Unbeknown to us at the time, in achieving that success we were inadvertently wrecking the Bosnians' deep operation. Small wonder then that they loathed our deployment to Pale. All in all, the meddlesome UN wrecked the Serbs' as well as the Bosnians' plan. Curiously, the Serbs were never able to operate at that deep mental level. They ignored the most vital weapon of war, the media. Their weapon was brute force – *"nothing to boast of, when you have it, since your strength is just an accident arising from the weakness of others"*.* In that sense they were merely attritionalists, while the Bosnians, by virtue of their relative weakness, were forced to become manoeuvrists and conduct war at a cleverer mental level.

'At Staff College they bang on and on about Manoeuvre Warfare theory. It's not well understood. Manoeuvre is frequently confused with "movement". It's nothing of the sort. To be a successful manoeuvrist you necessarily have to be cunning, devious and sly. We weren't that in Bosnia. Mentally, we were attritional, responding to each crisis as it arose thus taking our eye off the ball. We simply couldn't see the wood for the trees.

'None of this is surprising when you analyse it. Lying, cheating, deception, manipulation and a belief in the rule of force was the lingua franca of the warring factions. Unless you're able to speak that same language you'll get absolutely nowhere. One's much vaunted and highly proclaimed "moral high ground" means nothing to a bunch of Tartars. As they pass by your "moral hillock" on their way to torch another village, recognising that self-delusory "high ground" to be a product of hypocrisy, they simply sneer at you and laugh their heads off. Their moral frame of reference is diametrically opposed to our Western one. In the conduct of military operations we're shackled by our Just War Doctrine, underpinned as it is by illusory notions of muscular Christianity and neo-chivalry. It is inconceivable to us to stab our opponent in the back when he's not looking. We're enslaved by the Marquess of Queensberry's rules – no gouging, kicking or biting. Our culture makes us attritionalists mentally and physically. When we meet the

---

* Joseph Conrad, *Heart of Darkness,* p. 20, Penguin Books.

Tartars, be they Aideed's gunmen or Balkan warlords, we come up against people who can operate beyond the moral laws that shackle us. They will always beat us, and they did out there. In the final analysis we Westerners simply did not have the necessary mental architecture to deal effectively with the problem.

'In some respects General Rupert Smith managed to remove the ball and chain. It is not the case that he got into a mess over hostages: he simply ignored that "moral constraint", called the Serbs' bluff and spoke their lingo – force.'

'Just a moment, Milos. Earlier you seemed to come out against the use of air strikes. They weren't complementary to the peace effort, is what you said. Aren't you contradicting yourself?'

'Of course I am. All I can do is make observations. But so what if I'm contradicting myself? That war was laced with contradictions and hypocrisy . . . mainly Western. It's perfectly correct to suggest that bombing brought an end to hostilities and dragged the warring factions to Dayton. But there really is a confusion of thought concerning the definition of measure of success. Peace in Bosnia-Hercegovina was the much-trumpeted end-state. But, let's be clear about one thing. Peace is not defined as the absence of war. The UN's Charter for Peace defines it, amongst other things, as people practising tolerance with one another as good neighbours. That seems not to be the case in Bosnia-Hercegovina, divided as it is by Dayton into three nationalistic mini-states, trapped in the Purgatory of "no war, no peace". That's no great measure of success, no great vindication of bombing. Now you can do the hard work and try and resolve that contradiction.

'As for hypocrisy, that's a subject in its own right. I could talk to you all day on that alone. How can you have a battalion of Turkish peacekeepers wearing blue berets sitting in Zenica and representing the ideals of the United Nations while at the same time the Turkish army is shelling the shit out of the Kurds and being roundly condemned for it by the United Nations. I'm not just singling the Turks out; you could point the finger at any UN peacekeeping contingent and do the same. Moral high ground! And if that's not bad enough, then there's the issue of racism. Why the extraordinary efforts in the Balkans? Why all the hand-wringing? Why the expense? All quite disproportionate to similar such efforts around the globe where the suffering was worse. Could it be the case that the West simply can't stomach the sight of "honkies" slaughtering each other, but is stricken with myopia when it's blacks who are suffering? It really doesn't surprise me that Alexander Solzhenitsyn's parting two-fingers-up-at-the-West as he went back to Russia in disgust was that article in *The Times* – "The March of the Hypocrites". He's right, in the Computer Age we really are still living by the law of the Stone Age: the man with the biggest club is right. In that sense, ironically, the Serbs and NATO had identical philosophies – a belief in brute force. Nothing to boast of, standing as we do on the cusp of the twenty-first century.'

'So where does the blame lie?'

'For this Bosnian mess, this Purgatory? The Serbs for saying no to the Contact Group Plan. The Contact Group for drawing a line in the sand. The international community for not moving on the "global solution", which would have given the Muslims far more than they eventually got. The international community, again, for failing to move and exploit the COHA and for fuelling a return to hostilities and taking the easy option of resorting to the rule of force rather than the force of peace. Net result: NATO first, Croats second, Serbs third, Muslims fourth and UN last. Ironic, isn't it? The winner in a peace support operation is a warfighting machine. The loser is the peace organisation. And, the very people the international community was hell-bent on helping came last in the local league. All this because we, the UN and the West's negotiators, were incapable of operating at anything other than the superficial level.

'But at what cost? The saddest thing of all was that it was a betrayal of all those UNites, hundreds who had lost their lives and limbs following the peace ethos. I include also the locals who worked for the UN or for other NGOs. And there were other casualties too. The US administration was and is vicious in its pursuit of anyone who didn't toe its line. I don't just mean the propaganda war they waged against Rose. I mean the Little Folk who couldn't defend themselves, who just got tossed aside and smeared by all this.'

'How do you mean?'

'There's a long list of people who got shafted but one casualty of this insidious, dirty stag fight between NATO and the UN that I will always remember is a mate of mine, a Norwegian officer. His case puts it all in a nutshell.

'Remember I told you about the strange aircraft landings at Tuzla airbase in February, what was believed to be the covert re-supplying of arms to the Muslims? Oivind Moldestad was our G3 Helicopter Ops man in BH Command. He was the most senior Norwegian in theatre, bar the doctor, and was responsible for co-ordinating helicopter operations. More than that, he'd spent years in Bosnia and had been in Sarajevo in the bad old days of 1992 and therefore knew what was what. He was the bloke who saw the two fighters circling above Tuzla as decoys; he was the one who reported it and who was told to keep quiet about what he had seen. NATO sent an "investigation team" over to Sarajevo, a "truth suppression team" is a better term. They interviewed everyone who claimed to have seen anything and did their best to debunk their claims. While that was going on Oivind was attending a flight safety conference in Vicenza in Italy. The American running it started off by making a joke about the whole thing and said that he'd like to meet the man who had sparked it off. Imagine his shock when Oivind stuck his hand in the air and said, "Actually, it was me."

'That put them into a flat spin. After the conference Oivind was in with the UN LO in Vicenza explaining what had happened and these Americans virtually dragged him out of the office and frog-marched him into another office to face a panel of American officers. They tried to debunk his story and, as he left, they shouted after him, "Remember, we're here to protect you!" Well, what the fuck is that if it's not a shabby threat? The long and the short of it is that Oivind's name became mud. His integrity and honour had been turned to dust by these people. Basically, he was branded a liar. When he returned to Norway he received no support from his own people – too scared of the Americans, you see – and he eventually resigned. So, Oivind Moldestad – liar, fabricator, cheat. That's what happened to him and that's how he'll be remembered.

'But that's not how I remember him. I remember him for something entirely different. There was a young six-year-old girl in Srebrenica called Fauda Sukic. She was dying of some sickness and needed quick evacuation to save her life. Oivind organised a NORAIR Arapaho to fly in and pick her up. The Serbs agreed and in went the heli. But there was a fuck-up. The Dutch hadn't picked her up and the aircraft was left sitting on the football pitch. At the same time Rose was conducting an air strike against the Serbs elsewhere. The strike went in and Oivind, fearing retaliation from the Serbs, was forced to recall the helicopter. It returned to Tuzla without the girl.

'As the day wore on the situation became tenser. The Serbs had closed down all their checkpoints and were generally making life impossible for the UN. Reports were reaching Oivind that the girl was close to death. He did his best to get a second clearance from the Serbs but they refused point-blank. Eventually he gave up and accepted that Fauda Sukic would die. For some reason he phoned home that afternoon and spoke to his six-year-old daughter, happy and safe in Norway. This nearly drove him mad with desperation to do something about the girl in Srebrenica.

'Totally frustrated, he came to me and begged me to ring the Serbs and try and get clearance for the flight. I was up to my eyeballs trying to sort out some of the other dramas resulting from the air strike. The Serbs were barely speaking to me. I tried to put him off as I thought nothing could be done, but he wouldn't have any of that, wouldn't go, wouldn't stop pestering me. Eventually, I caved in. For two hours we sat together while I rang around anyone I could. I think it was Mladic I eventually spoke to. The flight went in. Fauda Sukic was evacuated to Tuzla where she was treated in hospital and lived.

'That is what Oivind Moldestad should be remembered for – for his sheer determination to do something for a little girl whom he'd never met, knew nothing about, and would never meet again. That's what it was all about out there, surely? The Little People. It's nothing short of a disgrace that he was treated in the way he was by the Americans and, worse still, by his own countrymen. Instead of shunning him, the Norwegians should be proud of him. I've no time for those smart-arsed bastards, those laptop bombardiers, those lizard-like armchair warriors espousing one theory after another from the hushed, cloistered safety of academia, or the sterile environment of Ministries. They weren't there.

'Oivind was the UN and the UN was Oivind. On that one day alone, for Fauda Sukic and for Oivind Moldestad, the UN mission was a success. Not a failure. I suppose the consequence of operating at the superficial level, shackled as we were by moral constraint, is that faced with an indiscernible problem, efforts to find a solution which were met with Tartar manipulation, we tended to seek solace in small acts of humanitarian kindness. These reinforced our position on the "moral hillock" but were largely inconsequential in solving the problems of the war at the deep operational level. Certainly, there are people alive today who might otherwise not be. To the beneficiaries these were huge matters and so one should neither diminish nor pour scorn on those who went out of their way to help others at the superficial level.'

I've hardly noticed the time pass. We've been at it all night, me gabbling away about Bosnia, right through the night. Talk, talk, talk. Beyond the window the sea is flat, not a ripple. There's a pink hue in the east and not a cloud in the pre-dawn sky. It's calm and light out there.

'You know, Ian. Since this so-called investigation began I've had to re-live all that again. I've had to open the lid on the box, empty out its horrid contents and look at them anew. I lie awake at night thinking about this or that. I dream it again. I have the luxury now of choosing which nightmare I belong to. I examine and re-examine every aspect of what went on out there. I search for a clue, for something to latch onto, something to wish changed or undone. But, try as I may, after going round and round in circles I come back to the beginning. The answer is always the same. Above and beyond the physical cost of the war to the United Nations and locals in terms of lost lives and limbs there was and still is an altogether darker, grimmer and hidden price that was paid.

'It's a ghastly realisation, this product of forced self-analysis. I've tried to hide from it. I've tried to deny it. But it lurks in the shadows of my memory. It stalks me with the persistence of a predator. As I twist and turn away it circumvents me and confronts me with what I have now come to understand, and finally accept, to be the Truth of the matter.

'The difficulties I encountered in my last three months had nothing to do with the newcomers, with Smith's New Order of things. The seeds of that troubled time lay in the past, with the Old Order. That transitional period from Old to New Order had been difficult for totally unforeseen and unpredictable reasons. General Smith brought with him a measure of military calm and order. His edict to refer to proper military ranks was symptomatic of a need to change chaos into near-order, at least in the Outer Office and among the Team.

'It's hardly surprising that the newcomers came in and, boggle-eyed, found the remnants of those of us who'd stayed behind close to a state which they referred to as *"out of control"*. Did they in fact mean *"unsound method"*? If we'd been out of control it's simply because there'd been little or no control exerted. The wilder excesses of the Old Order and its collective behaviour had all but disappeared. In that sense, although the job didn't change at all, although the situation outside was deteriorating, there reigned a thoughtful calmness which took a longer view, and was less knee-jerk and less driven by immediate crises.

'This came as a huge shock to me and was difficult to accept at the time – this desolation. Now, pursued relentlessly by this primeval predator called Truth and with the luxury of hindsight and time to reflect, I've been able to put the Old Order in its rightful box and can now rationalise what happened to us all out there.

'The New Order brought in military sensibility and ousted the ghosts of an ego-driven cult of the personality, during which we'd become lackeys; unquestioningly, unthinkingly, spaniel-like, pursuing every order and instruction, however absurd – zealots all, driven by a mesmerising, masochistic and self-flagellating fascination with the personality. In many respects we'd become an extension of that ego, aping its ways, accepting as perfectly normal, behaviour which was not just unorthodox but, worse still, beyond orthodoxy itself.' *Unsound method? No! No method at all!*

'Our days as lackeys were over. The Outer Office ceased in every way to be a "university common room". In a perverse and nostalgic way I missed the abuse. I was adrift. Being treated normally came as an immeasurable shock. I don't think I ever really got used to it, which put me at loggerheads with the New Order.

'I suppose the only way to explain what happened to us collectively out there is to suggest that every war throws up its very own Kurtz. Bosnia's and ours had been the Old Order. When it departed it took with it, and, in part, left behind, the tattered vestiges of what amounted to near-pagan ideology. Small wonder then that outsiders peering in through the looking glass were aghast at what they found in Bosnia's heart of darkness – Horror! The horror! . . . of our mad souls.'

Toronto 5 April 1995

Our dear friend Milos,

We hope that you will not be surprised that we call you friend since we hardly know each other. In spite of that, because of everything you have done for us we simply have to consider you a friend. You, Nick and your friends helped us to escape from that hell of Sarajevo, thus saving our lives. And, one can only consider as friends those who were prepared to sacrifice themselves to save others. Once again, we would like to thank you for everything you have done – you, Nick, your friends and, of course, the great humanitarian General Rose, who allowed you to help us. When you have a chance, please pass on our gratitude to the General for everything he has done for us as well as for our fellow countrymen in Sarajevo and Bosnia–Hercegovina. We often recall those ugly times in Sarajevo and they still make us shudder with horror; but then we remember those of you, who enabled us to live again the life of a worthy human being.

Best regards,

Ranko, Jasna and Maja Pandurevic

PART THREE

Reflections

CHARTER FOR PEACE

We the peoples of the United Nations are determined:

To save successive generations from the scourge of war,
Which has brought untold sorrow to mankind.

To reaffirm faith in fundamental human rights,
In the dignity and worth of the human person,
In the equal rights of men and women
And of nations large and small.

To establish conditions under which justice and respect
For international obligations can be maintained.

To promote social progress, standards of life and greater freedom.

To practise tolerance with one another as good neighbours, to
Live together in peace.

To unite our strength to maintain international peace and security.

To ensure that armed force shall not be used, save in the common interest.

To promote the economic and social advancement of all peoples.

AMERICAN FOOTBALL

A Reflection upon the Gulf War

Hallelujah!
It works.
We blew the shit out of them.

We blew the shit right back up their own ass
And out their fucking ears.

It works.
We blew the shit out of them.
They suffocate in their own shit!

Hallelujah.
Praise the Lord for all good things.

We blew them into fucking shit.
They are eating it.

Praise the Lord for all good things.

We blew their balls into shards of dust,
Into shards of fucking dust.

We did it.

Now I want you to come over here and kiss me on the mouth.

Harold Pinter, 1991

Glossary

A 10

US tank-busting aircraft built around a 30mm Gatling gun

ABiH

Armija Bosne i Hercegovine – Army of Bosnia and Hercegovina. Also
ARBiH – Army of the Republic of Bosnia and Hercegovina

AG

Adjutant General – a four-star British Army general on the Army Board

AK

Avtomat Kalazhnikova – 7.62mm Soviet assault rifle designed in 1947.
Hence AK47. Tens of millions have been produced and are ubiquitously
in service with many armies

AMERICARES

US NGO (see below for NGO) with a reputation for unilaterally flying
medical supplies and aid into war zones

AOCC

Air Operations Co-ordination Cell

AOR

Area of Responsibility given to a military unit or formation within a theatre
of operations

APC

Armoured Personnel Carrier – wheeled or tracked. Affords protection to
crew and troops but is not a fighting vehicle itself

ARSK

Army of the Republic of Srpska Krajina – (see RSK, UNCRO and UNPAs
below)

ATAF

Allied Tactical Airforce – A NATO military organisation. The 5th Allied
Tactical Airforce (5 ATAF – based in Italy) provided the aircraft in support
of UN operations in the Balkans. See Op DENY FLIGHT and Op BLUE
SWORD below

ATS
Auxiliary Territorial Service – British Army's Second World War uniformed female service. Precursor to the Women's Royal Army Corps

AWAC
Airborne Warning and Control aircraft – typically E3 'Sentry' or US E2 'Hawkeye'. Equipped with wide area coverage radar, these aircraft remain airborne for protracted periods identifying hostile aircraft movement and directing friendly aircraft

BDUs
Battledress Utilities – US military terminology for camouflage field clothing

Bergen
British Army term for a backpack or rucksack

BG
Bodyguard

BHC
Bosnia Hercegovina Command – UN Command in Bosnia

BiH also BH
Bosna i Hercegovina – Bosnia and Hercegovina. The Army of the Republic of Bosnia and Hercegovina was frequently referred to by the 'internationals' as 'The BiH', while Bosnia and Hercegovina was referred to in slang as 'BH'

BLUE SWORD
See Op BLUE SWORD below

Bluey
HM Forces slang for issued aerogramme letters

BRITBAT
British Battalion – UN designation for the British Battalion in Vitez; similarly SPANBAT, Spanish Battalion, FREBAT, French Battalion etc.

BRITDET
British Detachment

BRITFOR
British Force – The collective term for the British contingent to the UN in Bosnia Hercegovina. HQ BRITFOR was established in Divulje barracks near Split in Croatia and was based on a British armoured brigade's headquarters from Germany whose commander became COMBRITFOR (see below)

BSA
Bosnian Serb Army

C130
Multi-engined Lockheed C130 Hercules transport aircraft. Mainstay of most Western airforces and the Sarajevo Airlift (see Op CHESHIRE below). Slang: Herc

CAPSAT
A portable laptop computer email/fax system which sends data via satellite rather than through a ground telephone system. Used by ECMM monitors and UNMOs (see below)

CHOSC
Commando Helicopter Operations Support Cell – Royal Navy Fleet Air Arm organisation based at the Royal Naval Air Station at Yeovilton, Somerset. Co-ordinates the helicopter support to the Royal Marines

CINCSOUTH
Commander in Chief South – Commander in Chief Allied Forces Southern Command. Naples-based four-star NATO officer, usually a US admiral

CO
Commanding Officer – The senior responsible officer in overall command of a unit (British infantry battalion, armoured regiment, artillery regiment or logistics battalion). Always a lieutenant colonel. Not to be confused with OC (Officer Commanding), the designation given to the CO's subordinate sub-unit commanders (majors) of infantry companies, armoured squadrons and artillery batteries

COHA
Cessation of Hostilities Agreement – Signed between the warring factions in BH on 31 December 1994

COMBRITFOR
Commander British Forces – Split and later Gornji Vakuf-based British brigadier, responsible to the United Kingdom's JHQ (see below) in Wilton, Wiltshire. National chain of command link with BRITBAT

CSM
Company Sergeant Major – The most senior NCO in a rifle company. Works closely with the Company Commander

Crab
British Army and Royal Navy derogatory slang for Royal Air Force personnel. So called because the colour chosen in 1919 for the uniform of the newly created Royal Air Force (previously the Army's Royal Flying Corps) matched the colour of paint used on Royal Navy warships – crab blue

CVR (T)
Combat Vehicle Reconnaissance (Tracked)

Daysack
A smaller version of a bergen, usually of about thirty litres capacity

DETALAT
Détachement de l'Air d'Armée de Terre – French Army Aviation detachment of Puma and Gazelle helicopters based at Divulje barracks, Split, alongside their British counterparts 845 NAS (see below)

DF
Defensive Fire – adjusted and recorded targets on the ground for defensive indirect fire (artillery and mortars). Hence term 'to be DFed', i.e. to be subjected to indirect enemy fire
DMZ
Demilitarised Zone
DS
Directing Staff – On military courses the 'teachers' are known as the Directing Staff or DS. DS-ing is military slang for students being critiqued by the DS
DZ
Drop Zone
ECM
Electronic Counter Measures – a suite of electronics carried on board aircraft and helicopters designed to detect and to electronically confuse/ defeat a missile or radar directed gun threat. Such measures include the automatic release of decoy flares (see RWR below)
ECMM
European Community Monitoring Mission
FAMAS
Current French assault rifle
FCO
Foreign and Commonwealth Office – British Ministry of State
FIBUA
Fighting in Built-up Areas – urban offensive combat operations, as opposed to DIBUA, Defence in Built-up Areas
FMED 8
Form Medical 8 – British Army medical form for psychiatric evaluation. 'To FMED 8 a soldier' – slang for psychiatric evaluation with a view to consigning the individual to the 'loony bin'
FOD
Foreign Object Damage – the curse of all pilots. Any form of litter which might get ingested into the engine of an aircraft and cause engine failure.
FN
Fabrique Nationale – common designation for the ubiquitous 1960s vintage 7.62mm assault rifle on which the British Army's former self-loading rifle was based
FORCE COMMANDER
A three-star command in Zagreb at HQ UNPROFOR responsible for the command and control of all three UN commands in the Balkans: the UNPROFOR 2 Bosnia-Hercegovina Command in BH, the UNPROFOR 1

Command, later renamed UNCRO (see below) in Croatia, and the UN force in FYROM. Force Commander acted as military advisor to the SRSG (see below)

FRY

Former Republics of Yugoslavia also **Federal Republic of Yugoslavia**

FYROM

Former Yugoslav Republic of Macedonia

G staff branches

Functional areas within the Army at Unit and Formation level are divided into staff branches. Each branch is designated by a G plus the number to which the functional area applies. The five most common are: **G1** – Personnel Administration including discipline; **G2** – Intelligence and Security; **G3** – Operations and Training; **G4** – Logistics support; and **G5** – Civil/Military relations. A brigade's Chief of Staff (COS, a major) co-ordinates the G2 and G3 functions while the Deputy Chief of Staff (DCOS, a major) co-ordinates the G1 and G4 functions. Both are responsible to the Commander, a brigadier. These functional areas are no different from those found in civilian companies where G1, for example, is commonly expressed as 'Human Resources' (see also J staff branches below)

GMC

General Motors Company – US automobile manufacturer. The vehicle belonging to the BH Command's head of Civil Affairs, Victor Andreyev, was an armoured GMC estate

GPMG

General Purpose Machine Gun

GV

Gornji Vakuf

HDZ

Hrvatska Demokratska Zajednica – Croatian Democratic Union, the political party of the Bosnian Croats

HLS

Helicopter Landing Site

HOS

Hrvatske Odbrambene Snage – Croatian Defence Forces, ultra-nationalist extremist organisation/unit in the HV (see below)

HQ BHC

Headquarters Bosnia-Hercegovina Command – UN headquarters in Bosnia-Hercegovina. From 1992 to 1993 its Main HQ was in Kiseljak with a Tactical HQ in the Residency in Sarajevo. 1994–1995, Main HQ was still in Kiseljak, Forward HQ (an expanded Tactical HQ) was at the Residency while the Rear HQ was in Split. HQ BHC reported to and was commanded by HQ UNPROFOR in Zagreb

Hummer

US Army slang for **HMMWV – High Mobility Medium Wheeled Vehicle,** which replaced the Jeep. An armoured version was sometimes used as a backing vehicle to Commander BHC's Range Rover (see Range and Snatch, below)

HV

Hrvatska Vojska – Croatian Army (in Croatia, not Bosnia)

HVO

Hrvatsko Vece Odbrane – Croatian Defence Council, i.e. Bosnian Croat army

ICFY

International Conference on the Former Yugoslavia – co-chaired (initially) by Lord Owen and Cyrus Vance, and latterly by Lord Owen and Thorvald Stoltenberg. First steering committee was in Geneva on 3 September 1992

ICRC

International Committee of the Red Cross

IFOR

Implementation Force – NATO force of 60,000 troops which succeeded UNPROFOR (see below) in BH in December 1995 after the signing of the Dayton Accord

INMARSAT

International Maritime Satellite – insecure satellite telephone system used throughout the Former Yugoslavia by international agencies and UN forces alike

ISO Containers

Large, rectangular standard-sized steel shipping containers used for moving goods about the world by container ship

J staff branches

The J staff branch functions are exactly the same as the G staff branch functions (see above). The 'J' denoting 'Joint' is used wherever the Army, Navy and Air Force are involved in a joint operation; staff functional areas within a headquarters are shared out between officers of all three services (see JHQ below)

JA

Jugoslav Army – Redesignated from JNA (see below) and refers to the army of rump Yugoslavia, i.e. Serbia and Montenegro

JCO

Joint Commission Observer Officers and Non Commissioned Officers drawn on a voluntary basis from across all three Services who served in Bosnia in support of the Joint Commission (of Bosnian Muslims and Bosnian Croats chaired by the UN) established in March 1994 after the

Washington Accord ended the war between those two parties in Central Bosnia. The JCOs subsequently became the eyes and ears of Commander BHC and were tasked directly by him

JCSC & JDSC

Junior Command and Staff Course, part of the **Junior Division of the Staff College.** A mandatory five-month British Army course for career junior officers (captains) which prepares them for appointments in staff branches (see G and J above) of units and formations as Grade 3 (captains) staff officers

JHQ

Joint Headquarters – during the UN operation in FRY the controlling national headquarters for all UK military personnel deployed to the Balkans was located at HQ United Kingdom Land Forces (later renamed HQ Land) at Wilton in Wiltshire. The staff branches within JHQ were filled by personnel from all three Services (hence 'Joint'), on a somewhat ad hoc basis. Recognising that all future operational commitments are likely to be 'Joint', a Permanent Joint HQ (PJHQ) has been formally established at Northwood in Middlesex

JNA

Jugoslav National Army – the army of Tito's unified Yugoslavia. Now fractionalised into smaller independent national armies (see JA, HV, HVO, ABiH, BSA)

Kilo 1, K1

Bosnian Croat (HVO) checkpoint on the land route Sarajevo–Kiseljak

LO

Liaison Officer

LI

Light Infantry

M113

US **Vietnam vintage tracked APC** (see above) found in service with some NATO & non-NATO countries

MA

Military Assistant – a senior grade staff officer who runs the Outer Office for the Commander (of General rank). The MA is usually a lieutenant colonel

MAOT

Mobile Air Operations Team – a small team of military personnel equipped with the necessary radio communications which controls the arrival and departure of helicopters from ad hoc HLSs (see above)

MASH

Mobile Army Surgical Hospital

MILOB

Military Observer – UN observers in UNIKOM (see below)

MP5

    Heckler Koch Machine Pistol 5 – A robust and reliable German 9mm sub-machine gun favoured by many countries' special forces, police & bodyguards

MP5K

    A shortened (kurtz) version of the MP5

MRE

    Meals Ready to Eat – US military combat rations

MSF

    Médicines Sans Frontières – a highly efficient international NGO (see below)

MST

    Mobile Surgical Team – part of BRITBAT at Vitez offering operating facilities

NAS

    Naval Air Squadron – numbered designations for Royal Navy Fleet Air Arm squadrons. 845 NAS, operating Sea King helicopters, was based at Divulje barracks at HQ BRITFOR near Split, in Croatia, providing helicopter support to UN operations alongside DETALAT (see above). 845 NAS's normal role, along with 846 NAS, is to provide helicopter support to the Royal Navy's Royal Marine Commandos. In slang, both squadrons are known as 'junglies'

NBC

    Nuclear, Biological and Chemical warfare – Individual protective suits are known as 'Noddy' suits

NFZ

    No Fly Zone – in December 1992 mandated by a UNSCR (see below) a No Fly Zone was established over Bosnia-Hercegovina with the aim of ensuring that the parties to the conflict (particularly the Serbs) did not use fixed wing aircraft or helicopters in support of their combat operations (see Op DENY FLIGHT below)

NGO

    Non Governmental Organisation – aid and other humanitarian organisations not sponsored by any national government, i.e. HALO Trust, MSF, PSF etc

NSE

    National Support Element – the BRITFOR logistics support base at TSG (see below) which kept BRITBAT in Vitez, GV and Tuzla supplied. The NSE was based on a logistics battalion and an engineer regiment of the Royal Engineers

OP

    Observation Post – either overt or covert position from which information on 'enemy' troop movements etc is obtained through observation

Op

    Operation – within the British military culture operations are always desig-
nated by a single, randomly chosen name. Unlike US operational code
names, which comprise two words and reflect the desired nature of the
outcome of the operation (Op PROVIDE COMFORT, Op RESTORE
HOPE), British code names are single words having no relevance whatsoever to the nature of the operation (Falklands War – Op CORPORATE)

Op BLUE SWORD

    The code name given to Close Air Support by aircraft of Op DENY FLIGHT
in response to requests by Commander BHC. The mission typically was to
engage and hit a specific target (tank or artillery piece) which was either
endangering UN troops or acting in violation of the Safe Areas or TEZs
(see below). BLUE SWORD should not be confused with the term 'Air
Strike' which denotes wider, unrestricted bombing of ground targets of
NATO's choosing and timing

Op CABINET

    Unofficial BRITFOR code name given to the escorting by BRITBAT of
UNHCR convoys coming from the UNHCR warehouse in Belgrade. The
convoys had to cross the BSA/BiH front line at Kalesija before delivering
to the UNHCR warehouse in Tuzla

Op CHESHIRE

    The British (RAF's) contribution of C130s to the Sarajevo airlift

Op DENY FLIGHT

    NATO's 5 ATAF (see above) combat air patrol operation over Bosnia-
Hercegovina's NFZ (see NFZ above) in support of the UN operation (see
also Op BLUE SWORD above)

Op GRAPPLE

    The deployment in October 1992 of British forces to the UN operation in
Bosnia-Hercegovina

Op HANWOOD

    The 1992 deployment of a British Army medical battalion (BRITMEDBAT)
to Zagreb

Op SHARP GUARD

    Mandated by a UNSCR in 1992 an arms embargo was imposed on all
countries of FRY. Op SHARP GUARD was the NATO code name given
to the fleet of NATO warships in the Adriatic whose mission was to prevent
gun-running into the Balkans by sea

Op SLAVIN

    Unofficial BRITFOR code name given to the escorting by BRITBAT of
UNHCR aid convoys crossing from Bosnian Serb territory over the confrontation line at Turbe into Central Bosnia bound for the UNHCR warehouse
at Zenica

PInfo
>Public Information – UN/press interface. Each UN unit had a PInfo cell or officer

PTT
>Post, Telegraph and Telecommunications building in Sarajevo which served as the UN (French run) Sector Sarajevo headquarters

PWO/1PWO
>1st Battalion, The Prince of Wales's Own Regiment of Yorkshire

QM
>Quartermaster – Responsible to the CO of a unit for logistic supply

Range
>Slang for Range Rover. Commander BHC's vehicle was an armoured version

RARDEN Cannon
>A 30mm cannon fitted to Scimitar CVR(T) and Warrior Infantry Combat Fighting Vehicles. A direct fire weapon with a range of 2000 metres, it fires a number of ammunition natures, including AP (Armour Piercing) shot

RB44
>Renault Bowden 44 – A small military truck

R&R
>Rest and Recuperation – a short spell of leave taken during a six-month operational tour. During Op GRAPPLE a two-week R&R leave period was given to each service person. R&R flights back to the UK or Germany were provided by the RAF

REME
>Royal Electrical and Mechanical Engineers

REMF
>Rear Echelon Motherfuckers: US slang in common use in the British Army

RJC
>Regional Joint Commission, established in Tuzla and GV in January 1995

RS
>*Republika Srpska* – Serb Republic; the self-styled breakaway Bosnian Serb republic in Bosnia–Hercegovina

RSK
>*Republika Srpska Krajina* – Republic of Serbian Krajina; the self-styled breakaway Croatian Serb republic in Croatia, designated by UNPAs (see below)

RSM
>Regimental Sergeant Major – the senior Non Commissioned Officer in an infantry/logistics battalion, armoured regiment or artillery regiment. With the rank of Warrant Officer 1st Class he works closely with the CO (see above) and is largely responsible for discipline and good order in a unit

RWR

Radar Warning Receiver – part of the ECM (see above) suite carried on 845 NAS Sea Kings. Energy from hostile missile or gun tracking radars is detected by the RWR, giving warning and direction of the threat

SAM

Surface to Air Missile

SDA

Stranka Demokratske Akcije – the Party of Democratic Action in Bosnia Hercegovina. Party leader: Alija Izetbegovic (also President of BiH). The party has always been dominated by hard-line Muslims

SDS

Srpska Demokratska Stranka – the Serbian Democratic Party of the Bosnian Serb breakaway Republika Srpska. Party leader: Dr Radovan Karadzic

SF base

Security Force base – Northern Ireland terminology

SG

Secretary General of the United Nations

Shamagh

A broad sheet of patterned cloth comprising Arab headwear. Black and green versions are favoured by British troops on exercise or operations. A non-issued informal garment. Issued only on operations in desert regions

Sitrep

Situation Report

Snatch

Slang for armoured Land Rovers, which were used in Northern Ireland as snatch vehicles during riots. The snatch was usually the backing vehicle for Commander BHC's Range (see above)

SO2 G2

Staff Officer Grade 2 (i.e. Major) running the G2 (Intelligence) branch of a headquarters. (See G Staff branches above)

SOE

Special Operations Executive – a British Second World War organisation of agents and saboteurs whose function was to organise local resistance in Nazi-occupied countries and to 'set Europe ablaze'. Volunteers were frequently fluent in a second language and/or had been brought up in, or had a background from, the country to which they were sent on operations

SOP

Standard Operating Procedure – an operational procedure laid down in manuals for the conduct of operations. Army slang for 'standard practice'

SQMS

Staff Quartermaster Sergeant – Warrant Officer in a unit responsible for catering

SRSG

Special Representative of the Secretary General – the most senior UN individual in FRY. His office was located at HQ UNPROFOR in Zagreb where the Force Commander (see above) acted as his military adviser

TACSAT

Tactical Satellite radio

TAOR

Tactical Area of Responsibility (see AOR above)

TEZ

Total Exclusion Zone – a twenty-kilometre radius TEZ was established around Sarajevo at the end of February 1994. The purpose was to exclude the use of all heavy weapons within that zone. Heavy weapons of all parties to the conflict were either to be removed out of the TEZ or corralled in heavy weapons Weapon Collection Points supervised by the UN. Violations of the TEZ by all parties were frequent. A similar but smaller three-kilometre radius TEZ was established around the town of Gorazde at the peace talks in Geneva in June 1994

Theatre

Theatre of operations. Military term

TOW missile

Ground or air-launched wire guided anti-task missile. Range 3750 metres

TSG

Tomislavgrad

UDI

Unilateral Declaration of Independence

UDBA

Uprava Drzavne Bezbednosti – Department of State Security. Tito's Communist Yugoslav organ of state security which extended its arm beyond the country in the conduct of assassinations of 'enemies of the state', i.e. anti-Communist Yugoslavs living in the West. The 'A' of UDBA was a colloquial addition used when referring to the organisation, which is pronounced Udba

UH1

Utility helicopter. US Vietnam era – Commonly called a 'Huey'

UKLF

United Kingdom Land Forces. HQ UKLF is in Wilton, Wiltshire, now renamed HQ Land Forces Command

UKLO

United Kingdom Liaison Officer

UNCRO

United Nations Croatia – the UN force in the UNPAs in Croatia. Originally this force was called UNPROFOR 1. Because the force was seen by the Croatians to be protecting the integrity of the Croatian Serb breakaway Republika Srpska Krajina, it was referred to as 'SERBPROFOR'. This resulted in part in the redesignation of the force to UNCRO

UND
UN Department in the FCO

UNHCR
United Nations High Commissioner for Refugees – the lead aid agency in FRY

UNIKOM
United Nations Iraq Kuwait Observer Mission – UN observer mission establishing a 240-kilometre DMZ between Kuwait and Iraq after the Gulf War of 1991

UNMO
United Nations Military Observer

UNPA
United Nations Protected Area – the UNPAs were established by the UN after the cessation of the six-month war in Croatia in 1991 during which the Croatian Serbs of the Krajina border regions adjoining Bosnia–Hercegovina seceded and established their breakaway RSK (see above). The UNPAs were superimposed on top of and largely conformed to the territory held by the Krajina Serbs. The four UNPAs were called UN Sectors East, West, North and South. The UNPAs and RSK existed until 4 August 1995 when the Croatian Army (HV) mounted Operation STORM, reclaiming the UNPAs for Croatia

UNPROFOR
United Nations Protection Force – For UNPROFOR 1 see UNCRO above. UNPROFOR 2 was the UN operation in Bosnia–Hercegovina controlled by HQ UNPROFOR in Zagreb

UNSC
United Nations Security Council

UNSCR
United Nations Security Council Resolution

VADs
Voluntary Aid Detachments – Volunteer nurses in the British Army during the First World War

VOPP
Vance–Owen Peace Plan of 1993

VSAT
UN insecure satellite non-portable desk-top telephone system

VSI, VVSI
Very Seriously Injured and Very Very Seriously Injured

WFP

World Food Programme – UN organisation which spent donor countries' money to buy food and aid for the humanitarian relief effort in FRY which UNHCR delivered. Headquarters in Rome

Warrior

The British Army's tracked Armoured Infantry Fighting Vehicle. Unlike an APC (see above) it is armed with a 30mm Rarden cannon and a 7.62mm chain gun. It offers an offensive capability, high mobility off road and high levels of protection. It has a crew of three (driver in front, commander and gunner in the turret) and a section of seven infantry soldiers in the back

WCPs

Weapon Collection Points – established in and around Sarajevo when the Sarajevo TEZ came into existence (see TEZ above)

WHO

World Health Organisation – UN organisation

Wren

Member of the Women's Royal Naval Service (WRNS)

Index